P9-CNB-664

	DATE DUE	
AUG 2 8 1997		
SEP 0 5 1998		
APR 0 6 1999		

F
Doyle, Roddy
The Barrytown Trilogy
The Commitments, The Snapper,
The Van

WALKER'S POINT
PUBLIC LIBRARY

The Barrytown Trilogy

by the same author

Brownbread
War

THE
BARRYTOWN
TRILOGY

THE COMMITMENTS
THE SNAPPER
THE VAN

Roddy Doyle

Secker & Warburg
LONDON

The Commitments
First published in Great Britain 1988
by William Heinemann Limited

Copyright © Roddy Doyle 1987

Thanks to Mick Boland, John Condon, Enda Farrelly,
Darren Gallagher, Louise Hamilton, Caroline Jones,
Lorraine Jones, Kenneth Keegan, Kevin McDonald,
Brian McGinn, Jimmy Murray and Michael Sherlock.

The Snapper
First published in Great Britain 1990
by Martin Secker & Warburg Limited

Copyright © Roddy Doyle 1990

The Van
First published in Great Britain 1991
by Martin Secker & Warburg Limited

Copyright © Roddy Doyle 1991

This collection first published in Great Britain 1992
by Martin Secker & Warburg Limited
Michelin House, 81 Fulham Road, London SW3 6RB

Reprinted 1992 (twice), 1993 (three times)

A CIP catalogue record for this book
is available from the British Library

ISBN 0 436 20121 6

This book is a work of fiction and the characters
and events all came out of the author's own head.
Any resemblance to real events, places or people,
living or dead, it purely coincidental.

Printed in England by Clays Ltd, St Ives plc

Contents

THE COMMITMENTS

This book is dedicated to

My Mother and Father

Honour thy parents, Brothers and Sisters.
They were hip to the groove too
once you know. Parents are soul.

Joey The Lips Fagan

Acknowledgements

When a Man Loves a Woman, words and music by C. Lewis/
A. Wright, © 1966 Pronto Music Inc./Quinvy Music Publishing
Company; and *Knock on Wood*, words and music by Eddie Floyd/
Steve Cropper, © 1966 East Publishers Inc., reproduced by kind
permission of Warner Bros Music Limited.

Superbad, words and music by James Brown, © 1970 Crited Music;
Get Up, I Feel Like Being a Sex Machine, words and music by James
Brown/Bobby Byrd/Ronald L. Lenhoff, © 1970 Dynatone
Publishing Co.; and *It's a Man's Man's Man's World*, words and music
by James Brown/Betty Mewsome, © 1966 Dynatone Publishing
Co., reproduced by kind permission of Intersong Music Limited.

Out of Sight, words and music by James Brown, and *Night Train*,
words and music by Washington/Simpkins/Forrest, reproduced
by kind permission of Carlin Music Corp.

Walking in the Rain, words and music by Spector/Mann/Weil,
© 1964 Screen Gems–EMI Music Inc., USA, sub-published by
Screen Gems–EMI Music Ltd, London WC2H 0LD. Reproduced
by permission.

I'll Feel a Whole Lot Better, words and music by Gene Clark,
© 1965 Lakeview Music Publishing Co. Limited, 19/20 Poland
Street, London W1V 3DD. International Copyright Secured. All
Rights Reserved. Used by Permission.

Reach Out I'll Be There, words by B. Holland, L. Dozier,
E. Holland, © 1966 Jobete Music Co., Inc, JOBETE MUSIC (UK)
LTD. All Rights Reserved. Used by Permission. International
Copyright Secured.

What Becomes of the Broken Hearted?, words by P. Riser, J. Dean,
W. Weatherspoon, © 1966 Jobete Music Co., Inc, JOBETE MUSIC
(UK) LTD. All Rights Reserved. Used by Permission. International
Copyright Secured.

Chain Gang, words and music by Sam Cooke, reprinted by
permission of ABKCO Music Ltd.

—SOMETIMES I FEEL SO NICE—

GOOD GOD————
I JUMP BACK——

I WANNA KISS MYSELF————!
I GOT—
SOU—OU—OUL—
AN' I'M SUPERBAD————

     James Brown, *Superbad*

—We'll ask Jimmy, said Outspan. —Jimmy'll know.

Jimmy Rabbitte knew his music. He knew his stuff alright. You'd never see Jimmy coming home from town without a new album or a 12-inch or at least a 7-inch single. Jimmy ate Melody Maker and the NME every week and Hot Press every two weeks. He listened to Dave Fanning and John Peel. He even read his sisters' Jackie when there was no one looking. So Jimmy knew his stuff.

The last time Outspan had flicked through Jimmy's records he'd seen names like Microdisney, Eddie and the Hot Rods, Otis Redding, The Screaming Blue Messiahs, Scraping Foetus off the Wheel (—Foetus, said Outspan. —That's the little young fella inside the woman, isn't it?

—Yeah, said Jimmy.

—Aah, that's fuckin' horrible, tha' is.); groups Outspan had never heard of, never mind heard. Jimmy even had albums by Frank Sinatra and The Monkees.

So when Outspan and Derek decided, while Ray was out in the jacks, that their group needed a new direction they both thought of Jimmy. Jimmy knew what was what. Jimmy knew what was new, what was new but wouldn't be for long and what was going to be new. Jimmy had Relax before anyone had heard of Frankie Goes to Hollywood and he'd started slagging them months before anyone realized that they were no good. Jimmy knew his music.

Outspan, Derek and Ray's group, And And And, was three days old; Ray on the Casio and his little sister's glockenspiel,

Outspan on his brother's acoustic guitar, Derek on nothing yet but the bass guitar as soon as he'd the money saved.

—Will we tell Ray? Derek asked.

—Abou' Jimmy? Outspan asked back.

—Yeah.

————Better not. Yet annyway.

Outspan was trying to work his thumb in under a sticker, This Guitar Kills Fascists, his brother, an awful hippy, had put on it.

—There's the flush, he said. —He's comin' back. We'll see Jimmy later.

They were in Derek's bedroom.

Ray came back in.

—I was thinkin' there, he said. —I think maybe we should have an exclamation mark, yeh know, after the second And in the name.

—Wha'?

—It'd be And And exclamation mark, righ', And. It'd look deadly on the posters.

Outspan said nothing while he imagined it.

—What's an explanation mark? said Derek.

—Yeh know, said Ray.

He drew a big one in the air.

—Oh yeah, said Derek. —An' where d'yeh want to put it again?

—And And,

He drew another one.

—And.

—Is it not supposed to go at the end?

—It should go up his arse, said Outspan, picking away at the sticker.

* * *

Jimmy was already there when Outspan and Derek got to the Pub.

—How's it goin', said Jimmy.

—Howyeh, Jim, said Outspan.

8

—Howayeh, said Derek.

They got stools and formed a little semicircle at the bar.

—Been ridin' annythin' since I seen yis last? Jimmy asked them.

—No way, said Outspan. —We've been much too busy for tha' sort o' thing. Isn't tha' righ'?

—Yeah, that's righ', said Derek.

—Puttin' the finishin' touches to your album? said Jimmy.

—Puttin' the finishin' touches to our name, said Outspan.

—Wha' are yis now?

—And And exclamation mark, righ'? ——And, said Derek. Jimmy grinned a sneer.

—Fuck, fuck, exclamation mark, me. I bet I know who thought o' tha'.

—There'll be a little face on the dot, righ', Outspan explained.

—An' yeh know the line on the top of it? That's the dot's fringe.

—Black an' whi'e or colour?

—Don't know.

—It's been done before, Jimmy was happy to tell them. —Ska. Madness, The Specials. Little black an' whi'e men. ——I told yis, he hasn't a clue.

——Yeah, said Outspan.

—He owns the synth though, said Derek.

—Does he call tha' fuckin' yoke a synth? said Jimmy.

—Annyway, no one uses them annymore. It's back to basics.

—Just as well, said Outspan. —Cos we've fuck all else.

—Wha' tracks are yis doin'? Jimmy asked.

—Tha' one, Masters and Servants.

—Depeche Mode?

—Yeah.

Outspan was embarrassed. He didn't know why. He didn't mind the song. But Jimmy had a face on him.

—It's good, tha', said Derek. —The words are good, yeh know ——good.

9

—It's just fuckin' art school stuff, said Jimmy.

That was the killer argument, Outspan knew, although he didn't know what it meant.

Derek did.

—Hang on, Jimmy, he said. —That's not fair now. The Beatles went to art school.

—That's different.

—Me hole it is, said Derek. —An' Roxy Music went to art school an' you have all their albums, so yeh can fuck off with yourself.

Jimmy was fighting back a redner.

—I didn't mean it like tha', he said. —It's not the fact tha' they went to fuckin' art school that's wrong with them. It's —(Jimmy was struggling.) —more to do with —(Now he had something.) ——the way their stuff, their songs like, are aimed at gits like themselves. Wankers with funny haircuts. An' rich das. ——An' fuck all else to do all day 'cept prickin' around with synths.

—Tha' sounds like me arse, said Outspan. —But I'm sure you're righ'.

—Wha' else d'yis do?

—Nothin' yet really, said Derek. —Ray wants to do tha' one, Louise. It's easy.

—Human League?

—Yeah.

Jimmy pushed his eyebrows up and whistled.

They agreed with him.

Jimmy spoke. —Why exactly ——d'yis want to be in a group?

—Wha' d'yeh mean? Outspan asked.

He approved of Jimmy's question though. It was getting to what was bothering him, and probably Derek too.

—Why are yis doin' it, buyin' the gear, rehearsin'? Why did yis form the group?

—Well ——

—Money?

—No, said Outspan. —I mean, it'd be nice. But I'm not in it for the money.

—I amn't either, said Derek.

—The chicks?

—Jaysis, Jimmy!

—The brassers, yeh know wha' I mean. The gee. Is tha' why?

————No, said Derek.

—The odd ride now an' again would be alrigh' though wouldn't it? said Outspan.

—Ah yeah, said Derek. —But wha' Jimmy's askin' is is tha' the reason we got the group together. To get our hole.

—No way, said Outspan.

—Why then? said Jimmy.

He'd an answer ready for them.

—It's hard to say, said Outspan.

That's what Jimmy had wanted to hear. He jumped in.

—Yis want to be different, isn't tha' it? Yis want to do somethin' with yourselves, isn't tha' it?

—Sort of, said Outspan.

—Yis don't want to end up like (he nodded his head back) —these tossers here. Amn't I righ'?

Jimmy was getting passionate now. The lads enjoyed watching him.

—Yis want to get up there an' shout I'm Outspan fuckin' Foster.

He looked at Derek.

—An' I'm Derek fuckin' Scully, an' I'm not a tosser. Isn't tha' righ'? That's why yis're doin' it. Amn't I righ'?

—I s'pose yeh are, said Outspan.

—Fuckin' sure I am.

—With the odd ride thrown in, said Derek.

They laughed.

Then Jimmy was back on his track again.

—So if yis want to be different what're yis doin' doin' bad versions of other people's poxy songs?

That was it. He was right, bang on the nail. They were very impressed. So was Jimmy.

—Wha' should we be doin' then? Outspan asked.

—It's not the other people's songs so much, said Jimmy. —It's which ones yis do.

—What's tha' mean?

—Yeh don't choose the songs cos they're easy. Because fuckin' Ray can play them with two fingers.

—Wha' then? Derek asked.

Jimmy ignored him.

—All tha' mushy shite abou' love an' fields an' meetin' mots in supermarkets an' McDonald's is gone, ou' the fuckin' window. It's dishonest, said Jimmy. —It's bourgeois.

—Fuckin' hell!

—Tha' shite's ou'. Thank Jaysis.

—What's in then? Outspan asked him.

—I'll tell yeh, said Jimmy. —Sex an' politics.

—WHA'?

—Real sex. Not mushy I'll hold your hand till the end o' time stuff. ——Ridin'. Fuckin'. D'yeh know wha' I mean?

—I think so.

—Yeh couldn't say Fuckin' in a song, said Derek.

—Where does the fuckin' politics come into it? Outspan asked.

—Yeh'd never get away with it.

—Real politics, said Jimmy.

—Not in Ireland annyway, said Derek. —Maybe England. But they'd never let us on Top o' the Pops.

—Who the fuck wants to be on Top o' the Pops? said Jimmy.

Jimmy always got genuinely angry whenever Top of the Pops was mentioned although he never missed it.

—I never heard anyone say it on The Tube either, said Derek.

—I did, said Outspan. —Your man from what's their name said it tha' time the mike hit him on the head.

Derek seemed happier.

Jimmy continued. He went back to sex.

—Believe me, he said. —Holdin' hands is ou'. Lookin' at the moon, tha' sort o' shite. It's the real thing now.

He looked at Derek.

—Even in Ireland. ———Look, Frankie Goes To me arse were shite, righ'?

They nodded.

—But Jaysis, at least they called a blow job a blow job an' look at all the units they shifted?

—The wha'?

—Records.

They drank.

Then Jimmy spoke. —Rock an' roll is all abou' ridin'. That's wha' rock an' roll means. Did yis know tha'? (They didn't.) —Yeah, that's wha' the blackies in America used to call it. So the time has come to put the ridin' back into rock an' roll. Tongues, gooters, boxes, the works. The market's huge.

—Wha' abou' this politics?

—Yeah, politics. ———Not songs abou' Fianna fuckin' Fail or annythin' like tha'. Real politics. (They weren't with him.) —Where are yis from? (He answered the question himself.) —Dublin. (He asked another one.) —Wha' part o' Dublin? Barrytown. Wha' class are yis? Workin' class. Are yis proud of it? Yeah, yis are. (Then a practical question.) —Who buys the most records? The workin' class. Are yis with me? (Not really.) —Your music should be abou' where you're from an' the sort o' people yeh come from. ———Say it once, say it loud, I'm black an' I'm proud.

They looked at him.

—James Brown. Did yis know ———never mind. He sang tha'. ———An' he made a fuckin' bomb.

They were stunned by what came next.

—The Irish are the niggers of Europe, lads.

They nearly gasped: it was so true.

—An' Dubliners are the niggers of Ireland. The culchies have fuckin' everythin'. An' the northside Dubliners are the niggers o' Dublin. ———Say it loud, I'm black an' I'm proud.

He grinned. He'd impressed himself again.

He'd won them. They couldn't say anything.

—Yis don't want to be called And And exclamation mark And, do yis? Jimmy asked.

—No way, said Outspan.

—Will yeh manage us, Jimmy? said Derek.

—Yeah, said Jimmy. —I will.

They all smiled.

—Am I in charge? Jimmy asked them.

—Yeah.

—Righ' then, said Jimmy. —Ray isn't in the group annymore.

This was a shock.

—Why not?

—Well, first we don't need a synth. An' second, I don't like the cunt.

They laughed.

—I never have liked him. I fuckin' hate him to be honest with yis.

————I don't like him much meself, said Outspan.

—He's gone so?

He was gone.

—Wha' sort o'stuff will we be doin'? Derek asked.

—Wha' sort o'music has sex an' politics? Jimmy asked.

—Reggae, said Derek.

—No, not tha'.

—It does.

—Yeah, but we won't be doin' it. We'll leave the reggae to the skinheads an' the spacers.

—Wha' then?

—Soul.

—Soul?

—Soul?

—Soul. Dublin soul.

Outspan laughed. Dublin soul sounded great.

—Another thing, said Jimmy. —Yis aren't And And And annymore.

14

This was a relief.

—What are we Jimmy?

—The Commitments.

Outspan laughed again.

—That's a rapid name, said Derek.

—Good, old-fashioned THE, said Jimmy.

—Dublin soul, said Outspan.

He laughed again.

—Fuckin' deadly.

* * *

The day after the formation of The Commitments Jimmy sent an ad into the Hot Press classifieds:

—Have you got Soul? If yes, The World's Hardest Working Band is looking for you. Contact J. Rabbitte, 118, Chestnut Ave., Dublin 21. Rednecks and southsiders need not apply.

* * *

There was a young guy who worked in the same shop as Jimmy. Declan Cuffe was his name. He seemed like a right prick, although Jimmy didn't know him that well. Jimmy had heard him singing at the last year's Christmas Do. Jimmy had just been out puking but he still remembered it, Declan Cuffe's voice, a real deep growl that scraped against the throat and tongue on its way out. Jimmy would have loved a voice like it.

Jimmy was going to see if he could recruit Declan Cuffe. He took his tray and went over to where he was sitting.

—Sorry, eh ——Declan, said Jimmy. —Is there annyone sittin' here?

Declan Cuffe leaned over the table and studied the chair.

Then he said: —It doesn't look like it.

Normally Jimmy would have upended the slop on the tray over him (or at least would have wanted to) but this was business.

He sat down.

—What's the soup like? he asked.

—Cuntish.

—As usual, wha'.

There wasn't an answer. Jimmy tried a different angle.

—What's the curry like?

—Cuntish.

Jimmy changed tactics.

—I'd say yeh did Honours English in school, did yeh?

Declan Cuffe stared across at Jimmy while he sent his cigarette to the side of his mouth.

—You startin' somethin'? he said.

The woman from the Information Desk at the table beside them started talking louder.

—Ah, cop on, said Jimmy. —I was only messin'.

He shoved the bowl away and slid the plate nearer to him.

—You were righ' abou' the soup.

He searched the chicken curry.

—Tell us an' annyway. Are yeh in a group these days?

—Am I wha'?

—In a group.

—Doin' wha'?

—Singin'.

—Me! Singin'? Fuck off, will yeh.

—I heard yeh singin', said Jimmy. —You were fuckin' great.

—When did you hear me singin'?

—Christmas.

—Did I sing? At the dinner dance?

—Yeah.

—Fuck, said Declan Cuffe. —No one told me.

—You were deadly.

—I was fuckin' locked, said Declan Cuffe. —Rum an' blacks, yeh know.

Jimmy nodded. —I was locked meself.

—I must of had abou' twenty o' them. Your woman, Frances, from the Toys, yeh know her? She was all over me. ——Dirty bitch. She's fuckin' married. ——I sang then?

—Yeah. It was great.

16

—I was fuckin' locked.
—D'yeh want to be in a group?
—Singin'?
—Yeah.
—Are yeh serious?
—Yeah.
——Okay. ———Serious now?
—Yeah.
—Okay.

*   *   *

The next night Jimmy brought Declan Cuffe (by now he was
Deco) home from work with him. Deco had a big fry cooked
by Jimmy, five slices of bread, two cups of tea, and he fell in
love with Sharon, Jimmy's sister, when she came in from
work.

—What age is Sharon? Deco asked Jimmy.

They were up in Jimmy's bedroom. Deco was lying on the
bottom bunk.

—You're wastin' your time.

—What age is she?

—Twenty, said Jimmy. —But you're wastin' your time.

—I wonder would she fancy goin' out with a pop star.

The door opened. It was the rest of the group, Outspan and
Derek. They smiled when they got in and saw Deco on the
bunk. Jimmy had told them about him.

—That's Deco, said Jimmy.

—Howyeh, said Outspan.

—Howyeh, said Deco.

—Pleased to meet yeh, Deco, said Derek.

—Yeah, ———righ', said Deco.

Deco got up and let Outspan and Derek sit beside him on
the bunk.

—How did Ray take the news? Jimmy asked.

—Not too bad, said Derek.

—The cunt, said Jimmy.

—He wasn't too happy with the eh, And And And situation either. Or so he said.

—Yeah. So he said, said Jimmy. —Me arse.

—He's goin' solo.

—He doesn't have much of a fuckin' choice.

They laughed. Deco too.

—Righ' lads, said Jimmy. —Business.

He had his notebook out.

—We have the guitar, bass, vocals, righ'? We need drums, sax, trumpet, keyboards. I threw an ad into Hot Press. Yis owe me forty-five pence, each.

—Ah, here!

—I'll take American Express. ——Now. D'yis remember your man, Jimmy Clifford?

—Tha' fuckin' drip!

—That's him, said Jimmy. —D'yis——

—He was JAMES Clifford.

—Wha'?

—James. He was never Jimmy. What's your name? James Clifford, sir.

—Righ', said Jimmy. —James Clifford then. He——

—Tha' bollix ratted on us, d'yis remember? said Derek. —When I stuck the compass up Tracie Quirk's hole. —They had me da up. Me ma——

—Derek——

—Wha'?

—Fuck up ——Annyway, said Jimmy, —his ma used to make him do piano lessons, remember. He was deadly at it. I met him on the DART there yesterday——

—No way, Jimmy, said Outspan.

—No, hang on, listen. He told me he got fucked ou' o' the folk mass choir. ——D'yis know why? For playin' The Chicken Song on the organ. In the fuckin' church.

—Jaysis!

They laughed. This didn't sound like the James Clifford they'd known and hated.

—Just before the mass, Jimmy continued. —There were

18

oul' ones an' oul' fellas walkin' up the middle, yeh know. An' he starts playin' The fuckin' Chicken Song.

—He sounds okay, said Deco.

No one disagreed with Deco.

—I'll go round to his gaff an' ask him tomorrow, will I?

Outspan and Derek looked at each other.

—Okay, said Outspan.

—So long as he doesn't start rattin' on us again, said Derek.
—When we're all gettin' our hole.

—He'll be gettin' his too sure, said Outspan.

—Oh, yeah, said Derek. —That's righ'.

—Does he still wear tha' jumper with the sheep on it?

—They weren't sheep, said Derek. —They were deers.

—They were fuckin' sheep, said Outspan.

—They weren't. ——I should know. I drew a moustache on one o' them.

—Is he workin'? Outspan asked.

—He's a student, said Jimmy.

—Oh, fuck.

—He'll be grand, said Jimmy. —He'll have plenty o' time to rehearse. ———Hang on.

Jimmy put a record on the deck. He'd brought the deck and the speakers up from the front room. He turned to them again.

—D'yis know James Brown, do yis? he asked.

—Was he in our class too? Outspan asked.

They laughed.

—The singer, said Jimmy. —Blackie. He's deadly. ——Did yis see The Blues Brothers?

Outspan and Derek had seen it. Deco hadn't.

—I seen the Furey Brothers, said Deco.

—Fuck off, said Jimmy. —D'yis remember the big woman singer in the coffee place? (They did.) —Tha' was Aretha Franklin. D'yis remember the blind guy in the music shop? (—Yeah.) Tha' was Ray Charles. D'yis remember the preacher in the church? (—No.) —Well, th' was James ———No? (—No.) —In the red cloak? ———The black fella? (—No.) —Yeh have to. ——Derek?

—I don't remember tha' bit.

———Well, tha' was James Brown, said Jimmy. —Hang
on ———Rocky IV. Livin' in America, remember? Tha' was
him.

—Tha' header!

—Yeah.

—Tha' was a shite film, said Derek.

—He was good but, said Jimmy.

—Ah, yeah.

—Annyway, listen to this. It's called Get Up, I Feel Like
Being a Sex Machine.

—Hold on there, said Derek. —We can't do tha'. Me ma
would fuckin' kill me.

—What're yeh on abou'? said Outspan.

—I Feel Like a fuckin' Sex Machine, Derek explained.
—She'd break me fuckin' head if I got up an' sang tha'.

—You won't be singin' it, son, said Deco. —I will. An',
pesonally speakin', I don't give a fuck wha' MY ma thinks.
———Let's hear it, Jimmy.

—We won't be doin' this one, Derek, said Jimmy. —I just
want yis to hear it, yeh know, just to get an idea, to get the
feel o' the thing. ———It's called funk.

—Funk off, said Deco.

Outspan hit him.

Jimmy let the needle down and sat on the back of his legs
between the speakers.

—I'm ready to get up and do my thang, said James Brown.

A chorus of men from the same part of the world as James
went: —YEAH.

—I want to, James continued, —to get into it, you know.
(—YEAH, said the lads in the studio with him.) —Like a,
like a sex machine, man (—YEAH YEAH, GO AHEAD.)
—movin', doin' it, you know. (—YEAH.) —Can I count it
all? (—YEAH YEAH YEAH, went the lads.) —One Two
Three Four.

Then the horns started, the same note repeated (—DUH
DUH DUH DUH DUH DUH DUH) seven times and then

James Brown began to sing. He sang like he spoke, a great voice that he seemed to be holding back, hanging onto because it was dangerous. The lads (in Jimmy's bedroom) smiled at each other. This was it.

—GET UP AH, sang James.

A guitar clicked, like a full stop.

—GET ON UP, someone else sang, no mean voice either.

Then the guitar again.

—GER RUP AH——

Guitar.

—GET ON UP——

—STAY ON THE SCENE, sang James.

—GET ON UP——

James had the good lines.

—LIKE A SEX MACHINE AH——

—GET ON UP——

The lads bounced gently on the bunks.

—YOU GOT TO HAVE THE FEELING———

SURE AS YOU'RE BORN AH———

GET IT TOGETHER——

RIGHT ON—

RIGHT ON———

GET UP AH, sang James.

—GET ON UP——

Then there was a piano break and at the end of it James went: —HUH. It was the best Huh they'd ever heard. Then the piano got going again.

—GER RUP AH——

—GET ON UP——

The guitar clicked away.

And the bass was busy too, padding along. You could actually make it out; notes. This worried Derek a bit. He'd chosen the bass because he'd thought there was nothing to it. There was something to this one. It was busier than all the other instruments.

The song went on. The lads bounced and grinned. Deco concentrated.

—Bobby, James Brown called. (Bobby must have been the man who kept singing GET ON UP.) —Bobby, said James. —Shall I take them to the bridge?

—Go ahead, said Bobby.

—Take 'em all to the bridge.

—Take them to the bridge, said Bobby.

—Shall I take them to the bridge? James asked.

—YEAH, the lads in the studio, and Outspan and Derek, answered.

Then the guitar changed course a bit and stayed that way. James shouted and huh-huhhed a while longer and then it faded out.

Jimmy got up and lifted the needle.

A roar arrived from downstairs.

—Turn down tha' fuckin' radio!

—It's the stereo, Jimmy roared at the floor.

—Don't get snotty with me, son. Just turn it down.

The lads were in stitches laughing, quietly.

—Stupid bollix, said Jimmy. —Wha' did yis think o' tha'?

—Brilliant.

—Fuckin' brilliant.

—Play another one, said Outspan.

—Okay, said Jimmy. —I think yis'll be playin' this one.

He put on Night Train for them. It was even more brilliant than Sex Machine.

—We'll change the words a bit to make it —more Dubliny, yeh know, Jimmy told them.

They were really excited now.

—Fuckin' deadly, said Derek. —I'm goin' to get a lend o' the odds for the bass.

—Good man.

—I'd better get a proper guitar, said Outspan. —An electric.

Jimmy played It's a Man's Man's Man's World.

—I'm goin' to get a really good one, said Outspan. —Really fuckin' good.

—Let's go, said Jimmy.

They were off to the Pub.

Deco stood up.

He growled: —ALL ABOARD——

THE NIGHT TRAIN.

On the way down the stairs they met Sharon coming up.

—Howyeh, Gorgeous, said Deco.

—Go an' shite, said Sharon.

* * *

Jimmy spent twenty minutes looking at his ad in Hot Press the next Thursday. He touched the print. (—J. Rabbitte.) He grinned.

Others must have been looking at it too because when he got home from work his mother told him that two young fellas had been looking for him.

—J. Rabbitte they said.

—That's me alrigh', said Jimmy.

—Who d'yeh think yeh are with your J.? Your name's Jimmy.

—It's for business reasons, ma, said Jimmy. —J. sounds better. Yeh never heard of a millionaire bein' called Jimmy.

* * *

Things were motoring.

James Clifford had said yes. Loads of people called looking for J. Rabbitte over the weekend. Jimmy was interested in two of them: a drummer, Billy Mooney from Raheny, and Dean Fay from Coolock who had a saxophone but admitted that he was only learning how to Make It Talk. There were more callers on Monday. Jimmy liked none of them. He took phone numbers and threw them in the bin.

He judged on one question: influences.

—Who're your influences?

—U2.

—Simple Minds.

—Led Zeppelin.

—No one really.

They were the most common answers. They failed.

—Jethro Tull an' Bachman Turner Overdrive.

Jimmy shut the door on that one without bothering to get the phone number. He didn't even open the door to three of them. A look out his parents' bedroom window at them was enough.

—Who're your influences? he'd asked Billy Mooney.

—Your man, Animal from The Muppets.

Dean Fay had said Clarence Clemons and the guy from Madness. He didn't have the sax long. His uncle had given it to him because he couldn't play it any more himself because one of his lungs had collapsed.

Jimmy was up in his room on Tuesday night putting clean socks on when Jimmy Sr., the da, came in.

—Come 'ere, you, said Jimmy Sr. —Are you sellin' drugs or somethin'?

—I AM NOT, said Jimmy.

—Then why are all these cunts knockin' at the door?

—I'm auditionin'.

—You're wha'?

—Aud-ish-un-in. We're formin' a group. ——A band.

—You?

—Yeah.

Jimmy Sr. laughed.

—Dickie fuckin' Rock.

He started to leave but turned at the door.

—There's a little fucker on a scooter lookin' for yeh downstairs.

When Jimmy got down to the door he saw that his da had been right. It was a little fucker and he had a scooter, a wreck of a yoke. He was leaning on it.

—Yeah? said Jimmy.

—God bless you, Brother J. Rabbitte. In answer to your Hot Press query, yes, I have got soul.

—Wha'?

—And I'm not a redneck or a southsider.

—You're the same age as me fuckin' da!

—You may speak the truth, Brother Rabbitte, but I'm

24

sixteen years younger than B. B. King. And six years younger than James Brown.

—You've heard o' James Brown—

—I jammed with the man.

—FUCK OFF!

—Leicester Mecca, '72. Brother James called me on for Superbad. I couldn't give it my best though because I had a bit of a head cold.

He patted the scooter.

—I'd ridden from Holyhead in the rain. I didn't have a helmet. I didn't have anything. Just Gina.

—Who's she?

—My trumpet. My mentor always advised me to imagine that the mouthpiece was a woman's nipple. I chose Gina Lollabrigida's. A fine woman.

He stared at Jimmy. There wasn't a trace of a grin on him.

—I'm sure you've noticed already, Brother Rabbitte, it was wild advice because if it had been Gina Lollabrigida's nipple I'd have been sucking it, not blowing into it.

Jimmy didn't know what was going on here. He tried to take control of the interview.

—What's your name, pal?

—Joseph Fagan, said the man.

He was bald too, now that he'd taken his helmet off.

—Joey The Lips Fagan, he said.

—Eh ————Come again?

—Joey The Lips Fagan.

—An' I'm Jimmy The Bollix Rabbitte.

—I earned my name for my horn playing, Brother Rabbitte. How did you earn yours?

Jimmy pointed a finger at him.

—Don't get snotty with me, son.

—I get snotty with no man.

—Better bleedin' not. ————An' are YOU tryin' to tell me that yeh played with James Brown?

—Among others, Brother.

—Like?

—Have we all night? —————Screaming Jay Hawkins, Big Joe Turner, Martha Reeves, Sam Cooke, poor Sam, Sinatra. ——Never again. The man is a thug. ——Otis Redding, Lord rest his sweet soul, Joe Tex, The Four Tops, Stevie Wonder, Little Stevie then. He was only eleven. A pup. ——More?

—Yeah.

—Let's see. ——Wilson Pickett, Jackie Wilson, Sam an' Dave, Eddie Floyd, Booker T. and the MGs of course, Joe Tex.

—Yeh said him already.

—Twice. Em ——an unusual one, Jimi Hendrix. Although, to be honest with you, I don't think poor Jimi knew I was there. ——Bobby Bland, Isaac Hayes, Al Green.

—You've been fuckin' busy.

—You speak the truth, Brother Rabbitte. And there's more. Blood, Sweat and Tears. The Tremeloes. I know, I know, I have repented. ——Peter Tosh, George Jones, The Stranglers. Nice enough dudes under the leather. I turned up for The Stones on the wrong day. The day after. They were gone.

—Yeh stupid sap, yeh.

—I know. ——Will that do? ——Oh yeah, and The Beatles.

—The Beatles, said Jimmy.

—Money for jam, said Joey The Lips. —ALL YOU NEED IS LOVE——DOO DUH DOO DUH DOO.

—Was tha' you?

—Indeed it was me, Brother. Five pounds, three and sixpence. A fair whack in those days. ——I couldn't stand Paul, couldn't take to him. I was up on the roof for Let It Be. But I stayed well back. I'm not a very photogenic Brother. I take a shocking photograph.

By now Jimmy was believing Joey The Lips. A question had to be asked.

—Wha' do yeh want to join US for?

—I'm tired of the road, said Joey The Lips. —I've come home. And my mammy isn't very well.

Jimmy knew he was being stupid, and cheeky, asking the next question but he asked it anyway.

—Who're your influences?

—I admit to no influences but God My Lord, said Joey The Lips. —The Lord blows my trumpet.

—Does he? said Jimmy.

—And the walls come tumbling down.

Joey The Lips explained: —I went on the road nine, no ten maybe eleven years ago with a gospel outfit, The Alabama Angels, featuring Sister Julie Bob Mahony. They brought me to God. I repented, I can tell you that for nothing, Brother Rabbitte. I used to be one mother of a sinner. A terrible man. But The Lord's not a hard man, you know. He doesn't kick up at the odd drink or a swear word now and again. Even a Sister, if you treat her with proper respect.

Jimmy had nothing to say yet. Joey The Lips carried on.

—The Lord told me to come home. Ed Winchell, a Baptist reverend on Lenox Avenue in Harlem, told me. But The Lord told him to tell me. He said he was watching something on TV about the feuding Brothers in Northern Ireland and The Lord told the Reverend Ed that the Irish Brothers had no soul, that they needed some soul. And pretty fucking quick! Ed told me to go back to Ireland and blow some soul into the Irish Brothers. The Brothers wouldn't be shooting the asses off each other if they had soul. So said Ed. I'm not a Baptist myself but I've a lot of time for the Reverend Ed.

Jimmy still had nothing to say.

—Am I in? Joey The Lips asked.

—Fuck, yes, said Jimmy. —Fuckin' sure you're in. ——Are yeh on the phone?

—Jesus on the mainline, said Joey The Lips, —tell him what you want. 463221.

Jimmy took it down.

—I'll be in touch with yeh. Definitely. The lads'll have to see ——to meet yeh.

Joey The Lips threw the leg over his scooter. His helmet was back on.

—All God's chillun got wings, he said, and he took off out the gate, over the path and down the road.

Jimmy was delighted. He knew now that everything was going to be alright. The Commitments were going to be. They had Joey The Lips Fagan. And that man had enough soul for all of them. He had God too.

* * *

The Commitments used the garage of Joey The Lips' mother's house for meeting and rehearsing. The house was a big one on the Howth Road near Killester and the garage was big too.

When they all got there the first time Joey The Lips had it filled with chairs and rugs. They sat back while Joey The Lips counted them for tea-bag purposes.

—Strong tea, Brothers? he asked.

There wasn't an answer so he threw fifteen bags into the pot.

They were all there, their first time together.

Jimmy Rabbitte; manager.

Outspan Foster; guitar.

Deco Cuffe; vocals.

Derek Scully; bass. (He'd bought one, fourth-hand —he thought it was second —for £60. The amp and cabinet were £40 extra and sounded it. He'd made a deal with his ma. She'd paid for the bass and gear and he had to pay the video rental for the next eighteen months. There were no flies on Derek's ma.)

James Clifford; piano.

Billy Mooney; drums.

Dean Fay; sax.

And Joey The Lips.

This was the first time they'd seen Joey The Lips, and they weren't happy. He looked like a da, their da; small, bald, fat, making tea. He was wearing slippers, checked fluffy ones. One thing made him different though. He was wearing a Jesse Jackson campaign T-shirt.

—Is this the entire band here, Brother Jimmy? Joey The Lips asked.

He was handing out mugs.

—This is it, said Jimmy.

—And what have you been listening to? ——You said my man, James Brown, didn't you?

—Yeah, said Jimmy. —We'll be doin' Night Train.

—I like what I hear. ——And?

—Eddie Floyd. Knock On Wood, yeh know.

—Ummm.

—Percy Sledge, said Jimmy.

—When a Man Loves a Woman?

—Yeah.

—Lovely.

—That's all so far really, said Jimmy.

—A good start, said Joey The Lips. —I have some Jaffa Cakes here, Brothers. Soul food.

When they heard that they started to tolerate him. When he took out his trumpet and played Moon River for them they loved him. Jimmy had been annoying them, going on and on about this genius, but now they knew. They were The Commitments.

When they'd finished congratulating Joey The Lips (—Fair play to yeh, Mr Fagan.

—Yeah, tha' was deadly.

—The name's Joey, Brothers.) Jimmy made an announcement.

—I've some backin' vocalists lined up.

—Who?

—Three young ones.

—Young ones. ——Rapid!

—Are they foxy ladies, Jimmy? Joey The Lips asked.

They all stared at him.

—Fuckin' sure they are, said Jimmy.

—Who are they? said Outspan.

—Remember Tracie Quirk?

—She's fuckin' married!

—Not her, said Jimmy. —Her sister.

—Wha' one? Derek asked.

—Imelda.

—Wha' one's she? Hang on —————Oh Jaysis, HER! Fuckin' great.

—Which one is it? said Outspan.

—You know her, said Derek. —Yeh fuckin' do. Small, with lovely tits. Yeh know. Black hair, long. Over her eyes.

—Her!

—She's fuckin' gorgeous, said Derek. —Wha' age is she?

—Eighteen.

—She lives beside you, James.

—So I believe, said James.

—Is she anny good at the oul' singin'?

—I haven't a clue, said Jimmy.

—Who're the others? Deco asked.

—Two of her mates.

—That's very good management, Brother, said Joey The Lips. —Will they be dressed in black?

—Yeah —————I ——I think so.

—Good good.

* * *

The time flew in.

Those Commitments still learning their instruments improved. The ones ready were patient. There was no group rehearsing. Jimmy wouldn't allow it. They all had to be ready first.

Derek's fingers were raw. He liked to wallop the strings. That was the way, Jimmy said. Derek found out that you could get away with concentrating on one string. You made up for the lack of variety by thumping the string more often and by taking your hand off the neck and putting it back a lot to make it look like you were involved in complicated work. He carried his bass low, Stranglers style, nearly down at his knees. He didn't have to bend his arms.

Outspan improved too. There'd be no guitar solos, Jimmy

said, and that suited Outspan. Jimmy gave him Motown compilations to listen to. Chord changes were scarce. It was just a matter of making yourself loose enough to follow the rhythm.

Outspan was very embarrassed up in his bedroom trying to strum along to the Motown time. But once he stopped looking at himself in the mirror he loosened up. He chugged along with the records, especially The Supremes. Under the energy it was simple.

Then he started using the mirror again. He was thrilled. His plectrum hand danced. Sometimes it was a blur. The hand looked great. The arm hardly budged. The wrist was in charge. He held his guitar high against his chest.

He saved money when he could. He wasn't working but on Saturday mornings he went from door to door in Barrytown selling the frozen chickens that his cousin always managed to rob from H. Williams on Friday nights. That gave him at least a tenner a week to put away. As well as that, he gave the man next door, Mr Hurley, a hand with his video business. This involved keeping about two hundred tapes under his bed and driving around the estate with Mr Hurley for a few hours a couple of times a week, handing out the tapes while Mr Hurley took in the money. Then, out of the blue, his ma gave him most of the month's mickey money. He cried.

He had £145 now. That got him a third-hand electric guitar (the make long forgotten) and a bad amp and cabinet. After that they couldn't get him away from the mirror.

Deco's mother worried about him. He'd be eating his breakfast and then he'd yell something like Good God Y'Awl or Take It To The Bridge Now. Deco was on a strict soul diet: James Brown, Otis Redding, Smokey Robinson and Marvin Gaye. James for the growls, Otis for the moans, Smokey for the whines and Marvin for the whole lot put together, Jimmy said.

Deco sang, shouted, growled, moaned, whined along to the tapes Jimmy had given him. He bollixed his throat every night. It felt like it was being cut from the inside by the time he got to the end of Tracks of My Tears. He liked I Heard It through the Grapevine because the women singing I HEARD IT THROUGH THE GRAPEVINE NOT MUCH LONGER WOULD YOU BE MY BABY gave him a short chance to wet the stinging in his throat. Copying Marvin Gaye meant making his throat sore and then rubbing it in.

He kept going though. He was getting better. It was getting easier. He could feel his throat stretching. It was staying wet longer. He was getting air from further down. He put on Otis Redding and sang My Girl with him when he needed a rest. He finished every session with James Brown. Then he'd lie on the bed till the snot stopped running. He couldn't close his eyes because he'd spin. Deco was taking this thing very seriously.

All his rehearsing was done standing up in front of the wardrobe mirror. He was to look at himself singing, Jimmy said. He was to pretend he had a microphone. At first he jumped around but it was too knackering and it frightened his mother. Jimmy showed him a short video of James Brown doing Papa's Got a Brand New Bag. He couldn't copy James' one-footed shuffle on the bedroom carpet so he practised on the lino in the kitchen when everyone had gone to bed.

He saw the way James Brown dropped to his knees. He didn't hitch his trousers and kneel. He dropped. Deco tried it. He growled SOMETIMES I FEEL SO GOOD I WANNA JUMP BACK AND KISS MYSELF, aimed his knees at the floor and followed them there.

He didn't get up again for a while. He thought he'd knee-capped himself. Jimmy told him that James Brown's trousers were often soaked in blood when he came off-stage. Deco was fucked if his would be.

There was nothing you could teach James Clifford about playing the piano. Jimmy had him listening to Little Richard. He got James to thump the keys with his elbows, fists, heels. James was a third-year medical student so he was able to tell Jimmy the exact, right word for whatever part of his body he was hitting the piano with. He was even able to explain the damage he was doing to himself. He drew the line at the forehead. Jimmy couldn't persuade him to give the piano the odd smack with his forehead. There was too much at stake there. Besides, he wore glasses.

Joey The Lips helped Dean Fay.

—My man, that reed there is a nice lady's nipple.

For days Dean blushed when he wet the reed and let his lips close on it.

—Make it a particular lady, someone real.

Dean chose a young one from across the road. She was in the same class as his brother, third year, and she was always coming over to borrow his books or scab his homework. It didn't work though. Dean couldn't go through with it. She was too real. So the saxophone reed became one of Madonna's nipples and Dean's playing began to get somewhere.

Joey The Lips was a terrific teacher, very patient. He had to be. Even Joey The Lips' mother, who was completely deaf, could sense Dean's playing from the other side of the house.

After three weeks he could go three notes without stopping and he could hold the short notes. Long ones went all over the place. Joey The Lips played alongside him, like a driving instructor. He only shouted once and that was really a cry of fright and pain caused by Dean backing into him while Joey The Lips still had his trumpet in his mouth.

Billy Mooney blammed away at his drums. His father was dead and his brothers were much younger than him so there was no one in the house to tell him to shut the fuck up.

Jimmy told him not to bother too much with cymbals and to use the butts of the sticks as well as the tips. What he was after was a steady, uncomplicated beat: —a thumping back-beat, Jimmy called it. That suited Billy. He'd have been happy with a bin lid and a hammer. And that was what he used when he played along to Dancing in the Streets. Not a bin lid exactly; a tin tray, with a racehorse on it. The horse was worn off after two days.

The three backing vocalists, The Commitmentettes, listened to The Supremes, Martha and the Vandellas, The Ronettes,

The Crystals and The Shangri-las. The Commitmentettes were Imelda Quirk and her friends Natalie Murphy and Bernie McLoughlin.

—How yis move, yeh know ——— is more important than how yis sing, Jimmy told them.

—You're a dirty bastard, you are.

Imelda, Natalie and Bernie could sing though. They'd been in the folk mass choir when they were in school but that, they knew now, hadn't really been singing. Jimmy said that real music was sex. They called him a dirty bastard but they were starting to agree with him. And there wasn't much sex in Morning Has Broken or The Lord Is My Shepherd.

Now they were singing along to Stop in the Name of Love and Walking in the Rain and they were enjoying it.

Joined together their voices sounded good, they thought. Jimmy taped them. They were scarlet. They sounded terrible.

—Yis're usin' your noses instead of your mouths, said Jimmy.

—Fuck off slaggin', said Imelda.

—Yis are, I'm tellin' yeh. An' yis shouldn't be usin' your ordin'y accents either. It's Walking in the Rain, not Walkin' In De Rayen.

—Snobby!

They taped themselves and listened. They got better, clearer, sweeter. Natalie could roar and squeal too. They took down the words and sang by themselves without the records. They only did this though when one of them had a free house.

They moved together, looking down, making sure their feet were going the right way. Soon they didn't have to look down. They wiggled their arses at the dressing-table mirror and burst out laughing. But they kept doing it.

* * *

Jimmy got them all together regularly, about twice a week, and made them report. There, always in Joey The Lips' mother's garage, he'd give them a talk. They all enjoyed Jimmy's lectures. So did Jimmy.

They weren't really lectures; more workshops.

—Soul is a double-edged sword, lads, he told them once.

Joey The Lips nodded.

—One edge is escapism.

—What's tha'?

—Fun. ——Gettin' away from it all. Lettin' yourself go. ——Know wha' I mean?

—Gerrup!

Jimmy continued: —An' what's the best type of escapism, Imelda?

—I know wha' you're goin' to say.

—I'd've said that a bracing walk along the sea front was a very acceptable form of escapism, said James Clifford.

They laughed.

—Followed by? Jimmy asked.

—Depends which way you were havin' your bracing walk.

—Why?

—Well, if you were goin' in the Dollymount direction you could go all the way and have a ride in the dunes. ——That's wha' you're on abou', isn't it? ——As usual.

—That's righ', said Jimmy. —Soul is a good time.

—There's nothin' good abou' gettin' sand on your knob, said Outspan.

They laughed.

—The rhythm o' soul is the rhythm o' ridin', said Jimmy. —The rhythm o' ridin' is the rhythm o' soul.

—You're a dirty-minded bastard, said Natalie.

—There's more to life than gettin' your hole, Jimmy, said Derek.

—Here here.

—Listen. There's nothing dirty abou' it, Nat'lie, said Jimmy. —As a matter o'fact it's very clean an' healthy.

—What's healthy abou' gettin' sand on your knob?

—You just like talkin' dirty, said Natalie.

—Nat'lie ——Nat'lie ——Nat'lie, said Jimmy. —It depresses me to hear a modern young one talkin' like tha'.

—Dirty talk is dirty talk, said Natalie.

—Here here, said Billy Mooney. —Thank God.

—Soul is sex, Jimmy summarized.

—Well done, Jimmy, said Deco.

—Imelda, said Jimmy. —You're a woman o' the world.

—Don't answer him, 'melda, said Bernie.

Jimmy went on. —You've had sexual intercert, haven't yeh?

—Good Jaysis! Rabbitte!

—O' course she has, a good-lookin' girl like tha'.

—Don't answer him.

But Imelda wanted to answer.

—Well, yeah ——I have, yeah. ——So wha'?

There were cheers and blushes.

—Was it one o' them multiple ones, 'melda? Outspan asked.
—I seen a yoke abou' them on Channel 4. They sounded
deadly.

Derek looked at Imelda.

—Are yeh serious?

He was disappointed in Imelda.

Deco tapped Imelda's shoulder.

—We could make beautiful music, Honey.

—I'd bite your bollix off yeh if yeh went near me, yeh
spotty fuck, yeh.

There were cheers.

Imelda ducked her shoulder away from Deco's fingers.

—I might enjoy tha', said Deco.

—I'd make ear-rings ou' o' them, said Imelda.

—You're as bad as they are, 'melda, said Bernie.

—Ah, fuck off, Bernie, will yeh.

—I thought we said slaggin' complexions was barred, said
Jimmy. —Apologise.

—There's no need.

—There is.

———Sorry.

—That's okay.

—Spotty.

—Ah here!

Deco grabbed Imelda's shoulders. Bernie was up quick and grabbed his ears.

—Get your hands off o' her, YOU.

—As a glasses wearer, said James, —I'd advise you to carry ou' Bernie's instructions. Yeh might need glasses yourself some day and a workin' set of ears will come in handy.

—That's a doctor gave yeh tha' advice, remember.

Deco took the advice. Bernie gave him his ears back. Imelda blew him a kiss and gave him the fingers.

—Annyway, Imelda, said Jimmy. —Did yeh enjoy it?

—It was alrigh', said Imelda.

More cheers and blushes.

—This lady is the queen of soul, said Joey The Lips.

—Wha' 're you the queen of? Imelda said back.

—Then you agree with us, Jimmy asked Imelda.

—It's oney music, said Imelda.

—No way, 'melda. Soul isn't only music. Soul ——

—That's alrigh' for the blackies, Jimmy. —They've got bigger gooters than us.

—Speak for yourself, pal.

—Go on, Jimmy. ——At least we know tha' Imelda does the business.

—Fuck off, you, said Imelda, but she grinned.

Everyone grinned.

—Yeh said somethin' about a double-edged sword, said James.

—I s'pose the other side is sex too, said Derek.

—Arse bandit country if it's the other side, said Outspan.

—I'm goin' home if it is, said Dean.

—Brothers, Sisters, said Joey The Lips. —Let Brother Jimmy speak. Tell us about the other side of the sword, Jimmy.

They were quiet.

—The first side is sex, righ', said Jimmy. —An' the second one is ————REVOLUTION!

Cheers and clenched fists.

Jimmy went on.

37

—Soul is the politics o' the people.

—Yeeoow!

—Righ' on, Jimmy.

—Our people. ——Soul is the rhythm o' sex. It's the rhythm o' the factory too. The workin' man's rhythm. Sex an' factory.

—Not the factory I'm in, said Natalie. —There isn't much rhythm in guttin' fish.

She was pleased with the laughter.

—Musical mackerel, wha'.

——Harmonious herring.

—Johnny Ray, said Dean, and then he roared: —JOHNNY RAY!

—Okay —Take it easy, said Jimmy.

—Cuntish cod, said Deco.

——Politics. ——Party politics, said Jimmy, —means nothin' to the workin' people. Nothin'. ——Fuck all. Soul is the politics o' the people.

—Start talkin' abou' ridin' again, Jimmy. You're gettin' borin'.

—Politics ——ridin', said Jimmy. —It's the same thing.

—Brother Jimmy speaks the truth, said Joey The Lips.

—He speaks through his hole.

—Soul is dynamic. (—So are you.) —It can't be caught. It can't be chained. They could chain the nigger slaves but they couldn't chain their soul.

—Their souls didn't pick the fuckin' cotton though. Did they now?

—Good thinkin'.

—Fuck off a minute. ——Soul is the rhythm o' the people, Jimmy said again. —The Labour Party doesn't have soul. Fianna fuckin' Fail doesn't have soul. The Workers' Party ain't got soul. The Irish people ——no. ——The Dublin people —fuck the rest o' them. ——The people o' Dublin, our people, remember need soul. We've got soul.

—Fuckin' righ' we have.

—The Commitments, lads. We've got it. ——Soul. God told the Reverend Ed ——
—Ah, fuck off.

* * *

They loved Jimmy's lectures. His policy announcements were good too.
—What're they? Derek asked after Jimmy had made one of these announcements.
—Monkey suits, said Jimmy.
—No way, Rabbitte.
—Yes way.
—No fuckin' way, Jim. No way.
—I had one o' them for me mot's debs, said Billy. —It was fuckin' thick. The sleeves were too long, the trunzers were too fuckin' short, there was a stupid fuckin' stripe down ———
—I puked on mine at our debs, remember? said Outspan.
—Some of it got on mine too, Derek reminded him.
—Oh, for fuck sake! said Dean. —I'm after rememberin'. ———I forgot to bring mine back. It's under me bed.
—When was your debs? Bernie asked him.
—Two years ago, said Dean.
They started laughing.
—Yeh must owe them hundreds, said Outspan.
—I'd better leave it there so.
—Jimmy, said James. —Are yeh seriously expectin' us to deck ourselves out in monkey suits?
—Yeah. ———Why not?
—Yeh can go an' shite, said Billy.
—Well said.
—Yis have to look good, said Jimmy. —Neat ——Dignified.
—What's fuckin' dignified abou' dressin' up like a jaysis penguin? Outspan asked.
—I'd be scarleh, said Derek.
Deco said nothing. He liked the idea.
—Brothers, Sisters, said Joey The Lips. —We know that

soul is sex. And soul is revolution, yes? So now soul is
——Dignity.

—I don't understand tha', said Dean.

—Soul is lifting yourself up, soul is dusting yourself off, soul is ——

—What's he fuckin' on abou'?

—Just this, Brother. ——Soul is dignity. ——Dignity, soul. Dignity is respect. ——Self respect. ——Dignity is pride. Dignity, confidence. Dignity, assertion. (Joey The Lips' upstretched index finger moved in time to his argument. They were glued to it.) —Dignity, integrity. Dignity, elegance. ——Dignity, style.

The finger stopped.

—Brothers and Sisters. ——Dignity, dress. ——Dress suits.

—Dignity fuck dignity off dignity Joey.

—Dignity slippers, dignity cardigan.

—Ah, leave Joey alone, said Natalie.

Joey The Lips laughed with them.

Then Jimmy handed out photocopies of a picture of Marvin Gaye, in a monkey suit. That silenced them for a while.

——He's gorgeous, isn't he? said Imelda.

—Yeah, said Natalie.

Joey the Lips looked up from his copy.

—He's up there watching, Brothers.

—Now, said Jimmy when they all had one. —What's wrong with tha'?

—Nothin'.

—He looks grand, doesn't he?

——Yeah.

—We'll get good ones. Fitted. ——Okay?

Outspan looked up.

—Okay.

* * *

One of the best was the night Jimmy gave them their stage names.

40

—What's wrong with our ordin'y names? Dean wanted to know.

—Nothin', Dean, said Jimmy. —Nothin' at all.

—Well then?

—Look, said Jimmy. —Take Joey. He's Joey Fagan, righ'? ——Plain, ordin'ry Joey Fagan. An ordin'ry little bollix.

—That's me, Brother, said Joey The Lips. —I'm the Jesus of Ordinary.

—But when Joey goes on-stage he's Joey The Lips Fagan.

—So?

—He's not ordin'y up there. He's special. ——He needs a new name.

—Soul is dignity, Joey The Lips reminded them.

—What's dignified abou' a stupid name like The fuckin' Lips?

—I bleed, said Joey The Lips.

—Sorry, Joey. Nothin' personal.

Joey the Lips smiled.

—It's part o' the image, said Jimmy. —Like James Brown is the Godfather of Soul.

—He's still just James Brown though.

—Sometimes he's James Mr Please Please Please Brown.

——Is he? said Outspan. —Sounds thick though, doesn't it?

—Ours won't, said Jimmy.

He took out his notebook.

—I've been doin' some thinkin' abou' it.

—Oh fuck!

—Listen. ——Okay, we already have Joey The Lips Fagan, righ'. Now ——James, you'll be James The Soul Surgeon Clifford.

There were cheers and a short burst of clapping.

—Is tha' okay? Jimmy asked.

—I like it, said James.

He liked it alright. He was delighted.

—The Soul Surgeon performs transplants on the old piano, he said.

—That's it, said Jimmy. —That's the type o' thing. Every-one in the group becomes a personality.

—Go on, Jimmy.

They were getting excited.

—Derek.

—Yes, Jimmy?

—You're Derek The Meatman Scully.

They laughed.

—Wha' the fuck's tha' abou'? Derek asked.

He was disappointed.

—Are you fuckin' slaggin' me?

—You're a butcher, said Jimmy.

—I know I'm a fuckin' butcher.

—Yeh play the bass like a butcher, said Jimmy.

—Fuckin' thanks!

—It's a compliment, it's a compliment. ——Yeh wield the axe, ——know wha' I mean?

—I'll wield your bollix if yeh don't think of a better name.

—Hang on. —You'll like this. ———Over in America, righ', d'yeh know wha' meat is?

—The same as it is here.

—'cept there's more of it.

—No, listen, said Jimmy. —Meat is slang for your langer.

There were cheers and screams.

—That's fuckin' disgustin', said Natalie.

—Hang on a minute, said Derek. —Is Meatman the Ameri-can way o' sayin' Langerman?

—Yeah.

—Why not call him Langerman then?

—Or Dickhead, said Deco.

—Fuck off, you, said Derek.

He wasn't happy at all.

—Listen, he said.

This wasn't going to be easy, especially with the girls there.

—There's nothin' special abou' my langer.

—YEEOOW, DEREK!

—Gerrup, Derek, yeh boy yeh!

42

—A bit of quiet please, Brothers, said Joey The Lips.

—It's the image, said Jimmy. ———Annyway, nobody'll know wha' the name stands for till we break it in the States.

—It's a good name, said Joey The Lips. —Every band needs its Meatman.

———I don't know, said Derek. —Me ma would kill me if she knew I was called after me gooter.

—She won't know.

—I'll tell her, said Outspan.

—Fuck off.

—Righ', said Jimmy. —Next ———Deco.

—Can I be Meatman too, Jimmy?

—No, said Jimmy. —You're Declan Blanketman Cuffe.

—That's a rapid name, said Outspan.

—Politics an' sex, said Jimmy. —Wha' d'yeh think, Deco?

—Yeah, said Deco.

—Billy.

—Howyeh.

—Billy The Animal Mooney.

—Ah deadly! Animal. ———Thanks, Jimmy.

—No sweat. ———Okay, Dean next. ———Dean.

Dean sat up.

—You're Dean Good Times Fay.

Cheers.

—That's grand, said Dean.

—Wha' abou' us? said Imelda.

—Hang on, said Jimmy. ———Outspan, we can't call yeh Outspan.

—Why not?

—It's racialist.

—WHA'!

—It's racialist. ———South African oranges.

—That's fuckin' crazy, Jimmy, said Billy.

—It's me jaysis name, said Outspan.

—Not your real name.

—Even me oul' one calls me Outspan.

—No she doesn't, said Derek.

43

—Fuck off you or I'll trounce yeh.

—I saw a thing on telly, said Dean. —It said they make black prisoners, righ', pick the oranges.

—I don't make annyone pick fuckin' oranges! said Outspan.

—Soul has no skin colour, Brothers and Sisters, said Joey The Lips.

—I don't even like oranges, said Outspan. ———'cept them satsumas. ——They're nice.

—Does soul eat oranges, Joey?

—Leave Joey alone, Fuckface, said Jimmy. —Listen, ——your name's Liam, righ'?

—I fuckin' know tha', thanks, said Outspan.

—It's not a very soulful name.

—Aah ——fuckin' hell! I can't even have me real name now.

—Shut up a minute. ——What's your second name?

—Wha' d'yeh mean, like?

—I'm James Anthony Rabbitte. What're you?

—Liam, said Outspan.

He went scarlet.

——————Terence Foster.

—Howyeh, Terence, Imelda waved across at him.

He was going to tell her to fuck off but he didn't because he fancied her.

(Along with Jimmy, Derek, Deco, Billy, James and Dean, Outspan was in love with Imelda.)

—Righ', said Jimmy. —You are L. Terence Foster. —Listen to it, said Jimmy. —It sounds great. L. Terence Foster, L. Terence Foster. Doesn't it sound great?

—It sounds deadly, said Derek. —Better than bleedin' Meatman.

—Swap yeh, said Outspan.

—No way, said Jimmy.

—Wha' abou' us? said Bernie.

—Righ', said Jimmy. —Are yis ready, girls? ——Yis are ——Sonya, Sofia, an' Tanya, The Commitmentettes.

The girls screamed and then laughed.

44

—I bags Sonya, said Imelda.
—I'm Sofia then, said Natalie. —Sofia Loren.
—With a head like tha'?
—Fuck yourself, you.
—You've the arse for it anyway, Nat'lie.
—Fuck yourself.
—Wha' abou' me? said Bernie.
—She'd forgotten the last name.
—You're Fido, said Deco.
—Fuck yourself, said Natalie.
—Fuck yourself, Deco said back at her.
Natalie spat at his face.
—Here! Stop tha', said Jimmy.
—Hope yeh catch AIDS off it, said Natalie.
Deco let it go because he was in love with Natalie too.
—You're Tanya, Bernie, said Jimmy.
—Why can't I be Bernie?
—It's the image, Bernie.
—You'll always be Bernie to us, Bernie, said James.
—I must say, Jimmy, said Joey The Lips. —You've got a
great managerial head on your shoulders.
—Thanks, Joey, said Jimmy.
—Brothers, Sisters, said Joey The Lips. —Would you please
put your hands together to show your appreciation to Brother
James Anthony Rabbitte.
They clapped, all of them.

*　*　*

Then, after months, they were ready to rehearse.
Joey The Lips got rid of some of the chairs to make room in
the garage. They had the amps, speakers and mikes in position,
and Joey The Lips' mother's upright piano.
They stood around feeling excited but stupid, embarrassed,
afraid.
Joey The Lips went around listening to the instruments. He
frowned and turned knobs, listened again, nodded and went

on to the next instrument. He impressed the others. Here was a man who knew what he was doing.

Jimmy was lost here. He hadn't a clue how to get the rehearsal started.

Joey the Lips took over.

—Brothers, Sisters. I thank The Lord Jesus for today.

—Fuck off, Joey.

—We'll start with an easy one. Have yaw'l ——

—Yaw'l! For fuck sake!

—Have YOU ALL been listening to What Becomes of the Broken Hearted?

—We sure have, Massa Joey sir boss.

—Whooee!

Joey The Lips played the tape for them. They listened, frightened, to Jimmy Ruffin. They could never do that. Only Deco thought he could do better.

Joey The Lips turned the tape off.

—Alright, Sisters, let's have the Ooh ooh oohs at the beginning.

—God, I'm scarleh, said Imelda.

—Brother James, would you play the girls in please?

—Certainly, Joseph, said James.

Four times James tried to lead the girls but they couldn't follow.

—They're all lookin' at us, said Bernie.

—Hurry up, for Jaysis sake, said Deco.

—No, Declan, said Joey The Lips. —We're in no rush. Rome wasn't built in a day.

—Dublin was though, wha'.

—A fuckin' hour.

This time the girls followed James.

—UUH — UUH — UUH

They were shaking. They all heard the shaking in their voices but they didn't look at anybody and kept going.

—UUH — UUH — UUH —

　　　　　　　　　UUH — UUH — UUH

—That was terrific, ladies, said Joey The Lips. —The Commitmentettes.

—Well done, girls, said Jimmy.

—Right now, said Joey The Lips. —Let's hear The Blanketman.

Deco had the words on a sheet of paper. James donk donk donked, the girls UUH UUH UUHed and then Deco held the mike in his hand and sang. And sang well.

—AS I WALK THIS LAND
  OF BROKE —
            EN DREE — EE — EAMS ———

Deco lifted his voice for single words, then brought it back down again. He stopped before a word (—THIS) and thumped it. He slapped his thigh and tapped the heel of his right foot.

—I HAVE VISIONS O' MANY THING —
                                        INGS—

—Sisters, Joey The Lips shouted.

—Wha'? said Natalie.

—I want you to come in there, okay?

—How?

—Joey The Lips sang: —OF MANY THINGINGS. After Declan sings it, okay? ——Right, Brother Deco. ——I have visions.

—I HAVE VISIONS O' MANY THING —
                                      INGS —

—Sisters!

—OF MANY THINGINGS, sang the girls.

—Good good.

—BUT ——HAPPINESS IS JUST AN ILLU —
                                    SHUN —

—Sisters!

—JUST AN ILLUSION —

—Good.

—FILLED WITH SADNESS AN' CON —
                              FEU —
                              SHUN —

—Go with him, girls.

—WHA' BECOMES O' THE BROKE —

                      EN HEARTED —

WHO —

   HAVE LOVES THA' ARE NOW DE-

                    PAR — TED ——

I KNOW I'VE GOT TO FIND —

SOME KIND O' PEACE O' MIND ——

BAY —

      BEEE —

—Right, girls.

—UUH — EEE — UUH.

—Wonderful, Joey The Lips shouted.

He meant it. It had been woeful, but it was a start. Joey The Lips believed in starts. Once you had the start the rest was inevitable. The Lord made sure of that.

It was three in the morning when they stopped. They concentrated on the same song.

There were problems. Joey The Lips spent half the night twiddling knobs and yelling at the rest to get away from the amps. There were shrieks and groans and wails from the speakers.

Billy kept drumming too fast. At half-twelve they found out he'd been messing. Jimmy stepped in and told him off in no uncertain terms. (—You're a cunt, Mooney.) Derek was lost for a while but Joey The Lips told him just to do what James was doing. That was grand, just the same note three times, one and then the other two together, then the same again, and again right through.

The girls were suffering by two o'clock. Joey The Lips had to tune Outspan's guitar for him.

Jimmy had to take Deco aside and tell him to be patient.

—Give them a while, said Jimmy. —They're not ALL naturals.

—I'll try, Jimmy, said Deco. —It's just——I'm ready, know wha' I mean?

Jimmy nodded.

48

—There's somethin' in me tryin' to get ou', know wha' I mean?

—I know, said Jimmy. —Take it easy though, okay?

—Okay.

—Fuckin' eejit, said Jimmy. (To himself.)

—Brothers and Sisters, said Joey The Lips at about three. —We have done the good work tonight. Would you all form a circle here, please? You too, Jimmy.

They were too tired to object. They made a circle and, without being told to, held hands.

—Good, said Joey The Lips. —Now drop hands.

They did this.

—Turn right.

They did this too. They were still a circle. Each of them was looking at a back. Joey The Lips was in the circle too. He lifted both his hands.

—Now, Brothers and Sisters, we pat ourselves on the back for a job well done.

They laughed as they patted.

* * *

It was the next rehearsal.

—Okay, James, my man, said Joey The Lips. —Take us there.

James looked around. Everyone was at battle stations. He started.

—DUM—DUMDUM—

Joey The Lips pointed to Billy.

—CLAH—CLAHCLAH—

To Derek.

—THUM—THUMTHUM—

Once Derek was in James could be a bit more adventurous. He went along with the girls.

—UUH — UUH — UUH —
          UUH — UUH —
                    UUH — UUH — UUH ——

Joey The Lips clicked his fingers. Outspan was off.

49

—CHI—CHICHI—

Then Deco started to sing.

—AS I WALK THIS LAND

O' BROKE —

EN DREE—EE—EAMS——

It was going well, no mistakes.

Deco would have to be spoken to again. He'd started spinning the mike over his head.

The girls were good. Their step was simple; one step right, then back, then right again. They moved together. And they looked well, about the same height and size. Natalie clapped her hands, shook her head, bared her teeth.

Most of the other Commitments looked comfortable enough.

Dean looked petrified.

—I'LL BE SEARCHIN' EVERYWHERE—

JUST TO FIND SOMEONE TO CARE—

I'VE BEEN LOOKIN' EVERY DAY—

I KNOW I'M GOIN' TO FIND A WAY—

NOTHIN'S GOIN' TO STOP ME NOW—

I WILL FIND A WAY SOMEHOW——

They all stopped. The record faded quickly there. They didn't know how they were going to end it.

Deco kept singing.

—I'LL SEARCH FOR YOU DOWN ON THE DOCKS

I'LL WAIT UNDER CLERY'S CLOCK——

They cheered.

Deco stopped.

—Wha' was tha' abou'? Jimmy asked.

—A bit o' local flavour, said Deco.

—Tha' was deadly, said Derek.

—Yeh said we were goin' to make the words more Dubliny, said Deco.

—It's just——yeh should've warned us, said Jimmy.

—It's good though, said Billy.

—Very soul, said James.

—Soul is the people's music, said Joey The Lips.

50

—Only culchies shop in Clery's but, said Billy.

—Oh yeah, said Derek. —But, hang on. The clock's hangin' off the outside o' the shop. On the street.

—Soul is street, said Joey the Lips.

—That's alrigh' then, said Jimmy. —The clock stays.

They walked home. Seven of the ten Commitments worked. Four of them made it into work the next morning.

* * *

The Commitments rehearsed three times a week. After the first few nights they stopped before half-eleven for the last bus.

Joey The Lips kept them on the easier, less frantic numbers. Chain Gang became their favourite for a while.

The girls would lift their hammers above their heads, and bring them down:

—HUH——

And again:

—HAH——

And again:

—HUH——

Derek got to sing too.

He'd growl: —WELL DON'T YOU KNOW before Deco sang:

—THAT'S THE SOUND O' THE MEN —
WORKIN' ON THE CHAIN ——
            GA — EE — ANG ————
THAT'S THE SOUND O' THE MEN —
WORKIN' ON THE —
            CHAIN GANG ——

Deco closed his eyes a lot for this one.

—ALL DAY THEY'RE SAYIN'—
MY MY MY MY MY MY MY
            MY WORK IS SO HARD —
GIVE ME GUINNESS —
I'M THIRSTY ——
    MY — Y — Y —

51

                    MY WORK IS SO HARD
        OH OH MY MY MY —
                                    SWEET JAYSIS —
        MY WORK IS SO HARD ——
—HUH, went the girls.
—HAH, went the girls.
—HUH, went the girls.
Derek wrapped it up.
—WELL DON'T YOU ———
                                    KNOW.

                    *   *   *

Joey The Lips had them standing in a circle.

—What're we doin' today, Joey? Dean asked him.

—Well, Brother, said Joey The Lips. —I think we're going to bring our Soul Sisters to the front.

—Oh Jesus, said Natalie. —I'm scarleh.

—Hang on, said Deco. —What's this?

—The Sisters are going to sing, said Joey The Lips. —Like the birds of the air.

—They're supposed to be backing vocalists.

—Ah, fuck off, Cuffe, said Billy. —The cunt's jealous, so he is.

—Yeah, said Outspan.

—Sap, said Imelda.

—Grow a pair o' tits, pal, an' then yeh can sing with them, said Billy.

—Are you startin' somethin'?

—Don't annoy me.

—Here! said Jimmy. —None o' tha'.

The time was right for a bit of laying down the law.

—No rows or scraps, righ'.

—Well said, Jim.

—An' annyway, said Jimmy. —The girls are the best lookin' part o' the group.

—Dirty bastard, said Natalie.

—Thanks very much, Jimmy, said Imelda.

—No sweat, 'melda, said Jimmy.

—What'll we sing? Bernie asked Joey The Lips.

—You know Walking in the Rain?

—Lovely.

—I WANT HIM, Imelda sang.

—It doesn't exactly have a strong feminist lyric, does it? said James.

—Soul isn't words, Brother, said Joey The Lips. —Soul is feeling. Soul is getting out of yourself.

—But it's corny.

—You're not singin' it, Specky, said Imelda.

—It's wha' yeh'd call crossover music, Jimmy explained. —It appeals to a wider market. Black an' whi'e. Redneck an' Dub.

—An' it's good, said Natalie.

—You speak the truth, Sister, said Joey The Lips.

———We need rain and thunder. ——Brother Billy, you can supply us with the meteorological conditions?

—The wha'?

—Rain and thunder?

—I don't know abou' the rain but I can give yeh all the fuckin' thunder yeh want.

He attacked the kit.

—Fuckin' hurricane if yeh want it.

Jimmy spoke. —Can yeh rattle one o' the cymbals gently?

—Gently? ——Jaysis, I don't know. ———How's this?

—Grand, said Jimmy. —That's the rain.

—Good thinkin'.

The girls were practising a move. They crossed their arms over their chests every time they sang HIM.

—The wall of sound. Mr Spector's Wall of Sound here, Brothers, said Joey The Lips. —Brother Outspan, you're the main man on this one.

—Fuck! Am I?

—Stay cool, said Joey The Lips. —Let's hear it.

—CHUNGHA—CHUNGHA—CHUNGHA—CHUNGHA—

—Terrif, said Joey The Lips. —Sisters.

The Commitmentettes got ready.

—Rain, Joey The Lips shouted.

Billy gave him rain.

—Thunder. ————A bit less.

He nodded to the girls.

—DOO DOO DOO DOO DOO —

                                         DOOO—

DOO DOO DOO DOO DOO —

                                       DOOOooo—

Natalie, in the middle, stepped forward.

—I WANT HIM —

—Get up!

—That's not funny, Brother, said Joey The Lips. —We start again.

—Sorry.

—Rain. ————Now thunder.

—DOO DOO DOO DOO DOO —

                                       DOOO—

DOO DOO DOO DOO DOO —

                                       DOOOooo—

I WANT HIM ——

AN' I NEED HIM ——

AN' SOME DAY —

                            SOME WAY —

WOO OH WOO O —

                        O —

                        OH —

                                  I'LL SEE HIM—

Bernie and Imelda stepped up to join Natalie. They sang together now.

—HE'LL BE KIND O' SHY — Y —

Imelda started laughing but they didn't stop.

—AN' REAL GOOD LOOKIN' TOO —

                                  OOO ——

AN' I'LL BE CERTAIN —

                                  HE'S MY GUY —

COS THE THINGS —
                    HE'LL——
                    LIKE——
                    TO——
                    DOO——
—Thunder, Joey The Lips roared.
A cymbal hopped off its stand.
—LIKE WALKIN' IN THE RAIN, Natalie sang.
—LIKE WALKIN' IN THE RAIN, Bernie and Imelda
sang.
Then they were together again.
—AN' WISHIN' ON THE STARS ——
                         UP ABOVE—
AN' BEIN' SO —
                    IN LOVE.
If Outspan had broken one string it wouldn't have mattered.
But he broke two so they had to stop till he replaced one of
them and Joey The Lips tuned it.
—Tha' was smashin', girls, said Jimmy. —Fair play to yis.
They'll be eatin' chips ou' o' your knickers.
—You're fuckin' sick, you are.

                    *   *   *

Things were going very well.
    There were mistakes, rows, a certain amount of absenteeism
but things were going well. Joey The Lips was a calming
influence on them. It must have been his age. As well as that,
they now knew about his past. They'd seen the photographs
of Joey The Lips with the stars:
Joey The Lips and Otis Redding on horses, on Otis' ranch,
Joey The Lips said.
Joey The Lips on-stage lying on his back, behind him James
Brown's legs, one of them blurred.
Joey The Lips, with hair, in the studio, Gladys Knight,
headphoned, smiling at him.
Joey The Lips and Marvin Gaye, both in skull caps and
caftans, standing in front of a pile of rubble, Detroit.

There was even one of Joey The Lips with B. P. Fallon, Fallon with his arm around Joey The Lips' shoulders, half of Yoko Ono's head in the background.

And Jimmy had found Joey The Lips' name in the credits on a few of his albums. (—Is tha' our Joey? Outspan asked.

—Yep, said Jimmy.

—Fuckin' hell, said Outspan.

He read the list to Derek.

—Berry Gordy, Smokey Robinson, Lamont Dozier, Joey Irish Fagan, Steve Cropper, Martha Reeves, Diana Ross and The Lord, Jehovah. ———Who's he?) When they saw Joey The Lips looking pleased they knew they were doing alright. And Joey The Lips always looked pleased.

* * *

Or, Joey The Lips nearly always looked pleased. He looked shocked when Dean found Natalie kissing him.

Dean wasn't looking for them when he found them. He was shutting the garage door and they were behind it. He pulled the door in towards him and there they were, Joey The Lips the one up against the wall, which struck Dean as unusual when he thought about it later. Natalie jumped back, leaving Joey The Lips' right hand holding air. Dean was going to put the door back but Joey The Lips spoke. Natalie had dashed back inside.

—Do I look different? said Joey The Lips.

—No, Joey.

—Good good, said Joey The Lips. —Because you fairly ruffled my savoir faire there, Dean, my man.

—I, said Dean. ———I thought yeh were goin' for chips.

—I am gone, Dean.

If that was a hint or a plea or an order Dean didn't know it because he told the lads when he got back inside. He wasn't ratting. He needed to hear himself saying it. Then he'd be able to believe it.

—FUCK OFF! said Outspan.

—Honest to God, said Dean.

56

—Where? said Derek.

—Ou' there, said Dean. ——Behind the door.

—It's not fuckin' dark yet.

—I know.

—My Jaysis, wha'!

—Fuckin' hell!

—HEY, YOU! Deco roared across the garage at Natalie.

Natalie was filling the girls in on how she'd got on with Joey The Lips.

—Were you havin' it off with Joey behind the door?

—Fuck yourself.

—Were yeh?

—What's it to you if she was? said Bernie.

—You're fuckin' taller than him! Deco shouted.

This went against nature.

—So?

None of the lads could answer that one. It was ridiculous, but it hurt too. Natalie was a good looking, a lovely looking young one, younger than them. Joey The Lips was a baldy little bollix nearly fifty. He wore slippers——

For a few minutes The Commitments broke up.

But Jimmy snapped out of it. It happened when he went from the general to the particular. It wasn't Imelda Joey The Lips had got off with. It was Natalie. He didn't fancy Natalie. It was cool.

—It's a free country, lads, said Jimmy.

—God though, said Derek.

—It's not on, said Deco.

He hit the wall, not too hard.

Billy looked from one face to the next for some sign of hope.

—It's like doin' it with your fuckin' da, he said.

—Wha'? said Dean. ——Nat'lie, like? ——Oh, now I get yeh. ——Yeah.

Outspan asked Dean a question.

—Tongues?

—O' course.

—I'm goin' to be sick.

—That's fuckin' cat, tha' is, said Derek.

—Come on, lads, said Jimmy.

He slapped his hands together.

—Cop on, come on. ——Joey's one o' the lads.

—He's a fuckin' oul' fella.

—He's not like other oul' fellas.

—He's exactly like other oul' fellas.

—Do other oul' fellas play in groups? said Jimmy. —Did your oul' fella play with The Beatles?

—My da's got better taste than tha'.

Dean laughed.

—Look, said Jimmy. ——Look. ——He's older than us, righ'. But he's not married, remember. So he's as entitled to move in on a bird as we are. ——An' fair fucks to him.

He meant it.

—Jimmy's righ', men, said James. —It's horrible, but true.

—It's not——fair though, sure it's not?

—I suppose it's not, said James.

—O' course it's fuckin' fair, said Jimmy. —Look, righ', you could've tried to click with her yourself. But yeh didn't. An' Joey did. So fair fucks to him.

——Still, though, said Derek.

Deco called across to the girls.

—Did he force yeh to? ——Cos if he did——

The girls screamed laughing.

—Yeh stupid prick, yeh, said Natalie.

—Na'hlie got off with HIM, said Bernie.

They still laughed.

—Why? Outspan asked gently. ——Why, Nat'lie?

—Yeh fuckin' slut! Deco roared.

They all turned on him. Jimmy pointed a finger at him.

—Take it easy.

James and Derek held Outspan back. Dean helped. Outspan stopped struggling. They let him go. Then Outspan jumped at Deco. They pulled him away. He let them. He'd made his point.

James had a psychology exam coming up in a few weeks.

—You moved in on Joey, Nat'lie? he asked.

—Yeah. ——I did.

The girls laughed again.

—Yis're disgusted, aren't yis? said Imelda. —She likes him, yis stupid fuckin' saps.

—We all like him, said Outspan. —But we're not queuein' up to get off with him.

They all laughed. Outspan had to think back to see why, but then he grinned.

Natalie grinned.

—No.

She laughed.

—He's nice though. ——He's funny.

—An' he's done all those things, said Bernie.

—That's it! said Deco. —Heh! that's it. She's a fuckin' groupie.

—Well, wha' did you ever do? said Bernie. —Besides wank yourself.

—Bernie! said Imelda.

—Well!——said Bernie.

—She's a bleedin' groupie. Just cos he——For fuck sake!——That's pathe'ic, tha' is.

—You'd get off with Madonna, wouldn't yeh? said Natalie. —Wouldn't yeh? ———Fuckin' sure yeh would.

—She's not behind the garage door too, is she? said Billy.

—Or Joan Collins, said Imelda. —She's fifty.

—Older, said Dean.

—I'd be into Joan in a big way meself, said Jimmy. —I must admit.

—Tina Turner's a granny, said Natalie. —Yeh'd get off with her, wouldn't yeh?

—Well, he got off with his own granny, said Billy. —He might as well have a bash at Tina.

—An' your woman tha' reads the News, said Imelda. — Yeh'd get off with her just cos she reads the News.

—He'd try to get off with Bosco, said Outspan.

When Joey The Lips opened the door they were laughing.

—Soul food, said Joey The Lips.

They stopped laughing and looked awkward, and away from Joey The Lips.

————————Good man, Joey, said Outspan. —I'm fuckin' starvin'. I haven't eaten ann'thin' since me dinner.

Jimmy grabbed Deco's arm.

—Not a word, righ'. Not a fuckin' word, righ'?

Deco freed his arm.

————Righ'.

—You're a randy little bollix all the same, aren't yeh, Joey? said Billy.

They laughed through their shock and embarrassment.

—The soul man's libido, Brother, Joey The Lips explained.

* * *

By now The Commitments had about a quarter of an hour's worth of songs that they could struggle through without making too many mistakes. They could sound dreadful sometimes but not many of them knew this. They were happy.

Joey The Lips told them that they were ready for the funkier uptempo numbers, the meaner stuff.

—Rapid!

He didn't say it but Joey The Lips wanted to loosen up Dean, to get him swinging. Dean was the only one still suffering. He stood rigid and even though so far he'd only had three or four note changes at the most per song they usually came too quickly for him and they'd hear him saying Sorry yet again as the rest of them kept going.

A funkier number would force Dean into the open. It would do him good.

Deco was excited. This was where he'd come into his own. He was jumping up and down. He'd started wearing tracksuit bottoms during rehearsals. He swallowed teaspoons of honey whenever he wasn't needed for singing.

—Come on, come on, Deco shouted. —Let's go.

—Wha' 're we doin', Joey? Outspan asked.

Jimmy handed the lyrics to the girls and Deco.

—Knock on Wood.

—Deadly!

—I know this one, said Imelda.

—Not the disco version, said Jimmy.

—Aaah!

—No way, said Jimmy. —Use the butt-ends of your sticks
for this one, Billy.

—Yes, sir.

They listened to the tape of Eddie Floyd.

—You and me together, Dean, said Joey The Lips. —Let's
show these dudes what a horn section does for a living.

—Jaysis, Joey, I don't know.

Outspan got a chord and hit it.

—THI — THI —

—Is tha' abou' righ', Joey? he asked.

—That's about right. ——Now, Dean, make that baby
squeal.

—How?

—We did this one together before.

Joey The Lips put the trumpet to his mouth.

—DUHHH ——
             DU —
                    DUHHH ——

—Remember?

—Oh yeah.

—Good boy. ——Right. ——That's a nipple you've got
there.

—Wish it was.

—Ready?

—S'pose so.

—DUHHH ——
             DU —
                 DUH — DEHHH ——
               DE —
                    DEHHH —

—Good good, said Joey The Lips. —And that's where

Brother Deco comes in. ——Are we ready, cats?

They were ready.

—A one, a two.

Joey The Lips and Dean blew the intro again.

Billy joined in.

—THU — UNG UNG UNG — THU — UNG UNG UNG —

—I DON'T WANNA LOSE — HUH —

—Stop.

—Why ——— What's wrong?

—Brother Deco, said Joey The Lips. —Leave the Huhs till later on, okay. We don't want to alienate our white audience.

—I DON'T WANNA LOSE —

Outspan: —THI — THI —

THIS GOOD THANG ——

Billy: —THU — UNG UNG UNG

THA' I'VE GOT ——

IF I DO ——

—DUH DAA DOOHHH, blew Joey The Lips and Dean, very successfully.

—I WOULD SURELY ——

SURELY LOSE THE LOT ——

Dean wiped his face.

—COS YOUR LOVE —   —THI — THI —

IS BET HA —   THU—UNG UNG UNG

THAN ANNY LOVE I KNOW — OW —

The Commitmentettes joined in here.

—IT'S LIKE THUNDER —

—DUH UH UHHH, went the horns.

—LIGH' —

NIN' —

—DEH EH EHHH, went the horns.

—THE WAY YEH LOVE ME IS FRIGH'NIN' ——

I'D BET HA KNOCK —

Billy: THU THU THU THU

—ON WOO — O — OOD —

BAY —
BEEE ——
The horns: —DUHHH ——
DU —
DUH — DEHHH ——
DE
DEHHH —
Dean didn't sleep too well that night.

He'd got through his solo in Knock on Wood. When they were going through it the third time before going home Dean had arched his back and pointed the sax at the ceiling. He'd walloped his nose but it had been great. He couldn't wait for the next rehearsal.

* * *

The Commitments were looser and meaner the next night, three days later.

—NOW I AIN'T SUPERSTITIOUS, Deco yelled.

—THI — UH THI, went Outspan's guitar.

—ABOU' YEH —

Billy: —THU — UNGA UNG UNG —

—BUT I CAN'T TAKE NO CHANCE ——

Outspan: —THIDDLE OTHI — UH THI —

—YOU'VE GOT ME SPINNIN' —
YOU BRASSER ——
BABY ——
I'M IN A TRANCE ——

The Commitmentettes lifted their arms and clicked their fingers while they waited to sing. Derek bent his knees as he bashed away at his string. Dean was wearing shades. James hit the keys now and again with his elbows. Joey The Lips approved and gave James a thumbs-up. Jimmy grinned and danced his shoulders.

—IT'S LIKE THUNDER —

The horns: —DUH UH UHHH —

—LIGH' —
NIN'—

63

The horns: —DEH EH EHHH —
—IT'S VERY FUCKIN' FRIGH'NIN' ——
   I'D BET HA KNOCK
Billy: —THU THU THU THU
—ON WOO — O — OOD —
   BAY —
        BEEEE ——
The Commitmentettes: —OOOOHH —
The horns: —DUHHH——
            DU —
                  DUH — DEHHH ——
                      DE —
                          DEHHH ——

* * *

A week later The Commitments were taking five.

Jimmy was talking to Joey The Lips.

—Have yeh been to any o' the music pubs in town?

—No, said Joey The Lips. —Not my style.

—We prefer somewhere a bit more quieter, don't we, Joey? said Natalie.

—Behind the garage door, like? said Jimmy.

—Fuck yourself, you.

Natalie went over to Imelda, Bernie and Derek.

Joey The Lips looked straight at Jimmy.

—Rescue me.

—Wha'?

—Rescue me. ——I am a man in need of rescue.

—What're yeh on abou'?

Jimmy looked behind him.

—That woman is driving me fucking crazy, said Joey The Lips. —She won't get off my case.

—I think that's the first time I ever heard yeh say Fuckin', Joey.

—She won't leave me alone.

—Well, Jaysis now, Joey, yeh shouldn't of gotten off with her then.

—I had no choice, Brother, Joey The Lips hissed. —She had me pinned to the wall before I could get on my wheels.

—Wha' abou' tha' soul man's ludo yeh were on abou'?

——————What's the smell?

—Wha' smell? ——Hang on.

—Weed, said Joey The Lips.

He looked around, frowning.

—It's hash. ——Here, Jimmy shouted. —Who has the hash?

—Me, said Billy.

Deco, Outspan, Dean and James were with him, over at the piano.

—No way, Billy. ——No way.

—Wha'? said Billy.

The joint, a very amateur job, stopped on the way back to his mouth.

—Hash is out, said Jimmy.

—Why? said Deco.

He was next on it.

—It fucks up your head, said Jimmy.

—Jimmy, said James. —It's been medically proven ——

—Fuck off a minute, James, sorry, said Jimmy. —Yis won't be able to play.

—We'll be able to play better, said Deco.

—It'll wreck your voice.

That shut Deco up while he decided if it was true.

Billy took a long drag and held the joint out for any takers.

—BLOW THA' OU', BILLY, Jimmy roared.

Billy exhaled.

—I'd die if I didn't, yeh fuckin' eejit.

He still held the joint up in his fingers.

—What's wrong with it? Outspan asked.

Jimmy was doing some thinking. What had annoyed him at first was the fact that they hadn't got the go-ahead from him before they'd lit up. He needed a better reason than that.

—For one thing, he said. —Righ' ——Yis're barely able to play your instruments when yis have your heads on yis.

—Ah here!

—Are you sayin' I can't sing, son?

—Second, said Jimmy. ——We're a soul group. Remember tha'. Not a pop group or a punk group, or a fuckin' hippy group. ——We're a soul group.

—Wha' d'yeh mean, WE'RE? said Deco.

—Fuck up, you.

Jimmy was grateful for the interruption. It gave him more time to think of something.

—If you're not happy with the way I'm doin' things then ——

—We love yeh, Jimmy. Keep goin'.

—Righ'. ——Where was I? ——Yeah. ——We're a soul group. We want to make a few bob but we have our principles. It's not just the money. It's politics too, remember. We're supposed to be bringin' soul to Dublin. We can't do tha' an' smoke hash at the same time.

—It's oney hash.

—The tip o' the fuckin' iceberg, Billy. Dublin's fucked up with drugs. Drugs aren't soul.

—Wha' abou' drinkin'?

—That's different, said Jimmy. —That's okay. The workin' class have always had their few scoops.

—Guinness is soul food, said Joey The Lips.

—That's me arse, Jimmy, said Outspan.

—Listen, said Jimmy. —For fuck sake, we can't say we're playin' the people's music if we're messin' around with drugs. We should be against drugs. Anti drugs. Heroin an' tha'.

—Yeah, but——

—Look wha' happened to Derek's brother.

—Leave my brother ou' o' this, said Derek.

He nearly shouted it.

—Okay, sorry. But yeh know wha' I mean.

—Wha' happened to Derek's brother? Billy asked.

—Forget it.

—Wha' happened your brother?

—Forget it, Billy.

66

—I was oney askin'.

—Annyway, said Jimmy. —Do yis agree with me?

—Ah yeah ——o' course, oney ——

—We'll get a Heroin Kills banner for behind the drums, said Jimmy.

—Hang on, said Deco. —Wha' abou' the niggers in America, the real soul fellas, wha' abou' them? They all smoke hash. ——Worse.

This was Joey The Lips' field.

—Not true, Brother. Real Soul Brothers say No to the weed. All drugs. ——Soul says No.

—Wha' abou' Marvin Gaye?

—Wha' abou' him? said Jimmy.

—He died of an overdose.

—His da shot him, yeh fuckin' sap.

—A bullet overdose, said Billy.

—Sam Cooke then, said Deco.

—I don't know wha' happened him. ——Joey?

—Died under very mysterious circumstances, said Joey The Lips. —A lady.

—Enough said.

—I'm sure he was lookin' for it, said Imelda.

—Phil Lynott, said Deco.

—Fuck off, said Jimmy. —He wasn't soul.

—He was black.

—Ah, fuck off an' don't annoy me. ——Get ou' o' my life. ——Annyway, do yis agree abou' the hash? An' the heroin, like?

—Yeah

They all nodded or stayed quiet.

—Can we smoke it after the rehearsal, Jimmy? Billy asked.

—Yeah, sure. No problem.

* * *

It was another week later.

James was late so Joey The Lips was going to put Deco through a new song, James Brown's Out of Sight.

—You're sure you know it now?

—O' course I'm sure.

—Okay then. Off you go. ——A one——

Deco put his hands to his ears.

Outspan nudged Derek.

—Fuckin' tosser.

Deco sang.

—YOU GOT YOUR HIGH HEELED
SNEAKERS ON ——
    YOUR STUFF IS NEW ——
    YOU GOT YOUR HIGH HEELED
SNEAKERS ON —
    SIMON HARTS —
    YOUR GEAR IS NEW ——
    YOU'RE MORE THAN ALRIGH — HI —
HIGH' ——
    YEH KNOW —
            YOU'RE OU' O' SIGH' ——Fuck!

Jimmy had come in and made it obvious he wanted The Commitments to notice him when he threw an empty 7-up can at Deco's head.

—Wha' was tha' for? Deco shouted.

—I don't like yeh, said Jimmy. —An' I've a bit o' news for yis.

—So yeh hit ME?

—It didn't hurt, an' neither will me bit o' news.

—Ooh! said Imelda. —Sounds good.

—It is, 'melda, it is indeed. An' you're lookin' lovely tonigh'.

—Thank you, Jimmy. An' you're lookin' horrible as ever.

—The news, said Joey The Lips.

—Are we goin' to have The Angelus first or somethin'? said Outspan.

James came in.

—Sorry. ——Puncture.

—Jimmy's got news, James, said Bernie.

—But he's keepin' it to himself, said Imelda. (And she sang this bit.) —BECAUSE HE'S A BOLLIX.

—Are yis ready?

—Ah stop, Jimmy.

—Well, I've been busy for the last couple o' nights.

—Yeh dirty man, said Deco.

Billy thumped him.

—I've been negotiatin', said Jimmy.

—Janey!

—That'll make yeh deaf.

They laughed, but only for a little while.

—I've got us a venue for our first gig.

—Fuckin' great!

There were cheers and grins.

—When?

—Tomorrow week.

—Fuckin' hell!

—It has to be then, said Jimmy. —Because the bingo caller ——yeh know Hopalong——him, he's goin' into hospital for the weekend to get a tap put into his kidneys or somethin', so it's the only nigh' the place is free.

—The community centre?

—Yeah.

—Tha' kip!

—From little acorns, Brothers and Sisters, said Joey The Lips.

—Barrytown Square Garden, wha', said Outspan.

—Hang on, said Derek. —No slaggin'. It'll do for a start. ——Thanks, Jimmy.

—Yeah. Thanks, Jim.

—No sweat.

—We bring the music to the people, said Joey The Lips. —We go to them. We go to their community centre. That's soul.

—No one goes there, Joey, said Outspan. —'cept the oul' ones tha' play the bingo.

—An' the soccer. They change there, said Derek. —An' the operetta society, an' the Vinny de Paul.

—An' Hopalong, said Natalie.

—He's stickin' it into your woman from the shop, Colette, did yis know tha'?

—He is NOT, said Bernie.

—He fuckin' is.

—Good Jesus, that's disgustin'.

—No wonder he limps, wha'.

—Our first gig, said Dean. ———Our first gig.

—Who did yeh have to talk to abou' the hall, Jimmy? James asked.

—Father Molloy.

—Oh fuck! Father Paddy, said Outspan. —The singin' priest, he explained to the lads who weren't from Barrytown.

Derek began to sing.

—MOR —
        NIN' HAS —
                BROKE —
                        EN —
LIKE THE FIRST MOR —
                HOR — HOR — NIN' —
BLACK BIRD ON —
                TREE TOP —
HAS HAD ITS FIRST CRAP —

—The folk mass, Outspan explained to the lads. —Fuckin' desperate.

—Oh yeah, said Billy. —Is tha' the one you got flung ou' of?

—That's it, said James.

—Did he brown yeh, Jimmy? Outspan asked.

—No. He just ran his fingers through me curly fellas.

—Aah!! Stop tha'! said Natalie.

—How much is it goin' to cost? Deco asked.

—Nothin'.

—That's super.

—How come?

70

—I told him it was part o' the Anti-Heroin Campaign.

—Yeh fuckin' chancer, yeh.

They all stood back and admired Jimmy.

—Well, it is, said Jimmy. —We'll have our Heroin Kills banner. Me little brother, Darren——he's an awful little prick——he's goin' to do it in school. An art project, like. An' a few posters for the walls an' things.

—Good man, Jimmy.

—There's one thing but, said Jimmy. —I told Father Molloy we'd do a folk mass for him.

—No way!

—Only messin'. ——Northside News are sendin' someone ou' to see us. An' a photographer.

—How come?

—I told them abou' it. Phoned them up.

—Jaysis, fair play to yeh.

—I'll be scarleh, said Bernie.

—I haven't saved enough for me suit, said Derek.

—We can hire them for this one, said Jimmy. —We'll get the bread back on the door.

—Bread! said Billy. —Yeh fuckin' hippy.

—Fuck up.

—Well, Brothers and Sisters, said Joey The Lips. —Let's hear it for our manager, Brother J. Rabbitte, and let's hear it for Brother Hopalong's kidneys too.

The Commitments clapped.

—Brother Hopalong's kidneys are soul.

* * *

The Commitments rehearsed every night of the last week. They began to shout and throw the head when someone made a mistake and they had to start all over again. But Joey The Lips kept them short of panic stations. He said Stay Cool a lot during the week.

—Stay cool, my man, said Joey The Lips.

Deco had just roared at Billy who had just knocked over the snare drum.

71

—He's a fuckin' eejit, Joey, Deco shouted.

—Joey, said Billy. —I said it before, it's one o' the risks yis have to take. It's part o' me style. These sort o' accidents are likely to happen. I told yis tha'.

He now addressed Deco.

—An' here, you, George Michael. If yeh ever call me a fuckin' eejit again you'll go home with a drumstick up your hole. The one yeh don't sing ou' of.

He started to pick up the drum.

—The one yeh talk ou' of.

—That'll be the day, pal.

—It's comin'. I'm tellin' yeh.

—Maybe.

—Yeh'd want to have your vaseline with yeh the next time.

——Can we continue now, can we, please?

He began to play.

—THU — CUDADUNG CUDADUNG CUDADUNG
 THU — CUDADUNG CUDADUNG CUDADUNG

The horns: —DUUH — DU DUHH —

DUUH DU DUHH —

DEH —

DU DU DUUH —

Outspan and Derek followed that.

—DONG CADDA DONG CADDA DONG CADDA DONG —

The horns: DUUH — DU DUHH —

DUUH DU DUHH —

DEH —

DU DU DUUH —

—OOH WHEN YEH FEE — IL LIKE YEH CAN'T

GO —

OH ON—

The Commitmentettes: — CAN'T GO OHON —

—JUST COS ALL O' YOUR HOPE IS —

GOHON

—Ah fuck! Wha' now?

—Me string's gone again, said Outspan.

—Fuck you an' your string.
—Stay cool, said Joey The Lips.

* * *

There was a little saxophone in each corner of the poster.
—Saturday, 24 March, it said across the top. —In The Community Centre, The Hardest Working Band In The World, The Saviours Of Soul. The Commitments. Admission: £2 (Unwaged: £1). Bringing The People's Music To The People.

* * *

—I hate him, said Billy.
—We all do, for fuck sake, said Jimmy.
—Really, I mean——I really hate him.
—We all do, I'm tellin' yeh.
—Enough to kill him?
——Maybe not tha' much.
—I'd fuckin' kill him. I fuckin' would.
—Who'd do the singin' then?
——Good thinkin'.

* * *

—It's a pity we don't do anny songs of our own, isn't it? said Outspan, during a break.
—Yeah.
—A song belongs to no man, said Joey The Lips. —The Lord holds copyright on all songs.
—Me arse, said Outspan.
—We have the Dublin bits, said Derek.
—True.

* * *

—We'll need a Brother to do the mix, said Joey The Lips.
—We have one, said Jimmy.
—Who?
—Me.

73

—Good good.

—Wha' do you know abou' it? said Outspan.

—Fuck all, said Jimmy. —But I got an honour in science in me Inter.

* * *

Deco had bought his suit. He bought the shirt and bow on the Thursday before the gig. The other Commitments managed to get into town to hire their suits.

Joey The Lips got one of his dress suits dry-cleaned. Dean crawled in under his bed and found the one he'd flung under there. He soaked the jacket till the muck was nearly all gone. Then he brought it down to the cleaners.

Black shoes were polished or bought or borrowed.

* * *

Friday was a dress rehearsal.

Joey The Lips was already dressed when The Commitments got there.

—Oh my Jaysis, Joey, wha'! said Outspan.

—Yeh look like Dickie Davis, said Dean.

—I don't know the dude, said Joey The Lips. —But I accept the compliment. Thank you, Brother.

—Yeh look gorgeous, Joey, said Imelda.

—Joey? said Outspan. —How do yeh get your hankie to go like tha'? I can't get mine like tha'.

Joey The Lips let the girls into the kitchen to change. The lads changed in the garage. There was a lot of slagging of underpants and so on. None of them played football so it was a good while since they'd dressed in this way. They enjoyed it.

—Jaysis, look at those skid marks.

—Fuck off.

—Come here till I ride yeh, yeh lovely young fella, yeh.

—Fuck off, will yeh.

—Where's it gone? said Outspan.

—Wha'?

74

—Me knob. ——I could've sworn I tucked it into me sock before I came ou'.

James joined in the crack too.

—Do yeh know wha' the Latin is for tha' weapon yeh have on yeh there?

The small door to the kitchen was knocked.

—Can we come in? Imelda asked.

The lads cheered, and thumped and kicked each other.

Deco cupped his crotch in both hands (although one could have done) and roared: —I've a bugle here yeh can blow on, 'melda.

—Fuck yourself, Natalie roared.

—Jaysis, Cuffe, take it easy. For fuck sake!

—I've an arse here yeh can kiss, Imelda shouted back from behind the door. —Can we come in?

—No.

—Enter, Sisters.

—Well, we're comin'.

Deco cheered.

Imelda was first (—Good fuck!), then Natalie (—Fair fuckin' play to yis girls), then Bernie.

—I'm scarleh, said Bernie.

The girls were stunning; very tight black skirts to just above the knee with an extension at the back so they could walk, black sleeveless tops, hair held up, except the fringe, as near to the Ronettes as they could manage, black high heels, loads of black eye shadow, very red lipstick.

They were blushing.

Joey The Lips applauded.

Jimmy spoke. —Well, as James says, It don't mean nothin' without a woman or a girl.

—I never said tha', said James.

—James Brown, yeh dick.

The girls admired the suits. There was lots of giggling and redners.

Joey The Lips did their breast pocket hankies for them.

One of Billy's trouser legs was longer than the other.

75

—Ah, fuck tha', he said.

He looked very disappointed.

—You'll be behind the drums.

—They'll still see me legs.

—I'll fix it up for yeh tomorrow, said Natalie.

—Will yeh?—Thanks.

They played better in the suits. They were more careful, and considerate. Deco's suit seemed to pin him more to one spot. This was good. In his tracksuit he hopped around the garage and got in the way and on the nerves. Dean swapped jackets with Jimmy. (—Why have you got a suit? Outspan asked Jimmy.

—Soul is dignity, said Jimmy.

—This is a great fuckin' group, said Outspan. —I must say. Even the skivvies wear fuckin' monkey suits.

—I'm no skivvy, said Jimmy. —I'm your fuckin' manager, pal.

—An' don't you forget it, said James.

—Fuckin' righ', said Jimmy.) There was more room in Jimmy's jacket so Dean could still lift the sax up high. Billy didn't knock over any drums.

Joey The Lips showed Jimmy how to use the mixer.

—So all I have to do is push these lads up or down a bit when the sound's a bit gammy?

—That's correct, said Joey The Lips.

—That's great, said Jimmy. —There's nothin' to it. Anny fuckin' dope could do tha'. I might even pull a few birds this way, wha'. Wha' d'yeh think? Blind them with science, wha'.

—It works, my man. ——It works.

They finished early, got back into their civvies, and went for a drink.

*　*　*

Kick-off was at half-seven.

The Commitments said they'd meet at the hall at six. Jimmy was there at five, his dress suit hidden by a snorkel jacket he hadn't worn since he'd left school.

Billy arrived soon after with Dean. Billy had his van from work. They got the gear out but they left Joey The Lips' mother's piano in the van until some more arrived to help them.

At half-five the caretaker appeared out of a door beside the stage.

Wha' do youse want? the caretaker asked.

He saw the drums.

—That's not the bingo stuff.

—There's no bingo tonigh', pal, said Jimmy.

—It's Sahurday but, said the caretaker.

He took his Press out of his jacket pocket and looked at the date.

—Yeah. ———Sahurday.

Jimmy explained. —Hopa——The fella tha' calls the numbers is in hospital so Father Molloy said we could have the hall for the nigh'.

—He told me nothin' abou' it, said the caretaker. —So yis can take your bongos off o' the stage there an' the rest o' your tackle with it an' get ou'. As far as I'm concerned there's bingo tonigh'. Until I'm officially told otherwise.

—Why don't yeh go across an' ask him? said Jimmy.

Father Molloy's house was right across the road.

—I will not, said the caretaker. —It's not my job to go across an' ask him.

—Wha' is your job? Billy asked.

—I'm the caretaker, said the caretaker.

—You're not very good at it, are yeh? said Billy. —The state o' the place.

—Shut up a minute, Billy, said Jimmy. —Look. ——If I go across to Father Molloy will tha' do?

—Yis'll have to get your gear ou' first. I want nothin' in here till I'm officially informed.

Jimmy looked at Billy and Dean.

They started to gather the drums.

—It's our church collection money goes to pay your wages, Billy told the caretaker.

77

—I wouldn't get very far on the money you'd put in the collection, so I wouldn't, said the caretaker.

—Well, yeh'll be gettin' tenpence less from now on.

—Make tha' twenty, said Dean.

—That's no problem, said the caretaker. —I put in fifty meself. I'll oney put in thirty from now on.

They were beginning to like each other. The caretaker carried two mike stands for them.

—It's a cushy one, I'd say, is it? said Billy.

—Wha'?

—Your job.

—Oh, it is alrigh', the caretaker admitted. —I do fuck all to be honest with yeh. I watch a few women polishin' the floor on Tuesdays. An' I put ou' the chairs for the bingo. An' I open the windows to get rid o' the smell o' the footballers. That's abou' it. ——Mind you, the pay's useless.

—I s'pose so, said Billy.

He took a cigarette from the packet the caretaker held out.

—The soccer fellas are much smellier than the gaelic ones, said the caretaker. —I think it's because the soccer mammies don't wash their gear as much.

—The gaelic mas would all be culchies, said Dean. —They're always washin' clothes.

—That's very true, said the caretaker. —Will yis be wantin' the chairs ou'?

—No, said Billy. —It's stand–up.

—That'll be great, said the caretaker. —I'll sneak home for Jim'll Fix It. Yis'll be alrigh' by yourselves for a while.

Jimmy came back.

—Father Molloy says it's alrigh'.

—That's great, said the caretaker. —I'll give yis a hand to bring your stuff back in. ——D'yeh think I could have a go on the drums?

—No problem.

—I'll show yeh me saxophone, said Dean.

—Oh lovely.

The rest of The Commitments began to arrive.

Joey The Lips and Bernie arrived together, holding hands. Bernie had a crash helmet.

—What's the fuckin' story there? Outspan asked.

—Mind your own business, you, said Imelda.

—Tha' chap's a little rabbit, said Outspan.

—Wha' would you know abou' it? said Natalie.

—I was thinking there, Brother Jimmy, said Joey The Lips.

The girls were in the caretaker's room, changing. The caretaker had gone off home. The lads were sitting or shuffling around the stage, excited, nervous and uncomfortable.

—We need the hard men, bouncers.

—That's all organized, said Jimmy.

—How? Derek asked.

—Mickah Wallace is goin' to go the door for us.

—Oh, good fuck! said Outspan.

He had a small scar on his forehead, courtesy of Mickah Wallace.

—Tha' cunt! He'll fuck off with the money.

—He won't, said Jimmy. —Mickah's alrigh'.

—He's a fuckin' savage, said Derek.

—Who is he? said Deco.

—Wha' is he, yeh mean, said Outspan.

—He got fucked ou' o' our school, righ', Derek told them,—because he beat the shi'e ou' o' the Dean o' Girls. —— Girls! He kicked her up an' down the yard when she snared him smokin' an' she tried to take the pack off o' him.

—See tha'?

Outspan thought he was pointing to his scar but his finger was on the wrong side.

—He done tha'. Fucked a rock at me durin' a match. He was the goalie an' I oney had him to beat, the cunt. An' he fucked the rock at me.

—Jaysis!

—I still scored though.

—Yeh didn't, said Derek.

—I fuckin' did.

—Yeh were offside.

—I fuckin' wasn't.

—Fuck up, youse, said Jimmy. —Tha' was years ago. We were all fuckin' eejits then.

Outspan wasn't finished yet.

—He got up on the roof o' Mountjoy when he was in there cos the other guy in his cell had AIDS an' he thrun slates down at the screws.

—That's not true, said Jimmy.

—It is.

—Yeh just said it was him.

Jimmy explained to the rest.

—It was on the News. Some tossers up on the roof. An' Outspan just said one o' them was Mickah.

—I recognized him.

—They had their jumpers wrapped round their faces.

—I recognized his jumper.

—Fuck off. ——He's doin' bouncer an' that's it. He'll be grand.

—Who else? Derek asked.

—We won't need annyone else, said Jimmy. —Nobody's goin' to act the prick with Mickah here.

James spoke. —Mickah's okay.

—How would you know?

—I meet him a lot. ——He lent me a few books.

—Yeh still read Ladybird books, do yeh? said Outspan.

—Don't let Mickah hear yeh sayin' tha', said Jimmy.

—Let us tune up, Brothers, said Joey The Lips.

The girls came out.

—Yis rides, yis, said Deco.

He stuck his tongue out at them and jiggled it.

—Fuck yourself, said Natalie.

The male Commitments changed.

It was seven o'clock. The caretaker came back.

—Suits, he said.

—Yeah, said Jimmy.

—Monkey suits.

—D'you approve?

—Oh, very nice. It's a long, long time since I seen a band all dressed the same.

He went over to the girls.

—I know your daddy, he said to Imelda.

—So? said Imelda.

She raised her eyes to heaven.

—You're just like him, said the caretaker. —A cheeky little fucker.

Mickah Wallace arrived.

—How's it goin', Mickah, said Outspan.

—Alrigh', said Mickah. —An' yourself?

—Alrigh'.

—Guitar, wha'.

—Yeah.

—Are yis anny good?

—Alrigh'.

—The best, said Jimmy.

The ones not from Barrytown studied Mickah. He wasn't what they'd expected; some huge animal, a skinhead or a muttonhead, possibly both. This Mickah was small and wiry, very mobile. Even when he was standing still he was moving.

—I haven't a bad little voice meself, yeh know, Mickah told Jimmy. —Give us tha', please, pal.

He took Deco's mike. Deco stood back.

—Don't worry, said Mickah. —Your job's safe.

He bashed the mike into his forehead.

—That's a good strong mike, tha'. Quality's very rare these days.

He tapped the mike.

—Testin' one two, testin'. Time now, ladies an' gentlemen, plea-se.

He tapped again.

—An' it's Ben Nevis comin' in on the stand side, Lester's ou' o' the saddle. Come on, Ben Nevis, come on, come on. ——Shi'e! He's fallen over an' croaked.

They were afraid to laugh.

—Now I'll sing for yis.

He coughed.
—RED RED —

      WIY —

          YUN ——

STAY CLOSE TO —

         ME —

            EE YEAH ———

Wha' comes after tha'?

He gave the mike back to Deco.

—Howyeh, James, he said. —Did yeh read tha' one I gave yeh?

—I'm halfway through it.

—It's better than Catch 22, isn't it?

—I don't think so, Mickah.

—Fuckin' sure it is, said Mickah. —How much in, Jimmy?

—Two lids.

—Tha' all? Yis mustn't be anny good.

—Time will tell, Brother, said Joey The Lips.

—It told on you annyway, pal, said Mickah.

He was noticing Joey The Lips for the first time.

—The fuckin' state of yeh.

Imelda laughed.

Bernie stared her out of it.

—Can we come in?

A small boy stood at the door.

—No, Mickah shouted down to him.

—When?

—When I say so. Now shut the fuckin' door.

Mickah jumped off the stage. He landed in front of the caretaker, back in a clean shirt.

—I need a table, son, said Mickah.

Mickah and the caretaker took the table to the door. They sat behind it. Jimmy drew the stage curtain, a manky red thing. The Commitments took turns at peeking through it into the hall. The caretaker got an empty tin for the money.

—Righ', said Mickah.

He slipped down in his chair and stretched so he could swing the door open with his foot.

—Get in here, he shouted.

There were about twelve of them outside, all kids, brothers and sisters of The Commitments, and their friends.

The caretaker took the money. Mickah laid down the rules as each of them passed the table into the hall.

—Anny messin' an' I'll kill yeh, righ'.

—I've oney a pound, said one boy.

The caretaker looked to Mickah.

—Let him in, said Mickah.

Jimmy was standing behind them.

—How long are yis on for? Mickah asked him.

—Abou' an hour.

—I'll throw him ou' after half, said Mickah.

—I'm unwaged, said another boy with his pound held out.

—Yeh weren't this mornin' when yeh were deliverin' the milk, said Mickah.

—He sacked me after you seen me.

—Go on.

The caretaker took the pound.

It wasn't a big hall but three hundred could have stood in it. There was room for two hundred and seventy more at half-seven.

Mickah looked outside.

—There's no more ou' there.

Jimmy looked at the crowd. Four mates of himself, Outspan and Derek leaned against the back wall. He'd let them in for nothing. Ray Ward (ex And And! And) was with them. He'd paid in. There were six other older ones, in their late teens or early twenties, mates, he supposed, of Deco or Billy or Dean. There were three girls, pals of Imelda, Natalie and Bernie. The rest were kids, except for one, Outspan's mother. The caretaker got her a chair and she sat at the front, at the side.

Outspan looked again. He dropped the curtain.

—Fuck her, he said. —She promised me she wouldn't come.

—I'm scarleh for yeh, said Bernie.

—Soul has no age limits, said Joey The Lips.

—Fuck off, Joey, said Outspan.

—She's wearin' her fur, Imelda told them.

She was at the curtain.

—Fuck her annyway, said Outspan. —I'm not goin' on.

—If yeh don't go on, said Deco, —I'll tell your pal, Mickah.

Outspan looked at him.

—My ma could beat the shi'e ou' o' Mickah Wallace anny day.

At ten to eight Jimmy shut the door. The numbers had risen by three, his brother Darren and his mates.

Jimmy grabbed Darren's shoulder.

—Come here, you, bollox. There's only one E in Heroin.

He thumped Darren's ear.

—Make them all go up to the front, Mickah, will yeh. It'll look better.

—Righto. ——That's good thinkin'.

—We don't want the group demoralized.

—Fuck, no.

Mickah went along the back. He shoved everyone forward.

—Get up there an' clap or I'll fuckin' crease yis.

He was obeyed. Mickah followed them.

—Cheer when the curtain opens, righ'. ——An' clap like fuck. Great gig, Missis Foster, he shouted to Outspan's mother.

Billy stood back and looked at the banner.

—That's not how yeh spell heroin.

Imelda looked at it.

—Oh, look it, she said. —That's brilliant.

—The syringe is very good though, isn't it? said Dean.

—It'll do, said Derek. —It's grand. ——None o' those cunts ou' there knows how to spell an'annyway.

Jimmy was back-stage.

—If we do tha' dance in Walkin In The Rain we'll fall off the fuckin' stage, said Natalie. —It's much smaller than Joey's garage.

—Yis'll be alrigh', said Jimmy. —You're professionals.

84

—Janey!

The Commitments were all at their positions.

Jimmy stood at the side of the stage. He had a mike in one hand and the curtain cord in the other. He nodded to them. They looked at themselves and each other and stood, ready, very serious.

This was it. Even if there were only thirty-three in the hall. James Brown had played to less. Joey The Lips said so.

—Ladies an' gentlemen, Jimmy said to the mike.

There was a cheer, a big one too, from the other side of the curtain.

—Will yeh please put your workin' class hands together for your heroes. The Saviours o' Soul, The Hardest Workin' Band in the World, ——Yes, Yes, Yes, Yes——The Commitments.

He dropped the mike and pulled the cord. The curtain stayed shut.

—Wrong rope, son, said the caretaker.

—Yeh fuckin' sap, said Imelda.

The caretaker got the curtain open. There was another cheer. (Jimmy dashed down to the mixing desk. —Get away from tha', youse.) The house lights were still on. The crowd wasn't even two deep in some places. The caretaker went to turn off the lights.

The clapping stopped. The lights went off. There were a few cheers, but no music.

—Hurry up, a boy shouted.

—Who said tha'? said Mickah. —Which one o' yis said tha'? They watched him tearing along the front, grabbing shoulders.

—Billy, said Joey The Lips.

—Yeah?

—I Thank You.

—Wha' ——Oh fuck, yeah! Sorry.

—THUH THUH — DAH THUH — THUH THUH — DAH THUH —

   THUH THUH — DAH THUH — THUH THUH — DAH THUH —

Deco stepped up and walked along the front of the stage. He looked down at his audience.

—I want everybody to get up off o' your seats an' (—Wha' fuckin' seats? Mickah shouted.) —an' get your arms together an' your hands together an' give me some o' tha' Ooold Soul Clappin'.

Billy: — THUH THUH — DAH THUH — THUH THUH — DAH THUH —

Derek got going on the bass.

Deco sang.

— YEH DIDN'T HAVE TO LOVE ME LIKE YEH DID BUT YEH DID BUT YEH DID —

Joey The Lips and Dean: — TRUP —

Deco and The Commitmentettes: —AND—

I — THANK — YOU ——

—YEH DIDN'T HAVE TO SQUEEZE ME —

The girls squeezed themselves.

—Get up! someone roared.

—LIKE YEH DID BUT YEH DID BUT YEH DID —

The horns: — TRUP —

—AND —

I — THANK — YOU ——

A small hand grabbed Bernie's shoe. She stepped on it and turned.

—AAAH! ——Oh mammy! ——— yeh cunt, yeh. —Jaysis!

—EVERYDAY —

THERE'S SOMETHIN' NEW ——

YEH PULL OU' YOUR BAG AN' YOUR BATH IS DUE —

Imelda sniffed under her arm. Someone whistled.

—YEH GOT ME TRYIN' —

NEW THANGS TOO —

JUST —

SO —

I —

CAN KEEP UP WITH YOU ——

YEH DIDN'T HAVE TO SHAKE IT —

The Commitmentettes shook it.
                —LIKE YEH DID BUT YEH DID BUT YEH
          DID—
The horns: — TRUP —
—AND —
                I — THANK — YOU ——
YEH DIDN'T HAVE TO MAKE IT —
A mike screeched.
—Sorry 'bou' tha', they heard Jimmy shout. —My fault.
——Won't happen again.
It did though.
So far Outspan hadn't played a chord. He stood looking at
the boards, stiff. Deco was prancing up and down (he was
used to his suit by now) and Joey The Lips and Dean had been
forced back, up against the drums. Natalie's shoes were
digging into her. Bernie's hair was coming down.
But they were getting away with it. The thirty-three and
Mickah were enjoying the show. They were also expecting
Deco to fall off the stage any time now.
So they didn't need Mickah's prompting when I Thank You
ended.
—Clap. Go on. ——Clap.
They were clapping already. Mrs Foster was out of her seat.
She hadn't noticed that her son hadn't done anything yet.
—Hello, Barrytown, said Deco.
—Hello, Deco!
Deco rubbed his arm across his forehead.
—I hope yis like me group, said Deco.
Those watching the other Commitments saw them stiffen-
ing, and Billy making a rude gesture at Deco's back with one
of his sticks.
—This one's called Chain Gang.
—HUH ——————
    HAH ——————
    HUH ——————
    HAH ——————
Outspan turned so that he was looking away from his

87

mother. That helped. He began to play, the same chord, but it was a start.

Derek sang.

—WELL DON'T YEH KNOW —

Deco stepped in front of him.

Deco: — THAT'S THE SOUND O' THE MEN —

WORKIN' ON THE CHAIN ——

GA — EE — ANG ——

They were dancing. The audience was dancing, a lot of them, little mods and modettes, shaking, turning in time together, folding their arms, turning, folding their arms, turning. Mickah tried to stop them.

—Just listen, righ'.

But this was their kind of music. Jimmy saw Outspan's mother dancing with them. Mickah had to leave them alone.

Two heavy metallers were leaning against the wall at the side. Mickah went over to them.

—Get dancin', youse.

They started to head-bang.

—Not like tha'.

Mickah stopped them.

—Like them over there.

Back on-stage, an accident was going to happen. It was James' solo and Deco was killing time, swinging the mike over his head. The mike was rising to his right and swooping to his left. It swooped into the back of Bernie's head. She was sent flying forward and she had to jump off the stage.

The Commitments stopped.

There were disappointed Aahs from the crowd and then clapping, Mickah inspired.

Joey The Lips jumped off the stage. There were cheers. Jimmy was down there too, helping them find the heel that had broken off Bernie's shoe. The search kept her mind off the pain at the back of her head.

On-stage, Deco was being given out to.

—Yeh stupid cunt, yeh.

Imelda kicked out at him, and connected. Billy threw a stick at him. It hit his shoulder.

—Yeh were told not to do tha', said Derek.

—I forgot.

—Another thing, said Billy. —It's not YOUR fuckin' group.

—Okay okay, said Deco.

He stood at the edge of the stage. Outspan was looking mean.

—I'm sorry, I'm sorry, righ'.

Bernie came back. She left her shoes and heel in Jimmy's hands. Imelda and Natalie took their shoes off.

—Good girls, Sisters, said Joey The Lips.

He stopped on his way past Deco.

—You apologize very, very nicely to Bernadette or you get my trumpet up your ass.

Deco couldn't believe this. This little baldy fuck was threatening him.

—Move! Joey The Lips roared.

Deco hopped to it.

—Listen, Bernie. ——Sorry, righ'. ———Really.

—Yeah. ———Well, said Bernie.

—Wha' Bernie's tryin' to say, said Imelda,—is tha' you're a stupid bollix.

Mickah was singing from behind the crowd.

—WHY ARE WE —

WAI —

TIN' ——

—Okay, said Deco into the mike. —Thanks a lot. Tha' one was dedicated to the lads in jail. Mountjoy an' tha', who're in for drugs ——like ——because it must be like a chain gang for them. ———We hope they get better an'——because, like the banner says, Heroin Kills.

—So do you.

—Who said tha'?——Come here, you.

They watched Mickah picking up a child and carrying him to the door.

89

—It's not spelt righ', a boy took advantage of Mickah's absence.

—Fuck off, Smartarse, said Deco. —An'annyway, if you're ever tryin' to give up the drugs yeh can always reach ou'.

Nothing happened.

—Billy.

—Wha'?

—Reach Ou'.

—Oh yeah!

—THU — CUDADUNG CUDADUNG CUDADUNG

—THU — CUDADUNG CUDADUNG CUDADUNG

Outspan was happier now. Derek had his eyes closed. Dean wiped his face with his hankie. A drum fell over. Billy kept going.

———JUST LOOK OVER YOUR SHOULDER, Deco yelled.

The Commitmentettes looked over their shoulders.

  —THU — CUDADUNG CUDADUNG CUDADUNG

  —THU — CUDADUNG CUDADUNG CUDADUNG —

  —I'LL ——

        BE THERE ——

           TO LOVE AN'CHERISH —

              YOU —

                 HOU —

                    OU —

  I'LL ——

        BE THERE ——

    WITH A LOVE THA' IS SO —

              TRUE —

                HUE —

                  UE ——

Derek jumped as he thumped at the string and he walked backwards into the piano. James found his fingers on the wrong keys. The piano had moved, bashed into the backdrop, the operetta society's South Pacific scenery (last year's Sound of Music scenery with a very yellow palm tree painted onto one of the hills).

The song was over. The audience didn't know this until Mickah told them to clap.

The caretaker assessed the damage.

—No harm done. ——It's a crummy bloody thing annyway. A spa could paint better than tha', he told Jimmy as the two of them got off the stage.

—How yis doin' ou' there? Deco asked his audience.

—Very well, thanks, said Mrs Foster.

—Okay, said Deco. —This one's for the lads in CIE.

—What's he on abou'? Billy asked James.

He was putting the drum back.

—I just do not know, said James.

—ALL ABOARD, said Deco. —THE NIGHT TRAIN.

The little mods and modettes knew this one. They cheered. They formed a train as The Commitments got going. Joey The Lips and Dean pointed their horns at the lighting. Derek and Outspan shuffled in time together. Deco chugged up and down the front of the stage. The girls went off-stage to have a look at Bernie's shoe. Billy lobbed a stick into the crowd.

No one caught it because everyone was part of the train, Mickah the caboose, going round and round the centre of the hall.

—OH YEAH, Deco started.

OH YEAH ——

He swung his arms.

—MIAMI FLORIDA ——

ATLANTA GEORGIA ——

RALEIGH NORTH CAROLINA ——

WASHIN'TON D.C. ——

He went off the tracks for a second.

—SOMEWHERE THE FUCK IN WEST VIRGINIA ——

BALTIMORE MARYLAND ——

PHILADELPH — EYE — AY ——

NEW YORK CITY —

HEADIN' HOME ——

91

BOSTON MASSACHU — MASSATUST — YEH
KNOW YOURSELF ——
AN' DON'T FORGET NEW ORLEANS THE HOME
O' THE BLUES ——
OH YEAH ——
THE NIGH' TRAIN ——
THE NIGH' TRAIN ——
COME ON NOW —
THE NIGH' TRAIN ——
THE NIGH' TRAIN ——
NIGH' TRAIN ——
CARRIES ME HOME —
NIGH' TRAIN ——
CARRIES ME HOME ——

Deco let the other Commitments go on without him. The important part was coming.

Dublin Soul was about to be born.

He wiped his hands on his trousers. Joey The Lips gave him the thumbs-up. The Commitmentettes came back on-stage.

Joey The Lips and Dean were bringing the train back round towards Deco.

Deco growled: — STARTIN' OFF IN CONNOLLY ——

The train in the hall stopped as they waited to hear what was going to follow that.

Deco was travelling north, by DART.

—MOVIN' ON OU' TO KILLESTER ——

They laughed. This was great. They pushed up to the stage.

—HARMONSTOWN RAHENY ——

They cheered.

—AN' DON'T FORGET KILBARRACK — THE HOME O' THE BLUES —

Dublin Soul had been delivered.

—HOWTH JUNCTION BAYSIDE ——

THEN ON OU' TO SUTTON WHERE THE RICH FOLKS LIVE ——

OH YEAH ——

NIGH' TRAIN ——

His voice went but he got it back.

—EASY TO BONK YOUR FARE ——

Wild, happy cheers.

—NIGH' TRAIN ——

    AN ALSATIAN IN EVERY CARRIAGE ——

    NIGH' TRAIN ——

    LOADS O' SECURITY GUARDS ——

    NIGH' TRAIN ——

    LAYIN' INTO YOUR MOT AT THE BACK ——

    NIGH' TRAIN ——

    GETTIN' SLAGGED BY YOUR MATES ——

    NIGH' TRAIN ——

    GETTIN' CHIPS FROM THE CHINESE CHIPPER——

    OH NIGH' TRAIN ——

    CARRIES ME HOME —

    THE NIGH' TRAIN ——

    CARRIES ME HOME ——

Two boys invaded the stage and jumped up and down and went to jump off again. Deco grabbed one of them and stuck the mike under his mouth.

—Sing.

—No way.

—Go on. NIGH' TRAIN —

The little mod squealed: NIGH' TRAIN.

More of them climbed up on the stage and became a little choir around the mike-stand.

—NIGH' TRAIN, they roared.

—NIGH' TRAIN, they roared.

—NIGH' TRAIN.

It eventually stopped. The cheering went on for minutes. Derek let himself cry.

Jimmy called them off.

From the side Jimmy spoke into the mike.

—Ladies an' gentlemen, let's hear it for——Yes, Yes, Yes, The Commitments. ——The Commitments, ladies an' gentle-men. ——The Hardest Workin' Band in the World. ——— The Commitments —— bringing soul to Dublin ——Bringing

the People's Music to the People. ——Yes, Yes, Yes, Yes —
The Commitments.

Mickah dug his finger into backs.

—Shout for more. Go on. ——More.

—MORE!

—More!

—We can't hear yis, said Jimmy.

—Where d'yeh think you're goin'? said Mickah.

—Home, said a boy.

—Get back up there an' cheer. ——Go on.

—I have to go home. ——Me ma will burst me.

—I'll burst yeh if yeh don't get back.

—We can't hear yis, said Jimmy.

He put his hand over the mike.

—What Becomes of the Broken Hearted, then the girls do
Stoned Love, then yis come off again, then Knock on Wood,
righ'? ——Got tha'?

—Wha' abou' Man's World?

—They're too young, said Jimmy.

—When a Man Loves a Woman?

—Too slow, said Jimmy. —They'd get bored. They're too
young. A couple o' fast ones is enough for them.

—But we rehearsed loads more, said Derek.

—Brother Jimmy speaks the truth, said Joey The Lips. —A
short, sharp shock works best with the very young Brothers
and Sisters.

The caretaker arrived.

—There's a fella at the back, from tha' Northside News
thing.

—Fame, said James. —I'm gonna live till Tuesday.

—Janey! said Natalie. —Does he have a camera?

—Yeah, he does, said the caretaker. —He's a bag full o'
them. Flashes an' ——yeh know.

Jimmy spoke into the mike.

—They're comin' back, ladies an' gentlemen, The Commitments are comin' back.

He pointed to James.

94

—Clap hands clap hands for James The Soul Surgeon Clifford.

Deco pushed James onto the stage. James stood there.

—The man performs transplants on the piano, ladies an' gentlemen. ——Soul Surgeon Clifford.

James went over to the piano.

—On drums, Billy The Animal Mooney.

Billy jumped on-stage and gorilla-walked to his drums.

One at a time Jimmy sent them back. Joey The Lips got the biggest cheer.

The girls were last.

—Last, said Jimmy. —The girls.

There were screams. The girls looked at one another and raised their eyes to heaven.

—Sonya ——Sofia ——An' Tanya. ———The Commitmentettes, ladies an' gentlemen.

They strolled onto the stage. Natalie ducked when she saw something fly up and out of the darkness. It landed behind them, a little pair of light blue underpants.

The Commitments cracked up. Deco kicked the underpants off the stage. They came back. Deco kicked them across to Jimmy.

—Okay, y'awl, said Deco to the fans. —Let's take it to the bridge.

—I'll get them back for yeh after, righ', said Mickah. —When it's over.

—Yeh said yeh'd give me a pound, the boy reminded him.

—I'll let yeh in for nothin' the next time, said Mickah.

This injustice stunned the boy for a while. He'd just made a sap of himself, flinging his kaks at your women on the stage and now he wasn't even going to be paid for it. Then words came back to him.

—Yeh fuckin' bollix, yeh.

Mickah gave him a good dig, then felt guilty and gave the boy fifty pence, and another dig.

Most of the encore went well. The little mods recognized

95

What Becomes of the Broken Hearted and they cheered when Deco sang the bit about waiting under Clery's clock.

—Thank you, little Brothers and Sisters, said Joey the Lips. —The Lord Jesus smiles down on you. Thank you. ——Now the Sisters, Sonya, Sofia and Tanya, are going to cut loose. ——Brothers and Sisters, The Commitmentettes.

—Whooo! said Deco. —Let's take it to the bridge.

—Wha' fuckin' bridge?

—Who said tha'? Mickah roared.

—Matt Talbot bridge.

—Who said tha'?

Deco wouldn't get out of the girls' way. He stood his ground at the front, leering at his audience.

Billy shouted: —Get ou' o' the fuckin' way.

—Stay cool, said Deco.

He handed the mike to Imelda. She stung his ear with it.

And they were off. Against The Commitments' best ever, tightest thumping back-beat, the girls bleated Stoned Love. They swayed, clapped their hands, stopped. And before the crowd could start screaming, they started again. Jimmy had to climb up onto the stage to gently shove the small boys and girls back off.

Deco came back on and Knock on Wood began. It ended early when he knocked over the horn section's mike and half the horn section gave him an almighty kick up the hole.

Deco wasn't going to be able to sing again for a good few minutes so Jimmy drew the curtain. James and Billy looked at Deco kneeling on the floor, bent forward.

—Tha' took him to the bridge, said Billy.

—Quite, said James.

—He was lookin' for it, Dean was explaining to Jimmy.

—Could yeh not have waited till he stopped singin'? said Jimmy. —Or least till he got to the end o' the sentence.

Outspan laughed.

The first gig was over.

Mickah's head appeared from under the curtain.

—Hey, Jimmy, he said. —There's a sap here from ——
Hang on.

Mickah was gone. And back.

—The Northside News. ——He wants a word.

When Jimmy drew the curtain back they all saw the sap
from Northside News. He was tall, young, with tinted glasses.

—Great gig, said the sap from the Northside News.
—Who's in charge?

—I'm the singer, Deco told him.

—For the time being, said Jimmy.

—Well said, Jimmy, said Outspan.

—Pack the gear, lads, said Jimmy. —Keep the suits on but.
——For the snaps. ——Joey, come on.

Jimmy jumped off the stage. He shook the sap's hand.

They introduced themselves.

—An' this is Joey The Lips Fagan, said Jimmy.

—Hi.

—Good evening, Brother.

—Will we be in next Friday's one? Mickah asked the sap.

—Give Billy a hand with his kit, will yeh, Mickah.

Mickah grabbed Jimmy's fringe.

—Say please.

—Please, Mickah.

Mickah grinned.

—Certainly. ——No problem.

—Our security man, Jimmy explained.

—The price of fame, said Joey The Lips.

—Right, said the sap.

He had a notebook.

—When were you formed?

—Some months back, said Joey The Lips.

—How did the band come about?

Jimmy spoke. —Well, I put an ——

—Destiny, said Joey The Lips. —It was destined to happen.

Jimmy liked the sound of that so he let Joey The Lips keep
talking.

97

—My man, said Joey The Lips. —We are a band with a mission.

—A mission?

—You hear good and you hear right.

The sap looked to Jimmy but Jimmy said nothing.

—What kind of mission d'you mean?

—An important mission, Brother.

Jimmy leaned over to Joey The Lips and whispered: —Don't mention God.

Joey The Lips smiled.

—We are bringing Soul to Dublin, Brother, he said. —We are bringing the music, the Soul, back to the people. ——The proletariat. ——That's p,r,o,l,e,t,a,r,i,a,t.

—Thanks a lot.

Jimmy spoke. —We're against racial and sexual discrimination an' heroin, isn't tha' righ', Joey?

—That is right, said Joey The Lips.

—We ain't gonna play Sun City, said Jimmy.

—Tell the people, Joey The Lips told the sap, —to put on their soul shoes because The Commitments are coming and there's going to be dancing in the streets.

—This'll make good copy, said the sap.

—And there'll be barricades in the streets too, said Joey The Lips. —Now you've got great copy.

—Wow, said the sap. —Nice one. ——When's your next gig?

—My friend, said Joey The Lips. —We are the Guerrillas of Soul. We do not announce our gigs. We hit, and then we sink back into the night.

Jimmy tapped the sap's shoulder.

—I think there's a U in Guerrillas.

—Oh yeah. ——Thanks a lot.

—Do yeh want to take a few photographs?

—Yeah, right.

—Joey, make sure their ties are all on straigh', will yeh?

—I obey.

Joey The Lips sat on a chair. The Commitments kneeled

and stood around him. Bernie sat on his knee. Imelda lay in front of him, leaning on an elbow, chin in her hand, hair in her eyes. Natalie did the same, in the opposite direction. Jimmy, Mickah, the caretaker and Mrs Foster stood at the sides, like football managers and magic-sponge men. That way they all fitted.

*　*　*

There was nothing for a few weeks.

The Commitments rehearsed.

Jimmy did the round of the music pubs in town. One of them only did heavy metal groups. The manager explained to Jimmy that the heavy metal crowd was older and very well behaved, and drank like fish.

A barman in another one told Jimmy that the manager only booked groups that modelled themselves on Echo and The Bunnymen because they were always reviewed and the reviews usually included praise for the manager and his pioneering work.

On the fourth night Jimmy found a pub that would take The Commitments for one night, a Thursday, no fee, but three free pints each. The head barman was a big Motown fan and he and the Northside News headline (Soul Soldiers of Destiny) convinced the owner.

Jimmy couldn't figure out how it got the name The Regency Rooms. There was only one room, about ten times bigger than his bedroom. The walls were stained and bare. The floor was stained and bare. The stools and chairs showed their guts. The stage was a foot-high plywood platform.

—They won't all fit, said Mickah.

—I know tha', said Jimmy. —Billy will, an' the girls an' Outspan an' Derek. Put the piano over there at the jacks door, righ', an' Joey an' Dean can go over there an' Deco in the middle. An' the mixer on the table there.

—Good thinkin'.

When the head barman came in to work he went for Jimmy.

—You didn't tell us it was a fuckin' orchestra we were bookin', he screamed.

99

—I thought yeh'd know, said Jimmy. —Yeh said yeh were a Motown fan.

—The wife has The Supremes' Greatest Hits. ———It's the same size as any other record.

—We've squashed them all in, said Jimmy.

—Yeah. ——An' yis still take up half the fuckin' pub. ——Look. The piano. ——Yeh'd usually get abou' twenty into tha' corner.

—Yeh would in your bollix, said Mickah. —Fuckin' leprechauns maybe. ——Or test-tube babies.

—Mickah.

—Wha'?

—The drums.

—Okay.

—Anyway, said the head barman when Mickah was a safe distance away,—this is the last time yis'll be playin' here. Nothin' personal now but we can't afford the space. We usually do groups with just three in them.

He thought of something else.

—Another thing. ——There's no way we're givin' yis three pints each. We couldn't. ——One'll have to do.

—Ah, fuck tha'! said Jimmy.

—There's millions of yis, said the head barman. ——You can have the three though. Just make it look like you're payin' me.

Jimmy looked around him.

—Okay. ——Done.

There was a good crowd. Thirty would have been a great crowd in this place. The room was packed solid. The ones standing up had to hold their glasses up above their shoulders.

—An older bunch this time, Jimmy pointed out. —This'll be a better concert ——gig. More adult orientated. Know wha' I mean?

The Commitments stood around the platform waiting for the go ahead from the head barman.

—These people have votes, said Jimmy. —This is our real audience.

Outspan stood on the platform searching the crowd for his mother. He didn't think she'd have the neck to come to this one but he wanted to make sure.

Jimmy picked his way over to Mickah.

—Listen, he said. —They have their own bouncer here so——just enjoy the show, righ'.

—I was talkin' to him, Mickah told him. —He's goin' to give me a shout if there's anny messin'.

—That'll be nice, said Jimmy.

He got behind his desk. A mike screeched.

It was half-nine. The head barman gave Jimmy the nod. Jimmy got up and took Deco's mike.

—Ladies an' gentlemen, The Regency Rooms presents, all the way from Dublin (that didn't get the laughs he'd been expecting), The Hardest Workin' Band in the World, The Saviours of Soul ——Yes, Yes, Yes, Yes, ——The Commitments.

They were sharper this time. Billy knew what he was doing. Outspan didn't have his ma gawking up at him. Deco was hemmed in by tables on three sides and by Dean and Joey The Lips behind him. He couldn't budge. There'd be no accidents tonight.

Natalie fell off the platform. But it wasn't an accident. Imelda pushed her. They were only messing.

The songs were going down well. They were sticking to the classics, the ones everyone knew. The Dublined lyrics were welcomed with laughter and, towards closing time, cheers and clapping. The Commitmentettes were whistled at, but politely.

One man roared: —Get them off yeh!

Mickah advised him to stay quiet.

Deco's between-songs chat was better. Jimmy and Joey The Lips had been coaching him.

He was still a prick though, Jimmy had to admit to Mickah.

Night Train was a very big hit. There wasn't room for an audience train but the ones standing rocked up and down and the ones sitting stood.

It was over. The Commitments couldn't leave the stage,

unless they all piled into the jacks, so they stayed at the
platform while the audience clapped and cheered, and waited
for Jimmy to take over.

—More!

—Yes, Yes, Yes, ladies an' gentlemen —— comrades.
You've heard the people's music tonight. ———The Com-
mitments, ladies an' gentlemen. ——The Saviours o' Soul.
——Do yis want to hear more?

They wanted more.

Jimmy handed Deco the mike.

—Introduce the lads.

—Okay, said Deco into the mike. —I'd better introduce the
rest. ——On drums, Billy Mooney. ——On guitar ——If yeh
could hear it, ha ha ——Outspan sorry, L. Terence Foster.
Derek, there on bass. ——James Soul Surgeon Clifford is the
specky guy on the joanna.

Each Commitment was being clapped but The Commitments weren't hearing it. All Commitment eyes were burning
Deco. This wasn't what they'd rehearsed, at all.

—Dean Fay on the sax there, righ', an' Joey The Lips Fagan
on the trumpet. Joey on the horn, wha'. ——An' they're
Tanya, Sonya an' Sofia, The Commitmentettes. I'm Deco
Blanketman Cuffe and we are The Commitments. This one's
called When a Man Loves a Woman.

Deco climbed up on a vacant stool.

—THU —CUDADUNG CUDADUNG CUDADUNG —

Billy blammed out the Reach Out — I'll Be There beat, then
stopped. He got out from behind the drums and went across
to the jacks.

James played, then Derek, then Deco started to sing.

—WHEN A MA — HAN LOVES A WO —

MAN ——

CAN'T KEEP HIS MIND ON NOTHIN' EH — ELSE

——

HE'LL CHANGE THE WORLD —
FOR THE GOOD THINGS HE'S FOU —HOUND ——

IF SHE'S BA —HAD HE CAN'T SEE —
                              IT ———
SHE CAN DO NO WRO — O — ON — NG ——
TURN HIS BACK ON HIS BEST FRIEND IF HE PUT
HER DOWN ———

It was beautiful. Jimmy blinked. The Commitments were for-
giving Deco. Billy was still in the jacks though. The head barman sent a fourth pint over to Jimmy, and even one for Mickah.

—WHEN THIS —
                    MAN LOVES THIS WO —
                              MAN ———

Outspan's rhythm playing was just right here, light and
jangly.

—AN' GIVES HER EVERYTHING ON EARTH ———

Outspan swayed.

—TRYIN' TO HOLD ONTO ——
YOUR —
CROCK O' GOLD ——
BABY—
PLEASE DON'T —
TREAT ME BA — AA — AA — AAD ———

The crowd oohed.

—WHEN A MA — HAN LOVES A WO —
                              MAN ——
HE'LL BUY HER LOADS O' SWE — EE — EETS
———

HE'LL EVEN BRING HER TO STUPID PLACES
LIKE THE ZOO — OO ——
HE'LL SPEND ALL HIS WAGES ON —
                              HER ——
BUT DON'T LET HIM SEE YEH LOOKIN' AT
HER ——
COS HE'LL GET A HAMMER AN' HE'LL FUCKIN'
CREASE YOU ———

No one laughed. It wasn't funny. It was true.

—YES WHEN A MA —HAN LOVES A
                    WO — MAN —

I KNOW EXACTLY HOW HE FEEL — YELLS —
COS —
BABY —
BABY —
BABY
    I LOVE YOU ———

It was over. The lights went off and on and off and on. Friends came up to congratulate The Commitments.

—You've a great voice, a woman told Deco.

—I don't need you to tell me tha', said Deco.

Billy came out of the jacks. Before he could be asked if he was alright, he'd made it over to his drums and picked up a stick. He stepped over to Deco and started to hit him on the neck and shoulders with it.

He chanted as he walloped.

—I'm Billy—— The Animal Mooney, d'yeh ———hear me? Billy The —— Animal Mooney an' we all ———have stage names an' you know fuckin' ———well wha' they are, yeh lousy ——bollix yeh, we're not your group, we're ———not your fuckin' ——group ——

Mickah held his arms down. Deco got out from under him.

—Yeh were lookin' for tha', said Jimmy.

—Wha' did I do now? Deco asked.

—Oh look it! said Bernie. —He's after burstin' one of his plukes.

Most of The Commitments laughed.

—Yeh didn't introduce the group properly, said Jimmy.

  I forgot.

—Fuck off!

—I was oney jokin'. Yis have no sense o' humour, d'yis know tha'?

—An' you have? Outspan asked.

—Yeah.

—You've a big head too, pal.

—You're just jealous——

—Fuck off.

—All o' yis.

—Enough, said Joey The Lips.

—Jealous o' you? ——Huh ——

—Enough.

—Joey's righ', said Jimmy. —We'll meet tomorrow nigh' an' have this ou'.

Deco left.

—Watch ou' for the fans, Derek shouted after him.

Mickah let go of Billy.

—He's ruinin' everythin', Jimmy, said Billy. —I'm sorry abou' tha', yeh know. But I'm sick of him. It was great an' then he —— He's a fuckin' cunt.

—That's an accurate description, said James.

—I'll kill him the next time, said Billy. —I will. ——I will now.

—He's not worth it, said Derek.

—He is, Billy, said Imelda. —Kill him.

—Ah, for fuck sake! said Jimmy.

—I'm oney messin', said Imelda. —Don't kill him, Billy.

—Yeah, said Natalie. —Just give him a hidin'.

—I'll do tha' for yis if yeh want, said Mickah.

—Brothers, said Joey The Lips.

His palms were lifted. The Commitments were ready to listen to him.

—Now, Brother Deco might not be the most likeable of the Brothers ——

—He's a prick, Joey.

—He is, Brother Dean. I admit I agree. Brother Deco is a prick. He is a prick. But the voice, Brothers and Sisters. ——His voice is not the voice of a prick. That voice belongs to God.

No one argued with him.

—We need him, Brothers. We need the voice.

—Pity abou' the rest of him.

—Granted.

—I'll talk to him tomorrow at work, said Jimmy.

—Tell him I'll kill him.

* * *

The Commitments got a mention in the Herald.

—The Commitments, said the mention,—played a strong Motown(ish) set. New to the live scene, they were at times ragged but always energetic. Their suits didn't fit them properly. My companion fell in love with the vocalist, a star surely in the ascendant. I hate him! (—Oh fuck! said Jimmy.) Warts and all, The Commitments are a good time. They might also be important. See them.

* * *

Armed with this and the Northside News article, Jimmy got The Commitments a Wednesday night in another pub, a bigger one, The Miami Vice (until recently The Dark Rosaleen). It was a bit on the southside, but near the DART.

The Commitments went down well again. Deco stuck to the rehearsed lines. Everyone went home happy.

They were given a month's residency, Wednesdays. They could charge two pounds admission if they could fill the pub the first night.

They filled it.

A certain type of audience was coming to see them. The crowds reminded Jimmy of the ones he'd been part of at the old Blades gigs. They were older and wiser now, grown-up mods. Their clothes were more adventurous but they were still neat and tidy. The women's hairstyles were more varied. They weren't really modettes any more.

A good audience, Jimmy decided. The mods and ex-mods knew good music when they heard it. Their dress was strict but they listened to anything good, only, mind you, if the musicians dressed neatly.

The Commitments were neat. Jimmy was happy with the audience. So was Joey The Lips. These were The People.

Another thing Jimmy noticed: they were shouting for Night Train.

—NIGH' TRAIN, Deco screeched.

OH SWEE' MOTHER O' JAYSIS —

NIGH' TRAIN —

OH SWEE' MOTHER O' FUCKIN' JAYSIS —
NIGH' TRAIN —
NIGH' TRAIN —
NIGH' TRAIN ——
COME ON ——
The Commitmentettes lifted their right arms and pulled the whistle cords.
—WHHWOO WOOO —
—NIGH'
Deco wiped his forehead and opened his neck buttons.
—TRAIN.
—More!
—MORE!
They shouted for more, but that was it. Three times in one night was enough.
—Thank y'awl, said Deco. —We're The Commitments. ——Good nigh' an' God bless.
—We should make a few shillin's next week an' annyway, wha', said Mickah.
He was collecting the mikes.
—Brother Jimmy, said Joey The Lips. —I'm worried. —— About Dean.
—Wha' abou' Dean?
—He told me he's been listening to jazz.
—What's wrong with tha'? Jimmy wanted to know.
—Everything, said Joey The Lips. —Jazz is the antithesis of soul.
—I beg your fuckin' pardon!
—I'll go along with Joey there, said Mickah.
—See, said Joey The Lips. —Soul is the people's music. Ordinary people making music for ordinary people. ——Simple music. Any Brother can play it. The Motown sound, it's simple. Thump-thump-thump-thump. ——That's straight time. Thump-thump-thump-thump. ——See? Soul is democratic, Jimmy. Anyone with a bin lid can play it. ——It's the people's music.

—Yeh don't need anny honours in your Inter to play soul, isn't tha' wha' you're gettin' at, Joey?

—That's right, Brother Michael.

—Mickah.

—Brother Mickah. That's right. You don't need a doctorate to be a doctor of soul.

—Nice one.

—An' what's wrong with jazz? Jimmy asked.

—Intellectual music, said Joey The Lips. —It's anti-people music. It's abstract.

—It's cold an' emotionless, amn't I righ'? said Mickah.

—You are. ——It's got no soul. It is sound for the sake of sound. It has no meaning. ——It's musical wanking, Brother.

—Musical wankin', said Mickah. —That's good. ——Here, yeh could play tha' at the Christmas parties. ——Instead o' musical chairs.

—What's Dean been listenin' to? Jimmy asked.

—Charlie Parker.

—He's supposed to be good but.

—Good! Joey The Lips gasped. —The man had no right to his black skin.

Joey The Lips was getting worked up. It was some sight. They stood back and enjoyed it.

—They should have burnt it off with a fucking blow lamp.

—Language, Joey!

—Polyrhythms! Polyrhythms! I ask you! That's not the people's sound. ——Those polyrhythms went through Brother Parker's legs and up his ass. ——And who did he play to? I'll tell you, middle-class white kids with little beards and berets. In jazz clubs. Jazz clubs! They didn't even clap. They clicked their fingers.

Joey The Lips clicked his fingers.

—Like that. ——I'll tell you something, Brothers. —— I've never told anyone this before.

They waited.

—The biggest regret of my life is that I wasn't born black.

—Is tha' righ', Joey?

—Charlie Parker was born black. A beautiful, shiny, bluey sort of black. ——And he could play. He could play alright. But he abused it, he spat on it. He turned his back on his people so he could entertain hip honky brats and intellectuals. ——Jazz! It's decadent. ——The Russians were right. They banned it.

Joey The Lips was calmer now. He stopped picking at his sleeve.

—The Bird! he spat. ——And that's what poor Dean is listening to.

—Sounds bad alrigh'.

—Oh, it's bad. ——Very bad. Parker, John Coltrane —— Herbie Hancock —— and the biggest motherfucker of them all, Miles Davis.

——————Em, why does it worry you, exactly?

—We're going to lose him.

—Wha' d'yeh mean?

—Dean is going to become a Jazz Purist.

The words almost made Joey The Lips retch.

—He won't want to play for the people any more. Dean has soul but he's going to kill it if he listens to jazz. Jazz is for the mind.

—Wha' can we do? said Jimmy.

—We can give him a few digs, said Mickah.

—Mickah.

—Wha'?

—The drums.

—Okay.

*　*　*

Hot Press came to the second gig of the residency, and paid in because Mickah wouldn't believe him.

—I'm from the Hot Press.

—I'm from the kitchen press, said Mickah. —It's two quid or fuck off.

Mickah took in one hundred and twenty pounds. It made a great bulge in his shirt pocket. He showed it to James.

—The big time, wha'.

Jimmy studied Dean for tell-tale signs. There weren't many, but they were there. Dean hunched over the sax now, protecting it. He used to throw it up and out and pull himself back, to let everyone see its shininess. It wouldn't be long before he'd be sitting on a stool when he was playing. The stool definitely wasn't soul furniture. Jimmy was upset. He liked Dean.

Deco was his usual self. It was a pity his voice was so good. Jimmy didn't pay much attention to Billy.

This was a pity. Because Billy left The Commitments, just before the encore.

—On yeh go, Bill, said Jimmy.

—I can't, said Billy.

—Why not?

—I've left.

A long gap, then —Wha'?

—I've left. I'm not goin' back on. ——I've left.

—Jaysis! said Jimmy.

When a Man Loves a Woman didn't need drums.

—James, Jimmy roared. —Fire away.

—Now, said Jimmy. —Tell your Uncle Jimmy all abou' it.

—I just ——

Jimmy could see Billy thinking.

—It's just ——I hate him, Jimmy. I fuckin' hate him ——I can't even sleep at nigh'.

Billy's face was clenched.

—Why's tha'?

—I stay awake tryin' to think o' better ways to hate him. ——Imaginin', yeh know, ways to kill him.

Billy looked straight at Jimmy.

—I phoned his house yesterday. Can yeh believe tha'? I never done ann'thin like tha' before. No way. ——His oul' one —I s'pose it was his oul' one annyway ——answered. I said nothin'. ——I just listened.

—Yeh'd want to get a grip on yourself, son. You're talkin' like a fuckin' spacer.

—I know, I fuckin' know. Do yeh not think I know? ——— That's why I've left. I never want to have to look at the cunt again. ——Want to get him ou' o' me life, know wha' I mean? ——I made up me mind durin' I Thank You. The way he was shovin' his arse into your women at the front. It was fuckin' disgustin'. ——Annyway I've left, so ———I've left.

—He's not worth hatin'.

—He fuckin' is, yeh know.

Jimmy looked at Billy. He'd left alright. There was no point trying to talk him back in. That made Jimmy angry.

—Annyone can play the drums, Billy. ——So fuck off.

—Ah, Jimmy!

—Go an' shite.

—I want me drums.

—After the gig.

—It's my van, remember.

—We'll hire a van. No, we'll buy one. A better one than your scabby van.

Jimmy was going over to the platform but he turned back to Billy.

—A light blue one with The Commitments written on the side in dark blue. An' Billy The Animal Mooney Is A Bollox on the back, righ'.

Billy said nothing.

When a Man Loves a Woman was over. They were going to do Knock on Wood now.

Jimmy got a drum stick and stood behind a snare drum.

The others watched.

—Righ', said Jimmy. —Are yis righ'?

—BLAM —

—Come on.

—BLAM —

—James, come on.

—BLAM —

By the end of Knock on Wood Jimmy thought he'd proved his point: anyone could play the drums.

It had been a great gig, Hot Press told Jimmy. Dublin

needed something like The Commitments, to get U2 out of its system. He'd be doing a review for the next issue. Then he asked for his two pounds back.

*　*　*

The Commitments didn't see Billy again. He didn't live in Barrytown.

Mickah called for Jimmy on Friday. There was a rehearsal in Joey The Lips' mother's garage. When they got to the bus stop Mickah spoke.

—Jimmy, have I ever asked yeh for annythin'?

—Yeah.

Mickah hadn't banked on that answer.

—When?

—Yeh asked me for a lend o' me red biro in school. To rule a margin because E. T. said as far as he was concerned your homework wasn't done till it had a margin.

—Jimmy, said Mickah. —I'm bein' serious. Now will yeh treat me with a little respect, okay. Now have I ever asked yeh for annythin'?

—No.

—That's better. ——Well, I'm goin' to ask yeh for somethin' now.

—I've no money.

—Jimmy, said Mickah. —I'm tryin' me best. But I'm goin' to have to hit yeh.

He was leaning into Jimmy.

—Wha' is it? said Jimmy.

—Let me play the drums.

—I was goin' ——

—Let me play the drums.

—Fair enough.

*　*　*

So Mickah was the new drummer. He even had a name for himself.

—Eh, Washin'ton D. C. Wallace.

112

The Commitments laughed. It was good.

—The D. C. stands for Dead Cool, said Mickah.

—Oh yeah, said Imelda. —That's very clever, tha' is.

They were waiting for Dean and James.

Joey The Lips spoke. —We have lost The Animal, Brothers and Sisters. We'll miss him. But we have a good man in his place, a city of a man. Washington D. C.

Jimmy took over.

—We've had our first crisis, righ', but we're over it. We're still The Commitments. An' we're reachin' our audience. Yeh saw tha' yourselves on Wednesday.

Jimmy let them remember Wednesday for a bit. It had been a good night.

—We'll dedicate our first album to Billy.

—We will in our holes, said Outspan.

—Ahh ——why not? said Bernie.

—We'd have to pay him.

—Would we?

—Fuck him so.

Joey The Lips went into the house to answer the phone.

Dean arrived while Joey The Lips was gone. He'd had his hair cropped.

—Jaysis, Dean, wha'.

He was wearing his shades.

—Dean, your shirt's gorgeous.

—Thanks.

Joey The Lips came back.

—Brother James on the telephone, Brothers. He can't make it. He has a mother of an examination. ——Tomorrow.

Joey The Lips had just seen Dean.

—Is the wattage of the bulb too strong for you, Dean?

Outspan and Derek laughed.

—It's the flowers on his shirt he's protectin' his eyes from, said Deco.

—Leave him alone. It's lovely.

Jimmy clapped his hands.

—Let's get goin'. ——Come on. We'll keep it short.

—Yeah, said Bernie. —Rehearsals are borin'.

—We need some fresh tunes, said Joey The Lips.

He patted Bernie's shoulder.

—Let's break Mickah in first, said Jimmy.

—That's Washin'ton D. C. durin' office hours, said Mickah.

He was behind the drum. There was only the one.

—Can we call yeh Washah for short? said Outspan.

—Yeh can, said Mickah, —but you'll get a hidin' for yourself.

—Washin'ton D. C., said Derek. —That's a deadly name, Mickah.

Mickah smacked the drum.

—Nothin' to it.

He smacked it again.

—That's fuckin' grand. ———Child's play.

—Try it with both sticks.

He did.

—There. ——How was tha'?

—Grand.

—Can we go home now? said Mickah.

Mickah was a good addition. The Commitments liked him and his enthusiasm came at the right time. They enjoyed his mistakes and his questions. They rehearsed again on Monday night. They wanted Mickah ready for Wednesday.

Mickah took the drum home with him. His da, the only harder man than Mickah in Barrytown, burned the sticks. His ma bought him a new set.

* * *

The Commitments were a revitalized outfit on the third Wednesday of the residency. They all arrived on time. The Commitmentettes had new tights, with little black butterflies behind the ankles. Mickah wore Jimmy's suit. James had a bottle of Mister Sheen. He polished the piano.

—More elbow grease there, said Outspan.

Jimmy took in the money at the door, one hundred and forty-six pounds. That meant thirteen more people than the week before. And that didn't include Hot Press and the three others with him he'd let in for nothing.

The Commitments played well.

Outspan and Derek had become very confident. The Commitmentettes were brilliant. They looked great, very glossy, and their sense of humour showed in their stage movements.

They were enjoying themselves.

Mickah tapped and thumped happily on the drum, sometimes using his fingers or his fist, once his forehead. His shoulders jumped as he drummed, way up over his ears.

One thing spoiled Jimmy's enjoyment: Dean's solo in Stop in the Name of Love. The Commitmentettes were at their best. They raised their right hands every time they sang STOP. Then they'd spin quickly before they continued with IN THE NAME OF LOVE. Mickah kept his eyes on them and his timing and their timing were perfect.

Dean's solo was good. It was really good, but it was new. It wasn't the one he'd always done.

Joey The Lips explained what was wrong with it later.

—Soul solos have corners. They fit into the thump-thump-thump-thump. The solo is part of the song. Are you with me?

—No.

—Strictly speaking, Brother, soul solos aren't really solos at all.

—Ah, Jaysis, Joey ——

—Shhh ——There are no gaps in soul. If it doesn't fit it isn't used. Soul is community. As Little Richard says, If It Don't Fit Don't Force It. Do you understand now?

—Sort of.

—Dean's solo didn't have corners. It didn't fit. It spiralled. It wasn't part of the song. ——It wasn't part of anything. It was a real solo. Washington D. C.'s drumming wasn't there as far as it was concerned. ——That's jazz, Brother. That's what jazz does. It makes the man selfish. He doesn't give a fuck about his Brothers. That's what jazz is doing to Dean, said Joey The Lips. —Poor Dean.

The Commitments finished with It's a Man's Man's Man's World. Mickah stood back. James gave the beat out here.

—DOOM — DAH DAH DAH DAH DAH —

DOOM — DAH DAH DAH DAH DAH —

Deco sang: —THIS IS A MAN — AN'S WORLD ——

The Commitmentettes shook their heads.

—DOOM — DAH DAH DAH DAH DAH —

DOOM — DAH DAH DAH DAH DAH —

—THIS IS A MA — AN'S WORLD ——

The girls shook their heads again. Some men in the audience cheered.

—BUT IT WOULDN'T BE NOTHIN' —

NOTHIN' ——

WITHOU' ——

A WOMAN OR A GURL ——

The Commitmentettes nodded. They turned to look at Deco. He was facing them.

—YEH KNOW ——

MAN MADE THE CAR —

THA' TAKES US ONTO THE RO — OAD ——

MAN MADE THE TRAY — AY — YAIN —

TO CARRY THE HEAVY LOAD——

—DOOM — DAH DAH DAH DAH DAH —

DOOM —— DAH DAH DAH DAH DAH ——

The Commitmentettes turned their backs on Deco. He pleaded with them.

—MAN MADE THE 'LECTRIC LIGH' ——

The girls looked over their shoulders at him.

—TO TAKE US OU' O' THE DA — HARK ——

MAN MADE THE BOAT FOR THE WAT — HAH ——

LIKE NOAH MADE THE AH — ARK ——

Outspan plucked the guitar like a harp.

—COS IT'S A MAN'S —

MAN'S —

MAN'S WORLD ——

BUT IT WOULDN'T BE NOTHIN' —

NOTHIN' ——

WITHOU' A WOMAN OR A GURREL ——
The girls swayed and nodded. Mickah swayed and nodded.
—YEH SEE ——
Deco was still singing to the girls.
—MAN DRIVES THE BUSES ——
    TO BRING US ROUN' AN' ABOU — OU' ———
    AN' MAN WORKS IN GUINNESSES ——
    TO GIVE US THE PINTS O' STOU — OUT ——
The crowd began to clap here. Deco raised his hands, and
the clapping stopped.
    —AN' MAN —
    MAN HAS ALL THE IMPORTANT JOBS ——
    LIKE HE COLLECTS ALL THE TAXES ———
    BUT WOMAN —
    WOMAN ONLY WORKS UP IN CADBURY'S —
    PUTTIN' CHOCOLATES INTO BOXES —
    SO —
    SO —
    SO —
    IT'S A MAN'S —MAN'S WORLD —
    BUT IT WOULD BE NOTHIN' —
    NOTHIN' —
    FUCK ALL ———
    WITHOU' A WOMAN OR A GURREL ——
This time they wouldn't stop cheering and clapping, so It's
a Man's Man's Man's World was over.
The Commitments were clearing the stage after closing
time.
Derek spoke. —Tha' Man's World is a rapid song, isn't it?
—Fuckin' brilliant.
Deco took the bottle from his mouth.
—Yeah, he said. —I'm thinkin' o' doin' it on Screen Test.
——Tha' or When a Man Loves a Woman. They're me best.
Outspan dropped everything.
—There's no way we're goin' on Screen Test. No fuckin'
way.
—Yeah, said Derek.

117

—I know tha', said Deco. —Yis didn't hear me.

He took a mouthful from the bottle.

—Did I not tell yis? ——I thought I did. ——No, I'm goin' on Screen Test. On me own, like. I got me ma to write in for me.

Derek roared. —JIMMY! COME EAAR!

Then he stared at Deco.

Jimmy was just outside on the path, thanking Hot Press for coming. He heard the roar.

—Good fuck! I'd better get in. ——Migh' see yeh again next week so?

—Right, yeah.

—An' see if yeh can bring your man along, righ'. I'll buy him a pint.

—Will do.

Jimmy trotted in. He had good news.

He forgot it when he saw the story; The Commitments standing away from one another, Deco in the middle.

—Wha' now?

—Tell him, said Derek.

Deco told Jimmy.

—Yeh bad shite, yeh, said Jimmy.

—Wha'!

—Are yeh serious?

—Yeah. ——I am.

—What is this Screen Test? Joey The Lips asked.

Outspan told him.

—It's a poxy programme on RTE. A talent show like.

—It's fuckin' terrible, Joey, said Derek.

—Sounds uncool, said Joey The Lips.

—Why didn't yeh tell us? Jimmy asked Deco.

—I did tell yis.

No one backed him up.

—I remember tellin' some o' yis. ——I told you, James.

—No.

—I must've. ——I meant to.

Mickah came out of the jacks.

118

—Sorry abou' tha', said Deco. —Yeah ——annyway, the ma wrote in for me.

Deco decided to get all the confessing over with.

—I applied to sing in the National Song Contest as well.

—Oh ——my——Jaysis!

—I don't believe yeh, said Dean.

The Commitmentettes were starting to laugh.

—Well, said Deco. —Let's put it this way. ——I've me career to think of.

Mickah started laughing. Deco didn't know if this was good or bad.

James laughed too.

—Have yeh no fuckin' loyalty, son? said Jimmy. —You're in a fuckin' group.

—A Song for Europe! said Outspan. —Fuckin' God! —Wha'.

Imelda sang: —ALL KINDS —
OF EVERYTHIN' —
REMINDS ME —

OF —
YOU.

—Ah, fuck off, said Deco. —Look. ——The group won't last forever.

—Not with you in it.

—Look. ——Be realistic, will yeh. ——I can sing, righ'. ——

—That's not soul, Brother, Joey The Lips told Deco.

—Fuck off, you, said Deco, —an' don't annoy me.

That's when Mickah stitched Deco a loaf, clean on the nose. It wasn't broken but snot and blood fell out of it at a fierce speed.

Outspan got Deco to hold his head back. Natalie dammed the flow with a couple of paper hankies.

—That's not soul either, Brother, Joey The Lips told Mickah.

—Probably not, said James.

—He shouldn't o' talken to yeh like tha'. ——I'm sorry, righ'.

—Tell Brother Deco that.

—I will in me ——

—Tell him.

——I'm sorry, righ'.

—Okay, said Deco. —Don't worry abou' it.

Deco's nose was under control.

Jimmy remembered the good news.

—There might be an A an' R man comin' to see us next week.

—Sent from The Lord, said Joey The Lips.

He held his palms out. Jimmy slapped them. Then Joey The Lips slapped Jimmy's palms.

—What's an A an' R man? Dean asked.

—I don't know wha' the A an' R stand for but they're talent scouts for record companies. They look at groups an' sign them up.

The Commitments whooped and smiled and laughed and hit each other. They were all very happy, even Deco.

—A and R means Artists and Repertory, said Joey The Lips.

—I thought so, said Mickah.

—Wha' label?

—A small one, said Jimmy.

—Aaaah! said Imelda. —A little one. ——That's lovely.

They laughed.

—Independent, said Jimmy.

—Good, said Dean.

—Wha' are they called?

—Eejit Records. ——They're Irish.

They liked the name.

—They'd want to be fuckin' eejits to want us.

—They're only comin' to see us, Jimmy warned.

—Don't worry, Jim, said Outspan. —We'll introduce them to Mickah.

—Good thinkin', said Mickah. —They'll fuckin' sign us alrigh'.

—Plenty o' lipstick next week, girls, said Jimmy.

—Fuck yourself, you, said Natalie.

* * *

Jimmy hoped the good news would keep The Commitments going. But he was worried. He was losing sleep. Having problems with them one at a time was bad, but now both Dean and Deco were getting uppity. And James was worried about his exams, and Mickah was a looper.

He didn't organize a rehearsal for the weekend, to give James time to study and to keep them away from each other so there'd be no rows before Wednesday.

Jimmy called to Dean's house on Friday. He wanted to talk to him and maybe even catch him in the act, listening to jazz.

Dean was watching Blankety Blank.

They went up to Dean's room. Jimmy eyed the wall for incriminating posters. Nothing; just an old one of Manchester United (Steve Coppell and Jimmy Greenhoff were in it) and one of Bruce Springsteen at Slane. But maybe Dean's wall hadn't caught up with Dean yet.

—Did yeh come on the bus? Dean asked Jimmy.

—I haven't gone home yet, said Jimmy. —I went for a few scoops with a few o' the lads ou' o' work. ——Bruxelles. ——D'yeh know it?

—Yeah.

—It's good. ——Some great lookin' judies.

—Yeah.

—Eh ——I was thinkin' we could have a chat abou' the group.

—Wha' abou' it?

—Wha' d'yeh think of it?

—It's okay.

—Okay?

—Yeah. Okay. ——Why?

——How is it okay?

—Jaysis, Jimmy, I don't know. ——I like ——the lads, yeh know, Derek an' Outspan, an' James. An' Washin'ton D. C.

An' Joey's taught me a lot, yeh know. ——I like the girls. They're better crack than most o' the young ones I know. —— It's good crack.

—Wha' abou' the music?

—It's okay, said Dean. ———It's good crack, yeh know. —It's good.

—But?

—Ah, Jaysis, Jimmy. I don't want to sound snobby but —— fuck it, there's not much to it, is there? ——Just whack whack whack an' tha' fuckin' eejit, Cuffe, roarin' an' moanin' ——an' fuckin' gurglin'.

—Forget Cuffe. ———What's wrong with it?

Jimmy sounded hurt.

—Nothin'.

Dean was glad this was happening, although he was uncomfortable.

—Don't get me wrong, Jimmy. ———It's too easy. It doesn't stretch me. ——D'yeh know wha' I mean? Em, it was grand for a while, while I was learnin' to play. It's limitin', know wha' I mean? ———It's good crack but it's not art.

—Art!

—Well ——yeah.

—You've been listenin' to someone, haven't yeh?

—No.

—Watchin' Channel fuckin' 4. Art! Me arse!

—Slag away. Sticks an' stones.

—Art! said Jimmy. (Art was an option he'd done in school because there was no room for him in metal work and there was no way they could get him into home economics. That's what art was.) —Cop on, Dean, will yeh.

—Look, Jimmy, said Dean. ——I went through hell tryin' to learn to play the sax. I nearly jacked it in after every rehearsal. Now I can play it. An' I'm not stoppin'. I want to get better. ———It's art, Jimmy. It is. I express meself, with me sax instead of a brush, like. That's why I'm gettin' into the jazz. There's no rules. There's no walls, your man in The Observer said it ——

—I knew it! The Observer, I fuckin' knew it!

—Shut up a minute. Let me finish.

Dean was blushing. He'd let the bit about The Observer slip out. He hoped Jimmy wouldn't tell the rest of the lads.

—That's the difference between jazz an' soul. There's too many rules in soul. ——It's all walls.

—Joey called them corners.

—That's it, said Dean. —Dead on. ——Four corners an' you're back where yeh started from. D'yeh follow me?

—I suppose so, said Jimmy. —Are yeh goin' to leave?

—The Commitments?

—Yeah.

—No, Jaysis no. No way.

Jimmy was delighted with the way Dean answered him.

—How come? he said.

—It's good crack, said Dean. —It's good. The jazz is in me spare time. That's okay, isn't it?

—Yeah, sure.

—No, the soul's grand, Jimmy. It's good crack. It's just the artist in me likes to get ou' now an' again, yeh know.

—Yeah, righ'. I know wha' yeh mean. I'm the same way with me paintin'.

—Do you paint, Jimmy?

—I do in me bollix.

Dean was happy now. So he kept talking, to please Jimmy.

—No, I wouldn't want to leave The Commitments. It's great crack. The lads are great. ——You're doin' a good job too. An' ——Keep this to yourself now.

—Go on.

——I fancy Imelda a bit too, yeh know.

—Everyone fancies 'melda, Dean.

—She's great, isn't she?

—Oh, she is indeed. ——A grand young one. ——Wha' abou' Joey's ideas abou' soul bein' the people's music an' tha'?

—Don't get me wrong, said Dean. —Joey's great. ——He's full o' shi'e though. ——Isn't he?

—I suppose he is a bit now tha' yeh mention it, ——Brother

Dean. ——But go easy on the solos though, righ'.
—Okay.

* * *

Now that Jimmy thought of it, Imelda might have been holding The Commitments together. Derek fancied her, and Outspan fancied her. Deco fancied her. He was sure James fancied her. Now Dean fancied her too. He fancied her himself.

Imelda had soul.

* * *

There was no review in Hot Press. That was a disappointment. But they were in the Rhythm Guide.
—Your Regular Beat . . .
What's Happening In Residencies.
Wednesdays.
Carlow, Octopussys: The Plumbers.
Cork, Sir Henrys: Asthmatic Hobbit Goes Boing.
Dublin, Baggot: The Four Samurai.
Dublin, Ivy Rooms: Autumn's Drizzle.
Dublin, Miami Vice: The Commitments.
Jimmy cut it out and stuck it on his wall.

* * *

The Commitments all arrived on Wednesday. They all helped with the gear. They all looked well. Deco's hooter was back to normal.
—Is he here yet? James asked.
He stood behind Jimmy. Jimmy was sitting at a table at the door, taking in the money.
—Who?
—The man from Eejit.
—Not yet. I'd say he'll come though.
—I sure as hell hope so, Massa Jimmy, said James. —I'll have to piss off righ' after, okay. I've another oral tomorrow afternoon.
—Fair enough, said Jimmy. —Count tha' for us.

124

Hot Press arrived, with someone else.

—He's here, Jimmy told James. —Tell the others, will yeh.

—Goodie goodie, said James.

—Howyis, lads, said Jimmy.

—Hi there, said Hot Press. —The review'll be in the next issue, okay. We were out of space. A big ad, you know.

—No problem, said Jimmy.

—This is Dave I was telling you about last week, remember?

—Oh, yeah, said Jimmy. —Howyeh, Dave. ——Jimmy ——Rabbitte.

He shook Dave's hand.

—Hi, Jimmy, said Dave. —Maurice tells me your guys are good, yeah?

—He's righ' too, said Jimmy. —They have it alrigh'. —— Go on ahead in, lads. I'll be with yis in a minute. I'll just rob a few more punters.

Jimmy was shaking.

The Commitments were great. Everything was right. They looked great too. Each one of them was worth watching.

They started with Knock on Wood. Mickah was cheered every time he loafed the drum. Then they did I Thank You. Then Chain Gang, Reach Out — I'll Be There and then they slowed down with Tracks of My Tears. After that, What Becomes of the Broken Hearted. Then The Commitmentettes took over with Walking in the Rain, Stoned Love and Stop in the Name of Love.

Once the crowd knew that The Commitmentettes were finished they began to shout for Night Train.

They got it four songs later.

—ALL ABOARD, said Deco. —THE NIGH' TRAIN.

There was pushing. Someone fell, but was up quickly. Nothing serious happened. They swayed and bopped as Deco did the roll call of American cities.

The crowd was waiting, getting ready.

—AN' DON'T FORGET NEW ORLEANS — THE HOME O' THE BLUES ——

OH YEAH ——

WE'RE COMIN' HOME ——

All the Commitments could see now after the front rows was hands in the air, clapping, and a few women on boyfriends' backs. Outspan grinned. Derek laughed. This was great.

—THE NIGH' TRAIN —

CARRIES ME HOME ——

THE NIGH' TRAIN —

CARRIES ME HOME —

SHO' NUFF IT DOES ——

Jimmy looked at Dave from Eejit. He was smiling.

Deco and the girls chugged while The Commitments brought the train around for the home stretch.

Deco broke away from the girls.

He growled: —STARTIN' OFF IN CONNOLLY —

Screams, roars and whistles.

—MOVIN' ON OU' TO KILLESTER—

Everyone jumped in time, including Dave from Eejit. And Jimmy.

—HARMONSTOWN RAHENY —

AN' DON'T FORGET KILBARRACK —

THE HOME O' THE BLUES ——

HOWTH JUNCTION BAYSIDE —

GOIN' HOME —

THEN ON OU' TO SUTTON WHERE THE SNOBBY BASTARDS LIVE —

OH YEAH ——

OH YEAH ——

The crowd sang with Deco.

—NIGH' TRAIN —

COMIN' HOME FROM THE BOOZER —

NIGH' TRAIN —

COMIN' HOME FROM THE COMMITMENTS —

NIGH' TRAIN —

GETTIN' SICK ON THE BLOKE BESIDE YEH —

NIGH' TRAIN —

BUT IT DOESN'T MATTER COS HE'S ASLEEP —

NIGH' TRAIN —

WE'RE COMIN' HOME

CARRIES ME HOME —
NIGH' TRAIN —
CARRIES ME HOME —
NIGH' TRAIN —
TO ME GAFF —
NIGH' TRAIN —
CARRIES ME HOME ———
OH YEAH ——
OH YEAH ——

Then The Commitments did it all over again. There wasn't time for an encore but it didn't matter.

The Commitments were delighted with themselves.

—You're professionals, Brothers and Sisters, said Joey The Lips. —You ooze soul.

—That's a lovely thing to say, Joey. You ooze soul too. —I blush.

Dave from Eejit came over to the platform.

—Great show, said Dave.

—Thanks, pal, said Mickah.

—Very visual, said Dave.

—Didn't sound bad either, did it? said Mickah.

—It sounded great, said Dave. ———Ladies, wonderful. Amazing.

—Thanks very much, said Natalie.

—Yeah, said Bernie, —thanks.

—See now, said Natalie. —We're wonderful.

—Amaaazing, said Imelda.

Dave went over to Jimmy.

—Can we talk, em?

—Jimmy.

—Jimmy, right. Can we talk? Over here, yeah?

They went into a far corner. Hot Press came with them.

—Did yeh like tha', Dave? Jimmy asked.

—Great, terrific. ———Great.

—They're not bad at all, sure they're not, Dave? said Jimmy. —They need a bit o' polishin' maybe.

—No, no, said Dave. —That'd ruin them. Leave them as they are. Raw, you know.

—Fair enough. Wha'ever yeh say. You're the expert.

—The senior citizen. The trumpet, yeah? He's a terrific idea.

—That's Joey The Lips Fagan.

—Yeah.

—He played with James Brown.

—Right.

—Among others.

—The ladies too. ——Great visuals.

Jimmy nearly laughed. He hid behind his glass. Then he asked Dave a question.

——Would yeh be interested in us, Dave?

—Yeah, right. Definitely.

Jimmy held his glass to his chest. He knew it would rattle if he put it on the table.

Dave continued.

—We release singles only. At the moment. We're small, and happy that way, yeah? We're not in it for the lucre, yeah? You heard the Reality Margins single? Trigger Married Silver and Now They're Making Ponies? From the Fanning session?

Jimmy lied.

—Yeah. ——It was very good.

—That was Eejit. ——It didn't get the airplay. They were scared of it, you know. ——We sign bands for one single, yeah? No fee, sorry. We pay for the studio time so long as it's not more than a day, and the producer. We do the package. A good picture cover. You've seen the label?

—Yeah, said Jimmy.

He wasn't lying this time.

—It's good ——very nice.

Hot Press spoke. —Dave set up Eejit as a springboard for new bands. The Eejit record is meant to be the first step on the ladder. The idea is that the major labels hear it and if they like you they sign you. The Eejit single is to help you get a proper contract. It gives you a voice.

—That's right, said Dave.

—Tha' sounds fair enough, said Jimmy. —That'd be great. Has it worked so far?

—Yes and no, yeah? said Dave. —Reality Margins are before their time.

Hot Press laughed.

Dave explained.

—My little brother plays percussion for Reality Margins, yeah? But you know The Baby Docs?

—Yeah. ——Bitin' the Pillow. ——Yeah, it's good, tha'.

—CBS and Rough Trade are sniffing there, said Dave.

—That's good, said Jimmy. —I hope it works ou' okay for them now.

—So, Jimmy, said Dave. —Tell me. ——Would The Commitments be interested in recording Night Train for us?

—I'd say they would, yeah, said Jimmy. (And to himself: —Yeh fuckin' budgie, yeh!)

—You don't know for sure?

—We're a democratic group, Dave, said Jimmy. —Soul is democracy.

—Right, said Dave. —We could put that on the sleeve.

—Good thinkin'.

—I see a double A-side, said Dave. —Side A, the studio Night Train. The other side A, the live Night Train.

—I like it, said Hot Press.

—I'd buy tha', said Jimmy.

—It'd get the airplay, said Dave. —It'd sell. It'd chart, yeah? It's good, unspoilt roots stuff, you know. ——Pure. ——And very fuckin' funny.

Jimmy washed his giggles back with the last of his pint.

——Would we have to pay you annythin', Dave? he asked.

—No, said Dave. —It's cool. ——We're funded by the Department of Labour, yeah? Youth employment, yeah? They pay me. Any profit goes back into Eejit.

—Go 'way! said Jimmy. —That's grand.

—I suppose I'm just a hippy, you know, said Dave. —And my parents are rich. ——Are The Commitments on the dole?

——Some o' them.

—That's good, said Dave. —The Department will like that.
Hot Press laughed.
—We'd have to sign somethin', wouldn't we? said Jimmy.
—Right, yeah. A simple, one-off contract, yeah?
—We could do tha' annytime.
—Right.
—Yeh don't have one on yeh, I suppose?
—Tomorrow.
—Okay, righ'. ——I'll see if I can talk the group into it.
Will we have to meet annyone?
—No.
—No one from Eejit?
—I'm Eejit.
Hot Press laughed again.
—Just yourself?
—Just myself, said Dave.
He pretended to type.
—I'm even the secretary, yeah?
—Fair play to yeh, Dave, said Jimmy.
Jimmy went to the door with them. They said their good-
byes and arranged to meet the next night in The Bailey.
Jimmy took some deep breaths.
That was perfect. The Commitments wouldn't be tied to a
little gobshite label run by hippies. Just the one single (Night
Train would be a big hit in Dublin) and the big boys would be
queuing up for The Commitments, readies in hand. Jimmy
wondered if they should wait a bit before they gave up their
jobs.
Jimmy took one more long breath, clapped his hands,
rubbed them, and went back inside to tell The Commitments.
But they didn't exist any more. Somewhere in the quarter
of an hour Jimmy had been negotiating with Dave from Eejit,
The Commitments had broken up.
Outspan and Derek were the only ones still at the platform.
The rest were gone.
Jimmy leaned against the wall.
——Wha'?

—They all fucked off, said Outspan.

He was explaining how it had happened.

—Why?

—I'm not sure, said Outspan. —It was over before I copped on tha' ann'thin, was happenin'. ——Do you know, Derek?

—I think it was when Deco seen Joey kissin' 'melda.

—Imelda?

—Yeah.

—Wha' abou' Bernie?

—She didn't seem to mind.

—For fuck sake! said Jimmy. ——Real kissin', like?

—Oh yeah, said Derek. —They were warin' alrigh'. Over where you are.

—I seen tha' bit alrigh' said Outspan.

He shook his head.

—Nearly puked me ring.

—Then Deco said he was sick o' this, said Derek, —an' he pulled Joey away from her, righ'. An' he called 'melda a prick teaser. An' tha' wasn't on cos she isn't, so I went to give him a boot, righ'. But then Deco had a go at Joey. I think he fancied 'melda, d'yeh know tha'? ——He gave Joey a dig. Hurt him. Then Mickah went for Deco. He got him a few slaps an' Deco ran ou' an' he said The Commitments could fuck off an' Mickah went after him.

—How come I didn't see annythin'? Jimmy asked.

—It happened very fuckin' fast, said Outspan. —I didn't seen ann'thin' either an' I was here, sure.

—Where's James?

—He had go to, remember?

—That's righ'. ——Dean?

—Dean took it very badly, Jim, said Derek.

—I heard this bit, said Outspan. —He ——Listen to this now. ——He said he was fucked if he was goin' to waste his time jammin' — Jammin'! — jammin' with a shower o' wankers tha' couldn't play their instruments properly. —— Tha' wasn't on. ——I gave him a dig. An' he fucked off. I think he was cryin'. ——Spa!

——Fuckin' great, said Jimmy.

—D'yeh know wha'? said Derek. —I think Dean fancies 'melda too. It's a gas really when yeh think abou' it.

—It's a fuckin' scream, said Jimmy. —Where's Joey?

—He went to the hospital. He thinks his nose is broke. The girls went with him but I don't think he wanted them to. He was tryin' to get away from them. They had to run after him.

Jimmy sat down on the platform.

Derek continued.

—It's funny. ——I think Joey was the oney one of us tha' didn't fancy Imelda an' he's the oney one of us tha' got off with her. Fuckin' gas really, isn't it?

Jimmy said nothing for a while. He looked at the ground. Outspan and Derek reckoned that he was thinking, thinking things out.

Then he spoke. —Fuck yis annyway. ——Fuck the lot o' yis.

—We didn't do ann'thin'! said Outspan.

——Fuck yis, said Jimmy, quietly. ——Yis bastards.

The head barman came out of the room behind the bar.

—Why aren't yis gone? he shouted.

—Most of us are gone, pal, said Outspan.

—Fuck yis, said Jimmy to the floor. —Just ——

He swept his hand over his knee.

—Fuck yis.

—Come on, said the head barman.

—Hang on a sec, said Derek.

He bent down to Jimmy.

—Sorry 'bou' tha', Jimmy, he said.

He put his hand on Jimmy's shoulder.

—Still. ——It was good while it lasted, wasn't it?

—Ah fuck off! said Jimmy.

That sort of talk gave Jimmy the pip.

* * *

Jimmy phoned Joey The Lips about a week after The Commitments broke up.

He hadn't tried to get them together again. He hadn't

132

wanted to. They were fuckin' saps. He'd watched telly all week. It wasn't too bad. He'd gone for a few scoops with the lads from work on the Friday. That was his week.

He hadn't gone into The Bailey to meet Dave from Eejit.

He hadn't played any soul.

Now, a week after, he thought he was over it. He'd nearly cried when he was in bed that night. He'd have loved to have seen that Commitments single, with them on the cover, and maybe a video for Anything Goes. But now he was okay. They were tossers. So was Dave from Eejit. He had better things to do with his life.

But he was phoning Joey The Lips, just to say cheerio, and good luck, because Joey The Lips wasn't like the others. Joey The Lips was different. He'd taught them all a thing or two.

Joey The Lips answered.

—The Fagan household.

—Joey? ——Howyeh. This is Jimmy.

—Jimmy! My main man. How are you, Brother?

—Grand. How's your nose?

—It's still hanging on in there.

—Tha' was a fuckin' terrible thing for Deco to do.

—Forget it, forget it. ——When I was leaving the hospital they were bringing Brother Declan in.

—Wha'?

—On a stretcher.

—Go 'way! ——Funny. I haven't seen him since. I'd forgot he works where I work.

—Have you seen the other Brothers and Sisters?

—No way. I don't want to.

—Hmm. ——A pity.

——Wha' are yeh goin' to do now?

—America calls, Brother. I'm going back. Maybe soul isn't right for Ireland. So I'm not right. I'm going back to the soul.

—When?

—The day after tomorrow. Joe Tex called me. You've heard Joe Tex?

—I've heard the name alrigh'. ——Hang on. He had a hit there. Ain't Gonna Bump No More with No Big Fat Woman.

—Correct. ——Joe wants me to tour with him again.

—Fair play to yeh. ——Annyway, Joey, I phoned yeh to thank yeh for everythin', yeh know. ——So ——thanks.

—Oh, I blush. Thank The Lord, not me.

—You thank him for me, okay?

—I will do. ——Will you continue the good work, Jimmy?

—No way. I've learnt me lesson.

————Hang on one minute.

—Okay.

Joey The Lips was back.

—Howyeh, said Jimmy.

—Listen to this. ——O sing into the Lord, a new song, for he hath done marvellous things. Make a joyful noise unto the Lord, all the earth make a loud noise, and rejoice, and sing praise. ——Psalm Number 98, Brother Jimmy.

—Fuck off, Joey. Good luck.

Jimmy was in the kitchen filling the kettle when he remembered something, something he'd read a while back. Joe Tex died in 1982.

* * *

Jimmy met Imelda about a week after that. She had her sister's baby with her. Jimmy cutchie-cutchie-cooed it. It stared out at him.

—Is it a young one or a young fella?

—A young fella. ——Eddie. He's a little fucker, so he is. He's always cryin'. Aren't yeh a little fucker, Eddie?

Eddie belched.

—No manners, he hasn't. ——Wha' have yeh been doin' with yourself since an' annyway? Imelda asked Jimmy.

—Nothin'. ——Nothin' much.

—Have yeh seen anny o' the others?

—No.

—Have yeh seen Joey?

—Have YOU not? said Jimmy. —He's gone back to America.

—Has he? The little fucker.

—Wha'?

—He never said bye bye or ann'thin'.

Jimmy had decided not to mention Joe Tex to anyone.

—He's tourin' again. With The Impressions, I think he said.

—That's lovely, for some. ——D'yeh know wha', Jimmy? ——Don't tell annyone this now.

Jimmy said nothing.

—Promise not to tell.

—I promise, said Jimmy.

—I think Joey left because of us.

—Wha' d'yeh mean?

—Me an' Bernie an' Nat'lie.

—Because yis all got off with him, d'yeh mean?

—Yeah. Sort of. ——He was scared of us.

—D'yeh reckon? ——D'yeh mind if I ask? said Jimmy. —How come yis all got off with him?

—Ah, we were messin', yeh know. We did not like him but. It wasn't just messin'. ——It became a sort of joke between us. To see if we could all get off with him.

—Lucky Joey, wha'.

—Wha'? ——oh yeah.

She laughed a bit.

—I suppose he was really. ——The three of us. She laughed again.

—I think I went a bit too far though.

—How, like?

—I told him I thought I was pregnint.

—GOOD JAYSIS!

Jimmy roared laughing.

—Yeh fuckin' didn't!

—I did, Jimmy. ——Me others were late.

Jimmy fought back a redner.

—How long?

—A few days, a week nearly.

—Ah Jaysis! Imelda! ——Poor Joey.

He laughed again.

—I didn't really think I was pregnant. I shouldn't o' done it. I just wanted to see wha' he'd do.

—He fucked off to America.

—I know, said Imelda. —The shi'e.

Jimmy giggled. So did Imelda.

—He hadn't much willpower, d'yeh know wha' I mean? said Imelda. —He was a bit of a tramp, Joey was.

They both laughed.

—Come 'ere, said Imelda. —If you're startin' another group let us be in it, will yeh? It was brilliant crack.

—I won't be, said Jimmy.

—Sonya, Tanya an' Sofia, said Imelda. —It was fuckin' brilliant.

* * *

—Righ', said Jimmy. —Are yis righ'?

—Fire away, Jimmy, said Mickah.

Outspan and Derek were sitting beside him on the bunk.

—This is The Byrds, righ', said Jimmy. —I'll Feel a Whole Lot Better.

He let the needle down and sat on the back of his legs between the speakers.

There was a bit of a crackle (it was a second-hand album), then a guitar jangled and then they were surrounded by jangling guitars. They'd no time to get ready.

—THE REASON WHY — EE ——

OH I CAN'T STAY — AY — Y ——

I HAVE TO LET YOU GO BAY —AYBE ——

AND RIGHT AWAY — AY — Y ——

AFTER ALL YOU DID ————

I CAN'T STAY OH — H — H — ON —

AND I'LL PROBABLY —

Two high-pitched men joined in here.

—FEEL A WHOLE LOT BETTER —

WHEN YOU'RE GOH — ON —

The lads weren't bouncing up and down on the bunk for this music. They were throwing their heads and chests out and back, out and back. Their feet didn't tap: they slammed. Outspan strummed the air.

—BABY FOR A LONG TIME —

The other Byrds repeated the line.

—BABY FOR A LONG TIME —

—YOU HAD ME BELIE — IE — IEVE —

The others: —YOU HAD ME BELIEVE —

—THAT YOUR LOVE WAS ALL MI — I — I — INE —

The others: — YOUR LOVE WAS ALL MINE —

—AND THAT'S THE WAY IT WOULD BE ————

EE — EE —

The others: —LAA —

AAH —

AAH —

AAAAAH ————

Thirty seconds into the song the lads wanted to be The Byrds. They'd been demolished by the rip-roaring guitars and Gene Clark's manly whinge. It was sweet and rough at the same time. The guitars raced each other.

It was the best they'd ever heard. They didn't just hear it either. They were in its way. It went through them. Man's music.

—AFTER WHAT YOU DI — I — ID —

The other Byrds: —AFTER WHAT YOU DID —

—I CAN'T STAY ON — OH — ON —

The others: —I CAN'T STAY ON —

All The Byrds: —AND I'LL PROBABLY —

FEEL A WHOLE LOT BETTER —

WHEN YOU'RE GOH — ON ——

OH WHEN YOU'RE GOH — ON ——

OH WHEN YOU'RE GOH — ON ——

OH WHEN YOU'RE GOH — ON ——

More jangling guitars winding down and it was over.

Jimmy got the needle up quickly. The next track, The Bells

of Rhymney, was a piece of hippy shite and he didn't want the lads to hear it.

—Tha' was fuckin' rapid, said Outspan. —Play it again, Jimmy.

—Deadly, wasn't it? said Derek.

—Listen to this, said Mickah.

—BABY FOR A LON TAM ——

YEH HAD ME BEL — EE — EE — EE — EVE —

—My Jaysis, Mickah! ———— Fair play to yeh.

—We've a singer, said Jimmy.

—An' you could play the drums, Jimmy, said Derek.

—Yeah, said Outspan. —Just the four of us, wha'. No pricks.

—Is tha' wha' we want? Jimmy asked them.

That was what they wanted.

—Bass, guitar, drums an' Mickah, said Derek. —Rapid.

—Play it again, said Outspan.

—Hang on, said Jimmy. —Could you play like tha'?

—No problem to me, said Outspan.

—The bass sounds easier than for soul, said Derek.

—We'll need two guitars.

—We will in our arses, said Outspan. —I'll use both hands.

—Good thinkin'.

—Wha' abou' James?

—We'll let him in when he's a doctor, said Mickah. —Tha' comes first.

—Tha' won't be for ages.

Jimmy spoke. —He'll be a doctor abou' the same time we're puttin' our third album together. An' we'll need a gentler sound, righ', a new direction, like, after the first two cos they'll be real country-punk albums. James' piano will fit in nicely then.

—That's grand. ———— Will we tell him?

—No. We'll keep it as a surprise for him.

—Play it again, said Outspan.

—Wha' abou' the girls? said Derek.

—Wha' abou' them?

138

—Will we let them in?

—Ah, yeah, said Outspan. —The girls are sound.

—I know, said Mickah. —They could wear tha' Dolly Parton sort o' clobber. Yeh know, the frilly bits on the elbows an' tha' sort o' shi'e.

—Do we want the girls? Jimmy asked.

They did.

—They could give us a rest, said Derek. —They could sing a few slowies. For the oul' ones.

—An' the young ones.

—That's the lot though, righ', said Jimmy. —No fuckin' politics this time either. ———But, yeh know, Joey said when he left tha' he didn't think soul was righ' for Ireland. This stuff is though. You've got to remember tha' half the country is fuckin' farmers. This is the type o' stuff they all listen to. —— Only they listen to it at the wrong speed.

—We'll put them righ' though, wha'. Play it again, Jimmy, will yeh.

—Will we have names? Derek asked.

—Ah Jaysis, no, said Jimmy. —Not tha' shi'e again. This is different.

Outspan agreed with him.

—Would yis mind, said Mickah, —if I had a bit of a name?

—Wha'?

—Tex.

They laughed. They liked it.

—Tex Wallace. ——It sounds righ', doesn't it? said Mickah.

Jimmy was putting the needle down when he thought of something else.

—Oh yeah, he said. —We don't have a name. ——Anny ideas?

—Well, said Derek. —Yeh know the way they're The Byrds an' Bird is another name for a girl, righ'? ——Couldn't we be The Brassers?

It was a great name.

—Dublin country, said Jimmy. —That's fuckin' perfect. The Brassers. ———We're a Dublin country group.

—That's an excellent name, Derek, said Outspan.

—Ah———I just thought of it, yeh know.

Jimmy put the needle back on its stand.

—Another thing I forgot to tell yis. ——I was in touch with your man, Dave, from Eejit Records, remember? I asked him would he be interested in a country-punk version o' Night Train, an' he said he migh' be.

—That's brilliant, said Derek.

—Hang on, said Mickah.

—STARTIN' OU' IN MULLINGAR

MOVIN' ON OU' TO KINNEGAD —— Somethin' like tha'?

—That's very good, said Jimmy.

They laughed.

—That's very good, alrigh', said Outspan. —I like tha'. Fair play.

Jimmy had the needle ready.

—Righ', lads, give us a month an' this'll be us.

He let the needle down.

—Deadly, said Derek.

* * *

THE SNAPPER

This book is dedicated to

Belinda

—You're wha'? said Jimmy Rabbitte Sr.

He said it loudly.

—You heard me, said Sharon.

Jimmy Jr was upstairs in the boys' room doing his D.J. practice. Darren was in the front room watching Police Academy II on the video. Les was out. Tracy and Linda, the twins, were in the front room annoying Darren. Veronica, Mrs Rabbitte, was sitting opposite Jimmy Sr at the kitchen table.

Sharon was pregnant and she'd just told her father that she thought she was. She'd told her mother earlier, before the dinner.

—Oh —my Jaysis, said Jimmy Sr.

He looked at Veronica. She looked tired. He looked at Sharon again.

—That's shockin', he said.

Sharon said nothing.

—Are yeh sure? said Jimmy Sr.

—Yeah. Sort of.

—Wha'?

—Yeah.

Jimmy Sr wasn't angry. He probably wouldn't be either, but it all seemed very unfair.

—You're only nineteen, he said.

—I'm twenty.

—You're only twenty.

—I know what age I am, Daddy.

—Now, there's no need to be gettin' snotty, said Jimmy Sr.

—Sorry, said Sharon.

She nearly meant it.

—I'm the one tha' should be gettin' snotty, said Jimmy Sr.

Sharon made herself smile. She was happy with the way things were going so far.

—It's shockin', said Jimmy Sr again, —so it is. Wha' do you think o' this?

He was talking to Veronica.

—I don't know, said Veronica.

—Is tha' the best yeh can do, Veronica?

—Well, what do YOU think?

Jimmy Sr creased his face and held it that way for a second.

—I don't know, he said. —I should give ou', I suppose. An' throw a wobbler or somethin'. But ——what's the point?

Veronica nodded. She looked very tired now.

Jimmy Sr continued.

—If she was —

He turned to Sharon.

—You should've come to us earlier —before, yeh know —an' said you were goin' to get pregnant.

The three of them tried to laugh.

—Then we could've done somethin' abou' it. ——My God, though.

No one said anything. Then Jimmy Sr spoke to Sharon again.

—You're absolutely sure now? Positive?

—Yeah, I am. I done —

—Did, said Veronica.

—I did the test.

—The test? said Jimmy Sr. —Oh. —Did yeh go in by yourself?

—Yeah, said Sharon.

—Did yeh? Fair play to yeh, said Jimmy Sr. —I'd never've thought o' tha'.

Sharon and Veronica looked at each other, and grinned quickly.

146

Jimmy Sr got down to business.

—Who was it?

—Wha'? ——Oh. I don't know.

—Ah now, Jaysis —!

—No, I do know.

—Well, then?

—I'm not tellin'.

Jimmy Sr could feel himself getting a bit angry now. That was better.

—Now, look —

They heard Jimmy Jr from up in the boys' room.

—THIS IS JIMMY RABBITTE – ALL – OVER – IRELAND.

—Will yeh listen to tha' fuckin' eejit, said his father.

—Leave him alone, said Veronica.

Jimmy Sr stared at the ceiling.

—I don't know.

Then he turned to Sharon again.

—Why won't yeh tell us?

Sharon said nothing. Jimmy Sr saw her eyes filling with water.

—Don't start tha', he told her. —Just tell us.

—I can't, Sharon told the table.

—Why not?

——I just can't, righ'.

Jimmy Sr looked across at Veronica and shook his head. He'd never been able to cope with answers like that. If Sharon had been one of the boys he'd have walloped her.

Veronica looked worried now. She wasn't sure she really wanted to know the answer.

—Is he married? Jimmy Sr asked.

—Oh my God, said Veronica.

—No, he's not! said Sharon.

—Well, that's somethin', I suppose, said Jimmy Sr. —Then why —

Veronica started crying.

—Ah Veronica, stop tha'.

Linda ran in.

—Daddy, Darren's after hittin' me.

She was getting ready to cry.

—Jesus! Another one, said Jimmy Sr.

Then he spoke to Linda.

—I'll go in in a minute an' I'll hit Darren an' you can watch me hittin' him.

—Can I?

—Yeah, yeh can. Now get ou' or I'll practise on you first.

Linda squealed and ran away from him. She stopped at the safe side of the kitchen door.

—Can Tracy watch as well? she asked.

—She can o' course. Now, your mammy an' Sharon an' me are havin' a chat, so leave us alone.

Jimmy Sr looked at the two women. The crying had stopped.

—THIS IS JIMMY RABBITTE — ALL — OVER — IRELAND.

—Oh good Jesus, what a house! ——Is he queer or wha' is he? Jimmy Sr asked Sharon.

—No, he's not. He's alrigh'; leave him alone.

—I don't know, said Jimmy Sr. —Tha' gear he wears. He had his trous —

—That's only the fashion.

—I suppose so. But, Jaysis.

He looked at Veronica. She just looked tired again.

—This is an awful shock, Sharon, he said. —Isn't it, Veronica?

—Definitely.

—Make us a cup o' tea there, love, will yeh.

—Make it yourself, said Veronica.

—I'll make it, said Sharon.

—Good girl, said Jimmy Sr. —Mind yourself against the table there. Good girl. ——You're sure now he's not married?

—Yeah, he's not, said Sharon, at the sink.

—Then why won't yeh tell us then?

—Look, said Sharon.

She turned to face him.

—I can't, an' I'm not goin' to.

148

She turned back to plug in the kettle.

—Will he marry you? Jimmy Sr asked her.

—No. I don't think so.

—The louser. That's cheatin', tha' is.

—It's not a game! said Veronica.

—I know, I know tha', Veronica. But it's his fault as much as Sharon's. Whoever he is. ——It was his flute tha'—

—Daddy!

—Well, it was.

—It's no wonder they all talk the way they do, Veronica gave out to Jimmy Sr.

—Ah, lay off, Veronica, will yeh.

They heard a scream from the front room.

—Hang on till I sort this young fella ou', said Jimmy Sr.

He marched out of the kitchen.

—He's taking it well, said Veronica.

—Yeah, said Sharon. —So are you.

—Ah sure —

—I was afraid you'd throw me ou'.

—I never thought of that, mind you. ——It's not right though, said Veronica.

She looked straight at Sharon.

—I suppose it's not, said Sharon.

Jimmy Sr came back, rubbing his hands and calling Darren a sneaky little bastard. He sat down and saw the tea waiting for him.

—Aah, lovely.

He sipped.

—Fuck! ——Sorry, Veronica; excuse me. It's very hot.

—He's started saying Excuse me. After twenty-two years.

—Good luck, Jimmy Jr roared from the front door, and then he slammed it.

—He shuts the door like a normal man annyway. That's somethin', I suppose.

—He's alrigh', said Sharon.

Jimmy Sr now said something he'd heard a good few times on the telly.

—D'yeh want to keep it?

—Wha' d'yeh mean?

—D'yeh —d'you want to keep it, like?

—He wants to know if you want to have an abortion, said Veronica. —The eejit.

—I do not! said Jimmy Sr.

This was true. He was sorry now he'd said it.

—There's no way I'd have an abortion, said Sharon.

—Good. You're right.

—Abortion's murder.

—It is o' course.

Then he thought of something and he had to squirt his tea back into the cup. He could hear his heart. And feel it.

He looked at Sharon.

—He isn't a black, is he?

—No!

He believed her. The three of them started laughing.

—One o' them students, yeh know, Jimmy Sr explained. —With a clatter o' wives back in Africa.

—Stop that.

Jimmy Sr's tea was finished.

—That was grand, Sharon, thanks, he said. —An' you're def'ny not goin' to tell us who it is?

—No. ——Sorry.

—Never mind the Sorry. ——I think you should tell us. I'm not goin' to kill him or annythin'.

Sharon said nothing.

Jimmy Sr pushed his chair back from the table.

—There's no point in anny more talkin' then, I suppose. Your mind's obviously made up, Sharon.

He stood up.

—A man needs a pint after all tha', he said.

—Is that all? said Veronica, shocked.

—Wha' d'yeh mean, Veronica?

—It's a terrible —Veronica started.

But she couldn't really go on. She thought that Sharon's news deserved a lot more attention, and some sort of punishment. As far as Veronica was concerned this was the worst thing that had ever happened the family. But she couldn't really explain why, not really. And she knew that, anyway, nothing could be done about it. Maybe it wouldn't be so bad once she got used to it.

Then she thought of something.

—The neighbours, she said.

—Wha' abou' them? said Jimmy Sr.

Veronica thought for a bit.

—What'll they say? she then said.

—You don't care wha' tha' lot says, do yeh? said Jimmy Sr.

——Yes. I do.

—Ah now, Veronica.

He sat down.

Sharon spoke.

—They'll have a laugh when they find ou' an' they'll try an' guess who I'm havin' it for. An' that's all. ——An' anyway, I don't care.

—An' that's the important thing, Jimmy Sr told Veronica.

Veronica didn't look convinced.

—Sure look, said Jimmy Sr. —The O'Neill young ones have had kids, the both o' them. An' —an' the Bells would be the same 'cept they don't have anny daughters, but yeh know wha' I mean.

—Dawn O'Neill had her baby for Paddy Bell, Sharon reminded him.

—She did o' course, said Jimmy Sr.

He stood up.

—So there now, Veronica, he said. —Fuck the neighbours.

Veronica tried to look as if she'd been won over. She wanted to go up to bed. She nodded.

Jimmy Sr had a nice idea.

—Are yeh comin' for a drink, Sharon?

—No thanks, Daddy. I'll stay in tonigh'.

—Ah, go on.

—Alrigh', Sharon smiled.

—Good girl. Yeh may as well ——Veronica?

—'M? ——Ah no, no thanks.

—Go on.

—No. I'm goin' up to bed.

—I'd go up with yeh only I've a throat on me.

Veronica smiled.

—You're sure now? said Jimmy Sr.

—Yep, said Veronica.

Sharon went for her jacket.

—Will I bring yeh home a few chips? Jimmy Sr asked Veronica.

—I'll be asleep.

—Fair enough.

Jimmy Sr stopped at the front door and roared back to Veronica.

—Cheerio now, Granny.

Then he laughed, and slammed the door harder than Jimmy Jr had.

* * *

Jimmy Sr came back with the drinks and sat in beside Sharon. He hated the tables up here, in the lounge. You couldn't get your legs in under them. Sharon couldn't either. She sat side-saddle.

—Thanks a lot, Daddy, said Sharon when she'd poured the Coke in with the vodka.

—Ah, no problem, said Jimmy Sr.

He'd never had a drink with Sharon before. He watched his pint settling, something he never did when he was downstairs in the bar. He only came up here on Sundays, and now.

He turned to Sharon and spoke softly.

—When's it due an' annyway?

—November.

Jimmy Sr did a few quick sums in his head.

—You're three months gone.

—No. Nearly.

—Yeh should've told us earlier.

—I know. ——I was scared to.

—Ah, Sharon. ——I still think you should tell us who the da is.

—You can think away then.

Jimmy Sr couldn't help grinning. She'd always been like that.

—I thought your mammy took it very well, he said.

—Yeah, Sharon agreed. —She was great.

—Cos she's a bit ol' fashioned like tha'. Set in her ways.

—Yeah. No, she was great. So were you.

—Ah, now.

They said nothing after that for a bit. Jimmy Sr could think of nothing else to say. He looked around him: kids and yuppies. He sat there, feeling far from home. The lads would all be downstairs by now. Jimmy Sr had a good one he'd heard in work for them, about a harelip in a spermbank. He loved Sharon but, if the last five minutes were anything to go by, she was shocking drinking company.

He noticed Jimmy Jr up at the stools with his pals.

—There's Jimmy, he said.

—Yeah, said Sharon.

—That's an awful lookin' shower he hangs around with.

—They're alrigh'.

—The haircuts on them, look.

—That's only the fashion these days. Leave them alone.

—I s'pose so, said Jimmy Sr.

And they stopped again.

There was only an hour to closing time but Jimmy Sr wasn't sure he'd be able to stick it.

—Wha' does Jimmy be doin' up there when he's shoutin', yeh know, abou' bein' all over Ireland? he asked Sharon.

—He wants to be a D.J.

—A wha'?

—A D.J. A disc jockey.

—Wha'; like Larry Gogan?

—Yeah. Sort of.

—Jaysis, said Jimmy Sr.

He'd had enough.

He'd spotted a gang of Sharon's friends over past Jimmy Jr and his pals.

—There's those friends o' yours, Sharon, he said.

Sharon knew what he was at.

—Oh yeah, she said.

—D'yeh want to go over to them?

—I don't mind.

—They'd be better company than your oul' fella annyway, wha'.

—Ah no.

—Go on. Yeh may as well go over. I don't mind.

—I can't leave you on your own.

—Ah sure, said Jimmy Sr. —I can go down an' see if there's annyone downstairs.

Sharon grinned. So did Jimmy Sr. He still felt guilty though, so he got a fiver out and handed it to Sharon.

—Ah, there's no need, Daddy.

—There is o' course, said Jimmy Sr.

He moved in closer to her.

—It's not every day yeh find ou' you're goin' to be a granda.

He'd just thought of that now and he had to stop himself from letting his eyes water. He often did things like that, gave away pounds and fivers or said nice things; little things that made him like himself.

He patted Sharon's shoulder. He was standing up, but he stopped.

—Hang on a sec, he said. —I'll wait till your man passes.

Sharon looked.

—Who?

—Burgess there, the bollix. Excuse me, Sharon. I can't stand him.

—I've seen yeh talkin' to him loads o' times.

—He traps me. An' Darren's his goalie this year. He'd drop him if I got snotty with him.

—Oh. Yeah.

—It's alrigh' now, said Jimmy Sr, and he stood up again. —The coast's clear. See yeh later.

Jimmy Sr trotted out, and down to the lads in the bar. Sharon took her vodka and her jacket and her bag and went across to Jackie O'Keefe, Mary Curran and Yvonne Burgess, her friends; the gang.

—Hiyis, she said when she got there.

—Oh, howyeh, Sharon.

—Hiyeh, Sharon.

—Howyeh, Sharon.

—Hiyis, said Sharon.

—Put your bag over here, Sharon, look, said Yvonne.

—Thanks, said Sharon. —Hiyeh, Jackie. Haven't seen yeh in ages.

—She's been busy, said Mary.

Yvonne sniggered.

—How's Greg? Sharon asked Jackie.

Yvonne sniggered again.

—Fuck off, you, said Jackie. —He's grand, Sharon.

—They're goin' on their holliers together, Mary told Sharon.

—Dirty bitch, said Yvonne.

They laughed.

—Fuck off, will yeh, said Jackie. —We're not goin' for definite.

She explained.

—He mightn't be able to take the time off.

—Yeh see, Sharon, said Yvonne. —You've got to understand, Greg's a very important person.

—Fuck off, Burgess, said Jackie, but she was grinning.

—Where're yeh goin'? Sharon asked Jackie.

—Rimini. In Italy.

—Lovely.

—Yeah.

—Yeh can go for a swim with the Pope, said Yvonne.

They laughed.

—Cos there'll be fuck all else to do there, Yvonne finished.

—She's just jealous, said Mary.

—Of wha'? said Yvonne ———

Mary changed the subject.

—Anny news, Sharon? she asked.

—No, said Sharon. —Not really.

* * *

Sharon told no one else yet.

She bought a book in Easons and read about the first fourteen weeks of pregnancy and waited for the changes to happen; the breasts swelling, the urinating, the nausea and that. She looked at herself in her parents' wardrobe mirror. She looked the same. And from the side; the same as well. She was ten weeks and two days pregnant. She didn't bother including the hours and minutes, but she nearly could have. The book said that the real changes started after the tenth week. And that was now.

Her nipples were going to get darker. She didn't mind that too much. The veins in her breasts would become more prominent. Sharon didn't like the sound of that. That worried her. She wondered would they be horrible and knobbly like her Auntie Mona's varicose veins. The joints between her pelvic bones would be widening. She hoped they wouldn't pinch a sciatic nerve, which ran from her arse down through the back of her legs, because she had to stand a lot of the time in work and a pinched sciatic nerve would be a killer. She read about her hormones and what they were doing to her. She could picture them; little roundy balls with arms and legs. She hoped her bowel movements stayed fairly regular. Her uterus would soon be pressing into her bladder. What worried her most was the bit about vaginal secretions. They'd make her itchy, it said. That would be really terrible in work, fuckin' murder. Or when she was out. She'd have preferred a pinched sciatic nerve.

She hoped these changes came one at a time.

She read about eating. Nearly everything she normally ate was wrong. She decided she'd follow the instructions in the book. She wasn't getting sick in the mornings but she started having dry toast for her breakfast, just to be on the safe side.

It was good for morning sickness. She ate raw carrots. She took celery home from work and chewed that. Jimmy Sr banned the carrots and the celery when the telly was on, except during the ads. If she didn't go easy on the carrots, he said, she'd give birth to a fuckin' rabbit. And there were enough bunnies in the house already.

She ploughed through her book, about three pages a night. It was hard going, and frightening. There was a lot more to being pregnant than she'd thought. And there was so much that could go wrong.

She didn't feel pregnant yet, not really.

She read about the feelings she might have at this stage. She might, she read, feel increased sensuality. She looked that up in Darren's dictionary and that wasn't how she felt at all. She might feel like she was in love: no way. She might feel great excitement: ——no.

She was sitting between Jimmy Sr and Veronica a few days after she'd told them the news. Blankety Blank was over. The panel were waving out at them. Jimmy Sr stuck his fingers up at them. Darren laughed.

—Your man, Rolf Harris, is an awful gobshite, said Jimmy Sr. —I've always said it.

—He's a great painter, said Veronica.

—He is in his hole a great painter, said Jimmy Sr. —He slaps a bit o' paint around an' if it looks like somethin' he says it an' if it doesn't he starts singin' Two Little Boys Had Two Little Toys. To distract us.

—He's good for the kids, said Veronica.

—He's good for the bowels, said Jimmy Sr. —You don't like him, do yeh, Darren?

—No way.

—I don't like him either, said Tracy.

—I don't like him either, said Linda.

—There now, Veronica, said Jimmy Sr.

—What's perception? Sharon asked.

—Wha?

—What's perception?

—Sweat, Jimmy Sr told her. —Why?

Sharon whispered to Jimmy Sr.

—It says my perception might be heightened when I'm pregnant.

—Yeh smell alrigh' from here, love, said Jimmy Sr.

He leaned over.

—What's the buke abou'?

—Pregnancy.

—Jaysis, d'yeh need a buke to be pregnant these days?

—I didn't have a book, said Veronica.

—Shhh! went Jimmy Sr.

—You wouldn't've been able to read it, Ma, said Darren.

The remote control hit his shoulder and bounced off his head.

—Wha' was tha' for!? he cried.

His hand tried to cover both sore spots.

—Mind your own business, you, said Jimmy Sr. —Don't look at me like tha', son, or I'll ——Say you're sorry to your mother.

—I was on'y —

—SAY YOU'RE SORRY.

———Sorry.

—PROPERLY.

—I'm sorry, Ma.

—You don't look it, said Veronica.

—I can't help it.

—You get that from your father.

—It's not all he'll get from his father, said Jimmy Sr. —Turn on Sky there, he barked at Darren, —for the wrestlin'.

—His master's voice, said Veronica.

—No chips for you tonigh', Jimmy Sr told her.

—Aw.

Jimmy Sr pointed at a diagram in Sharon's book.

—What's tha' supposed to be? he asked her.

—The inside of a woman, said Sharon, softly.

—Jaysis, said Jimmy Sr. —Sky, I said. That's RTE 2. Look

at the wavy lines, look. That's RTE 2. It's one o' their farmin' programmes.

Linda and Tracy giggled.

Jimmy Sr studied the diagram.

—Where's it all fit? he wanted to know. —Is this an Irish buke, Sharon?

—No. English.

—Ah, said Jimmy Sr.

—Is Sharon havin' a baby? Linda asked.

—No! said Jimmy Sr.

—Are yeh, Sharon?

—Are yeh havin' a baby, Sharon? said Tracy.

—NO, I SAID.

—Sharon, are yeh?

—Aaah! said Jimmy Sr.

—No, I'm not, Sharon told them. —A friend o' mine is, that's all.

—Ah, said Tracy, very disappointed.

—Ma? said Linda.

—Mammy, said Veronica.

—Mammy. Will you be havin' more babies?

—Oh my Jaysis, said Jimmy Sr. —Here. Here. Come here.

He dug into his pockets. He'd no change, so he gave Linda a pound note.

—Go ou' an' buy sweets. ——Say Thank —

But they were gone. Jimmy Sr saw Darren looking at him.

—What're you lookin' at? ——Here.

It was a pound.

—Thanks, Da. Rapid.

—Get ou'. ——I think yeh'd better read tha' buke up in your room, Sharon. I can't afford to do tha' every nigh'.

—D'yeh think they know? Sharon asked him.

—Not at all, said Jimmy Sr. —They'll have forgotten all abou' it once they have their faces stuffed with —with Trigger Bars an' Cadbury's fuckin' Cream Eggs.

—Stop that.

—Sorry, Veronica. ——Annyway sure, we'll have to tell them some time annyway, won't we?

—Yeah. I suppose so. ——Yeah. I hadn't thought o' tha', said Sharon.

—I have, Veronica told her.

Sharon brought the book upstairs.

She read on. She might feel shock: no, not now. She might feel a loss of individuality. She might feel she didn't matter: no. Like a vessel: no. Loveless: yeah ——not really. Scared: a bit. Sick: not yet. Not ready for pregnancy: sort of, but not really.

What she really felt, she decided later in bed, was confused. There was so much. And she wouldn't have really known that if she hadn't bought the bleedin' book.

But she wanted to know. She wanted to know exactly what was going to happen, what was happening even now. She put her hand on her stomach: nothing.

* * *

She felt a bit impatient too. Sometimes she didn't think anything was going to happen. She hoped the changes came soon. She was ready for it; getting bigger, backache, and the rest of it. In a way she wanted it. She didn't mind people knowing she was pregnant —as long as no one knew who'd helped her —but she couldn't go around telling everyone. She could never have done that. Once she started getting bigger, then they'd know. Then they could laugh and talk about it and try and guess who she'd done it with, and then leave her alone.

Though she'd have to tell her friends, Jackie and them.

* * *

Jimmy Sr woke up. His neck was killing him. He hated falling asleep sitting on the couch, but he'd had a few pints with the lads after the pitch and putt, so he didn't know he was falling asleep till now, after he'd woken up. He tried to stretch, and lift his head up.

—Ah —! ——fuck——

He shook himself. His chin was wet, and a bit of his shirt.

—Ah Jaysis, he gave out to himself. —Yeh fuckin' baby, yeh.

He looked at the telly. Cricket.

—Ah, fuckin' hell.

He always got angry the minute he saw cricket. It really annoyed him, everything about it; the umpires, the white gear, the commentators, the whole fuckin' lot.

He couldn't find the remote control, so he had to stand up. When he got to the telly he didn't bother looking to see if there was anything else on. He just turned it off.

His mouth and throat were dry. He needed Coke, or anything fizzy and cold.

Veronica was in the kitchen, at the table, cutting material.

—Is it still Saturday? said Jimmy Sr.

—The dead arose, said Veronica.

Jimmy Sr went to the fridge. He bent down and took out a large yellow-pack bottle, empty.

—Fuck it annyway!

—Now now.

—There was loads in it this mornin'. I only had a few slugs.

—Jimmy had the rest of it before he went to work, Veronica told him. —He didn't look very well.

—Fuck'm, said Jimmy Sr. —Why can't he buy his own?

—Why can't you buy your own?

—I bought this one!

—Excuse me. I bought it.

—With my fuckin' money.

Veronica said nothing. Jimmy Sr sat down. He shouldn't have shouted at her. He felt guilty now. He'd send one of the kids to get her a choc-ice when one of them came in.

—What's tha' you're makin', Veronica? he asked.

Veronica glanced at him over her glasses.

—A skirt. For Linda, she said.

—No one'll run her over in the dark annyway, wha', said Jimmy Sr.

The material was very bright, shiny red.

—Ha ha, said Veronica. —It's for their majorettes.

—Their wha'?

—Majorettes. You know. Marching to music.

—Wha'? Like in American football?

—That's right.

This worried Jimmy Sr.

—They're a bit young for tha', aren't they?

—Don't be stupid, said Veronica. —They're doing it in school.

—Oh, fair enough so, said Jimmy Sr. —What's for the dinner?

—You had your dinner, Veronica reminded him.

She put the scissors down on the table. That was that for one day. Her eyes were sore.

—For the tea, said Jimmy Sr.

————A fry, said Veronica.

—Lovely, said Jimmy Sr. —An' some fried bread maybe?

Veronica looked across. There was one full sliced pan and most of another one.

—Right, she said. —Okay.

—Veronica, said Jimmy Sr. —I love yeh.

—Umf, said Veronica.

The back door opened and Les charged through the kitchen. They heard him walloping the stairs as he ran up to the boys' room.

—Don't say hello or ann'thin'! Jimmy Sr roared.

There wasn't an answer. The door slammed.

—No one just closes doors annymore, said Jimmy Sr. —Did yeh ever notice tha', Veronica?

Veronica had her head in the fridge. She was wiping some dried milk off the inside of the door.

—They either slam them or they leave the fuckin' things open, said Jimmy Sr. —I went into the jacks there this mornin' an' Linda was sittin' in there readin' a comic. Or it might've been Tracy.

—You should have knocked, said Veronica.

—The door was open, said Jimmy Sr. —An open jacks door

means the jacks is empty. Everywhere in the world except in this house. Walk into the jacks in this house an' you'll find a twin, or Jimmy pukin', or Leslie wankin' —

—Stop that!

—Sorry. ——That's the sort o' stuff they should be teachin' them in school. Not Irish or —or German. Shuttin' jacks doors an' sayin' Hello an' tha' sort o' thing. Manners.

—Will you look who's talking about manners, said Veronica, and she stabbed a sausage a couple of times and turned it, and stabbed it again.

Jimmy Jr came in, from work.

—Howyis, he said.

—Get stuffed, you, said Jimmy Sr.

—Manners! said Veronica.

—Listen here, you, said Jimmy Sr. —You're not to be drinkin' all the Coke in the mornin', righ'. Buy your own.

—I put me money into the house, said Jimmy Jr.

—Is tha' wha' yeh call it? Yeh couldn't wipe your arse with the amount you give your mother.

He pointed at the sausages.

—D'you know how much they cost, do yeh?

—Do you know? Veronica asked him.

Darren came in the back door, and saved Jimmy Sr.

—Did yeh win, Darren? he asked.

—Yeah, said Darren. —I saved a penno.

—Did yeh? Ah, good man. Good man yourself. Wha' score?

—Two-one.

—Yeh let one in.

—It wasn't my fault.

—Course it wasn't.

—Muggah McCarthy let it through his legs an' —

Veronica looked at Darren.

—Get up, you, and wash some of that muck off you.

The twins came in as Darren went out.

—Ma, Da, said Linda. —Can we keep this?

It was a pup, a tiny black wad of fluff with four skinny legs

163

and a tail that would have looked long on a fully grown dog. It was shaking in Linda's hands, terrified.

—No, said Veronica, and —Yeah, said Jimmy Sr at the same time. —Yeh can o' course.

—Not after the last one, said Veronica. —They never stopped crying after Bonzo got run over. And Darren and Sharon.

—And you, said Jimmy Sr.

—Ah, Mammy. We won't cry this time. Sure we won't, Tracy?

—Yeah, said Tracy. —We'll tie the gate so he can't get ou'.

—No, I said.

—Ah, Ma-mmy! Let's.

—Who'll feed it? Veronica wanted to know.

—Wha' is it? said Jimmy Sr.

—A dog, said Linda. —It'll grow bigger.

—Will it? said Jimmy Sr. —That's very clever.

Veronica laughed. She couldn't help it.

Tracy pounced.

—Can we keep it, Mammy? Can we?

——Alright, said Veronica.

Jimmy Sr beamed at her.

—When was the last time you brushed your teeth? she asked him.

—This mornin'!

—With Guinness, was it?

She looked at the twins.

—You're to feed it, the two of you. ——An' it's not to come into the house.

—The 'Malley's dog had it, Linda told them. —He had loads o' them.

—Can we get another one, Ma? One each.

—No!

—Aah.

—No.

—One'll do yis, said Jimmy Sr. —Show us it here.

Linda handed the pup to Jimmy Sr.

Jimmy Jr walked back in.

—What's tha'? A rat?

—It is not a rat, Jimmy Rabbitte, said Tracy. —It's a dog.

—It's a dog, righ', said Linda.

It was warm and quivering. Jimmy Sr could feel its bones.

—Wha' sort of a dog is it but? he asked.

—Black, said Tracy.

—Go 'way! said Jimmy Jr.

—I'm your new da, Jimmy Sr told it.

They all laughed.

—An', look it. There's your mammy makin' the tea.

He made its paw wave at Veronica. Linda and Tracy were delighted. They couldn't wait to do that.

—Give us it, said Linda, and she pulled at it.

—Easy! ——for Jaysis sake, said Jimmy Sr. —You'll break the poor little bastard.

He lifted it up by the skin at the back of its neck and looked under it.

—It's a young fella, he told Veronica.

—Thank God, said Veronica.

—How do yeh know tha'? Tracy wanted to know.

—It's written there. Look.

—It isn't. ——Where is it?

Then the pup puked on Jimmy Sr's shoulder.

—Oh, look it, said Linda.

She tried to rub it off before her mammy saw it and changed her mind.

—Leave it, leave it, said Jimmy Sr. —What're you laughin' at?

—Nothin' much, said Jimmy Jr.

—Put it in the back, said Veronica.

Jimmy Sr put the pup on the table so he could get to the sink and clean his shoulder. It stood there, rattling, its paws slipping on the formica, and pissed on it.

Tracy grabbed it and ran for the door and Jimmy Sr had the piss in a J-cloth and under the tap before Veronica had time to turn from the cooker to see what had happened.

Jimmy Sr studied his shoulder.

—That's grand.

—Change it, said Veronica.

—Not at all, said Jimmy Sr. —It's grand.

Tracy came back in with the pup clinging to the front of her jumper.

—Look it. He's hangin' on by himself.

—What're yis goin' to call him? Jimmy Sr asked.

—Don't know.

—Wha' abou' Larry Gogan? said Jimmy Sr.

He looked across at Jimmy Jr, but Jimmy Jr didn't know he was being slagged.

—That's stupid, said Linda.

—It's thick, said Tracy.

—No, it's not, said Jimmy Sr. —Listen. How many —?

—Call him Anthrax, said Jimmy Jr.

—They will not, said Veronica.

—Look it, said Jimmy Sr when he'd stopped laughing. —If yis call him King or Sultan or somethin' like tha' an' yis shout ou' his name half the dogs in Barrytown'll come runnin' at yis; d'yeh see? But if yis call him Larry Gogan he's the only one that'll come to yis cos there's not all tha' many dogs called Larry Gogan as far as I know.

—It's an excellent name, said Jimmy Jr.

The girls looked at each other.

—Okay, said Linda. —We were goin' to call it Whitney.

—It's a boy, said Jimmy Sr, laughing.

—Yeah.

—Your name's Larrygogan, Tracy told the pup.

Larrygogan didn't look all that impressed.

—Howyeh, Larrygogan.

—Will yis do a message for me, girls?

—Yeah, said Linda.

Jimmy Sr always paid them for messages.

—Get a choc-ice for your mammy —

—I want a Toblerone as well, said Veronica.

—Certainly, Veronica, said Jimmy Sr. —A choc-ice an' a small Toblerone, an' you can have choc-ices as well.

—Can we just have the money?

—No way. Choc-ices. An', come here, I want to see yis eatin' them.

—Not till they've had their tea, said Veronica.

—Did yis hear tha'? said Jimmy Sr. —An' get one for Darren an' as well.

—Wha' abou' me? said Jimmy Jr.

—Buy your own.

—Aaah! He's gorgeous!

Sharon had just walked in and seen Larrygogan.

—There's Sharon, said Jimmy Sr. —D'yeh want a choc-ice, Sharon?

—Yeah thanks, Daddy.

—A celery one, is it?

—Very funny, I don't think.

Sharon patted Larrygogan.

—God, he's only a skeleton.

—He's from Ethiopia, said Jimmy Jr.

Jimmy Sr, Linda, Tracy and Sharon laughed but Veronica didn't. They heard a bang from above them. The bunk beds in the boys' room had hopped. Les and Darren were fighting.

—STOP THA', Jimmy roared at the ceiling. ——There.

He gave three pound notes to Linda.

—We'll bring Larrygogan, said Tracy.

Sharon laughed.

—Is tha' wha' yis're callin' him?

—That's righ', said Jimmy Sr.

He winked at her.

—Don't bring him, he told the twins. —He'll have to have his shots. If yis bring him ou' before he has his shots he'll catch diseases.

—What's shots?

—Injections.

—Ah no!

—They're nice injections. They don't hurt. They'll tickle

167

him. An' annyway, if he doesn't have them he'll catch all sorts o' diseases. An' then Jimmy here'll catch them off o' him an' give them to all his pals.

—I'll wear a johnny, Jimmy Jr whispered to Sharon.

—Oh Jesus! Sharon laughed.

—Take it easy, said Jimmy Sr.

—Right, said Veronica. —Ready. Sharon, give me a hand here.

—Dash, girls, Jimmy Sr told the twins.

And they did.

And Larrygogan fell into the sink.

* * *

On the Tuesday morning after Larrygogan joined the family, in the middle of week eleven, Sharon got an awful fright when she was climbing out of bed, just waking up. Her period had started.

—Oh no! ——Oh God ——

She'd been robbed.

But then she remembered: she'd read in the book that this could happen. It wasn't a real period. It probably wasn't a real period.

She stayed at home in bed and waited. She lay there, afraid to move too much. She tried to remember the Hail Mary but she couldn't get past Hello Be Thy Name, and anyway, she didn't believe in it, not really; so she stopped trying to remember the rest of it. It was just something to do. She wanted to turn on her side but she was afraid to. She just lay there and she started saying Please please please please all the time to herself. She kept everything else out of her mind. She concentrated on that.

—Please please please please.

The book was right. It didn't last long. It wasn't the same. It wasn't a real period at all. She was still pregnant.

* * *

168

—Aah! Jaysis!!

Veronica put the skirt on the table and got up to see what was wrong in the hall. But before she got to the door Jimmy Sr came hopping into the kitchen with one of his leather slippers in his hand.

—What happened? said Veronica.

—The dog's after shitein' in the fuckin' hall an' I fuckin' stood in it, that's wha' happened.

—On the floor?

—No. On the fuckin' ceilin'. Jesus!

He hopped over to the sink and put the slipper under the tap. Veronica came back from the hall.

—It's comin' off alrigh', Jimmy Sr told her.

—What about the carpet?

—The twins'll be cleanin' tha', don't worry. An' the sink here.

—It's disgusting, said Veronica.

Jimmy Sr inspected the slipper. It was grand and clean again. He threw it on the floor and stepped into it.

—Ah, he's only a pup, he said.

—He'll have to go. They're not training him properly.

—Give him a chance, Veronica. You'll be expectin' the poor little bollix to eat with a knife an' fork next.

Veronica gave up and got back to the skirt. She was just finishing Linda's and then she had Tracy's to do.

Jimmy Sr saw the twins out in the back. They were trying to get Larrygogan to catch a burst plastic football but Larrygogan was having problems staying upright. If the ball landed on him Jimmy Sr thought it would kill him. The grass needed cutting. Larrygogan kept disappearing in it.

Jimmy Sr opened the back door.

—Get in here, you–is!

* * *

Sharon woke up and she knew she was going to be sick.

She was hunched down at the toilet bowl. There was sweat,

169

getting cold, on her face. She shivered. More puke, not much now —hardly any —rushed into her mouth.

—Yu —hh ——!

It dropped into the water and she groaned. She squeezed her eyes shut. She wiped them, then her nose, and her eyes again. She stood up carefully. She was cold.

—Are yeh alrigh' in there, Sharon?

It was Jimmy Sr.

—Yeah, she said. —Ou' in a minute.

—No hurry, Jimmy Sr assured her. —I was in already.

Sharon rubbed her arms. A wave of horribleness ran through her.

She gagged. She really felt terrible, and weak. She leaned against the wall. It was cool; nice. She knew she wasn't going to be sick again. This morning.

She thought about nothing.

—Are yeh stayin' in there, or wha'?

It was the other Jimmy.

Sharon unlocked the door.

—What's your fuckin' hurry? she said.

Jimmy Jr looked at her face.

—Wha' were you drinkin' last nigh'? he asked.

Sharon passed him. She was going back to bed. That was where she wanted to be.

The twins looked at her.

—Are yeh not well, Sharon? Linda asked her.

—No, said Sharon.

—That'll be the flu, said Linda.

Tracy agreed with her.

—There's a bug goin' around, she said. —Cover yourself up properly.

They went downstairs to get a cup of tea and a bit of dry toast for Sharon. Sharon rubbed her legs. Only her forehead was cold now.

Well, she was pregnant now alright. She pressed her stomach gently: still nothing, but she was on her way. She smiled, but she hoped to God it wasn't going to be like this every morning.

When she took her hand away from her stomach —probably because she didn't feel sick any more —she noticed that her skin there was kind of sore, a bit like sunburn but not nearly as bad. She pressed again: yeah, the same. She tried her tits.

—Ouw! —

She'd been half-aware of that soreness for a few days but it was only now, because she'd just been sick, that she paid proper attention and linked it to being pregnant. They used to get a bit sore before her periods, but now —God, it was all starting to happen.

She'd have to tell her friends now; no, soon.

Jesus.

Tracy ran in.

—Ma said to say if yeh keep not goin' to work you'll be sacked an' jobs don't grow on trees.

—Tell her I'll be down in a little while.

Linda came in. She had Larrygogan with her.

—Larrygogan wants to say Howyeh.

She brought him over to Sharon's bed so he could lick Sharon's face. Sharon lifted her head for him.

—Hiyeh, Larry.

He stared at her. Linda put him right up to Sharon's nose.

—Kiss her, she said.

Nothing happened.

—Kiss her, will yeh.

—Give us a kiss, Larry, said Sharon.

—Daddy said we're to call him his whole name so he'll know who he is, said Tracy.

—He kisses us, Linda told Sharon. —Tracy, doesn't he?

—Yeah.

—He doesn't really know me yet, that's all, said Sharon. —Bring him back down now, will yeh.

—Okay. Come on, Larrygogan.

Linda ran out.

—Tracy, will yeh tell Mammy I'm gettin' up now, said Sharon.

She sat up.

—Ah, said Tracy. —Do yeh not have the flu?

—No.

—Ah janey.

She sounded very disappointed.

—Wha'? said Sharon.

—I wanted to catch it off yeh, an' so did Linda.

Sharon laughed.

—Why?

—Don't want to do the majorettes annymore, said Tracy. —It's stupid.

—I thought yis liked it.

—No. We used to. But it's stupid.

—Why is it? Sharon asked.

—It's just stupid, said Tracy. —She won't let us be in the front.

—Why won't she?

—Don't know. ——She hates us. It's prob'ly cos Daddy called her a wagon at tha' meetin'.

Sharon laughed. She got out of bed.

—He didn't really call Miss O'Keefe a wagon, she told Tracy. —He was only messin' with yeh.

Tracy continued.

—Nicola 'Malley's in the front an' she's nearly always droppin' her stick an' me an' Linda only drop ours sometimes.

—It's not fair, sure it's not, said Sharon.

Tracy followed her into the bathroom.

—No, she agreed. —The last time Nicola 'Malley threw her stick through the fuckin' window.

Sharon nearly bit the top off her toothbrush.

—Tracy!

—It just came ou'. ——She did though, Sharon.

—An' is she still in the front row?

—Yeah. It's not fair. ——An' the music's stupid.

They were back in the bedroom.

172

—What is it? Sharon asked.

—Don't know. A woman singin' Moll-ee My Irish Moll-ee, or somethin'. Miss O'Keefe thinks it's brilliant but it's thick.

Jimmy Sr shouted from downstairs.

—Are yeh ready for a lift, Sharon?

—Nearly.

—Make it snappy, will yeh.

He strolled back into the kitchen. Veronica was the only one still in there.

—Cummins is comin' ou' to have a look at the plasterin' this mornin' an' we've still got one o' the rooms to do, Jimmy Sr told her.

—Did you mention about a job for Leslie to him? Veronica asked him.

—Not yet. I will but. Today.

—Mm, said Veronica.

—I will now, Jimmy Sr assured her. —Scout's honour. Is he up yet?

—Not at all.

—We'll have to put a stop to tha'.

He picked up his sandwiches.

—Wha' are they? he asked.

—It's a surprise.

—It's not Easy Slices, is it?

Veronica turned to the sink.

—Is it? It is. Ah Jaysis, Veronica! How many times —!?

Linda came in from the back.

—Does the dog like sandwiches, does he? Jimmy Sr asked her.

And he lobbed the tinfoil pack out the door into the back garden.

*   *   *

It was the thirteenth week of Sharon's pregnancy and the middle of May, but it was cold.

—It's fuckin' freezin', said Jimmy Sr, and he was right.

173

Any time now, Sharon knew, and the real swelling would start. But she kept putting off telling the girls. Twice in the last week she'd gone down to the Hikers and she was definitely going to tell them. But she didn't. She couldn't.

She could've told them she was pregnant. That wouldn't have been too bad, not all that embarrassing really. But it was the big question that would come after that —WHO? —that was what she couldn't face.

But she'd have to tell them sooner or later and, judging by what she'd been reading, it would have to be sooner.

She struggled through her book. She read forward into the weeks ahead. Parts of it terrified her. She learned that the veins in her rectum might become painful. She was sure she felt a jab just after she'd read that.

She might get varicose veins. Or nosebleeds. Better than iffy rectum veins, she thought. Oedema sounded shocking. She could see herself filling up with water and bouncing around. Larrygogan would claw her and she'd have a puncture.

All these things were bad but when she read about eclampsia she went to the toilet and got sick. She shook and shivered for ages after it. She read it again: protein in the urine —blurred vision —severe headaches —hospital —swelling of face and fingers —she read it very slowly this time ——eclampsia ——convulsions ——coma ——death. She was going to catch it, she knew it. She always got the flu and colds when they were going around. She didn't mind the protein in her urine, or even the blurred vision so much. It was the word Convulsions that got to her.

So much could go wrong. Even when it was okay there seemed to be nothing but secretions and backache and constipation. And she'd thought there was no more to it than getting bigger and then having it and maybe puking a few times along the way.

Still, nothing was going wrong so far. The book said there might be vomiting in the mornings, and there was —not every morning though. The book said her breasts would be tender. She'd always thought that that was another word for Good when you were talking about meat but she looked for it in Darren's dictionary and that was what her tits were alright. They were still the same colour though. Her nipples were the same colour as well, although it was hard to tell for sure. They changed colour every day in the bathroom mirror.

She started doing sit-up exercises and touching her toes when she got home from work. They'd make carrying the extra weight easier. As well as that the exercises helped to squeeze water from the pore spaces in her blood vessels. But the book didn't say what happened to the water after that. Sometimes she forgot about the exercises though, and sometimes she just didn't feel like it; she was too knackered. Anyway, she was tall and quite strong and she always walked straight, so she didn't think the exercises mattered that much. She really did them because she wanted to do everything right, and the book said she should do them.

She was drinking a lot of milk. She was eating oranges. She kept reminding herself to go to a chemist's and get vitamin pills. She was eating All-Bran four times a week.

—What's tha' stuff like, Sharon? Jimmy Sr asked her one morning she'd the time to eat her breakfast sitting down.

—Horrible, said Sharon.

—Does it work?

—Sort of, yeah.

—Ah well, that's the main thing, isn't it? ——You don't need it, sure yeh don't?

He was talking under the table to Larrygogan.

She kept eating the celery and the carrots. The right food was hard and boring and it took ages to eat but Sharon thought she was doing things the right way, and that pleased her. And excited her. She felt as if she was getting ready, packing to go somewhere —for good. And that frightened her a bit.

She felt her stomach. It was harder and curved, becoming like a shell or a wall.

She'd definitely have to tell the girls.

* * *

It was Tuesday morning. It was raining. There was war going on downstairs in the kitchen.

Linda and Tracy put the table between themselves and their mother.

—What's wrong now? Jimmy Sr wanted to know. —Can a man not eat his bit o' breakfast in peace?

—It's stupid, Ma, said Linda.

—Yeah, said Tracy.

—Mammy! said Veronica.

—Mammy, said Linda. —It's stupid.

—I don't care, said Veronica. —I spent hours making those skirts for you two little rips —

—They're stupid, said Linda.

She hadn't meant to say that. She knew she'd made a mistake but she hated those skirts, especially her own one.

Veronica roared.

—Aaah!

The hours she'd wasted; cutting, clipping, sewing, making mistakes, starting again.

Jimmy Sr threw his knife and fork onto the plate.

—Wha' kind of a fuckin' house is this at all? he asked the table.

He looked at Veronica. She was deciding if she'd throw the marmalade at the twins.

—A man gets up in the mornin', said Jimmy Sr. —an' —an' —

—Oh shut up, said Veronica.

—I will not shut up, said Jimmy Sr. —A man gets up —

—Hi-dee-hi, campers, Jimmy Jr greeted them all when he came into the kitchen.

—Fuck off, Jimmy Sr shouted.

Jimmy Jr looked down at Jimmy Sr.

—Do yeh not love me annymore, Daddy?

—Yeh sarcastic little prick, yeh, said Jimmy Sr. —If —

—Stop that language, said Veronica.

—I'm only startin', said Jimmy Sr.

—Miss O'Keefe said yeh should be ashamed of yourself, Linda told Jimmy Sr.

This interested Jimmy Sr.

—What? said Veronica.

Darren came in and sat down and started eating Sugar-Puffs.

—They're ours, said Tracy.

—So? said Darren.

—When did, eh, Miss O'Keefe say tha' to yis? Jimmy Sr asked.

—Last week.

—Yeah, said Tracy.

—WHY did she say it? Veronica asked.

—Yeh took the words righ' ou' of me mouth, said Jimmy Sr.

—When Tracy said wha' you said, Linda told him.

—You said it as well! said Tracy.

—I did not!

—Girls, girls, said Jimmy Sr. —Wha' happened? Exactly.

He looked at Veronica. She looked away.

—She told everyone to say wha' our mammies an' our daddies said to each other tha' mornin'.

—Oh my God! said Veronica.

Jimmy Jr started laughing. Darren was listening now as well.

—An' it was real borin' cos they were all sayin' things like Good mornin' dear an' Give us the milk. ——An' Tracy said wha' you said to Mammy.

She looked at Tracy. Tracy was going to kill her.

Veronica sat down.

—An' would yeh by any chance remember wha' I said to your mammy? Jimmy Sr asked.

——Yeah.

—Well? What was it?

—Yeh pointed ou' the window ——at the rainin' —

She pointed at the window.

—An' then yeh said ——

Jimmy Jr laughed. He remembered.

—Go on, said Jimmy Sr.

—You said It looks like another fuck of a day.

Jimmy Jr howled. So did Darren. Jimmy Sr tried not to.

Veronica put her hands to her face and slowly dragged her fingers down over her cheeks. Her mouth was open.

—Oh sweet Jesus, she said then, to no one.

Sharon came in.

—Hiyis, said Sharon. —What're yis laughin' at?

—There's Sharon, said Jimmy Sr. —How are yeh, Sharon?

—Grand.

—Good. ——Good.

He started laughing.

—Serves her righ', the nosey brasser.

Jimmy Jr, Darren and the twins laughed. Jimmy Sr grinned at Veronica.

—Listen, he said to the twins. —If she asks yis again today tell her —

—No!

That was Veronica.

The Rabbittes laughed.

—What're yis laughin' at? Sharon still wanted to know.

—You, said Jimmy Jr.

Sharon gave him a dig.

—Mammy, you can give the skirts to the poor people, said Linda.

This tickled Jimmy Sr.

—What's this? said Jimmy Jr.

—None o' your business, said Jimmy Sr.

—What poor people? said Veronica.

—The Ethiopians, said Jimmy Jr.

Linda and Tracy giggled.

—I think that's a lovely idea, Linda, said Jimmy Sr. —Fair play to yeh.

—Stop encouraging them, said Veronica.

—Stop? said Jimmy Sr, shocked. —Well now, I hope Miss O'Keefe doesn't hear abou' this. My God, wha'. The twins's

178

mother won't let them show a bit o' charity to those less
fortunate than —

—Stop that!

Darren was in stitches. He loved it when his da talked like
that.

—I'm sure there's a couple o' piccaninnies —

—Daddy!

The boys laughed, cheering on Jimmy Sr. The twins were
still giggling, and looking at their mammy.

——in a refugee camp somewhere that'd love a couple o'
red lurex majorette's dresses. An' the sticks as well.

—You're not fit to be a father, said Veronica.

—Not now maybe, Jimmy Sr admitted.

He patted his gut.

—I used to be though, wha'.

He winked at Veronica. She growled at him. Jimmy Sr
looked at the boys and raised his eyes to heaven.

—Women, wha'.

He lowered the last of his tea. Then he heard something, a
scraping noise.

—What's tha'?

—Larrygogan, said Tracy. —He wants to come in.

Linda opened the door. Larrygogan, even smaller than usual
because his hair was stuck down by the rain, was standing on
the step.

—Come on, Larrygogan, said Linda.

Larrygogan couldn't make it. He fell back twice. They
laughed.

—The poor little sappo, said Jimmy Sr.

Linda picked him up and carried him in and put him down
on the floor. He skidded a bit on the lino, then shook himself
and fell over.

Then he barked.

The Rabbittes roared laughing. Jimmy Sr copied Larrygogan.

—Yip! Yip!

He looked at his watch.

—Oh good shite!

He was up, and grabbed his sandwiches.

—Are yeh righ', Sharon? ——Wha' are they, he asked
Veronica.

—Corned beef.

—Yippee. ——Good luck now. See yeh tonigh'.

He wondered if he should kiss Veronica on the cheek or
something because they were both in a good mood at the same
time. But no, he decided, not with the boys there. They'd slag
him.

—Da, can I've a bike for me birth'y? Darren asked him.

—Yeh can in your hole, said Jimmy Sr.

—Ah, Da!

—Forget it, Sunshine.

Jimmy Sr waited for Sharon to go out into the hall first.

—Good girl.

He followed her.

—Hang on a sec, he said, at the front door.

He gave Sharon the keys of the van.

—Let yourself in.

Les thought it was a heart attack. He tried to scream, but he
couldn't.

Jimmy Sr's hand was clamped tight over Les's face. He
waited till Les was awake and knew what was happening.

—That's the front o' me hand, Jimmy Sr told Les.

He pushed Les's head deeper into the pillow.

—If yeh don't get up for your breakfast tomorrow like I
told yeh you'll get the back of it. D'yeh follow?

Jimmy Sr took his hand off Les's face.

—Now get up, yeh lazy get, an' don't be upsettin' your
mother.

He stopped at the door.

—I want to talk to you tonigh', righ'.

Downstairs, Jimmy Jr and Darren heard a snort. They
looked and saw their mother crying. It was terrible. She was
wiping tears from her eyes before they could get to her
cheeks.

But she wasn't crying. She was laughing. She tried to explain why.

—They're not —

She started laughing again.

—They're not corned beef at all.

A giggle ran through her, and out.

—They're Easy Slices.

They didn't know what she was on about but they laughed with her anyway.

*   *   *

Sharon was in bed. She'd decided: tomorrow. She'd been half-thinking of doing it tonight but then Jackie had come in with the big news: she'd broken it off with Greg. So they'd had to spend the rest of the night slagging Jackie and tearing Greg apart. It'd been brilliant crack.

So Jackie would be there when she told them all tomorrow. That was good because the two of them always defended one another when the slagging got a bit serious. She was going to tell the rest of the family first, after the tea —that would be easy —and then the girls, later in the Hikers.

That was it, decided. But she wasn't a bit sleepy now. She had been when she got into bed but once she'd made up her mind she was wide awake again.

What was she going to tell them; how much? Only that she was pregnant. But what was going to happen after that, and what they were going to ask and say, and think; that's what was worrying her.

—Go on, Sharon, tell us. Who was it?

There was no way she was going to tell them that. If they ever found out ——God, she'd kill herself if that happened, she really would. She couldn't think of a good enough lie to tell them, one that would stop them from asking more questions. She could say she didn't know who he was but they wouldn't believe her. Or if they did, if Sharon told them she'd been so pissed she couldn't remember, they'd help her remember and they wouldn't give up till they'd found someone.

—Was it him, Sharon, was it? And if Sharon said, No, it wasn't him, they'd say, —How d'yeh know if yeh can't remember? It must've been him then.

She'd just have to tell them that she wasn't going to tell them.

But they'd still try and find out.

She didn't blame them. She'd have been the same. It was going to be terrible though. She wouldn't be able to really relax with them any more.

—There's Keith Farrelly.

—Yeah.

—He's a ride, isn't he?

—He's alrigh'.

—D'yeh not like him?

—He's alrigh'.

—I thought that yeh liked him.

—Fuck off, will yeh. It wasn't him.

It was going to be fuckin' terrible.

She felt a bit lonely now. She'd have loved someone to talk to, to talk to nonstop for about an hour, to tell everything to. But —and she was realizing this now really —there was no one like that. She'd loads of friends but she only really knew them in a gang.

It hadn't been like that in school. Jackie had been her best friend for years but now that was only because she saw her more often than the others, not because she knew her better. She'd never have been able to tell Jackie all about what had happened. They'd often talked about fellas; what he did and how he did it and that sort of thing, but that had only been for a laugh; messing. They hadn't spoken seriously about anything to do with sex since —since Sharon had her first period. Or they'd pretended it wasn't serious. It was always for a laugh. Giggling, roaring, saying things like, —I swear, Jackie, I was scarleh. ——She really had something to be scarlet about now and it wasn't even a little bit funny. And she couldn't tell it to Jackie. And anyway, Jackie had been going with Greg until last weekend so she hadn't seen her that much since —she knew the date —the twentieth of February.

That was always the way when one of the gang was going with someone. She'd disappear for a while, usually a couple of months, and come back when one of them broke it off. She'd come back to the pub and they'd all be delighted to see her and she'd have to slag the fella —it always happened —about how he was always farting, or how he kept trying to tear the tits off her, or how his tongue always missed her mouth in the dark and he slobbered all over her make-up (Sharon giggled as she thought of that one. Yvonne Burgess had said that about a fella in the army who'd gone off to the Lebanon without telling her. —I hope he's fuckin' kilt, said Yvonne. —By an Arab or somethin'. D'yeh know wha' his ma said when I phoned? He's gone to the Leb. The Leb! I thought it was the name of a pub or somethin' so I said to her, D'yeh know wha' time he'll be back at? I'm tellin' yis now, I swear, I was never so mortified in —my —life. I wasn't. And they'd screamed laughing), and after that it was like she'd never been gone. It was back to normal till the next time they went to Saints or Tamangos or one of the places in town and one of them got off with a fella she liked and disappeared again for another couple of months. She'd often read in magazines and she'd seen it on television where it said that women friends were closer than men, but Sharon didn't think they were. Not the girls she knew. ——Anyway, if she couldn't tell Jackie the whole lot —and she couldn't —then she couldn't tell anyone.

She'd have to be careful and not get too drunk again so she wouldn't blabber, and make sure she wasn't caught looking at him and try not to vomit if anyone mentioned his name and Jesus, it was going to be terrible.

If they ever found out! She tried to imagine it. But all she could do was curl up and groan. It was ——

Years ago —four years ago —when she'd been a modette, she'd gone with this young fella called Derek Cooper who spent all of his money on clothes and then never washed them and was dead now, and the two of them missed the last DART from town so they got the last bus instead. She'd been really pissed. She was only a kid then. She'd gotten the money she got for doing the pre-employment in school the day before so she'd been loaded. She paid for his drink as well. Anyway, she was pissed and she fell asleep on the bus and she woke up and she'd wet herself and she had to tell him and she made them stay on till the last stop, Howth. It was horrible remembering it. Even now. She'd never been able to laugh about it. She'd nearly been glad when she found out that Derek Cooper had been killed in that crash, but she'd made herself cry.

But this —this was far worse than that.

Sharon didn't even bother closing her eyes. There was no point. She waited for the time to get up.

It was mad, but she wished she'd had sex a lot more often. Doubts about the father would have been very comforting; lovely. But the last time she'd done it with a fella she'd really liked —who'd turned out to be a right fuckin' bastard —was six months before.

Before ——Jesus!

She was glad she didn't remember much about it. The bits she did remember were disgusting. It wasn't a moving memory, like a film. It was more like a few photographs. She couldn't really remember what happened in between. She'd been really drunk, absolutely paralytic. She knew that because she remembered she'd fallen over on her way back from the toilets. She bumped into loads of people dancing. It was the soccer club Christmas do, only it was on in February because they weren't able to get anywhere nearer to Christmas. She'd made it back to her table and she just sat there, trying not to think about getting sick. She remembered Jackie was asking her was she alright. Then it was blank. Then she was by herself at the table. Jackie was getting off with a fella in front of her. That was Greg. She could remember the song: The Power of Love, the Jennifer Rush one. She wasn't sure if it was then or after but she was very hot, really sweating. She was going to be sick. She rushed and pushed over the dance floor, past the toilets, outside because she wanted cold air. It was blank again then for a bit but she knew that she didn't puke. The air had fixed her. She was leaning against the side of a car. She was looking at the ground. It was just black gravel so she didn't know why she was looking at it; maybe because she'd thought she was going to get sick earlier. Anyway, she was shivering but she didn't move; go back in. Pity. She couldn't move really. Then there was a hand on her shoulder. —Alrigh', Sharon? he'd said. Then it was blank and then they were kissing rough —she wasn't really: her mouth was just open —and then blank again and that was it really. She couldn't remember much more. She knew they'd done it —or just he'd done it —standing up because that was the way she was in the next bit she remembered; leaning back against the car, staring at the car beside it, her back and arse wet through from the wet on the door and the window and she was wet from him too. She was very cold. The wet was colder. He was gone. It was like waking up. She didn't know if it had happened. She wanted to be at home. At home in bed. Her knickers were gone. And she was all wet and cold there. She wanted to get into bed. She went straight home. She staggered a lot, even off the path. She wanted to sleep. Backwards. To earlier. She was freezing but she didn't go back for her jacket.

Jackie brought it and her bag home for her the day after.

—What happened yeh?

—Jesus, I was pissed, Jackie, I'm not jokin' yeh. I just came home. I woke up in me clothes.

—Yeh stupid bitch yeh.

—I know.

She'd wondered a few times if what had happened could be called rape. She didn't know.

That was as much as she remembered. She wished she didn't remember more. ——When he sat down white skin poked out from between the buttons of his shirt.

There was one more thing she remembered; what he'd said after he'd put his hand on her shoulder and asked her was she alright.

—I've always liked the look of you, Sharon.

Sharon groaned.

The dirty bastard.

* * *

Les was nearly crying. So was Veronica.

—Shut up! The lot o' yis! said Jimmy Sr.

—You started it, Jimmy Jr reminded him.

—Good Jesus!!

—I'm goin' to smash your fuckin' records, Les told Jimmy Jr.

This time Veronica slapped him hard across the head.

—Wha'!?

—Don't Wha' me, said Veronica, and she slapped him again. —Don't think you can stroll in and out of here when you feel like it and shout language like a —like a knacker.

She drew her hand back, Les ducked, and then she slapped him.

Linda and Tracy were giggling.

—Don't start, youse! Jimmy Sr roared at them.

—You never hit THEM, do yeh? said Les.

He was crying now.

—I'm not takin' this.

He slammed the back door.

Jimmy Sr was going after him.

—Leave him out there, said Veronica. —It's going to rain in a minute. That'll bring him back.

Jimmy Sr couldn't leave it just like that. He'd lost, in front of Darren, the twins, Sharon —them all. He was the head of the fuckin' house!

—Come here, you, he said to Jimmy Jr. —If you ever behave like that again in this house yeh can pack your belongin's. Your groovy clothes an' your shampoo an' —an' your bras an' yeh can fuck off to somewhere else, righ'. Is tha' clear?

—I don't know, said Jimmy Jr. —I'll have to discuss it with my solicitor.

186

A laugh burst out of Darren. He'd have loved the neck to say something like that.

—Don't YOU start!

Darren stopped.

And Jimmy Sr felt a bit better.

—Now, he said. —Sharon has a bit o' news for yis.

Veronica started laughing.

—Sorry, she said. —I can't help it.

—Darren, said Jimmy Sr. —We live in a mental home.

Darren laughed.

—Sorry, Sharon, said Veronica. —Go on, love.

Sharon grinned at Veronica. She looked at the twins when she spoke.

—I'm goin' to be havin' a baby.

* * *

Jimmy Sr and Veronica were alone in the kitchen. Jimmy Sr was having the cup of tea he always had before he went out.

—These yokes aren't as nice as they used to be, said Jimmy Sr. —Sure they're not?

He put the rest of the Jaffa Cake on the table.

—That doesn't stop you eating them.

—I didn't say they weren't nice, Veronica. Wha' I said was —

—Right. Right. I agree with you.

—Are yeh tired, Veronica?

—Mm, said Veronica.

—Will yeh go on up to the bed?

—Mm.

—That's the place to be. ——It went well, didn't it?

—I suppose it did, said Veronica.

—They took it very well, I thought.

—Ah Jimmy, for Christ's sake. What did you expect? Did you think the girls would be outraged or something?

——No.

He grinned at her.

—I didn't think they'd go tha' wild. Poor Sharon won't have any peace now. Inside —

He nodded at the door.

—watchin' the telly there, Sharon yawned an' Tracy asked her was she havin' the baby. ——Tha' Jimmy fella's a righ' pup though. He said somethin' to Sharon, yeh know, cos I saw her hittin' him. She gave him a righ' wallop.

—They get on very well, those two.

—I don't know, said Jimmy Sr.

He sighed.

—You were exactly like him, said Veronica.

—Veronica, please. It's been a rough day. Now, lay off.

—Remember that Crombie you had?

—No.

—You do so. You used to keep it spotless. Except for your dandruff.

—I didn't have dandruff!

—Excuse me, you did so. My Uncle Bob used to say that we needed a Saint Bernard dog to find everyone after you'd been in the house.

Jimmy Sr laughed.

—He was an oul' bollix, tha' fella. A right oul' bollix. I bought tha' fucker a brandy at the weddin', I did. ——Annyway, we didn't have those special shampoos. Timotei. So mild you can wash your hair as often as yeh like! As if yeh didn't have better things to be doin' than washin' your fuckin' hair all day. As often as yeh like!

—What happened that coat?

—I don't know! I threw it ou'.

—You did not. After you bought it you stopped trying to get me to go into the fields with you. It was the best contraceptive ever invented, that coat.

—Veronica!

—That's what they should give every young lad these days. A nice new coat.

Jimmy Sr laughed.

They said nothing for a while. Then Veronica spoke.

—Jimmy.

—Yes, Veronica?

—Do you not think —? —You'll probably shout at me for saying it. ——I think we should tell the twins that what Sharon did was wrong.

—Wha'?

—No, listen. I don't want to turn them against her or anything —

—An' the baby, remember.

—Yes, I know that. But —

—Wha'?

—I think we should tell them. Without, you know. We should tell them that they should only have babies when they're married.

—They wouldn't understand wha' you were on abou'.

—Oh they would, you know.

—Maybe they would. ——It's a bit young but, isn't it? Wha' were yeh thinkin' o' tellin' them?

He was flicking fluff and specks off his jumper. That meant he was on his way out.

—Do you not think we should? Veronica asked him.

—Well, whatever you think yourself, Veronica, said Jimmy Sr. —They'd only laugh at me. I'm only their da. Anyway, it'd sound better comin' from a woman, wouldn't it? ——Maybe leave it till they're a bit older.

—But by then —

She couldn't finish. There was no tidy way of saying what she thought. She gave up. Maybe she'd talk to Sharon about it.

Jimmy Sr was standing up, ready to go. But he didn't want to leave Veronica unhappy.

—Times've changed, Veronica, he said.

—I suppose so, said Veronica. —But do we have to keep up with them?

Jimmy Sr didn't like questions like that.

—D'yeh want to come? he asked Veronica.

—Ah no.

—Up to the bed?

—Mm; yeah.

—That's the place. See yeh later.

—Bring your Crombie. It might rain.

—Ha fuckin' ha.

* * *

—How much did it cost yeh, Jackie? Yvonne asked.

She dipped two wetted fingers into her crisp bag and dredged it for crumbs.

—Fifteen pound, ninety-nine, said Jackie.

—Really? said Yvonne. —That's brilliant, isn't it?

—Is it hand wash, Jackie? said Mary.

—Yeah, it is.

—It's very nice now.

—Thanks.

Yvonne wiped her fingers on the stool beside her.

Sharon saw this as she walked over to join them so she parked herself on the stool opposite Yvonne.

—Hiyis, she said.

—Hiyeh, Sharon.

—Ah howyeh, Sharon.

—Hiyis, said Sharon.

—Are they new, Sharon?

—No, not really.

A lounge boy was passing. Sharon stopped him.

—A vodka an' a Coke, please, she said.

—Don't bother abou' the Coke, Sharon, said Jackie. —I've loads here, look it.

—Okay. Thanks, Jackie. A vodka just, she told the lounge boy.

—Anyway, Jackie, said Mary.

The real business of the night was starting.

—Will yeh be seein' Greg again?

—Tha' prick! said Jackie.

They laughed.

Jackie had given Greg the shove the Saturday before —or so

she said anyway —in one of those café places in the ILAC Centre, after he'd accused her of robbing the cream out of his chocolate eclair. —An' I paid for the fuckin' thing! she'd told them the night before.

She was in good form tonight as well. She tapped the table with her glass.

—If he was the last man on earth I wouldn't go with him.

She took a fair sip from the glass.

—I'd shag the Elephant Man before I'd let him go near me again, the prick.

They roared.

—Yis should've seen him with that fuckin' eclair. I was so embarrassed, I was scarleh, I'm not jokin' yis, I was burnin'. In his leather jacket an' his fuckin' keys hangin' off his belt, yeh know, givin' the goo goo eyes to a fuckin' eclair. It was pat'etic, it was.

—Were yeh goin' to break it off annyway? Sharon asked her.

—Yeah, said Jackie. —I was thinkin' about it alrigh'. I was givin' the matter, eh, my serious consideration.

They laughed.

—Then when I saw him sulkin'; Jesus!

—He was very good lookin' though, wasn't he? said Yvonne. —Very handsome.

—Not really, said Jackie. —Not when yeh got up close to him. D'yeh know what I mean?

—Beauty is only skin deep, said Mary.

—It wasn't even tha' deep, Mary, Jackie told her. —He had loads o' little spots on his chin. Tiny little ones now. Millions o' them. You only noticed them when you were right up against him, an' then you'd want to throw up. ——There was nothin' under the leather jacket really. That's all he was now that I think of it.

Jackie sighed and took a slug from her glass.

—A leather jacket. ——He was thick as well.

—Come here, Jackie, said Mary. —Was he passionate?

—No, said Jackie. —But he thought he was. Yeh know? He was just a big thick monkey.

191

—Lookin' for somewhere to stick his banana, wha', said Yvonne.

They screamed.

—Yvonne Burgess!

Sharon wiped her eyes.

—He stuck his tongue in me ear once, Jackie told them when they'd settled down again. —An', I'm not jokin' yis, I think he was tryin' to get it out the other one. I don't know what he fuckin' thought I had in there.

She laughed with them.

—He licked half me brains ou'. Like a big dog, yeh know.

They roared.

Jackie waited.

—His sense o' direction wasn't the best either, d'yis know what I mean?

They roared again.

—Jesus!

—Jackie O'Keefe! You're fuckin' disgustin'!

—Wha'?

More vodkas and Cokes and a gin and a tonic were ordered. And crisps.

Then Sharon told them her bit of news.

—I'm pregnant, did I tell yis?

Mary laughed, but the others didn't. Then Mary stopped.

—Yeah, well, said Sharon. —I am.

—She's fuckin' serious, said Yvonne.

No one said anything for a bit. Sharon couldn't look anywhere. The others looked at one another, their faces held blank. Sharon picked up her glass but she was afraid to put it to her mouth.

Then Jackie spoke.

—Well done, Sharon, she said.

—Thanks, Jackie.

She put the glass down. She was starting to shake. Suddenly she couldn't breathe in enough air to keep her going.

—Yeah, Sharon. Congrats, said Mary.

—Thanks, Mary.

—Well done, Sharon, said Yvonne. —Yeh thick bitch yeh.

Then they all started laughing. They looked at one another and kept laughing. Sharon was delighted. They were all blushing and laughing. The tears were running out of her and the snot would be as well in a minute. She took up her bag from the floor to look for a hankie.

The laughing died down and became fits of the giggles. They all blew their noses and wiped their eyes.

—Jesus though, Sharon, said Jackie, but she was grinning.

Sharon reddened again.

—I know, she said. —It's terrible really.

Some questions had to be asked.

First an easy one.

—How long are yeh gone, Sharon? Yvonne asked her.

—Fourteen weeks.

They converted that into months.

—Jesus! Tha' long? said Mary.

They looked at Sharon.

—You don't look it, said Yvonne.

—I do, said Sharon.

—I won't argue with you, said Yvonne. —You're the expert.

They screamed.

—I'm only messin', said Yvonne.

Sharon wiped her eyes.

—I know tha'.

—You look the same, said Mary.

—I'll start gettin' bigger in a few weeks.

—Well, said Jackie, —you can start hangin' round with someone else when tha' happens. No fellas'll come near us if one of us is pregnant.

They laughed.

—Sharon, said Yvonne. —Who're yeh havin' it for?

Your fat da, thought Sharon.

—I can't tell, she said. —Sorry.

She looked at her drink. She could feel herself going red again.

—Ah, Sharon!

She grinned and shook her head.

—Meany, said Jackie.

Sharon grinned.

—Give us a hint.

—No.

—Just a little one.

Nothing.

—Do we know him?

—No, said Sharon.

—Ah Sharon, go on. Tell us.

—No.

—We won't tell annyone.

—Leave Sharon alone, said Jackie. —It's none o' your fuckin' business. Is he married, Sharon?

—Oh Jesus! said Mary.

—No, said Sharon.

She laughed.

—You're scarleh. He must be.

—He's not. I swear. He's not —

—Are yeh gettin' married? Mary asked.

—No. I mean —I mean I don't want to marry him.

—Are yeh sure we don't know him?

—Yeah.

—Is he in here?

—Jesus, said Jackie. —If we don't know him he isn't here. An' anyway, would you do it with annyone here?

—I was only fuckin' askin', said Yvonne.

She looked around. The lounge was fairly full.

—You're righ' though, she said. —It was a stupid question. Sorry for insultin' yeh, Sharon.

—That's okay.

—Serious though, Sharon, said Mary. —Do we really not know him?

—No. I swear to God.

—I believe yeh, thousands wouldn't, said Yvonne.

—Where did yeh meet him?

194

—Ah look, said Sharon. —I don't want to talk about it annymore; righ'?

—Let's get pissed, will we? said Jackie.

—Ah yeah, said Sharon.

—Hey! Jackie roared at the lounge boy. —Get your body over here.

They laughed.

The lounge boy was sixteen and looked younger.

—Three vodkas an' two Cokes an' a gin an' tonic, said Jackie. —Got tha'?

—Yeah, said the lounge boy.

—An' a package o' crisps, said Yvonne.

—Ah yeah, said Sharon. —Two packs.

—Do yeh have anny nuts? Mary asked him.

—Jesus, Mary, yeh dirty bitch yeh!

They screamed.

—I didn't mean it tha' way, said Mary.

The very red lounge boy backed off and headed for the bar. Yvonne shouted after him.

—Come back soon, chicken.

—Leave him alone or he'll never come back, said Jackie.

—Who's goin' to sub me till Thursday? said Yvonne.

—Me, said Sharon. —I will. A tenner?

—Lovely.

—He'll be nice when he's older, won't he? said Mary.

—Who? The lounge boy?

Jackie looked over at him.

—He's a bit miserable lookin'.

—He's a nice little arse on him all the same, said Yvonne.

—Pity there's a dickie bow under it, said Jackie.

They stopped looking at the lounge boy.

—Annyway, Sharon, said Jackie. —What's it like? Are yeh pukin' up in the mornin's?

—No, said Sharon. —Well, yeah. Only a couple o' times. It's not tha' bad.

—I'd hate tha'.

—Yeah. It's bad enough havin' to get up without knowin' you're goin' to be vomitin' your guts up as well.

—It's not tha' bad, said Sharon.

—Are you goin' to give up work? Mary asked her.

—I don't know, said Sharon. —I haven't thought about it really. I might.

—It's nice for some, said Yvonne. —Havin' a job to think abou' givin' it up.

—Ah, stop whingin', said Jackie.

—I wasn't whingin'.

—Would you really like to be doin' wha' Sharon does, would yeh? Stackin' shelves an' tha'?

—No.

—Then fuck off an' leave her alone.

—Are you havin' your periods or somethin'?

—Yeah, I am actually. Wha' about it?

—You're stainin' the carpet.

The row was over. They nearly got sick laughing. The lounge boy was coming back.

—Here's your bit o' fluff, Mary, said Sharon.

—Ah stop.

—Howyeh, Gorgeous, said Jackie. —Did yeh make your holy communion yet?

The lounge boy tried to get everything off the tray all at once so he could get the fuck out of that corner.

He said nothing.

—Wha' size do yeh take? Yvonne asked him.

The lounge boy legged it. He left too much change on the table and a puddle where he'd spilt the Coke. Mary threw a beer-mat on top of it.

—Jesus, Sharon, said Jackie. —I thought you were goin' to have a miscarriage there you were laughin' so much.

—I couldn't help it. —Wha' size d'yeh take.

They started again.

—I meant his shirt, said Yvonne.

They giggled, and wiped their eyes and noses and poured the Coke and tonic on top of the vodka and gin.

—Are yeh eatin' annythin' weirdy? Mary asked Sharon.

—No, said Sharon.

—Debbie ate coal, Jackie told them.

—Jesus!

—I wouldn't eat fuckin' coal, said Sharon.

—How d'you eat coal? Mary asked.

—I don't know! said Jackie. —The dust, I suppose.

—My cousin, Miriam. Yeh know her, with the roundy glasses? She ate sardines an' Mars Bars all squashed together.

—Yeuhh! Jesus!

—Jesus!

—That's disgustin'.

—Was she pregnant? said Jackie.

—Of course she ——Fuck off, you.

They all attacked their drinks.

—He won't come back, said Jackie. —We'll have to go up ourselves.

—Come here, Sharon, said Yvonne. —Was it Dessie Delaney?

—No!

—I was on'y askin'.

—Well, don't, said Sharon. —I'm not tellin', so fuck off.

—Was it Billy Delaney then?

Sharon grinned, and they laughed.

Sharon put her bag under her arm.

—Are yeh comin', Jackie?

—The tylet?

—Yeah.

—Okay.

Jackie got her bag from under the table. They stood up. Sharon looked down at Yvonne and Mary.

—Me uterus is pressin' into me bladder, she told them.

—Oh Jesus!

They roared.

* * *

197

—Annyway, said Bimbo. —I gave him his fiver an' I said, Now shag off an' leave me alone.

—A fiver! said Paddy. —I know wha' I'd've given the cunt.

—I owed him it but.

—So wha'? said Paddy. —Tha' doesn't mean he can come up to yeh outside o' mass when you're with your mot an' your kids an' ask yeh for it.

—The kids weren't with us. Just Maggie an' her mother.

—Jimmy!

—Wha'? said Jimmy Sr from the bar.

—Stick on another one, said Paddy. —Bertie's here.

Bertie saluted those looking his way and then sat down at the table with Paddy and Bimbo.

—There y'are, Bertie, said Bimbo.

—Buenas noches, compadre, said Bertie.

—How's business, Bertie? said Paddy.

—Swings an' roundabouts, said Bertie. —Tha' sort o' way, yeh know.

—Tha' seems to be the story everywhere, said Bimbo. —Doesn't it?

—Are you goin' to nigh' classes or somethin'? said Paddy.

Bertie laughed.

—Ah fuck off, you now, said Bimbo. —Every time I open me mouth yeh jump down it.

—There's plenty o' room in there annyway, said Bertie, —wha'.

They heard Jimmy Sr.

—D'yis want ice in your pints?

He put two pints of Guinness down on the table, in front of Paddy and Bimbo. There was a little cocktail umbrella standing up in the head of Bimbo's pint.

Jimmy Sr came back with the other two pints.

—How's Bertie?

—Ah sure.

—It's the same everywhere, isn't it? said Paddy.

Bertie sniggered.

Bimbo was spinning the umbrella.

198

—Mary Poppins, said Jimmy Sr.

—Who? said Bimbo. —Oh yeah.

He held the umbrella up in the air and sang.

—THE HILLS ARE A—

Paddy squirmed, and looked around.

—LIVE WITH THE SOUND O' —no, that's wrong. That's not Mary Poppins.

—It was very good, all the same, said Jimmy Sr.

—It fuckin' was, alrigh', Bertie agreed. —Yeh even looked like her there for a minute.

Bimbo stuck his front teeth out over his bottom lip, and screeched.

—JUST A SPOONFUL OF SHUGEH —

HELPS THE MEDICINE ——GO DOWN —

THE MEDICINE ——GO DOW —

WOWN —

THE MEDICINE ——GO DOWN —

—Are yeh finished? said Paddy.

—Do your Michael O'Hehir, said Jimmy Sr.

—Ah, for fuck sake, said Paddy. —Not again. All o' them horses are fuckin' dead.

—Weuahh!

That was Bertie.

—Jesus! ——fuck!

He gasped. His mouth was wide open. He shook his face. He was holding his pint away from his mouth like a baby trying to get away from a full spoon.

He pointed the pint at Jimmy Sr.

—Taste tha'.

—I will in me hole taste it. What's wrong with it?

—Nothin', said Bertie.

And he knocked back a bit less than half of it.

—Aah, he said when he came up for air. —Mucho good.

Bimbo put the umbrella into his breast pocket.

—Wha' d'yeh want tha' for? said Paddy.

—Jessica, said Bimbo. —She collects them. Maggie brings all hers home to her.

199

Paddy looked across to Jimmy Sr and Bertie for support. Jimmy Sr grinned and touched his forehead.

—Oh yeah, said Bertie.

He'd remembered something. He picked the bag he'd brought in with him off the floor and put it on his lap.

—You don't follow Liverpool, said Paddy.

—It's Trevor's, said Bertie. —I had to take all his bukes an' copies ou' of it cos I'd nothin' else. There was a lunch in the bottom of it an', fuckin' hell. Did yis ever see blue an' green bread, did yis?

—Ah fuck off, will yeh.

—The fuckin' meat. Good Christ. It stuck its head ou' from between the bread an' it said, Are The Tremeloes still Number One?

He put his face to the opening and sniffed.

—Yeh can still smell it. The lazy little bastard. Annyway, Jimmy, he said. —Compadre mio. How many bambinos have yeh got that are goin' to school.

—Eh ——three. Why?

Bertie took three Casio pocket calculators in their boxes out of the bag.

—Uno, dos, tres. There you are, my friend. For your bambinos so tha' they'll all do well for themselves an' become doctors.

—Are yeh serious? said Jimmy Sr.

He picked up one of the calculators and turned it round.

—Si, said Bertie.

He explained.

—There's a bit of a glut in the calculator market, yeh know. I took three gross o' them from a gringo tha' we all know an' think he's a fuckin' eejit —

—An' whose wife does bicycle impressions when he isn't lookin'?

—That's him, said Bertie. —I gave him fuck all for them. I was laughin' before I'd the door shut on the cunt, yeh know. Only now I can't get rid o' the fuckin' things. No one wants them. I even tried a few o' the shops. Which was stupid. But

200

they were gettin' on me wick. I can't live with failure, yeh know. So I'm givin' them away. Righ', Bimbo. How many do you need?

—Five, said Bimbo.

—Five!?

—He only has four, said Jimmy Sr. —He wants one for himself.

Bimbo held up his left hand. He pointed to his little finger.

—Glenn.

He moved on to the next finger.

—Wayne.

The middle one.

—Jessica.

—Okay okay, said Bertie. —There'll be six by the time you've finished.

He dealt the boxes out to Bimbo.

—Uno, dos, tres, four, five.

—Thanks very much, Bertie.

—No problem, said Bertie. —See if yeh can get them to lose them, so I can give yeh more. I still have two gross in intervention. A fuckin' calculator mountain. ——Cal-cul-ators! We don't need your steenking cal-cul-ators! I speet on your cal-cul-ators! ——Paddy?

—Wha'?

—How many?

—I don't want your charity.

Bertie, Jimmy Sr and Bimbo laughed. Paddy was serious, but that made it funnier.

—None o' those kids he has at home are his annyway, said Jimmy Sr.

The stout in Bimbo's throat rushed back into his mouth and bashed against his teeth.

—My round, compadres, said Bertie.

He stood up.

—Three pints, isn't that it? he said.

They looked up at him.

—Do yeh want me charity, Paddy, or will yeh stay on your own?

—Fuck off.

—Four pints, said Bertie.

Jimmy Sr and Bimbo laughed and grinned at each other. Paddy spoke.

—Fuck yis.

Bertie took two more calculators out of the bag.

—For my amigos, the barmen.

When he got back from the bar Bimbo had one of the calculators out of its wrapper.

—The round costs five pound, forty-four, he told them.

—Go 'way! said Jimmy Sr.

—That's very fuckin' dear all the same, isn't it? said Bimbo.

—It was just as dear before yeh got the calculator, said Bertie.

—I know, I know tha'. It's just when yeh see it like tha' in black an', eh, silvery grey it makes it look worse. ——I think annyway.

—My Jaysis, said Paddy.

He looked at Bertie.

—Fuckin' hell, said Bimbo. —If there was six of us the round'd cost —

—Put it away, Bimbo, for fuck sake, said Jimmy Sr.

—I've got two kids in school, Paddy told Bertie.

—Is tha' righ'? said Bertie.

—Yeah.

—Well, I hope they're good at their sums, said Bertie. —Cos they're not gettin' anny calculators.

—Young Sharon's after gettin' herself up the pole, Jimmy Sr told them.

He rubbed his hands and picked up his pint.

—Is tha' YOUR Sharon, like? said Bimbo.

—That's righ', said Jimmy Sr. —Gas, isn't it?

—One calculator for Sharon, said Bertie, and he passed one across to Jimmy Sr, and then another one. —And one for the bambino. A good start in life.

—She's not married, said Bimbo.

—I know tha'! said Jimmy Sr.

—Is tha' the tall girl tha' hangs around with Georgie Burgess's young one? Paddy asked.

—That's righ', said Jimmy Sr.

—Is she gettin' married? said Bimbo.

—No, said Jimmy Sr. —Why should she? They've more cop-on these days. Would you get married if you were tha' age again these days?

—I think I'm goin' to cry, said Bertie.

—I'd say I would, yeah, said Bimbo.

—What're yeh askin' him for, for fuck sake? said Paddy. —He brings home little umbrellas for his kids. He goes to meetin's. He brought his mot to the flicks last week.

—Only cos her sister's in hospital, said Bimbo. —She usually goes with her sister, he told Jimmy Sr. —The Livin' Daylights, we went to. The James Bond one.

—Is it anny good?

—Ah it is, yeah. It's good alrigh'. ——There's a lovely lookin' bird in it. Lovely.

—Oh, I've seen her, said Bertie.

—Isn't she lovely?

—Oh si. Si. A little ride.

—Ah no. She's not. She's the sort o' bird, said Bimbo, —that yeh wouldn't really want to ride. D'yeh know wha' I mean?

—No.

Paddy shook his head and looked at Bertie, and grinned.

—Is she a cripple or somethin'?

—No! said Bimbo. —No. ——She's TOO nice, yeh know?

—You'd give her little umbrellas, would yeh?

—Fuck off, you, said Bimbo.

Bertie put a calculator in front of Bimbo.

—Give her tha' the next time yeh see her.

—Who did the damage? Paddy asked Jimmy Sr.

—We don't know, to tell yeh the truth, said Jimmy Sr. —She won't tell us.

—Well, you'd want to fuckin' find ou', said Paddy.

—What's it you who it is? said Bimbo.

—I couldn't give a fuck who it is, said Paddy. —It's Jimmy. I'm not goin' to be buyin' food for it, an' nappies an' little fuckin' tracksuits. Jimmy is.

—I am in me hole, said Jimmy Sr. —Hang on though. Maybe I will be.

He thought about it.

—So wha' though. I don't care.

—Good man, said Bimbo.

—An' she'll have her allowance, said Bertie.

—Will she? said Jimmy Sr. —I don't know. I s'pose she will. I don't care.

—Of course yeh don't, said Bimbo. —Such a thing to be worryin' abou'! Who's goin' to pay for it!

—Will yeh listen to him, said Paddy. —The singin' fuckin' nun.

—Fuck off.

—I believe Gerry Foster's young fella's after puttin' some young one from Coolock up the stick, Bertie told them.

—Wha'? said Jimmy Sr. —Jimmy's pal? What's this they call him? Outspan.

—Yeah. Him.

Jimmy Sr laughed.

—I'd say tha' made his hair go curly.

—Is he marryin' her? Bimbo asked.

—Yes indeed, said Bertie. —A posse came down from Coolock. Mucho tough hombres. They hijacked the 17A. Take us to Barrytown, signor.

They laughed.

—I believe the poor fucker's walkin' around with half an 8 iron stuck up his arse.

—Where's he goin' to be livin'?

They knew the answer they wanted to hear.

—Coolock, said Bertie.

—There's no need for all tha' fuss, said Jimmy Sr, when they'd stopped laughing. —Sure there's not?

204

—Not at all, said Bimbo. —It's stupid.

Bertie agreed.

—Thick, he said.

—It's only a baby, said Bimbo. —A snapper.

—Doctor Kildare, Bertie said to Paddy.

—That's it, said Paddy.

—Fuck off, youse, said Bimbo.

—I wouldn't want Sharon gettin' married tha' young, said Jimmy Sr.

—She's her whole life ahead of her, said Bimbo.

—Unless she drinks an iffy pint, said Bertie.

—Annyway, said Jimmy Sr.

He lifted his glass.

—To Sharon, wha'.

—Oh yeah. Def'ny. Sharon.

Bertie picked up his pint.

—To the Signorita Rabbeete that is havin' the bambino out of wedlock, fair play to her.

He gave Jimmy Sr another calculator.

—In case it's twins.

—Stop, for fuck sake.

Bimbo filled his mouth, swallowed, filled it again, swallowed and put his glass back on its mat.

—Havin' a baby's the most natural thing in the world, he said.

Jimmy Sr loved Bimbo.

—D'you know wha' Sharon is, Jimmy? said Bimbo.

——Wha'?

—She's a modern girl.

—Oh good fuck, said Paddy.

* * *

Sharon was lying in bed.

Well, they knew now. They'd been great. It'd been great.

She was a bit pissed. But not too bad. She shut her eyes, and the bed stayed where it was.

She'd never laughed as much in her life. And when Yvonne

205

had pinched the lounge boy's bum, the look on his face. And Jackie's joke about the girl in the wheelchair at the disco. It'd been brilliant.

Then, near closing time, they'd all started crying. And that had been even better. She didn't know how it had started. Outside, they'd hugged one another and said all sorts of stupid, corny things but it had been great. Mary said that the baby would have four mothers. If she'd said it any other time Sharon would have told her to cop on to herself but outside in the car-park it had sounded lovely.

Then they'd gone for chips. And Jackie asked the poor oul' one that put the stuff in the bags how she kept her skin so smooth.

Sharon laughed —

Soon everyone would know. Good. She could nearly hear them.

—Sharon Rabbitte's pregnant, did yeh hear?
—Your one, Sharon Rabbitte's up the pole.
—Sharon Rabbitte's havin' a baby.
—I don't believe yeh!
—Jaysis.
—Jesus! Are yeh serious?
—Who's she havin' it for?
—I don't know.
—She won't say.
—She doesn't know.
—She can't remember.
—Oh God, poor Sharon.
—That's shockin'.
—Mm.
—Dirty bitch.
—Poor Sharon.
—The slut.
—I don't believe her.
—The stupid bitch.
—She had tha' comin'.
—Serves her righ'.

206

—Poor Sharon.

—Let's see her gettin' into those jeans now.

Sharon giggled.

Fuck them. Fuck all of them. She didn't care. The girls had been great.

Mister Burgess would know by tomorrow as well. He probably knew now. He might have been up when Yvonne got home. ——Fuck him too. She wasn't going to start worrying about that creep.

She couldn't help it though.

* * *

—There's Stephen Roche, said Darren.

—Wha'? said Jimmy Sr.

He looked over his Press.

—Oh yeah.

The Galtee cheese ad was on the telly.

—That's a brilliant bike, Da, look.

—No, said Jimmy Sr, back behind the paper.

—Ah, Da!

—No.

Jimmy Sr put the paper down.

—I'll tell yeh what I will do though, he told Darren. —I'll buy yeh a box o' cheese. How's tha'?

Darren wouldn't laugh.

—What's on now? said Jimmy Sr.

He was sitting between Veronica and Sharon on the couch. He nudged Veronica.

—Leave me alone, you.

Jimmy Jr stuck his head into the room.

—Are yeh finished with the paper?

—No, said Jimmy Sr. —What's on, Sharon?

—Top o' the Pops, said Sharon.

—Oh good shite! said Jimmy Sr. —Where's the remote?

Sharon was getting up.

—Where're yeh off to now? he asked her nicely.

—The toilet.

207

—Again!? Yeh must be in a bad way, wha'.

Sharon sat down again. She whispered to Jimmy Sr.

—Me uterus is beginnin' to press into me bladder. It's gettin' bigger.

Jimmy Sr turned to her.

—I don't want to hear those sort o' things, Sharon, he said. —It's not righ'.

He was blushing.

—Sorry, said Sharon.

—That's okay. Who's tha' fuckin' eejit, Darren?

—Can you not just say Eejit? said Veronica.

—That's wha' I did say! said Jimmy Sr.

Darren laughed.

Veronica gave up.

—Da, said Darren.

—No, yeh can't have a bike.

Darren got up and left the room in protest. That left Jimmy Sr and Veronica by themselves.

—There's Cliff Richard, said Jimmy Sr.

Veronica looked up.

—Yes.

—I'd never wear leather trousers, said Jimmy Sr.

Veronica laughed.

Jimmy Sr found the remote control. He'd been sitting on it.

—He's a Moonie or somethin', isn't he? he said as he stuck on the Sports Channel. —And an arse bandit.

—He's a Christian, said Veronica.

—We're all tha', Veronica, said Jimmy Sr. —Baseball! It's worse than fuckin' cricket.

He looked at it.

—They're dressed up like tha' an' chewin' gum an' paint on their faces, so you're expectin' somethin' excitin', an' wha' do yeh get? Fuckin' cricket with American accents.

Jimmy Jr stuck his head round the door.

—Finished with the paper yet?

—No.

—You're not even lookin' at it.

208

—It's my paper. I own it. Fuck off.

Jimmy Sr switched again; an ad for a gut-buster on Sky.

—Jesus!

—You've got the foulest mouth of anyone I ever knew, Veronica told him. —Ever.

—Ah lay off, Veronica.

The front door slammed and Darren walked past the window.

—It's not his birthd'y for months yet, said Jimmy Sr. —Sure it's not?

—A bike's much too dear for a birthday, said Veronica.

—God, yeah. He has his glue ——What's tha' ANCO thing Leslie's signed up for, again?

—He's only applied, said Veronica. —He doesn't know if he'll get it. ——Motorbike maintenance.

—Wha' good's tha' to him? He doesn't have a motorbike.

—I don't know, said Veronica. —It lasts six months, so there must be something in it.

—But he doesn't have a motorbike. An' he's not gettin' one either. No way.

—You don't have to have a car to be a mechanic, said Veronica.

—That's true o' course, said Jimmy Sr. —Still, it doesn't sound like much though.

—It's better than what you got him.

—That's not fair, Veronica.

—He says he'll be able to fix lawn-mowers as well.

—We'll have to buy one an' break it so.

—Ha ha.

—He might be able to do somethin' with tha' alrigh', said Jimmy Sr. —Go from door to door an' tha'.

—Yes, said Veronica.

—Get little cards done, said Jimmy Sr. —With his name on them.

—Yes, said Veronica. —That sort of thing.

—Leslie Rabbitte, lawn-mower doctor.

—Ha ha.

—He won't get much business round here. Everyone gets a lend o' Bimbo's.

—He can go further.

—That's true. ——It'll get him up with the rest of us annyway. An' a few bob. ANCO pays them.

—Yes.

—The EEC, Jimmy Sr explained. —They give the money to ANCO.

—An' who gives the money to the EEC? Veronica asked.

—Em, said Jimmy Sr. —I've a feelin' we do.

—There now, said Veronica.

Jimmy Sr stayed quiet for a while. He switched back to the baseball.

—Look at tha' now, he said. —Your man there swingin' the bat. You'd swear somethin' great was goin' to happen, but look it.

He switched through all nine channels, back to the baseball.

—There. He hasn't budged. It's fuckin' useless. What's tha' you're knittin'?

—A jumper.

—I don't like purple.

—It's not purple and you won't be wearing it.

—Who will?

—Me.

—Good. 'Bout time yeh made somethin' for yourself. You have us spoilt.

—And then you never wear them.

—I do so. What's this I have on?

—That's a Dunnes one.

—It is in its hole.

—Can I buy the paper then?

It was Jimmy Jr.

—No!

Veronica picked the paper off the floor.

—Here.

Jimmy Jr grabbed it.

—Thanks, Ma.

And he was gone.

Veronica turned to Jimmy Sr.

—Do you think I stitch St Bernard tags and washing instructions on the jumpers when I've finished knitting them?

—No, Veronica. I don't think that at —

Veronica grabbed the tag that was sticking up at the back of Jimmy Sr's jumper.

—What's that? she said.

—Take it easy! said Jimmy Sr. —You're fuckin' stranglin' me.

Linda and Tracy ran in.

—Get tha' dog out o' here, Jimmy Sr roared.

—Ah! —

—Get him ou'!

He pressed the orange button and the telly popped off.

—Yeh can always tell when it's comin' up to the summer, he said. —There's nothin' on the telly.

—There's never anything.

—That's true o' course. But in the summer there's absolutely nothin'.

He was restless now and it wasn't even half-seven yet. He said it before he knew he was going to.

—I suppose a ride's ou' of the question.

—Hang on till I get this line done, said Veronica.

—Are yeh serious?

—I suppose so.

—Fuckin' great, said Jimmy Sr. —It's not even dark yet. You're not messin' now?

—No. Just let me finish this.

Jimmy Sr stood up.

—I'll brush me teeth, he said.

—That'll be nice, said Veronica.

* * *

—It doesn't really show yet, said Jackie.

—It does! said Sharon. —Look.

Sharon showed Jackie her side.

Jackie was sitting on Linda and Tracy's bed while Sharon got out of her work clothes.

—Oh yeah, said Jackie. —You'd want to be lookin' though.

—Everyone's lookin', Jackie.

They laughed.

Sharon went over to Jackie.

—Put your hand on it.

Jackie did, very carefully.

—Press.

—Fuck off, Sharon, will yeh.

—Go on.

Jackie pressed gently.

—God, it's harder than I thought, she said. —Oh Jesus, somethin's movin'!

She took her hand away. Sharon giggled. Jackie put her hand back.

—It's funny, she said.

Then she took her hand down.

—Thanks, Sharon, she said.

Sharon laughed.

—I won't show yeh the state of me nipples, she said.

—Aah Jesus, Sharon!

—Ah, they're not tha' bad, said Sharon. —They're just a funny colour, kind of. I can't wear these jeans annymore, look.

—Why not? ——Oh yeah. Yeh fat bitch yeh.

—These are grand though. Where'll we go?

—Howth?

—Yeah. Get pissed, wha'.

—Yeah.

* * *

—Jaysis, Sharon, said Jimmy Sr as he moved over on the couch to make room for her. —You'll soon be the same shape as me, wha'.

* * *

212

—Sharon, let's touch the baby.

—No!

—Aah!

—Alrigh'. Quick but. Daddy's waitin' on me.

* * *

—There's an awful smell o' feet in here, said Jimmy Sr. —It's fuckin' terrible.

—It's the dog, said Jimmy Jr.

—He's wearin' shoes an' socks now, is he? said Jimmy Sr. —Where is he?

—Ou' the back, said Darren.

Jimmy Sr, Jimmy Jr and Darren were in the front room, watching the tennis.

—It can't be him so, said Jimmy Sr. —An' it's not me.

—Don't look at me, said Jimmy Jr.

They both looked at Darren. He was stretched out on the floor. Jimmy Sr tapped one of his ankles.

—Get up there an' change your socks an' wash your feet as well. Yeh smelly bastard yeh.

—Ah Da, the cyclin's on in a minute.

—I amn't askin' yeh to amputate your feet, said Jimmy Sr. —I only want yeh to change your fuckin' socks.

—But the —

—Get ou'!

—Come here, said Jimmy Jr as Darren was leaving the room. —Don't go near my socks, righ'.

—I wouldn't touch your poxy socks.

—Yeh'd better not.

—It's those fuckin' runners he wears, said Jimmy Sr.

—Yeah, said Jimmy Jr.

—His feet can't breathe in them.

—Yeah.

—Who's your one?

—Gabriella Sabatini.

—Jaysis, wha'.

—She's only seventeen.

213

—Fuck off. ——Are yeh serious?

—Yeah.

—Is she winnin', is she?

—Yeah.

—Good.

* * *

—Jesus, I wouldn't like tha', said Yvonne. —Some dirty oul' bastard with a rubber glove.

—It was a woman, said Sharon.

—Yeah?

—Yeah. She was very nice. Doctor Murray. She was real young as well. It took bleedin' ages though.

—How long abou'? Mary asked her.

—Ages. Hours. Most of it was waitin' though. All fuckin' mornin', I'm not jokin' yeh. She said it was because of the cutbacks. She kept sayin' it. She said I should write to me TD.

—The stupid bitch, said Jackie.

They laughed.

—Ah, she was nice, said Sharon. —Come here though. I nearly died, listen. She said she wanted to know me menstrual history an' I didn't know what she talkin' abou' till she told me. I felt like a right fuckin' eejit. I knew what it meant, like, but I was —

—Why didn't she just say your periods? said Yvonne.

—Doctors are always like tha', said Mary.

—Menstrual history, said Jackie. —I got a C in that in me Inter.

They roared.

* * *

—Mammy, said Linda.

Tracy stood beside her.

—What? said Veronica.

—Me an' Tracy are doin' ballroom dancin'.

Veronica opened her eyes and sat up on the couch and put her feet back into her slippers.

214

—Ballroom dancing, she said. —Is that not a bit old-fashioned for you?

—No, it's brilliant, said Tracy.

—Yeah, said Linda.

—Where are my glasses? said Veronica.

She wanted to see the twins properly.

—There, look.

Both girls went to get Veronica's glasses for her but Veronica got to them first. She put them on.

—How much? she said.

—Nothin'!

—There's a competition, said Linda, ——an' that's ten pounds but it isn't on for ages.

—Well, I know you want something, said Veronica. —So you might as well tell me what it is.

—We have to have dresses.

—Oh God, said Veronica.

* * *

Sharon bought some pants with elastic waists, baggy things that would get bigger as she got bigger. She wouldn't have been caught dead in them if she hadn't been pregnant but now, when she looked at herself in them, she thought she looked okay. She'd have looked stupid and pathetic in what she usually wore. She was happy enough with her new shape. She walked as straight as she could although now and again she just wanted to droop.

She was sweating a lot. Like a pig sometimes. She knew she would, but it was embarrassing one day when she was putting jars of chutney on a high shelf in work and she felt a chill and looked, and under her arms was wringing. She felt terrible. She didn't know if anyone else had seen but she wanted to go around and tell everyone that she'd washed herself well that morning. As far as she knew she had a choice: she could drink a lot and sweat or she could stop and become constipated. Some choice. She kept drinking and wore a jumper in work.

She looked at her face. Was it redder or was it just the light? She thought she looked as if she'd just been running.

She met Mister Burgess once. It wasn't a real meeting because she crossed the road to the shops when she saw him coming round the corner and she looked at the girls playing football on the Green while he went past. He just went past, and that was what she wanted.

* * *

Jimmy Sr got out of the house earlier than usual because Veronica was in her moods again. Anyway, they were all watching Miami Vice at home and he couldn't stand it. It was like watching a clatter of Jimmy Jr's pals running around and shooting each other.

Bimbo was with him.

—Now, Bimbo continued, —there mightn't be annythin' in this.

He took a mouthful from his new pint.

—That's grand. ——It's a bit embarrassin' really —

He waited till Jimmy Sr was looking at him.

——But I heard him talkin' abou' Sharon. Your Sharon, like, on Sunday. Yeh know the way they all come in after the mornin' match.

—An' take over the fuckin' place; I know. Wha' was he sayin' abou' Sharon? Jimmy Sr asked, although he'd already guessed the answer.

——He said she was a great little ride.

——My God ——said Jimmy Sr, softly.

His guess had been way wrong.

—What a ——I'll crease the fucker. Would yeh say he's upstairs?

Bimbo was shocked.

—Yeh don't want to claim him here, he said. —You'd be barred.

He lifted his glass.

—An' me.

Jimmy Sr was breathing deeply.

—You're right o' course, he said. —That's wha' he'd want.

He whacked his glass down on the counter. It didn't break. He gripped the ashtray. The two barmen braced themselves for some kind of action.

He took his hand away from the ashtray.

Bimbo was appalled when he heard, then saw, that Jimmy Sr was crying.

—He'd no right to say tha', Bimbo, said Jimmy Sr.

—I know, said Bimbo.

—Just cos —

He snuffled.

In a way, Bimbo felt privileged, even though it was terrible. He knew that Jimmy Sr would never have cried in front of the other lads.

It had gone very quiet in the bar.

—Yeh wouldn't want to be listenin' to tha' fella, Bimbo told Jimmy Sr. —I only told yeh cos ——I'm not sure why I told yeh.

—You were righ', Bimbo, said Jimmy Sr.

—It's pat'etic really, said Bimbo. —A grown man sayin' things like tha'.

—Exactly.

—Just cos she's pregnant.

—Exactly.

—It's stupid.

—Yeah.

—It's not worth gettin' worked up abou'.

—Still though, said Jimmy Sr.

They looked around. There was no one looking at them.

Bimbo put his glass down.

—Sure, that's wha' we were put down here for. To have snappers.

—You should know, said Jimmy Sr.

—Ah here.

—Two pints, chop chop, Jimmy Sr called.

Bertie came in.

—Three pints!

217

—Buenas noches, lads, said Bertie.
—There y'are, Bertie, said Bimbo.
—Howyeh, Bertie, said Jimmy Sr.
—The rain she pisses down, Bertie told them.
Something was still eating Jimmy Sr.
—Why did he say it THA' way? he asked Bimbo.
—Wha'? said Bertie.
—Nothin', said Jimmy Sr.
—Okay; be like tha'.
—I will.
—Fuck you, amigo.
—Go an' shite, amigo.
—Here's the pints, said Bimbo.
Jimmy Sr looked at them.
—Get back there an' put a proper head on them pints, he told Dave, the apprentice barman. —Jaysis.

* * *

Sharon wasn't asleep.
—Sharon, are yeh awake?
She didn't answer.
He didn't know which side of the room he should have been talking into. He hadn't been in here in eight years, the last time he'd wallpapered the room.
—Are you awake, Sharon?
—Daddy, said Sharon. —Is tha' you?
—Yeah.
—Daddy, is tha' you? said Linda.
—Yes, pet. Go back to sleep. I want to talk to Sharon.
—Daddy, is tha' you? said Tracy.
—Yes, pet, said Linda. —Go back to sleep.
They laughed and giggled.
—Will yeh come down to the kitchen for a minute, Sharon? said Jimmy Sr.
He was making a sandwich for himself when Sharon got downstairs.
She was worried. She'd never been called out of bed before.

218

—Yeh might as well have a cup o' tea now you're up, said Jimmy Sr.

—Okay.

—Good girl.

Jimmy Sr sat down. Sharon went back to the sink and filled the kettle.

—Is somethin' the matter? she asked.

—Not really, no, Sharon. ——It's just, I heard somethin' tonigh'. An' I wanted to warn yeh.

Then he started eating his sandwich, a lemon curd one.

Sharon turned off the tap.

—Warn me?

She was really worried now. The kettle was heavy enough to hide the shakes. She took it over to the socket, and then went back to wash two cups.

—Well, yeah, said Jimmy Sr. —Warn.

He took a drop of lemon curd off the table with his finger, thought twice about licking it and rubbed it into his trousers.

—Yeh know your man, George Burgess?

Sharon was facing the kitchen window. She leaned over the sink and coughed. She turned on the tap.

—Are yeh alrigh' there? said Jimmy Sr.

—Yeah. I'll be fine.

—I thought yis only did tha' sort o' thing in the mornin's.

——Sometimes in the night as well.

—Is tha' righ'? God love yis.

Sharon felt a bit better. He was being too nice. He didn't know anything.

—What abou' Mister Burgess? she said.

—Ah, he was sayin' things abou' yeh.

—Wha' was he sayin' about me?

—Not to me face. He wouldn't fuckin' want to. It was Bimbo tha' told me. He said ——He was sayin' things abou' you, bein' pregnant.

—So wha'?

—Good girl.

—Wha' did he say?

—Ah ——He said you were a great little ride. So Bimbo says annyway.

—Mister Reeves wouldn't make somethin' like that up.

—God no, not Bimbo. Never.

—An' who's your man Burgess callin' little? I'm bigger than he is.

Jimmy Sr laughed, delighted.

—That's righ'. You're not upset or annythin'?

—No!

She filled the cups and worked at the teabags with a spoon.

—Really, bein' called a ride is a bit of a compliment really, isn't it?

—Jaysis, said Jimmy Sr. —I don't know. ——Thanks.

He took his cup.

—I suppose it is.

He tried the tea.

—That's grand, good girl. ——Still though, he'd no righ' to be sayin' things like tha'.

—Sure, fellas —men —are always sayin' things like tha' abou' girls.

—Ah yeah, but. Not daughters though.

—Don't be thick, Daddy. All girls are daughters.

—Well, not my fuckin' daughter then.

—That's hypocritical.

—I don't give a fuck what it is, said Jimmy Sr. —He has young ones of his own. Tha' pal o' yours —?

—Yvonne.

—That's righ'. ——It's shockin'. Annyway, I'm not havin' some fat little fucker insultin' any of my family. Specially not you.

—You're my knight in shinin' armour.

—Don't start.

He grinned. So did Sharon.

—I just thought tha' I should tell yeh, yeh know, said Jimmy Sr.

—Thanks.

—No problem.

220

—I'm goin' back up now, righ'?

—Okay. Night nigh', Sharon.

Les got tired and cold waiting out the back for his da to go to bed so he filled his lungs and opened the back door.

—Good Jaysis! Where were you till now?

—Ou'.

Les got past Jimmy Sr, behind his chair. Standing up quickly was always a problem for Jimmy Sr.

—Get back here, you.

But Les didn't come back. Jimmy Sr heard the boys' bedroom door being opened and closed. He'd get him in the morning. He started looking for a few biscuits.

Larrygogan yelped in his sleep.

—Shut up, you, said Jimmy Sr.

Sharon heard the boys' door as well. She was deciding what to do about Mister Burgess. It was simple: she'd go over to his place and tell him to stop saying things about her or she'd tell Missis Burgess, or something. She didn't really know him but she thought that that would give him a big enough fright. Simple. Not easy though; no way. She hated the idea of having to go over and talk to him, and look at him; and him looking at her. Still though, she had to shut him up.

She'd do it tomorrow.

The stupid prick.

* * *

It was half-six and Sharon was home from work. She was standing on the Burgess's front step. She was afraid she was making a mistake but she rang the bell again before she could change her mind.

Pat Burgess slid back the aluminium door.

—Yeah?

—Is Mister Burgess there?

—Yeah.

—Can I see him for a minute?

—He's still havin' his tea.

—Only for a minute, tell him.

Sharon looked in while she was waiting. It was a small hall, exactly the same as theirs. There were more pictures in this one though, and no phone. Sharon could hear children and adult voices from the kitchen. She could see the side of Missis Burgess's back because she was sitting at the end of the table nearest the door. Then she saw Missis Burgess's face. And then she heard her voice.

—Is it George you want, Sharon?

God! thought Sharon.

—Yes, please, Missis Burgess. Just for a minute.

She wanted to run. Jesus, she was terrified but she thought Mister Burgess probably was as well. The kitchen door closed for a second and when it opened again Mister Burgess was there. There was a napkin hanging from his trousers. He looked worried alright. And angry and afraid. And a bit lost.

Looking at him, Sharon felt better. She knew what she was going to say: he didn't. She wasn't disgusted looking at him now. She just couldn't believe she'd ever let him near her.

Mister Burgess came towards her.

—Yes, Sharon? he said. To Missis Burgess.

—I want to talk to you, Sharon said quickly when he got to the door.

He wouldn't look at her straight.

—Wha' abou'?

—YOU know.

—I'll see yeh later.

—I'll tell Missis Burgess.

Mister Burgess looked back into the hall. A lift of his head told her to come in.

—Come into the lounge, Sharon, he shouted. —Sharon's here abou' Darren.

—Hiyeh, Sharon.

It was Yvonne, from somewhere in the kitchen.

—Hiyeh, Yvonne, Sharon called back.

—See yeh later.

—Yeah, okay.

She walked into the front room. Mister Burgess shut the door. He was shaking and red.

—Wha' do yeh think you're up to, yeh little bitch, he hissed.

—Wha' d'yeh think YOU'RE up to, yeh little bastard?

He didn't hiss now.

—Wha'?

—Wha' were yeh sayin' about me to your friends? said Sharon.

—I didn't say ann'thin' to annyone.

It was an aggressive answer but there was a tail on it.

—You said I was a ride. Didn't yeh?

George Burgess hated that. He hated hearing women using the language he used. He just didn't think it was right. It sounded dirty. As well as that, he knew he'd been snared. But he wasn't dead yet.

—Didn't yeh? said Sharon.

—Are yeh mad? I did not.

—I can tell from your face.

It wasn't the first time he'd been told that. His mother had said it; Doris said it; everyone said it.

—I was only jokin'.

—I'm a great little ride.

The word ride made him snap his eyes shut.

—I didn't mean anny harm. I only —

—Wha' else did yeh say about me?

—Nothin'.

—Maybe!

—I swear. I didn't. On the Bible. I didn't say annythin'. Else.

She was nearly feeling sorry for him.

—Yeh stupid bastard yeh.

He looked as if he was being smacked.

She went on.

—You got your hole, didn't yeh?

He shut his eyes again. He got redder.

—Wha' more do yeh want?

—I swear on the Bible, Sharon, I didn't mean anny harm, I swear. True as God now.

—Wha' did yeh say?

—Ah, it was nothin'.

—I'll go in an' tell her.

He believed her.

—Ah, it was silly really. Just the lads talkin', yeh know.

Sharon knew that one step towards the door would get her a better explanation, so she took one.

—We —they —we were havin' a laugh, abou' women, yeh know. The usual. An' the young lads, the lads on the team, they were goin' on abou' the young ones from around here. ——An' that's when I said you were a —I said it.

He looked at the carpet.

—Yeh dope. Wha' did yeh say tha' for?

—Ah, I don't know.

He looked up.

—I was showin' off.

——Wha' else?

—Nothin', I swear. They laughed at me. Some o' them didn't even hear me. They'd never believe that I got me ——have —Off you.

He was looking at the carpet again.

—They thought tha' I was jokin'.

He jumped when the door was opened by Missis Burgess.

—There y'are, love, he roared at her.

—Hello, Sharon, said Missis Burgess.

—Hiyeh, Missis Burgess, said Sharon. —I was just tellin' Mister Burgess abou' Darren.

—That's righ', Mister Burgess nearly screamed.

—Is somethin' wrong with Darren?

—He has a bit of a cold just.

—A cold, said Mister Burgess.

—Maybe flu.

—We'll just have to hope he's better for Saturday, said Mister Burgess. —God knows, we'll need him.

—I didn't know there was flu goin' around, said Missis

Burgess. —I hope there isn't, ——now. Will you tell your mammy I was askin' for her?

—I will, yeah, Missis Burgess.

—When are yeh due, Sharon? Missis Burgess asked.

—November. The end.

—Really? You look sooner. ——D'you want a boy or a little girl?

—I don't mind. A girl maybe.

—One of each, wha', said Mister Burgess.

Missis Burgess looked at Mister Burgess.

—I'm off to my bingo now, George.

—Good, said Mister Burgess. —That's great. Have you enough money with yeh, Doris?

—My God, he's offerin' me money! He's showin' off in front of you, Sharon.

Sharon smiled.

—Bye bye so, Sharon, said Missis Burgess.

—See yeh, Missis Burgess.

—Don't forget the grass, George.

—No, no. Don't worry.

—Remember to tell your mammy now, Missis Burgess told Sharon.

Then she was gone.

Sharon knew what he was going to say next.

—Phew, he said. —Tha' was close, wha'.

—It'll be closer the next time if yeh don't stop sayin' things abou' me.

—There won't be a next time, Sharon, I swear to God. I only said it the once. I'm sorry. ——I'm sorry.

—So yeh should be. ——I don't mind bein' pregnant but I do mind people knowin' who made me pregnant.

——So ——you're pregnant, Sharon?

—Fuck off, Mister Burgess, would yeh.

They stood there. Sharon was looking at him but he wasn't looking at her, not really. She wanted to smile. She'd never felt power like this before.

—Sorry, Sharon.

Sharon said nothing.

She was going to go now, but he spoke. His mouth was open for a while before words left it.

——An', Sharon —

He rubbed his nose, on his arm.

—Yeah?

—I never thanked yeh for —yeh know. Tha' nigh'.

He was looking at the carpet again, and fidgeting.

—I was drunk, said Sharon.

She wanted to cry now. She'd forgotten That Night for a minute. She was hating him again.

—I know. So was I. I'd never've ——God, I was buckled.

——Em —

He tried to grin, but he gave up and looked serious.

—You're a good girl, Sharon. We both made a mistake.

—You're tellin' me, said Sharon.

—Hang on a sec, Sharon, he said. —I'll be back in a minute.

He went to the door.

—Wait there, Sharon.

Sharon waited. She was curious. She wasn't going to cry now. She heard Mister Burgess going up the stairs, and coming down.

He slid into the room.

—That's for yourself, Sharon, he said.

He had a ten pound note in his hand.

Sharon couldn't decide how to react. She looked at the money.

She wanted to laugh but she thought that that wouldn't be right. But she couldn't manage anger, looking at this eejit holding out his tenner to her.

—Do you think I'm a prostitute, Mister Burgess?

—God, no; Jaysis, no!

—What're yeh givin' me tha' for then?

—It's not the way yeh think, Sharon. Shite! ——Em, it's a sort of a present —

The tenner, he knew now, was a big mistake.

—Yeh know. A present. No hard feelin's, yeh know.

—You're some fuckin' neck, Mister Burgess, d'yeh know tha'?

—I'm sorry, Sharon. I didn't mean it the way you're thinkin', I swear. On the Bible.

He was beginning to look hurt.

—We made a mistake, Sharon. We were both stupid. Now go an' buy yourself a few sweets —eh, drinks.

Sharon couldn't help grinning. She shook her head.

—You're an awful fuckin' eejit, Mister Burgess, she said. —Put your tenner back in your pocket.

—Ah no, Sharon.

He looked at her.

—Okay, sorry ——You're a good girl. And honest.

—Fuck off!

—Sorry! ——Sorry. I'll never open me mouth about you again.

—You'd better not.

—I won't, I swear.

Then he remembered something.

—Oh yeah, he said.

He dug into his trousers pocket.

—I kept these for yeh. Your, em, panties, isn't tha' what yis call them?

He was really scarlet.

—Me knickers!

Sharon was stunned, and then amused. She couldn't help it. He looked so stupid and unhappy.

She put the knickers in her jacket pocket. Mister Burgess, she noticed, wiped his hand on his cardigan. She nearly laughed.

—Wha' were yeh doin' with them? she asked.

—I was keepin' them for yeh. So they wouldn't get lost.

He was purple now. His hands were in and out of his cardigan pockets. He couldn't look at her.

—Don't start again, said Sharon. —Just tell us the truth.

—Ah Jaysis, it was stupid really. Again. ——A joke —I was goin' to show them to the lads.

—Oh my —!

—But I didn't I didn't, Sharon! I didn't.

He coughed.

—I wouldn't.

Sharon went to the door.

—I've changed me mind, she said. —Give us the tenner. I deserve it.

—Certainly, Sharon. Good girl. There y'are.

Sharon took the money. She stopped at the door.

—Remember: if you ever say annythin' about me again I'll tell Missis Burgess wha' yeh did.

—Yeh needn't worry, Sharon. Me lips are sealed.

—Well —Just remember. ——Bye bye.

—Cheerio, Sharon. Thanks, ——very much —

She was a great young one, George decided as Sharon shut the door after her. And a good looker too. But, my God ——! He sat down and shook like bejaysis for a while. She'd do it; tell Doris. No problem to her. He'd have to be careful. Think but: he'd ridden her. And he'd made her pregnant. HE had.

—Jaysis.

He was a pathetic little prick, Sharon thought as she went back across the road to her house. He was pathetic. He wouldn't yap anymore anyway. He'd be too scared to.

* * *

Bertie put his pint down.

—Caramba! he said. —That's fuckin' lovely.

—It is alrigh', Bimbo agreed. —Lovely.

—Is it a new bike? Jimmy Sr asked Bertie.

—Nearly, yeah, said Bertie.

—Fuck off now, said Jimmy Sr. —How old is it?

—A few months only.

—Any scratches?

—Not at all, said Bertie. —It's perfect.

Bimbo shifted to one side and farted. They started laughing.

—My Jaysis, said Paddy. —You're fuckin' rotten.

228

—There's somethin' dead inside you, d'yeh know tha'? said Jimmy Sr, waving his hand in the air and leaning away from Bimbo.

Bimbo wiped his eyes with his fist.

—Yeh can smell it from here, said a voice from a distant corner.

That got them laughing again.

—They sound great in these chairs, Bimbo explained.

—Yeah, said Bertie. —Tha' stuff's great.

—Leatherette.

—Si.

—I don't believe I'm hearin' this, said Paddy.

—Ah fuck off, Paddy, said Jimmy Sr. —Annyway, it's your twist.

Jimmy Sr turned back to Bertie.

—Okay, he said. —You're on.

—Good, said Bertie. —Mucho good. Are yeh sure now you'll be able to get me the jacks?

—No problem to me.

—An' one o' those yokes for washin' your arse? A bidet.

—No problem.

—Wha' would yeh want one o' them for? Bimbo asked.

—For washin' your arse, yeh fuckin' eejit, said Paddy.

—Yeah, but wha' would yeh want to do tha' for? Bimbo wanted to know. —Puttin' your arse wet back into your knickers.

—You've got a point there, said Jimmy Sr.

—It's a buyer's market, Bimbo, compadre mio, said Bertie. —My client he wants to wash his hole, so ——I'll wash it for him meself if he pays me enough. Fawn? he asked Jimmy Sr.

—Okay. No problem.

—What's fawn? Bimbo asked.

—The colour!

—Oh yeah.

—Jesus, said Paddy.

*　*　*

—Wha' did yeh say to him? Yvonne asked.

—I said I couldn't help it, said Sharon.

—He must be a righ' fuckin' bastard, said Jackie. —I know what I'd've told him.

—I said I couldn't help it if I had to keep goin' to the toilet. He blushed, yeh should've seen him. Just cos I said Toilet.

—Jesus, are yeh serious? He must be red all the time, is he?

—He's a fuckin' eejit, said Sharon. —He said it wasn't fair on the other girls. An' I said they didn't mind. They don't annyway. Most o' them prefer the check-out. Cos they can sit down. ——'Cept when it's really busy. But you'd swear stackin' shelves was a fuckin' luxury, the way he talked. That's all he is annyway. A shelf stacker in a suit. He's not a real manager at all. He's only one o' them trainee ones. Paddy in the bakery called him tha' to his face once, a shelf stacker in a suit. It was fuckin' gas.

—Is he good lookin', Sharon? Mary asked.

—Are yeh jokin' me! said Sharon. —Yeh know Roland the Rat? Well, he looks like him. Only not as nice.

They laughed.

—Jesus then, listen, said Sharon.

She'd remembered something else.

—He asked me why I wasn't wearin' me uniform, an' I —

She did it as she said it.

—stuck me belly out an' I said, It doesn't fit me. Yeh should've seen his face, I'm not jokin' yis.

They screamed.

—Ah, said Jackie. —The poor chap must've been embarrassed.

—Yeah, Sharon, said Mary. —You're mean.

They laughed again.

—Well ——said Sharon. —I was only standin' up for me rights.

—You were dead right, Sharon, said Yvonne. —Yeh should've stuck one o' your tits in his mouth as well.

—Jesus!!

They really screamed now.

—Oh look it, said Yvonne when they'd recovered.
—There's your chap, Mary.

They looked across at the lounge boy.

Yvonne waved at him.

—Come here!

—Is he comin'?

———No.

They started laughing again.

* * *

A few Sundays after Sharon had sorted out George Burgess, at a quarter to seven, Jimmy Sr was standing in the bar jacks, tucking a bit of shirt back into his fly. The lads had all gone home for their tea and to bring their wives back later —because it was Sunday. Jimmy Sr was going home now himself to collect Veronica.

He decided to wash his hands. They'd installed a new hand dryer and he wanted to have a go on it.

He had his hands in under the dryer and was wondering how long more it would take when he saw George Burgess in the mirror, coming in. George walked behind Jimmy Sr and put his hand on his shoulder. He smiled at Jimmy Sr in the mirror.

—How's it goin', Jimmy? he said.

Jimmy Sr shrugged violently.

—Get your fuckin' hands off me, Burgess.

George was very surprised, and worried.

——What's wrong with YOU? he asked, still looking at the mirror.

—You know fuckin' well what's wrong with me.

Jimmy Sr turned.

—I haven't a clue, Jim, said George.

He stepped back a bit, to make room for Jimmy Sr.

—Don't start, said Jimmy Sr. —If you're goin' to start tha' then we'll go outside an' have it ou' now.

George hadn't been in a fight since 1959, in Bray. He'd lost it, and two of his teeth. And, he was only realizing it now that this was Sharon's father he was having a row with.

—Look, Jimmy, I don't know wha' you're talkin' abou' so you'll have to tell me.

—I'll tell yeh alrigh'. You were sayin' things abou' Sharon.

Jimmy Sr's face dared George to deny it.

—I said nothin' abou' Sharon, Jimmy. I —

Jimmy Sr gave George's chest a good dig. It was loud but not too hard; a warning.

—Yeh fuckin' did, pal, said Jimmy Sr. —Cos Bimbo heard yeh.

—I didn't mean anny harm, for fuck sake; it was only a joke —

Jimmy Sr thumped him again, harder. George stayed put. He wasn't going to let himself be pinned to the urinal wall. He'd his good suit on him.

—You've got it wrong, Jim.

—Wrong me bollix!

—Yeh have, I swear.

—Me bollix.

Jimmy Sr was pressing into George by now.

—Just cos the poor young one's pregnant, he said.

—Look —

George was up against the wall. He had to get up onto the step.

—Look, I'm sorry, Jimmy.

—Yeh'd fuckin' want to be.

—I am, I sw —

—Yeh should be ashamed of yourself, a man o' your age sayin' things abou' young girls like tha'.

—I know —

—Yeh bastard, yeh. —You're not worth hittin'.

That, thought George, was good news.

—I'm sorry, Jimmy. Really now. On the Bible. I was just messin' with the lads, yeh know.

—The lads! said Jimmy Sr. —Yeh sound like a fuckin' kid.

Jimmy Sr turned away and went to the door. He wanted to whoop. He'd won. He stopped at the door.

—Come here, you, he said. —If you ever say another word abou' Sharon again I'll fuckin' kill yeh. Righ'?

—Righ', Jimmy. I won't. Yeh needn't worry. I'm not, eh —

George looked like a beaten man. And that chuffed Jimmy Sr a bit more.

—An' come here as well, he said. —If yeh drop Darren off the team cos o' this I'll kill yeh as well.

—Jaysis, Jimmy, I'd never drop Darren!

* * *

Darren walked into the kitchen.

—Happy birthd'y, son.

—Happy birthday, Darren.

—Happy birth'y, Darren.

—Good man, Darren, said Jimmy Sr. —There y'are.

He handed Darren a thin cylindrical parcel.

—Wha' is it?

—It's your birthd'y present, Jimmy Sr told him.

—It's not a bike.

—I know tha', said Jimmy Sr.

—What is it?

—Open it an' see, son.

Darren did.

—It's a pump.

—That's righ', said Jimmy Sr. —It's a good one too.

Darren didn't understand. He looked at his da's face.

—I'll get yeh a wheel for your Christmas, said Jimmy Sr. —An' the other one for your next birthd'y. An' then the saddle. An' before yeh know it you'll have your bike. How's tha'?

Darren looked at the pump, then at his da. His da was smiling but it wasn't a joking smile. He looked at his ma. She had her back to him, at the sink. Now he understood. He understood now: he'd just been given a poxy pump for his

233

birthday. And he was going to be getting bits of bike for the rest of his life and ——But the twins were giggling. And now so was Sharon.

His brother, Jimmy, stood up and was putting on his jacket.

—Yeh can pump yourself to school every mornin' now, he said.

—Yis are messin', said Darren.

He laughed. He knew it. He had a bike. He knew it.

—Yis are messin'!

Jimmy Sr laughed.

—We are o' course.

He opened the back door and went out, and came back in with a bike, a big old black grocer's delivery bike with a frame over the front wheel but no basket in it.

—Get up on tha' now an' we'll see how it fits, said Jimmy Sr.

—Wha'? said Darren.

His mouth was wide open. Veronica was laughing now.

—It's a Stephen Roche special, said Jimmy Sr.

Darren was still staring at the bike. Then he noticed the others laughing.

He looked around at them.

—Yis are messin'.

He laughed, louder now than before.

—Yis are still messin'.

—We are o' course, said Jimmy Sr.

He patted the saddle.

—This is Bimbo's.

He wheeled it out, and wheeled in the real present. Larry-gogan followed it in.

—Ah rapid! Da ——Ma —. Thanks. Rapid. Ah deadly.

He held the bike carefully.

—A Raleigh! Deadly. ——Ten gears! Great. Muggah's only got five.

Jimmy Sr laughed.

—Only the best, he said.

—Raleighs aren't the best, Darren told him. —Peugeots and Widersprints are.

He was looking at his new bike and adoring it; its thinness, neatness, shininess, the colour, the pedals with the straps on them and, most of all, the handlebars.

—Yeh ungrateful little bollix, said Jimmy Sr. —Give us tha' back.

He grabbed the bike and pushed Darren away from it.

Darren was lost. He didn't know what he'd done. He didn't know. His eyes filled. He just stood there.

Jimmy Sr pushed the bike back to him.

—There.

——Thanks, Da. Thanks, Ma.

—Mammy.

—Mammy. It's brilliant.

He wolfed his breakfast, then cycled across the road to school.

* * *

It was about six o'clock the same day, Jimmy Sr, washed and ready, sat down at the kitchen table. But the dinner wasn't ready.

—How come? he wanted to know.

—I started on the girls' dresses, said Veronica.

—Wha' dresses?

—Ballroom.

—Jaysis.

—Stop that. ——Anyway, I forgot the time.

Jimmy Sr was in good form.

—Ah well, he said. —Not to worry. I'll have a slice o' bread. That'll keep me goin'.

He didn't bother with the marge.

—How ——are yeh today, Veronica? he asked.

—Okay. Grand. I'm tired now though.

—Cummins said he might have somethin' for Leslie in a few weeks.

—I'll believe it when I see it, said Veronica.

—I suppose so, said Jimmy Sr. —He said he'll ask round an'

see if anny of his pals have annythin' for him. Yeh know, the golf an' church collection shower.

—You wouldn't want to be relying on them.

—True.

He began to demolish another couple of slices.

—Still ——what else can we do? ——I had five fuckin' jobs to choose from when I got thrun out o' school. Where is he?

—Who?

—Leslie.

—I don't know. Out.

—I haven't seen him in ages. Weeks —Yeah, weeks. Wha' does he look like?

Veronica laughed.

—He's not hangin' round the house annyway, said Jimmy Sr. —Gettin' under your feet.

—No.

—That's somethin'. But he should have his breakfasts an' his dinners with the rest of us. The family tha' eats together ——How does it go?

Veronica was prodding the potatoes.

Darren came in, on his way out. He was wearing a Carrera cycling jersey Jimmy Jr had just given him. It nearly reached his knees. He was trying to rub the creases out of it. When he looked down the zip touched his nose.

—That's a great yoke, Darren, Jimmy Sr told him —It'll fit yeh properly in a couple o' months, wha'.

—It'll be too small, said Veronica, —the way he's growing. Where d'you think you're going to?

—Ou', said Darren.

—Not till after your tea you're not, said Veronica.

—Ah Ma. Round the block only?

—Let him go, said Jimmy Sr. —He wants to show off his jersey to the young ones.

Darren was out the door.

Jimmy Jr came into the kitchen.

—Was tha' jersey yoke dear? Jimmy Sr asked him.

Jimmy Jr tapped the side of his nose with a finger, and

winked. Jimmy Sr raised his eyebrows. He looked at Veronica. She was turning the chops.

—Did no one actually buy the poor fucker a present? he whispered.

Jimmy Jr grinned, and went upstairs to change.

Sharon came in from work.

—There's Sharon, said Jimmy Sr. —How are yeh, Sharon?

—Grand.

—Good. That's the way to be. Your face is nice an' pink.

—Thanks very much!

—Very healthy lookin'. Is he kickin'?

—He's doin' cartwheels.

—We'll have to get him a bike like Darren's so.

Sharon sat down.

—That's righ', Sharon, said Jimmy Sr. —Sit down.

The twins were in the hall.

They heard Linda.

—Slow – Slow – Quick – Quick – Slow. ——Ah, watch it! You're supposed to be the man, yeh fuckin' eejit.

—Tell them to stop that language, said Veronica.

—Stop tha' language, Jimmy Sr shouted.

—Linda said it, said Tracy from the hall.

—You made me.

—I didn't.

—Did. ——Come on. Your fingers are supposed to be at righ' angles to my spine. ——Slow – Slow – Quick – Quick – Slow.

—What's goin' on ou' there? said Jimmy Sr.

He leaned back so he could see out into the hall. He grinned as he watched Linda and Tracy going through their steps. They hit the stairs.

—You're doin' it wrong, he said. —Look.

He got up and went into the hall.

Sharon grinned.

Veronica was dividing the food onto the plates.

—D'yeh need a hand, Mammy? said Sharon.

—No.

237

They heard Jimmy Sr.

—Now. Are yis watchin'? Yeh put your feet slightly apart, d'yeh see? Like this. ——Now, I put my weight on me left foot. An' wha' foot do you put your weight on?

—The righ' one, said Linda.

—Good girl, said Jimmy Sr. —Cos you're the lady. ——Then, look it, I side-step like tha' —an' we're off. Step – Step – Cha Cha Cha – Step – Step – Cha Cha Cha —

Sharon laughed.

—I didn't know Daddy could dance like tha', she said.

—Neither did I, said Veronica. —Now, where is everyone? Why do they all disappear just when their dinner's ready?

They heard Jimmy Sr.

—Step – Step – Cha Cha Cha —An' there we go. Your turn, Tracy. ——No, wrong foot. You're the lady. Good girl. An' off we go. Two – Three – Four —an' One – Two – Three – Four —an' One – Step – Step – Cha Cha Cha. It's all comin' back to me.

—Dinner, Veronica roared.

Jimmy Jr came in.

—Has Da been drinkin'?

Jimmy Sr was in after him, followed by Linda and Tracy.

—Do we still have tha' Joe Loss LP, Veronica? ——Wha' are you grinnin' at?

He was talking to Jimmy Jr.

—LP, Jimmy Jr sneered. —It's an album.

—Oh, said Jimmy Sr. —I forgot. We've Larry fuckin' Gogan here with us for the dinner. Spinnin' the discs, wha'. ——It's an LP, righ'.

—Fair enough, Twinkletoes.

—I'll fuckin' —

—Shut up and eat your dinner, said Veronica.

—Certainly, Veronica, said Jimmy Sr.

He looked down at his dinner.

—My God now, tha' looks lovely. I'm starvin' after all tha' dancin'. I could eat the left leg o' the Lamb o' ——

—Don't! said Veronica.

238

Jimmy Sr chewed, and swallowed.

—Mind you, girls, he told the twins. —I always preferred the Cucarachas to the Cha Cha Cha. You can really swing your lady in the Cucarachas.

Jimmy Jr laughed. So did Sharon.

—Fuck yis, said Jimmy Sr.

Darren dashed in. He had news for them.

—Pat said his da's after runnin' away from home.

Jimmy Sr looked up from his dinner.

—Pat who?

—Burgess.

Jimmy Sr burst out laughing. Jimmy Jr and the others joined in.

—Is Georgie Burgess after runnin' away? said Jimmy Sr.

—Yeah, said Darren. —Pat said he fucked —ran off last nigh'. His ma's up to ninety. He's says she's knockin' back the Valiums like there's no tomorrow.

—She would, said Veronica.

—Poor Doris, said Jimmy Sr. —That's a good one though.

—Here, said Jimmy Jr. —He's prob'ly gone off to join the French Foreign Legion.

—That's righ', yeah. Where's he gone, Darren?

—Don't know. Pat doesn't know. He said he just snuck ou'.

—Sneaked, said Veronica.

—Yeah, righ'.

—That's a good one all the same.

Jimmy Sr was delighted.

—Where's Sharon gone?

—She must be gone to the jacks.

—She's always in there.

—Leave her alone. She can't help it, said Jimmy Sr. ——Ran away, wha'. ——That's a lovely chop.

—That's a lovely chop, said Linda.

—Don't start, you, said Jimmy Sr.

He grinned.

—Who'll be managin' yis now, Darren?

—Don't know, said Darren. —He might come back.

—Jaysis, I hope not.
Jimmy Sr filled his mouth again.
——Ran away, wha'.
—Yeah, said Jr.
—Tom Sawyer, said Jimmy Sr.
He laughed.

* * *

Sharon was in her parents' bedroom, looking out across at the Burgess's.

It was frightening. She was sure Mister Burgess running away had something to do with her but she hadn't a clue what. And she was sure as well that this wasn't the end of it; there was more to come.

What though? She didn't know. Something terrible, something really terrible ——

Oh God ——

She'd have to wait and see.

She stood up off the bed. The bad shakes were gone. Her chest didn't hurt as much. She'd go down and finish her dinner.

On the way down she went into the toilet and flushed it.

* * *

—Tom Sawyer, wha', said Jimmy Sr.
—Exactly, said Bimbo.
They all laughed again.
—That's the best ever, said Bimbo. —Gas.
—He must have a mot hidden away somewhere, said Paddy.
—Si, Bertie agreed.
—Who'd fuckin' look at HIM? Jimmy Sr wanted to know.
—The state of him.
—Have yeh looked at yourself recently? Paddy asked him.
—I'm not runnin' away, am I? said Jimmy Sr. —Fuckin' off an' —an' shirkin' my responsibilities.
—Shirkin'? said Bertie.
—Fuck off.

—He's not tha' bad, said Bimbo.

—Yeh fancy him yourself, do yeh?

—No!

Bertie and Paddy laughed.

—Bimbo goes for the younger lads, Jimmy Sr told them.
—Isn't tha' righ'?

—Ah lay off, will yeh. ——I can't understand it. Yeh know,
the way queers —like each other.

—D'yeh think about it much? Paddy asked him.

—No! ——Nearly never. Lay off.

Bertie put his pint down.

—So the Signor Burgess has vamoosed, he said.

—An' shirked his responsibilities, said Paddy.

—Fuck off, you, said Jimmy Sr.

—Poor Doris an' the kids, said Bimbo.

—Why don't you adopt them? said Paddy.

—Would you ever leave me alone, said Bimbo.

—Tell him to fuck off, said Jimmy Sr.

—I will, said Bimbo. —Fuck off.

—Make me.

* * *

What WAS he up to anyway?

Sharon pulled on her other boot. She sat up slowly. God
Jesus, her back really hurt her when she did that, after being
bent down. She put her hands on her belly. She could feel it
shifting.

What was he fuckin' up to?

The baby butted her.

—Take it easy, will yeh, said Sharon.

She got her money off the bed and put it in her bag. She
hoped to God Yvonne wouldn't be there tonight. Maybe she'd
be better off staying at home ——

—Ah fuck this, she said.

And she got up and went out.

* * *

241

—Jesus; poor Yvonne though, said Jackie.

—Yeah, said Mary and Sharon.

—Maybe we should go round to her, said Jackie.

—Ah no, said Sharon.

—Yeah, said Mary. —I'd be too embarrassed.

—Mm, said Jackie. —Can yeh imagine it? Jesus!

—Jesus, yeah.

* * *

She waited. She knew she'd have to get up and go to the toilet at least once more.

He was going to do something really stupid, she was certain of that.

She sat up. She'd go to the toilet now.

Something really, really stupid.

She'd just have to wait and see, that was all. ——People were going to find out ——her mammy and daddy ——! Oh God, if that —!

She'd just have to wait and see.

She got back into bed.

* * *

Sharon wasn't long waiting and seeing. Linda woke her up. This was the night after Darren had broken the big news.

—Sharon, said Linda.

She was scared.

—There's someone throwin' things at the window.

—Yeah, said Tracy.

She wouldn't get out of the bed.

—Who's throwin' things? said Sharon.

—Don't know.

—Yeah.

—Let's see, said Sharon.

—I'm not lookin', said Linda.

Sharon went over to the window. Just before she reached it there was a neat little bang.

—Oh janey! said one of the twins.

Someone had flung something at it. That frightened Sharon.

She parted the curtain a little bit. The bedroom light was out but she could see nothing in the garden.

But then she saw someone, behind the hedge at the back, in the field. He —it looked like a man —was bent down. Then he stood up and came through the gap in the hedge, over the wire, and it was Mister Burgess.

Sharon nearly died.

He stood there in the middle of the garden at the place where Les was supposed to do the digging. He was looking up at her window. —How did he know? —Then she saw his hand move up from his side, the palm towards her. Then there was another bang.

She jumped. He'd just lobbed a little stone at the window. She let go of the curtain.

—Who is it, Sharon?

—Just young fellas, said Sharon. —Messin'.

—Messin'! said Tracy. —At this hour o' night.

—I'll get them tomorrow, said Sharon.

—Wha' young fellas? said Linda.

Sharon parted the curtain again. Mister Burgess wasn't there. She didn't think he was behind the hedge or the trees in the field either.

—They're gone now, she said.

—Let's see, said Linda.

She looked.

—They're gone, Tracy, she said.

—Night nigh', said Sharon.

She was back in bed.

—Nigh' nigh', said Linda.

Tracy was sleeping.

Was Mister Burgess getting all romantic on her? Sharon wondered. Jesus, that was disgusting. Maybe he'd gone weird, like one of those men on the News ——

She'd have to wait and see a bit more.

She lay there, wide awake.

* * *

243

Jimmy Sr turned the sound down a bit.

—I'll never lay a hand on the twins again, he told Sharon.

—Wha'?

—The twins, said Jimmy Sr. —I'll never touch them again.

—Did you hit them?

—No! ——No; it's all tha' child abuse stuff goin' on over in England. Were yeh not watchin' it?

—No. I was miles away.

—On the News there, Jimmy Sr explained. —It looks like yeh can't look at your own kids over there. They'll take them away from yeh. An' inspect their arses —

—Daddy!

—It's true, Jimmy Sr insisted.

They were by themselves in the front room.

—Half the fuckin' doctors in England are spendin' their time lookin' up children's holes.

—You're disgustin'.

—It's not me, Sharon, said Jimmy Sr. —Yeh can't turn on the fuckin' telly or open a paper or ——there's somethin' abou' child abuse. The kids must be scared stiff.

—But it happens, said Sharon.

—Maybe it does, I don't know. I suppose it does. ——I'd kill annyone tha' did somethin' like tha' to a child. A little kid. They do it to snappers even. I'd chop his bollix —excuse me, Sharon —off. I would. Then hang him. Or shoot him. ——At least it's not goin' on over here.

—You'd never know, said Sharon.

—Would yeh say so? said Jimmy Sr. —Maybe you're righ'. Jaysis. ——It's shockin'. How could annyone —

Darren came in.

—Good man, Darren, said Jimmy Sr. —Have yeh come in for your cyclin'?

—Yeah, said Darren.

He sat down on the floor.

—Channel 4, said Jimmy Sr. —Let's see now.

He studied the remote control.

—Number one.

244

He pressed it.

—Ads, he said. —That's it. How's Kelly doin', Darren?

—Alrigh'.

——He's gettin' old, said Jimmy Sr. —The oul' legs. Wha' abou' Roche?

—Fourth.

—He hasn't a hope, said Jimmy Sr.

—He has so.

—Not at all, said Jimmy Sr. —He's too nice, that's his problem. He doesn't have the killer instinct.

—He won the Giro, Darren reminded him.

—Fluke, said Jimmy Sr. —Hang on, here it is.

He turned up the sound.

—The music's great, isn't it?

—Yeah, said Darren and Sharon.

—Good Jaysis, said Jimmy Sr. —Look at those mountains. Roche is fucked. There's no mountains like tha' in Ireland.

—Ah shut up, Da, will yeh.

—I'm only expressin' me opinion.

—Yeh haven't a clue.

Jimmy Sr nudged Sharon. Then he switched channels.

—Aaah!

—Sorry. Sorry, Darren. Me finger slipped, sorry——There; that's it back. There's Roche now. He's strugglin', look it. I told yeh. He's not smilin' now, wha'.

—Da!

Jimmy Sr grinned and nudged Sharon again.

* * *

Sharon got home from work a bit early on Monday, five days after she'd seen Mister Burgess throwing stones at the window. She hadn't been feeling well, like as if she'd eaten too much chocolate, and the bottom of her back was killing her.

She took a box of cod steaks from her bag.

—I got these out o' work, she told her mother.

—You'll get caught, said Veronica.

—No, I won't, said Sharon.

245

—It's not right. There's a letter over there for you.

—For me?

The envelope was white and the address was in ordinary writing. Sharon had never got a real letter before.

—That's a man's writing, said Veronica.

Sharon looked at her.

—I didn't open it.

—I never thought yeh did, Mammy, said Sharon.

But she went upstairs to read it. Linda and Tracy were down watching the telly or practising their dancing. Something had been written on the back of the envelope but it had been rubbed over with the same pen. She couldn't make it out. She opened the envelope carefully, afraid she'd rip what was inside. She gasped, then groaned, —Oh my God, and sat down on her bed when she saw what the letter was about. She should have guessed it, but she hadn't; not really.

There was no address or date.

Dear Sharon,

I hope you are well. Please meet me in the Abbey Mooney in town at 8 o'clock on Tuesday night. I want to talk to you about something very important. I am looking forward to seeing you.

Yours sincerely
George Burgess.

There was a P.S.

The paper is my sisters.

The writing paper was pink. There was a bunny rabbit in the top left corner, sitting in some light blue and yellow flowers.

Sharon sat there. She just sat there.

Then she sort of shook herself, and realized that she was angry.

The fucker.

There was no way she was going to meet him, no fuckin'

246

way. She lifted the flap of the envelope up to the light coming through the window. She could make out the shapes of the rubbed-out writing on the flap now. They were capital letters.

S.W.A.L.K.

—Oh, the fuckin' eejit! said Sharon.

* * *

Bertie came in.

—There y'are, Bertie, said Bimbo.

—Howyeh, Bertie.

—Buenas noches, compadres, said Bertie.

—It's your round, Paddy told him.

—Give us a chance, for the sake of fuck.

As Bertie said this he sat down and lifted his hand, showing four fingers to Leo the barman.

—How's the Jobsearch goin', Bertie? Jimmy Sr asked him.

—Don't talk to me abou' Jobsearch.

He pretended to spit on the ground.

—I speet on Jobsearch.

Bimbo and Jimmy Sr laughed and Paddy grinned.

—D'yis know wha' they had me doin' today, do yis? Yis won't believe this.

—Wha'? said Bimbo.

—They were teachin' us how to use the phone.

—Wha'!?

—I swear to God. The fuckin' phone.

—You're not serious.

—I am, yeh know. I fuckin' am. The gringo in charge handed ou' photocopies of a diagram of a phone. I think I have it ——No, I left it back at the Ponderosa. I'll show it to yis tomorrow. ——A fuckin' phone.

—Don't listen to him.

—It's true, I'm tellin' yeh. I was embarrassed for him, the poor cunt. He knew it was fuckin' stupid himself. You could tell; the poor fucker tellin' us where to put the tenpences. One chap told him where he could stick the tenpences an' then he walked ou'.

WALKER'S POINT PUBLIC LIBRARY

247

They laughed.

—Then he was tellin' us, Bertie continued, —wha' we should an' shouldn't say when we're lookin' for work.

—Wha' should yeh not say? Bimbo asked.

—Anny chance of a fuckin' job there, pal.

They laughed.

—It was the greatest waste o' fuckin' time, said Bertie. —You should always tell the name o' the paper yeh saw the ad in. There now. An' there's no job ads in the Mirror. Unless it's the manager o' Spurs or Man United or somethin'. ——I wouldn't mind, compadres, but I've abou' thirty fuckin' phones in cold storage. Mickey Mouse an' Snoopy ones.

—Jessica'd like a Snoopy one, said Bimbo. —For her birth'y.

—You don't have a phone, said Paddy.

—So?

—So a Snoopy one won't be much use to Jessica, will it?

—For an ornament, I meant. For her bedside locker.

—Her wha'?

—Her bedside locker.

—I bet yeh you made it yourself.

—No! ——I bought it an' put it together.

Paddy raised his eyes to heaven.

—Do anny of yis ever hit your kids? Jimmy Sr asked them all.

He lowered a third of his latest pint while they looked at him.

—Never, said Bimbo.

—Now an' again, said Paddy.

—Well, yeah, said Bimbo. —Now an' again, alrigh'. When they're lookin' for it. Specially Wayne.

—It's the only exercise I get, Bertie told them. —I wait till they're old enough to run but. To give them a fair chance, yeh know.

Bimbo knew he was joking, so he laughed.

—I'm dyin' to give Gillian a good hidin', said Bertie. —But she never does annythin' bold. She'd give yeh the sick. Trevor's great though. Trevor's a desperado.

WALKER'S POINT
PUBLIC LIBRARY

Jimmy Sr took control of the conversation again.

—Yis'd want to be careful, he told them.

—Why's tha', compadre?

—Cos if you're caught you're fucked.

—What're yeh on abou'? said Paddy.

—Child abuse, said Jimmy Sr.

—Would yeh ever fuck off, said Paddy. —Givin' your kids a smack for bein' bold isn't child abuse.

—No way.

—I don't know, said Jimmy Sr. —It looks to me like yeh can't look crooked at your kids now —

—Don't be thick, said Paddy. —You're exaggeratin'. Yeh have to burn them with cigarette butts or —

—I'm not listenin' to this, said Bimbo.

—Don't then, said Paddy. —Or mess around with their —

—SHUT UP.

It was Bimbo. Paddy stopped.

—You're makin' a joke of it, said Bimbo.

—I'm not.

—Yeh are.

—Whose twist is it? said Bertie. —Someone's shy.

—Four pints, Leo, Jimmy Sr shouted. —Like a good man. ——Maybe you're righ', he said to both Bimbo and Paddy. —It's shockin' though, isn't it? The whole business.

—Fuckin' terrible, said Bimbo.

—Come here, said Bertie. —Guess who I spied with my little eye this mornin'.

—Who?

—Someone beginnin' with B.

—Burgess!

—Si.

—Great. Where?

—Swords.

—How was he lookin'? said Jimmy Sr.

—Oh, very thin an' undernourished, said Bertie. —An' creased.

—Yahaah!

Jimmy Sr rubbed his hands.

—I nearly gave the poor cunt twopence, Bertie told them.

They liked that.

—There mustn't be another mot so, said Paddy. —If he's in rag order like tha'.

—Unless she's a brasser.

—Were yeh talkin' to him? Bimbo asked.

—No, said Bertie. —I was on me way to learn how to use the phone.

—Now, Leo called. —Four nice pints over here.

—Leo wants yeh, Paddy told Jimmy Sr.

Jimmy Sr brought the pints down to the table and sat down. Bertie picked up the remains of his old pint.

—To the Signor Horge Burgess, he said.

—Oh def'ny, said Bimbo.

They raised their glasses.

—The fuckin' eejit, said Jimmy Sr.

—Ah now, said Bertie. —That's not nice.

* * *

Sharon was nowhere near the Abbey Mooney at eight o'clock on Tuesday.

She lay in bed later, half expecting stones to start hitting the window. Or something.

* * *

It was that Sharon Rabbitte one from across the road. She was pregnant. She'd come to the house. She was the one; she knew it.

Dear Doris,
        I hope you are well——

People probably knew already. They always did around here. Oh God, the shame; the mortification. She'd never be able to step out of the house again.

I am writing to you to let you know why I left you last week —

If he'd died and left her a widow it would've been different, alright; but this wasn't fair. He was making her feel ashamed, the selfish bastard, and she hadn't done anything.

Doris, I've been having a bit of an affair with a girl. This girl is expecting —

The Rabbitte one; it had to be.

I am very sorry —

It had to be.

I hope you will understand, Doris. I cannot abandon this girl. She has no one else to look after her —

The next bit was worse.

I still love you, Doris. But I love this girl as well. I am, as the old song goes, torn between two lovers. I will miss you and the children very much —

Oh God!
He was her husband!
Twenty-four years. It wasn't her fault.

P.S.
I got a lend of the paper.

Doris sniffed.
He'd always been an eejit. She'd never be able to go out again. ——Men got funny at George's age. She'd noticed the same thing with her father. They went silly when there were girls near them; when her friends had been in the house. They

tried to pretend that they weren't getting old and made eejits out of themselves. And, God knew, George had a head start there.

The Rabbitte one probably took money off him as well.

* * *

Veronica made out Doris Burgess's shape through the glass. The hair was the give-away.

She opened the door.

—Doris, she said.

—Is Sharon in? said Doris.

—She's at work. Why?

Veronica knew; before she had it properly worked out.

Doris tried to look past Veronica.

—Why do you want her? said Veronica.

Now Doris looked at Veronica.

—Well, if you must know, she's been messin' around with George. ——He's the father.

—Get lost, Doris, said Veronica.

—I will not get lost now, said Doris. —She's your daughter, isn't she?

There were two women coming up the road, four gates away.

—Of course, said Doris, —what else would you expect from a —

Veronica punched her in the face.

* * *

—What happened yeh, Doris? said Mrs Foster.

—Tha' one hit her, said Mrs Caprani. —Yeh seen it your-self.

—I mean before that.

Doris wanted to get out of Rabbitte territory. She pulled herself away from the women and ran out the gate. She stopped on the path.

—What happened, Doris? Mrs Foster asked again.

She tried to get to Doris's nose with a paper hankie.

252

More people were coming.

—Veronica Rabbitte's after givin' poor Doris an awful clatter, Mrs Caprani told them. —In the nose.

Doris was still crying.

—I'll do it —it myself.

She took the hankie.

—Wha' happened yeh, Doris?

——Sh —Shar —

—Shar, Doris? What shar?

* * *

Inside, Veronica sat in the kitchen, putting sequins onto Linda's dancing dress.

* * *

Sharon lay on her bed. She couldn't go downstairs, she couldn't go to the Hikers, or anywhere. She was surrounded. She was snared. If she went anywhere or ——she couldn't. All because of that stupid fucker.

—The fucker, she said to the ceiling.

The baby was nothing. It happened. It was alright. Barrytown was good that way. Nobody minded. Guess the daddy was a hobby. But now Burgess —He'd cut her off from everything. She'd no friends now, and no places to go to. She couldn't even look at her family. God, she wanted to die; really she did. She just lay there. She couldn't do anything else.

She was angry now. She thumped the bed.

The bastard, the fucker; it wasn't fuckin' fair. She'd deny it, that was what she'd do. And she'd keep denying it. And denying it.

* * *

Veronica and Jimmy Sr were down in the kitchen.

—Desperate, so it is, said Jimmy Sr quietly. —Shockin'.

Veronica put the dress down. She couldn't look at another sequin.

253

—That's about the hundredth time you've said that, she told
him.

—Well, it is fuckin' desperate.

They heard Linda and Tracy coming up the hall.

—Slow – Slow – Quick – Quick ——Slow.

——Get ou'! Jimmy Sr roared.

—We know where we're not wanted, said Linda. —Come
on, Tracy.

—Slow – Slow – Quick —

They danced down the hall, into the front room to annoy
Darren.

Jimmy Sr was miserable.

—Poor Sharon though.

——Poor Sharon! said Veronica. —What about poor us?

—Don't start now, said Jimmy Sr.

He was playing with a cold chip.

—I suppose ——She could've been more careful, he said.

—She could've had more taste, said Veronica.

—That's righ', said Jimmy Sr, glad to be able to say it.
—You're right o' course. That's what's so terrible about it.
George Burgess. ——Georgie Burgess. Jesus, Veronica, I
think the cunt's older than I am.

He threw the chip at the window, and then felt stupid. He
was feeling sorry for himself; he knew it. And now he was
letting his eyes water.

—It's only yourself you're worried about, Veronica told
him.

—Ah ——I know, said Jimmy Sr. —But poor Sharon as
well.

He rubbed his eyes quickly.

—I can't even go ou' for a fuckin' pint.

—It's about time you stayed in.

—Is there annythin' good on?

—I don't know.

——George fuckin' Burgess.

Then they heard the voice from upstairs.

—THIS IS JIMMY RABBITTE – ALL – OVER – IRELAND.

—Oh fuck, no, Jimmy Sr pleaded. —Not tonigh'. Please.

* * *

Jimmy Sr gave Sharon a lift to work the next morning. They didn't say much. Jimmy Sr asked a question.

—How —?

— It wasn't him.

—I never —

—It wasn't him, righ'.

—Okay. ——Okay.

That was it.

* * *

Jimmy Sr scooped out the teabag and flung it into a corner. His shoulders were at him. He felt shite. He wanted to go home.

It wasn't him, she'd said.

He didn't know. He tried it again: it wasn't him. He believed her of course, but ——If it wasn't Burgess then who the fuck was it? She'd have to tell them. He had to know for certain that it was definitely someone else; anyone. She'd just have to fuckin' tell them.

Or else.

He tried the tea. It was brutal.

* * *

—There's no fuckin' way, Jackie. You know tha'.

Jackie was sitting on the twins' bed. Sharon was sitting on her own bed. She looked at the steam rising up off her tea, so she didn't have to look at Jackie.

—I know, said Jackie.

It wasn't enough, Jackie knew; not nearly. It didn't sound as if she'd meant it enough.

—I know tha', she said; better this time, she thought.

—Jesus, the state of him. There's no way you'd've —

—Don't say it, said Sharon. —I'll get sick, I swear.

Jackie tried to laugh. They looked at each other and then they really laughed. Sharon thought the happiness would burst out of her, through her ribs, out of her mouth.

—Can yeh imagine it! she said.

—Tha' dirty big belly on top o' yeh!

—Stop it!

They said nothing for a bit, and the giggling died. Sharon's nails dug into her palms.

—I KNOW WHA' YOU'RE THIN —KIN', she sang.

Jackie laughed, at the floor.

—Fuck off, she said. ——Are yeh tellin'?

—S'pose I'd better.

——Jesus, Sharon, come on.

—It was one o' them Spanish sailors.

—Wha'?

—Yeh know, said Sharon. —Yeh do. In the Harp, I met him.

—Oh, now I get yeh. Jesus, Sharon.

—There was loads o' them there, yeh know. There was a big boat, yeh know; down in the docks for two days, I think it was.

She had this bit off by heart.

—He was gorgeous, Jackie, I'm not jokin' yeh.

—Was he? Jesus. ——Yeh never mentioned him before.

—No. I didn't want to. ——Yeh know. It was only for one night.

—Yeah. Do yeh know his address?

—I don't even know his fuckin' name, Jackie.

Manuel was the only Spanish name she could think of.

—Jesus, said Jackie. —Go on annyway.

—Ah, I just met him. In the Harp, yeh know. His English was brutal. ——Come here, he had a sword.

She'd just thought up that bit.

—I'd say he did alrigh', said Jackie, and they roared laughing.

—That's disgustin', Jackie.

—Where did yis —do it? Jackie asked.

She was smiling. She was enjoying herself now.

—In his hotel. The Ormond, yeh know.

—Was he not supposed to sleep in his ship?

—No, not really. They let them ou' for the night.

—Oh yeah. ——Like Letter To Brezhnev.

—God, yeah, said Sharon. —Jesus, I never thought o' tha'.

She was sure her nails had gone through the skin.

—Was he nice?

—Fuckin' gorgeous. Anyway, I wouldn't've done it with him if he hadn't o' been, sure I wouldn't?

—No way.

—He was very dark.

She hoped to God the baby wouldn't have red hair.

—Was he good?

—Fuckin' brilliant. He had me nearly screamin', I'm not jokin' yeh.

—Oh —

—We did it in the bath as well.

—God, I'd love tha'.

—It was brilliant.

—Yeah, said Jackie. —Yeh lucky bitch yeh, Sharon. I'm goin' to go to the Harp from now on. ——Come here, did he give you his cap?

—Wha'?

—His cap. Yeh know. His uniform.

—Ah, no.

—Did he not? ——Yeh know Melanie Beglin? She has two o' them. A German an' a Swedish.

—Does she?

—Yeah. She's a slut, tha' one. ——Jesus, sorry, Sharon! I didn't mean —

Sharon laughed.

—She is though, said Jackie. —I hate her. Come here, Sharon, though. Why did Mister Burgess run away?

—I don't know!

—I know it wasn't ——because. Yeh know. But —Let's go an' get pissed.

—Ah —

—Go on, Sharon. Howth. A bit o' buzz.

—Okay. Where's me shoes?

—There, look it. I'll get them.

—No, it's alrigh'. Jesus, me fuckin' back. ——How's Yvonne takin' it?

——

—Will yeh tell her about the sailor? said Sharon.

—Okay.

—Thanks.

*   *   *

—I'll be blinded by these bloody sequins, said Veronica.

—Wha'? said Jimmy Sr.

—Look it, said Veronica. —I'm still on Linda's one.

She held up the dress.

—It looks like I've only started.

——That's shockin', said Jimmy Sr. —Why couldn't they just play basketball or somethin'? It looks very nice though, Veronica.

—Mm.

Jimmy Sr wriggled around on the couch. It was past his going out time.

—D'yeh know wha', Veronica? I'm nearly afraid to go down to the pub ——because of —

—Oh, shut up.

——Do you believe her, Veronica?

—Shut up.

*   *   *

There was a bunch of kids, boys Darren's age, sitting on the wall at the bus-stop when Sharon got off. They all stared at her as she went past them. When she'd gone about three gates one of them shouted.

—How's Mister Burgess?

She didn't turn or stop.

—Yeh ride yeh.

258

She kept walking.

They were only kids.

Still, she was shaking and kind of upset when she got home and upstairs. She didn't know why really. Men and boys had been shouting things after her since she was thirteen and fourteen. She'd never liked it much, especially when she was very young, but she'd looked on it as a sort of a stupid compliment.

Tonight was different though. Being called a ride wasn't any sort of a compliment anymore.

* * *

—What're YOU fuckin' lookin' at? Jimmy Sr asked Paddy.

He was serious.

—Nothin'.

—D'yeh think I have fuckin' cancer or somethin'?

—No!

—Ah lads, now, said Bimbo. —There's no need for tha' sort o' shite.

—I didn't do annythin', Paddy insisted.

—You were starin' at me, said Jimmy Sr. —Annyway, he said out of nowhere. (They'd been talking about Stephen Roche.) —It wasn't Burgess. It was a Spanish sailor.

* * *

—She thinks he was Spanish annyway, Jackie told Mary.

—Where? said Mary.

—The Harp.

—Oh, yeah. ——D'you believe her?

——Yeah. It couldn't have been —

—No.

—Will Yvonne believe it, d'yeh think? Jackie asked.

—Emm ——she might.

—She won't, sure she won't?

—No. ——She might though.

* * *

259

Two nights after Sharon told Jackie about the Spanish sailor George Burgess was waiting for her outside work.

—God! said Sharon. —How did you know where I worked?

—Did yeh not see me at the vegetables?

He was having problems holding up his smile.

—What d'you want, Mister Burgess?

—George.

—Mister Burgess.

—Yeh didn't turn up on Tuesday.

—I know I didn't. Wha' d'yeh want?

—I want to talk to yeh, Sharon.

—That's a pity now, Mister Burgess, cos I don't want to talk to you.

—Ah Sharon, please. I have to talk.

The smile was gone.

—I'm tormented.

—You're tormented! Yeh prick yeh. Who's been flingin' rocks at my window? An' how did yeh know it was my window annyway? An' sendin' me stupid fuckin' letters. Well?

——You've made me the laughin' stock o' Barrytown, that I can't even go ou' without bein' jeered. You're tormented! Fuck off, Mister Burgess.

She started to walk around him. He was going to stop her, but then he didn't. He walked with her.

—Look, Sharon, I swear I'll leave you alone. On the Bible; forever. If yeh just listen to me for a minute. I swear.

—Fuck off.

—Please, Sharon. Please.

—Get your fuckin' hands off me!

But she stopped.

—Wha'? she said.

—Here?

—Yeah.

—Can we not go into a pub or —or a coffee place or somethin'?

—No, we can't. Come on, I'm in a hurry.

—Okay.

She was watching Mister Burgess blushing.

—Sharon, he said. —Sharon ——I love you, Sharon. Don't laugh; I do! I swear. On the —— I love you. I'm very embarrassed, Sharon. I've been thinkin' about it. ——I think I —I want to take care of you —

—You took care of me five months ago. Goodbye, Mister Burgess.

She walked on.

—It's my son too, remember, said George.

—Son!?

—Baby, I meant baby.

—Your baby?

She couldn't stop the laugh coming out.

—You've got it bad, haven't you, Mister Burgess?

—I have, Sharon; yeah.

He sighed. He looked at the ground. Then he looked at her for a second.

— I've always liked yeh, Sharon; you know tha'. I ——Sharon, I've been livin' a lie for the last fifteen years. Twenty years. The happily married man. Huh. It's taken you to make me cop on. You, Sharon.

—Did you rehearse this, Mister Burgess?

—No. ——Yeah, I did. I've thought o' nothin' else, to be honest with yeh. I've been eatin' an' drinkin' an' sleepin' —sleepin' it, Sharon.

—Bye bye, Mister Burgess.

—Come to London with me, Sharon.

—Wha'!?

—I've a sister, another one, lives there an' —

—Would you ever —

—Please, Sharon; let me finish. ——Thanks. Avril. Me sister. She lives very near QPR's place, yeh know. Loftus Road. She'd put us up no problem, till we get a place of our own. I'll get a —

—Stop.

Sharon looked straight at him. It wasn't easy.

—I'm not goin' annywhere with yeh, Mister Burgess. I'm

stayin' here. An' it's not YOUR baby either. It's not yours or annyone else's. Will yeh leave me alone now?

—Is it because I'm older than yeh?

—It's because I hate the fuckin' sight of yeh.

—Oh. ——You're not just sayin' tha'?

—No. I hate yeh. Will I sing it for yeh?

—What abou' the little baby?

—Look; forget about the little baby, righ'. If yeh must know, you were off-target tha' time annyway.

—I was not!

That was going too far.

—Yeh were. So now.

Then she remembered.

—An' anyway, it was a Spanish sailor, if yeh must know.

——Spanish?

—Yeah. I sleep around, Mister Burgess. D'yeh know what I mean?

—I find tha' hard to believe, Sharon.

Sharon laughed.

—Go home, Mister Burgess. George. Go home.

—But —

—If yeh really want to do me a favour —

—Annythin', Sharon. You know I'd —

—Shut up before yeh make an even bigger sap of yourself. Sorry. ——Don't ever talk abou' wha' we did to annyone again; okay?

—Righ', Sharon; okay. It'll be our —

—Bye bye.

She went.

He didn't follow.

—I'll always remember you, Sharon.

Sharon laughed again, quietly. That was that out of the way. She hoped. She felt better now. That poor man was some eejit.

* * *

Sharon grabbed the boy. She held him by the hood of his sweatshirt.

—Let go o' me!

She was twice as big as him. He wriggled and elbowed and tried to pull away from her but he wasn't getting anywhere. They heard cloth ripping.

—You're after ripping me hoodie, said the boy.

He stopped squirming. He was stunned. His ma had only bought it for him last week. When she saw it she'd —

Sharon slapped him across the head.

—Wha'!

—Wha' did yeh call me? said Sharon, and she slapped him again.

—I didn't call yeh ann'thin'!

Sharon held onto the hood and swung him into the wall. There was another rip, a long one.

—If you ever call me annythin' again I'll fuckin' kill yeh, d'yeh hear me?

The boy stood there against the wall, afraid to move in case there was another tear.

—D'yeh hear me?

He said nothing. His mates were at the corner, watching. Sharon looked down quickly to see if there was room. Then she lifted her leg and kneed him.

—There, she said.

She'd never done it before. It was easy. She'd do it again.

For a while the boy forgot about his ripped hoodie and his ma.

Sharon looked back, to make sure that he was still alive.

He was. His mates were around him, in stitches.

* * *

—She's a fuckin' lyin' bitch, said Yvonne. —I don't care wha' yeh say.

* * *

Jimmy Sr was in the kitchen. So were Sharon and Veronica. Veronica wished she wasn't.

So did Sharon.

—D'yeh expect us to believe tha'? Jimmy Sr asked her, again. —Yeh met this young fella. Yeh —yeh clicked with him. An' yeh went to a hotel with him an' —an' yeh can't even remember his fuckin' name.

—I was drunk I said, said Sharon.

—I was drunk when I met your mother, said Jimmy Sr. —But I still remember her name. It's Veronica!

—Don't shout, said Veronica.

—Ah look, I was really drunk, said Sharon. —Pissed. Sorry, Mammy.

—How do yeh know he was Spanish then? said Jimmy Sr.

He had her.

—Or a sailor.

He had her alright.

—He could've been a Pakistani postman if you were tha' drunk. ——Well?

Sharon stood up.

—Yis needn't believe me if yeh don't want to.

There wasn't enough room for her to run out so she had to get around Jimmy Sr's chair as quick as she could. Jimmy Sr turned to watch her but he didn't say anything. He turned back to the table.

—Wha' d'yeh think? he asked Veronica.

Veronica was flattening the gold paper from a Cadbury's Snack —she always had a few of them hidden away from the kids for when she wanted one herself —with a fingernail.

—I think, she said, —I'd be delighted if the father was a Spanish sailor and not George Burgess.

—God, yeah, said Jimmy Sr.

—Why don't you leave her alone then?

—Wha' d'yeh mean, Veronica?

—If she says he was a Spanish sailor why not let her say it?

—An' believe her?

Veronica shrugged.

264

—Yeah.

—I don't know, said Jimmy Sr. —It'd be great. ——If she'd just give us a name or somethin'.

—Does it matter?

—Wha'? ——Maybe you're righ'.

He stood up.

—Fuck it annyway. ——I'll, eh, give it some thought.

—You do that, said Veronica.

* * *

Tracy stayed at the bedroom door. She had something she had to ask Sharon.

She got it out.

—Sharon, sure the baby won't look like Mister Burgess?

—Aaah! No, he won't! He's not the daddy, Tracy; I told yeh.

She eyed Tracy.

—Who said that annyway?

—Nicola 'Malley, said Tracy.

—Well, you tell Nicola 'Malley ——to fuck off.

They grinned.

—I did already, said Tracy.

—Good.

—An' I scraped her face as well.

—Good.

—An' Linda scribbled all over her sums.

Sharon laughed.

—Brilliant.

* * *

They were nearly finished talking about Bertie's shirt and tie and jacket and why he was wearing them. He'd done a mock interview that afternoon.

—He said he'd've given me the job if there'd been a real job goin', Bertie told them.

—Did he say yeh did annythin' wrong? Paddy asked him.

265

—Yes, indeed. He said I'd have to stop scratchin' me bollix all the time.

They laughed, but Jimmy Sr didn't.

—Jimmy, said Bertie. —Compadre mio.

—Wha'?

—I just said somethin' funny. Why didn't yeh laugh?

—Sorry, Bertie. I wasn't listenin'. ——I was just lookin' at the soccer shower over there. I think they were laughin' at me.

—Ah cop on, will yeh, said Paddy.

—No; they were, said Jimmy Sr. —Lookin' over, yeh know, an' laughin'.

—No one's laughin' at yeh, said Bertie.

—Not at all, said Bimbo. —They'd want to try.

—Ah sorry, lads. —— It's just —

—You're alrigh', said Bertie.

Jimmy Sr forced himself to smile. They said nothing for a short while.

—She says that it was a Spanish sailor now, said Jimmy Sr. —Sharon.

—So yeh said.

—Why did Burgess fuck off then? Paddy wanted to know.

His wife at home wanted to know as well. So did Bertie and Bimbo.

—That's it, said Jimmy Sr. —I don't fuckin' know. If I knew tha' I'd be able to ——yeh know?

—He must've had some reason, said Paddy.

—Tha' doesn't mean tha' Sharon was the reason, said Bimbo. —It could've been annythin'. Your mot left you for a bit, remember.

—Tha' was different.

—Annyone'd leave him, said Bertie.

—Fuck off, you, said Paddy.

—The way I see it, said Bimbo, —just cos Georgie Burgess ran away an' said he got some young one pregnant an' Sharon is pregnant, yeh know, tha' doesn't mean it has to be Sharon.

He drank.

—That's wha' I think annyway.

266

—Si, said Bertie.

—Sharon's a lovely lookin' young one, Bimbo told Jimmy Sr. —She'd have young lads queuin' up for her. Burgess wouldn't get near her. I'd say it was the sailor alrigh'.

—This hombre, he speaks the truth, said Bertie.

—A good lookin' young lad, yeh know, said Bimbo. —A bit different as well, yeh know. Dark an' tall. An' —

—Exotic, said Bertie.

—Exactly, said Bimbo.

—An' a hefty langer on him, said Bertie.

They all laughed, even Jimmy Sr.

—Christopher Columbus, said Bertie.

They roared.

—You believe her, don't yeh? said Bimbo.

Jimmy held his glass up to the light so he wouldn't have to look at Bimbo or the other two.

—I'd —, he began.

—Course yeh do, said Bimbo.

—Yeah, said Jimmy Sr. —I suppose I do. I def'ny would if I knew —Veronica says I should believe her whether it's true or not.

—She's righ', said Bimbo.

—Yeah, said Jimmy Sr. —Yeah. Whose round is it?

* * *

Sharon wasn't sure, but she thought they'd all swallowed it. It made more sense anyway, the lie; it was more believable. No one would ever have believed that herself and Mister Burgess had —she couldn't think of any proper name for it —except for she was pregnant and Mister Burgess had told Missis Burgess that he'd got a young one pregnant. But everyone would easily believe that she'd got off with a Spanish sailor.

So it made more sense. But she knew this as well: everyone would prefer to believe that she'd got off with Mister Burgess. It was a bigger piece of scandal and better gas. She'd have loved it herself, only she was the poor sap who was pregnant.

Yeah definitely, Sharon and Mister Burgess was a much better story than Sharon and the Spanish sailor.

So that was what she was fighting against; Barrytown's sense of humour. She'd keep telling them that it was the Spanish sailor and they'd believe her alright, but every time they thought about Mister Burgess with his trousers down and pulling at her tits and watering at the mouth they'd forget about the Spanish sailor.

She should have given him a name. It was too late now. Anyway, her daddy would have been down to the Spanish embassy looking for his address then.

She hated this time of the day, when there weren't enough customers and some of the girls on the check-out had to do the shelves. She was straightening the ranks of shampoo and then she was going to do the same with the soap so she wouldn't have to bend down too much because they were on the middle and top shelves.

She'd keep at it anyway, telling them about her Spanish sailor. She was sorry now she hadn't thought of this earlier, before Mister Burgess ran away and started writing letters to everyone. It was a pity. None of this would have happened then.

—Ah cop on, Sharon, she told herself.

It was a good idea and it was working. Jackie believed her. Jackie said Mary believed her as well. Her mammy believed her. She wasn't so sure about her daddy. But she'd keep at him, telling him until she believed it herself. She'd have loved that, to believe it herself.

She'd been noticing all the Spanish students that were always upstairs on the buses at this time of year. They looked rich —their clothes were lovely —and snotty. There were a lot of fat ones. But most of them had lovely skin and hair. Black eyes and black hair.

Sharon was fair. Mister Burgess was —pink and white. His hair was like dirty water.

Maybe she should have said it was a Swedish sailor.

Too late now.

She'd have to start eating polish or something.

She grinned although she didn't really feel like it. The shampoos were done and now she crossed the aisle to the soap.

—Fuck it annyway.

The Palmolives were nearly all gone and Simple section was empty. She'd have to fill them and that meant she'd have to bend down.

* * *

It wasn't fair on the lads either, Jimmy Sr told Bimbo at his gate a few nights later, after closing time.

—I should stay at home maybe.

—Don't be thick, said Bimbo.

Jimmy Sr reckoned they'd been talking about him. He knew it. Nothing surer. Let's be nice to Jimmy. He's having it rough. Don't mention babies or Burgess or Sinbad the fuckin' Sailor. It was terrible. He'd had a good one tonight about a young lad getting up on an oul' one but he couldn't tell it. They'd have laughed too loud.

—They're just bein', eh, considerate, said Bimbo. —It'll pass.

—I suppose you're righ', said Jimmy Sr. —But I felt like a leper tonigh' the way they were smilin' at me.

—Bertie an' Paddy wouldn't smile at a leper, Jimmy. Cop on now. They just see that you're not the best these days so ——It'll pass. It'll pass. They're just bein' nice.

—I don't like them nice. I prefer them the other way; bollixes. ——Did yeh see the way the other shower were gawkin' over at me?

—Ah Jaysis, Jimmy. ——You're not startin' to get sorry for yourself, are yeh?

—Go home to bed, you.

—I will.

He yawned.

—Nigh' now, Jim.

—Good luck.

—See yeh.

Jimmy Sr had chips for Veronica but they were cold so he ate them on the step, looking across at the Burgess's, and then he went in.

* * *

It was Thursday night and Sharon was going upstairs after work. Jimmy Jr was coming down.

—Howyeh, Larry, said Sharon.

—Ah, don't start, Sharon.

—How's the practice goin'?

—Shite, to be honest with yeh. The tape sounds woeful. I sound like a fuckin' harelip. ——I'm thinkin' o' gettin' elocution lessons.

Sharon screamed.

—You!

—Yeah; why not. Don't tell Da, for fuck sake.

Sharon laughed. Jimmy grinned.

—It'd be worth it, he said, still grinning.

—How much?

—Don't know. I'm only thinkin' about it. Don't tell him but; righ'?

—Don't worry, said Sharon.

Sharon had asked about him and listened so Jimmy thought he'd better ask about her, and listen.

—How are yeh yourself an' annyway? he said.

—Grand.

—Gettin' big, wha'.

He nodded at her belly.

—Yeah, said Sharon.

—Does it hurt?

—No! ——I do exercises for the extra weight an' tha'.

—Yeah?

—Yeah. Sometimes only.

—Nothin' wrong then?

—No. Not really.

—D'yeh get sick?

—No. Not annymore.

—That's good. I was in bits meself this mornin'.

—Were yeh?

—Yeah. The oul' rum an' blacks, yeh know.

—Oh Jesus.

—I know. Never again. I puked me ring; Jesus. And me lungs. The oul' fella was batterin' the door. ——Come here, d'yeh eat annythin' funny?

—No.

—I saw yeh eatin' tha' long stuff; what's it ——celery.

—That's not funny.

—S'pose not. Never ate it.

—It's nice.

—Mickah's ma ate coal when she was havin' him.

—Jesus!

—He says annyway. She said she used to nibble it when no one was lookin'.

—That's gas ——

Jimmy looked at his watch. It wasn't there.

—Bollox! I've left me watch in work again.

—I'm goin' to me check-up tomorrow, Sharon told him.

—Yeah?

—Yeah. Me second one, it is.

—That's great. I'm —

—Not a complete physical this time. Thank God. It took fuckin' ages the first time, waitin'. They even checked me heart to see if I have a murmur.

She didn't know why she was telling Jimmy all this. She just wanted to.

—I'd a murmur once, said Jimmy. —But a lorry splattered it.

—Ha ha. Anyway, it's at eleven.

—Wha'?

Sharon looked at the ceiling.

—Me antenatal check-up, yeh simple-head yeh.

—Oh yeah. That's great.

He looked at where his watch usually was.

—Meetin' the lads, yeh know. See yeh, righ'.

271

—Yeah. See yeh.

He stopped a few steps down.

—An' come here, he said.

He was reddening a bit.

——Abou' Burgess bein' the da an' tha'.

—He's not!

—I know, I know tha'. No; I mean —IF he was.

—He's not.

—I fuckin' know. Will yeh shut up a minute. ——There's people tha' still say he is, righ'.

He was getting red again.

—An' they'll prob'ly always say it. ——I couldn't give a shite who the da is. D'yeh know what I mean?

—Yeah. ——Thanks.

—No; I wanted to say tha'. An' the lads couldn't give a fuck either.

Sharon grinned.

—Mickah says it's great.

Sharon laughed.

—He says there's hope for us all if fuckin' Burgess can —

—Jimmy!

They laughed.

—Seriously, Jimmy, though, said Sharon. —They don't really think it was him, do they?

—No, not really. It's just, yeh know —funnier.

—Yeah.

—Good luck.

He had the door open.

—Jimmy.

—Wha'?

Sharon looked over the landing rail.

—How. Now. Brown. Cow.

—Fuck off, said Jimmy Jr. —You're the only brown cow around here.

—Thanks very much!

* * *

272

—I'm not takin' this, said Jimmy Sr.

He pushed his chair back and stood up and walked away, towards the bar.

—What's he on abou'? Bimbo asked Bertie.

—Don't know, compadre, said Bertie.

They got up to follow Jimmy Sr.

* * *

—These are reheats, Jackie complained, but she kept eating them.

—Mine aren't too bad, said Sharon. —Look it. That's a lovely one.

She held up a huge, healthy-looking chip.

—Come here, said Jackie. —I wouldn't mind seein' tha' on a young fella.

—Jesus, Jackie!

They screamed laughing.

They were going across the Green to Jackie's house. It hadn't rained in ages so the ground was nice and hard.

—I shouldn't be eatin' these, said Sharon.

—Wha' harm can they do yeh?

—They're all fat an' things. I don't know; things that'll clog me up, I can't remember. ——She asked me did I eat chips an' tha', your woman this mornin'.

—None of her fuckin' business.

—Yeah. I said I didn't. Ah, she's nice though. She says I have the right kind o' nipples.

—Lezzer.

—Ah stop; for breast feedin'. Me blood pressure's grand.

—I'm very happy for yeh.

—Fuck off, you.

They got to Jackie's gate.

—Come here, Jackie, said Sharon. —Did Yvonne say anny-thin' else about me?

They'd been talking about Yvonne Burgess before they bought the chips.

—Only; she said you led him on.

—God, said Sharon. —Poor Yvonne. Still, I'll break her head for her if I see her.

—Yeh know wha' else though? said Jackie. —She said he paid yeh.

—He did, said Sharon.

Then she laughed.

Jackie looked at her, and then she laughed as well.

—I'm pissed, d'yeh know tha', said Sharon.

She patted the lodger.

—He's playin' fuckin' tennis in there.

—He's prob'ly eatin' your chips, said Jackie.

—Yeuuh; stop.

Jackie remembered what she'd wanted to ask Sharon earlier but she'd been a bit afraid to. Now, with a few vodkas inside her, she was still afraid but it was easier.

—Come here, Sharon, she said. —Why didn't yeh tell me earlier? Yeh know; abou' your sailor.

—Aah. I don't know —

Sharon couldn't tell her the truth: because I only made it up a few days ago and you ARE the first person I told. Or the realler truth: because we're not that close; or weren't anyway.

—I just ——I was too embarrassed. Sorry; I should've.

—No, it's okay. I was only —

—Here, I'll tell yeh the next time, righ'.

They screamed again, but quieter because people were in bed.

* * *

Jimmy Sr came in with a bloody nose. The blood was dry and there wasn't much of it but it was there to be seen. He put a brown paper bag with grease marks down on the table.

Veronica took off her glasses and scooped up the loose sequins and poured them into a tobacco tin. She put the lid on the tin. Then she saw Jimmy Sr and his nose.

—Where in the name of God did you get that?

—Hang on till I have a look at it, said Jimmy Sr.

He pointed at the bag.

—I got yeh a burger as well.

—You didn't go into the chipper with that nose!

—No; I got them from the van.

—You can eat them yourself then. Who hit you?

Jimmy Sr had the curtain pulled back and he was trying to get a good look at himself in the kitchen window. He was leaning over the sink.

—It doesn't look too bad. From here annyway.

—Who hit you?

Veronica was eating the chips but she wasn't going to go near the burger.

—Ah, I'll live, said Jimmy Sr.

—More's the pity, said Veronica. —Who hit you? I want to thank him.

—You would too. Are yeh not eatin' tha' burger?

The inspection was over. There was no real damage done. He hadn't even got any of it on his shirt or his jacket. He'd wash his nose before he went to bed. He took a good bite out of the burger in case Veronica said, Yes, she was eating it.

—I'll tell yeh one thing though, said Jimmy Sr. —I gave back better than I got.

—Aren't you great?

—Tha' soccer shower, said Jimmy Sr. —Yeh know the bunch o' wankers tha' hang —used to hang around with Georgie Burgess. They were laughin', yeh know. The whole gang o' them. They've been at it since —yeh know. The bollixes.

—How d'you know they were laughing at you, for God's sake?

Jimmy Sr ignored the question. Bimbo had asked it already and he hadn't answered it then either.

—I got Larry O'Rourke when he was up at the bar an' I told him if, righ', if they were laughin' at me I'd fuckin' kill them. Every —

Jimmy Sr liberated the rest of the burger.

—Every —'scuse me, Veronica —every jaysis one o' them. He said they wouldn't bother their bollixes —pardon,

275

Veronica —bother laughin' at me, an' I said they'd better not. For their own sakes.

—You're —

—An' —sorry —I gave him a bit of a dig —nothin' much now —when he was tryin' to get past me. Bimbo an' Bertie got in between us. Just as well.

He wiped his fingers with the bag.

—I'd've destroyed him.

Veronica didn't know what to say. And he was too old to be slapped.

Jimmy Sr continued.

—I'm not goin' up there annymore. I don't care. I only have to walk in an' they're —

He saw Veronica looking at him.

—I can't enjoy me pint under those conditions.

Veronica was still looking at him.

—It's fuckin' desperate, so it is.

—God almighty, said Veronica.

Jimmy Sr sat down. He tried to explain again.

—If it was annyone else. I don't care abou' the age, annyone. But Georgie Burgess! Jesus.

—Oh, shut up. I'm sick of it. Why won't you believe her?

—Oh, I do believe her. Only —I don't know. I —

They heard the door. Sharon was coming in.

—Wash your nose, said Veronica.

—There's no point.

—You want her to see it, don't you?

—That's offside, said Jimmy Sr.

It was true though.

He got up too late to be at the sink by the time Sharon came in.

—Hiyis.

—Look, Sharon, said Veronica. —Your father's been defending your honour. Isn't he great?

—What happened yeh, Daddy?

—Nothin', Sharon, nothin'. Don't listen to your mother. She's been at the sherry bottle again, ha ha.

Jimmy Sr was at the sink again. He studied the J-cloth, threw it back and rooted in his pockets for a paper hankie. He turned on the cold tap.

—Were you in a fight? Sharon asked him.

—No, no. Not really.

—He was defending your honour, I told you, said Veronica.

—Shut up, Mammy, will yeh.

—Don't —

—Shut up!

Veronica did. Sharon looked like she was going to kill Jimmy Sr and that was alright with Veronica.

Sharon was angry. Something unfair was going on.

—Wha' did yeh do? she asked Jimmy Sr.

—Ah —

—Yeah?

—They were sayin' things about yeh, Sharon, said Jimmy Sr.

His nose was clean now.

—You didn't hear them, said Veronica.

—I know wha' I heard, said Jimmy Sr. —I'm not goin' to stand by an' let annyone —annyone, I don't care who, jeer Sharon.

—You're a fuckin' eejit, Daddy, said Sharon. —Why couldn't yeh just ignore them?

—I'm not like tha', said Jimmy Sr.

He was nearly crying.

—I'm not goin' to let them jeer yeh.

He was liking himself now.

—Why not, for fuck sake?

Veronica tut-tutted.

Jimmy Sr thumped the table.

—Because you're my daughter an' —well, fuck it, you're my daughter an' as long as yeh live in this house I'm not goin' to let bollixes like them say things about yeh.

—Maybe I should leave then.

That hit like a thump.

—Ah no, Sharon.

—Maybe I will if you're goin' to get into fights all the time.

—No, Sharon, Jimmy Sr assured her. —It was just the once. Something had gone wrong.

—I'm not goin' there again.

That wasn't the right thing to say, he realized. He changed it.

—I'm not goin' to listen to them annymore. ——They're only a shower o' shites. They're not worth it.

He felt like a right fuckin' eejit now. He couldn't look at Veronica.

—Well —, said Sharon. —Look; I know you mean well —

—I know tha', Sharon.

—I can fight my own fights, on my own.

—I know tha'.

—No better girl, said Veronica.

—Anyway, said Sharon. —They've nothin' to jeer me about. Now tha' they know I'm not havin' the baby for Mister Burgess.

—You're right o' course.

Sharon went to bed.

All Jimmy Sr had wanted was value for his nosebleed. But something had gone wrong. A bit of gratitude was all he'd expected. He'd felt noble there for a while before Sharon started talking about leaving, even though he'd been lying. But she'd attacked him instead.

There was more to it than that though.

—She put you back in your box, didn't she? said Veronica.

Veronica went to bed.

Jimmy Sr stayed there, sitting in the kitchen. He was busy admitting something: he was ashamed of Sharon. That was the problem. He was sorry for her troubles; he loved her, he was positive he did, but he was ashamed of her. Burgess! Even if there WAS a Spanish sailor ——Burgess! ——

There was something else as well: she was making an eejit of him. She wasn't doing it on purpose —there was no way she'd have got herself up the pole just to get at him. That wasn't what he meant. But, fuck it, his life was being ruined because of her. It was fuckin' terrible. He was the laughing stock of Barrytown. It wasn't her fault —but it was her fault as well. It wasn't his. He'd done nothing.

Jimmy Sr stood up. He was miserable. He'd admitted shocking things to himself. He'd been honest. He was ashamed of Sharon. He was a louser for feeling that way but that was the way it was. He could forgive her for giving him all this grief but it would still be there after he'd forgiven her. So what was the point?

He did forgive her anyway.

A bit of gratitude would have been nice though. Not just for himself; for Veronica as well.

Jimmy Sr went up to bed.

*   *   *

Sharon nearly died.

Her heart stopped for a second. It did.

She was just getting to her gate and there was Yvonne Burgess, coming out of her house, across the road.

She must have seen her.

Sharon threw the gate out of her way and dashed up the path. She nearly went head–first through the glass in the front door. She hadn't her key with her. Oh Jesus. She rang the bell. She couldn't turn around. She rang the bell. She was bursting for the toilet. She rang the fuckin' bell. And she wanted to get sick. She rang the —The door opened. She fell in.

—I nearly gave birth in the fuckin' hall, Jackie, she said. —I'm not jokin' yeh.

*   *   *

—When will they be finished, Mammy? said Tracy.
—When they're ready, said Veronica.
—When?
—Get out.
Linda spoke.
—We have to have them —
—Get out!

Veronica felt Larrygogan at her feet. She gave him a kick and she didn't feel a bit guilty about it after.

* * *

Jimmy Sr got moodier. He wouldn't go out. He sat in the kitchen. He roared at the twins. He walloped Darren twice. He'd have hit Les as well but he didn't see Les. He stayed in bed, didn't go to work two mornings the next week. He listened to the radio and ate most of a packet of Hobnobs one of the mornings and Veronica nearly cut herself to ribbons on the crumbs when she got into bed that night. He couldn't have been that sick, she said. It wasn't his stomach that was sick, Jimmy Sr told her. What was it then? He didn't answer.

But she'd guessed it and she wanted to box his ears for him.

Jimmy Sr knew he could snap out of it but he didn't want to. He was doing it on purpose. He was protesting; that was how he described it to himself. He'd been wronged; he was suffering and he wanted them all to know this. Especially Sharon.

What he was doing was getting at Sharon. He wanted to make her feel bad, to make her realize just how much she'd hurt her father and the rest of the family.

He couldn't tell her. That wasn't the way to do it. She'd have to work it out herself —he didn't know; say Sorry or something; admit —something.

He sat in the kitchen by himself. He was dying to go in and watch a bit of the American Wrestling on the Sports Channel —he loved it; it was great gas and he always ended up feeling glad that he lived in Ireland after he'd watched it —but he didn't want them to see him enjoying himself.

He looked down at the Evening Press crossword.

8 across. Being a seaman he requires no bus. ——What did that fuckin' mean?

He looked at the pictures of the women's faces on the Dubliner's Diary page and decided how many of them he'd ride. ——All of them.

He drew moustaches on some of them, and then glasses.

Bimbo called.

—He's in the kitchen, said Darren.

—There y'are, said Bimbo.

—Howyeh, Bimbo, said Jimmy Sr. —I'm not comin' ou'.

—Ah, why not?

—Ah, said Jimmy Sr. —I'm not well. ——I'm fed up, Bimbo. I've had it up to here.

—Wha' has yeh tha' way?

—Ah —, said Jimmy Sr.

He was saying nothing.

—I know wha' you need, said Bimbo. —An' so do you. A kick up the hole an' a few nice pints.

—No way, said Jimmy Sr.

—Go on, said Bimbo. —Yeh must be constipated, yeh haven't had a pint in ages. Bertie says your shite must be brown by now.

Jimmy Sr grinned.

—Hang on till I get me jacket.

He was only human.

* * *

Sharon noticed. It wasn't hard. Her daddy stopped talking to her during the drives into work. He stopped saying Thanks Sharon when she handed him things at the table. He stopped asking her how she was and saying There's Sharon when she came in from work or in the mornings. He said Howyeh to her as if it cost him money.

At first she didn't know why. He'd been great before; bringing her out, giving her lifts, telling her not to mind what people said. He'd helped her. He'd been brilliant. But now he didn't want anything to do with her.

It annoyed her.

She caught him looking at her belly when she turned from the cooker. She let him know he'd been snared.

—I'm gettin' very big, amn't I? she said.

—S'pose so, he answered.

That was all; no joking, no smile, not even a guilty look.

He just stared at the cinema page of the Press. He never went to the pictures.

She knew now for definite what was eating him: she was. There he was, sitting there, pretending to read the paper. For a second she thought she was going to cry, but she didn't. She would have a few weeks ago, but not now. She had no problem stopping herself. A few weeks ago she wouldn't have blamed him for being like this. But —she flattened her hands on her belly —it was a bit late to be getting snotty now.

She'd have to do something.

* * *

What though? What could she do?

She didn't know.

But she did know that she wasn't going to put up with it. He probably didn't believe her about the sailor. Why couldn't he, the oul' bastard? Everyone else did. There was nothing she could do to make him believe her —at least she didn't think there was —but she wasn't going to let him go on treating her like shite. The twins might start copying him; and Darren. And then she'd be having the baby in —in ten weeks —Jesus —and if it didn't look a bit Spanish they'd all gang up on it before it was even fully out of her.

There was nothing in the book about snotty das. She was on her own.

She took all her clothes off and locked her parents' bedroom door and looked at herself in the wardrobe mirror and the dressing table mirror. Jesus, she looked terrible. She was white in one mirror and greeny-pink in the other one. Her tits were hanging like a cow's. They weren't anything like that before. A fella she'd gone with —Niall, a creep —once said that she should have been in the army because her tits stood to attention. She looked like a pig. In both the mirrors.

She washed her hair but the shampoo stayed in it and it looked worse. Now she wanted to cry. She tried to think of something to set her off. She thought of everything but she couldn't cry. A few drinks would have got her going; bawling.

But she'd no money. And now the baby was throwing wobblers inside of her.

—Ah, lay off, will yeh, she said.

She sat down on her bed and slumped and stayed that way for ages.

* * *

Jimmy Sr began to time his moods. This gave him the best of both worlds. He could enjoy his depression when Sharon was around or when he thought she was around and he could enjoy his few pints with the lads as well. Sharon didn't go up to the Hikers any more —she went to Howth or Raheny or into town —so he let her believe that he didn't go there either. He didn't announce it or anything. He just hinted at it. He wondered out loud where he'd go tonight or he waited till she went out before he went out. Or he stayed in. He wanted her to think she'd robbed his local off him.

Now and again guilt got to him. He felt like a bollix and he thought he should leave her alone and get back to normal. He'd have liked that. But every time he saw one of the soccer shower looking his way or when Georgie Burgess came into his head he decided to keep it up. Anyway, it was for her own good. She had to be made to realize all the trouble she'd caused, the consequences of her messing around.

One time at the dinner he came within that, an inch, of giving the twins a few quid to go and get choc-ices for everyone. It was a lovely day, a scorcher. But he'd stopped himself just in time.

Mind you, he bought one for himself later on his way up to the Hikers.

* * *

Now was as good a time as any.

—What —, Jimmy Sr started.

Bertie, Bimbo and Paddy paid attention.

—What, said Jimmy Sr, —is hard an' hairy on the outside —

283

Bimbo started giggling. Hairy was a great word.
—is soft an' wet on the inside —
They were laughing already.
—begins with a C —
—Oh Jaysis! said Bimbo.
—ends with a T, an' has a U an' an N in it?
They sat there laughing, Jimmy Sr as well.
Paddy knew he was going to be wrong.
—A cunt, he said.
—No, said Jimmy Sr. —A coconut.
They roared.

* * *

—Hey Daddy, said Linda. —Will yeh watch us for a bit to tell us wha' we're doin' wrong?
    Jimmy Sr looked up at her.
—Can't yeh see I'm readin' me paper? he said.

* * *

Veronica was looking in the dressing table mirror, hunting an eyelash that was killing her. She was leaning over the stuff on the table so she could get right in to the mirror. She saw Jimmy Sr's head floating behind her shoulder. She felt his hand go down between the cheeks of her bum. His finger pressed into her skirt.
—You're still a great lookin' —
—Get away from me, you, she barked at the mirror.
She clouted his arm with the hairbrush.
—Oh Jesus! Me fuckin' ——There was no need for tha'.
The face was gone from the mirror.
She'd been wanting to do something like that for days. Weeks.

* * *

Sharon asked Jackie to back her up.
—Yeah, said Jackie. —No problem.
—Is that alrigh' then?

284

—Yeah. It is, said Jackie. —An', come here. If nothin' happens an' he's still actin' the prick, we'll go ahead an' do it, okay?

—Are yeh serious?

—Yeah. Why not?

They were sitting in the front room of Jackie's house.

—I hate this fuckin' room, said Jackie.

Sharon laughed.

—Yeh can't open the door without trippin' over one of her ornaments, said Jackie.

* * *

He wasn't in the kitchen. She looked in the front room. He was in there by himself, watching MTV with the sound down. He only turned the sound up when he recognized the singers or when he liked the look of them. Veronica had been in bed since just after the tea. It had been a bad day. The twins and Darren were in bed. The twins were asleep. Darren was listening to Bon Jovi on Jimmy Jr's walkman. Jimmy would kill him when he caught him but it was worth it: Bon Jovi were brilliant. Jimmy Jr was in Howth, trying to get into Saints. Mickah Wallace was with him so it wasn't easy. Les was out. Larrygogan was in the coal shed.

Jimmy Sr didn't go to bed these days until Sharon got in.

—Hiyeh, said Sharon.

Jimmy Sr didn't answer. He kept his eyes on Curiosity Killed the Cat.

—I said Hiyeh, Daddy, said Sharon.

—I heard yeh.

—Then why didn't yeh answer me?

—Wait a —

—An' why haven't yeh answered for the last —weeks?

She got the pouffe and sat in front of him.

—You're in me way, look it, he said.

She said it louder.

—Why haven't yeh answered me?

—Get lost, will yeh; I have.

285

Jimmy Sr'd been taken by surprise. He tried to look around Sharon. She leaned back —it wasn't easy —and turned off the telly.

—Yeh haven't, she said. —Yeh haven't said hello to me properly in ages.

Jimmy Sr was never going to admit anything like that.

—You're imaginin' things, he said.

—No, I'm not.

She looked straight at him. There wasn't any shaking in her voice. She just spoke. She was a bit frightening.

—I'll tell yeh the last time yeh spoke to me.

—I said hello to yeh yesterday.

—Yeh didn't. Not properly. The last time yeh said hello to me properly was before the night yeh got hit in the nose.

—Now listen; that's not true.

—It is. An' you know it.

Jimmy Sr wondered if he'd be able to get past her and up to bed. He thought she was capable of trying to stop him.

—Are yeh goin' to tell me why? Sharon asked him.

He looked as if he was going to get up. She didn't know what she'd do if he did that. She'd follow him.

—There's nothin' to tell, for fuck sake, said Jimmy Sr.

—It's me, isn't it?

—Go up to bed, will yeh.

—It is, said Sharon. —I can tell.

Sharon nearly had to stop herself from grinning as she asked the next question.

—Did I do somethin' to yeh?

Jesus, she was asking him had she done something: had she done something! She could sit there and —

—You've done nothin', Sharon.

—I'll tell yeh what I've done.

Her voice had softened. The bitch; he couldn't have a proper row with her that way.

—I'm pregnant. ——I saw yeh lookin' at me.

Jimmy Sr said nothing yet.

—I've disgraced the family.

—No.

—Don't bother denyin' it, Daddy. I'm not givin' out.

The look on his face gave her the sick for a minute.

—I've been stupid, she said. —An' selfish. I should've known. An' I know tha' you still think it was Mister Burgess an' that makes it worse.

—I don't think it was —

—Ah ah! she very gently gave out to him. ——You were great. Yeh did your best to hide it.

—Ah, Sharon —

—If I leave it'll be the best for everyone. Yeh can get back to normal.

—Leave.

—Yeah. Leave. Go. Yeh know what I mean.

She stopped herself from getting too cheeky.

—I'm only bringin' trouble for you an' Mammy, so I'm ——Me an' Jackie are goin' to get a flat. Okay?

—You're not goin'?

—I am. I want to. It's the best. Nigh' night.

She went upstairs.

—Ah Sharon, no.

Sharon got undressed. She wondered if it would work; what he was thinking; was he feeling guilty or what. The face on him when she was talking to him; butter wouldn't melt in his fuckin' mouth, the bastard. She got into bed. She wondered if she'd be here next week. God, she hoped so. She didn't want to move into a flat, even with Jackie. She'd seen some. She didn't want to be by herself, looking after herself and the baby. She wanted to stay here so the baby would have a proper family and the garden and the twins and her mammy to look after it so she could go out sometimes. She didn't want to leave. What was he thinking down there?

Jimmy Sr sat back and stretched.

Victory: he'd won. Without having to admit anything himself, he'd got her to admit that she was the one in the wrong. She was to blame for all this, and he'd been great. She'd said it herself.

Jimmy Sr stretched further and sank down in the couch. He punched his fists up into the air.

—Easy! Easy! he roared quietly.

He'd won. He'd got what he wanted.

—Here we go, here we go, here we go!

He stood up.

He could get back to normal now. He'd drive her all the way to work on Monday, right up to the door. He'd bring her out for a drink at tea-time on Sunday, up to the Hikers. He'd insist.

He switched on the telly to have a quick look and see if there was a good video on. There was a filthy one they sometimes showed after midnight. No; it was only some shower of wankers running down a beach. He switched it off.

He was glad it was over. He preferred being nice. It was easier.

Sharon had been great there, the way she'd taken the blame. Fair play to her. She was a great young one; the way she'd just sat there and said her bit, and none of the fuckin' water works that you usually got. Any husband of Sharon's would have his work cut out for him.

Tomorrow he'd tell her not to leave.

* * *

He told her when she came down for her breakfast. Veronica was there too but she was determined not to have anything to do with it. She was sick of the two of them.

—No, Daddy, said Sharon. —Thanks, but I've made me mind up.

—But there's no need, Sharon.

—No; you've been great. So have you, Mammy.

—I know.

—Hang on, Veronica; this is serious. You can't go, Sharon. I won't let yeh.

—Try fuckin' stoppin' me.

—Now there's no need for tha' now. We want yeh to stay here with us an' have it —

288

He nodded and pointed.

—the baby there, with us. Don't we?

Veronica didn't look up from Tracy's ballroom dress.

—Yes, she said.

Sharon stopped spreading the Flora on her brown bread.

—I'm goin'.

Jimmy Sr believed her.

—When?

—After dinner.

—Wha'!? Today?

—Yeah.

—Ah, for fuck sake, Sharon —

Jimmy Jr walked in. He wasn't looking the best. He headed for the fridge.

—Why aren't you in work? said Jimmy Sr.

—Wha'?

Jimmy Jr's head came out of the fridge.

—It's alrigh'. I'll phone in. I'll work me day off. Is there anny Coke?

—No.

—Or annythin' with bubbles in it?

—Go down to the shops, said Veronica.

—I'd never make it.

He sat down carefully and stared at the table.

Sharon was cursing him. Now she'd have to start again.

—It's the best thing to do, she said.

—What's tha'? said Jimmy Sr. —No. Fuck it, Sharon; this is your home.

His voice didn't sound right. It was shivery. He coughed.

—You should stay —stay with your family.

Sharon smiled.

—Now maybe. But, look it.

She patted her belly.

—It's goin' to be gettin' bigger an' yeh won't be able to get out of its way an' stop lookin' at it. It'll keep remindin' you of Mister Burgess. No, it will; even though he's not —So, yeh see, it's best for us all if I go.

She stood up. She smiled. She patted his shoulder.

—I'll go upstairs an' pack.

Jimmy Sr was afraid to say anything. He didn't know what it would sound like. He'd never felt like this before.

Sharon was planking going up the stairs. She hoped she hadn't been too convincing. He mightn't bother trying to stop her. She didn't even have a suitcase or anything. She'd just pile her stuff on the bed.

Jimmy Sr didn't know what to do. It was terrible. Sharon was leaving because of him. That wasn't what he'd wanted at all.

It was wrong.

Jimmy Jr's face distracted him.

—Jaysis, he said.

Jimmy Jr was still staring at the table. Veronica looked up from the dress.

—Get up, quick!

Jimmy Jr stood up and fell across to the sink. He dropped his head and vomited —HYUHH —uh —— fuck —— HYY——YUUH! —onto the breakfast plates and cups.

That was it, Jimmy Sr decided. There was no way Sharon could go. She was the only civilized human being in the whole fuckin' house.

Veronica had her face in her hands. She shook her head slowly.

Jimmy Sr stood up.

—Veronica, he said. —She's not goin'.

Veronica looked up at him. She still had her hands to her face but she nodded.

—An' come here, you, he bawled across to Jimmy Jr. —Wash up them dishes, righ'.

Jimmy Jr groaned.

Sharon heard the stairs creaking. She threw a bundle of knickers onto the bed.

Jimmy Sr knocked, and came in.

—Are you alone?

—Yeah.

—Where're the twins?

—Camogie, I think.

—They do everythin', don't they?

—Yeah.

—Fair play to them. Don't go, Sharon.

—I have to.

She stopped messing with the clothes.

—Yeh don't have to ——

Jimmy Sr looked across, out the window. His eyes were shiny. He kept blinking. He gulped, but the lump kept rising.

—I'm cryin', Sharon, sorry. I didn't mean to.

He pulled the sleeve of his jumper over his fist and wiped his eyes with it.

—Sorry, Sharon.

He looked at her. She looked as if she didn't know how she should look, what expression she should have on.

—Em —I don't know wha' to fuckin' say. ——That's the first time I cried since your granny died. Hang on; no. I didn't cry then. I haven't cried since I was a kid.

—You cried last Christmas.

—Sober, Sharon. Drunk doesn't count. We all do stupid things when we're drunk.

—I know.

—Fuck, sorry; I didn't mean it like tha'!

He looked scared.

—I know tha', said Sharon.

—Sorry. ——Annyway, look —I've been a righ' bollix, Sharon. I've made you feel bad an' that's why you're leavin'. Just cos I was feelin' hard done by. It's my fault. Don't go, Sharon. Please.

Sharon was afraid to say no. She didn't want to start him crying again.

—But I'll only keep remindin' yeh —

—Sorry, Sharon. For interruptin' yeh. ——This isn't easy for me. I wanted to make you feel bad cos I was feelin' sorry for myself. I can't look at yeh, sayin' this. It's very fuckin' embarrassin'.

He tried to grin but he couldn't.

—I behaved like a bollix, I realize tha' now. ——I didn't think you'd leave. Don't leave. We need you here. Your mammy —Your mammy's not always the best. Because of —Yeh know tha' yourself. I'm a fuckin' waster. Jimmy's worse. D'yeh know what he's at now?

—Wha'?

—He's down there gettin' sick into the sink. On top o' the plates an' stuff.

—Oh my God.

—Poor Veronica. ——The fuckin' dinner might be —what's the word —steepin' in the sink for all I know. Believe me, Sharon, we need you. The twins, they need you.

Sharon was nearly crying now. She was loving this.

—What abou' the baby?

Jimmy Sr breathed deeply and looked out the window, and looked at Sharon. His eyes were shiny again.

—I feel like a fuckin' eejit. ——I love you, Sharon. An' it'll be your baby, so I'll love it as well.

—Wha' —what if it looks like Mister Burgess?

Jimmy Sr creased his forehead. Then he spoke.

—I don't mind what it looks like. I don't give a shite.

—It's easy to say tha' now —

—I don't, Sharon, I swear I don't. Not now, fuck it. I don't mind. If the first words it says are On the Bible, Jim, on the Bible, I won't mind. I'll still love it.

Sharon was laughing.

—If it looks like Burgess's arse I'll love it, Sharon. On the Bible.

They were both laughing. They'd both won. Both sets of eyes were watery. Sharon spoke.

—What if it's a girl an' she looks like Mister Burgess?

—Ah well, fuck it; we'll just have to smother it an' leave it on his step.

—Ah Daddy!

—I'm only messin'. I suppose I'll still have to love her. Even if she does have a head on her like Georgie Bur —

He couldn't finish. He had an almighty fit of the giggles.

—She'll be lovely, said Sharon.

—She'd fuckin' better be. We're a good lookin' family. 'Cept for Jimmy, wha'. An', come here, an' anyway; it won't look like Burgess cos he isn't the da. ——Isn't tha' righ'?

—Yeah.

—Unless your Spanish sailor looked a bit like him, did he?

——Just a little bit.

—Ah well, said Jimmy Sr after a small while. —Your poor mammy. I'd better go down an' see if your man's still spinnin' the discs in the sink. ——Good girl, Sharon.

—See yeh in a minute. I'll just put me stuff back.

—Good girl.

He was gone, but he came back immediately.

—Eh, sorry; Sharon?

—Yeah?

—Don't tell Jimmy yeh saw me cryin' there, sure yeh won't?

—Don't worry.

—Good girl.

He grinned.

—He looks up to me, yeh know.

*　*　*

—Ah, said Jimmy Sr to the twins. —There yis are. An' there's Larry with yis.

He bent down and patted the dog's head.

—He's growin', he said. —He'll soon be makin' his communion. Yis must be thirsty after your camogie, are yis?

—Yeah, said Linda and Tracy.

—Yes! said Veronica.

—Yes, said Linda.

—There, said Jimmy Sr.

It was a pound.

—Get yourselves some 7 Ups. Or the one tha' Tina Turner drinks. Pepsi.

—What about me?

—A Toblerone?

—And a Flake.

Jimmy Sr's hand went back into his pocket.

—Can we have a Flake instead of the 7 Up? said Tracy.

—No! ——Oh, alrigh'.

The twins legged it.

Jimmy Sr smiled over at Veronica.

—Are yeh well, Veronica?

—I'm alright, said Veronica.

—Good, said Jimmy Sr. —Good.

* * *

It was a few weeks later.

Jimmy Sr dropped the book onto the couch. He was the only one in the front room.

—Wha' in the name o' Jaysis was tha'? he said out loud to himself although he knew what it was.

Veronica had just screamed. What Jimmy Sr really wanted to know was, why? He struggled out of the couch. It hadn't sounded like a scream of pain or shock. It'd been more of a roar.

—No peace in this fuckin' house, he sort of muttered as he went down to the kitchen.

Tracy and Linda were in there with Veronica.

—What's goin' on here? said Jimmy Sr.

He saw the way Veronica was glaring at the twins and the twins were trying to glare back, keeping the table between themselves and their mother. They looked at Jimmy Sr quickly, then back at Veronica in case she did something while they were looking at Jimmy Sr.

—What's wrong? said Jimmy Sr.

Veronica picked up the dress from her lap and clutched it in front of her, nearly hard enough to tear it.

—Are you after upsettin' your mammy? said Jimmy Sr.

—No, said Linda.

—No, said Tracy.

Jimmy Sr was going to shout at them.

—We on'y told her somethin', said Linda. —Tracy said it.

—You did as well! said Tracy.

—Shut up! Jimmy Sr roared.

They jumped. They didn't know where to move. If they got away from their daddy that would mean getting closer to their mammy and she had the scissors on the table in front of her.

Veronica spoke.

—All those ——fuckin' sequins, she said, softly. —Oh my sweet Jesus.

Jimmy Sr could have murdered Linda and Tracy. They saw this, so they both answered promptly when he asked them what they'd said to their mother.

—Tracy said —

—Linda said I was —

—Shut up!

Tracy started crying.

Jimmy Sr pointed at Linda.

—Tell me.

—Tracy said —

Jimmy Sr's pointed finger seemed to get closer to her although he didn't move. She started again.

—We on'y told her we weren't doin' the dancin' annymore.

—Oh good fuck, said Jimmy Sr, not loudly.

He looked at Veronica. She was staring at a little pile of sequins in front of her.

—Yis ungrateful little brassers, he said.

—It's stupid, said Linda. —I'm sick of it. It's stupid.

Veronica came back to life.

—They're not giving it up, she said.

—That's righ'.

—Ah Mammy —

—No! said Veronica.

—But it's stupid.

—You heard your mammy, didn't yeh? said Jimmy Sr. —DIDN'T YEH?

——Yeah.

—An' wha' did she say?

———

—ANSWER ME.

——We have to keep doin' it.

—That's righ', said Jimmy Sr. —An', what's more, yis'll enjoy it. An' if I hear anny whingin' out o' yis yis'll need an operation to get my foot ou' of your arses. ——Now, say you're sorry.

——Sorry.

—Not to me.

——Sorry.

—Now go inside an' practise, said Jimmy Sr.

They got past Jimmy Sr without touching him. He heard Tracy when they'd got out of the kitchen.

—I don't care, I'm not doin' it.

Jimmy Sr rushed out and grabbed her and, without intending to, lifted her.

—Wha' did you say?

—Aah! —Nothin'!

—Are yeh sure?

She was rubbing her arm and deciding whether to cry or not.

—Yeah, she said.

—Good, said Jimmy Sr. —Now get in there an' cha cha cha.

Darren was coming in the back door when Jimmy Sr got back to the kitchen.

—Again? said Jimmy Sr.

—Yeah, said Darren.

He'd crashed again. One side of his face was grazed, the darkest, reddest scrape along his cheekbone.

—Look.

Darren showed them where his jersey was ripped.

—Look it.

He showed them the big, wide scrape down his leg. He was delighted.

Jimmy Sr remembered having a gash like that, only bigger,

296

when he was a young fella. He was going to tell Darren about it but he decided not to, not with Veronica there.

—Wha' happened yeh? he said instead.

Sharon came in from work.

—Hiyis.

—There's Sharon. Do us a favour, love. Talk to the twins, will yeh. ——They're talkin' abou' wantin' to give up the oul' dancin', yeh know?

He nodded at Veronica. Sharon looked at her.

—Okay, she said.

—Good girl. They're in with the telly. Practisin'.

Sharon saw Darren.

—God, wha' happened yeh?

—I came off me bike.

He smiled.

—Sharon'll sort them ou', Jimmy Sr told Veronica. —Are we havin' the dinner?

Veronica put the dress on the table. She stood up and looked around her, as if she'd just woken up with a fright.

—It'll have to be from the chipper, she said.

—Grand, said Jimmy Sr. —Darren can go an' show off his war wounds, wha'.

Darren laughed.

—How'd it happen? Jimmy Sr asked him.

—I was blemmin' down Tonlegee Road.

—Jaysis! Was it a race?

—Yeah, but I didn't give up. I got on again an' I finished it.

—Good man, said Jimmy Sr. —Course yeh did. Did yeh win?

—No. I was last but Mister Cantwell says I showed the righ' spirit.

—He's dead righ'.

He turned to Veronica.

—Just like his da, wha'.

He turned back to Darren.

—Did yeh know I met your mammy when I fell off me bike?

—Did yeh?

—He was drunk, said Veronica.

—It was love, said Jimmy Sr. —Love knocked me off me bike.

Darren spoke.

—Mister Cantwell says we're not to bother with young ones cos they'll only distract us.

Jimmy Sr laughed.

—Fair play to Mister Cantwell. He's dead righ'. ——Cantwell. He's your man from across from the shops, isn't he?

—Yeah.

—He does the church collection.

—Yeah.

—Isn't he great? said Veronica.

Jimmy Sr grinned at her.

—An' he's your manager, is he?

—Yeah.

—Good. What're yis called?

—The Barrytown Cyclin' Club.

—Go 'way! That's very clever.

—Don't mind him, Veronica told Darren. —He's just being smart. Wash your cuts and then you're to go to the chipper.

—I don't need to wash —

—Do wha' your mammy tells yeh.

Darren did.

Jimmy Sr looked at Veronica.

—How're yeh feelin', love?

—Ah ——

Linda and Tracy came in.

—Yes? said Jimmy Sr.

The twins looked at each other. Then Linda spoke.

—Ma, we're sorry.

—Mammy.

—Mammy. We're sorry.

—It's not tha' bad, said Tracy. —It's not really stupid.

—Won't yeh keep makin' our dresses? said Linda.

—She will o' course, said Jimmy Sr.

—I'll think about it, said Veronica to Jimmy Sr.

—She'll think abou' it, said Jimmy Sr.

He clapped his hands.

—The few chips'll go down well, he said.

He went over to the bread bin.

—I'll butter a few slices, will I? For butties.

—You think of nothing except your stomach, said Veronica.

—It's the family's stomachs I'm thinkin' of, Veronica, me dear.

He rolled up two slices and shoved them into his mouth. He winked at Veronica and then he went back to the front room. Sharon was in there, alone. She was sitting on the couch, and reading Jimmy Sr's book.

—Who's readin' this? she asked Jimmy Sr when she saw him.

He shouldn't have left it there.

—I am, he said.

—You!

The book was Everywoman.

—Yeah. ——Why not?

He sat down beside her.

—What're yeh readin' it for? Sharon asked him.

—Aah ——Curiosity. I suppose.

—Where d'yeh get it?

—Library.

He looked at Sharon. He took the book from her.

—I didn't know there was so much to it, yeh know.

—Yeah.

—It's like the inside of a fuckin' engine or somethin'. 'Cept engines don't grow.

Sharon grinned.

—D'yeh get cramps, Sharon? said Jimmy Sr.

Sharon laughed a bit.

—No. Not yet annyway.

—Good. Good. I'd say they'd be a killer. We'll have to keep our fingers crossed. ——Anythin' else?

—Wrong?

—Yeah.

—No.

—Good. That's good.

—I went to me antenatal check-ups.

—Yeh did o' course. ——An' wha' were they like?

—Grand.

—Good. ——Good. Darren's gone to the chipper, for the dinners.

—Yeah.

—That's some knock he got.

—Yeah.

—He got up though, fair play to him. ——I was lookin' at another chapter there.

He opened the book and closed it and opened it again and looked at a diagram and closed it.

—The one abou' ——doin' the business, yeh know.

—Sex?

—Yeah. Exactly. ——Jaysis, I don't know —It's very fuckin' complicated, isn't it?

Sharon laughed, and felt her face getting hot.

—I can't say I don't know, she said.

—Wha'? Oh yeah. ——I'd say Georgie Burgess was a dab hand at the oul' —wha' d'yeh macall it —the foreplay, wha'?

—Daddy!

—Sorry. Sorry, Sharon. It wasn't Burgess, I know. I just said it for a laugh. But ——abou', yeh know, ridin' an' tha' —I thought it was just ——D'yeh know wha' I mean?

—I think so.

—Jaysis, Sharon. I don't know —

—I'd better warn Mammy.

—Wha'? Oh yeah. Very good. Yeah. ——Annyway, I was lookin' at another bit here. Look it.

Les saved Sharon by sticking his head round the door. Jimmy Sr felt the draught and looked up.

—Jaysis!

—Howyeh.

—Leslie. How are yeh?

300

—Alrigh'.

—Good man. How're the jobs goin'?

—Alrigh'.

—Good man. Gardens?

—Yeah.

—An' windows.

—Yeah.

—Good. Gives yeh a few bob annyway, wha'. Are yeh havin' your dinner with us?

—Yeah.

—My God. We'll have to kill the fatted cod for yeh.

—Wha'?

—Darren's gone to the chipper.

—He's back.

—Is he?

—Yeah.

—Why didn't yeh tell us? I'm fuckin' starvin'. ——Hang on. He took the book.

—I'll put this upstairs, he said to Sharon. —I wouldn't want Darren to see it. ——Or Jimmy.

Sharon laughed.

—I could blackmail yeh now.

—Yeh could indeed. Yeh could alrigh'.

* * *

They heard the radio being turned up.

—Righ' now, said Jimmy Sr. —Listen now.

He looked up at the ceiling. Sharon and Veronica looked up at the ceiling.

Alison Moyet was singing Is This Love. The sound dropped.

—Now, said Jimmy Sr.

They listened.

—THIS IS JOMMY ROBBITTE – ALL – OVER – ORELAND.

Then the sound went up again.

—There, said Jimmy Sr. —Doesn't he sound different?

* * *

301

—Sorry, Sharon, said Jimmy Sr. —Sorry for interruptin' yeh.

Sharon wasn't doing anything really. She hadn't the energy even to get up. She was lying on the couch, flicking through the channels.

Jimmy Sr was at the door.

—Wha'? said Sharon.

She was getting really tired of her da; all his questions.

—How many weeks are yeh pregnant, exactly? said Jimmy Sr.

—Thirty-five. Why?

—Just checkin'.

—What're yeh lookin' at?

—Your ankles. They don't look too swollen.

—They're not.

—Good.

Sharon hoped that was that.

It wasn't.

—I was just readin' there, said Jimmy Sr. —Abou' what's goin' on, yeh know. It made me a bit worried.

Sharon said nothing. She flicked to BBC 2; two hippies talking.

—Pain is mentioned a bit too often for my likin'. ——Are yeh in pain, Sharon?

—No.

—None?

—No.

—At all?

—No!

—Good. ——I'll leave yeh to your telly. Sorry for disturbin' yeh.

—Okay.

He was becoming a right pain in the neck. He'd be down again in a few minutes with more questions. Last night he'd told Darren and the twins to get out of the room and then he asked her if her shite was lumpy!

He came home earlier in the week with two new pillows for her so she could prop herself up in bed.

—It'll take some o' the pressure off the oul' diaphram, Sharon.

Was she in pain, he asked her. The fuckin' eejit; she'd give him pain if he didn't get off her case. It was her pregnancy and he could fuck off and stay out of it. If he came in once more, once more she'd —

She felt fuckin' terrible.

The screen became blurred.

She was sweating and wet and she'd gone over herself with the hairdryer an hour ago only and she was still sweating and wet. Her hair was dead and manky. She could hardly walk. She was really hot and full; full like the way she used to be on Christmas Day when she was a kid; stuffed. It was brutal. She was a fat wagon, that was what she was.

She hoped Jackie'd call down because she wanted to see her but she couldn't be bothered getting up. ——She'd been like this all her life.

Ah fuck it; she tried to get up.

The heat made her sleepy. She hated sleeping this way. It wasn't right. Only oul' ones did it.

She thought she heard her daddy's voice.

—Good girl, Sharon.

*   *   *

—What d'you think you're doing down there? Veronica asked Jimmy Sr.

—Hang on a minute. ——How's tha', Veronica?

—I'm cold. ——Aah!

—What's wrong?

—Your fingernail! Get up here; I'm freezing.

—Okay. ——I love you, Veronica.

—Jesus. Get out and brush your teeth. No; hang on. Do that again.

—Wha'? Tha'?

—Yeah.

—There. D'yeh like tha', Veronica?

—It's alright.

She grabbed his hair.
—Where did you learn it?
—Ah, let go!
—Where!?
—In a buke! Let go o' me!

* * *

Her face was wet. She pushed the blanket and the sheet off and the nice cool air hit her and made her feel awake, and that was what she wanted.

Bits of the dream clung. She'd had a miscarriage, in an empty bath. She kept having miscarriages; like going to the toilet. And they all lived, hundreds of them, all red and raw and folded over. All crawling all over her. And she lay there and more of them climbed out of her.

It was only half-five but she got out of bed. By the time she'd got downstairs to the kitchen her head was clear and the dream wasn't part of her any more. She just remembered it. It was stupid.

She hadn't thought about what the baby would be like before; only if it would be a boy or a girl. God, she hoped it would be normal and healthy and then she nearly stopped breathing when she realized she'd just thought that. What if it wasn't? Jesus. What if it was deformed, or retarded like Missis Kelly's baby down the road; what then? And she'd been worrying that it might look like Mister Burgess!

She was kind of looking forward to being a mother but if —

The kettle was boiling.

It might be a Down's Syndrome baby. It would never be able to do anything for itself. It wouldn't grow properly. It would have that face, that sort of face they all had.

The baby nudged her.

She'd seen a programme about dwarfs. It said that there were ten thousand of them in Britain. The ones on the programme seemed happy enough.

She started laughing. She'd suddenly seen her mammy making a ballroom dress for a dwarf.

This was stupid. If she kept on like this something was bound to go wrong. That was what always happened.

It had gone wrong already —it was too late —if anything HAD gone wrong, if there was something wrong with it.

She spread her hands over her dressing gown.

What was in there?

The baby bounced gently off the wall of her uterus. She opened her dressing gown and put her hands back on her belly. It moved again, like a dolphin going through the water; that was the way she imagined it.

—Are yeh normal? she said.

She wished to fuck it was all over. She was sick of it, and worried sick as well.

—Soon, she said.

*   *   *

—Specially with a few chips, said Bertie.

They howled.

—I'm fuckin' serious, righ', said Jimmy Sr.

He was getting furious.

—It IS a fuckin' miracle.

—Fuckin' sure it is, Your Holiness, said Paddy.

Bimbo was wiping his eyes.

—You're a sick bunch o' fuckers, said Jimmy Sr.

Bertie pointed at Jimmy Sr, and sang.

—MOTHER OF CHRIST —

STAR OF THE SEA—

Jimmy Sr mashed a beer mat.

*   *   *

—Sharon, said Jimmy Sr.

Sharon looked up from her Bella.

Not again.

—Yeah? she said.

—D'yeh know your hormones?

305

—Wha'?

—Your hormones, said Jimmy Sr.

Sharon was interested.

—What abou' them?

—Are they givin' yeh anny trouble?

—Eh ——wha' d'yeh mean?

—Well —

He shifted his chair.

—I was just readin' there yesterday abou' how sometimes your hormones start actin' up when you're pregnant an' tha'. An' yis get depressed or, eh, snotty or —yeh know?

Sharon said nothing. She didn't know she'd been asked a question.

—Don't get me wrong now, Sharon, said Jimmy Sr. —Hormonal changes are perfectly normal. Part an' parcel of the pregnancy, if yeh follow me. But sometimes, like, there are side effects. Snottiness or depression or actin' a bit queer.

—I'm grand, said Sharon.

—Good, said Jimmy Sr. —Good girl. That's good. I thought so myself. I just wanted to be on the safe side, yeh know.

—Yeah, said Sharon. —No, I'm grand. I feel fine. I'd another check-up. Me last one, I think.

—An' no problems?

—No.

—Good. All set so.

Sharon got back to her magazine, but Jimmy Sr wasn't finished yet.

—I was lookin' at this other buke there an' ——It was abou' wha' happens —

He pointed at the table, just in front of Sharon.

—inside in the woman for the nine months. The pictures. Fuckin' hell; I don't know how they do it. There was this one o' the foetus, righ'. That's the name o' —

—I know what it is, Daddy!

—Yeh do o' course. ——I'm a stupid thick sometimes.

—Ah, you're not.

—Ah, I am. Annyway, it was only seven weeks, Sharon. Seven weeks. In colour, yeh know. It had fingers —

He showed her his fingers.

—Ah, Jaysis, everythin'. An' the little puss on him, yeh know.

—Yeah, it's incredible, isn't it?

—It fuckin' is, said Jimmy Sr. ——It got me thinkin'. I know it sounds stupid but —

He was blushing. But he looked straight at her.

—Youse were all like tha' once, said Jimmy Sr. —Yeh know. Even Jimmy. ——I was as well long, long ago.

He belched.

—'Scuse me, Shar —

He belched again.

—Sharon. Tha' fried bread's a killer. ——Wha' I'm tryin' to say is ——when yeh look at tha' picture, righ', an' then the later ones, an' then the born baby growin' up —Well, it's a fuckin' miracle, isn't it?

—I s'pose it is, said Sharon.

—It's got to be, said Jimmy Sr. —Shhh!

Veronica came back into the kitchen. She'd been upstairs, lying down.

—There's Veronica, said Jimmy Sr. —Yeh may as well fill the oul' kettle while you're on your feet.

—God almighty, said Veronica. —You'd die of the thirst before you'd get up and do it yourself.

—That's not true, said Jimmy Sr. —I'd say I'd've got up after a while.

The front door was opened and slammed. Jimmy Jr came in from work.

—Hoy, said Jimmy Jr.

Jimmy Sr studied him.

—Ahoy, he said. —Shiver me timbers. It's Jim lad, me hearties. Hoy! Is there somethin' wrong with your mouth?

—Fuck off.

—That's better.

—Fuck off.

—Better still. Ahoy, Veronica. There's the kettle.

—I'll get it, said Sharon.

—Now don't be ——Only if you're makin' one for yourself now.

Jimmy Sr looked up at Jimmy Jr. Then he sang.

—JUST A MINUTE —

THE SIXTY SECOND QUIZ —.

—Fuck off.

—That's lovely language from a DJ.

The front room door opened and they heard the music of Victor Sylvester and his orchestra.

—Ah now, said Jimmy Sr. —There's music. Listen to tha', wha'.

He tapped the table.

—Oh my Jaysis, said Jimmy Jr. —This is embarrassin'.

Sharon laughed. Veronica smiled. Jimmy Sr closed his eyes and nodded his head and kept tapping the table.

Linda and Tracy had danced into the hall. Sharon and Veronica went to the door to watch them.

—They're very good, aren't they? said Sharon. —You can nearly hear their bones clickin' when they turn like tha'.

Jimmy Sr was impressed.

—They're good enough for the Billie Barry kids, he said. —Too fuckin' good.

They heard the doorbell.

Linda came running down, into the kitchen.

—Da, Mister Cantwell wants yeh.

—Cantwell? Wha' does he want?

He stood up.

—Don't know, said Linda.

—It must be abou' Darren. Where is he?

—He's out, said Veronica.

—Oh God.

Jimmy Sr dashed out to the front door. The others stayed where they were.

—Hope he's not hurt, said Sharon.

—Shut up, for God's sake! said Veronica.

She sat down and lined up a row of sequins.

Victor Sylvester was still playing.

Jimmy Sr came back. He was pale.

—What did he want; what's wrong?

—Wha'? said Jimmy Sr. —Oh. It wasn't abou' Darren. Is Leslie in?

—Don't be stupid.

They all relaxed, except Jimmy Sr. He put a painted cement gnome on the table.

—Ah, look it, said Tracy.

—He says tha' Leslie threw tha' thing through his window. His, eh, drawin' room window.

They all studied the gnome. It had a red cap and trousers and a yellow beard. Jimmy Jr laughed.

—Don't start, said Jimmy Sr. —It's not funny. ——Would Leslie do tha'?

—Did he see him?

—No.

—Well then.

—Did he dust it for fingerprints? said Jimmy Jr.

—Wha'? ——Oh yeah. No. He says he'll let me deal with it this time but if it happens again he'll have to get the guards. He said Leslie's always hangin' around outside his house. Loiterin', he said.

—Did you not say annythin' back? said Sharon.

—I know wha' yeh mean, said Jimmy Sr. —I should've. He's no proof. I'll go round an' have it ou' with him later. On me way to the Hikers. But, he explained, —I got a terrible fuckin' fright.

They waited for more.

—Look at its face, said Jimmy Sr.

They did.

—It's the spit o' George Burgess.

It was.

* * *

Darren had news for them the next day at tea time.

—Pat Burgess said his da's after comin' back.

Jimmy Sr put his knife and fork down.

—I knew it, he said. —I fuckin' knew it. I told yis. When I saw tha' gnome yoke's face. ——Where is it?

—Out on the windowsill, said Veronica.

—Well, it's goin' in the bin the minute I've liberated these fishfingers.

He shovelled one into him.

—So he's back, he said.

He looked at Sharon.

—I don't care, she said.

—Good girl, said Jimmy Sr. —Course yeh don't. He's only a bollix, isn't tha' righ'?

—Yeah.

*   *   *

Darren had more news later.

—I've been dropped.

He sat down on the arm of the couch and looked like he'd just seen his dog being splattered.

—From the soccer? said Jimmy Sr.

—No, said Darren.

Fuck the soccer, his face said.

—The cyclin'.

—Ah no. Why?

—Cos —cos you won't pay for Mister Cantwell's window an' yeh called him names.

—I didn't call him names, said Jimmy Sr.

—You told me you called him a little Virgin Mary, said Veronica.

—Now, Veronica. Please. ——Let me talk to Darren.

Darren couldn't stop the tears any more.

—Why won't yeh pay him? he asked Jimmy Sr.

—Why should I? said Jimmy Sr. —Listen, Darren; he's lookin' for twenty-five quid an' he doesn't even know for definite tha' Leslie broke the window. He only thinks he did.

D'yeh expect me to cough up every time the man thinks Leslie done somethin'?

—All ——all I know is —

—Ah Darren, sorry. But it's a matter o' principle. I can't pay him. It's not the money —

—It is!

—It isn't! ——It's not the money, Darren. Fuck the money. It's the principle o' the thing. If he even said he saw Leslie runnin' away I'd pay him. But Leslie says he didn't do it an', fuck it, I believe him.

Darren's voice hurt Jimmy Sr.

—I'll never get back on the team now.

Jimmy Sr thought about this. Darren was probably right. He didn't know Cantwell but he looked like that sort of a small-minded bollix.

—We'll form our own club.

—Wha'?

—We'll form our own fuckin' club, said Jimmy Sr.

He laughed and rubbed his hands and looked around him, laughing.

—You're messin', said Darren.

—I'm not, Darren, I can assure you. I've been thinkin' that I should get involved in somethin' ——for the kids ——an' the community.

—Oh my God, said Veronica.

—A cyclin' club, Darren. Wha' d'yeh say?

—Are yeh not messin'?

—I'm deadly serious, said Jimmy Sr. —Cross me heart, look it, an' hope to die. You are attendin' the inaugural meetin' of the new cyclin' club.

—Wha'?

—This is the club's first meetin'.

Darren studied his da's face.

—Ahh, rapid!

Jimmy Sr beamed.

—Is tha' alrigh' then? he asked.

—Ah Da; yeah. Fuckin' —sorry —brilliant!

Veronica was pretending to watch Today Tonight.

—Darren's joined a new club, Veronica, Jimmy Sr told her.

—That's nice.

—We'll be wantin' sequins on our jerseys, isn't tha' righ', Darren?

—No way. ——Oh yeah! Yeah.

Darren gasped, keeping the laugh in. Jimmy Sr nudged Darren. Darren nudged Jimmy Sr. Snot burst out of Darren's nose because he was trying not to laugh, but Jimmy Sr didn't mind. His cardigan was due a wash anyway.

Veronica flicked through the channels while the ads were on.

—How's this for a name, Darren? ——The Barrytown Wheelies.

—Brilliant!

Darren couldn't stay sitting any more.

—Better than the oul' Barrytown Cyclin' Club, wha'.

—Ah yeah!

—I'll tell yeh wha'. Go an' see if yeh can get a few o' your chums to join. All o' them. The more the merrier. We'll poach them.

He laughed.

—That'll teach the bollix.

Darren dashed to the door.

—You'll never keep it up, said Veronica.

—Won't I? said Jimmy Sr. —Who says I won't? I'm serious abou' this, yeh know. I've been doin' a lot o' thinkin' these days an', well ——I'm his father an' —

Darren jumped back in.

—Da.

—Yes, Darren?

—Can girls be in the club?

Jimmy Sr looked at Darren. He wanted to give him the right answer. He guessed.

—Yeah ——probably.

—Rapid! Thanks.

Darren was gone again. Jimmy Sr turned back to Veronica.

312

—That's mah boy, he said.

—Are you crying?

—No, I amn't! ——Jaysis! ——It's the smoke.

—What smoke?

—Fuck off an' stop annoyin' me.

*　*　*

Sharon was passing her before she saw her. She'd been too busy thinking about wanting to get out; she felt really squashed in and surrounded and sticky. Then she saw her and before she had time even to say, Jesus, it's her, she said —Hiyeh, Yvonne.

Yvonne Burgess saw who it was. She turned back quickly and continued to flick through the rack of skirts.

Sharon stayed for a second, half deciding to force Yvonne to talk to her.

Yvonne spoke.

—Terrible smell in here, isn't there, Mary?

Sharon then saw that Mary Curran —she hadn't seen her in months —was on the other side of the rack. She wasn't exactly hiding but that was what she was doing all the same.

Mary didn't say anything.

Sharon stood there a bit more, then went on.

She heard Yvonne again, louder.

—They shouldn't let prostitutes in here, sure they shouldn't, Mary?

Sharon grinned.

God help her, she thought. She couldn't blame her really. At least she hadn't tried to beat her up or anything. That Mary one was a right cow though, pretending she hadn't seen her.

Spotty bitch. Even Mister Burgess wouldn't have gone near her.

*　*　*

—What's tha' shite? said Jimmy Sr. —What's tha' under the hedge there? ——A hedgehog, is it? The head on it, wha'.

—It's David Attenborough.

—It looks like a hedgehog, said Jimmy Sr.

313

They laughed.

—It's abou' hedgehogs, said Sharon. —Wildlife On One.

—Ah yeah. Jaysis, look at him! The speed of him. Where's the remote till we hear wha' David's sayin'.

—Oh look it, said Sharon. —There's two o' them now.

Jimmy Jr came in.

—Typical, said Jimmy Sr. —Walkin' in just when the nookie's startin'.

Jimmy Jr sat down, on the other side of Sharon.

—What's thot? he said.

—A hudgehog, said Jimmy Sr. —Two hudgehogs. Roidin'.

—Fuck off.

—Keep your feet up there, Sharon, said Jimmy Sr. —You'll get cramps.

—I'm goin' to the toilet.

—Oh, fair enough. ——So that's how they do it. That's very clever all the same. Off he goes again, look it. Back into the hedge. Didn't even say goodbye or thanks or ann'thin'. That's nature for yeh.

Jimmy Jr was bored. He didn't like nature programmes or things like that. But he wanted to talk to Sharon so he stayed where he was.

Jimmy Sr sniffed.

—Are you wearin' perfume?

—Fuck off.

Sharon came back and sat between the Jimmys.

—Feet up, Sharon, said Jimmy Sr. —That's righ'.

—Come here, said Jimmy Jr.

But Jimmy Sr got to her first.

—Only a few more weeks to go now, wha'.

—Yeah, said Sharon.

—Sharon, said Jimmy Jr.

—Wha'?

—Do us a favour, will yeh.

—I was just lookin' at your, eh, stomach there, Jimmy Sr told Sharon. —It's movin' all over the place.

—Wha'? Sharon asked Jimmy Jr.

—I can't tell yeh here —

—Do you mind! said Jimmy Sr.

—Wha'? said Jimmy Jr.

—I was talkin' to Sharon.

Jimmy Jr leaned out so he could see past Sharon.

—So?

—So fuck off. Go upstairs an' spin your discs.

Sharon was laughing.

Jimmy Sr was looking at his watch. He stood up.

—You've got three minutes, he said. —I'll check an' see if Veronica's fixed Darren's jersey yet.

—Did he crash again?

—No. The fuckin' dog was swingin' off it when it was on the line.

He was gone. Jimmy Jr stood up and shut the door.

—I've a gig in a few weeks; Soturday, he told Sharon.

—Stop talkin' like tha', will yeh.

——I'm tryin' to get used to it.

—It makes yeh sound like a fuckin' eejit.

—Here maybe, but not on the radio, said Jimmy.

—Anywhere, said Sharon.

—The lessons cost me forty fuckin' quid, said Jimmy.

—You were robbed, said Sharon. —Yeh sound like a dope. ——Roight?

—Fuck up a minute. I've a gig on, Soh-Saturday fortnight.

—Wha' gig?

—On the radio, said Jimmy.

She looked as if she didn't believe him.

—The community radio. You know. ——Andy Dudley's garage.

—Tha'!

—Yeah; tha'!

Sharon roared.

—Don't start, said Jimmy. —Wacker Mulcahy —he calls himself Lee Bradley on Saturdays —he has to do best man at his brother's weddin'. So Andy said I can have his slot.

—His wha'?

—His slot.

—That's disgustin'.

—Oh yeah.

They both laughed.

—Annyway, listen.

He switched on his new accent.

—Hoy there, you there, out there. This is Jommy Robbitte, Thot's Rockin' Robbitte, with a big fot hour of the meanest, hottest, baddest sounds arouuund; yeahhh. ——How's tha'?

—Thick.

—Fuckin' thanks.

—No, it's good. Rockin' Rabbitte, I like tha'.

—Do yeh? ——I was thinkin' o' callin' meself Gary ——eh, Gary Breeze.

Sharon had a hankie in her sleeve and she got it to her nose just in time.

—I'll stick to Rockin' Rabbitte, will I? said Jimmy.

He grinned. Sharon nodded.

—Yeah.

Jimmy Sr was back.

—Hop it.

—Righ'. Thanks, Sharon.

Jimmy Jr left.

—Was he annoyin' yeh? said Jimmy Sr.

—Ah no.

—You've enough on your plate withou' that eejit hasslin' yeh. ——Righ'. Annyway, Sharon, what I wanted to say was: how're yeh feelin'?

—Grand.

—You're not nervous or worried or ann'thin'?

—No, she lied. —Not really.

—Three weeks.

—Twenty days.

—That's righ'. ——I've been thinkin' a bit, said Jimmy Sr. —An', well; if yeh want I'll —

The twins charged in, just like the cavalry.

—Daddy, said Linda. —Mister Reeves says you're to hurry

up an' he says if we get you ou' of the house in a minute he'll give us a pound.

Jimmy Sr patted Sharon's leg.

—I'll get back to yeh abou' tha', he said.

—Okay, said Sharon.

About what? she wondered.

—Righ', girls, said Jimmy Sr. —Let's get this pound off o' Bimbo.

That left Sharon alone. She laughed a bit, then closed her eyes.

* * *

She didn't wait at her usual bus-stop, across from work. She kept going, around the corner to the stop with the shelter. There was no one else there.

She couldn't stop crying. She wasn't trying to stop.

She leaned her back against the shelter ad. She gulped, and let herself slide down to the ground. She fell the last bit. She didn't know how she'd get up again. She didn't care.

She gulped, and gulped, and cried.

* * *

Sharon tried to explain it to Veronica.

—I'm sick of it, she said.

She tried harder.

—I hate it, watchin' the oul' ones countin' their twopences out o' their purses an' lookin' at yeh as if you were goin' to rob them. An' listenin' to them complainin' abou' the weather an' the prices o' things.

Her mother was still looking hard.

—And anyway, said Sharon. —Me back's really killin' me these days an' I'm always wantin' to go to the toilet an' —

She was crying.

—tha' bastard Moloney is always houndin' me. He's only a shelf stacker in a suit, an' Gerry Dempsey —prick! —he put his arm round me. In front of everyone, an' he said to give

317

him a shout if I was havin' anny more babies. ——An' I'm
sick of it an' I'm not goin' back. I don't care!

Veronica wanted to go around to Sharon and hold her
but —

—Sharon, love, she said. —A job's a job. Could you not
wait —

—I don't care, I'm not goin'. You can't make me.

Veronica let it go.

—You'd love to make me go back, wouldn't yeh? said
Sharon. —Well, I'm not goin' to. I don't care. ——All you
care abou' is the money.

Veronica got out of the kitchen. She sat on the bed in her
room.

* * *

—Yeh did righ', Sharon, said Jimmy Sr.

—Yeah ——well —

—No; you were dead righ'.

—It was just —Sharon started; then stopped.

—I shouldn't have paid any attention to them, she said.
—I'd only the rest of the week to go anyway. I'll go back
tomorrow an' —

—You won't, said Jimmy Sr. —If yeh don't want to.

—Sure, me maternity leave; I've three months off after
Saturday annyway.

—Well, you've the rest o' your life off if yeh want it, wha'.

—Wha' abou' Mammy?

—Your mammy's grand, said Jimmy Sr. —She doesn't
want you to go back there if you don't want to either. She was
just a bit worried abou' you havin' no job after you have the
baby ——but —She's grand. She doesn't want you to go in
an' be treated like tha' ——by thicks.

—Ah —said Sharon.

She'd been thinking about it.

—They ARE fuckin' thick, she said. —If he'd said it —half
an hour earlier even I'd've told him to feck off or I'd've

laughed or —But when he said it ——an' they all started laughin', I just —If he said it now ——

—We'd feed the bits of him to the dog, wha'.

—Yeah.

—You're not goin' back so.

It was sort of a question.

—No.

—Good.

—I'd like to go back just ——An' walk ou' properly, yeh know?

—I do, yeah. ——The lady o' leisure, wha'.

—Yeah.

—Wish I was.

* * *

—Ah fuck this, said Jimmy Sr.

He let go of the lawn-mower. He looked at his palms. He was sure he'd ripped the skin off them. But, no, it was still there, and a bit redder but alright. That meant he'd have to keep going.

—Fuck it, he said.

Jimmy Sr was cutting the grass, the front. Last night Bimbo had called Jimmy Sr's house Vietnam because of the state of the front garden. Jimmy Sr had laughed. But when Bimbo told him that everyone called it that Jimmy Sr'd said, Enough; fuck it, he'd cut the grass tomorrow, the cunts.

—Give us a lend o' your lawn-mower, Bimbo, he'd said.

—No way, Bimbo'd said.

—Ah go on, he'd said, —for fuck sake. I'll give it back to yeh this time.

—Okay, Bimbo'd said.

—Good man, he'd said.

So here he was trying to cut the grass. In November.

—Fuck Bimbo, he said to himself.

The grass was too long for the mower. And it was damp, so the mower kept skidding. He'd have to get the shears to it first. Bimbo'd insisted that he take the shears as well when he'd called for the mower. That was why he said Fuck Bimbo.

He'd have to get down on his hunkers now. But it had to be done.

He was a changed man, a new man. That trouble a while back with Sharon had given him an awful fright and, more important, it had made him feel like a right useless oul' bollix. He'd done a lot of thinking since then. And a lot of reading, and looking at pictures. Those little foetuses all curled up ——with their fingers, and the lot.

There was more to life than drinking pints with your mates. There was Veronica, his wife, and his children. Some of his own sperms had gone into making them so, fuck it, he was responsible for them. But, my Jaysis, he'd made one poxy job of it so far. Bimbo'd said he was being too hard on himself; his kids were grand, but Jimmy Sr'd said that that was just good luck and Veronica because he'd had nothing to do with it. But from now on it was going to be different. Darren and Linda and Tracy, and even Leslie, were still young enough, and then there'd be Sharon's little snapper as well. A strong active man in the house, a father figure, would be vital for Sharon's snapper.

—Vital, Bimbo. Vital.

—Oh God, yes, Bimbo'd agreed.

So cutting the grass was important. The new short grass would be a sort of announcement: there's a new man living in this house, so fuck off and mind your own business.

Jimmy Sr looked at the garden. For a small garden it grew a terrible lot of grass. The Corporation should have cut it; he'd always said it. But they were useless.

It was up to him.

He chose a spot to put his knees. It looked soft.

There was a problem but. Any minute now Darren would come flying around the corner, down the road and past the house and he'd be expecting Jimmy Sr to shout out how long the lap had taken him. Because, as well as cutting the grass, Jimmy Sr was training the Barrytown Wheelies Under 14 squad; Darren and three of his pals. They had a team time trial at the weekend and Darren had said that they'd have to be ready and Jimmy Sr agreed with him. So he had them doing laps of the estate, and he was pretending to time them. He was only pretending because he couldn't get the hang of the stop-watch Bertie'd got him. He couldn't admit this to the team because it would've been bad for morale. The last thing a new, breakaway, very keen team needed to know was that their manager couldn't operate the stop-watch.

He'd wait till they cycled past, then he'd do a few minutes shearing and he'd be waiting for them when they came around again.

He leaned on the wall and held the stop-watch ready. It looked like an easy enough yoke to use. He was sure it was. He'd bring it up to the Hikers and see if one of the lads could figure it out.

—How's it goin', Mister Rabbitte?

Jimmy Sr looked. It was one of Jimmy Jr's pals, Mickah Wallace.

—Howyeh, Mick, said Jimmy Sr. —He's upstairs doin' his DJin'. Or shavin' his legs or somethin'. No fear of him givin' me a hand here an' annyway, that's for fuckin' certain.

—Wha'; holdin' the wall up?

—Wha' ——No. No; I'm cuttin' the grass. Hang on, here they come.

Darren was first. He came out of Chestnut Drive onto Chestnut Avenue. He was slowing but he still had to go up on the far path to get a wide enough angle to turn. Then he was through two parked cars, back onto the road and across to the proper side and towards Jimmy Sr and Mickah, picking up speed again. Two more followed Darren across the road, onto the path. One of them got too close to the wall and must have scraped his knee. The last lad was on an ordinary bike, the poor little sap. No gears or nothing. Jimmy Sr would've loved to have got him a proper bike, if he'd had the money. But he didn't have it. And anyway, he was the manager. He had to be ruthless. If he didn't have gears he'd just have to pedal faster. He was part of a team.

Darren raced past him. Jimmy Sr stared at the stop-watch. He pressed one of the black twirly knobs at the top.

He roared.

—Thirteen seconds faster! Good man, Darren!

But Darren was gone.

—Thirteen seconds up, lads! Good lads!

Mickah admired their yellow jerseys. They had The Hiker's Rest —Pub Grub printed across the backs.

The last one, Eric Rickard, was suffering.

—Come on, Paddy Last, Jimmy Sr roared as Eric came up to them. —Catch up with him. Come on.

His face was white. His legs weren't really long enough for the bike. He had to shift from side to side as he pedalled. The bollix must've been torn off him.

But he was pedalling away like bejaysis.

—Good lad, good man, good man. ——Poor little fucker.

Mickah was laughing. He'd enjoyed all that.

—The hurlin' helmets look deadly, he said.

—Yeah, said Jimmy Sr. —Your man, the Hikers' manager, bought them for us as well. One for me even as well.

—Fair play. Jimmy's inside an' anyway?

—Yeah. Spinnin' the discs.

Jimmy Sr looked down at the grass.

—Fuckin' hell.

He was bending his knees experimentally.

—Wish I was younger.

Mickah was still there.

—A good bit younger, said Mickah.

—Fuck off, you, said Jimmy Sr. —He's up in his room. Go on ahead in.

Jimmy Sr got down on his knees.

—Oh, bollix to it.

Mickah stood there with his hands in his pockets, his head tilted a bit to one side.

—Wha'? said Jimmy Sr.

—Just lookin'.

—Are you actin' the prick?

322

—No! No; it's just I've never seen yeh doin' annythin' before, yeh know. Can I watch?

—Fuck off ou' o' tha'. It's hard enough without havin' bollixes like you gawkin' at —

—Watch ou'!

Darren was coming.

Jimmy Sr got up and ran to the wall.

—Seven seconds down, Darren! Seven seconds! Come on now. —Come on, lads; yis're laggin' behind. Nine seconds down. Come on now. Good lads. One last drive. Come on.

There was no sign of Eric. Jimmy Sr turned back to Mickah.

—Tha' was close.

Mickah ran around Jimmy Sr and ducked in behind the wall. Jimmy Sr looked around, and saw George Burgess coming down his path to the gate.

Then Mickah started singing.

—OH ——TIE A YELLOW RIBBON —

ROUND THE OLD OAK TREE —

George looked over at Jimmy Sr.

—Don't look at me, Burgess!

—IT'S BEEN THREE LONG YEARS —

DO YEH STILL WANT ME —

DA RAH DA RAH—

Jimmy Sr held up the shears.

—Yeh know wha' I'd like to do with these, Burgess, don't yeh?

—Go on, Mister Rabbitte, said Mickah, still crouched behind the wall. —Have him ou'. Go on. I'll back yeh up.

Eric cycled by.

—Good man, Eric! Good man, son. One more now, one more, then we'll call it a day. Good lad. ——Hope he doesn't die on us.

George kept walking. He didn't look back. Mickah stood up. They both looked at George walking down Chestnut Avenue.

—You SHOULD knock the shite ou' of him though, Mickah told Jimmy Sr.

—Why? said Jimmy Sr. —He didn't do annythin' to me.

Mickah thought about this. He studied Jimmy Sr carefully.

—Maybe he didn't, he said. —But yeh should still give him a hidin'.

—Why?

—Cos you'd beat him.

Jimmy Sr got down on his knees at the edge of the grass.

—That's why I couldn't be bothered, he said. —Jaysis, look it!

—Wha'?

Jimmy Sr held up a well mauled and weathered ten pound note.

—Nice one, said Mickah.

—It was in the grass, said Jimmy Sr. —Just there. That's gas.

He stood up.

—What're yeh goin' to do with it? Mickah asked him.

—Well, said Jimmy Sr. —I'm goin' to give five of it to Leslie. After he's cut this fuckin' grass.

—Good thinkin', said Mickah.

—An' maybe a nice set o' handlebars for poor Eric.

—Ah, said Mickah. —Nice one.

* * *

Sharon got Linda to open the window a bit before she went down for her breakfast. Now she was alone in the bedroom. She sat up against all the pillows, and listened. The room was at the back of the house but she could still hear enough. She'd heard about five cars starting, including her daddy's —it always coughed before it got going. She could hear kids shouting, going into the school. She heard a front door slamming, and back ones —the sound was different. But best of all was the clicking of heels. That meant girls dashing to work, and she wasn't one of them.

It was brilliant. She'd been doing this every morning since she'd given up work.

She didn't care much about the money. The pay had been useless anyway. She'd be getting her allowance after the baby was born and her daddy was going to give her some money every week, once he'd sorted it out with her mammy. She'd only have to stay in the house a bit more often and she'd be doing that anyway because of the baby. So it was great.

Her back wasn't hurting her that much. The baby's head had settled and sometimes it felt like she wasn't pregnant any more. But never for long. She was dry and clean. She was nice and tired. She wanted to go to the toilet but not enough yet to get up. She was going to read a bit of her book, Lace II —it was a bit thick but she liked it and she liked being able to get through the pages fast. Then she'd go down and have her breakfast. She'd see if she could get her mammy to come out for a walk or something. She'd watch a bit of telly as well; there'd be videos on Sky and Super.

She couldn't make her mind up about the name. Fiona or Lorraine; she liked them. Mark, if it was a boy. Or maybe James. Her daddy would love that. But then he might take over the baby, the way he was these days. And there'd be three Jimmys in the house. She didn't know.

It had gone quiet outside. There were no cars. Everyone was gone.

Her belly button was like a real button now; inside out. She didn't like it that way. It felt dangerous.

She heard something; someone was running and wheezing, and the steps weren't very fast. The wheezing must have been really bad if she could hear it from the back of the house. And now it was raining again. She hoped it was Mister Burgess out there. Not really though.

It was nice.

But she still couldn't stop worrying. It could happen any time. She was having these —painless contractions the book called them —all the time, now and again, but they weren't really painless at all because they made her really nervous because the next one might be painful, and she waited and waited for the next one until she ached.

She got up. She wanted to be in the kitchen.

* * *

—Oh Jesus! said Sharon.

—What's wrong? said Jimmy Sr.

He jumped up off the couch.

—Is it comin', is it?

—No, said Sharon.

She shifted, to get the cushions behind her again.

—Sorry. I was just fallin' asleep an' I didn't know it, em —Sorry.

Jimmy Sr looked disappointed. He sat down, but he was ready to get up again.

—Yeh can't be too careful abou' this sort o' thing, he said.

Veronica climbed out of the armchair and stood up.

—We don't want you bursting your waters all over the furniture, isn't that right, Jimmy dear? They're new covers.

She went out, into the kitchen.

Jimmy Sr sat there, appalled. That was the dirtiest, foulest thing he'd heard in his life. And his wife had said it!

Sharon was laughing.

—Jaysis, Sharon, I'm sorry, said Jimmy Sr. —Tha' was a terrible thing for Veronica to say. Terrible.

—Ah, stop it, said Sharon. —She was only jokin'.

—No, no, said Jimmy Sr. —There's jokin' an' jokin' but tha' was no fuckin' joke. I'm just glad the twins weren't here to hear it.

—Ah Daddy!

—No, Sharon, Jimmy Sr insisted. —This is no laughin' matter.

He pointed at Sharon's belly.

—Do yeh not realize tha' there's a livin' bein' in there? he said. —A livin' ——thing.

—Ah, feck off, Daddy. Cop on.

—Don't start tha' raisin' your eyes to heaven shite with me. An' don't start chewin' tha' fuckin' celery when I'm talkin' to yeh.

Sharon tapped Jimmy Sr on the head with her celery.

—Yes, Daddy.

She gulped.

—The livin' bein' in here is givin' me terrible fuckin' indigestion, she said.

—That's cos your stomach's flattened, Jimmy Sr told her. —Yeh prob'ly ate too much.

—I didn't.

—Yeh should only eat small amounts.

—Ah, shag off.

—It looks like there's only one person takin' this thing seriously, an' that's me.

—Excuse me! said Sharon. —I am takin' it seriously. I'm the one carryin' it around with me all the time.

—You're gettin' snotty now cos o' your hormones, Jimmy Sr told her. —I'll talk to yeh later.

Sharon laughed at this.

—There's nothin' wrong with my hormones.

—I didn't say there was annythin' wrong with them, said Jimmy Sr. —No, there's nothin' wrong. As such. Wrong's the wrong word. Imbalance is the term I'd use.

—Thanks very much, Doctor Rabbitte.

—Fuck off.

Then he grinned. Then he stopped grinning, and coughed.

—When, he said. —When your mammy ——Times have changed, d'yeh know tha'?

Sharon smiled.

—When your mammy was havin' Jimmy I was in work. An' when she was havin' you I was in me mother's. When she had Leslie I was inside in town, in Conways, yeh know, with the lads. The Hikers wasn't built then. For Darren, I was —I can't remember. The twins, I was in the Hikers.

—You've a great memory.

—Nowadays the husbands are there with the women, said Jimmy Sr. —That's much better, I think. I'd ——

He scratched his leg.

—Because he can hold her hand an' help her, an' encourage her, yeh know, an' see his child bein' born.

There wasn't even a car going past. The pipes upstairs weren't making any noise.

—Sharon, I'll —Only if yeh want now ——I wouldn't mind stayin' with you when ——you're havin' it.

—Ah no.

——Okay.

* * *

—Stop pushin' her, will yeh!

Sharon and Jackie were in Howth, on stools at the bar. It was busy and getting busier.

—I'm tryin' to get tha' prick of a barman to serve me, said the young fella in the black polo neck and glowing dandruff who'd pushed Sharon's back. He was wedged between Sharon and one of the poles that held up the ceiling, on his toes and clicking his fingers.

—Look at her condition, will yeh, said Jackie.

He did, still clicking his fingers.

—She doesn't look tha' bad, he said.

—She's pregnant, yeh fuckin' sap.

—Fuck, sorry!

—Yeah; so yeh should be. ——I'll get the barman for yeh. Raymond!

Raymond was there before she'd finished calling him.

—Yeah?

—He wants yeh.

—Oh. ——Yeah?

—He fancies yeh, said Sharon.

—I know, said Jackie. —He nearly dribbles all over me. Did yeh see him there? His fuckin' tongue was hangin' ou'.

She copied Raymond.

—Yeah? Yeah? Yeah?

Sharon laughed.

—Ah stop. He's not tha' bad.

—I suppose he isn't. He's still a spa though.

Sharon laughed again.

—You're a terrible fuckin' wagon, Jackie. ——I'm pissed.

—So am I, said Jackie. —Raymond!

—Yeah?

—Same again, chicken.

—Yeah.

He ran over to the optics.

—Yeah, said Jackie.

She lifted herself up a bit so she could see all of Raymond.

—He's got a nice arse on him all the same.

She sat down again.

—Pity abou' the rest of him.

—I'm pissed, Jackie, said Sharon.

—So am I, said Jackie.

Sharon looked down.

—I shouldn't be doin' this.

—Wha'?

—Drinkin'.

—Ah, don't be thick, Sharon. Yeh need to get pissed now an' again. There's no harm in it.

—Yeah, said Sharon.

She tried to sit up.

—Thank you, Raymond, said Jackie. —You're the best little barman in the world.

—An' the best lookin', said Sharon.

—Oh def'ny, said Jackie.

Raymond grinned and blushed and dropped tenpence into Jackie's glass, and decided not to try and get it out after he'd already put two of his fingers into the vodka.

—I want another one, said Jackie. —I'm not takin' tha'.

—Okay, said Raymond. —Sorry abou' tha'.

He went over to the optics, got the tenpence out, filled a new glass, but left it on the counter and brought Jackie back her old one.

—There, he said.

—Thank you, Raymond. I'll have my change now. If you don't mind.

—Oh yeah.

Sharon couldn't stop laughing. Her hand shook when she poured the Coke in on top of the vodka.

—Thank you very much, Raymond, said Jackie when

Raymond came back with the tenpence. —Better late than never.

Sharon pushed the tears off her nose.

—Is me mascara alrigh'? she asked.

—Ah yeah, said Jackie. —Yeh'd want to be lookin'.

—Me back's fuckin' killin' me. We shouldn't've sitten here. I need somethin' to lean against.

—The pole, said Jackie.

—Yeah, said Sharon.

She came down off her stool.

—Jesus! ——God, I'm pissed, d'yeh know tha'.

She straightened up.

—Jesus.

She picked up the stool.

—'Xcuse me. Out o' me way.

She shoved the stool between the bar and a man who was waiting at it, and reached the pole. Jackie followed her. They got back onto the stools. Sharon leaned back. The pole was cold through her clothes.

—That's lovely.

—What're YOU lookin' at? Jackie asked a spotty young fella.

—Nothin'!

—Better not be. ——Where's me drink? Jesus, I'm finished already.

—My turn, said Sharon.

She knocked back the rest of hers.

—You call him, okay? she said to Jackie.

—Raymond!

—Same again?

—Yeah, said Jackie. —Yeah.

—Oh fuh-fuck, said Sharon. —I've got the hic-coughs.

She put her hand on her chest, to feel for any approaching hiccups.

—Jesus, I'm scuttered. ——They're gone.

—Wha'?

—The hi-hi —Fuck it, they're back.

There was a new song on the jukebox.

330

—Oh, I love this one, said Jackie.

—Yeah, said Sharon. —He's a ride, isn't he?

—He is, yeah, said Jackie. —A riyed! I'd love to dig me nails —

—Talkin' abou' rides, lo-look who's behind yeh, Jackie. Don't turn.

But she'd turned already.

—Where?

—There.

—Where!

—There. Look it, yeh blind bitch. Beside your woman.

—Who is it? ——Oh Jesus Christ!

It was Greg, Jackie's ex, the fella she'd blown out in the ILAC Centre because the cream in his eclair had gone missing.

Jackie turned back and faced the bar.

—Is he lookin' this way?

—Yeah, said Sharon. —He's seen yeh. Oh Jesus, he's comin' over, Jackie.

—I won't talk to him, I don't care. I fuckin' won't.

—He's takin' somethin' ou' of his trousers. Oh my God, Jackie!

Jackie had copped on by now. She turned and saw the back of Greg's head way over on the other side of the lounge.

—You're a fuckin' cunt, Rabbitte.

She hoped she hadn't sounded too disappointed. She laughed with Sharon, just in case.

—I think I'm goin' to be sick, said Sharon.

Her face was really white.

—Oh Jesus, said Jackie. —Come on.

She slid off her stool.

Sharon shook her head.

—I won't make it.

She grabbed her bag from the counter. She unclasped and opened it quickly. It wasn't a big bag but she got as much of her head as she could into it; her chin, her mouth and her nose. Then she puked. It was a quick rush of vodka and Coke and a few little things. Then up with her head and she shut the bag.

Jackie gave her a paper hankie. She wiped her mouth and opened the bag a bit and threw the tissue in on top of the vodka and the rest. She held the bag up.

—It should hold, she said. —I'll bring it ou' and empty it in a minute.

They both laughed. Sharon felt much better already. She gave herself a test burp: grand; there was no taste off it or anything.

—Did annyone see me? she said.

—Yeah, said Jackie. —I think so. Your man there, look. He was lookin' at yeh.

—Him? Specky Features? I wouldn't mind him.

—You were very fast, said Jackie.

—There wasn't tha' much, said Sharon.

They drank to it. The vodka put up no fight going down. Sharon relaxed. She dropped the bag onto the floor.

—Squelch, said Jackie.

—I'm fuckin' pissed.

—Hiyis.

Mary Curran was standing between them.

—Mary! said Jackie. —Howyeh.

—Hiyis, said Mary. —Haven't seen yis in ages.

—Yeh saw me a few weeks ago, said Sharon.

—When, Sharon?

—You know fuckin' well when, Mary. In Dunnes with Yvonne.

—I didn't see yeh, Sharon.

—Yeh did so.

—I didn't Sharon; when?

—Ah, who cares when? said Jackie. —Yeh see each other now, don't yis?

—Yeah —— Well —

—Jesus, Sharon, sorry.

—Yeah. —— Sorry for shoutin' at yeh.

—Your hair's lovely, Mary, said Jackie.

—Yeah, said Sharon.

—Thanks. How are yeh, Sharon, an' annyway?

—Alrigh', said Sharon. —Grand.

—She's pissed, said Jackie.

—Fuck off, you. I am not.

—You look fabulous, Mary told Sharon.

—Thanks.

—When're yeh due?

—Monday.

—Jesus, that's brilliant.

—But it'll be late prob'ly.

—Yeh must be thrilled, are yeh?

—Ah yeah.

They were struggling, but they tried.

—Who're yeh with, Mary? said Sharon.

—A fella.

—Who?

—You know him, Jackie. Greg.

Sharon looked at Jackie.

—Does he still like eclairs? said Jackie.

—Pardon?

—Nothin'. Tell him I was askin' for him, will yeh.

—Yeah. ——I'd better go back.

—Yeah. See yeh, Mary.

—See yeh, Jackie. See yeh, Sharon. I'll come in to see yeh when you're in the hospital.

—Thanks. See yeh.

—See yeh, Mary. Bye bye. ——Yeh fuckin' cow yeh. She's a titless bitch, isn't she?

They laughed.

—I never liked her, said Jackie.

—Jesus, I'm pissed.

—My turn, said Jackie. —Raymond!

—Yeah? Same again?

—S'il vous plait.

—Yeah.

—Yeah. ——Wha' did yeh think of her fuckin' hair?

Sharon slid off the stool, and nearly fell.

—I'm goin' home, she said.

333

—Are yeh alrigh'?
—Yeah, I think —I'd better go home.
Jackie picked up their bags.
—Come on, she said.

* * *

She was afraid to close her eyes. She didn't want to get sick
again. She was glad she was home. She wouldn't go out again,
even if the baby was weeks late.

Even in the taxi, before it moved even, she knew that
nothing was going to happen. But she didn't tell Jackie that.
She just wanted to get home. She'd sort of panicked; thought
she'd felt something, a real contraction or something, and the
heat and the smoke and the crowds got to her and she had to
get out of the pub and come home. She'd been sick twice since
she got home but she wasn't going to be again. As well as that
though, she'd wanted to go to the toilet really badly, like she
had the runs, but she hadn't gone nearly as much as she
thought she'd needed to but she still felt like she wanted to go,
and that was supposed to be a sign that the labour would be
starting soon, so it was just as well that she was here at home.

Could it start when you were asleep? she wondered. She'd
wake up. Wouldn't she? Anyway, she didn't think she'd be
able to sleep. She was terrified.

She'd felt better the minute she got into the taxi. The driver
had been nice, telling them he was going to charge them for
three because of the size of Sharon. And Jackie told him to
hurry up or he'd be charging for three alright, and paying for
the cleaning. It'd been nice. And then when Sharon opened
her bag to pay him!

She wished she'd someone to talk to.

It was going to hurt. Jesus, it was like waiting to be stabbed,
knowing for definite you were going to be, but not when,
only soon. It wasn't fair. It was cruel. She'd never do this to
anyone.

* * *

334

—They're a bit smelly, Jimmy Sr admitted. —But they're not
too bad.

He threw the jerseys on the floor.

—Are yeh alrigh', Sharon?

—Yeah.

—Sure?

—Yeah!

—Are yeh constipated at all?

—Lay off, Daddy, will yeh.

—Fair enough. I was only askin'.

—Well, don't.

———Tea, said Jimmy Sr.

He went over to the kettle and looked at it.

—You get the water from the tap, said Veronica, who'd just
come in.

—Ha ha, said Jimmy Sr.

He put the kettle under the tap, and sang.

—OH YEH–HESS —

I'M THE GREAT PRE–TE–HENDER —

DO DOO —DO DOO —DO —

The twins came barging in the back door. They had their
dancing dresses on under their anoraks.

—There's the girls, said Jimmy Sr. —How 'd yis get on,
girls?

—We didn't come last, Tracy told them.

—Course yeh didn't, said Jimmy Sr. —We didn't either.
Darren, eh, acquitted himself very well. An' buckled his
wheel.

—Teresa Kelly's shoe broke an' she fell, said Linda.

—Yeah, said Tracy. —An' she said somethin' rude an' they
disqualified her.

—Yeah, an' her ma dragged her —

—Mammy!

—Her mammy dragged her ou' an' yeh could hear her dress
rippin'.

Jimmy Sr laughed. He switched the kettle on.

—There. ——Poor Teresa.

—We hate her, said Linda.

—Course yeh do, said Jimmy Sr. —When's the big one? Next week, is it?

—Yeah.

—We'll all have to go to tha'.

—You're not to, said Linda. —Only if yeh want to.

—You can hold our coats an' our handbags, said Tracy.

—Thanks very much, said Jimmy Sr.

—What handbags? said Veronica.

—Missis McPartland says we've to have —

—No!

—Ah now, Veronica, said Jimmy Sr. —Maybe Santy'll come a bit early.

—Ah, no way, said Linda. —I don't want a handbag from Santy.

—We'll see wha' happens.

Sharon had gone upstairs for her radio. She had it ready.

—Listen, she said.

She turned it on. Alexander O'Neal was singing Fake.

—Wha'? said Jimmy Sr.

—Shut up an' listen a minute, said Sharon.

Fake was ending. Then they heard him.

—THOT WAS OLEXONDER O'NEAL WITH FAKE. THERE'S NOTHIN' FAKE ABOUT THIS ONE. HERE'S THE GODFATHER OF SOUL. ———JAMES BROWN, YIS SIMPLEHEADS YIS.

James Brown sang Living in America. Sharon turned it down.

—Was tha' Jimmy? said Jimmy Sr.

—Yeah, said Sharon.

—Was it, Sharon? said Tracy.

—Yeah.

—Janey.

—Jimmy on the radio.

—Wha' station is it? Jimmy Sr asked.

—Radio 2, Sharon lied.

—Go 'way. Jimmy?

—Yeah. He's fillin' in for someone on their holidays.

336

—Go 'way. ——Jimmy, wha'. Turn it up.

He listened to James Brown.

—We're some family all the same, wha'.

He smiled at Veronica, and nodded at the radio.

—Cyclin', ——dancin', DJin on the radio. Havin' babies. ——Y'alrigh', Sharon?

—Yeah ——

She looked shocked, and scared.

——I think I'm startin'.

—Sure?

—Yeah. ——Yeah.

—Up yeh go, girls, an' get Sharon's bag for her, said Jimmy Sr.

—Are yeh havin' the baby, Sharon?

—Get up!

—And —Ah! —an' me toothbrush, Tracy.

—ROIGHT. ROCKIN' ROBBITTE COMIN' AT YOUUU, FILLIN' IN FOR LEE BRADLEY. HOW'S YOUR WEEKEND GOIN'? ——TOUGH.

—We're some family alrigh', said Jimmy Sr.

He grinned at Sharon.

—Come on, Sharon.

—THIS ONE'S FOR ANTO AN' GILLIAN WHO WERE SNARED BEHIND THE CLINIC LAST NIGHT BY FATHER MOLLOY. YEOW, ANTO!

Jimmy Sr was out starting the car, so he didn't hear that bit.

* * *

—The lights are turnin' green for us, look it, said Jimmy Sr.

—Yeah.

—That's the second one. Must be a good sign, wha'.

—Yeah.

—Soon be over.

—Yeah.

—Don't worry, love. ——God, wait'll yeh have it in your arms, wha'. Jaysis, women have all the luck. ——Y'alrigh'?

—Yeah.

—Good girl. Don't hold the handle so tight there, Sharon. You might fall ou'.

—Sorry.

—No problem. ——Shite; they've turned red up here. Can't expect them all to be green, I suppose.

He slowed the car, then gripped Sharon's hand.

—Good girl. It's only the oul' cervix dilatin'. ——It could happen to a bishop, wha'.

He got the car going again.

—Here, Sharon. Look it; here's me watch. Yeh can time the contractions so you'll be able to tell them when we get there. They'll be impressed. ——Oh, God help yeh. Sit back, Sharon, good girl. Take deep breaths, good girl. Good deep breaths. That's wha' I always do, wha'.

He was going to turn on the radio.

—Let's listen to Jimmy.

—He'd be over by now.

—Ah well. He was very good, wasn't he? ——Did yeh time tha' one, Sharon?

—Ye-yeah. ——Thirty-seven seconds, ——abou'.

—That's grand, said Jimmy Sr. —Nearly there now. Summerhill, look it. Straight down now an' we're there. Green again up here, look it.

—Yeah.

—That's great. Is it God or the Corporation, would yeh say?

——————

—Tha' place has changed its name again, look it. ——Good girl, sit back. Good girl. Deep breaths. ——Get ou' of me way, yeh fuckin' ——! Gobshite; I should have run over him. The thick head on him, did yeh see it? Good girl. ——Here we are, Sharon, look.

* * *

The nurse, the nice one, wiped Sharon's face.

—Th-thanks. ——Will it hurt anny more?

—Not really, love. We're nearly there now.

—How long more —

—Quiet, Sharon. Come on; breathe with me. ——In ——

338

The breath became a gasp and a scream as Sharon let go of
it.
—No, Sharon. Don't push! ——It's too early; don't —
She wiped Sharon's face.
—Don't push yet, Sharon.
Sharon gasped again.
—When!?
—In a little while. ——In ——Out ——
Sharon had to scream again, and gulp back air.
—It —it hurt more.
—Not much.
—Yes, much! Jeeesus!

*   *   *

They were all in the hall, watching Veronica, waiting. She was
taking ages.
—Ah no, she said. ——Ah no; the poor thing.
She wouldn't look at them.
—Is she alright? ——Will you come home now? ——Get a
taxi, Jimmy. You must be exhausted. ——That's terrible.
——Okay. In a while. Bye bye, love.
She put the phone down, and turned to them.
—A girl, she said.
—Yeow!
—Alive? said Darren.
He was crying.
—Yes!
—I thought —The way you were talkin' —
He started laughing.
The twins hugged Darren and Jimmy Jr and Veronica and
Larrygogan. Les was out.
—What'll we call her? said Linda.
Veronica laughed.
—Hey, Larrygogan, said Tracy. —We've a new sister.
—She's not your sister, said Jimmy.
—Why?
—You're her auntie, he told her.

339

—Am I? Janey!

—So am I then, said Linda.

—That's righ', said Jimmy.

—I'm tellin' Nicola 'Malley, said Linda. —She thinks she's great just cos her ma lets her bring her sister to the shops. ——Come on, Tracy.

They were gone.

—Well, Darren, said Veronica. —Do you like being an uncle?

—Ah yeah, said Darren. —It's brilliant.

* * *

Sharon was able to look at her in the crib there without having to lift her head. That was nice.

There she was, asleep; red, blotched, shrivelled and gorgeous; all wrapped up. Tiny. And about as Spanish looking as —

She didn't care.

She was gorgeous. And hers.

She was fuckin' gorgeous.

Georgina; that was what she was going to call her.

They'd all call her Gina, but Sharon would call her George. And they'd have to call her George as well. She'd make them.

—Are yeh alrigh', love?

It was the woman in the bed beside Sharon.

—Yeah, said Sharon. —Thanks; I'm grand.

She lifted her hand —it weighed a ton —and wiped her eyes.

—Ah, said the woman. —Were yeh cryin'?

—No, said Sharon. —I was laughin'.

* * *

340

THE VAN

This book is dedicated to

John Sutton

Thanks to
Brian McGinn and Will Moore
for their help, advice and recipe for batter

Acknowledgments

Let's Twist Again (Mann/Appell) used by permission of Carlin Music Corporation, Iron Bridge House, 3 Bridge Approach, London NW1 8BD. *Barbara Ann* (Fassert) © Warner Chappell Music Ltd. Reproduced by permission. *Hippy Hippy Shake* (Chan Romero) © 1959, Jonware Music Corp, USA. Reproduced by permission of Ardmore and Beechwood Ltd, London WC2H OEA. *California Girls* (Brian Wilson) © Irving Music Inc. Used by permission of Rondor Music (London) Ltd. *Give It a Lash, Jack* used by permission of GOAL.

Jimmy Rabbitte Sr had the kitchen to himself. He felt a draught and looked up and Darren, one of his sons, was at the door, looking for somewhere to do his homework.

—Oh—, said Darren, and he turned to go back into the hall.

—D'yeh need the table, Darren? said Jimmy Sr.

—Eh —

—No, come on. Fire away.

Jimmy Sr stood up. His arse had gone numb on him.

—Jesus —!

He straightened up and grinned at Darren.

—I'll go somewhere else, he said.

—Thanks, said Darren.

—Not at all, said Jimmy Sr.

Jimmy Sr left Darren in the kitchen and went out to the front step and sat on it. Christ, the step was cold; he'd end up with piles or the flu or something. But there was nowhere else to go until after the dinner. All the rooms in the house were occupied. He rubbed his hands; it wasn't too bad. He tried to finish the article in the Press he'd been reading, about how people suffered after they got out of jail, with photographs of the Guildford Four.

A car went by. Jimmy Sr didn't know the driver. The sun was down the road now, going behind the school gym. He put the paper down beside him on the step and then he put his hands in under the sleeves of his jumper.

He was tempted to have a bash at the garden but the grass

was nearly all gone, he'd been cutting it so often. He'd have looked like a right gobshite bringing the lawn-mower for a walk around a baldy garden, in the middle of November. There were weeds in under the hedge, but they could stay there. Anyway, he liked them; they made the garden look more natural. He'd painted the gate and the railings a few months back; red, and a bit of white, the Liverpool colours, but Darren didn't seem to care about that sort of thing any more.

—Look, Darren. Your colours.

——Oh yeah.

Jimmy Sr'd noticed small patches where some dust and bits of stuff had got stuck to the wet paint. He'd go over it again, but not today. It was a bit late.

The car went by again, the other way this time. He got a better look at the driver but he still didn't know him. He looked as if he was searching for a house he didn't know. He was only looking at the even numbers across the way. He might have been the police. That would've been good, watching the guards going in and arresting Frano Traynor again. It had been great gas the last time they'd done it, especially when Chrissie, Frano's mot, started flinging toys down at them from the bedroom window and she hit Frano with Barbie's Ferrari.

—Jesus; sorry, love!

—You're alrigh', said Frano back, searching his hair for blood.

That would have killed the time till the dinner.

But the car was gone.

There was nothing else happening, no kids on the street even. He could hear some though, around the corner, and a Mr Whippy van, but it sounded a good bit away, maybe not even in Barrytown. He took his change out of his pocket and counted it: a pound and sevenpence. He looked at his watch; the dinner'd be ready soon.

* * *

348

Darren read the question he'd just written at the top of his page.

—Complexity of thought and novelty in the use of language sometimes create an apparent obscurity in the poetry of Gerard Manley Hopkins. Discuss this view, supporting the points you make by quotations from or references to the poems by Hopkins on your course.

Then he tore out the page and wrote the question out again, in red. He read it again.

Starting was the hard bit. He brought the poetry book in closer to him. He wrote Complexity, Language and Obscurity in the margin.

He could never start questions, even in tests; he'd sit there till the teacher said Ten minutes left and then he'd fly. And he always did alright. It was still a bit of a fuckin' drag though, starting.

He read the question again.

His ma would come in to make the dinner in a minute and then he'd have to find somewhere else.

He read one of the poems, That Nature is a Heraclitean Fire.

Darren didn't know when Tippex had been invented but Gerrah Manley Hopkins had definitely been sniffing something. He couldn't write that in his answer though.

Down to business.

—Right, he whispered. —Come on. Complexity.

He started.

—In my opinion the work of the poet and priest —

He crossed out And Priest.

—Gerard Manley Hopkins is —

Then he stopped.

—Fuck it.

He'd just remembered; he shouldn't have written In My Opinion. It was banned. Crosbie, their English teacher, wouldn't let them use it.

He tore out the page.

*   *   *

Upstairs in her bedroom Veronica, Darren's mother, was doing her homework as well.

The door was locked.

* * *

—You're not even inhalin' properly, said Linda.

—I am so, Linda; fuck off.

Tracy took another drag, held the smoke in her mouth for a bit, then blew it out, in behind the couch. She couldn't blow it out the window cos her daddy was out there sitting on the step. Linda grabbed the Major from her and took a drag, a real one, and held it much longer than Tracy had – and got rid of it when they heard the stairs creaking. She threw the fag into her Zubes tin and shut it and nearly took the skin off her fingers. They beat the air with their copy books.

They waited. They looked at the door.

But it didn't open.

—Get it before it goes ou', Tracy whispered.

Linda giggled, and so did Tracy. They shushed each other. Linda opened the tin.

—Jesus, she said. —I've crushed it.

—Let's see.

It was their last one.

—Ah Jesus, said Linda. —I'm gaspin'!

—So am I, said Tracy.

—Yeh can't be. You don't even inhale.

—I do, Linda.

—Yeh don't. Your smoke comes ou' too puffy.

—That's just the way I do it. It is, Linda. ——God, I'm gaspin'.

—Yeah, said Linda. —Does tha' look like Mammy's writin'?

Tracy looked at the writing on the inside cover of one of Linda's copies.

—Yeah, she said. —Sort of ——

—Look it, said Linda.

She took the copy from Tracy and showed her the other inside cover.

—That's wha' it was like when I started, she told Tracy.

She turned back to the first cover.

—This's much better, isn't it?

—Yeah, said Tracy, and she meant it.

She read it; Please Excuse, about ten times down the page, getting smaller and closer near the bottom, not like her mammy's yet but not like Linda's usual writing either, much smaller, hardly any holes in the letters.

—She'll kill yeh, Tracy told Linda.

—Why will she? said Linda. —I haven't done annythin'. I'm only experimentin'.

She wrote Please.

—Is tha' like it?

——Yeah, said Tracy.

They'd forgotten that they were gasping. Tracy crossed out History in her homework journal. She'd just finished it, five questions about the pyramids.

—Jesus, she said, reading what was next on the list. —Wha' Irish story are yeh doin', Linda?

—I'm not doin' anny, said Linda.

She showed Tracy another Please and a new Excuse.

—Is tha' like it?

*   *   *

—No.

—Ah but, Mammy —

—No, I said.

—Daddy —?

—Yeh heard your mammy, said Jimmy Sr.

—But —

—No buts.

The twins, Linda doing all of the talking, had just asked if they could get a new video for Christmas. They'd had none in the house since Jimmy Jr, the eldest, had taken his with him when he'd moved out a few months ago.

—No buts, said Jimmy Sr. —We can't afford it, an' that's that. And, we've no place to put it —

—With the telly —

—Don't interrupt me, righ'!

He was really angry, before he knew it; nearly out of his seat. It was happening a lot these days. He'd have to be careful. He stopped pointing at Linda.

——We're not gettin' one; end o' story. Now I want to enjoy me dinner. For a change.

Linda raised her eyes to heaven and shifted a bit in her chair, and thought about walking out of the kitchen in protest, but she stayed. She was hungry.

So was Gina, Sharon's little young one.

—Shut up, Sharon told her. —Wait.

She put the chips in front of Gina, then lifted them away.

—Now, if yeh throw them around, Sharon warned her, — I'll take them back off yeh, d'yeh hear me?

Gina screamed.

—An' Grandad'll eat them on yeh. Isn't tha' righ', Grandad?

—Wha'? said Jimmy Sr. —Chips, is it? Come here, I'll eat them now.

He leaned over to Gina's chair.

—Give us them here. Lovely.

Gina screamed, and grabbed the plate. Sharon managed to keep the chips on the plate but got ketchup on her hand.

—Ah, bloody —

—Buddy! said Gina.

Sharon wiped her hand on Gina's bib.

The Rabbittes got dug into their dinners.

—Lovely, said Jimmy Sr.

Tracy had an announcement.

—There's a piece o' paper hangin' up in the toilet an' yis are all to put a tick on it every time yis flush the toilet.

—Wha'? said Jimmy Sr.

Darren came in.

—Good man, Darren, said Jimmy Sr. —Were yeh watchin' abou' the Berlin Wall there?

—Yeah, said Darren as he sat down.

—Terrific, isn't it? said Jimmy Sr.

—Yeah, said Darren.

Jimmy Sr wondered, again, why Darren wouldn't talk to him properly any more.

—Darren, said Tracy. —Every time yeh flush the toilet you're to put a tick on the paper hangin' up on the wall.

—What's this abou'? Jimmy Sr still wanted to know.

—There's a biro for yeh to do it in the glass with the toothbrushes, Tracy told them.

—Okay, said Darren.

—Hang on, said Jimmy Sr. —What are we to do? Exactly.

Tracy raised her eyes.

—Jesus, she said to Linda.

—Don't Jesus me, you, said Jimmy Sr. —An' anyway, that's a curse. Swearbox.

—It's not a curse, said Tracy. —It's a name.

—Not the way you said it, said Jimmy Sr.

He picked up the marmalade jar with the slit in its lid and rattled it in front of her. The swearbox had been his idea, to force him to clean up his act in front of the baby.

—Come on, he said.

—I haven't anny money, said Tracy.

—Yeh have so, said Linda

—Fuck —

—Ah ah! said Jimmy Sr. —Double.

Veronica took over.

—That's the last time you'll use language like that in this house, she told Tracy. —D'you hear me? And you as well, she told Linda.

—I didn't say ann'thin'! said Linda.

—You know what I mean, said Veronica. —It's disgraceful; I'm not having it. In front of Gina.

Gina was busy with her chips.

—That's righ', said Jimmy Sr. —Yis know how quickly she's pickin' up things.

—I on'y said Jesus, said Tracy very quietly, standing up for her rights.

—I didn't say ann'thin', said Linda.

—You're becoming a right pair of ——

Veronica didn't finish. She stared at them, then looked away.

—Bitches, said Sharon. —If Gina starts usin' dirty language I'll kill yis.

—I didn't say ann'thin', Linda told her plate.

Jimmy Sr studied the piece of burger on his fork.

—Eh, he said. —Should it be this colour?

—Yes! said Veronica.

—Fair enough, said Jimmy Sr. —Just askin'.

He chewed and swallowed.

—Second time we've had these yokes this week, he said, sort of to himself.

Veronica let her knife and fork rattle off her plate. Jimmy Sr didn't look at her.

—Anyway, he asked Tracy, —why am I to put a tick on this piece o' paper when I go to the jacks?

—It's for school, said Tracy, as if he was some sort of a thick. —Geog'aphy.

—Wha' has goin' to the jacks got to do with geography?

—I don't know, said Tracy. —Somethin' to do with water. Miss Eliot says we're to do it.

—Why does Miss Eliot want to know how often I have a—

—Swearbox! said Linda.

—Starebock! said Gina.

—I didn't say it, said Jimmy Sr.

He turned back to Tracy.

—Why does she want to know how often I use the toilet facilities?

—Not just you, said Tracy. —All of us have to.

—Why?

—Geog'aphy.

—It's to see how much water all the class uses, Linda told him.

—Why? Darren asked.

—I don't know! said Linda. —It's thick. She's useless. Tracy's to do the toilet an' I'm to do the sink an' the washin' machine but I'm not goin' to. It's thick.

—Is that your homework? said Veronica.

—Yeah, said Linda.

—Then you're to do it.

Linda said nothing.

—I'd still like to know wha' Miss Eliot wants with all this information, said Jimmy Sr. —She might blackmail us; wha', Darren?

—Yeah. ——Yeah.

—The Rabbittes go to the jacks twice as much as everyone else, wha'. She'll want to know how often we change our underwear next; wait an' see.

—Stop that, said Veronica. —It's their homework.

Darren was beginning to grin, so Jimmy Sr continued.

—An' after tha' we'll find bits o' paper stuck up beside the beds, wha'.

—Stop!

Darren laughed. And so did Jimmy Sr. He spoke to Gina.

—We'd run ou' of paper if we had to tick off every time you go to the jacks, wouldn't we, Honey?

Gina threw a chip at him, and hit. He pretended he was dying. Sharon picked up the chip before the dog, Larrygogan, got to it and she made Gina eat it.

—There, she said.

But Gina didn't mind.

—Do you not do maps and stuff like that? Veronica asked Linda and Tracy.

—No, said Linda. —Sometimes only.

—Nearly never, said Tracy.

Veronica shrugged.

Jimmy Sr belched.

—Lovely dinner, Veronica, he said.

—You liked those yokes, did you? said Veronica.

—They were grand, said Jimmy Sr. —Much nicer than the ones yeh get in the chipper or the shops.

—Yeah, well, said Veronica. —When I start getting some proper money again you won't see them so often.

—No no, said Jimmy Sr. —They're grand.

They looked at each other.

Then Gina dropped her plate on Larrygogan.

—Ah Jesus, said Sharon.

—Starebock! said Gina.

Jimmy Sr stood on some chips when he was trying to wipe the ketchup off Larrygogan.

—Ah Jaysis —

—Starebock!

And Sharon slapped her.

—Ah leave her, leave her, said Jimmy Sr. —It's only chips.

—She does it on purpose.

Gina started some serious screaming. Sharon wanted to kill her, but only for a second. She lifted her out of her chair and rocked her. But Gina wasn't impressed.

—Jive Bunny, Gina, said Jimmy Sr. —Look it.

—OH —

He started twisting.

—Look at Grandad, Gina, said Sharon.

—LET'S TWIST AGAIN —

LIKE WE DID LAST Jaysis!

He slid on a chip and nearly went on his arse, saved by the table. Gina stopped screaming, to watch. Jimmy Sr, steadying himself and taking off his shoe, looked at Gina and sniffed victory. But Gina was getting ready to start again; he could tell by the way her cheeks were twitching.

—Righ', he said to the rest. —Hawaii 5-o.

He made a trumpet out of his fists and started.

—DEH DEH DEH DEH —

DEHHH DEH —

Linda, Tracy, Darren, even Veronica made trumpets and joined in. Gina danced in Sharon's arms and forgot about screaming. Larrygogan cleaned the chips off the floor and he cleaned the plate as well.

* * *

Jimmy Sr sat watching the television. There was no sound on. The three other lads watching it all had earphones but Jimmy

Sr couldn't see another pair anywhere. He could've asked the young one behind the desk over there what he'd to do to get a pair of earphones for himself but he didn't want to. She looked busy. Anyway, they mightn't have been free. And anyway as well, what was on didn't look that good; just fellas in togas talking; a play or something.

Jimmy Sr was in the ILAC library, in town.

It was terrific here, very nice.

He'd never been in here before. It was great. There was a lot more to it than just the books. You could get tapes or records out or even those compact discs, or just listen to them in here. He'd go over there, to the music part, after this. There was a language resource centre, a room where you could learn more than sixty languages in one of those booth things. Or you could use the computer – he looked at the brochure again – to enhance your computer literacy skills. There was even a reading machine for if you had sight problems. Having one of them beside the bed would have been very handy for when you came home scuttered at night.

He didn't drink much any more; just the few pints twice a week.

He'd go over and have a look at the machine in a minute.

He was definitely joining. He had his application cards here. It was lovely here. You could stay here for ages and never get bored. You could even borrow pictures and bring them home.

That was a bit fuckin' stupid when you thought about it; sticking a picture up on your wall for a fortnight and then having to bring it back again; on a bus or on the DART, sitting there like a gobshite with a big picture on your lap, of a woman in her nip or something.

Still though.

It was gas watching your men here watching the telly, and not being able to hear. One of them had laughed a minute ago, like he was trying not to, but the chaps on the telly had looked deadly serious. She'd asked him – your woman at the desk – if he was a householder when he'd asked her how you joined.

He didn't know.

357

He told her it wasn't for himself he was asking, and she gave him the cards and told him that he'd have to get a householder to sign the back of them.

He sort of knew. But the problem was, he didn't know – not exactly – if you actually had to own your house or if renting was enough. And he rented his, so if he'd said Yeah, I am a householder and he'd found out that he wasn't one when he was filling in the card at the desk he'd've felt like a right fuckin' eejit. In front of the young one there. She looked younger than Sharon.

Bimbo, one of his mates, owned his house. Jimmy Sr'd get him to sign it, to be on the safe side.

There was a thing he'd seen downstairs in the shopping part of the ILAC on his way up here; a studio, a small one you went into and sang a song – for six quid. The twins would've loved that.

Maybe they wouldn't have, but; not any more. They'd have been too embarrassed. There was a list of the songs you could sing along to. New York New York was one of them. That was his song; he always sang it at weddings and on bank holiday Mondays in the Hikers.

Six quid. Veronica would fuck him from a height if he came home with a tape of himself singing and she found out how much it'd cost.

He got up. He was going to have a look at the books. When he joined up he could take out three at a time and keep them for three weeks, but he'd only take out one or maybe two. He wasn't that quick of a reader. And anyway, he'd want to come here more than just once every three weeks so if he took out one book at a time he could come back more often than that.

There was a sign – a handmade one – on the desk that said that you could get an Action Pack for the Unemployed but there weren't any on the desk. You had to ask for one.

He wondered what was in them. Action Pack. Probably just leaflets.

And a compass and a fuckin' hand grenade and one of them cyanide tablets for if you were caught behind enemy lines.

He'd ask for one the next time. The young one was dealing with some people at the desk and one of them looked like he was going to start getting snotty with her.

She was a nice-looking young one, lovely; not what you'd have expected. With a few buttons open at the front, fair play to her.

He went over to the books. He wanted to find the Sports shelf. He was thinking of getting a couple of greyhounds.

* * *

Veronica and Jimmy Sr were alone, sitting on their bed. Jimmy Sr watched Veronica putting on socks and then her boots.

—We could always get a few bob from a lender, I suppose, said Jimmy Sr.

—No, said Veronica.

—A few bob only —

—No, said Veronica.

——You're righ'; you're right, o' course, Veronica, said Jimmy Sr. —We'd only be gettin' ourselves into —

—I'd die before I'd go looking for help from one of those crooks, said Veronica.

—You're dead right, yeah. I just thought ——Will Leslie come home, d'yeh think?

Veronica didn't want to answer this. But she did.

—I doubt it, she said.

——Yeah, said Jimmy Sr.

Les was in England, somewhere. They thought.

—What abou' Jimmy? said Jimmy Sr.

—Ah yeah, said Veronica.

She studied the soles of the boots.

—Where else would he go? said Veronica. —If I pushed a bit harder my fingers would come through, look it.

Well, don't push then, Jimmy Sr nearly said, but he stopped himself.

—Would he not go to – em – Aoife's parents' place? he said.

Aoife and Jimmy Jr were living in a bedsit in Clontarf.

—He'd better not, said Veronica. —If he does he needn't come home for his Sunday dinner again.

She stood up.

—With his washing.

—Yeah, said Jimmy Sr. —At least we won't have to buy anythin' for him.

—Something small, said Veronica.

—Very small, said Jimmy Sr. —So that's the twins an' Gina is all we have to get presents for really. An' Darren. An' somethin' small for Sharon as well. That's not too bad.

Veronica wasn't convinced.

—Well ——, she said.

She was at the dressing-table mirror now.

—What about all the food and the drink? There's a lot more than just the presents. And there's other presents as well, you know. Gerry's kids and —

—I'll tell Gerry and Thelma and Pat they're not to send ours any presents an' we won't send theirs any.

—God, said Veronica. —— I never —

—Sure, they can't afford it either, said Jimmy Sr.

He didn't want Veronica to finish. There was no point. He'd heard it before. It only made him angry now and he'd end up shouting. It wasn't fair.

—No one can, said Jimmy Sr.

Veronica said nothing.

—We were always broke at Christmas.

—After it though, said Veronica.

—Ah ——! said Jimmy Sr.

It wasn't fuckin' fair.

—Ah sorry, said Veronica.

She turned to look at him properly.

—I didn't mean anything.

—Ah, I know. —— I don't blame yeh. It's just ——

He looked at her looking at him.

—We'll manage, he said.

—Yes, said Veronica.

—I'll win the turkey in the pitch 'n' putt annyway, he said.

—You always do, said Veronica.

—An' maybe a hamper as well, wha'.

—That'd be great.

Neither of them wanted to talk any more about Christmas. It was still months away anyway; weeks. And Veronica had to go. She checked her folder.

—Eh ——how're the oul' classes goin', Veronica? said Jimmy Sr.

—Grand, said Veronica.

Veronica was doing night classes, two Leaving Cert subjects.

—Are yeh the oldest? said Jimmy Sr.

—No!

—I'd say the maths is hard, is it?

—It's not too bad, said Veronica.

That was a lie, only a small one though because it was getting easier. She was getting used to it, being in the classroom and having the teacher, a young lad Jimmy Jr's age, looking over her shoulder all the time. And Darren was going to give her a hand.

—I was thinkin' I might do a few classes meself, Jimmy Sr told her.

—You're too late, Veronica told him. —You'll have to wait till next year.

She wasn't sure if that was true – she thought it was: really – but she wanted to do it on her own, even going up to the school on her own and walking home; everything.

She had to go.

—Bye bye so, she said. —Are yeh stayin' up here?

—I am, yeah, said Jimmy Sr. —I'm goin' to read one o' me bukes.

The twins were in the front room – he could hear them – and Darren would be in the kitchen but he didn't mind staying up here. He'd lie back – it wasn't that cold; just nice – and read.

—I got three bukes ou', he told Veronica. —Look it.

But she was gone.

—See you later, she said from the hall.

—Okay, love, said Jimmy Sr. —Good luck. D'yeh have all your eccer done now?

But she didn't answer. She was gone. He heard the door.

Fair play to her.

He picked up one of his books. The Man in the Iron Mask. By Alexandre Dumas. Lousy cover. He could have drawn better himself.

He remembered something. He got his thumb-nail and dragged it across the plastic covering. It worked, left a line of little grooves across the plastic. He did it again. The sound was the same as well, as when he was a kid.

That was gas ——

He got up.

He'd make himself a cup of tea – it was just a bit chilly up here – and then he'd get going. Fifty pages before Veronica got home.

* * *

—Mind your house!

That wanker over there had been roaring that since the start of the match. He probably didn't even know what it meant, the stupid oul' bollix. The ball was down at the Barrytown goal, about the first time it had gone in that direction in the second half.

It was Saturday afternoon. Jimmy Sr was in St Anne's Park, watching the Barrytown Utd Under 18s; watching Darren.

Five-nil for Barrytown was the score. The opposition were useless. Jimmy Sr couldn't even remember what they were called. Darren didn't bother dashing back to help defend, and he was dead right. The last time this shower had seen the net shake was when their keeper farted.

The ball was coming back up. Darren went to meet it. No one came with him.

—Good man, Darren! Away yeh go!

Darren stopped the ball. Normally he'd have had two or three men up his arse by now or, with the ground this soggy, someone sliding towards his ankle. Now though, two of their defence ran around him on their way back as if they didn't want to get in his way because it was rude, so Darren held onto the ball for a while, turned and crossed where the centre line should have been.

—Give us a display of your silky skills, Darren!

That was the Barrytown keeper, Nappies Harrison.

The sweeper was waiting for Darren. That was what he'd called himself; the sweeper. —We're playin' three central defenders, he'd told Darren in the first half. —Like Arsenal. He was waiting for Darren on the other side of a puddle, hunched as if he was going to dive into it. Kenny Smith was to Darren's left, shouting for the ball. Darren lobbed the ball over the sweeper, ran around him (—Yeow, Darren!) and dug the ball out of the muck with his toe and sent it over to Kenny, hard so it wouldn't get stuck again.

—Good play, said their sweeper; Jimmy Sr heard him.

Darren knew he'd be praised after the match for his unselfish play (—That's the Liverpool way, lads) but he'd given the ball to Kenny because he couldn't be bothered bringing it any further himself. He heard the ironic cheer. They'd scored again; an Anto Brennan diving header that he hadn't really needed to dive for.

Darren strolled back across the line. He hated these sort of games, when they won without sweating. They'd be beaten next week; it always happened.

—Come on now, lads, the oul' guy at the side shouted. —Make the score respectable, come on.

—Will yeh listen to him, said Kenny.

—Yeah, said Darren. —Fuckin' pitiful.

Most of them wouldn't turn up for training on Tuesday night because of this win; their emphatic victory.

The ball was in the centre circle. The ref picked it up and blew his whistle; game over, ten minutes early.

—Thank fuck, said Pat Conlon. —It's fuckin' freezin'.

—I was goin' for me hat-trick, Kenny complained.

—Ah, fuck off complainin', said Pat. —Anyway, yeh'd never have got another two.

—No problem to me against these cunts.

The sweeper was waiting for Darren at the sideline, with his hand out.

—Good game, he said.

—Yeah, said Darren. —Thanks.

—Best team won.

—The pitch wasn't fit for playin' on, said Darren.

His da was waiting for him as well.

—Well done, Darren.

—Thanks, Da.

He ran along the edge of the gravel path to the gates of the park.

—Bring your ma with yis the next time, he heard Kenny telling the sweeper, and he heard his da laughing.

Darren got into the back of one of the three Barrytown cars.

—Push over, there, he said.

—Ahh! Hang on; me leg!

—Good man, Darren, said Mr Reeves, his da's friend; Bimbo. —Is that everyone now?

—No; Kenny.

—Kenny! Darren roared. —Come on.

—They were useless, weren't they? said Mr Reeves.

—Pitiful, said Darren.

Hurry up, he wanted to say. Hurry up!

Kenny climbed in the back on top of the three lads already in there. There were two more in the front, and Bimbo.

Darren got the door shut.

—Jaysis, said Bimbo. —We're nearly scrapin' the ground. Did yis have your dinners at half-time or somethin'?

They laughed. The car moved. They cheered.

But Bimbo braked.

Darren's da was at the front passenger window.

—Will youse go with Billy, lads? he asked Muggah McCarthy and Pat Conlon.

—Okay, said Muggah, and Darren's da got in when the two
of them got out.

—Off yeh go, he said to Bimbo.

Kenny leaned over (—Ah, Kenny! Watch it!) and rolled
down Darren's window. He roared at the other team as they
climbed into their mini-bus.

—Yis dozy cunts, yis!

—Here; none o' tha'! said Bimbo.

He braked again.

—Yeh can get ou' here if you're goin' to start tha'.

—Disgraceful behaviour, said Darren's da, and he winked
back at them.

——Sorry, said Kenny.

They nudged each other. Bimbo got the car going again.

—Did yeh get this yoke off the Vincent de Paul, Mr Reeves?
said Nappies.

They laughed.

—Yeah, said Kenny. —It's pitiful, isn't it, Darrah?

—Fuck off, said Darren.

His da laughed.

—Gettin' locked tonigh', men? said Anto.

—Fuckin' sure, said Kenny.

He started singing.

—HERE WE GO
HERE WE —

—Shut up in the back, said Bimbo.

The windows were steaming up. Darren rubbed his and
watched the people walking along the sea front, looking out
for young ones.

—D'yeh see her? said Kenny. —Jaysis.

He turned to look out the back window and kicked Anto in
the mouth.

—You're dead, said Anto.

He checked for blood. There wasn't any.

—That's pitiful behaviour, said Nappies. —Isn't it, Darren?

Darren gave Nappies the finger.

—Swivel, he said.

Nappies was sitting on Anto's lap. His right ear was nearly pressed to the roof.

—Hurry up, Mr Reeves, will yeh. Me neck's nearly broke.

—Well, men, said Anto. —Where're we goin' tonigh'?

—The Nep, said Nappies.

—No way. Yeh fuckin' hippy.

—There's nothin' wrong with the Nep, said Anto. —It's better than the field youse drink in.

—Yeah, man.

—Right on, Anto.

—Will yeh be wearin' your flares, Nappies?

—He's pitiful.

—Yis haven't a clue, Nappies told them.

—Where's the Nep? said Bimbo.

—Town, said Nappies.

—My God, said Bimbo. —Would yis go tha' far for a drink?

—Fuckin' eejits, said Jimmy Sr.

—It's cos they're afraid their oul' ones'll catch them if they drink in the Hikers, Anto told Bimbo and Jimmy Sr.

—Don't start, you, said Nappies. —My ma knows I drink.

—Yeah; milk.

—Fuck off.

—Does she know yeh smoke hash as well, Nappies?

Kenny got a couple of digs from Darren, to shut him up.

—Where do the rest of yis go? Bimbo asked them.

He wasn't being nosy.

—The Beachcomber, said Anto.

—Yeh do not, said Nappies. —Don't start. They wouldn't let yeh in.

—Would they not now? said Anto. —D'yis hear him?

—What's it like inside then? said Nappies, —if yeh've been in there. Tell us; go on.

—Better than the fuckin' Nep anyway.

—You were never in there; I knew it.

—Fuck off, you.

—Fuck off, yourself. The state o' yeh. You'd get drunk on a barman's fart.

—Fuck off.

—Language, lads. ——Do none of yis go up to the Hikers at all?

—I do, said Kenny.

—Yeh do in your brown, said Anto. —He asked yeh do yeh drink in the Hikers, not do yeh sit on the wall outside.

—Don't start, said Kenny. —I do drink there.

—When?

—Yeah; go on.

—With me da.

—Yeah; the day yeh made your Confirmation.

—Fuck off.

—Yeah, Kenny; your oul' lad drank your money on yeh.

Darren enjoyed this, even with his da there; the lads slagging each other. He rubbed the window. He couldn't open it because Kenny's feet were in the way. They were turning off the sea front. It was a bit fuckin' childish though; not the slagging, the subject matter. The theme.

—Anyway, said Kenny, —knacker drinkin's better than drinkin' in a pub. Specially if you've a free house.

—That's not knacker drinkin'! said Anto.

They didn't even shave, most of them in the car. Darren did, and he was younger than some of them. And he'd been in the Beachcomber. And the Hikers. It was no big deal. He was working tonight in the Hikers – but he'd drunk in there as well when he wasn't working – and then he was going on to the Grove. The Grove was a dump. It usen't to be that bad but there were just kids there now and the music was pitiful; it used to be great. But he was meeting Miranda there after work, so it was okay.

—Hey, Darren. Where're you goin' tonigh'?

—Workin', said Darren.

She was fifteen but she looked much older; she wasn't skinny at all. She'd done her Inter; six honours; two less than Darren. She'd great hair, black that went up and out and

367

down, and huge eyes and no spots, not in the light in the Grove anyway. He'd only seen her in the Grove so far. He wasn't really going with her.

—Here we are, lads.

They were outside the community centre.

—Thanks, Mr Reeves. You're a poxy driver.

Darren opened the door and Kenny fell out onto the road, on purpose; he always did it. Darren climbed out.

—Jesus; me legs.

—Yeah. We should have a bus.

—Will you get us one for Christmas? said Bimbo.

—Here, Mr Reeves, said Pat. —We'll rob the 17A for yeh.

The two other carloads had arrived. Their manager, Billy O'Leary, got out of his car.

—Righ', he said. —Yis listenin'?

He zipped up his bomber jacket and rubbed his hands. Bimbo and Jimmy Sr went over and stood beside him.

—Yis listenin'? ——Righ'; good win there but, let's face it, lads. They were spas.

He let them laugh, then frowned.

—Next week'll be a different kettle o' fish. Cromcastle are always a useful side so we can't afford to be complacent.

—Wha'? said Kenny.

—We're not to act the prick, Muggah told him.

Miranda was a bit of a Curehead —

—Darren, said Billy. —Terrific game, son.

—I thought he was pitiful, Pat whispered.

They sniggered.

—Fuck off, you, said Darren.

—Listen now, lads, said Bimbo.

—Terrific, said Billy. —One-touch stuff, he told the team. —Get the ball and give it to someone who can do more with it.

—That's the Liverpool way, Muggah whispered.

—I heard tha', said Billy. —And you're righ'; it is.

—Wha' abou' me, Billy? said Nappies. —Didn't I have a terrific game as well.

368

—Yeah, said Kenny. —Pullin' your wire.

—Yis listenin'!? said Billy. —Now listen, I want yis all at trainin' on Tuesday, righ'. No excuses. Annyone not goin' to be there?

No one's hand went up.

—Good, said Billy. —On time as well, righ'. I want to work on some set pieces for Saturday.

—Yeow, Billy!

—Fuck up a minute. Even if it's rainin' there's still trainin', righ'.

—Fair enough.

—Okay.

—Okay, boss.

—Righ'; off yis go home, an' fair play; yis were very good there today. I was proud o' yis.

—We're proud o' you as well, Billy, said Pat.

—Come here you, Bollockchops, said Billy.

They roared.

—What's happened your long throw, pal? Billy wanted to know. —My mother's cat could throw the fuckin' ball further than you did today.

They roared.

—Too much wankin', son, said Billy. —That's your problem.

He ran at Pat.

—Show us your palms there. Come on; hands ou'.

Darren watched Pat jumping over the low wall into the shopping centre carpark. Billy couldn't follow him over.

—See yis, said Darren, quietly.

He headed for home, still wearing his boots and gear. He hoped there'd be hot water. There often wasn't these days.

She was a bit of a Curehead but not that bad: she had a mind of her own. It was just the look, the image she followed, the hair and the Docs. She was into the Cure as well but not only the Cure.

He was walking on the Green, to keep his boots off the concrete.

369

She was into—

—There's Darren Rabbitte an' his legs.

It was Anita Healy from Darren's class, and her friend, Mandy Lawless.

—Howyis, said Darren.

He grinned and pretended to pull his jersey down over his legs.

—They're nicer than yours, Mandy, said Anita.

—That's true, said Darren. —Yours are hairier though, Mandy.

Anita screamed.

—Fuck off, you, Rabbitte, said Mandy.

She pretended to kick him and Darren grabbed her. She screamed Let go as if she didn't really mean it, and he did. They stood there for a bit.

He saw his da coming.

—Seeyis, he said.

—See yeh, Darren.

Anita shouted after him.

—Mandy said you're a ride, Darren!

—I did not, Anita. Fuck off.

Darren kept going.

Jesus. Mandy wasn't a bad-looking bird – woman. She was a bit Kylie-esque but she'd great legs, real woman's legs. And tits too. She often took her jumper off in school and wrapped it round her waist, even when it wasn't all that hot. Darren liked that, and it annoyed him as well sometimes.

He started to run.

* * *

It was Monday. Jimmy Sr was reading to Gina. He had her for the afternoon because Sharon had wanted to go into town. He had been going to play a round of pitch 'n' putt.

—Can yeh not bring her around with yeh in the buggy? Sharon had said. —From hole to hole.

—Are yeh jokin' me, Sharon? he'd said. —They wouldn't let me in. Ah, she'd be too much of a distraction. She'd be hit by a ball. Some o' the wankers tha' go down there are cross-eyed.

—Can yeh not play tomorrow instead? she'd said.

—I am playin' tomorrow, Sharon, he'd told her. —I have to. I'll have to win a turkey between now an' Christmas an' there's not tha' many weekends left when yeh add them up. I need all the practice I can get. —— Okay, okay. Give her to me here.

Veronica wouldn't take her. She had to read six chapters of Lord of the Flies and summarise them; that was her excuse.

—She won't stop yeh from readin', Veronica, for Jaysis sake.

—Take her with you or stay at home, she'd said. —I've other things to do.

So he was stuck with Gina. He didn't mind, not too much. The afternoon off would be good for Sharon. She wasn't looking the best these days, kind of pale and hassled looking. Give her a few hours in the shops and she'd be grand.

Gina was on his lap, trying to grab the book.

—The king is a beau, my good friend, he read. —An' so are you, too, wha'ever – Ah ah; just listen – wha'ever you may say abou' it. Porthos smiled triumphantly. Let's go to the king's tailor, he said —— I'll smack yeh if yeh do that again, Gina.

—Smack!

—Yeah. —— Now. —— An' since he measures the king, I think, by my faith! I may allow him to measure me.

He closed the book.

—I think, by my faith, it's a load o' bollix. —— Here.

He put Gina down and got up – Jaysis! – and picked her up.

—Up we get. You're a righ' little buster, aren't yeh?

—G'anda.

—That's me. We'll go for a walk, will we? an' find someone to annoy.

He picked up the book. Only thirty-nine pages gone and over four hundred to go still and it was shite. He was sure it was good, brilliant – a classic – but he fuckin' hated it. It

371

wasn't hard; that wasn't it. It was just shite; boring, he supposed, but Shite was definitely the word he was looking for. And he'd have to finish it because he'd told Veronica he was reading it, told her all about it, shown it to her; the fuckin' eejit.

—Better get your anorak, he told Gina.

She pushed his chest and he put her down. She ran to the door – they were in the front room – reached up and got the door open.

Jimmy Sr noticed her pile of video tapes on the shelf; Postman Pat, The Magic Roundabout – that was a great one – five of them, presents from people. And no video to play them in. God love her.

He walloped his leg with the book.

—The Man in the Iron fuckin' Mask.

Maybe he'd tell Veronica he'd finished it (—He escaped, Veronica) and start one of the other ones he'd got out of the library. He was useless; couldn't even read a book properly.

He went down to the kitchen, and the bell rang.

—Wha' now?

He went back up the hall. Veronica had no problem reading and finishing her books. He made out Jimmy Jr's shape through the glass.

—What's he doin' here?

He only came on Sundays, since he'd left and shacked up with that Aoife young one; a good-looking young one: too good for that waster.

He opened the front door.

—Howyeh, said Jimmy Jr.

He got past Jimmy Sr.

—Forgot me washin' yesterday, he said. —No kaks or nothin'.

Jimmy Sr followed him down the hall into the kitchen. It was empty; Veronica was swotting up in Sharon's room and the rest were still at school. Jimmy Jr held up the bag with his washing in it. It had Ibiza printed on the side of it, and a little map.

—Here, he said.

—Would Aoife not do your washin' for yeh? said Jimmy Sr.

—No way, said Jimmy Jr.

—Yis divide the work between yis?

—No, said Jimmy Jr. —She told me to fuck off an' do me own washin'.

They laughed a bit.

—She's dead righ', said Jimmy Sr.

—When was the last time you washed annythin'? Jimmy Jr asked him.

—Don't start. I do me fair share.

—Yeah, yeah, yeah. Course yeh do. ——I'd better go. I've to make the fuckin' dinner.

—My Jaysis, tha' young one has you by the bollix alrigh', said Jimmy Sr.

He followed Jimmy Jr to the door.

—Come here, said Jimmy Jr. —Could yeh use tha'?

It was a fiver.

—Eh —

—Go on, said Jimmy Jr.

He put it into his da's cardigan pocket.

—A few pints, he said.

——Thanks.

—No problem. See yeh.

—Thanks.

—Shut up, will yeh. See yeh.

—Okay. ——Good luck, son.

* * *

Sharon found him.

—Did yeh not hear me? she said.

Jimmy Sr was standing facing the door when she walked into the bedroom. He'd been in there since Jimmy Jr'd left.

—Wha'? said Jimmy Sr. —Were yeh lookin' for me, love?

—I was screamin' up at yeh nearly, Sharon told him. —From downstairs. Did yeh not hear me? she asked him again.

—I must have fallen asleep. Dozed off. I was just —

—Are yeh alrigh'?

He looked miserable, and small and kind of beaten looking.

—I'm grand, he said.

He looked around him, as if for a reason for being there.

—The tea's ready, Sharon told him.

—Oh, lovely.

—What's wrong?

—Nothin', Sharon. Nothin'. ——Nothin'.

He smiled, but Sharon kept gawking at him.

—There is somethin', isn't there? she said.

—Ah, look —

—I can tell from your —

—Get off me fuckin' back, will yeh!

—Sorry I spoke.

She grabbed the door on her way out.

—I'll be down in a minute.

—Please yourself, she said, and she slammed the door.

She heard wood splitting in the middle of the slam but she didn't stop. She went back downstairs.

In the bedroom Jimmy Sr opened his mouth as wide as he could and massaged his jaws. He was alright now. He'd thought his teeth were going to crack and break; he couldn't get his mouth to open, as if it had been locked and getting tighter. And he'd had to snap his eyes shut, waiting for the crunch and the pain. But then it had stopped, and he'd started breathing again. He felt weak now, a bit weak. He was alright though. He'd be grand in a minute.

He closed his mouth. It was grand now. He'd say sorry to Sharon for shouting at her. He stood up straight. He'd go down now. He took the fiver off the bed and put it in his pocket.

* * *

He had young Jimmy's fiver and two more quid Veronica'd given him so he could buy a round. If only Bimbo and Bertie were there the fiver would be enough and he'd be able to give Veronica her money back but if Paddy was there he'd need it.

374

It was a quarter past ten, early enough to get three or four pints inside him and late enough to make sure that his turn to put his hand in his pocket didn't come round again before closing time.

He came off the Green, crossed the road. The street light here was broken again. The glass was on the path. It was always this one they smashed, only this one.

It was funny; he'd been really grateful when young Jimmy had given him the fiver, delighted, and at the same time, or just after, he'd wanted to go after him and thump the living shite out of him and throw the poxy fiver back in his face, the nerve of him; who did he think he was, dishing out fivers like Bob fuckin' Geldof.

He was grand now though. He had the fiver and he was out on a Monday night.

—There's Jimmy, said Malcolm, one of the Hikers' bouncers.

—Howyeh, Malcolm, said Jimmy Sr.

—Chilly enough.

—Who're yeh tellin'.

He pushed the bar door, and was in.

—The man himself, said Bimbo.

He was pleased to see him; Jimmy Sr could tell. He had a grin on him that you could hang your washing on. There was just himself and Bertie up at the bar, new pints in front of them. Bertie turned and saw Jimmy Sr.

—Ah, he said. —Buenas noches, Jimmy.

—Howyis, said Jimmy Sr.

There was nothing like it, the few scoops with your mates.

—A pint there, Leo, Bimbo shouted down the bar, —like a good man.

Leo already had the glass under the tap. Jimmy Sr rubbed his hands. He wanted to whoop, but he put his hands in his pockets and looked around.

He nodded to a corner.

—Who're they? he said.

—Don't know, compadre, said Bertie. —Gringos.

They were looking over at three couples, all young and satisfied looking.

—They look like a righ' shower o' cunts, said Jimmy Sr.

—You don't even know them, sure, said Bimbo.

Bimbo fell for it every time.

—I wouldn't want to fuckin' know them, Jimmy Sr told Bimbo. —Look at them. They should be upstairs.

The Lounge was upstairs.

—I speet on them, said Bertie.

—Yeh can't stop people from comin' in if they want, said Bimbo. —It's a pub.

—'Course yeh can, said Jimmy Sr.

—He's righ', compadre, Bertie told Bimbo.

—How is he? said Bimbo. —A pub is a pub; a public house.

Leo arrived with Jimmy Sr's pint.

—Now, said Leo.

—Good man, Leo, said Jimmy Sr. —Fuck me, it looks lovely.

They agreed; it did.

The head of the pint stood higher than the glass, curving up and then flat and solid looking. The outside of the glass was clean; the whole thing looking like an ad. Jimmy Sr tilted the glass a little bit but the head stayed the way it was. They admired it.

—My Jaysis, said Jimmy Sr. —Wha'.

They got down off their stools and headed for an empty table.

—Anyway, said Bimbo. —Anyone should be able to come into a pub if they want.

—No way, said Jimmy Sr.

They sat down at their table and settled themselves in; sank into the seats, hooshed up their trousers, threw the dried-up, twisted beermats onto the table beside them – they were dangerous.

There wasn't much of a crowd in.

—Come here, Bimbo, said Jimmy Sr. —Do yeh think annyone should be allowed in here? Annyone now?

—Eh —, said Bimbo.

He didn't want to answer, but he had to.

—Yeah.

—Then what's Malcolm doin' outside then?

He had him.

—In the fuckin' cold, said Jimmy Sr.

—Si, said Bertie. —Poor Malcolm.

—He's gettin' well paid for it, Bimbo told Bertie.

Then he got back to Jimmy Sr.

—That's different, he said. —He's only there to stop messers from comin' in. He's not goin' to stop them just cos he doesn't like them.

—Me bollix, said Jimmy Sr. —How does he tell tha' they're messers?

He had him again.

——He can tell.

—How?

—Si.

—Ah look it, lads, said Bimbo. —Anyone – not messers now, or drug pushers or annyone like tha' – annyone tha' behaves themselves an' likes their pint should be allowed in.

They could tell by the way he spoke and looked at them that he wanted them to agree with him; he was nearly begging them.

—No way, said Jimmy Sr. —No fuckin' way.

Bertie agreed.

—Si, he said.

—Ah; why not?

—Look it, Jimmy Sr started, although he hadn't a breeze what he was going to say.

—Compadre, Bertie took over.

He sat up straight.

—Say we go into town, righ'; we go into town an' we try an' get into one o' those disco bars, righ'?

—Yeah, said Jimmy Sr.

—Would we be let in, would yeh say? Bertie asked Bimbo.

—I wouldn't want to go into one o' them, said Bimbo.

—Answer me question, said Bertie.

Bimbo thought about it.

It wasn't the pints Jimmy Sr loved; that wasn't it. He liked his pint – he fuckin' loved his pint – but that wasn't why he was here. He could do without it. He WAS doing without it. He only came up about two times a week these days, since he'd been laid off, and he never missed the drink, not really. Every night at about nine o'clock – when he heard the News music – he started getting itchy and he had to concentrate on staying sitting there and watching the News and being interested in it, but it wasn't the gargle he was dying for: it was this (he sat back and smiled at Bimbo); the lads here, the crack, the laughing. This was what he loved.

—Well? Bertie said to Bimbo.

Being on the labour wouldn't have been that bad if you could've come up here every night, or even every second night, and have got your batteries charged. But there you were; he'd a family to feed and that. He was only here now because one of his young fellas had given him a fiver.

—I wouldn't say we'd get in, said Bimbo.

—I agree with yeh, said Bertie. —The hombres at the door would tell us to vamoose an' fuck off. And——

He picked up his new pint.

—they'd be right.

He disappeared behind his pint. Jimmy Sr and Bimbo waited for him.

—Now, said Bertie, and he was looking at Bimbo, —why would they be righ'?

Jimmy Sr loved this.

Bimbo took up his pint, and put it down on the mat again.

—I give up, he said. —I don't know.

—Yeh do know, said Bertie. —It's because we've no righ' to be there. Amn't I righ'?

—Yeah, said Jimmy Sr.

—Disco bars aren't there for the likes of us, Bertie told Bimbo. —They're for young fellas an' signoritas. To go for a

378

drink an' a dance an' wha'ever happens after, if yeh get me drift.

They laughed.

—It's not our scene, said Bertie.

He swept his open hand up and across from left to right, and showed them the room.

—This is our scene, compadre, he said.

—Fuckin' sure, said Jimmy Sr.

Bertie was really enjoying himself. He pointed the things out to them.

—Our pints. Our table here with the beermat under it stoppin' it from wobblin'. Our dart board an' our hoops, over there, look it.

He stamped his foot.

—Our floor with no carpet on it. Our chairs here with the springs all stickin' up into our holes. We fit here, Bimbo, said Bertie. —An' those fuckers over there should go upstairs to the Lounge where they fuckin' belong.

—Ah well, said Bimbo after he'd stopped laughing. —I suppose you're righ'.

—Oh, I am, said Bertie. —I am.

—Yeh are, o' course, said Jimmy Sr. —Come here but, Bertie. You were in one o' them before, weren't yeh? In a disco bar.

—I was indeed, compadre, said Bertie.

—Were yeh? said Bimbo. —Wha' were yeh doin' in one them places?

—Watchin' the greyhound racin', said Jimmy Sr.

—Yeh know wha' I mean, said Bimbo. —Don't start now.

—Wha' d'yeh think he was doin' there, for fuck sake?

Bimbo ignored him.

—Excuse me, Bertie, he said. —Why were yeh in the disco bar?

—There was nowhere else, Bertie told him.

He waited.

—Wha' d'yeh mean?

379

—There was nowhere else to go cos all the other canteenas were shut; comprende?

—No. Not really.

—I got into Limerick after —

—Limerick!?

—Si.

—Wha' were yeh doin' there?

—Ah now, said Bertie. —It's a long story, an' it doesn't matter cos it's got nothin' to do with the disco bar.

—Yeah, but why were yeh in Limerick? Jimmy Sr asked him.

—You're beginnin' to annoy me, compadre, said Bertie.

—I was only askin', said Jimmy Sr. ——My round, lads.

—No, hang on, Jim, said Bimbo. —I'll get this one.

—It's my round but.

—You're alrigh', said Bimbo. —Don't worry 'bout it.

Bimbo stood up so that Leo could see him.

—No, hang on, said Jimmy Sr. —Sit down.

—Not at all, said Bimbo. —You're alrigh'.

—Sit down!

Bimbo didn't know what to do.

—I'll buy me own round, said Jimmy Sr. —Righ'?

People were looking over at them, and wanting something to happen. Leo was at the end of the bar, ready to jump in and save the glass.

Bimbo sat down.

—O' course, Jim, he said. —No problem. I just ——Sorry.

—You're alrigh', said Jimmy Sr.

He patted Bimbo's leg.

—Sorry for shoutin' at yeh, he said. —But I'll pay me own way, alrigh'.

—Yeh'd better, said Bertie.

Jimmy Sr smiled.

—Sorry, Jimmy, said Bimbo. —I didn't mean —

—No, Jimmy Sr stopped him.

He stood up.

—Three nice pints here, Leo!

He had a look at his watch on his way back down: he was safe; there wouldn't be time for another full round.

—Wha' were yeh doin' in a shaggin' disco bar? Bimbo asked Bertie. —Of all places.

—He told yeh, said Jimmy Sr.

—No, said Bimbo. —He didn't; not really. He only said he was in Limerick.

—Correction, said Bertie. —I told yeh, there was nowhere else to go to.

—Why was tha'?

—Jesus, he's thick, Jimmy Sr told Bertie.

—Everywhere else was shut, Bertie told Bimbo. —By the time I got my burro corralled an' I'd thrown a bit of water on me face an' dusted me poncho it was past closin' time; comprende?

—Yeah, said Bimbo.

—So, said Bertie. —There was this disco bar in the hotel —

—Did yeh stay in a hotel? Jimmy Sr asked him.

—Si.

—Jaysis, wha'.

—Nothin' but the best, said Bertie.

—Was it dear?

—Twenty-six quid.

—Are yeh serious? said Bimbo. —For the one night only?

—Oh, si.

—My God, said Bimbo. —Breakfast?

—Ah, yeah, said Bertie. —'Course.

—Was it one o' them continental ones, Bertie? Jimmy Sr asked him.

—Fuck, no, said Bertie. —I speet on your continental breakfast. A fry.

—Lovely, said Bimbo. —Was it nice?

—Alrigh', said Bertie.

—That's gas, said Bimbo. —Isn't it?

—Wha'? said Jimmy Sr.

—Bertie bein' in a hotel.

—I still want to know wha' he was doin' in fuckin' Limerick, said Jimmy Sr.

—Now, Leo shouted from the bar.

—That's me, said Jimmy Sr.

He was up and over to the bar in a second.

—Wha' was it like, an'annyway? Bimbo asked Bertie.

—What's tha'?

—The disco bar.

—Oh, tha'. Grand. It wasn't too bad at all.

Jimmy Sr was back.

—Get rid o' some o' them glasses there, Bimbo, will yeh. Good man.

He lowered the pints onto the table.

—Look at them now, wha'.

—Tha' man's a genius, said Bimbo.

—Si, said Bertie.

—How come they let yeh in? Bimbo asked Bertie.

—What's this? said Jimmy Sr.

—The disco bar.

—Oh, yeah.

—I was a guest, compadre, Bertie told Bimbo. —I was entitled to get in.

—Is tha' righ'?

—Si. I made a bit of an effort.

He held the collar of his shirt for a second.

—Know wha' I mean?

—Yeh brasser, yeh, said Jimmy Sr.

—Fuck off, you, said Bertie. —I'll tell yeh one thing. It works.

—Wha'?

—Makin' the effort. Dressin' up.

Jimmy Sr made his face go sceptical.

—I'd say it does alrigh', he said.

—I'm tellin' yeh, said Bertie.

—Maybe, said Jimmy Sr.

Bimbo was a bit lost.

—He's tryin' to tell us he got off with somethin', Jimmy Sr told him.

—Ah no, said Bimbo. —You're jokin'.

—He is, o' course, said Jimmy Sr.

—I'm sayin' nothin', said Bertie.

Bimbo was looking carefully at Bertie, making sure that he was only messing. Bimbo didn't like that sort of thing; Bertie was married. But he thought he was having them on; he could tell from Bertie's face, looking around him like he'd said nothing. He was definitely codding them.

Bertie caught Bimbo looking at him.

—A big girl, she was, he told him.

—Ah, get ou' of it, said Bimbo.

Jimmy Sr was looking at Bertie as well. He was the same age as Bertie, a few years older only. Bertie hadn't got off with any young one in Limerick; he could tell. But he kept looking.

*　*　*

Jimmy Sr was having problems with one of his laces. The knot was tiny and his fingernails weren't long enough to get at it properly. He'd have to turn the light on; he could hardly feel the knot now it was so small. He'd no nails left either, all bitten to fuck.

—Christ!

He didn't roar it or anything, but it exploded out. And he threw his head up because his neck felt like it was going to burst. He was sitting on the bed, bent over.

His nails usen't to be like this.

He tried to pull the fuckin' shoe off. His neck was getting sorer. He shut his eyes.

—Is that you?

Now he'd woken Veronica.

—Can't get me fuckin' poxy shoe off.

But it was good that she'd woken up. He slumped, then stretched and rubbed his neck.

—Sorry, he said.

—How was it?

383

—Grand.

—How are all the lads?

She always said Lads like they were kids, like he went out to play with them.

—Grand, he said. —Bimbo was askin' for yeh.

—And what did you tell him?

—Eh —

That was a hard one.

—I said yeh were fine, said Jimmy Sr.

—Did you cross your fingers when you said it?

—Ah, Veronica.

—Ah, Jimmy.

It was alright; she wasn't getting at him.

—I'll have to get into bed with the fuckin' shoe on; look.

Veronica sat up and turned on the lamp beside her.

—What's wrong? she said.

—Me shoe; look it.

She looked.

—Can you not tie your laces properly yet?

And she put his foot in her lap and got going on the knot. He nearly fell off the bed turning for her.

—You're useless, she said. —You really are.

For a split second he was going to straighten his leg quick and put his foot in her stomach, the way she spoke to him like that; for a split second only. Not really.

—There.

She had it done already.

It was nice as well sometimes, being mothered by Veronica.

—Thanks very much, he said.

* * *

He got up with the rest of them in the mornings, even though he didn't have to; got dressed and all. Only Darren and the twins had to get out of the house early these days, and not that early because the school was only up the road, but it was still mad in the kitchen. He liked it though. He knew chaps that wouldn't bother their arses getting up, and wives as well who

384

stayed in bed and let their kids get themselves off to school. He wasn't like that.

First thing, after he had a piss, he sneaked into Sharon's room and took Gina out of her cot. She'd be waiting for him. It was thick, but he held his breath when he was opening the door until he saw that she was still alive. Every morning; he couldn't help it. She grabbed his neck and the two of them sneaked back out of the room because they knew that they weren't to wake Sharon.

Then they'd hit the twins' room. Veronica stuck her head in and roared at them on her way down to the kitchen and his and Gina's job was to follow Veronica and make sure that they were getting up.

—Yis up, girls?

It was a stupid question because they never were. He'd put Gina down on the bed and she jumped on them and that made them stop pretending that they were still asleep. It was like having a bag of spuds hopping on you. Once, Gina's nappy had burst, and that had got them up quick. When he heard Linda or Tracy telling Gina to stop he got out of the room because they didn't like him to be there when they got out from under the blankets.

He went downstairs by himself. He looked into the front room to see that Darren was up. He didn't look in really; he just knocked. Darren had been sleeping in the front room since they'd decided that Sharon needed a room of her own, for Gina. It was terrible; there were two less in the house – Jimmy Jr and Leslie – and still poor Darren had to sleep on the couch. They'd been going to build an extension in the back; he kept meaning to find out if the Corporation would do it.

This morning Darren was coming out when Jimmy Sr got to the door.

—Howyeh, Darren.

—Howyeh.

—Y'alrigh'?

—Yeah.

—Good. Did yeh tidy up the blankets an' stuff yet?

385

—Yeah.

—Good man.

He got out of Darren's way and let him go into the kitchen first. Next he unlocked the back door and let Larrygogan in. The fuckin' hound had a hole bored through the door nearly, from scraping at it every morning to get in, and whining. But Veronica never let him in; she didn't seem to hear him. Jimmy Sr had watched her sometimes when the dog was crying and whining outside – it was fuckin' terrible, like a baby being tortured or something – but Veronica didn't notice it; he'd watched her.

When he opened the door the dog was all over him, hopping around him; thanking him, Jimmy Sr sometimes thought. The dog was no thick. He could nearly talk, the noises he made sometimes when he wanted a biscuit or a chip. He didn't just growl; he had different growls that he used, depending on how badly he wanted something, and whimpers and other stuff as well. And sometimes he just looked at you – just looked – and you couldn't help thinking of one of those starving kids in Africa. He was a great oul' dog, Larrygogan was.

—Ah Christ!

His fuckin' paws were wet, and dirty. He jumped at Jimmy Sr again. Jimmy Sr grabbed the dog's legs just before they landed on his trousers.

—Get his towel, Darren, will yeh.

—Okay, said Darren.

Jimmy Sr looked out the open door while Darren was getting him the dog's towel from under the sink. It was pissing out there, and cold. Not real wintery cold, but the stuff that got inside you and made every room in the house seem miserable, except the kitchen when it was full. The poor dog was wringing, like a drowned rat; half his normal size because his hair was all stuck to him. He barked. Then he shook himself. His back paws started slipping on the lino, so Jimmy Sr let go of his legs.

—Here.

Darren threw the towel to Jimmy Sr.

—Good man, said Jimmy Sr.

He opened the towel – it was manky but dry – and got ready to dry the dog's back, and this was the bit the dog loved. Jimmy Sr dropped the towel and missed Larrygogan by a mile because Larry was in under the kitchen table, sliding and barking.

—Come ou' till I dry yeh.

Larrygogan put his chin on the floor and barked at Jimmy Sr.

Jimmy Sr always thought that that bark, the real cheeky one, sounded like Get fucked. And the way his ears jumped up when he said it – not said it, not really; just barked – but he looked like he was saying it, giving cheek to Jimmy Sr, his master. It was gas.

—Come on ou' here, yeh renegade, yeh.

The dog barked again.

—Here, Darren; go round there an' shove him ou' to me.

Jimmy Sr stared at Larrygogan.

—You're fucked now, he said.

—Stop that, said Veronica.

—Sorry, Veronica, he said.

He loved this.

Darren was at the other side of the table. He got down on his knees and stretched in under the table and pushed Larry-gogan – Larrygogan was chin down, arse up – but Larrygogan pushed back against Darren's open hands. The dog's paws slid a bit but he stayed put, and Darren had to climb in under the table. He was bursting his shite laughing now, and so was Jimmy Sr.

—Mind he doesn't fart on yeh, he told Darren.

—Oh Jaysis, said Darren, and he couldn't push properly any more because he was laughing so much.

Larrygogan was winning.

—Ah, leave him, said Jimmy Sr.

He stood up.

—Let him catch his death. He deserves to die, the fuckin'
eejit of a dog.

Darren got out and up from under the table. They grinned
at each other but then Darren sat down and started reading his
book. Jimmy Sr shut the door. Larrygogan charged out to the
hall.

He still had a good breakfast these days, the fry and loads of
toast and a bowl of Cornflakes as well sometimes if he still felt
a bit empty. They used to have Sugar Puffs and the rest of
them; every time there was a new ad on the telly the twins had
to have a box of the new things. But they only had the
Cornflakes now. They were the best. Tea as well, loads of it.
He only had coffee later on in the day, and sometimes he
didn't bother. He didn't need it. Tea though, he loved his cup
of tea; twenty bleedin' cups.

He had a mug for work that he'd had for years; he still had
it. It was a big plain white one, no cracks, no stupid slogans.
He put two teabags into it; used to. My God, he'd never forget
the taste of the first cup of tea in the morning, usually in a bare
room in a new house with muck and dirt everywhere, freezing;
fuck me, it was great; it scalded him on the way down; he
could feel it all the way. And the taste it left; brilliant; brilliant.
He always used two bags, squeezed the bejesus out of them.
The mug was so big it warmed more than just his hands. It
was like sitting in front of a fire. After a few gulps he'd sip at
it and turn around and look at his work. He always got a few
walls done before he stopped for the tea. Even if the other lads
were stopping he kept going, till he felt he needed it; deserved
it. He'd look around him at the plastering. It was perfect; not
a bump or a sag, so smooth you'd never know where he'd
started. Then he'd gulp down the rest of the tea and get back
to it. The mug was outside in the shed, in a bag with his other
work stuff. He'd wrapped toilet paper around it.

—You'll get drenched goin' to school, Darren, he said.

—Yeah, said Darren.

—Still, said Jimmy Sr. —It'll save yeh the bother o' washin'
yourself, wha'.

—Yeah, said Darren.

Darren looked at the rain hitting the window.

—Jesus, he said.

—Stop that, said Veronica.

—That's the real wet stuff alrigh', Jimmy Sr told Darren.

—I've P.E. today, Darren told him.

—Is tha' righ'? said Jimmy Sr. —Ah, they'll never send yeh ou' in tha'; they couldn't.

—They did the last time.

—Did they, the cunts?

Veronica put his plate in front of him and then walloped him across the head.

—Sorry, he said.

He took out tenpence and dropped it in the swearbox.

—D'yeh want a note for the teacher? he asked Darren.

—He does not, said Veronica.

—No, said Darren. —I don't mind. It might stop.

—That's very true.

Darren got back to his book and his breakfast. Jimmy Sr picked up his knife and fork.

—Wha' have we here? he said.

Darren kept reading. Veronica was busy. So he just chopped a bit of sausage off, put it on a piece of toast, closed the toast over on it and bit into it. The marge was lovely and warm.

The twins came in.

—You're to sign this, Linda told Jimmy Sr.

—Get back upstairs and get that stuff off, said Veronica.

—Ah, Mammy —

—Go on! ——You too, she told Tracy.

Tracy followed Linda out into the hall.

—It's not fair! they heard Linda.

—Wha' was tha' abou'? Jimmy Sr wanted to know.

—They were wearing eye-shadow, said Veronica.

—Oh.

—They were sent home last week for having it on, said Veronica.

—It's crazy, said Darren. —It's pitiful.

Jimmy Sr wasn't sure.

—They're a bit young, he said.

—Sixth years aren't allowed to have it on either, Darren told Jimmy Sr.

—Ah then, said Jimmy Sr. —Then you're righ', Darren. That's just stupid.

—It's a school rule, said Veronica.

—That's right as well, o' course, said Jimmy Sr.

Darren was standing up, putting his book marker carefully into place so it wouldn't fall out.

—If everybody had that attitude, he said, —nothing would ever change.

Jimmy Sr didn't know what to do. He liked hearing Darren talk like that, but he was being cheeky as well; to his mother. There was something about the way Darren spoke since his voice broke that left Jimmy Sr confused. He admired him, more and more; he was a great young fella; he was really proud of him, but he thought he felt a bit jealous of him as well sometimes; he didn't know. Anyway, he wasn't going to be let talk like that to his mother. That was out.

But the twins were back.

—You're to sign this.

Linda had spoken to him.

—Wha'?

—Here.

—Yeah, said Jimmy Sr. —Why but?

He took Linda's homework journal from her.

—Don't know, said Linda. —You're to just sign it.

Jimmy Sr looked at the cover; Big Fun, Wet Wet Wet, Brother Beyond, Tracy loves Keith. He looked at the back; Linda loves Keith.

—Lucky Keith, he said. —Where am I to sign?

Linda took the journal and found the right page.

—Here, she said.

There was a page for each week, divided into sections for subject, homework and teachers' comments.

—You don't have to read them, said Linda.

—Homework not done, Jimmy Sr read. —Persisted in talking. ——Homework not done. Cheeky. Stabbed student with compass. ——Homework should be done at home.

He looked up.

—Fuckin' hell, he said. —An' that's only Monday.

—Let me see, said Veronica. ——My God.

Linda pointed at one of the comments.

—I wasn't cheeky. She just said I was but I wasn't. An' he – tha' one there – he hit me with his ruler so I had to get him back but she didn't see him hittin' me, she on'y seen —

—Saw, said Veronica.

—She only saw me gettin' him with the compass. An' I did not stab him. I on'y —

—Shut up! said Jimmy Sr.

He looked at Veronica.

—Give us a pen, he said to Linda. —Where's your journal till I see it, he said to Tracy.

—It's in school, said Tracy.

—Why's tha'?

—A teacher kept it.

—Why?

—He just did.

Jimmy Sr looked at Veronica again.

—You're grounded, he told the twins. —The two o' yis.

He saw Parent's Signature, and signed the dotted line.

—Till when? said Tracy.

—Till I say so, said Jimmy Sr. —Who told yeh to get me to sign this?

—Miss McCluskey.

—Elephant Woman, said Darren, on his way out.

—Don't start now, said Jimmy Sr.

He stared the twins out of it.

—I'm warnin' yis, he said. —If one o' yis laughs I'll tan your arses for yis.

Tracy started; she couldn't keep it in. And that got Linda going.

—Here, said Jimmy Sr.

He walloped her with the journal, but not too hard.

—I'm checkin' your homework every nigh', d'yeh hear me. An' —

He shouted after them.

—if I see anny more bad comments I'll —

The front door slammed.

—crucify yis! ——The pair o' them'll be pushin' buggies before they're fifteen.

—Oh God, said Veronica. —Don't.

He looked at Veronica, carefully.

—I'll check their eccers every nigh', don't worry. An' we won't let them out at all after their tea, an' that'll sort them ou', wait an' see, Veronica. Fair enough?

—Okay.

—I'll do everythin'. I'll even sleep in the same bed as them.

—Jesus, said Veronica. —We've enough trouble in the house without that as well.

Jimmy Sr laughed.

—Good girl, he said. —An' you can sleep with Darren. How's tha'?

He loved the breakfasts. Pity they went so quick.

He got up.

Where was Gina?

—No rest for the wicked, he said.

* * *

—They're not real computers annyway, sure they're not.

—Not at all, said Veronica. —They're only toys.

Jimmy Sr and Veronica were doing a bit of Christmas shopping. It was Thursday morning and more than three weeks to go, so Donaghmede Shopping Centre – where they were – wasn't too bad, not too crowded. They hadn't really said it, but they were looking for things that looked good and cost nothing. It reminded Jimmy Sr of when he was a kid and he used to walk along with his head down and pray, really pray, that he'd find money on the path, and he'd close his eyes

392

turning a corner and then open them and there'd be nothing on the ground in front of him.

—And they're very bad for your eyes, said Veronica.

—Is tha' righ'? said Jimmy Sr. —Oh yeah; I read somethin' abou' tha' somewhere, I think. ——Ah well, then. We'd be mad to get one for them.

They'd just been looking at the computers in a window. They were for nothing, dirt cheap; great value they looked. You linked them into the telly and then you could play all kinds of games on them. Jimmy Sr had played Space Invaders once, years ago; only the once, so he hadn't really got the hang of it, but he'd enjoyed himself. These things looked better; more colours and varieties. It would have been good to have one at home, a bit of gas. And, as well as that, it was a computer, after all; there were probably other things you could do with them, not just play games. Only they couldn't afford one of the fuckin' things. Last year now, last year they'd have bought —

—Sure, who'd we give it to? said Veronica.

—The twins. I suppose.

—They wouldn't be interested, said Veronica. —They'd hate you if you gave them one of them.

She laughed.

—I'd love to see the look on their faces if they thought they were getting a computer game for Christmas.

Jimmy Sr laughed as well now.

—Yeah, he said. —I just thought they looked the business, yeh know. Darren?

—He'd be insulted.

She was right.

—You'd be the only one who'd use it, said Veronica.

He made himself smile.

—True, he said.

—We'll get you an Airfix instead, said Veronica.

*   *   *

393

It was crying alright; she was crying.

Jimmy Sr was outside Sharon's room. He'd come up for his book.

Sharon snuffled.

Jimmy Sr held the door handle. He was going to go in.

But he couldn't.

He wanted to, but he couldn't. He wouldn't have known what to do any more.

He went back down to the kitchen very carefully, and stepped down over the stair with the creak in it.

* * *

Veronica had been in already to have a look at her. It was his turn now. One, two —

He grabbed the handle and went straight into the front room.

—Sorry, Darren; for bargin' in on yeh ——Oh, hello.

—Hi.

She smiled. God, she was lovely.

He held his hand out to her.

—Darren's da, he said. —Howyeh.

She blushed a bit; lovely.

—This is Miranda, Darren told Jimmy Sr.

—Sorry, said Jimmy Sr. —I didn't catch —

—Miranda, said Darren.

—Miranda, said Jimmy Sr. —Howyeh, Miranda.

—Fine, thank you, said Miranda.

—'Course yeh are, said Jimmy Sr.

—Were yeh lookin' for somethin' in particular? Darren asked him.

He had one of his smirks on him, one of his they-treat-me-like-a-kid ones. But he was chuffed as well, you could tell.

Jimmy Sr patted him on the head.

—I am indeed, Darren, son, he said. —I'm lookin' for Gina.

—She's not here.

—No, that's true, Jimmy Sr agreed. —But Miranda is, wha'. Bye bye, Miranda.

394

He shut the door after him. She was a cracker alright. Veronica'd said she was lovely but women always said that other women were lovely and they weren't; they hadn't a clue. Miranda though, she was a —

A ride; she was. It was weird thinking it; his son was going out with a ride; but it was true. He could've given himself a bugle now, out here in the hall, just remembering what she was like and her smile; no problem.

He'd never gone out with a young one like that.

He went back into the kitchen to tell Veronica he liked her.

* * *

There were days when there was this feeling in his guts all the time, like a fart building up only it wasn't that at all. It was as if his trousers were too tight for him, but he'd check and they weren't, they were grand; but there was a little ball of hard air inside in him, getting bigger. It was bad, a bad sort of excitement, and he couldn't get rid of it. It was like when he was a kid and he'd done something bad and he was waiting for his da to come home from work to kill him. He used to use his belt, the bollix. He didn't wear a belt; he only kept it for strapping Jimmy Sr and his brothers; under the sink he kept it, a big leather thing; he'd take ages bending over, looking for it and then testing it on the side of the sink and saying Ah yes as if he was pleased with it; and he'd stare at Jimmy Sr and make him stare back and then Jimmy Sr'd feel the pain on the side of his leg and again and again and it was fuckin' terrible and it was worse if he took his eyes off his da's eyes, the fuckin' sadistic cunt, so he had to keep staring back at him; it was agony, but not as bad as the waiting. Waiting for it was the worst part. If he did something early in the day and his mother said she was going to tell his da, that was it; she never changed her mind. He'd go through the whole day scared shitless, waiting for his da to come home, praying that he'd go for a pint first or get knocked down by a car or fall into a machine at work or get a heart attack, any fuckin' thing.

395

And that was how he sometimes – often – felt now, scared shitless. And he didn't know why.

* * *

—Did yeh ever read David Copperfield, Veronica? said Jimmy Sr.

—No, said Veronica.

She was reading Lord of the Flies at the kitchen table.

—Did yeh not? said Jimmy Sr. —Ah, it's very good.

The best thing he'd ever done was give up on that Man in the Iron Mask fuckology.

—Look at the size of it but, he said. —Eight hundred pages. More. Still though, it's the business. There's this cunt in it called Mr Micawber an', I'm not jokin' yeh – D'yeh want to read it after me, Veronica?

Veronica finished the note she was taking, about Piggy getting his head smashed. She knew what he wanted her to say.

—Okay, she said.

—Do yeh? said Jimmy Sr. —Fair enough. I'd better finish it quick so. I've to bring it back to the library on the twenty-first of December.

He checked the date.

—Yeah, he said.

—We've loads of time, said Veronica.

—'Course we have, said Jimmy Sr.

He was delighted. He didn't know why, exactly.

—Do you want this one when I'm finished with it? Veronica asked him.

—Okay, said Jimmy Sr. —That's a good idea. A swap, wha'.

—Yes, said Veronica.

He looked at her reading and stopping and taking her notes. He wondered if maybe he should take notes as well. He sometimes forgot what —

No; that would just have been thick; stupid.

396

—I'll go up an' get a few more chapters read before the tea, he told Veronica.

—Grand, said Veronica.

*   *   *

—They're stupid fuckin' things annyway, said Jimmy Sr.

—Ah – I know, but —

Veronica wasn't convinced.

Jimmy Sr picked up one of the cards.

—For instance, he said, —look at this one, look it. Dessie an' Frieda; they only live around the fuckin' corner, we see them every fuckin' day!

Veronica's face was the same.

—Annyway, said Jimmy Sr. —It's you says tha' we can't send any, not me.

Veronica's face hardened. Jimmy Sr got in before she could.

—You said we can't afford them, he said. —I don't mind.

—We can't afford them, said Veronica.

—There, said Jimmy Sr. —Yeh said it again. We can't afford them. So we won't send any. ——So wha' are yeh whingin' abou'? It's your idea.

Veronica sighed. She just looked sad again.

—That's not fair, she said.

—How is it not fair? Jimmy Sr wanted to know. —How is it not fair!?

Veronica sighed again.

—How!?

—You're blaming me, said Veronica.

—Yeah, said Jimmy Sr. —An' you're blamin' me.

—What d'you mean? said Veronica.

—Yeh are, said Jimmy Sr. —You've decided tha' we haven't the money to buy Christmas cards an' you're probably righ'. But then you put this puss on yeh ——It's not my fault we've no fuckin' money for your fuckin' Christmas cards!

—I never said it was.

—No, but yeh looked it; I have eyes, yeh know.

He stood up.

—Ah, Jimmy —

—Ah, nothin'; I'm sick of it; just ——fuck off!

* * *

Jimmy Sr was holding a bottle of Guinness. He had a can of
Tennents in his other hand and an empty glass between his
knees, so he was having problems. That was the worst thing
about not being at home; just that; you weren't at home, so
you couldn't do what you wanted. You had to watch yourself.

He was in Bimbo's house.

If he'd been in his own gaff he wouldn't have been sitting
like this, like a gobshite, too far back in the armchair – he
couldn't get out of the fuckin' thing because his hands were
full. He didn't want to put the can or the bottle on one of the
arms of the chair because the wood was at an angle like a ski
jump and very shiny; he could smell the polish. And Bimbo's
kids were flying around the place, in and out, like fuckin' –
kids. And this fuckin' tie he had on him, it was killing him; it
was sawing the fuckin' neck off him. It was the shirt, a new
one Veronica'd given him; she said he'd put on weight. It
wasn't fuckin' fair: he was drinking far less but he was getting
fuckin' fatter. She said he was anyway. She'd probably said it
because it was either that or admit that she'd bought him the
wrong size of a shirt. Anyway, he was fuckin' choking and he
couldn't loosen the poxy tie because his fuckin' hands were
full —

Jesus tonight!

It was Christmas morning. They did this every Christmas,
went to one of their houses and had a few scoops before the
dinner. It was good; usually. He wasn't sure, but he had a
good idea that it was really his and Veronica's turn to have the
rest of them in their house; he wasn't sure. Bimbo had just
said, Will yis all be comin' to our place for your Christmas
drinks? a few days ago and Jimmy Sr hadn't bothered saying
anything because there was no point; they hadn't the money
to buy the drink for them all.

They'd only a few cans for themselves at home, and Jimmy Jr was bringing some more. He was supposed to be anyway.

He leaned forward as far as he could go and put the Tennents on the floor; he could just reach it. That was better. Now he could organise himself a bit better. He rescued the glass from between his knees and held it for the Guinness.

Bimbo's mother-in-law was still looking over at him.

Let her, the bitch.

He wished Bertie would hurry up. He was good with oul' ones like that. He told them they were looking great and he wished he was a few years older and that kind of shite. Jimmy Sr was no good at that sort of thing, not this morning anyway.

She was still looking at him.

He smiled over at her.

—Cheers, he said.

She just looked at him.

Jesus, he didn't know how Bimbo could stick it. Where the fuck was Bimbo anyway? He was by himself in here, except for Freddy Kruger's fuckin' granny over there. He said he'd be back in a minute. And that was hours ago. He was playing with one of the kids' computers, that was what the cunt was doing; leaving Jimmy Sr here stranded.

Veronica was inside in the kitchen with Maggie, Bimbo's one.

—That's a great smell comin' from the kitchen, wha', said Jimmy Sr.

Her mouth moved.

—What's tha'? he said, and he leaned out.

Maybe she hadn't said anything. Maybe she couldn't help it; she couldn't control her muscles, the ones that held her mouth up. Ah Jaysis, this was fuckin' terrible; fuck Bimbo anyway.

He heard feet on the path.

—Thank fuck.

It was out before he knew it. And she nodded; she did; she'd heard him; oh Christ!

She couldn't have; no. No, she'd just nodded at the same

399

time, that was all. Because, probably, her neck wasn't the best any more, that was all. He hoped.

The bell rang; the first bit of Strangers in the Night.

She definitely hadn't heard him.

Stupid fuckin' thing for a bell to do, play a song. Anyway, they didn't even need a bell. This house was the exact same as Jimmy Sr's; you could hear a knock on the door anywhere in the house.

Bertie came in.

—Compadre!

Jimmy Sr got up out of the chair.

—Happy Christmas, Bertie.

They shook hands. Bertie's hand was huge, and dry.

Vera, the wife, was with him; a fine thing, Jimmy Sr'd always thought; still in great nick.

—Howyeh, Jimmy love, she said, and she stuck her cheek out, sort of, for him to kiss.

He kissed it. It wasn't caked in that powdery stuff that a lot of women wore when they were out. Mind you, Veronica didn't wear that stuff either.

The room was fuller now; Jimmy Sr, Vera, Bertie, Bimbo and two of his kids, and the mother-in-law over there in her corner. Jimmy Sr felt happier now.

—What'll yeh have, Vera? said Bimbo.

—D'yeh want a Tennents? Jimmy Sr asked Bertie.

—Oh si, said Bertie.

—Bimbo gave me one, Jimmy Sr explained, —an' then he asked me if I'd prefer a bottle o' stout an' I said Fair enough, so —

He picked the can up off the floor.

—I didn't open it or annythin'.

—Good man, said Bertie. —Gracias.

—Will yis have a small one with them? Bimbo asked Jimmy Sr and Bertie.

Jimmy Sr looked at Bertie and Bertie shrugged.

—Fair enough, yeah, said Jimmy Sr. —Good man.

This was the business now alright. He grinned at Vera, and lifted his glass.

—Cheers, wha'.

—What did Santy bring yeh, Jimmy? Vera asked him.

—This, said Jimmy Sr.

He showed her his new shirt.

—Very nice.

—It's a bit small.

—Ah no; it's nice.

Bertie had found Maggie's mother.

—Isn't she lookin' even better than last year? he said to them.

—Def'ny, said Jimmy Sr, but he couldn't look at her.

—They're in the kitchen, Jimmy Sr told Vera.

—Good for them, said Vera.

Bimbo came back with the small ones and Vera's drink, a gin or a vodka.

—The cavalry, said Bertie. —Muchos gracias, my friend.

—The girls are in the kitchen, Bimbo told Vera.

—Good, said Vera.

Jimmy Sr reckoned she'd had a few already. Maybe not though: she wasn't really like the other women, always making fuckin' sandwiches and tea and talking about the Royal Family and Coronation Street and that kind of shite. She kept their house grand though; any time Jimmy Sr had been in it anyway.

Bertie leaned in nearer to Bimbo.

—There's a funny whiff off your mammy-in-law, he told him.

Bimbo looked shocked.

—She might be dead, said Bertie.

Jimmy Sr burst his shite laughing. Poor Bimbo's face made it worse. Vera laughed as well. She just laughed straight out; she didn't cluck cluck like a lot of women would've, like Veronica would've.

—Go over, Bertie told Bimbo. —I'm tellin' yeh, compadre, the hum is fuckin' atrocious.

401

—My God, said Bimbo, dead quiet. —Is she after doin' somethin' to herself?

—Go over an' check, said Bertie. —It might have been just a fart, but —

Bimbo looked around, to make sure that none of the kids was around to witness this.

—Hang on, said Jimmy Sr. —I can smell somethin' meself now alrigh'.

—Isn't it fuckin' woeful? said Bertie.

—Oh God, said Bimbo.

—This could ruin your Christmas dinner, compadre, Bertie told Bimbo.

Bottled Guinness got up into Jimmy Sr's nose.

He went out into the hall to sort himself out and to laugh properly. This was great; this was the kind of thing you remembered for the rest of your life.

—You'll never get it out o' the upholstery, said Bertie.

Jimmy Sr wanted to go out into the garden and roar, really fuckin' howl.

One of Bimbo's kids – Wayne he thought it was – ran into the room to tell his da something —

—Get ou'! said Bimbo.

And then.

—Sorry, son; go in an' tell your mammy I need her.

—Tell her to bring a few J-cloths, said Bertie.

—No! don't, Wayne, said Bimbo. —Off yeh go.

Wayne came out, looking like he'd just changed his mind about crying, and galloped down to the kitchen walloping the side of his arse like he was on a horse.

When Jimmy Sr went back into the room Bimbo was over at his mother-in-law, pretending he was looking for something on the shelf behind her. Vera pointed at Bertie and whispered to Jimmy Sr.

—He did this to his brother last night, she said. —The exact same thing.

Bimbo came back. They got in together, to consult.

—I can't smell annythin', said Bimbo.

402

—Can yeh not? said Bertie.

—D'yeh have a cold? Jimmy Sr asked Bimbo. —It's gettin'
worse.

—It's not, is it? said Bimbo. —God, this is desperate.

Maggie and Veronica arrived, and most of Bimbo's kids.

—What's up? said Maggie. —Ah howyeh, Vera.

—Howyeh, Maggie. Happy Christmas. Happy Christmas,
Veronica.

—And yourself, Vera; happy Christmas.

—Never mind Christmas, said Bimbo.

He nodded his head back; he didn't want to look. He
whispered.

—We've an emergency on our hands.

—How come? said Maggie.

Jimmy Sr was having real problems keeping his face straight.
So was Vera. Bertie though, he looked like a doctor telling
you that you had cancer.

—Your mother —, said Bimbo.

—She has a name, you know, said Maggie.

—That's not all she has, signora, said Bertie.

That was it; Guinness, snot, probably some of his breakfast
burst up into Jimmy Sr's mouth and nose; it didn't get past his
teeth – he was lucky there – but something landed on his shirt;
he didn't care, not yet; his eyes watered —

—Fuck; sorry.

And he laughed.

Veronica had her handkerchief out and was trying to get the
snot off his shirt.

He laughed like he was dying of it; it was hurting him but it
was fuckin' great. Veronica was tickling him as well and that
made it worse.

Veronica started laughing at him laughing.

They were all laughing now, even Bimbo. He knew he'd
been had but he didn't mind; he never did; only sometimes.

Jimmy Sr felt a fart coming on, and he didn't trust himself
with it; he couldn't, not the way he was, helpless from the
laughing and sweating and that; he'd have ended up being the

one who'd ruined Bimbo's Christmas – by shiteing all over his new carpet.

—Eh, the jacks, he said.

—Off yeh go, said Bertie.

It took him ages to get up the stairs; he had to haul himself up them.

*   *   *

He had a piss while he was up there, and gave his hands a wash; he always did when he was in someone's house.

He was some tulip, Bertie; he was fuckin' gas.

Jesus, the water was scalding.

He dried his hands, and looked at his watch: half-twelve. That was good; they'd stay another hour and a half or so. The crack would be good.

Vera; she was a fine-looking bird. She looked after herself – whatever that meant. She looked healthy, that was it. She looked healthier than Veronica. She was a good bit younger than Veronica, maybe ten years. But she looked like she'd been a young one not so long ago and poor Veronica looked like she'd never been a young one. It wasn't just age though.

Bimbo had an electric razor.

He had two of them, two razors, the jammy bastard; an ordinary-looking one and a thin yellow one that didn't look like it could've been much good. Jimmy Sr picked up the yellow one: Girl Care. What the fuck —

She was a bit of a brasser, Vera, but Jimmy Sr liked that.

It was Maggie's, that was it; for her legs or – only her legs probably. He pressed a small rubber button, and it came on but there was hardly any noise out of it. He put his foot up on the bath and lifted his trouser leg and pulled down his sock a bit; new socks, from the twins.

—One from each o' yis, wha', he'd said when he'd unwrapped them, earlier at home.

He looked at the door; it was alright, it was locked.

He slowly put the Girl yoke down on top of a couple of long hairs, there on his shin: nothing. He massaged another

404

bit of his leg with it, and then felt it. It was smooth alright but – it was smooth there anyway. There was a clump of about ten hairs growing out of a sort of a mole yoke he'd had since he was a kid.

They were real wiry, these hairs, and blacker than the other ones. He wouldn't put the head of the razor straight down on top of them; he'd just run the thing over the mole quickly and see what it did.

He looked at the door again. Vera probably used one of these, when she was shaving her legs —

—Ah fuck this!

He threw the Girl Care back onto the shelf over the sink.

God, he was a right fuckin' eejit. Shaving his legs; for fuck sake!

He was sweating.

He'd better get back down to the others.

Shaving his fuckin' legs.

He felt weak, hopeless, like he'd been caught. Was something happening him?

He turned on the cold tap.

No, fuck it; he'd only been curious, that was all; he'd only wanted to see if the fuckin' thing worked, that was all.

The cold water was lovely on his face. Nice towel as well; lovely and soft. Maggie had probably put it into the bathroom just before they'd arrived, just for them. It wasn't damp and smelly, the way it would've been if the whole family had been through it that morning.

Fair play to Bimbo; and Maggie. They had the house lovely.

He felt better now. That hot wetness was gone. He was grand now.

He unlocked the door and went downstairs.

*   *   *

It was nice. The window was open and it wasn't cold at all. There was no one out on the road; no voices or cars. No one would've been out on Christmas Day night; there was nowhere to go, unless they'd been out visiting the mother or something and they were on their way home.

Veronica was asleep.

That was the first time they'd done the business in a good while; two months nearly. Made love. He'd never called it that; it sounded thick. Riding your wife was more than just riding, especially when yis hadn't done it in months, but – he could never have said Let's make love to Veronica; she'd have burst out laughing at him.

He wasn't tired. He hadn't drunk much. There hadn't been that much to drink, but that didn't matter; he wouldn't have wanted it anyway. Anyway as well, he'd had a snooze after they got back from Bimbo's while Veronica and Sharon were getting the dinner ready.

Veronica had caught him feeling her legs to see if they were smooth, to see if she shaved them.

—What're you doing?

—Nothin'.

She hadn't really caught him; he'd have been doing it anyway. But he'd had to keep feeling them up and down from her knees up to her gee after she'd said that, so she wouldn't think he'd stopped just cos she'd said it.

They were smooth, except on her shins. They were a bit prickly there.

Young Jimmy'd come for the dinner. In a taxi, no less. Fair play to him. And five cigars for Jimmy Sr from Aoife, his mot. That was very nice of her; he'd only met her the once. She was a nice young one, too nice for that —

That wasn't fair. He was alright, young Jimmy. He was staying the night, downstairs with Darren. And Darren was well set up as well, with a lovely-looking young one.

Aoife and Miranda.

Two lovely names. There was something about them; just thinking of the names, not even the girls themselves, got him going. They were models' names.

Veronica wasn't what you'd have called a sexy name. Or Vera.

Vera wasn't too bad though. There was no saint called Vera as far as he knew.

Veronica shifted and moved in closer to him. That was nice. He felt guilty now; not really though. He put his hand on her back.

That fucker Leslie hadn't got in touch; not even a card. Even just to tell them where he was; and that he was alive. He'd been caught robbing a Lifeboat collection box out in Howth. He hadn't even been caught, just seen by an off-duty cop who knew him. And that was why he'd left, for robbing a couple of quids' worth of fivepences and twopences. Last August that was. He'd spent two nights in Veronica's sister's in Wolverhampton, and that was it; they hadn't heard from him since. On the run. He was only nineteen. He'd have gone eventually anyway; he was always in trouble and never at home, and you couldn't be held responsible for a nineteen-year-old. They were better off without him. Jimmy Sr had taken the day off work to go with Leslie to court the first time, about five years ago now, for trespassing on the tracks.

Poor Veronica had bought a present for him, just in case; a jumper. But she hadn't put it under the tree. It was up in the wardrobe over there, all wrapped up. She hadn't said anything when he didn't turn up yesterday or even today. She'd been in good form all day. You never knew with Veronica.

Jimmy Sr would throw the little shitehawk out on his ear if he turned up now. No, though; he wouldn't.

Trespassing on the tracks. Then he'd gone on to the big time, robbing fuckin' poor boxes. He was probably sleeping in a cardboard box —

It hadn't been a bad day; not too bad at all. Fair enough, probably nobody got the present they'd really wanted – the faces on the poor twins when they'd seen their presents, clothes. They used to get new clothes anyway, their Christmas clothes; their presents had always been separate. Still, they were happy enough with the clothes. They'd been changing in and out of them all day. They were getting very big, real young ones. Gina was the only real child left in the house.

Jimmy Sr had got David Copperfield for Darren, and he'd liked it; you could tell. To Darren From His Father; that was what he'd written inside it. He saw Darren reading it after the tea.

They'd had their turkey as well, same as always; a grand big fucker. They'd be eating turkey sandwiches for weeks. He'd won it with two Saturdays to spare, and a bottle of Jameson. His game had definitely improved since he'd gone on the labour.

He got a tea-towel for Veronica, with Italia 90 on it. She liked it as well. She showed it to Sharon and the two of them laughed. He gave out to her later when he caught her using it to dry the dishes and she'd laughed again, and then he had as well. That was what it was for, he supposed. But she could have kept it for – he didn't know – a special occasion or something.

—Jimmy, love, she'd said. —Christmas is a special occasion.

Then she'd shown him how to use it; for a laugh. It had been a good oul' day.

* * *

You got used to it. In fact, it wasn't too bad. You just had to fill your day, and that wasn't all that hard really. And now that the days were getting a bit longer – it was January – the good weather would be starting soon and he'd be able to do things to the garden. He had plans.

The worst part was the money, not having any of it; having to be mean. For instance, Darren had gone to Scotland with the school when he was in second year, but the twins wouldn't be going anywhere. They'd come home soon and ask and he'd have to say No, or Veronica would; she was better at it.

Unless, of course, he got work between now and then.

Only, it was easier to cope if you didn't think things like that, getting work. You just continued on, like this was normal; you filled your day. The good thing about winter was that the day was actually short. It was only in the daylight that you felt bad, restless, sometimes even guilty. Mind you, the time went slower, probably because of the cold.

It hadn't been cold at all yet this winter, not the cold that made your nose numb. Inside in the house during the day, when they didn't have a fire going – when the kids were at school – and they didn't have any heaters on, except in Sharon's room for Gina, it was never really cold, just sort of cool, damp without being damp. It wasn't bad once you were dressed properly.

He'd had to take his jacket off a good few times when he was out walking with Gina it was so warm. He did that a lot, went out with Gina. He even took her to the pitch 'n' putt once, and some fuckin' clown had sent a ball bouncing off the bar of her buggy when Jimmy Sr was teeing up at the seventh, the tricky seventh. God, if he'd hit her he'd have killed her, and he'd only said Sorry and then asked Jimmy Sr did he see where his fuckin' ball had gone. Jimmy Sr told him where the fuckin' ball would go if he ever did it again. But it had scared him.

Mind you, at least he'd had something to tell Veronica when he got home, something genuine. Sometimes he made up things to tell her, little adventures; some oul' one dropping her shopping or some kid nearly getting run over. He felt like a right prick when he was telling her but he kind of had to, he didn't know why; to let her know that he was getting on fine.

He went into town and wandered around. He hadn't done that in years. It had changed a lot; pubs he'd known and even streets were gone. It looked good though, he thought. He could tell you one thing: there was money in this town.

—Si.

Bertie agreed with him, and so did Bimbo.

Young ones must have been earning real money these days as well; you could tell by the way they dressed. He'd sat on that stone bench with the two bronze oul' ones chin-wagging on it, beside the Halfpenny Bridge; he'd sat on the side of that one day and and he'd counted fifty-four great-looking young ones going by in only a quarter of an hour; brilliant-looking women now, and all of them dressed beautifully, the height of style; they must have paid fortunes for the stuff they had on them; you could tell.

He'd read three of your man, Charles Dickens' books now; they were brilliant; just brilliant. He was going to do some Leaving Cert subjects next year, next September; at night, like Veronica. He read the papers from cover to cover these days. He read them in Raheny Library, or Donaghmede if he felt like a change. He preferred Raheny. And he watched Sky News in the day. He couldn't keep up with what was happening these days, especially in the Warsaw Pact places. They were talking about it one day, him and Darren and Sharon and Veronica, and even the twins, at their dinner; they were talking about it and he'd noticed one thing: the twins called Thatcher Thatcher and Bush Bush but they called Gorbachev Mr Gorbachev: that said something. Because they could be cheeky little bitches when they wanted to be.

Sky News was good, better than their other poxy channel, Sky One. But he wouldn't pay for it when they had to start paying for it later in the year sometime. It wasn't worth it, although he didn't know how much they were going to charge. And that reminded him: there'd been a bill from Cablelink stuck up on the fridge door for weeks now. It could stay there for another few; fuck it.

He'd made a list of things to do in the house and he was doing one a week. He'd fixed the jacks yesterday, for example; tightened the handle. It was working grand again now. That sort of thing. But nothing mad. He wasn't going to become one of those do-it-yourself gobshites, fixing things that didn't need fixing, and then invading the neighbours and fixing their stuff as well, and probably making a bollix of it. Once the weather got better and the days got a bit longer, he'd be out there in the garden, ah yes; he wouldn't notice the days flying past him then. He had plans.

He had loads of things to keep him going. The money was the only thing. He'd be going past a pub in town and he'd have the gum for a pint – he always did when he heard the voices and the telly on – just one pint, but he couldn't go in; he couldn't afford it. Or he couldn't buy an ice-cream for Gina when they were out, not that he'd let her have an ice-cream in this weather, but that kind of thing; it was irritating. It was humiliating.

Still though, money wasn't everything. He was happy enough.

* * *

Bimbo was crying.

Jaysis.

Bimbo; of all —

—What's up? said Jimmy Sr.

But that sounded bad, like nothing big was happening. The man was crying, for fuck sake.

—What's wrong with yeh?

That was worse.

—Are yeh alrigh'?

Better.

He sat down, in front of Bimbo, at the other side of the table. He blocked Bimbo from the rest of the bar so no one could see him, unless they were looking.

—Ah, I'm —

Bimbo tried to smile. He wiped his cheeks with the outside of his hand.

—I'm grand.

It was like Bimbo remembered where he was. He sat up and lifted up his pint. Jimmy tasted his; it was fine, the first in five days.

—I got a bit o' bad news earlier, said Bimbo. —It knocked me a bit.

He shrugged.

Bimbo's parents were already dead. Jimmy Sr knew that because he remembered that they'd died very close to each other, a couple of weeks between them only. Maybe Maggie's mother had snuffed it but – Bimbo was a bit of a softy but he wouldn't break out crying in his local for Maggie's mother;

411

she'd been as good as dead for fuckin' years. One of the kids
—
Oh fuck. He wished Bertie was here.

Bimbo spoke.

—I was let go this mornin'.

—Wha'?

—Let go. ——I'm like you now, Jimmy, wha'. A man o'
leisure.

—You were —?

—Yeah; gas, isn't it?

He could see Bimbo's eyes getting watery again. Poor
Bimbo.

—How come? said Jimmy Sr, hoping that it might get
Bimbo talking instead of crying.

—Oh. Ten of us got letters. The oldest, yeh know. In the
canteen, on our way ou'.

Bimbo was a baker.

—The chap from the office said tha' they had to compete
with the big boys. That's wha' he called them, the big boys.
——The fuckin' eejit.

Bimbo hardly ever said Fuck.

—They need our wages to compete with the big boys
——wha'.

——That's shockin', said Jimmy Sr.

Bimbo was twirling the stout in his glass; he didn't know
what he was doing.

—Any chance they'll take yeh back when they've ——yeh
know?

—He said Yeah, the young fella from Personnel tha' gave us
the letters. I didn't believe him though. I wouldn't believe him
if he ——Tha' sort o' fella, yeh know.

Bimbo sat up straight again.

—Ah sure —

He grinned.

—We'll keep each other company anyway, wha'.

—Ah yeah, said Jimmy Sr. —Fuckin' sure.

There was that about it. He stopped himself from thinking that this was good news, but he nearly couldn't help it.

It was shocking though. Bimbo was younger than him and he was being fucked out on his ear because he was too old.

—My father, God rest him, got me in there, said Bimbo.

—That's righ'.

—His brother, me Uncle Paddy, he worked there.

—Yeah.

—I'll never forget comin' home the first week with me first wage packet. I ran all the way, nonstop all the way with me hand in me pocket to stop me money from fallin' ou'. An' a bag o' cakes tha' had been sent back. Fruit slices. Fly cemeteries. I was more excited abou' the cakes than I was abou' the money, that's how young I was. I knew I'd be king o' the castle when me sisters saw the fruit slices. Marie's little one has epilepsy, did I tell yeh?

Marie was one of Bimbo's sisters, the one Jimmy Sr liked.

—No; is tha' righ'?

—Yeah; Catherine. She's only six. Sad, isn't it?

—Jesus, yeah. ——Six?

Bimbo started crying again. His face collapsed. He rubbed his nose. He searched for a hankie he didn't have. He gulped. He smiled through it.

—What am I goin' to do, Jimmy?

* * *

They got locked, of course. Bertie was great when he arrived.

—That's great news, compadre, he told Bimbo. —You were always a poxy baker anyway, wha'.

And Bimbo burst his shite laughing; he was delighted. And Bimbo's laugh; when Bimbo laughed everyone laughed. Veronica always said that Bimbo's laugh lassoed you.

—Three nice pints, por favor, Bertie roared across to Leo, the barman. —An' John Wayners, lads?

—Jaysis, said Jimmy Sr.

He hadn't much money on him. Still though —

—Fair enough, he said.

—Okay, said Bimbo. —Me too.

—Good man, said Bertie. —An' Leo? he roared. —Three Jamesons as well.

And then Paddy turned up.

—How much of a lump sum will yeh be gettin'? Paddy asked Bimbo when he came in.

—Jesus Christ, said Jimmy Sr. —He isn't even sittin' down yet an' he wants to know how much money you're gettin'.

Bimbo laughed.

—I couldn't give a shite how much he's gettin', said Paddy.

—Then wha' did yeh ask him for then?

—I only asked him, said Paddy. —Fuck off.

—A couple o' thousand, said Bimbo.

—Don't tell him, said Jimmy Sr.

—Around three, said Bimbo. —I don't know. They're tellin' us on Monday.

—We'll meet up here at teatime on Monday so, said Bertie.

—Ah yeah, Bimbo assured them. —We'll have to have a few pints out of it alrigh'.

—You'll go to pieces without somethin' to do, Paddy told Bimbo.

—Shut up the fuck! said Jimmy Sr.

He gave Bimbo a quick look, but Bimbo didn't mind.

—You'd make a great doctor, Bertie told Paddy, —d'yeh know tha'. I can just see yeh. You have cancer, missis, your tit'll have to come off.

—Oh Jesus, said Bimbo.

—Yeah, said Jimmy Sr, when he'd stopped laughing. —Will he be alrigh', Doctor? No, missis, he's fucked.

They laughed again.

—Wha' will yeh do but? Paddy asked Bimbo.

—There's loads o' things he can do, said Jimmy Sr.

—Like?

—Doin' up his house, eh —

—His house is already done up, said Bertie. —It's already like Elvis's gaff; what's it – Graceland.

Bimbo laughed at that, but he was pleased.

414

—His garden, said Jimmy Sr.

—His garden's like —

—It's not like a human garden at all, said Bertie.

—There's loads o' things he can do, Jimmy Sr insisted.

—Yeah, said Paddy. —I'm sure there is. Wha' though?

—He can clean the church on Monday mornin's, said Bertie. They roared.

—Some oul' one tried to get Vera to start doin' tha', said Bertie. —Help cleanin' the fuckin' church on Monday mornin's.

—I wouldn't say that'd be Vera's scene exactly, said Jimmy Sr.

—Not at all, said Bertie. —She doesn't even help to dirty the fuckin' place on Sunday mornin's.

Bertie knocked back half of his pint.

—Ahh, he said.

—My turn, said Bimbo.

—The first of many, said Bertie.

—Leo, Bimbo shouted. —When you're ready. Three —

—Four, said Paddy.

—Four pints an' four small ones like a good man, please! They said nothing for a bit.

—Ah yes, said Bertie.

He was getting them ready.

—I know wha' I'd do if I got a lumpo sum like Bimbo's gettin', he said.

One of them had to say it. So —

—Wha'? said Jimmy Sr.

—I'd bring it into the Gem, righ'.

—Eh —, righ'.

—An' I'd wave it under Mandy's nose an' let her sniff it a bit.

Jimmy and Paddy started laughing.

—Then I'd bring her round the back, behind the fridge, righ'.

—Oh God.

Bimbo started laughing now.

—An' I'd ——die happy.

They laughed on top of what they were laughing already; Bertie sounded so sincere.

—My Jaysis, compadres, said Bertie when he'd recovered a bit, —I'm not jokin' yis.

Paddy nodded. He liked Mandy from the Gem as well.

They all liked Mandy.

—You're a dirty fucker, Jimmy Sr told Bertie.

—I said nothin' tha' yis don't all think when yis go into tha' shop. Tha' signorita. My fuckin' Jaysis.

—She's only sixteen, abou', said Bimbo.

—So?

Bimbo shrugged. It didn't matter; they were only messing.

—I was in there this mornin', said Bertie. —She is unfuck-inbelievable; isn't she? I was gettin' me Sun. She's as good lookin' as anny of them Page Three brassers.

—She's better lookin', said Jimmy Sr.

—Si, said Bertie, —She fuckin' is. I said it as well; I told her.

—Yeh didn't, said Paddy.

Bertie stared Paddy out of it for a second. Then he got back to Mandy.

—I opened it up at page three, righ', an' I showed it to her. Tha' should be you, I told her.

—Did she say ann'thin' back to yeh?

—Si. She told me to fuck off. But she was delighted, yeh could see.

—She's a lovely-lookin' girl alrigh', said Bimbo.

—I made her get a packet o' crisps for me as well, said Bertie. —I hate the fuckin' things.

They laughed. They knew what was coming next.

—Just to get her to bend over, yeh know. Caramba, lads, I nearly broke the counter with the bugle I had on me. When she gave them to me I said Salt an' vinegar so she had to do it again.

—She'll be fat by the time she's eighteen, said Paddy.

—No, said Jimmy Sr. —No, she won't.

—Why not?

—She's not like tha', said Jimmy Sr. —She's not like those young ones tha' look like women when they're fourteen an' then they're like their mothers before they're twenty. She's not like tha'.

He wondered if he should have been talking like this, if he was maybe giving something away. But Bertie agreed with him.

—Si, he said.

—My twist, said Jimmy Sr.

He wanted to get up. Halfway through talking there he'd felt dirty; kind of. And then stupid. Talking about young ones like that, very young ones. But when Bertie joined in it was safe. Darren was doing lounge boy tonight though. If he heard —

He stood up.

—Same again over here, Darren, please!

—Wha'?

—Leo knows. Just tell him the same again.

It was getting crowded. Leo was skidding up and down behind the bar.

—So annyway, Bimbo, said Bertie when Jimmy Sr was sitting back down. —Compadre mio, that's wha' I'd do if I was you.

—How though? said Paddy.

—Wha'?

—How would yeh do it?

—The same way I've always done it.

—No, I don't mean the ridin', Paddy explained. —I mean gettin' her to do it. How would yeh manage tha'?

—No great problem there, compadre, said Bertie. —I'd show her the money an' tell her I'll give her some of it if she'll say hello to the baldy fella; there'd be nothin' to it.

—Ah fuck off, said Jimmy Sr.

—Wha'? said Bertie.

—Yeh can't just do tha'.

—Why not?

—Cos the girl's not a fuckin' prostitute, that's why not.

—No, Bimbo agreed.

—Listen, compadre, said Bertie. —All women are prostitutes.

—Ah now —, said Bimbo.

—Will yeh listen to him, said Jimmy Sr.

—He's righ', said Paddy. —I had to buy my one a Crunchie before she'd let me ou' tonigh'.

Bertie addressed Bimbo.

—Don't misunderstand me, compadre, he said. —Not just women. All men are brassers as well.

—I'm no brasser, chum, said Jimmy Sr.

—Fuck up a minute, said Bertie. —Wha' I'm sayin' is, is tha' everyone has his price.

—Ah, is that all? said Bimbo.

—If you think —, said Jimmy Sr.

He was talking to Bertie.

—If you think tha' you can just walk into the shop an' put the money on the counter there an' Mandy will drop her —

—Watch it, Jimmy, here's Darren.

—Here's the cavalry, lads, said Bertie.

—Make room there, will yis, said Darren.

—Certainly, certainly.

They got all the dead glasses and put them on the table behind them, so Darren could put the tray on their table.

—D'yeh know Mandy from the Gem, Darren? said Bertie.

Jimmy Sr tried to kick him but he got Bimbo instead, but not hard.

—Yeh, said Darren. —Mandy Lawless.

—Nice, isn't she?

—She's alrigh', yeah.

—Keep the change, Darren, said Jimmy Sr. —Good man.

Darren took the money and counted it.

—You're a pound short, he told Jimmy Sr.

—Is tha' righ'? said Jimmy Sr.

He'd never get rid of him before Bertie opened his mouth again. He gave Darren a fiver.

—Yeh can pay me back later, he told him.

—No, said Darren. —I have it here.

Ah sufferin' Jesus!

But Bertie said nothing, and Paddy didn't either. He was looking around him, looking for something to moan about.

—There y'are, said Darren.

Jimmy Sr took the notes and left the silver and copper in Darren's hand.

—Good man.

—Thanks very much, Da.

—No problem.

—I'll tell yis though, said Jimmy Sr when Darren was gone. —Yis should see his mot. Darren's mot.

—Is she nice? said Bimbo.

—Lovely, said Jimmy Sr. —Fuckin' lovely.

—Go 'way. That's great.

—Miranda, her name is.

—Oh I like tha', said Bertie. —Mirr-andaah. Si; very nice. Is she a big girl, Jimmy?

—She's a daisy, said Jimmy Sr.

—An' you're a tulip, said Paddy.

—Fuck off, you, said Jimmy Sr.

—Lads, lads, now, said Bertie, and he leaned forward to get between Jimmy Sr and Paddy as if to break up a fight, even though there wasn't one. —Birds in their little nest, said Bertie.

—Wha' abou' them? said Paddy.

—They agree, said Bertie. —Righ'?

Paddy didn't argue with him.

—Now, said Bertie. —If yeh had, say, a thousand quid, righ' —

They sat up. They loved these ones.

—An', Bertie continued, —yeh knew for a fact tha' the most gorgeousest woman – now, the best fuckin' thing yeh'd ever seen in your life, righ'. An' yeh knew for a fact —

Bimbo started laughing.

—Shut up, you. —Yeh knew for a fact tha' she'd let yeh get up on her if yeh gave her it, the money. Would yis give her it?

—All of it? said Jimmy Sr.

—Si, said Bertie.

He looked around at them. They were thinking about it, even Bimbo.

—Wha' would she give me for half of it? Paddy asked him.

They roared.

*   *   *

—Where is it? said Jimmy Sr.

They were outside in the carpark, watching poor Bimbo getting sick. He was finished now, for the time being anyway. But he still looked very pale around the gills.

They'd been the last to leave; out of their trees, especially poor Bimbo. He could hardly talk. Darren had been giving the air a few squirts of Pledge, to let the manager think he'd done the cleaning.

—Tan ver muh, Darr-n, Bimbo'd said, and that was as much as he could manage.

They were outside now.

—Oh God, said Bimbo again, for about the thousandth time.

—You're alrigh', said Bertie.

—Terrible waste o' fuckin' money tha', said Paddy.

He was looking down at what had come out of poor Bimbo. Jimmy Sr had to agree with Paddy.

—Still though, he said. —He got the good ou' of it.

—True, said Paddy.

Jimmy Sr didn't feel too bad at all, considering he was out of practice. He was swimming a bit. He'd had to hold on to the wall there when he thought he was going to fall. He was pleased with himself though.

Bimbo straightened up.

—Are yeh alrigh' now, son? Bertie asked him.

—He is, o' course, said Jimmy Sr. —Aren't yeh?

Bimbo didn't say anything for a bit. Then he spoke.

420

——Yeah. ——Yeah —

—Are we goin' or wha'? said Paddy.

The plan was, they were all going down to the seafront with a couple of sixpacks. They'd decided this after Paddy had been complaining about all the kids that were down there every night.

—All ages, he'd told them. —Polluted out of their heads.

—That's shockin', Bimbo'd said.

And then Bertie'd said that they should go down there themselves after they were flung out of the boozer, and that was where they were going now. So —

—Are we goin' or are we? said Paddy.

—Lead the way, compadre, said Bertie.

—Ah, I don't —, said Bimbo. —I don't know if —

—Come on for fuck sake, said Jimmy Sr. —The fresh air will fix yeh.

—There —, said Bimbo. —There's nothin' wrong with me.

—Come on then, said Jimmy Sr.

—Are – Hey, lads, said Bimbo. —Are – are we goin' on a boat?

—Will yeh listen to him, said Paddy.

Bimbo started singing.

—Ah shite! said Paddy.

—WE COME ON THE SLOOP JOHN B —

—Ah si, said Bertie.

He liked this one, so he joined in with Bimbo.

—ME GRAN'FATHER AN' ME —

—Where's it gone? Jimmy Sr asked Paddy.

—Wha'?

—The chipper van, said Jimmy Sr.

—Wha' about it?

—Where is it?

—I don't know!

—LET ME GO HOME —

LEHHHHH' ME GO HOME —

—I want some fuckin' grub, said Jimmy Sr. —Shut up, will yis.

And then he joined in.

—I FEEL SO BROKE UP —

I WANNA GO HOME —

They were finished. Bimbo looked much better. He started again.

—BA BA BAH —

—Hang on a minute, Bimbo, said Jimmy Sr.

—BA BARBER ANN —

—Shut up!

Jimmy Sr nearly fell over, the shout had taken so much out of him.

—We've no fuckin' chipper, he told them.

—That's righ', said Bertie. —I thought there was somethin' missin' alrigh'.

There was always a van outside the Hikers, not just at the weekends either; always.

It wasn't there tonight though. Bimbo looked up and down the road for it, and behind him.

—He must be sick, said Bimbo.

—He must've eaten one of his own burgers, said Bertie.

—What'll we do? said Jimmy Sr.

—No problem, amigo. We'll go to the chipper.

He meant the real chipper, the one not on wheels; the one over the Green between the Gem and the place where the Bank of Ireland used to be.

—No, way, said Jimmy Sr.

He shook his head and nearly went on his ear again.

—What's wrong with yeh? said Bertie.

—WEEHHL —

THE WEST COAST FARMERS' DAUGHTERS —

—Shut up, Bimbo.

—The chipper's down there, said Jimmy Sr. —Righ'?

—Eh —si.

—An' the fuckin' seafront's up there, said Jimmy Sr.

—Si.

—So there's no way I'm goin' all the way down there, then all the way back up here again.

422

—Paddy'll go for us an' we'll wait for him.

—I will in me brown, said Paddy.

They sat on the carpark wall.

—May as well liberate these an' annyway, said Bertie, —wha'.

He got his sixpack out of its paper bag.

—While we're makin' up our minds. Alrigh', Bimbo?

——Yes, thank you.

—Annyone got an opener?

—I fuckin' told yeh we should've got cans, said Paddy. —I told yeh.

—Fuck off.

—The cans don't taste as nice, said Jimmy Sr.

—Si, said Bertie. —Correct.

He stood up and put the neck of the bottle to the edge of the wall.

—Let's see now, he said.

He tried to knock the cap off the bottle.

—You're goin' to break it, said Paddy.

—Am I? said Bertie.

He lifted the bottle and held it out so the froth ran over his hand but not onto his clothes.

—Well done, Bertie, said Jimmy Sr.

—There y'are, Bimbo, said Bertie, handing him the opened bottle.

—My turn next, said Jimmy Sr.

—Do your own, said Bertie.

He put the top of the bottle to the edge of the wall, then pulled it down but he missed the wall and scraped his knuckles and dropped the bottle.

—Shite!

—Watch it.

A Garda car was crossing the road towards them.

The guards didn't get out but the passenger opened his window.

—What's goin' on here?

Bertie took his knuckles out of his mouth.

—We're waitin' on your wife, he said.

Paddy started whistling the Laurel and Hardy music. Jimmy Sr nudged him but Paddy didn't stop.

—None of your lip, said the garda to Bertie.

Jimmy Sr didn't like this sort of thing.

Bertie went closer to the car and leaned down. He held his top lip.

—This one? he said.

Then his bottom lip.

—Or this one.

Paddy stood up now as well.

Bimbo whispered to Jimmy Sr.

—Do we know—know his wife?

Jimmy Sr didn't know what he'd do if the cops got out of the car. He'd never been in trouble with the guards, even when he was a kid; only through Leslie.

The driver spoke.

—Mister Gillespie.

Bertie bent down further and looked past the passenger.

—Buenas noches, Sergeant Connolly, he said.

Bimbo got down off the wall and started picking up the broken glass.

—You're looking grand and flushed, said Sergeant Connolly.

—That's cos we've been ridin' policemen's daughters all nigh', Sergeant, said Bertie.

Jimmy Sr wanted to get down and run.

Paddy leaned down beside Bertie to see the faces on the gardaí. He hacked, like he was getting ready to spit, but the passenger didn't budge. He wouldn't even look at him.

Sergeant Connolly spoke.

—You wouldn't know anything at all about a small bit of robbery of Supervalu in Baldoyle this afternoon, Mister Gillespie? he asked Bertie. —Would you, at all?

—Yeah, said Bertie. —I would.

—What?

—They got away, said Bertie.

The sergeant laughed. Jimmy Sr didn't like it.

—You can come over to me house now an' search it if yeh like, Bertie told the sergeant.

—We already did that, said the sergeant.

The passenger grinned.

—Wha' are you fuckin' grinnin' at? said Paddy.

Bertie moved forward a bit and crowded Paddy out of the way.

—Did yeh find annythin'? he asked Sergeant Connolly.

—Not really, said the sergeant. —But ——tell your lovely wife Thank you, will you, like a good man. ——I forgot to thank her myself. Good night now. Safe home.

The car moved away from the kerb and back across the road, and around onto Chestnut Avenue.

—The cunts, said Paddy.

—Where's there a bin? said Bimbo.

—Over here, Bimbo, said Jimmy Sr. —Look it.

He took Bimbo's arm and made him come with him. He wanted to get home – and get Bimbo home – before the cops came back.

—See yis, he told Bertie and Paddy.

—Where're you goin'? said Paddy.

—Home, said Jimmy Sr. —I'm knackered.

—Good nigh', compadre, said Bertie. —Here; bring one o' the sixpacks here, look it.

—No, said Jimmy Sr. —No, thanks, you're alrigh'. See yis.

He wanted to get the fuck home. He couldn't handle that sort of thing at all. He didn't want the guards thinking anything about him. And Bimbo; the two of them not working and that. Your man, Connolly, would start thinking that they were working for Bertie. And they'd raid the fuckin' house or something. Veronica —

—Are we goin' home, Jimmy? said Bimbo.

—Yeah.

—Good.

* * *

The next couple of weeks were great. He had to admit that. If he'd been looking for someone to be made redundant it would have been Bimbo. That didn't mean that he'd wanted Bimbo to get the sack; not at all. What he meant was this: he couldn't think of better company than Bimbo, and now that Bimbo wasn't working he could hang around with Bimbo all day. It was fuckin' marvellous.

He didn't think he was being selfish. At first – during the first week or so – he'd felt a bit guilty, a bit of a bollix, because Bimbo was so miserable and he was the opposite. He couldn't wait to get up and out in the mornings, like a fuckin' kid on his summer holliers. But he didn't think that way any more. Because he was helping Bimbo really. He wasn't denying that he was delighted that Bimbo wasn't working – not that he'd told anyone – but he didn't have to feel bad about it because, after all, he hadn't given poor Bimbo the sack and he'd never even wished it. And if Bimbo ever got his job back or got a new one he'd be the first one to slap him on the back and say Sound man. And he'd mean it as well.

But Bimbo was sacked; it was a fact. He was hanging around doing nothing. And Jimmy Sr was hanging around doing nothing, so the two of them might as well hang around and do fuckin' nothing together. Only, with the two of them, they could do plenty of things. Playing pitch and putt by yourself on a cold March morning could be very depressing but with someone else to go around with you it could be a great bit of gas. And it was the same with just walking along the seafront; and anything really.

Jimmy Sr hadn't felt bad, really bad, in a while; not since before Christmas. He hadn't felt good either, mind you; just – settled. Now though, he felt good; he felt happy. Bimbo was helping him and he was helping Bimbo. The day after the night they'd got locked – the day after Bimbo'd been sent home – Jimmy Sr called for him and took him out for a walk. Maggie patted Jimmy Sr's arm when he was going out the front door. It was a Saturday, a day when Bimbo would have been at home anyway, but he could tell that Bimbo didn't think it was an ordinary Saturday. He had a terrible hangover as well. But the walk had cheered him up and Jimmy Sr took him into Raheny library and got him to fill in a card and he showed him what books were where.

On Monday, the first real day, Jimmy Sr called for Bimbo at nine o'clock and made him come out for a game of pitch and putt. He had to threaten to hit him over the head with his putter if he didn't get up off his hole but he got him out eventually. He even zipped up his anorak for him. And Maggie filled a flask for them, which went down very well cos it was fuckin' freezing. They gave up after six holes; they couldn't hold the clubs properly any more because they'd no gloves, but they enjoyed themselves. And Jimmy Sr showed Bimbo what was wrong with his swing. He was lifting his head too early. They watched a bit of snooker in the afternoon, and played Scrabble with Sharon until Gina upended the board, the bitch, when they were looking at something in the snooker.

On Wednesday – it was pissing all day Tuesday – Jimmy Sr brought Bimbo into town. Bimbo had only been on the DART a couple of times before, so he enjoyed that. And some little cunt flung a stone at their carriage when they were going past the hospital in Edenmore, and that gave them something to talk about the rest of the way; that and the big new houses off the Howth Road in Clontarf that were so close to the tracks the train nearly went through them.

—Imagine payin' a fortune to live tha' close to the tracks, said Jimmy Sr.

—Thick, said Bimbo.

Jimmy Sr pointed out the houses he'd plastered.

He brought Bimbo up to the ILAC Centre and he got a young one behind the counter to put a programme about volcanoes on the telly and they watched a bit of that. They went for a cup of coffee, after Jimmy Sr had taken out a couple of books and he'd explained to Bimbo about the computer strip yokes inside the books and on Jimmy Sr's card and how the young lad at the check-out only had to rub a plastic stick across them to put the names of the books beside Jimmy Sr's name inside in the computer. They still stamped the date you had to bring them back by the old way.

They went for a coffee downstairs. The coffee was lovely there but Bimbo had insisted on having tea. He could be a cranky enough little fucker at times. Jimmy Sr was going to make him have coffee – because it WAS lovely – but then he didn't. They looked out at what was going on on Moore Street. They enjoyed that, watching the oul' ones selling their fruit and veg and the young ones going by. They saw a kid – a horrible-looking young lad – getting a purse out of a woman's bag. He'd done it before they knew what they were seeing, so there was nothing they could do. The woman didn't know yet either. She just walked on along, down to Parnell Square, the poor woman. The kid had probably done it to get drugs or something. They didn't say anything to each other about it. It made Jimmy Sr think of Leslie.

—Taste tha' now, Bimbo, said Jimmy Sr.

He held his mug out for Bimbo to take. Bimbo took it, and sipped.

—There. Isn't it lovely?

—Oh, it is, said Bimbo. —It is, alrigh'.

—Bet yeh regret you didn't get a mug of it for yourself now, wha', said Jimmy Sr.

They went home after that.

They did something every day nearly. The weather was weird. It was lovely one minute; they'd have to take their jackets off, and even their jumpers. And then it would start snowing – it would! – or hailstoning.

—Snow in April, said Bimbo, looking up at it.

He liked it, only he was cold. They were in under the shelter at the pond in St Anne's Park. Bimbo didn't want to lean against the wall because he could smell the piss; it was terrible. They had Gina with them, in her buggy.

—It's mad alrigh', said Jimmy Sr.

—It was lovely earlier, said Bimbo.

—That's righ', said Jimmy Sr. —It's the fuckin' ozone layer; that's wha' I think's doin' it.

—Is April not always a bit like this? said Bimbo.

—Not this bad, said Jimmy Sr. —No.

He made sure that Gina's head was well inside her hood.

—The greenhouse effect, he said.

—I thought tha' was supposed to make the world get warmer, said Bimbo.

—It does that alrigh', Jimmy Sr agreed with him. —Yeah; but it makes it go colder as well. It makes the weather go all over the shop.

—Yeh wouldn't know wha' to wear, said Bimbo. —Sure yeh wouldn't.

He put his hands up into his sleeves.

—Yeh'd be better off goin' around in your nip, said Jimmy Sr.

They laughed at that.

—At least yeh'd know where yeh stood then, wha', said Jimmy Sr.

—I'd need shoes though, said Bimbo.

—An' somewhere to put your cigarettes, wha'.

They laughed again.

—I'm never happy unless I have me shoes on me, said Bimbo. —Even on a beach.

—Is tha' righ'?

—Or slippers.

Then it stopped. And the sun came out nearly immediately and it was like it had never been snowing, except for the snow on the ground. But that was disappearing quick; they could see it melting and evaporating.

—I love lookin' at tha' sort o' thing, said Bimbo.

—Yeah, said Jimmy Sr.

He checked on Gina. She was still asleep.

—Just as well, wha', he said. —She makes enough noise, doesn't she, Bimbo?

—Ah sure, said Bimbo. —That's wha' they're supposed to do at her age. She's lovely.

—Isn't she but, said Jimmy Sr. —If the rest of her is as good as her lungs she'll be a fine thing when she grows up.

They got going. They had a read of the newspapers in the library, to get in out of the cold, on their way home. But they had to leave because Gina started acting up.

They didn't meet much at night; once or twice a week only. —Look, said Bimbo one morning.

He took something out of a brown envelope with a window in it.

Jimmy went over and turned so he could see it. Bimbo didn't really hold it up to him; he just held it.

It was his redundancy cheque.

—Very nice, said Jimmy Sr.

Bimbo put it back in the envelope and went into the kitchen and gave it to Maggie. Then they went out.

Bimbo put a lot of the lump sum into the house. He got aluminium windows for the back; they already had them in the front. And he put his name down for the gas conversion, the Fifty-Fifty Cash Back. Jimmy Sr helped Bimbo put new paper up in his kitchen and Veronica went through him for a short cut when she saw the paste in his hair and he told her how it had got there. He had to promise to do their own kitchen before she'd get off his back, but they didn't have the money to buy any paper or anything so it had been an easy enough promise to make.

They went out to Howth as well sometimes, and had a walk down the pier and along the front. They were going to get fishing rods.

Then a great thing happened. Bimbo helped out a bit with Barrytown United. He just went to the Under 13 matches cos Wayne, one of his young lads, was playing for them now; he was usually the sub, and Bimbo minded their gear and their money for them. And he sometimes drove some of the Under 18s to their matches, and home again. Anyway, he got a chance of two tickets to one of the World Cup warm-up matches, against Wales, in Lansdowne.

—Not two tickets exactly, he explained to Jimmy Sr.

—Wha' does tha' fuckin' mean? said Paddy.

—Was I talkin' to you? said Bimbo. —We get into the game for nothin', he told Jimmy Sr, —but we have to do a bit o' stewardin'. Nothin' much though.

—Wha'?

—I don't know, said Bimbo. —Exactly. Are yeh on?

—Okay, said Jimmy Sr.

—Ah good, said Bimbo.

—They'll fuckin' lose, Paddy told them. —Wait an' see.

—Fuck off you, said Jimmy Sr.

Jimmy Sr loved soccer but he hadn't been to a game in years, and now he could go to an international for nothing.

—The tickets are like gold dust, he told Veronica.

They got the DART straight across to Lansdowne. Jimmy Sr had Darren's Ireland scarf on him. Darren still went to all the matches but he didn't bother with the scarf any more. So Jimmy Sr had it.

—How many stops after Amiens Street is Lansdowne? Jimmy Sr asked Bimbo.

Bimbo looked up at the yoke with the stations on it over the window.

—Eh ——three ——, said Bimbo. ——Yeah; three.

—Good, said Jimmy Sr. —I could do with a slash.

They'd had a pint in the Hikers; just the two.

—We'll have one when we get there, said Bimbo.

—Grand, said Jimmy Sr. —No hurry.

—There's a big jacks under the stand.

—Grand, said Jimmy Sr.

When they got to Lansdowne they had to put on these white jackets with Opel on them and they followed this fat fella, and he brought them up into the East Stand and what they had to do was show people where their seats were. It was easy. You'd want to have been a fuckin' eejit not to have been able to find your own seat. He slagged Bimbo; said he'd buy him a torch and a skirt so he could get him a job in a cinema. —Can I help you, sir, he'd heard him saying to one fuckin' eejit who couldn't find his seat.

Then they went down to the side of the pitch just after the game started, inside the barriers – it was great – and they watched the game. It was a shite match, woeful; but he enjoyed it and the weather stayed good. He took off his Opel jacket and the fat fella told him to put it back on, but he said it nicely, so Jimmy Sr did put it back on. Coming up to full time the fat fella told them to turn around and face the crowd and stop any young fellas from climbing over the barriers when the whistle went. Then Ireland got a penno, and they had to watch that; and that gobshite, Sheedy, missed it – Southall saved it – and he turned back, and the crowd went fuckin' mad, and he turned back around and the new fella, Bernie Slaven, had scored a goal and Jimmy Sr'd fuckin' missed it. He had to watch it on the telly later on that night. He didn't know why he'd faced the crowd anyway; there was no way he was going to try and stop anyone from climbing over the barriers. They could chew their way through the barriers for all Jimmy Sr cared; it was none of his business. He enjoyed the whole day though. Mick McCarthy came over near to where himself and Bimbo were just before the end to take one of his famous long throws and Jimmy Sr nodded at him and said Howyeh, Mick, and McCarthy winked at him. He was a good player, McCarthy, a hard man.

They were going to get into the Russia game as well for nothing at the end of the month. That was definitely something to look forward to; it would be a much better match.

—Definitely, said Bimbo.

They were on the DART home.

—I don't know, said Jimmy Sr. —I'd say tha' glasnost shite has made them soft, d'yeh know tha'. They don't have to worry abou' bein' sent to the salt mines if they lose any more.

—We'll see, said Bimbo.

So they filled their time no problem. Sometimes that was all they did; fill it – they just fucked around doing nothing till they could go home for their dinner or their tea. That wasn't so good. And sometimes Jimmy Sr could tell that Bimbo had the blues. And sometimes as well he had the blues himself. But they were good for each other, him and Bimbo.

And now – today – all Bimbo's practice had paid off; he'd won the pitch and putt. And instead of winning a poxy voucher for the butchers or something he'd won a trophy, a huge one with a golfer on top of it; not cheap looking either, like a lot of them were. No, it was very nice, and Bimbo was fuckin' delighted; he was fuckin' glowing.

They'd had a few pints to celebrate and now they were going out to the van to get a few chips and a bit of cod, because they were too late for their tea and too hungry to wait for Maggie and Veronica to rustle up something for them.

—Are yeh righ'? said Jimmy Sr.

Bimbo was collecting his clubs and his trophy, trying to work out the handiest way to carry them all.

—Here, said Jimmy Sr. —Give us them.

He took the clubs from Bimbo. He was fuckin' starving.

—Seeyis now, said Bimbo.

He was saying goodbye to everyone.

—Will yeh come on! said Jimmy Sr. —For Jaysis sake.

They went out into the carpark. It was still bright; it was only eight o'clock. The sky was red over where the sun was.

—Isn't tha' lovely? said Bimbo.

—I'm havin' a burger as well, Jimmy Sr told him.

But the van wasn't there.

—Ah fuck it!

And then they remembered that the van hadn't been there in a long time; months in fact. They only missed it now when they wanted it.

They headed over the Green to the real chipper.

—Prob'ly just as well really, said Bimbo. —You never know wha' you were gettin', out o' tha' van. ——It's funny though —

He was having problems keeping up with Jimmy Sr.

—Tha' van was a little gold mine, he said.

Jimmy Sr agreed with him.

—Yeah, he said.

—Maybe he's sick, said Bimbo.

He nearly went through a puddle.

—Or maybe he's dead.

—Good, said Jimmy Sr.

—A little gold mine that place was, Bimbo said again.

—It can't have been tha' much of a gold mine if it's not there annymore, said Jimmy Sr.

—Maybe, yeah, said Bimbo. —I'd say he's just sick or dead.

—I'll be dead in a minute meself if I don't get a bit o' grub into me, said Jimmy Sr. —Come here, Bimbo, he said. —You'll have to be careful yeh don't get complacent just cos you've won once. I'm not bein' snotty now —

—I know tha'.

—It happens a lot o' fellas. They stop workin' at their game, just cos they've won one poxy trophy; no offence.

—Don't worry, Bimbo assured him. —It's not goin' to happen to me.

—Good man. ——We wouldn't want a job now, wha'. We're too busy.

Bimbo smiled back at him.

* * *

There were bad times as well, of course. Of course there were. Poor oul' Bimbo got the blues a bit, the way he used to himself before he got the hang of it, being a man of leisure. He – Bimbo – got the Independent every morning. It was supposed to be the best paper for jobs, and he went straight to the back pages. He hadn't a hope in shite of getting a job out of it, he knew it himself; they knew nobody who'd ever got a job out of a paper. But he still got it and went down the columns with his finger and got ink on it and then on his face, and then got depressed when there was nothing for him. God love him, Jimmy Sr had to stop him from writing away for a job in McDonalds; there was a huge ad for them in Saturday's paper.

Jimmy Sr called for him. They were playing against each

other in this week's pitch and putt. And he was at the kitchen table starting to write the letter.

Jimmy Sr read the ad.

—You're not serious, he said when he was finished.

Bimbo finished writing his address.

—You're not fuckin' serious, said Jimmy Sr.

—I knew yeh'd say tha', said Bimbo.

He kept his eyes on the paper but he wasn't writing anything. His address was the only thing on the paper so far.

—Wha' d'yeh think you're at? Jimmy Sr asked him. —Well?

He took care to make sure that what he said sounded just right, not too hard and not too sarcastic.

—I'm just writin', said Bimbo. —To see wha' they say, like.

—They won't want you, said Jimmy Sr. —They're lookin' for young ones an' young fellas tha' they can treat like shite an' exploit. Not grown up men like you, like us.

—I know, said Bimbo. —I know tha' —

—They wouldn't have a uniform to fit yeh.

Bimbo had something he wanted to finish saying.

—I want to see wha' they say, yeh know. Wha' they write back.

—They won't bother writin' back, said Jimmy Sr.

—They might, said Bimbo.

—Jaysis, Bimbo; for fuck sake. You're a fuckin' baker.

—There now, said Bimbo.

He pointed his biro at the paper.

—If I put tha' in the letter, that I'm a baker, they might be impressed – I don't know – not impressed; they might just think that I've experience an' – you'd never know.

—Ah Bimbo.

—I'm only writin' to them.

He stood up.

—I'm only writin' to them. ——I'll do it later.

Bimbo won; he won the pitch and putt.

—Yeh cunt yeh, said Jimmy Sr.

They didn't have a pint after; it was a bit early. They just went home.

Jimmy Sr knew Bimbo; if he was offered one of those jobs he'd take it. —It's a start, he'd say; and he wouldn't give a shite who saw him in his polyester uniform. He'd even wear the fuckin' thing to work and home, not a bother on him. And Veronica would ask him why he couldn't get a job like Bimbo – but that wasn't the reason he wanted Bimbo to cop on to himself. Veronica knew that if Jimmy Sr ever got offered proper work he'd jump at it, even if it was less than the dole. He couldn't let a friend of his – his best friend – allow himself to sink that low. A man like Bimbo would never recover from having to stand at a counter, wearing a uniform that didn't fit him and serving drunk cunts and snot-nosed kids burgers and chips. They weren't even proper chips.

They were at Bimbo's gate.

—You're not goin' to write tha' letter to McDonalds, said Jimmy Sr. —Are yeh?

—Ah —

—You'd just be wastin' the fuckin' stamp, for fuck sake.

—No, said Bimbo. —I don't think I'll bother.

—Good man, said Jimmy Sr. —See yeh later.

—See yeh, said Bimbo.

Jimmy Sr went on, to his own house. He wondered would the front room be free this afternoon. Darren was doing a lot of studying for the Leaving, and Jimmy Sr wasn't going to get in his way. Liverpool were playing Chelsea on RTE. Maybe Darren would be going out, meeting his mot.

He'd forgotten his key. He knocked on the glass. Bimbo probably would write off to McDonalds even though he'd said he wouldn't. He knocked again. He wouldn't rest until he got himself one of those fuckin' uniforms. He hid his eyes from the sun with his hand and looked in the window of the front room. There was no one in there. He knocked again. He should have got a knocker, one of those brass ones on the door. Bertie had one on his, and one of those spy-hole things. There was no one in.

—Fuck it annyway.

He'd go down to Bimbo's for a bit, and watch the – Hang on though, no; there was someone coming down the stairs. He could hear it, and now he could make out the shape. It was Veronica. She must have been asleep, or studying. She was doing the Leaving as well in a couple of weeks, God love her. Fair play to her though. He was going to do the same himself next year.

Veronica opened the door.

—Wha' kept yeh? said Jimmy Sr.

*   *   *

Jimmy Jr came around with four cans of Carlsberg, still lovely and cold from the off-licence fridge. Jimmy Sr put his nose to the hole in his can.

—I always think it smells like piss when yeh open it first, he said. —Not bad piss now, he explained.

—Yeah, Jimmy Jr agreed.

He got his jacket from behind the couch and took out two packets of Planter's Nuts and threw one of them to Jimmy Sr.

—Open them an' smell them, he said.

Jimmy Sr did.

—Well? said Jimmy Jr.

—They smell like shite, said Jimmy Sr.

—Yeah, said Jimmy Jr. —Fuckin' gas, isn't it? An' they still taste lovely.

Jimmy Sr took a swig and trapped the beer in his mouth and only let it down slowly. That way he didn't belch. The remote control needed a battery so Jimmy Sr couldn't turn up the sound without getting up, and he couldn't be bothered. He'd turned it down when young Jimmy had come, to ask how he was and that, and how Aoife was. There'd been one more goal since then; Ian Rush had scored it. He didn't need George Hamilton or Johnny Giles to tell him who'd scored it cos he'd seen it himself. He was sick of those two. Giles was always fuckin' whinging.

—They're a machine, said Jimmy Sr. —Aren't they?

437

—What's tha'?

—Liverpool, said Jimmy Sr. —They're like a machine. Brilliant.

—Yeah, said Jimmy Jr.

He didn't follow football much.

—A well-oiled machine, said Jimmy Sr. —There's nothin' like them.

—Yeah, said Jimmy Jr. —I'm gettin' married.

—They always do the simple thing, said Jimmy Sr. —It's obvious but no one else fuckin' does it.

—I'm gettin' married, said Jimmy Jr.

—I heard yeh, said Jimmy Sr.

—And?

—And is she pregnant?

—No, she fuckin' isn't!

—That's grand so, said Jimmy Sr.

He held out his hand to Jimmy Jr.

—Put it there.

He'd have killed him if he'd put her up the pole; she was too nice a young one to have that sort of thing happen to her, far too nice.

They shook hands.

—Did you tell your mother yet?

—No. No, I wanted to tell you first. There's another goal, look it.

—Barnes, said Jimmy Sr. —Brilliant. Pity he hasn't an Irish granny. ——Why?

—Why, wha'?

—Don't start, said Jimmy Sr. —Why did yeh want to tell me first?

Jimmy Jr was concentrating on the telly.

—I just did, he said. —Eh, I'll go in an' tell Ma.

—She'll be delighted.

—Yeah, said Jimmy Jr.

He got up and went out.

Liverpool had scored again but Jimmy Sr only noticed it

438

when the replay came on and even then he didn't really pay attention to it. He didn't know who'd scored it.

* * *

—What're her parents like? Sharon asked Jimmy Jr.

—Good question, said Jimmy Sr. —Look carefully at her mother cos that's wha' she'll end up lookin' like.

—Will you listen to him, said Veronica.

They were all having the dinner, Darren and the twins as well. It was very nice. Not the food – it was nice as well, mind you; lovely – the atmosphere.

Young Jimmy had brought a bottle of wine. He poured a glass for the twins as well, just a small one, and Veronica didn't kick up at all. Jimmy Sr looked at her. She couldn't keep her eyes off young Jimmy.

—They're alrigh', said Jimmy Jr.

He put down his knife and fork, making noise on purpose.

—No, they're not, now that I think of it, he said.

They cheered.

—He's a bollix —, said Jimmy Jr.

—Stop that, said Veronica.

—Sorry, ma, said Jimmy Jr. —He is though.

They laughed, Veronica as well.

—An' she's—, said Jimmy Jr. —I think she's ou' of her tree half the time.

—Go 'way, said Jimmy Sr. —Is tha' righ'? Drink?

—No, said Jimmy Jr. —I don't think so.

—Tippex, said Darren.

—Stop that, said Veronica.

—She looks doped, said Jimmy Jr. —When yeh go into the house she smiles at you abou' ten seconds after she's been lookin' at you, yeh know. It'd freak you ou'.

—Maybe she's just thick, said Jimmy Sr.

—You'll be meetin' her soon annyway, said Jimmy Jr, —so you'll be able to judge for yourself.

—That's righ', said Jimmy Sr. —Is she good lookin'?

—Who? Her ma?

439

—O' course! said Jimmy Sr. —Who d'yeh think I meant?
Her da?

They laughed.

—I couldn't give a shite wha' her da looks like, said Jimmy
Sr.

—Excuse me, said Veronica. —You'd better not give a shite
what her ma looks like either.

—Yeow, Ma!

They roared. Veronica was pleased.

Jimmy Sr really did want to know what Aoife's ma looked
like. He didn't know why; he just did – badly.

—Well? he said.

He put some more salt on his spuds. They were good spuds,
balls of flour.

—Is she?

—Yeah, said Jimmy Jr. —I s'pose she – No, not really —

—Ah Jaysis —

—It's hard to say. She an oul' one. She was probably nice
lookin' once alrigh'. Years ago but.

—Can she not be good looking if she isn't young? Veronica
asked Jimmy Jr.

—Eh —

—'Course she can, said Jimmy Sr.

—Yeah, Jimmy Jr agreed. —But she —

—Be careful wha' yeh say, son, Jimmy Sr warned him.

—Some old women are lovely lookin', said Sharon.

—That's true, said Jimmy Sr. —A few o' them.

He glanced over at Veronica.

—What abou' you? said Darren to his da. —Look at the
state o' you.

Jimmy Sr looked at Darren. Darren was looking back at
him, waiting for a reaction. Jimmy Sr wasn't going to take
that from him, not for another couple of years.

He pointed his fork at Darren.

—Don't you forget who paid for tha' dinner in front of you,
son, righ'.

—I know who paid for it, said Darren. —The state.

Jimmy Sr looked like he'd been told that someone had died.

—Yeh prick, Jimmy Jr said to Darren.

But no one said anything else. Linda and Tracy didn't look at each other.

Jimmy Sr took a sip from his wine.

——Very nice, he said.

Then he got up.

—Em ——the jacks, he said.

He had to sit down again and shift his chair back to get up properly.

—Back in a minute, he said.

—Yeh fuckin' big-headed little prick, yeh, Jimmy Jr called Darren when they heard Jimmy Sr on the stairs, going up.

—Stop that! said Veronica.

—Wha' did yeh go an' say tha' for? Sharon asked Darren, and wanting to slap the face off him.

—Stop, said Veronica.

—I was only jokin', said Darren.

It was true; mostly.

Jimmy Jr grabbed Darren's sleeve.

—Stop!!

Veronica looked around at them all.

—Stop that, she said. —Now, eat your dinners.

They did. Sharon kicked Darren under the table but didn't really get him.

Then Linda spoke.

—Are they rich, Jimmy?

—Who?

—Her ma an' da, said Linda.

—Yeah, said Jimmy Jr. —They are, kind of. ——Yeah. — —I suppose they are.

They were all listening for noise from upstairs.

—What did you do in school yesterday? Veronica asked Tracy.

Tracy was stunned.

—Eh —

—Nothin', said Linda.

—The usual.

—Tell us about it, said Veronica.

—Ah, get lost —

—Go on.

—Yeah, said Sharon. —Tell us.

—Well ——, said Linda.

She knew what was going on, sort of. They weren't to be waiting for her daddy to come down.

—Well, she said. —We had Mr Enright first class.

—Lipstick Enright, said Darren.

—Shut up, you, said Jimmy Jr.

—Linda fancies him, Tracy told them.

—I do not you, righ'!

Veronica started laughing.

—I used to —, said Linda. —I'm goin' to kill you, Tracy, righ'.

Jimmy Sr was coming down; they heard the stairs.

—Why did yeh stop? Sharon asked Linda. —Fancyin' him. Linda teased them.

—I just did, she said.

—She —, Tracy started.

—Shut up, Tracy, said Linda, —righ'. I'm tellin' it.

—Tellin' wha'? said Jimmy Sr.

He'd combed his hair.

—Why she doesn't fancy Mr Enright annymore, Sharon told him.

—Oh good Jaysis, he said.

They all laughed, hard.

* * *

He washed his face, put his hands under the cold tap and rubbed water all over his face and put them under again and held them over his eyes. God, he felt much better now. He was looking forward to going home. He had to wipe his face in his jumper because there was no towel. It was like when you ate ice-cream too fast and you had a terrible fuckin' headache, a real splitter, and it got worse and worse and you had to close your eyes to beat it – and then it was gone and you were grand, not a bother on you. For a while after the dinner, he'd had to really stretch his face to stop himself from crying. And that passed and he'd thought he was going to faint – not faint exactly —— He kept having to lift himself up, and sit up straight and open his eyes full; he couldn't help it. He didn't blame Darren; it was a phase young fellas went through, hating their fathers. He wouldn't have minded smacking him across the head though.

He was grand now, wide awake. The pint had helped, nice and cold, and the taste had given him something to think about. He was grand.

—Come here, you, he said to Bimbo when he got back from the jacks. —The only reason you beat me today was because I let yeh take your first shot again at the seventh.

—Oh, said Bertie. —The tricky seventh; si.

—I beat yeh by two shots, said Bimbo.

—So?

—So I'd still've beaten yeh.

—Not at all, said Jimmy Sr. —Yeh went one up at the seventh. D'yeh admit tha'?

—Say nothin', compadre, said Bertie.

—Yeah, Bimbo said to Jimmy Sr.

He was dying to know what Jimmy Sr was going to say next.

—Yeh went up after I let yeh take your shot again. Yeah?

—Yeah.

—Well, that had a bad psychological effect on me. I shouldn't've let yeh. I'd've hockied yeh if I'd won tha' hole like I should've. ——Like I really did when yeh think about it.

—Nick fuckin' Faldo, said Paddy.

—That's not fair now, said Bimbo.

He sat up straight.

—That's not fair, Jim, he said. —I beat yeh fair an' square.

—No, Bimbo, sorry; not really.

Bimbo was annoyed.

443

—Righ', he said. —Fair enough. ——I wasn't goin' to mention it but ——

—Wha'?

Jimmy Sr was worried now, but he didn't show it.

—Wha'? he said again. —Go on.

—I seen yeh kickin' the ball ou' o' the long grass on the ninth.

—Yeh cunt!

—I seen yeh, Bimbo insisted.

—Yeh poxbottle fuck yeh; yeh did not!

—I did, said Bimbo.

—Serious allegations, said Bertie after he'd stopped laughing.

—He's makin' it up, said Jimmy Sr. —Don't listen to him.

Bimbo tapped his face with a finger, just under his left eye.

—He's makin' it up, said Jimmy Sr. —It's pat'etic really. He's just a bad loser.

—I won, sure! said Bimbo.

—Not really, yeh didn't, said Jimmy Sr.

—You're the loser, excuse me, said Bimbo. —And a cheater.

—Yeh'd want to be careful abou' wha' you're sayin', Jimmy Sr told him.

He knew well they all believed Bimbo; he didn't give a fuck. He was enjoying himself.

—I'm only sayin' what I saw, said Bimbo. —Yeh looked around yeh an' yeh gave the ball a kick, then yeh shouted Found it! And then yeh said, I was lucky, it's landed nicely for me.

Bertie and Paddy were roaring.

—Fuck yeh, said Jimmy Sr. —Wha' were yeh lookin' at me for annyway?

—You'll have to buy a round because o' tha', compadre, Bertie said to Jimmy Sr.

—Fair enough, said Jimmy Sr.

He had a tenner that Jimmy Jr'd given him.

—Four pints over here, he roared at the young fella who

was going past them with a trayload of empty glasses. —I'd still have beaten yeh, he told Bimbo.

—But I won, said Bimbo.

—It's tha' baldy bollix, Gorbachev's fault. The grass should-'ve been cut there; he's useless. There's always dogshite in the bunkers as well.

—Annyone want a kettle jug? said Bertie.

—Free?

—No, said Bertie. —No, I'm afraid not. I can give it to yeh at a keen price though.

—How much? said Paddy.

—Fifteen quid, said Bertie. —Thirty-five in the shops. ——Two for twenty-five.

—How many have yeh? Jimmy Sr asked him.

—Ask no questions, compadre, said Bertie. —Not tha' many. A small herd. Well?

—No, said Jimmy Sr.

He looked around to see if there was anyone listening or watching.

—No, Paddy said. —We don't need one.

—No, Bimbo agreed.

—Fair enough, said Bertie. —No problem.

—Yeh wouldn't have a chipper van to sell, I suppose, said Bimbo, —would yeh, Bertie?

—No, said Bertie, like Bimbo'd just asked him if he'd any bananas.

Jimmy Sr and Paddy stared at Bimbo.

—Just a thought, said Bimbo.

And he left it at that.

Bertie loved a challenge.

—Wha' abou' a Mister Whippy one? Bertie asked Bimbo. —I think I could get me hands on one o' them.

—No, said Bimbo.

—You've your heart set on a chipper one?

—Yeah. ——Not really; just if yeh see one.

—Si, said Bertie. —I'll see what I can do.

Jimmy Sr looked at Bimbo. But Bimbo was just looking the

way he always did, friendly and stupid looking, no glint in his eye or nothing.

* * *

—Bimbo's talkin' abou' gettin' himself a chipper van, he told Veronica.

—I knew he liked his food, said Veronica. —But I didn't know he was that bad.

Jimmy Sr didn't get it at first.

——Ah yeah; very good.

* * *

Jimmy Sr had no luck trying to get anything out of Bimbo.

—It was just an idea, that's all.

That was about as much as he'd tell him.

They were in Jimmy Sr's front room watching Blockbusters.

—If Bertie finds one will yeh buy it? Jimmy Sr asked him.

—B M ——, said Bimbo.

The girls' team on the telly got to the answer before Bimbo.

—Are yeh listenin' to me? said Jimmy Sr.

—M T, said Bimbo.

—Mother Teresa, said Jimmy Sr.

—Let's see; ——you're righ'.

—'Course I'm righ'.

—They've won, look it. You'd've won if you'd o' been on it, Jimmy.

—What's the prize?

—A trip to somewhere.

—Would yeh take the van if Bertie found one for yeh? Jimmy Sr asked him again.

—Edinburgh; that's where it's to. That's not all tha' good, is it?

—Better than nowhere, said Jimmy Sr, defending the prize he could've won.

—That's right, o' course. They look happy enough with it annyway, don't they?

Jimmy Sr looked at the two girls on the telly.

—Wouldn't mind goin' with them, he said.

*   *   *

The weather was glorious. All week the sun had been blazing away, none of the chill that you often got when it was sunny in May.

They were sitting on Jimmy Sr's front step, Jimmy Sr and Bimbo, lapping up the sun. Bimbo had his eyes closed and his face shoved up to catch the sun, daring it to burn him.

—Lovely, he said.

—Fuckin' sure, said Jimmy Sr. —You can really feel it, can't yeh?

—God, yeah.

—Great drinkin' weather, said Jimmy Sr.

Bimbo didn't answer. He agreed with Jimmy Sr but he'd been talking with Maggie about them dipping into his redundancy money; they'd both been doing it, for clothes – Wayne had made his Confirmation two weeks ago – and Easter eggs and things that they'd always had. They'd taken all the kids to the pictures on Wayne's Confirmation day and that had set them back nearly forty quid after popcorn and ice-creams, forty quid that they didn't have, so it had come out of the lump sum. Maggie'd take a tenner out so they could have nice steak on a Sunday. And Bimbo'd been helping himself to the odd tenner so he could go up to the Hikers now and again. And the aluminium windows and the other bits and pieces. But it was stopping. This morning they'd had a meeting and they'd agreed that it had to stop or there'd be nothing left for when they really needed it. So the last treat they were giving themselves was three tickets for Cats, for himself and Maggie and her mother; they had them bought since last week, before the decision, so they were going to go ahead and go.

—Oh, here we go, said Jimmy Sr. —Look it.

Bimbo opened his eyes and looked at the ground till he got used to the light.

—Ah yes, said Jimmy Sr, nearly whispering.

There were three girls passing; girls about sixteen or seventeen. You could tell that they knew that Jimmy Sr and Bimbo were there. One of them looked in at them and away quickly. Bimbo felt sweaty suddenly and that annoyed him because it was Jimmy Sr that was really looking at them, not him.

—They're only young ones, he said.

—There's no harm, said Jimmy Sr.

He felt like a bollix now; he'd have to control himself – especially when the Child of fuckin' Prague was sitting beside him.

—They're goin' home for their tea, said Bimbo.

Jimmy Sr saw him shiver when he said it.

—An' to do their homework, said Bimbo.

—Those young ones aren't in school annymore. They left —

—I know, said Bimbo. —Those particular girls aren't goin' to school annymore but —

—They work in tha' sewin' factory in Baldoyle, said Jimmy Sr.

—They're still only young girls, said Bimbo. —Kids.

—Ah, rev up, said Jimmy Sr.

The sewing factory girls got a half day on Fridays. The first time Jimmy Sr'd looked at them on a Friday, from his bedroom window, he'd felt the blood rushing through his head, walloping off the sides, like he was watching a blue video and he was afraid that Veronica would come in and catch him. There was a gang of them – all of them seemed to be in denim mini-skirts – outside Sullivans. Derek and Ann Sullivan's daughter, Zena, worked in the sewing factory. There was about six of them laughing and hugging themselves to keep out the cold; it was months ago and young ones like that never dressed properly for the weather. All of them had haircuts like your woman, Kylie Minogue. Jimmy Sr liked that. He thought curly hair was much better than straight. He'd looked at them for ages. He even dived back onto the bed when one of them was looking his way. He'd been afraid to go back and look out the window. But he did, and then they went, their heels making a great sound; he'd always loved that sound – he always woke up when he heard it. He'd felt like a right cunt then, gawking out the window; like a fuckin' pervert.

But he was only looking, day dreaming maybe. There was no harm in it, none at all. He wasn't going to start chasing after them or following them or – he just liked looking at them, that was all.

They were coming back up the road. He could hear them, their heels. Bimbo'd been wrong; they weren't going home to their mammies for their tea. He'd tell him that when they went by, the fuckin' little altar boy.

They were two gates away now. He'd see them in a minute. He'd look the other way so Bimbo wouldn't think anything. Not that he cared what Bimbo thought.

He'd see them now if he looked.

He'd say something to Bimbo, just to be talking to him when they went by.

—Will Palace beat United tomorrow, d'yeh —

—Compadres!

It was Bertie. He stayed at the gates and looked at the young ones' arses when they'd gone by, not a bother on him; he didn't give a shite who saw him.

—How's Bertie? said Bimbo.

He wouldn't give out to Bertie for looking at the young ones, of course; no way.

Bertie stayed at the gate. He was wearing an Italia 90 T-shirt. He held the collar and shook it to put some air between him and the cloth.

—Are yis busy, compadres?

—What's it look like? said Jimmy Sr.

Bertie opened the gate and nodded at them to get up.

—Come on till I show yis somethin'.

* * *

It was filthy. He'd never seen anything like it. They walked around it. It was horrible to think that people had once eaten

449

chips and stuff out of this thing; it was a fuckin' scandal. There was no way he was going to look inside it.

He looked at Bimbo but he couldn't see his face. Bimbo was looking under the van now. For what, Jimmy Sr didn't know; acting the expert. The last place Jimmy Sr would have wanted to stick his face was under that fuckin' van; it would probably shite on top of you. It was like something out of a zoo gone stiff, the same colour and all.

It didn't even have wheels. It was up on bricks.

Bimbo stood up straight.

Bertie came out from behind the van, rolling a wheel in front of him.

—The wheels are new, compadres, he told them. —There's three more behind there, he said. —In perfect nick.

He let the tyre fall over onto the grass.

—Wha' d'yeh think? he asked Bimbo.

—Which end does it shite out of? said Jimmy Sr.

Bertie got in between Bimbo and Jimmy Sr. Bimbo was still looking at the van, moving a bit to the left and to the right like he was studying a painting or something. Jimmy Sr went over so he could get a good look at Bimbo.

Bimbo looked excited and disappointed, like a light going on and off. Jimmy Sr looked at the van again.

Ah Jesus, the thing was in fuckin' tatters. The man was fuckin' mad to be even looking at it. He couldn't let him do this.

—Maggie'll have to see it, Bimbo said to Bertie.

Thank God for that, thought Jimmy Sr. It saved him the hassle of trying to stop Bimbo from making a fuckin' eejit out of himself. Maggie'd box his ears for him when she saw what he was dragging her away from her work to see.

Bimbo's face was still skipping up and down.

—I'll get her, he said. —Hang on.

* * *

Jimmy Sr and Bertie waited in the garden while Bimbo went and got Maggie. The garden was in rag order, as bad as the

450

van. You could never really tell what state a house was in from the front. Jimmy Sr had walked past this house dozens of times – it was only a couple of corners away from his own – and he'd never noticed anything about it. He'd never noticed it at all really; it was just a house at the end of a terrace. It was only when you came round the back that you realised that there was a gang of savages living a couple of hundred yards away from you. It wasn't just poverty.

—I don't know how annyone can live like this, he said.

Bertie looked around.

—It's not tha' bad, he said. —A bit wild maybe.

—Wild! said Jimmy Sr.

He pointed at a used nappy on the path near the back door.

—Is tha' wild, is it? That's just fuckin' disgustin'.

He looked around nearer to him – he was sitting on one of the wheels – as if he was searching for more nappies.

—They should be ashamed of themselves, he said.

—It's not They, compadre, Bertie corrected him.

—Wha' d'yeh mean?

—It used to be They but now it's just He. ——She fucked off an' left him. An' the kids.

—Jaysis, said Jimmy Sr. —That's rough. Why?

—Why wha'?

—Why'd she leave him?

——I don't know, compadre, said Bertie after a bit. —He's an ugly cunt but.

—Did you ever see her? Jimmy Sr asked him.

—No, said Bertie. —But the kids are all ugly as well.

—Ah well then, said Jimmy Sr.

He had his back to the van, on purpose, kind of a protest. He looked over his shoulder at it.

—You've some fuckin' neck though, he told Bertie.

—Wha'? said Bertie.

—Tryin' to get poor Bimbo to throw his money away on tha' yoke, Jimmy Sr explained.

—I'm not trying to get Bimbo to throw his money away on

annythin', said Bertie. —He asked me to look ou' for a van for him an' that's what I did.

Jimmy Sr took his time answering Bertie. He had to be careful.

—How did yeh find it? he asked Bertie.

—I followed me nose, said Bertie.

They laughed.

Jimmy Sr knew now that Bertie wouldn't push Bimbo into buying it. Anyway, Maggie would never let Bimbo buy it.

—It hasn't been used in years, he said.

—No, Bertie corrected him. —No, it's not tha' long off the road. A year about only.

He looked at the van from end to end.

—She's a good little buy, he said. —Solid, yeh know. Tha' dirt'll wash off no problem.

Jimmy Sr changed his mind; the cunt was going to make Bimbo buy it.

—There's more than dirt wrong with tha' fuckin' thing, he told Bertie.

—Not at all, compadre, said Bertie, —I assure you.

—Assure me bollix, said Jimmy Sr.

—Hey! said Bertie.

He was pointing at Jimmy Sr. Jimmy Sr'd been afraid that this was going to happen. But sometimes you had to stand up and be counted.

—Hey, said Bertie again, not as loud now that he had Jimmy Sr looking at him. —Listen you, righ'. You ask annybody – annybody – that's ever dealt with me if they've anny complaints to make abou' their purchases an' what'll they tell yeh?

Jimmy Sr didn't know if he was supposed to answer.

—No signor, they'll say, said Bertie. —Quality, they'll say, is Bertie Gillespie's middle name. My friend Bimbo, he asks me to find him a chipper van an' I find him a fuckin' chipper van. It needs a wash an' its armpits shaved, but so wha'? Don't we all?

Jimmy Sr shrugged.

452

——I was only givin' me opinion, he said.

—Jimmy, said Bertie. —You've bought things from me, righ'? Many products.

—That's righ', said Jimmy Sr.

—Did annythin' I ever gave yeh stop workin' on yeh?

—Never, Bertie, Jimmy Sr assured him. —Linda's Walkman broke on her but tha' was her own fault. She got into the bath with it.

—Well then, said Bertie. —If I say it's a good van then it's a good fuckin' van. It's the Rolls-Royce o' fuckin' chipper vans; si?

——Okay, said Jimmy Sr. —Sorry.

—No problem, said Bertie. —What's keepin' Bimbo annyway?

He stood up and hitched his trousers back up over his arse. Jimmy Sr stood up and did the same thing with his trousers, although he didn't need to; he just did it – cos Bertie'd done it. He put his hands in his pockets and shoved the trousers back down a bit.

They looked at the van.

—Where's the window? said Jimmy Sr.

—You're beginnin' to annoy me, said Bertie, —d'yeh know tha'?

—No, I didn't mean it like —

—Who wants the van annyway? You or Bimbo? It's nothin' got to do with you, chum.

—I only fuckin' asked! said Jimmy Sr. —For fuck sake.

—Maybe, said Bertie.

—I only asked, said Jimmy Sr. —I did. I was only fuckin' curious. Where's the fuckin' window, that's all. It has to have one.

Bertie thought about this.

He went over to the van. He tapped it, at about chin level.

—No, he said.

He moved down a bit and tapped again.

—No, he said again.

He moved further down.

453

—It must be here somewhere, he said.

He tapped again.

—No.

He looked at his knuckles.

—Jesus, it's fuckin' dirty alrigh', he said.

He stepped back and looked carefully at the side of the van from left to right.

—It must be round the other side, he told Jimmy Sr.

—Does it have to have a window?

—'Course it does, said Jimmy Sr.

This was great; no fuckin' window.

—Why? said Bertie.

—How else can yeh serve the fuckin' customers? said Jimmy Sr. —Get up on the fuckin' roof?

—Oh, said Bertie. —You mean the hatch, compadre. It's round the back. A fine big hatch. Yeh could serve a small elephant through it.

—Ventilation, said Jimmy Sr.

—Que?

—Yeh'd want a window for ventilation, said Jimmy Sr.

—Me bollix yeh would, said Bertie. —Why would yeh? You've the hatch, for fuck sake. It's as big as a garage door.

—Doesn't matter a shite wha' size it is if there isn't a through draught.

—There's the door for gettin' in an' ou' as well, said Bertie. —That'll give yeh your through draught.

Jimmy Sr studied the van.

—I don't know, he said.

—Look it, said Bertie. —Let me at this point remind you of one small thing; uno small thing, righ'. It's a van for selling chips out of, not a caravan for goin' on your holidays in; comprende? It doesn't matter a wank if there's a window or not. Unless you're plannin' on—

—Oh God.

It was Maggie.

—Ah, said Bertie. —There yis are. Use your imagination,

454

signora, he told Maggie as he stepped aside to let her have a good look at the van.

Maggie stayed where she was, as if she was afraid to go closer to it. She brought her cardigan in closer around her shoulders. Bimbo was beside her, looking at her carefully, hoping, hoping.

Like a kid, the fuckin' eejit; buy me tha', Mammy, he'd say in a minute, the fuckin' head on him. If she did let him buy it Jimmy Sr'd – he didn't know what he'd do. Fuck them, it was their money.

Bertie's outstretched hand showed Maggie the van from top to bottom and back up again.

—A few minutes with a hose an' maybe, just maybe, a few hours with a paint scraper an' it'll be perfect. The Rolls-Royce o' chipper vans.

Jimmy Sr didn't know why he didn't want Bimbo to buy it. It just sort of messed things up, that was it. It was a shocking waste of money as well though.

—Have yeh looked inside it? Maggie asked Bimbo.

—Oh I have, yeah, said Bimbo. —No, it's grand. It's all there, all the equipment. It's a bit, eh—

—What abou' the engine? said Maggie.

Bertie got there before Bimbo.

—Wha' engine would tha' be, signora?

* * *

There was a window. They found it when they got it back to Bimbo's. Two days after he bought it.

It was like a procession, pushing and dragging the van through Barrytown, Bimbo and Jimmy Sr and some of their kids although the twins were no help at all, just worried about getting their clothes dirty. Mind you, you didn't even have to touch the van to get dirty from it, you only had to stand near it. It took them ages to get the wheels on it and then getting it around to the front without knocking a lump off the house took ages as well and it was nearly dark by the time they were on the road to Bimbo's. The weather was great, of course, and everyone on the left side of the street was out on their front steps getting the last of the sun and by the time they'd got to the corner of Barrytown Road there was a huge fuckin' crowd out watching them. Jimmy Sr kept his head down all the way, except when they were going down the hill just at the turn into Chestnut Avenue and he had to run up to the front to help Bimbo stop the van from taking off on its own, past the corner. They'd had to dig their heels in or else it would've gone over Bimbo and his young one, Jessica. He should have let it; that would have taught Bimbo a lesson about how to spend his money. Anyway, they got the useless piece of rusty shite to stop just after the corner and there was a really huge crowd by now and they cheered when they missed the corner, the cunts. They backed it back and Wayne, one of Bimbo's young fellas, got the steering wheel around; the sweat was running off the poor little fucker, and they got it onto Chestnut Avenue and the cunts at the corner cheered again. No fear of the lazy shites giving them a hand, of course.

There really was a huge crowd out. It was a bit like Gandhi's funeral in the film, except noisier. It was more like the Tour de France, the neighbours at the side of the road clapping and whooping, the cynical bastards.

—Hey Jimmy, are yeh pushin' it or ridin' it!?

And they all laughed, the eejits, like sheep.

—Yeow, Jimmy!

—Hey, look it! Mister Rabbitte's wearin' stripy kaks!

God, he wanted to kill someone when he heard that. Veronica was right; he should never have tucked his shirt inside his underpants; she'd been saying it for years. He tried to stand up straighter when he was pushing to make the underpants go back down in behind his trousers but he was probably too late, and he couldn't put a hand behind and shove them back down; that would only have been giving in to them.

—Here, lads, look at the skidmarks!

Some people would laugh at anything. A kid had his ghetto blaster on full blast; it was like a jaysis circus. Only a couple of gates left and they'd be at Bimbo's gate and it would be over. The worst part but, was earlier, going past the Hikers, not only because he'd have loved a pint but because loads of the lads came out with their pints and sat on the wall laughing and slagging them. Larry O'Rourke was offering 3/1 that Jimmy Sr would die before they got to Bimbo's. Ha fuckin' ha. By Jaysis, the next bank holiday that fucker got up with the band and started doing his Elvis impressions Jimmy Sr would let him know who he really sounded like; Christy fuckin' Brown.

—Come on, three to one Jimmy snuffs it. Anny takers?

—That's a fuckin' big pram he's pushin', isn't it?

Jimmy Sr looked up to see who'd said that and it was Bertie. He couldn't believe it. He'd only enough breath in him to say one thing back at them.

—Fuck yis.

He got a bit more air in.

—Yis cunts.

They were there. Just one last big push up onto the path and into Bimbo's drive and it was over.

Jimmy Sr couldn't stand up straight for a while, his back was killing him. The sweat was worse though. He was wringing. His shoes squelched, his shirt was stuck to him, his arse was wet. He sat down on the grass. The twins wanted money for helping.

—Get lost, he managed to say.

—Ah, that's not fair —

—Fuck off!

Jimmy Sr got the sweat out of his eyes and looked at Bimbo and Maggie looking at the van. Not a bother on Bimbo, of course; he didn't even look dirty. He had his arm around Maggie's shoulders and the two of them were gawking at the van like it was their first fuckin' grandchild. Bimbo was anyway; Maggie didn't look as delighted. You couldn't blame her. If her first grandchild was in the same state as the van she'd want to smother it, and nobody would object. Then they looked at each other and started laughing and then they looked at the van and stopped laughing, and then they started again. It was nice really, seeing them like that.

Then Bimbo noticed Jimmy Sr on the grass.

About fuckin' time.

—Tha' was great gas, wasn't it? he said.

—Eh ——yeah. Yeah.

—D'yeh know wha' I think? said Bimbo then.

And he waited for Jimmy Sr to give him the green light.

—Wha'? said Jimmy Sr.

—It doesn't look nearly as bad here, away from that other place.

He was talking through his arse, of course, but Jimmy Sr gave him the answer he was dying for.

—You're righ', yeh know, he said.

—The more I look at it, said Bimbo, —the more I think we're after gettin' a bargain; d'yeh know tha'.

Ah, thought Jimmy Sr, God love him.

—Yeh might be righ' there, he said.

—This sounds stupid now, said Bimbo.

Maggie had come over now as well.

—But I think that it's a godsend tha' there's no engine in it. We got it for nothin'.

—Umm, said Maggie.

They'd got it for eight hundred quid. Maggie'd put her foot down at seven hundred and fifty until Bertie'd introduced her to the owner with one of his motherless children, the youngest, in his arms.

—Poor Jimmy looks like he could do with a drink, Maggie told Bimbo.

—He's not the only one, said Bimbo. —Wait now till I do somethin' first.

He went through to the back of the house and came back with two bricks and put them behind the back wheels.

—There now, he said. —She's rightly anchored.

He tapped one of the bricks with his foot and it didn't budge.

—Tha' should hold it annyway, he said.

He was pleased with his work.

—I'll put a chain on the gate later, he told Maggie. —To make sure tha' no young fellas decide to rob it durin' the nigh'.

—Good thinkin' tha', said Jimmy Sr.

There actually were a few young fellas in Barrytown that nearly would have robbed even as worthless a pile of shite as poor Bimbo's van, just for the crack. They'd've robbed themselves if there was no one else, some of the little bastards around here.

Jimmy Sr was feeling normal again.

—Could yeh manage a pint, Jim? Bimbo asked him.

—It's abou' the only thing I could manage, said Jimmy Sr.

—Come on so, said Bimbo. —Wha' abou' yourself, Maggie?

—No, said Maggie. —Thirtysomething's on in a minute.

—She never misses it, Bimbo told Jimmy Sr when they were going to the gate. —She won't video it either. She has to watch it live.

That was when they found the window. Bimbo's kids were inside in the van exploring and Wayne put his foot through it. Bimbo got them all out and checked Wayne's foot. It was grand, no cuts or anything. Then he told the kids to stay out of the van cos it was dangerous until they got all the grease off the floor and, to the two youngest, that it was full of spiders that bit you and then he pretended to lock the door with one of his house keys.

He was good with the kids; they'd all listened to him.

—Now, he said when he'd done it.

He patted the door and wiped his hand on his trousers and they went up to the Hikers.

* * *

Jimmy Sr needed bubbles. Darren was working in the bar, collecting the glasses and that, and he recommended Budweiser. Jimmy Sr was looking suspiciously at the glass. He lifted it and took a sip, then a bigger one and then a much bigger one.

—It's not tha' bad, he said.

The seat was nice and cold against his back.

Bimbo was very giddy, looking around him all the time, shifting, waving at every wanker that walked in.

—Settle down, will yeh, said Jimmy Sr.

—Wha'?

—You're like a performin' flea there, Jimmy Sr told him. — You're makin' me fuckin' nervous.

—Sorry, said Bimbo. —It's just —. Ah, yeh know.

He lifted his pint.

—Well, Jim, cheers, he said for the third time.

—Yeah, said Jimmy Sr.

—Will yeh have another one? Bimbo asked him.

—There's no —

—Go on.

—Fair enough, said Jimmy Sr. —Thanks very much; there's no need. ——Make it Guinness but, will yeh.

—Good man, said Bimbo. —Darren! Two pints o' Guinness, like a good man, please.

—Poor Darren'll be doin' his Leavin' durin' the World Cup, Jimmy Sr told Bimbo. —Isn't tha' shockin'?

—Ah that's shockin', said Bimbo.

—Fuckin' terrible, said Jimmy Sr.

And Darren arrived with the pints and Jimmy Sr let him take the rest of the Budweiser.

—It's like drinkin' fuckin' Andrews, he sort of apologised to Bimbo.

—Not to worry, said Bimbo.

He gave Darren a big tip when he was going.

—I was thinkin', said Bimbo. —We'll have to have the van ready in time for the World Cup.

Jimmy Sr didn't like the sound of that. We'll.

He said nothing.

—The pubs'll be jammered, said Bimbo.

He still said nothing.

—An' there'll be no cookin' done, said Bimbo. —'Specially if Ireland do well.

—They will, said Jimmy Sr. —Don't worry.

—It's a great opportunity, said Bimbo. —Everyone'll be watchin' the telly for the whole month.

—So will I, said Jimmy Sr.

—Yeah, said Bimbo. —It should be smashin'.

They drank. It was good to be back on the Guinness. They'd have a chat now about the World Cup. Jimmy Sr felt good now. He sang softly.

—OLÉ——OLÉ OLÉ OLÉ——Did yeh hear tha' song yet, Bimbo?

—Which; the Ireland one?

—The official one, yeah.

—Ah, I did, yeah, said Bimbo.

—Isn't it brilliant? said Jimmy Sr.

—Terrific.

Jimmy Sr tried to do Jack Charlton.

—Put them uunder presheh.

—D'yeh want to be me partner, Jim? said Bimbo.

—Wha's tha'?

He'd heard Bimbo alright but he was confused.

—Would yeh think abou' becomin' me partner? said Bimbo.

He looked serious in a way that only Bimbo could look; deadly serious.

—We'd make a great team, said Bimbo. —I was talkin' to Maggie about it.

—Jaysis——, said Jimmy Sr. —Eh, thanks very much, Bimbo. I don't know —

—Will yeh think about it annyway? said Bimbo.

—I will, Jimmy Sr assured him. —I will. ——Thanks.

—No, said Bimbo. —You'd be doin' me a favour.

—Oh, I know tha', said Jimmy Sr.

They laughed, and that gave Jimmy Sr a chance to wipe his eyes. He said it again.

—Thanks very much.

He took a big breath.

——Fuckin' hell, he said then. —What a day.

Wait till Veronica heard.

—McDonalds can go an' fuck themselves, he said to Bimbo. —Isn't tha' righ'?

Bimbo laughed, delighted.

—That's righ'.

They laughed again.

—Bimbo's Burgers, said Jimmy Sr. —How does tha' sound?

Bimbo clapped his hands.

—I knew it! he said.

He held his hand out, and Jimmy Sr took it and didn't let go of it for ages.

Then he dropped Bimbo's hand.

—Hang on though, he said.

He looked very worried.

—Do I have to help you clean it?

He watched Bimbo deciding if he was joking or not and then the two of them roared and shook hands again.

* * *

Veronica was lying beside him, nearly asleep, God love her; she'd been studying all night for her exams. She'd told him how to make chips and it seemed easy enough.

These were good chips, the ones he was eating now. They always were in the summer. There'd be a terrible smell of vinegar in the bedroom in the morning though.

He'd bought a sausage-in-batter tonight as well. He held it up to the light coming in where the curtain stopped short of the wall, to get a decent look at it. He looked down at Veronica.

—Veronica? he whispered.

He didn't want to talk to her unless she was awake anyway.

—Mmmm? said Veronica.

—Are yeh awake?

—What?

—Only if you're awake.

—Go on, said Veronica.

—How do they make these? said Jimmy Sr.

462

He brought the sausage down to the pillow so she could see it properly.

Veronica snorted, kind of.

——I don't know, she said. —I don't think they make them. I think they just find them.

She found his knee and gave it a squeeze.

* * *

There was only a month to go to the start of the World Cup so, as Bimbo said, they had it all to do. It wasn't even a full month, a bit less than four weeks.

They walked around the van again.

—Righ', said Bimbo. —We'll never get it cleaned up by just lookin' at it.

So he went through the house to the back and got his hose and rigged it up to the tap in the kitchen and brought the hose out to the front through the hall.

—Wha' colour is it annyway? Jimmy Sr asked.

—White! said Bimbo.

—How d'yeh know?

—All chipper vans are whi'e, said Bimbo. —Stand back there, Jimmy.

He roared into the hall.

—Righ'! Turn her on.

Someone inside turned on the cold tap and Bimbo pointed the hose at the side of the van. The water came out in two gushes and then in a steady stream and Bimbo went up close so the water would drum against the wall of the van. It made an impressive sound, and brought some of the neighbours out to watch. Bimbo sprayed right across; he put his thumb to the nozzle and aimed at one spot and held the jet of water at it for ages – but he might as well have been pissing at it for all the good it did.

—Okay! Turn her off! ——Turn her off!!

He sounded annoyed.

The water slowed down and stopped altogether.

—Will yeh switch it on to the hot tap!? Bimbo yelled.

Maggie answered.

—I used up all the hot doin' the clothes.

—Ah, God almighty, Bimbo said quietly.

He let the hose drop. They studied the side of the van.

The dirt was still there, solid as ever, only shinier now because of the water. It looked even worse that way, almost healthy and alive.

—How did it get greasy on the fuckin' outside? Jimmy Sr asked.

—God knows, said Bimbo.

—Yeh could understand the inside, said Jimmy Sr.

—Yeah, said Bimbo. —Yeah.

—What'll we do now? Jimmy Sr wanted to know.

*   *   *

Bimbo scraped a clot of grease off with his fingernail.

—It does come off, he said.

Jimmy Sr did the same.

—Yeah, he said. —Fuckin' hell though, Bimbo. It's goin' to take fuckin' years.

—Not at all, said Bimbo.

They got paint scrapers, five of them, from Barney's Hardware and attacked the van with them, and then they started getting somewhere. Once you got the blade in under the grease and the dirt it came away easily enough. It was a little bit disgusting alright but at least they could see that it was working, the grease was coming off, and that made up for it. But the feel of it was horrible, and the smell; it was hard to describe, fuckin' terrible though. Jimmy Sr could smell it on his hands even after putting some of Veronica's Oil of Ulay all over them. And his clothes; he'd have roasted himself if he'd sat too close to the fire after a day's work. Veronica said she'd never seen dirt like it; she said it the first four days he came home, but she didn't say it like she was annoyed, more like she was fascinated.

They concentrated on the outside. They were both too scared to look carefully inside, but they didn't say anything.

They just did their work. They scraped all day and when they started sliding because of the grease on the ground they stopped and hosed the path and went at it with the yard brush. Bimbo got sawdust from the butchers and sprinkled it on top of the grease and that way they didn't have to interrupt the work too often. It was manky work though, messy and slow. But Maggie said it wouldn't go on for ever and she was right; it just felt that way. He'd get up at eight and go down to Bimbo's and look at the bit he'd done the day before and it was like he'd never touched it; it was still filthy and shiny. But, then again, he'd be scraping away, breathing through his mouth, listening to the radio or chatting with Bimbo, and he'd see that there was no more grease to scrape off in this part; he'd reached the end, there was just white paint, a small island of it.

He felt brilliant the first time that happened and he didn't stop working till eight o'clock.

They were getting there.

There was more than just the cleaning of the van, of course. They had to become chefs before the end of the month, which was no fuckin' joke. The first time he made chips, at home, he put far too much oil into the pan and nearly set fire to the fuckin' kitchen when he lowered the chips into it. It frightened the shite out of him. But Veronica was a good teacher, very patient; she even let him make the dinner one night, which was very decent of her. He made a bit of a bollix of it – burnt fuck out of the burgers; it was like eating little hubcaps – but no one complained. She showed him how to peel spuds without peeling the skin off your hands as well, how to always peel out, away from your body, so you didn't stab yourself.

He cut his wrist the first time he did it; not cut it exactly, more scraped, but it was very fuckin' sore all the same. He nearly went out the window when Veronica put Dettol on it but they laughed later in bed, imagining trying to kill yourself with a potato peeler scraping away till you hit an artery, and then start on the other wrist, quick before you fainted. They hadn't laughed together like that in ages. She'd a good sense of humour, Veronica had. The only time she got annoyed was when he peeled all the potatoes in the house, practising. He didn't blame her but, like he told her, they were running out of time. Another thing she showed him that he'd never known before; you put the chips you didn't want to use immediately in water to keep them fresh and the right colour.

—God, he said. —The simple things are the most ingenious, aren't they?

He caught Sharon grinning at him when he was practising his peeling.

—Fuck off, you, he said.

And he brought the bucket and the spuds up to the bedroom so he could do his practice in peace. Later on, Sharon asked him if she could work in the van some nights, when it was on the road. And he said Yeah.

It would do her good.

* * *

—She'd be a good worker, said Jimmy Sr.

He wanted to clout Bimbo, the way he was looking at him, like he'd farted at mass during the Offertory; that sort of look.

—I know tha', said Bimbo. —I never said different, Jimmy, now.

—Well then —?

—Staff appointments should be a joint decision, Jimmy. Between the two of us.

—It's only Sharon, for fuck sake.

—Still, though —

He was right really. But —

—D'yeh want me to sack her, is tha' it? Before she's even started.

—Ah, Jimmy —

—Ah, me arse.

But Bimbo was right, Jimmy Sr could see that. He just hated losing.

—I'll tell her we don't want her, Jimmy Sr told Bimbo, like he was giving in to him.

466

—Not at all, said Bimbo. —No way.

—Wha' then? said Jimmy Sr. —I'm fuckin' lost.

—Just, in future we'll make these decisions together, said Bimbo. —Is tha' alrigh'?

—Yeah, said Jimmy Sr. —No problem. Sorry abou' —

—Ah no, said Bimbo. —No. No.

They got back to work and didn't say anything to each other for a good while.

The roof wasn't as bad as the sides but it was very tricky. There was no grease up there but that didn't mean that you couldn't fall off. Bimbo did fall off but he landed on the grass, so it wasn't too bad; there was no real damage done. Still, the noise he made when he hit the ground was terrifying, like a huge thump. Jimmy Sr was on his hands and knees up there, afraid to budge. Maggie felt Bimbo hitting the ground from where she was in the house and she came out and got him up on his feet and gave out shite to him once she knew that he wasn't dying on her. Poor oul' Bimbo was a bit shook after it, so they called it a day. The only problem was getting down off the fuckin' roof. Jimmy Sr's leg couldn't find the ladder and he was shaking like fuck, but he got down eventually and he took Bimbo off for a pint. They took a look back at the van when they got out to the path, just to see what it looked like from a distance, and it didn't look too bad at all; it wasn't as white as it could've been, like new teeth, but it was definitely white.

They went on a reconnaissance mission. That was what Bimbo called it, but he was only messing. They went to a chipper; not the one they normally used cos the crowd in there were a snotty bunch of fuckers and Jimmy Sr hadn't got on well with them since Leslie threw a dead cat over the counter into the deep fat fryer. That was years ago, long before Leslie went to England, and they still held it against him. Actually, it was gas when it happened. Jimmy Sr and the lads had gone in after closing time and the old fella, the one the kids called the Fat Leper, told Jimmy Sr what Les had done with the cat and Bertie changed his order from a batter burger to a smoked

467

cod. —Just to be on the safe side, compadres, he said. Jaysis, they howled. And the Fat Leper barred the lot of them. And Bertie offered to buy the cat if that would make him feel any better, as long as he didn't expect him to eat it as well. Anyway, the barring order only lasted one night – they were cute fuckers, the Italians; you don't make your fortune by barring your best customers – but they still glared at Jimmy Sr. The Fat Leper didn't; he'd died last year, but the rest of them did. Even the ones that had been in Italy when it had happened.

So they went to a different chipper, one in Coolock. It was kind of exciting going in; stupid really, but Jimmy Sr couldn't help thinking that he was a bit of a thrill seeker. Bimbo went ahead of him. It was empty except for them.

—So far so good, said Bimbo.

There were two young fellas behind the counter, one of them opening the bags they put the chips into, putting a line of them on top of the counter, at the ready. Good thinking, thought Jimmy Sr, and he made a mental note of it. The other one was leaning against the back wall, scratching his hole. There were more of them inside, behind the yellow and red and blue plastic strips they always put over doorways in chippers but there was only the two lads on duty.

—Howyeh, lads, said Bimbo.

—Yeah? said the hole scratcher.

—Two singles, said Bimbo. —Like a good man, please.

—Large or small?

Bimbo looked at Jimmy Sr.

—A large'll do me, Jimmy Sr told him.

—Two large, said Bimbo.

They stood there at the low part of the counter, where they put the vinegar on the chips and took the money. They leaned over and tried to see the lads in action, but the chips were already done so all they did was bag them.

—That all? said the other one.

—Yeah, said Bimbo, —thanks. We're just after the dinner.

Jimmy Sr nudged him.

—Wha'?

—Go on, said Jimmy Sr. —Ask him.

It would be too late in a minute.

—Eh, lads —? said Bimbo.

They looked at him.

Jimmy Sr had to nudge Bimbo again; he was fuckin' useless.

—Where d'yis get your chips? Bimbo asked them. —Eh, if yeh don't mind me askin' now.

—In the ground, said the hole scratcher, the smartarsed little prick, and the two of them laughed.

Jimmy Sr had to drag Bimbo away from the counter.

—Come on.

—Wha' abou' the chips? said Bimbo.

—Fuck them, said Jimmy Sr.

He pushed Bimbo out the door. The two behind the counter were annoyed now because they'd two singles wrapped and ready and no home for them. Jimmy Sr gave them the fingers.

—Go back to your own country, he said. —Fuck the EEC.

He felt a lot better after that. He went back to give them more.

—An' bring Tony Cascarino with yis, he said. —He's fuckin' useless annyway.

And he left the door open, so one of them would have to come around and close it cos it was quite chilly out.

Bimbo told Maggie what had happened and she kind of took over that department.

—Joint decisions, me bollix said Jimmy Sr, but he didn't mind; he just said it to make Bimbo feel guilty, because he deserved it.

Maggie was brilliant. She got them a cash-and-carry card, no problem to her. Fellas Jimmy Sr knew would have killed their mothers for one of those cards, to get at the cheap drink, but Maggie went off one afternoon and came back with one. She'd a great business head on her.

—A revelation, said Bertie.

—Ah yeah, said Jimmy Sr. —Hats off to her.

Bimbo was chuffed.

She found out about permits and licences and that, stuff that Jimmy Sr couldn't've been bothered looking into, and Bimbo wouldn't've been able to. She said she'd organise the stock, and all they'd have to worry about was getting the van in order, and then manning it. She said she'd look after the whole legal side of the operation. It was a load off their minds, both Jimmy Sr and Bimbo agreed on that.

—I didn't even know yeh needed a fuckin' licence, Jimmy Sr admitted.

—Oh God, yeah, said Bimbo. —Yeh need a licence for nearly everythin', so yeh do.

Jimmy Sr supposed that it was only right; if you needed a licence for a dog or a telly it was only proper that you had to have one for a chipper van as well.

—It's not so much the van, said Bimbo. —It's more what yeh do in it, if yeh get me.

The outside of the van was looking well now. Bimbo's brother, Victor, was a panel beater and he was going to do a job on the dints, the worst ones anyway. There were a few bald patches but a lick of paint would make them hard to find. The neighbours still stopped and looked at them working, but they'd stopped slagging them.

—We've got it looking smashin', said Bimbo.

Jimmy Sr rubbed his fingers down the side, and there was no track left after it. He wouldn't have been able to do that last week; his finger would've got stuck.

—Now for the inside, said Bimbo.

—Oh fuck, said Jimmy Sr.

* * *

They all got together in Bimbo and Maggie's kitchen. Veronica came with Jimmy Sr so there was the four of them, and Maggie's mother. It was nice.

—Now, said Maggie. —What I thought we'd do tonight was finalise the menu.

—Wha' menu? said Bimbo.

—Yeah, said Jimmy Sr.

He was worried; he didn't want to be a fuckin' waiter.

Bimbo nearly whispered over the table to Maggie.

—It's only a van.

Veronica started laughing, and Maggie did as well.

Jimmy Sr wasn't sure what was happening, but he couldn't help thinking that he was being hijacked, himself and Bimbo.

—The menu, lads, said Maggie – a bit sarcastically, Jimmy Sr thought – is the list of things that the customer chooses from.

—Like on the wall behind the counter? said Jimmy Sr.

—Exactly, said Maggie.

Jimmy Sr nodded, like he'd known that all along; he was just checking.

They got down to business. Maggie had stuff already done in under the grill, like on a cookery programme on the telly. She divided a burger in five and they each had a little bit. Jimmy Sr thought that this was a bit mean, until he tasted it.

—Jesus!

Enough said; they all agreed with him. Maggie had a list; she even had one of those clipboard things. She put a line through the first name.

—Wha' are they called an' annyway? Jimmy Sr asked Maggie.

—Splendid Burgers, said Maggie.

—My God, said Veronica.

They tasted five more. Maggie's mother was still only on the second one when the rest of them had finished.

—Would annyone like a glass o' water? said Bimbo.

—Please, said Veronica.

—Yeah, me too, said Jimmy Sr. —I thought the third one was the nicest.

—I don't know if nicest is the word, said Veronica, —but —

—What abou' you, Bimbo? Jimmy Sr asked.

—Yeah. I think so, he said. —Not the last one annyway; the fifth one.

—Fuck, no.

Maggie's mother caught up with them.

—What do you think, Mammy? Maggie asked her.

—Very nice, she said.

—Which but? said Jimmy Sr.

—Oh, she said. —Is it a quiz?

And Veronica kicked Jimmy Sr's leg before he could say anything back.

—Will we go for the Champion Burger so? said Maggie.

—Is tha' the third one? said Jimmy Sr.

—Yeah.

—Def'ny then, said Jimmy Sr. —They were bigger as well.

—That's only because o' the way I cut it, said Maggie. —I gave you the biggest bit.

—Still though, said Jimmy Sr. —I thought it was head an' shoulders above the others.

—Champion? said Maggie. —Goin' once —— twice —— Champion, it is.

Jimmy Sr was delighted; he'd won. He knocked back his water and got up to get more.

—What's next? said Bimbo.

—Spice-burgers, said Maggie.

Herself and Veronica started laughing again.

They were all feeling a bit queasy by the time they'd finished – very fuckin' queasy actually – but it was great crack all the same. Fresh cod–in–batter, small bricks of the stuff, was next, followed closely by smoked cod–in–batter.

—It's not really smoked cod at all, yeh know, Maggie told them. —It's black mullet.

Veronica took her bit out of her mouth when she heard that but Jimmy Sr thought it was grand. His philosophy was that he didn't give a shite what it was so long as it tasted alright, and he made that point to the rest of them. Bimbo didn't agree with him.

—I don't think yeh should sell somethin' if it's really somethin' else, he said.

—Fair enough, said Jimmy Sr. —Put Black mullet-in-batter up on the, eh, menu an' see how many yeh sell.

—Maybe if we can't get real smoked cod we shouldn't sell it at all.

—Yes, said Veronica.

—People like smoked cod! said Jimmy Sr. —I love a bit o' smoked cod.

—But it isn't really smoked cod.

—So wha'?

Veronica wanted to say something.

—Does it have to be all these processed things? she asked. —Could you not get your fish in Howth and prepare it yourselves.

—Too dear, I'm afraid, said Maggie.

She consulted her clipboard.

—An' anyway, said Jimmy Sr. —As well as tha', how would we smoke the cod an' tha'? We don't know how. We're not —— fuckin' Amazon tribesmen or somethin'.

He took another hunk of the mullet and chewed fuck out of it.

—Well, I think it's fuckin' lovely, he said.

And bloody Veronica started laughing again.

Maggie was gas once she had a few scoops inside in her. She made her mother try out two different types of ketchup.

They watched her putting a little fingerload of the second ketchup onto her tongue.

—Now, Mammy, said Maggie. —Was tha' one any less disgustin' than the last one?

—Oh yes, she said. —Definitely.

They'd polished off the few cans that Bimbo had hidden under the stairs (—I'd've sworn tha' there was more in there), so they went for a few pints before closing time, to get rid of the taste of all the gunge and shite they'd been experimenting with all night.

Maggie's mother stayed at home.

—I think the last spice-burger must've floored her a bit, said Bimbo.

—Ah yeah; God love her, said Jimmy Sr.

Veronica burst her hole laughing when he said that. She was

really enjoying herself. Jimmy Sr held her hand for a bit when they were going up the road.

* * *

They were both nervous going in. The World Cup was only two and a bit weeks away now. They climbed in and stood there, sweating already before they'd done anything. They breathed through their mouths, air that hadn't been used in months; it smelt a bit like old runners, but far worse than that.

—No rust, said Bimbo, after a fair while.

—Everythin' else though, said Jimmy Sr.

——How'll we manage it? said Bimbo.

Jimmy Sr had an idea; he'd had it since he'd started sweating.

—A couple o' kids would be better in here than us, he said. —Much more effective.

Bimbo didn't look too keen.

—We'd just get them to take off the first layer, Jimmy Sr explained. —An' then we can do the rest ourselves easily. We won't be gettin' in each other's way.

It was Saturday; no school.

—I'll get Wayne up, said Bimbo.

—Good man, said Jimmy Sr. —Bribe him.

—I'll have to, said Bimbo. —Wayne loves his bed.

Wayne grew up that day; he earned his first day's wages. God, he was great. Early on, only a little while after he'd started, he got out of the van and got sick, and climbed back in again, not a bother on him. He didn't even want a glass of water when Bimbo said he'd get one for him. Bimbo got another of his young fellas, Glenn, when he came home from his football and that made two of them inside and Bimbo and Jimmy Sr outside handing buckets of hot water into them. It was a lovely day, the sun was powerful and a nice breeze as well. Wayne was small and Glenn was tiny.

—Made for this kind o' work, said Jimmy Sr.

Bimbo agreed with him.

—They're good in school as well though, Jimmy, he said. —Glenn is tops in his class.

474

—Yeh can see that alrigh', said Jimmy Sr. —He's a man's head on him.

He looked in at them again.

—D'yeh know wha'? he said. —If they'd been around a hundred years ago they'd've spent all their time up fuckin' chimneys.

Bimbo looked in as well; he couldn't help laughing, but he was beaming, delighted with himself.

—Now now, lads, he said.

They were throwing water at each other.

—D'yeh know what I was thinkin'? said Jimmy Sr.

They were sitting on the grass, keeping an eye on the lads.

—Wha'?

—We should have a big paintin' there beside the hatch, said Jimmy Sr. —An' another one to match it on the other side.

—What sort of a paintin'? said Bimbo.

—I don't know, said Jimmy Sr. —A burger or somethin', an' a few chips beside. Like an ad. Not a painting paintin' like the Mona Lisa or annythin'. A sign.

Glenn slid out of the van headfirst but he was going fast enough to miss the path and land on the grass. He laughed and got up to do it again. Bimbo grabbed him by the kaks; he was only wearing his runners and his underpants.

—No messin' now, Glenn.

But they were sliding around like Torvill and Dean in there, not on purpose; they couldn't help it. Then Bimbo had a brainwave. He got sheets of sandpaper – he had loads of them, of course – and tied them to the soles of their runners, and it worked.

He kept looking in at them and their feet.

—Take it easy, Bimbo, will yeh, said Jimmy Sr. —You're not after inventin' fuckin' electricity.

—You're only jealous, Bimbo told him.

—Fuck off, will yeh.

By the end of the day the two lads were shagged but they'd done a great job. Maggie gave out shite; she said she'd never be able to get the rings off the bath. She'd soaked the two of them till their skin was wrinkly and they still looked grey.

—Take a look at wha' they did though, said Bimbo.

Maggie looked into the van. And she had to admit it; they'd done a great job.

* * *

They climbed into the van.

—They did a smashin' job, didn't they? said Bimbo.

It was Monday morning, bright and early.

It was still manky, there was still a very funny smell – it was worse now that the van was much cleaner; more out of place – but it looked a hell of a lot better than it had two days ago.

The door was at the back of the van. The driver and passenger seats were separate; you had to get out and walk round to the back to get into the van bit. There was a step up to the door. When you came in the hatch was on your right. It was wide enough for two using their arms and elbows, with a good wide counter, although you'd have to lean out a bit to get the money. The door of the hatch was like the emergency exit at the back of a double-decker bus, but without the glass. You pushed it out and up. The hot-plate and the deep fat fryer were behind the hatch, on the other side of the van. There was a small window above them, without the glass since Wayne had put his foot through it. There was a sink at the back and not a lot else; a few shelves and ledges. The sink was behind where the passenger seat was.

—What's the sink for? Jimmy Sr wanted to know.

—For washin' stuff, o' course, said Bimbo.

—But there's no fuckin' water, said Jimmy Sr.

—Yeh'd have to have a sink, said Bimbo.

—But there's no fuckin' water, Jimmy Sr said again.

—Well, it's there for somethin', said Bimbo. —We'll figure it ou'. ——We'll go at it from the top down.

—Righto, said Jimmy Sr.

Bimbo was on the left wall and Jimmy Sr on the right, the one with the hatch in it. He'd skip over the hatch and finish before Bimbo and give out shite to him for being a slowcoach, for the laugh.

—Just a squirt gets the dirt, said Bimbo when they were starting.

It was a doddle compared to what they'd had to do outside.

—How much did yeh give the lads? Jimmy Sr asked Bimbo.

—Nothin' yet, said Bimbo. —Sure, they asked me could they do it again there yesterday. They had a great time, so they did.

They laughed.

—They'll learn, said Jimmy Sr. —Let's get a bit o' light in here, wha'.

He figured out how to open the hatch.

—Now.

He pushed it out, and it fell off and Jimmy Sr nearly fell out after it. It made an almighty clatter when it hit the ground. Bimbo nearly fell off his perch. He dropped his Jif into the deep fat fryer.

—God, me heart, he said.

Jimmy Sr was swinging off the counter. His legs found the floor and he felt safer.

—Fuck your heart, said Jimmy Sr. —I nearly had a shite in me fuckin' trousers. Come here, swap sides.

—No way!

* * *

They weren't happy with the look of the deep fat fryer. But they'd done their best with it.

—Still though, said Bimbo. —It might be dangerous.

—Not at all, said Jimmy Sr. —It's just wear an' tear, that's all.

They were in Bimbo's kitchen having their elevenses.

—The hotplate looks very well now, said Bimbo.

—It does alrigh', Jimmy Sr agreed. —Yeh'd ride your missis on it it's so clean.

—Shhh! said Bimbo.

Glenn was coming through with tins of pineapple rings.

477

—It's the man from Delmonte, said Jimmy Sr. —Good man, Glenn.

—These're the heaviest, Glenn told him.

—No problem to yeh, said Jimmy Sr.

Glenn ran out into the garden so he could get to the shed before he had to drop the tray of pineapple rings. They heard the clatter of tins hitting the path.

—He didn't make it, said Jimmy Sr.

Bimbo lifted himself up to look out the window.

—No, he said. —He did.

They'd two freezers out in Bimbo's shed – Bertie'd got them for them; grand big freezers, nearly new – and all the stuff went into them; the blocks of cod, the blocks of lard, the burgers, anything that would go bad.

The kids were bringing cartons of Twixes and Mars Bars out to Maggie now.

—I have them counted, she warned them.

Jessica went to the kitchen door and yelled out.

—There's nothin' left!

—Come here, said Maggie.

In a few seconds the kids came charging through with two Twixes and two Mars Bars apiece.

Bimbo made a grab at Glenn.

—Give us a Twix.

Glenn got away from him and into the hall, bursting his little shite laughing. Maggie shut the kitchen door. She threw a burger onto the table. It bounced; it was rock solid.

—What d'you think of tha'? she said.

—It's a bit hard, said Bimbo.

Jimmy Sr picked it up. It was the whole thing, the bun and all.

—What's the idea? he said.

—There's onion an' sauce an' a slice o' gherkin already in there, she said. —And you can get them with cheese as well.

She sat down.

—All yeh have to do is throw it in the microwave, she said.

—That's very good, said Bimbo.

—We don't have a microwave, said Jimmy Sr.

—Can't yis get—? said Maggie.

—We've no electricity, said Bimbo.

They looked at one another.

—Oh Christ—, said Jimmy Sr.

*   *   *

—Now, said Jimmy Sr. —Look at this now; there's nothin' to it. Anny fuckin' eejit could do it.

They were in the Rabbitte kitchen.

He had the mixing bowl on the table in front of him. He poured water from a milk bottle into the bowl.

—Water, he said.

He sprinkled some flour from a packet in on top of the water, then got a bit braver and poured half the packet in.

—An' flour, he said. —Yeh with me so far?

—Water an' flour, said Bimbo.

—Good man.

He picked up the whisk.

—This is the hard part, he said. —The hard work. I'm doin' it by hand, he explained, —cos that's the way we'll have to do in the van.

He attacked the mixture with the whisk, holding the bowl to him the way Veronica'd shown him.

—I'm tellin' yeh, he said. —It gets yeh sweatin'.

He stopped and looked.

—It's blendin' well there, d'yeh see? he said. —We need a bit more water though, to get rid o' the lumps.

Bimbo went to the sink and filled the milk bottle.

—Nearly there, said Jimmy Sr.

He poured in some more water, and prodded the lumps with the whisk and then his fingers.

—There's somethin' else supposed to go into it but I can't remember what it is.

He started whisking again.

—Doesn't matter though, he said. —This'll be grand.

He stopped and showed Bimbo the result.

479

—There, he said. —Batter. Not bad, wha'.

It looked right.

—Is tha' all there is to it? said Bimbo.

—That's it, said Jimmy Sr. —Except for the thing I'm after forgettin'. Let's see if it works now.

He'd already put an open can of pineapple rings on the table.

—Remind me to replace this one, will yeh, he said. —Veronica'll go spare if she goes to get it on Sunday and it's not there. ——Let's see now—

He took a ring out and let it down onto a sheet of kitchen roll.

—Yeh dry it first; that's important.

He dabbed the top of the ring with the edge of the roll.

—Tha' should do it.

He held up the ring and picked the bits of fluff off it.

—It's only the paper, he said. —Harmless.

—Yeah.

—Righ'; fingers crossed.

He lowered the pineapple ring into the batter, and let it sink in completely. He got a fork and searched for the ring, and found it.

—Our father who art in heaven —— Fuckin' brilliant! Look it; completely covered.

—That's great, said Bimbo.

—An' all yeh do then is drop it into the fryer. ——That's great now; the batter's just righ'. If it was too watery it wouldn't've stuck an' if it was too thick the hole in the ring would've disappeared. But that's just righ' now. Perfect.

* * *

—We'll cut them up into different sizes, said Jimmy Sr. — People prefer tha'.

That was what they were doing now, peeling the spuds and cutting them up and throwing them all into a big plastic bin full of water; out in the shed.

—When we've the money, said Jimmy Sr, —maybe we should get a chip machine like Maggie was talkin' abou' and just cut up a few o' the spuds by hand an' mix them in so people'll think they're all done tha' way.

—Yeah, said Bimbo.

Jimmy Sr looked into the bucket and gave it a kick to flatten out the chips.

—There's enough in there now, I'd say, he said.

—Good.

They took a handle each and carried the bin through the house out to the van. They'd a job getting it up the step, and in; the water made it very heavy and it was slopping over the sides. They were all set; tonight was the night. Everything in the van was gleaming; nearly everything. They'd had to buy some new equipment, some of the trays and the basket for the deep fat fryer. Bimbo bought it; Jimmy Sr hadn't a bean to his name. They put the bin under the sink. That was the best place for it, because it got in the way anywhere else and the sink was fuck all use to them.

—We should just pull it ou' altogether, said Jimmy Sr.

—Ah no, said Bimbo. —Not now annyway.

The thing got on Jimmy Sr's wick, a sink with no water; it was about as useful as an arse with no hole. He let it go though. They'd other things to do today.

—Will we put the rest of the stuff in? said Bimbo.

—We might as well, said Jimmy Sr.

They didn't want to leave anything in the van for too long. Some of the stuff from the freezers would go soft or even bad if they took it out too early. The timing was vital.

—The difference between a satisfied customer and a corpse, Jimmy Sr'd said.

They'd laughed, but it wasn't funny.

They got out, and stopped to look at the burger on the side of the van again. It was a huge big burger, a bunburger with BIMBO'S BURGERS above it and TODAY'S CHIPS TODAY under it.

The bottom bit was Maggie's idea.

—I still don't like tha' ketchup, said Jimmy Sr. —It's too like fuckin' blood. It'll put people off.

—Ah no, said Bimbo. —It's nice an' bright.

Maggie's brother's kid, Sandra, had done it; she went to some painting college or something.

—The bit o' meat stickin' ou' as well, said Jimmy Sr.

He pointed to it.

—It's like a fuckin' tongue hangin' ou'.

—Well, to be honest with yeh, Jimmy, said Bimbo. —I've never seen a tongue made o' mince.

—It's the same colour as—

—Look it, said Bimbo. —She put all those little black speckles on it to make it look like mince.

He went over and touched them, showing them to Jimmy Sr.

—They just make it look like it's gone off, said Jimmy Sr.

—It was your bloody idea in the first place, said Bimbo.

—D'yeh want to know why I don't like it? said Jimmy Sr. —An' annyway, I do like it. It's just the colours I don't like. D'yeh want to know why?

—Why then?

—Cos the young one tha' done it is a vegetarian, that's why.

He had him now. Sandra'd told him that, when he was talking to her while she was painting; a lovely-looking girl, she was, but a bit snotty; a good laugh though.

Bimbo looked lost.

—Sabotage, yeh dope, said Jimmy Sr.

——Wha'?

—Sabotage, said Jimmy Sr. —Animal rights.

—Wha' d'yeh mean?

—Is it not fuckin' obvious?

—Eh —— no.

—A vegetarian, righ', paints a picture of a burger an' wha' does she do? ——She paints it horrible colours to put people off buyin' anny.

—Sandra?

—They're all the same, said Jimmy Sr. —Fanatics, for fuck sake. Sure, they're puttin' bombs under people's cars over in England, just cos they experiment with animals.

—Hang on now, said Bimbo. —We're not experimentin' with animals.

—No, said Jimmy Sr. —But we're slappin' them up on the hot plate an' fryin' fuck ou' o' them. An' then gettin' people to eat them.

Bimbo gave this some thought. He looked at the burger.

——Ah, I don't think so, he said.

—Please yourself, said Jimmy Sr. —It's your fuckin' money. Come on or we'll be late.

They put the cartons of Twixes and Mars Bars in under the hot plate, and the cans of Coke and 7-Up. They put piles of spice-burgers on the shelf over the fryer. They had the flour and a line of milk bottles full of water for the batter, at the ready on the shelf beside the sink; they'd had to go scouting for real glass bottles. They'd a box for the money. Bimbo put the big red Kandee sauce bottle and the salt and vinegar on the counter. They had ten packs of Bundies. Maggie'd got them in Crazy Prices. Jimmy Sr opened a pack and took one out.

—These are the nicest part o' the burger, he said. —Aren't they?

—They're lovely alrigh', said Bimbo, and he took one as well. —We'd better not eat all of the supplies though.

—An army marches on its stomach, Jimmy Sr told him.

There was a ream of small bags on a piece of string, for the chips, and Jimmy Sr hung that on a hook beside the fryer, and put a pile of big brown bags on the counter. Bimbo folded up their aprons nice and squarely and put them on the counter beside the brown bags.

—It's not a fuckin' pinnie, Jimmy Sr'd said when Veronica caught him trying his one on up in the bedroom. —It's an apron, righ'.

Maggie'd got the aprons, World Cup ones. It was good thinking, and a lot better than those ones with recipes printed on them or something. These just had Italia 90 on them, and the cup.

—It's not a cup but, said Bimbo. —It's a statue. I never noticed that before.

483

—Look it, said Jimmy Sr. —Which sounds better; World Cup or World Statue?

—I get yeh, said Bimbo.

They kept the fish in the freezer till the last minute. If you didn't dip the cod in the batter when it was still like a piece of chipboard you ended up with a fuckin' awful mush that floated on the top of the cooking oil. They piled the rectangles of cod and black mullet onto the aluminium trays.

—Yeh'd nearly need gloves for this, said Jimmy Sr. —These things are fuckin' freezin'.

He walloped a piece of cod against the side of the freezer and examined it: there wasn't a mark on it.

—That's a good piece o' fish, tha', he said. —It won't let yeh down.

The trays were cold, but not that heavy. Still, they rushed through the house so they could put them down in the van and blow on their hands.

—Beep beep, said Bimbo, to get Maggie's mother out of his way as he barrelled through the kitchen, trying to carry his tray without having to use too firm a grip. He rested it against his chest and his shirt was getting wet.

Maggie followed them out.

—Good luck now, she said.

Jimmy Sr climbed up into the driver's seat. The van was hitched up to the back of Bimbo's jalopy with a bit of rope, in the driveway and halfway out onto the path. Bimbo had wrapped an old cardigan around his bumper, for a buffer. He'd wanted to use Wayne, with one foot on each bumper, but Maggie wouldn't let him. Bimbo got in and started the car. Maggie put her head down to him, he rolled down the window and she gave him a kiss.

—Jaysis, said Jimmy Sr, softly. —Come on, come on.

They were off.

Bimbo'd only gone a couple of feet and he had to stop cos there were two cars passing. The van rolled into the back of him, but only gently. Then they were out on the road, heading up to the Hikers. A couple of kids ran beside him, and one of them kicked the van. They disappeared; Jimmy Sr knew they were scutting on the back, the fuckers.

There was an awkward bit coming up, a bit of a dip just before they got onto the main road, Barrytown Road. If there was traffic coming Bimbo would have to stop for it and Jimmy Sr would go into him; it couldn't be helped. That was what happened, except it was worse. There was nothing coming so Bimbo kept going out across the main road turning to the right but this fuckin' eejit on a motor bike came out of nowhere from behind a parked van and Bimbo had to brake and Jimmy Sr couldn't brake, of course, so he went into Bimbo, and he heard stuff falling off the shelves behind him.

—Fuck it!

He listened.

Nothing else fell. Maybe it wouldn't be too bad.

Bimbo got going again and they made it to the Hikers without anything else happening. He started stopping about fifty yards before the Hikers, so that when he stopped he'd nearly stopped already anyway, going so slow that the van didn't bump into him at all this time.

Jimmy Sr listened to hear if there was anything rolling around inside in the back. He couldn't hear anything.

Bimbo got the bricks out from the back seat of the car and put them behind the wheels of the van. Jimmy Sr opened the door at the back.

—Ah, Christ.

Water fell onto his shoes, not much of it; most of it was at the back, on the floor, along with some of the spice-burgers and the fish. The bin hadn't turned over but there was an awful lot of water there, too much to call a puddle. The spice-burgers were the worst; the water had made them soggy and they were falling apart; they'd have to throw them out. The fish, though, weren't too bad.

They got the cartons up off the floor before the water could get at them. There was no other damage.

Still though, it was depressing.

Jimmy Sr leaned over and poked one of the fish with a finger. It was still good and hard.

——We need a mop, said Bimbo.

—We need a fuckin' engine, said Jimmy Sr. —Come on. We'll clean it up an' go in an' watch the match.

They cleaned up the mess, shoved all the bits of spice-burger and the water and the rest out onto the road with a bit of cardboard, and dried the floor with a tea-towel. Jimmy Sr gave the fish a good wash with some of the water from the milk bottles. He threw out the really dirty ones; where the dirt had got into the fish.

—There now, said Bimbo when they'd finished. —It wasn't as bad as it looked.

—Come on, said Jimmy Sr. —Or all the good places'll be taken.

* * *

——Sheedy gets it back —— and Sheedy shoots!

The place went fuckin' mad!

Ireland had got the equaliser. Jimmy Sr grabbed Bimbo and nearly broke him in half with the hug he gave him. Bertie was up on one of the tables thumping his chest. Even Paddy, the crankiest fucker ever invented, was jumping up and down and shaking his arse like a Brazilian. All sorts of glasses toppled off the tables but no one gave a fuck. Ireland had scored against England and there was nothing more important than that, not even your pint.

—Who scored it!? Who scored it?

—Don't know. It doesn't fuckin' matter!

They all settled down to see the action replay but they still couldn't make out who'd scored it, because they all went wild again when the ball hit the back of the net from one, two, three different angles, and looking at poor oul' Shilton trying to get at it, it was a fuckin' panic.

Word came through from the front.

—Sheedy.

—Sheedy got it.

486

—Kevin Sheedy.

—WHO PUT THE BALL IN THE ENGLISH NET —

SHEEDY—

SHEEDY—

God, it was great; fuckin' brilliant. And the rest of the match was agony. Every time an Irishman got the ball they all cheered and they groaned and laughed whenever one of the English got it; not that they got it that often; Ireland were all over them.

—Your man, Waddle's a righ' stick, isn't he?

—Ah, he's like a headless fuckin' chicken.

A throw-in for Ireland.

—MICK — MICK — MICK — MICK — MICK —

They all cheered when they saw Mick McCarthy coming up to take it. And there was Paddy Mick-Mick-Micking out of him and only an hour ago he'd been calling Mick McCarthy a fuckin' liability.

—OLÉ——OLÉ OLÉ OLÉ —

—OLÉ

—OLÉ —

There was ten minutes left.

—Ah Jaysis, me heart!

—No problem, compadre.

Jimmy Sr was about ten yards away from where he'd started when Sheedy'd scored. He didn't know how that had happened. He tried to get back to his pint.

—'Xcuse me. —— Sorry there; – thanks. —— 'Xcuse me. —— Get ou' o' me way, yeh fat cunt.

His pint was gone, on the floor, or maybe some bollix had robbed it. He looked over at the bar. He'd never get near it; it was jammered. Anyway, Leo the barman was ignoring all orders; he was looking at the big screen and praying; he was, praying.

—Look it, Jimmy Sr pointed him out to Bimbo.

He had his hands joined the way kids did, palm against palm, like on the cover of a prayer book, and his lips were moving. When everyone else cheered Leo just kept on praying.

—How much is there left?

—Five, I think.

—Fuck.

He looked around him. There were a lot of young ones in the pub. They hadn't been paying much attention to the match earlier but they were now. There was one of them, over near the bar; she was in a white T-shirt that you could see her bra through it and —

There was a big groan. Jimmy Sr got back to the match.

—What's happenin'?

—They have it.

Gascoigne got past two of the Irish lads and gave it to someone at the edge of the box and he fired – Jimmy Sr grabbed Bimbo's arm – but it went miles over the bar.

They cheered.

—Useless.

—How much left now?

—Two.

—Take your time, Packie!

—ONE PACKIE BONNER

THERE'S ONLY ONE PACKIE BONNER —

—Up them steps, Packie!

—Ah, he's a great fuckin' goalkeeper.

—ONE PACKIE BOHHHH-NER —

—He's very religious, yeh know. He always has rosary beads in his kit bag.

—He should strangle fuckin' Lineker with them, said Jimmy Sr, and he got a good laugh. —How much now, Bimbo?

Before Bimbo answered the Olivetti yoke came up on the screen and answered his question; they were into time added on.

They cheered.

—Come on, lads; go for another one!

—Ah, Morris; you're fuckin' useless.

—Fuck up, you. He's brilliant.

—ONE GISTY MORRIS

THERE'S ONLY ONE GISTY MORRIS —

—Blow the fuckin' whistle, yeh cunt yeh!

They laughed.

Jesus, the heat. You had to gasp to get a lungful; that and the excitement. He couldn't watch; it was killing him.

—OLÉ——OLÉ OLÉ OLÉ —

Jimmy Sr was looking over at the young one again when he got smothered by the lads. They went up – the ref had blown the whistle – and he stayed down. But he grabbed a hold of Bimbo and hung on. Everyone was jumping up and down, even Leo blessing himself. The tricolours were up in the air. He wished he had one. He'd get one for the rest of the matches.

Bertie was back up on the table doing his Norwegian commentator bit.

—Maggie Thatcher! – Winston Churchill! —

—WHO PUT THE BALL IN THE ENGLISH NET —

SHEEDY – SHEEDY —

—Queen Elizabeth! – Lawrence of Arabia! – Elton John! Yis can all go an' fuck yourselves!

They cheered.

Jimmy Sr was bursting; not for a piss, with love. He hugged Bimbo. He hugged Bertie. He hugged Paddy. He even hugged Larry O'Rourke. He loved everyone. There was Sharon. He got over to her and hugged her, and then all her friends.

—Isn't it brilliant, Daddy?

—Ah, it's fuckin' brilliant; brilliant.

—I love your aftershave, Mister Rabbitte.

—OLÉ——OLÉ OLÉ OLÉ —

—Jaysis, said Jimmy Sr when he got back to Bimbo. —An' we only fuckin' drew. Wha' would happen if we'd won?

Bimbo laughed.

Everyone in the place sang. Jimmy Sr hated the song but it didn't matter.

—GIVE IT A LASH JACK

GIVE IT A LASH JACK

NEVER NEVER NEVER SAY NO

IRELIN' – IRELIN' – REPUB–ILIC OF IRELIN'

—It's a great song, isn't it? said Bimbo.

—Ah, yeah, said Jimmy Sr.

It was that sort of day.

—We'd better get goin', I suppose, said Bimbo.

—Fair enough, said Jimmy Sr.

He was raring to go.

—Red alert, he shouted. —Red alert.

They came charging out of the pub, the two of them. Jimmy Sr let go of a roar.

—Yeow!!

His T-shirt was wringing. Fuck it though, he was floating.

Bimbo got the back door open and hopped in; really hopped now; it was fuckin' gas.

Jimmy Sr stopped.

—Listen, he said.

They could hear loads of cars honking. And there were people out on the streets, they could hear them as well.

He climbed into the van. Bimbo was fighting his apron.

It was getting dark. They had two big torch lights, the ones well-prepared drivers always had in case they had to change a tyre at night. Jimmy Sr turned them on.

—OLÉ——OLÉ OLÉ OLÉ. They're grand now, aren't they?

—Terrific, said Bimbo.

Bimbo had already rigged up the Kozengas canisters to the fryer and the hotplate. The canisters were outside, at the back beside the steps, cos there was no room for them inside. That made Jimmy Sr a bit nervous; he didn't like it. Kids were bound to start messing with them, disconnect them, or worse, start cutting the tubes and before you knew it Jimmy Sr, the van and half of Barrytown would be blown to shite. Still, there was no room for them in here. He had a quick look outside; there was no one at them.

—OLÉ——OLÉ OLÉ OLÉ —

Jimmy Sr got the box of matches and took one out. He didn't like this either. He stuck the match into the hollow tube of a biro. He got down on his hunkers in front of the hotplate.

490

He lit the match, turned on the gas, pressed in the knob and held the biro to the jet in under the hotplate. He heard the gas go whoosh and he got his hand to fuck out from under there. He'd never get used to doing that. The smell; fuck it, he'd singed his hair again.

—I fuckin' hate tha', he said.

He got the deep fat fryer going as well, but he didn't need the biro this time. He threw a slab of lard onto the hotplate and topped up the cooking oil in the fryer; everything under control.

—WE ARE GREEN — WE ARE WHI'E

WE ARE FUCKIN' DYNAMI'E

LA LA LA LA — LA LA LA — LA —May as well open the hatch, wha', he said.

—Righto, said Bimbo.

It was the moment they'd been waiting for but they pretended it wasn't. Bimbo was dipping the bits of fish into the deep fat for a few seconds to make the batter stay on them, a trick they'd picked up the last time they'd gone to a chipper; it made a lot of sense. You could pile them up and it didn't get messy and you could have the fish ready to fling back into the fryer whenever anyone ordered one. That was what Bimbo was doing when Jimmy Sr unfastened the hatch and pushed it back and got the steel poles in under it to hold it up and made sure that they were secure. Jimmy Sr concentrated on what he was doing. He didn't want to look too soon, to see how many were outside waiting.

There was no one.

They said nothing; they just kept doing their work. Jimmy Sr didn't have much to do. He spread the melted lard all over the hotplate. He was using one of the wallpaper scrapers they'd left over after cleaning the van. There was a hole in the corner of the plate where the fat dripped down through, onto the cans of drinks and the Mars Bars and Twixes.

—Oh shite, said Jimmy Sr when he saw what was happening.

He looked around for something, and took the cup off the

top of Bimbo's flask and put it under the hole, balanced on top of the cans. It worked. Jimmy Sr scraped some of the lard over to the hole and got down to check that it all dripped into the cup. It did. That was good.

He stood up; still no one outside. He couldn't hear honking horns any more. It was like a fuckin' ghost-town out there.

Still though, it was early days yet.

—Go easy on the fish there, Bimbo, he said. —We don't want to be stuck with a load of it at the end of the nigh'.

It was beginning to look like they'd be stuck with a lot more than just a couple of dozen cod. Still though —

—OLÉ——OLÉ OLÉ OLÉ —

Getting the fish to stay inside the batter was easier said than done. Bimbo'd just scooped out a smashing piece of batter, lovely and crispy; but it was empty. He was rooting around in the oil for the fish.

A couple of people, kids mostly, walked by and gawked in, and kept walking, the fuckin' eejits.

Jimmy Sr checked the fryer. It was ready and waiting. The chips were in the basket. He picked it up and shook it; just right. He got a burger and threw it on the hotplate, just to be doing something. The noise it made at the beginning was a bit like something screaming. He pressed it down hard with the fish slice, and it screamed again; it wasn't a scream really, more a watery crackle.

He turned to keep an eye on the hatch and caught Bimbo helping himself to a Mars Bar.

—Jesus Christ, Bimbo; could yeh not wait till we've sold somethin'!

The head on Bimbo, snared rapid.

—I was a bit hungry —

—Haven't yeh half Ireland's fuckin' fish quota over there with yeh?

He was joking but suddenly he was annoyed.

—I didn't want to touch them, said Bimbo. —In case —

—No one else fuckin' wants them, said Jimmy Sr.

He was thinking of something good, something nice to say

when – Jaysis! – there was a young fella at the hatch. He could
see the top of his head.

He jumped over to him.

—Yes, son?

—A choc-ice, said the young fella.

Sharon climbed into the van in time to hear her da.

—Wha'? —— Fuck off ou' o' tha' or I'll —

Sharon started laughing.

—Do yeh not sell choc-ices? said the young fella.

Bimbo looked out at him. The poor little lad was only about
ten.

Jimmy Sr leaned out and pointed.

—What's tha'? he asked the young fella.

He was pointing at the sign.

—A big burger, said the young fella.

—That's righ', said Jimmy Sr. —Wha' does it tell yeh?

—Bimbo's Burgers, the young fella read. —Today's chips
today.

—That's righ', said Jimmy Sr. —It doesn't say annythin'
abou' choc-ices, does it?

—No.

—No, it doesn't, sure it doesn't. So, fuck off.

Jimmy Sr went back to his burger. It was stuck to the
hotplate.

—Shite on it!

Bimbo took over at the hatch.

—We've no fridge, he explained to the little young fella.

—Yeh can get choc-ices an' stuff in other chippers, Mister,
the young fella told him.

—Yeah, said Bimbo; he was whispering —but we've no
fridge, yeh see. We've no electricity.

He looked around at Jimmy Sr. He was trying to get some
lard in under the burger so it would slide off the plate.

—Here, he said to the young fella.

He handed him down the rest of his Mars Bar, then shooed
him off.

—Thanks very much, Mister.

493

—Shhhh!

Jimmy Sr's neck was going to snap; that was how it felt. There were still little bits of the burger soldered to the hot-plate; the scraper kept sliding over them, the useless fuckin' thing! He'd get them off if it fuckin' killed him!

—Yeaahh!

Sharon and Bimbo kept well away from him. That wasn't easy in a space as big as two wardrobes. You couldn't go anywhere without someone getting out of your way first. Bimbo handed two milk bottles over Jimmy Sr's head to Sharon.

—We need more water, love, he told her.

Sharon was lost.

—Pop over the road an' she'll fill them for yeh, Bimbo told her. —Rita Fleming; Missis Fleming. D'yeh know which house she's in?

——Yeah.

She didn't do anything yet though. She thought she'd been told to go over to the Flemings with two milk bottles and ask Missis Fleming to fill them for her, but she wasn't sure.

—I asked her earlier, said Bimbo. —There's no problem. So long as it's not too late.

—Can I not just run home —

—Do wha' you're told, said Jimmy Sr.

—Who rattled your cage? said Sharon.

—Customers! said Bimbo. —Quick, love; off yeh go.

He said it just when Jimmy Sr got the last lump of burger off the hotplate; his timing couldn't have been better.

—Great stuff, said Jimmy Sr.

Sharon looked out the back door, and there was a gang of women coming towards the van, getting their money out of their handbags.

—There's loads of them, she said, and she ran across the road to Flemings.

Jimmy Sr got the basket of chips – he'd been waiting all night to do this – and dropped it into the oil, and nearly fuckin' blinded himself.

494

—Ahhh!!! —— Jaysis!! —— Me fuckin' ——

He thought he was blinded. Little spits of fat stung all his face; he kept his eyes clamped shut.

—Are yeh alrigh'?

Bimbo didn't sound all that worried.

—Me eyes, said Jimmy Sr.

—Oh, that's shockin', said Bimbo. —Here, he said. —Wash them.

He handed Jimmy Sr one of the milk bottles.

—Jesus, said Jimmy Sr.

He poured a small amount of the water into his palm and gave his face a wipe. That was better. The stinging was gone. It was no joke though; he'd have to be careful. He didn't want to end up like the Phantom of the fuckin' Opera.

He was ready. He lifted the basket and shook it, and carefully dropped it back in; he wasn't sure why but he'd seen it being done all his life; to check if the chips were done, he supposed.

—Nearly ready over here, he told Bimbo. —Action stations, wha'.

Sharon was back with the milk bottles, full.

—Good girl, said Jimmy Sr. —Yeh missed me accident.

—They're takin' their time, said Sharon.

She was talking about the women outside, who were still approaching the van very slowly.

—Oul' ones are always like tha', said Jimmy Sr. —Yeh'd swear it was fur coats they were buyin'.

—What'll I do now? Sharon asked.

—Help Bimbo with the orders, said Jimmy Sr. —I'd say. We'll have to play it by ear.

She nearly pushed him up onto the hotplate getting her apron on, but he said nothing.

—How're yis all? Bimbo said out the hatch, and Jimmy Sr went over to have a look at the oul' ones himself.

There was a big crowd of them alright, a good few quid's worth, if they ever made their fuckin' minds up. He could tell; they were coming home from bingo. They were real diehards.

495

Imagine: going to bingo on the night Ireland were playing their first ever World Cup match, and against England as well.

—Wha' are yis havin', girls? said Jimmy Sr.

No joy; they were still making their minds up. Jimmy Sr got back to his post. The chips were done. He gave the basket a good fuckin' shake, and another one for good measure, and emptied the chips into the tray. He'd another basket ready with more chips and he lowered that into the fryer, but he stood well back this time. The going was getting very hot though.

The women were up at the counter now.

—A fresh cod, Sharon called back to him.

—Yahoo! said Jimmy Sr, and he slipped the cod into the fryer. Jesus, the noise; like having your ear up to a jet engine.

—Another one.

—A smoked, said Bimbo.

They were in business now alright.

Another five cods, three smoked ones, a spice-burger and an ordinary burger; now they were working.

—Chips just, said Sharon.

—Comin' up.

He got the scoop in under the chips and got a grand big load into the bag, filled it right up. Good, big chips they were, and a lovely colour, most of them; one or two of them were a bit white and shiny looking.

—There yeh go.

He held them out for Sharon, and she dropped them.

——Not to worry, he said.

He filled another bag.

Bimbo was still taking orders.

—Three spice-burgers, two smoked cod —

Jimmy Sr sang.

—AN' A PAR-TRIDGE IN A PEAR TREE.

The fryer was getting very full now. Some of the yokes at the top were hardly in the cooking oil at all. He skidded on the chips Sharon had dropped and nearly went on his arse. He kicked them out the back door but some of them were stuck to the floor. The fuckin' heat, the sweat was running off him. There was too much for one man here.

—Gis a hand here, Sharon.

Sharon left Bimbo at the counter.

—Righ', Bimbo, shout ou' those orders again till we get them sorted ou'.

He heard Bimbo.

—Wha' was it you ordered, love?

—I told yeh, said some oul' wagon. ——A cod an' a small chips.

—Got yeh, Jimmy Sr called back. —Hope she fuckin' chokes on them, he said to Sharon.

Sharon was managing the chips and Jimmy was taking the other stuff out of the fryer. He had one of those tongs yokes but you had to be careful with it cos if you held the fish too tight it fell apart on you and if you didn't it dived back into the fryer and you had to jump back quick or suffer the fuckin' consequences. But he thought he had the knack of it. He dropped the cod into a small greaseproof bag and Sharon took it and put it into the big brown bag, along with the chips. They worked well together, Sharon and Jimmy Sr. They didn't bump into each other. It was like they were two parts of the same machine.

The only problem now was Bimbo. He was good with the oul' ones and he handled the salt and vinegar like a professional, but he couldn't count for fuck.

—A cod an' a small —— . Eh, —— that's, eh —

—One sixty-five, Sharon called back to him.

—Good girl, said Jimmy Sr.

They were nearly through with the oul' ones; there were no more orders coming in. It was coming up to closing time though and then there'd be murder, with a bit of luck.

—One eighty, Sharon called.

She was sharp, that girl. She didn't even have to think first.

He couldn't make up his mind if the last spice-burger was done yet. He blew on it and poked it with a finger; it left a mark.

—Grand.

He dropped it into its bag and gave it to Sharon.

—I'll give poor Bimbo a hand, he said.

Most of the women were still out there but away from the counter, up against the carpark wall eating their stuff. There were only a few left at the counter.

—Wha' was yours? he asked one of them.

—A chips an' a spicey burger.

She was tiny. He nearly had to climb out over the counter to see her.

—Large or small? said Jimmy Sr.

—Large, she said.

—An' why not, said Jimmy Sr.

This was good crack. Sharon handed him the bag.

—The works?

—Oh yes.

He did the salt first, shook the bag to make sure it went well in. He looked at the women. They were real bingo heads alright; all the same, like a gang of twenty sisters.

—That's enough, said the little woman.

He showed her the vinegar bottle.

—Say when, he said.

She had a nice enough face, he could see now.

—There y'are now, he said, and he held the bag for her to collect.

—Thanks v' much. How much is tha'?

—Eh —

—One twenty-five, said Sharon.

—One twenty-five, said Jimmy Sr.

He waited while she put tenpences and twentypences up on the counter.

—Sorry —

—No no, said Jimmy Sr. —Take your time.

—I want to get rid of my change.

—Well, yeh came to the righ' place, love.

There was a nice breeze coming in. Jimmy Sr held his arms out a bit, but nothing too obvious.

Bimbo was nearly having a row with the last of the women.

—D'you take butter vouchers? she asked him.

—No, he said. —God, no.

—They take them in the newsagents, she told him.

You couldn't help feeling sorry for her. She'd probably held back till the end so the other women wouldn't hear her. Still though, they weren't running a charity.

—Only money, Bimbo told her.

—Or American Express, said Jimmy Sr, and he gave Bimbo a nudge. —We'll give yeh a shout when we start sellin' butter, he told the woman, for a joke. She didn't laugh though, and he felt like a prick. His face was hot and getting hotter. Still, if she could afford to go to bingo then she could afford to pay for her supper.

That was it. They'd all been served, and they were all stuffing their faces, beginning to move away. Jimmy Sr, Bimbo and Sharon watched them.

—Tha' was grand, said Bimbo. —Wasn't it?

—Money for jam, said Jimmy Sr.

They looked around. The place was in bits already.

—I'll do more batter, said Bimbo.

—Good man, said Jimmy Sr. —But make it a bit stronger, will yeh. It keeps comin' off the fish.

Sharon got down and started wiping the mushed-up chips off the floor. One of the bingo women came back.

—Yes, Missis? said Jimmy Sr.

—D'yeh sell sweets? she asked him.

She was one of those culchie-looking women, roundy and red.

—Mars or Twix just, Jimmy Sr told her.

—A Twix.

—Comin' up, said Jimmy Sr.

He got the Twix out from under the hotplate and wiped the grease off it with his apron.

—There y'are, he said. —Best before April '92. You've loads o' time, wha'.

She laughed, and then Jimmy Sr saw it.

—Oh good shite.

It was a stampede, that was what it was, coming out of the Hikers.

—Yeh'd better be quick with tha' batter, he said to Bimbo.

—Why's tha'? said Bimbo, and he looked out.

—Oh, mother o' God.

Sharon looked.

—Jesus, she said. —I'm scarleh.

Jimmy Sr gave the woman her threepence change.

—Yeh'd want to get out o' the way there, he told her.
—You'll be fuckin' trampled on.

The woman did a legger.

There was an almighty crowd coming out, pouring out of the place, still going Olé olé olé olé. It was mostly the younger ones. There was suddenly a couple of hundred people in the carpark, and then one of them saw the van.

—Yeow!!

They stopped Oléing and looked at the van.

—Charge!

—Oh my fuck —, said Jimmy Sr. —Red alert; red alert.

It was like Pearl fuckin' Harbor. Jimmy Sr had half said — Form a queue there, when they hit the van.

—Oh, mother o' shite!

It hopped; they lifted it up off the road. One of the bars holding up the hatch skipped and Jimmy Sr just caught it before it fell and skulled someone outside.

—A cod an' a large!

—Curry chips, Mister.

—Howyeh, Sharon!

—OLÉ——OLÉ OLÉ OLÉ

—I was first!

—Are yis Irish or Italians or wha'?

—Yeow, Sharon!

—Sharon; here! We're first, righ'.

—Give us a C!!

Bimbo was covered in batter. Sharon was trying to get the spilt fat off her shoes.

—Give us a H!!

It was madness out there; pande-fuckin'-monium.

—Give us an I!!

There was a young one being crushed against the van. Her neck was digging into the counter.

Bimbo joined Jimmy Sr at the hatch.

—Back now! he roared. —Push back there! There's people bein' crushed up here!

—Fuck them!

Jimmy Sr pointed at the young fella who'd said that.

—You're barred!

They cheered, but they quietened after that.

—Give us a P!

The young one was rubbing her neck but she was alright. Jimmy Sr served her first.

—Wha' d'yeh want?

—Give us an S!

Jimmy Sr looked out over the crowd.

—Will somebody shut tha' fuckin' eejit up! he roared.

—Yeow!!

They cheered and clapped, and Jimmy Sr started to enjoy himself. He lifted his arms and acknowledged the applause — Thank you, thank you – and then got back to business.

—Wha' was tha'? he asked the young one.

—Curry chips, she said, raising her eyes to heaven.

—No curry chips, Jimmy Sr told her.

—Why not?

—Cos we're not fuckin' Chinese, said Jimmy Sr. —This is an Irish Chipper.

—That's stupih, said the young one.

—Next!

—Hang on, hang on! A large single an' – an' –

—Hurry —

—A spice-burger.

—A large an' a spice, Sharon, please!! Jimmy Sr roared over his shoulder. —Next. —You with the haircut there; wha' d'yeh want?

—World peace.

—You're barred. Next!

Sharon had a complaint.

—I can't do it all on me fuckin' own!

—Hold the fort there, Bimbo, said Jimmy Sr, and he went back to give Sharon a hand.

It was like that for over an hour after that. They got into a flow; Bimbo would shout back the order and Jimmy Sr and Sharon would pack it, and Bimbo would repeat the order out loud and Sharon would tell him how much it cost, and that way they started flying. The heat though; they were sorry now they'd got Victor, Bimbo's brother, to block up the window. They had to go the door now and again, Jimmy Sr and Sharon – Bimbo was alright; he had the hatch – and get some proper air. That was how Jimmy Sr caught a kid trying to disconnect the gas. Such a kick he sent at him, he was blessed that it had missed because he'd have killed the poor little fucker.

When the going got rough up at the hatch one of them would go up and help Bimbo, and when it got rough back at HQ one of them would come back from the hatch: they took turns. The only thing was the heat: Jimmy Sr's throat was dry and he didn't have time for a can of 7-Up. Anyway, there wasn't enough room to drink it comfortably; he'd have got an elbow in the neck. Jimmy Sr took off his apron, then his T-shirt, and put the apron back on.

—You should do this, Sharon, look.

—Ha ha.

He checked to make sure that his knickers were well into his trousers and then he was back to work, throwing the burgers onto the hotplate like there was no tomorrow. It didn't work though, taking the T-shirt off, not really; it just gave the flying fat more places to hit.

They'd serve two people and get them out of the way and three more would come out of the pub. It was a killer. Still though, this was what they'd wanted. There was money being made.

—Here! a young fella outside shouted. —These chips are raw!

—Yeh never said yeh wanted them cooked! said Jimmy Sr, and he dashed back to turn the burgers.

He was enjoying himself; the three of them were.

The older lads came out later, Bertie and Paddy and them, and it was more relaxed, a good laugh. It was nearly one o'clock. Jimmy Sr had lost weight, he could tell. He put his hand down the back of his trousers and there was much more room than usual, even with no shirt or vest in there. It was like working in a sauna. He liked the idea of losing a few pounds. He'd say nothing yet to Veronica about it, not for a few days. He'd do a twirl in front of her and see if she noticed.

The place was a mess, and getting dangerous. Sharon had fallen and Bimbo had scorched two of his fingers. It served him right for trying to pick up the burger with his hand cos Jimmy Sr was using the fish slice.

—Night nigh', compadres.

—Good luck, Bertie.

There was no one left. Jimmy Sr closed the hatch. He could see another gang coming up the road and he didn't want to have to start all over again. Anyway, they'd hardly anything left. There were a few chips in the bottom of the bin but they were a bit brown looking. Most of the water was on the floor. It could stay there. They were too shagged to do any cleaning. They made room for themselves on the ledges and shelves and sat up or leaned against them.

—Fuck me, said Jimmy Sr.

—Look at me shoes, said Sharon.

—Buy a new pair.

—Wha' with?

—This, said Bimbo.

He held up a handful of notes, then put them back in the box. He showed them the rest of the cash in the box. He had to squash it down to keep it from falling out; not just green notes either, brown ones as well, and even a couple of blueys.

—Fair enough, wha'.

Someone hit the hatch a wallop.

They ignored it, and stayed quiet.

It felt good, being finished, knackered. They were too tired to grin. Jimmy Sr's ears were buzzing with the tiredness. He got a can from under the hotplate and it slipped out of his hands because of the grease; the flask cup had flowed over.

—Ah Jaysis —

He held the can with his apron, opened it and took a slug: it was horrible and warm.

—Ah —— shi'e —

Bimbo got a can and held it up to make a toast.

—Today's chips today, he said.

Jimmy Sr nudged a chip on the floor with his shoe.

—Absolutely, he said.

It had been some day.

At the end of the week – next Friday – he was going to put money on the table in front of Veronica, and say nothing.

They went home.

* * *

—Look it.

Sharon showed Jimmy Sr, Veronica and Darren the spots on her left cheek all the way up to her eye, clusters of them in little patches. She'd just found them, up in the bathroom. Her left side was much redder than the right, horrible and raw looking; she couldn't understand it. She wanted to cry; she could feel them getting itchy.

—My God, said Veronica, and went to get a closer look.

Darren was a bit embarrassed.

Jimmy Sr leaned out from his chair to see.

—Gis a look, he said.

—It's some sort of a rash, said Veronica, —or – I don't know.

—That's gas, said Jimmy Sr. —I've them as well; look.

He showed them the right side of his face.

—I shaved over them, he said. —But yeh should be able to still see them.

He rubbed his cheek.

—They're still there alrigh'.

Veronica was confused but Sharon was beginning to understand.

—D'yeh know wha' it is? said Jimmy Sr. —It's the hotplate; the fat splashin' up from the hot plate.

He mimed turning a burger.

—I was on the righ' an' you were on the left, he told Sharon.

He grinned.

—Poor Bimbo must be in tatters, he said. —Cos he was in the middle.

Darren laughed.

* * *

By the time Ireland played Egypt, the Sunday after, they'd added sausages to the menu and Jimmy Sr was putting less lard on the hotplate.

Business was hopping.

On Friday they pitched their tent outside the Hikers earlier, at five o'clock, and stuck up posters – Jessica's work – all over the van: £1 Specials—Chips + Anything—5 to 7.30pm. It worked; the Pound Specials went down a bomb. Women coming out of Crazy Prices with the night's dinner read the posters and stopped and said to themselves Fuck the dinner; you could see it in their faces. They either bought the chips and anything immediately or went home and sent one of the kids out to get them.

It was Maggie's idea.

—Twelve Poun' Specials, Mister, said one little young one, and that was the record.

By seven, when they were having a rest, Jimmy Sr and Bimbo were talking seriously about getting an engine; then there'd be no stopping them. They'd have to get some sort of a flue put in as well. Even with the hatch and the door open, the fumes were gathering up in the back of the van. You noticed it when you went down there to get more chips from the bin; you came back crying. And the smell off your clothes; no amount of washing could get rid of it.

—It's an occupational hazard, Jimmy Sr told Veronica.

Spots, singed hair and smelly threads; Veronica said that he looked like something out of Holocaust.

—Ha fuckin' ha, said Jimmy Sr.

* * *

—A large an' a dunphy.

—Wha'? said Jimmy Sr.

He looked down at the customer, a young fella about young Jimmy's age, with his pals.

—Large an' a dunphy, he said again.

He was grinning.

—What's a dunphy? Jimmy Sr wanted to know.

—A sausage, said the young fella.

—Sausage, large, Jimmy Sr called over his shoulder to Bimbo.

He looked back at the young fella.

—Are yeh goin' to explain this to me? he asked.

—Sausages look like pricks, righ'?

—Okay; fair enough.

—An' Eamon Dunphy's a prick as well, said the young fella.

By Thursday of the second week, the night of the Holland game, the word Sausage had disappeared out of Barrytown. People were asking for a dunphy an' chips, please, or an eamon, a spice burger an' a small single. Some of them didn't even bother eating them; they just bought them for a laugh. Young fellas stood in front of the big screen in the Hikers and waved Jimmy and Bimbo's sausages in batter instead of big inflated bananas.

* * *

—This is where the real World Cup starts, said Paddy, when they'd settled down again after the final whistle.

—He's righ', said Jimmy Sr. —For once.

Ireland were through to the knock-out stages.

Jimmy Sr took another deep breath.

—Fuckin' great, isn't it?

They all agreed.

—After all these years, wha', he said.

—COME ON WITHOU'

COME ON WITHIN

YOU'VE NOT SEEN NOTHIN' LIKE THE MIGHTY QUINN —

Bertie summed up the campaign so far.

—We beat England one-all, we lost to Egypt nil-all, an' we drew with the Dutch. That's not bad, is it?

—OOH AH —

PAUL MCGRATH —

SAY OOH AH PAUL MCGRATH —

Jimmy Sr stood up.

—Yeh righ', Bimbo?

The van was outside waiting for them.

It was hard leaving the pub after all that, the match and the excitement: but they did, Bimbo and Jimmy Sr. You had to admire them for it, Jimmy Sr thought anyway.

* * *

The day after the Holland game Maggie brought home T-shirts she'd got made for them in town. They had Niall Quinn's head on the front with His Mammy Fed Him On Bimbo's Burgers under it. They were smashing but after two washes Niall Quinn's head had disappeared and the T-shirts didn't make sense any more.

* * *

It was great having the few bob in the pocket again. They didn't just count the night's takings and divide it in two. They were more organised than that; it was a business. There was stock to be bought, the engine to save for. Maggie kept the books. They paid themselves a wage and if business was really good they got a bonus as well, an incentive, the same way footballers got paid extra if they won. Jimmy Sr took home a hundred and sixty quid the first week. He had his dole as well. He bought himself a new shirt – Veronica'd been giving him grief about the smell off his clothes – a nice one with grey stripes running down it. He'd read in one of Sharon's magazines that stripes like that made you look thinner but that wasn't why he bought it; he just liked it. He handed most of the money over to Veronica.

—You're not to waste it all on food now, d'yeh hear, he said. —You're to buy somethin' for yourself.

—Yes, master, said Veronica.

* * *

The country had gone soccer mad. Oul' ones were explaining offside to each other; the young one at the check-out in the cash-and-carry told Jimmy Sr that Romania hadn't a hope cos Lacatus was suspended because he was on two yellow cards. It was great. There were flags hanging out of nearly every window in Barrytown. It was great for business as well. There were no proper dinners being made at all. Half the mammies in Barrytown were watching the afternoon matches, and after the extra-time and the penalty shoot-outs there was no time left to make the dinner before the next match. The whole place was living on chips.

—Fuck me, said Jimmy Sr. —If Kelly an' Roche do well in the Tour de France we'll be able to retire by the end o' July.

He'd brought home two hundred and forty quid the second week.

They were going to get a video.

—Back to normal then, said Jimmy Sr. —Wha'.

—Yep, said Veronica.

She was going to say something else, something nice, but Germany got a penalty against Czechoslovakia and she wanted to see Lothar Matthaeus taking it; he was her favourite, him and Berti, the Italian. Jimmy Sr liked Schillaci; he reminded him of Leslie, the same eyes.

* * *

508

—Ah, good Jesus, said Jimmy Sr.

He got up off the floor. His trousers were wringing, his back was killing him. He'd been going at the floor with sudsy water and a nailbrush for the last half hour and the floor still looked the wrong colour.

—We're fightin' a losin' battle here, I think, he said to Bimbo.

Bimbo was attacking the gobs of grease on the wall around the hotplate and the fryer. He was making progress but it was like the grease spots were riding each other and breeding, they were all over the wall. Bimbo took a breather. The thing about it was, even if you cleaned all day – and that was what they did for the first week or so – it would be back to dirty normal by the end of the night.

—Look it, said Jimmy Sr. —Tha' grease there —

He pointed at the grease above the fryer.

—It's fresh cos it only got there last nigh', cos it was clean there when we started last nigh'. D'yeh follow?

—Yeah, said Bimbo.

—So, said Jimmy Sr. —It's doin' no harm. It's fresh. It's grand for another couple o' days. Then it'll be gettin' bad an' we'd want to get rid of it cos it'd be a health hazard then, but it's fuckin' harmless now.

Bimbo didn't disagree with him.

—All we have to worry abou' every day before we start is the floor, said Jimmy Sr. —Cos we'll go slidin' an' split ourselves if it's not clean, but that's all.

Bimbo just wanted to check on one thing first. He opened the hatch and then got out of the van and went round to the hatch and looked in, to see if he could see the dirt from out there. He couldn't.

—Okay, he said. —I'm with yeh.

* * *

Bimbo couldn't watch, but Jimmy Sr could, no problem; he loved it. Nil-all after extra time, a penalty shoot-out.

—Pennos, said Paddy when they saw the ref blowing the final whistle.

—Fuckin' hell.

—Packie'll save at least one, wait'll yeh see.

—He let in nine against Aberdeen a couple o' weeks ago, remember.

—This is different.

—How is it?

—Fuck off.

It got very quiet. Jimmy Sr's heart was hopping, but he never took his eyes off the screen, except when the young one behind him screamed. She did it after the Romanians got the first penalty. Women had been screaming all through the match but this one stood out because when the ball just got past Packie's fingers there were a couple of hundred groans and only the one scream.

Bertie turned round to the young one.

—Are yeh like tha' in the scratcher? he said.

The whole pub erupted, just when Kevin Sheedy was placing the ball on the spot, like he'd scored it already. There was no way he'd miss it after that.

He buried it.

—YEOWWW!!

—One-all, one-all; fuckin' hell.

Houghton, Townsend, Tony Cascarino.

Four-all.

—Someone's after faintin' over there.

—Fuck'm.

They watched Packie setting himself up in his goal for the fifth time.

—Go on, Packie!

—ONE PACKIE BONNER —

—Shut up; wait.

—He has rosary beads in his bag, yeh know, said some wanker.

—They'll be round his fuckin' neck if he misses this one, said Jimmy Sr.

No one laughed. No one did anything.

Packie dived to the left; he dived and he saved the fuckin'
thing.

The screen disappeared as the whole pub jumped. All Jimmy
Sr could see was backs and flags and dunphies. He looked for
Bimbo, and got his arms around him. They watched the penno
again in slow motion. The best part was the way Packie got
up and jumped in the air. He seemed to stay in mid-air for
ages. They cheered all over again.

—Shhh! Shhh!

—Shhh!

—Shhh!

Someone had to take the last penalty for Ireland.

—Who's tha'?

—O'Leary.

—O'Leary?

Jimmy Sr hadn't even known that O'Leary was playing. He
must have come on when Jimmy Sr was in the jacks.

—He'll be grand, said someone. —He takes all of Arsenal's
pennos.

—He does in his hole, said an Arsenal supporter. —He
never took a penno in his life.

—He'll crack, said Paddy. —Wait'll yeh see.

Jimmy Sr nearly couldn't watch, but he stuck it.

—YEH —

David O'Leary put it away like he was playing with his kids
at the beach.

—YESSS!

Jimmy Sr looked carefully to make sure that he'd seen it
right. The net was shaking, and O'Leary was covered in
Irishmen. He wanted to see it again though. Maybe they were
all beating the shite out of O'Leary for missing. No, though;
he'd scored. Ireland were through to the quarter-finals and
Jimmy Sr started crying.

He wasn't the only one. Bertie was as well. They hugged.
Bertie was putting on a few pounds. Jimmy Sr felt even better.

—What a team, wha'. What a fuckin' —

He couldn't finish; a sob had caught up on him.

—Si, said Bertie.

They showed the penno again, in slow motion.

—To the righ'; perfect.

—Excellent conversion, said some gobshite.

Where was Bimbo?

There he was, bawling his eyes out. A big stupid lovely grin had split his face in half.

—OLÉ——OLÉ OLÉ OLÉ —

OLÉ——

OLÉ —

Jimmy Sr took a run and a jump at Bimbo and Bimbo caught him.

—ONE DAVE O'LEARY —

—OLÉ——OLÉ OLÉ OLÉ

—THERE'S ONLY ONE DAVE O'LEARY —

They stood there arm in arm and watched O'Leary's penalty again, and again.

—I'll tell yeh one thing, said Larry O'Rourke. —David O'Leary came of age today.

Jimmy Sr loved everyone but that was the stupidest fuckin' thing he'd ever heard in his life.

—He's thirty fuckin' two! he said. —Came of age, me bollix.

—ONE DAVE O'LEEEEARY —

He hugged Bimbo again, and Bertie and Paddy, and he went over and hugged Sharon. She was crying as well and they both laughed. He hugged some of her friends. They all had their green gear on, ribbons and the works. He wanted to hug Sharon's best friend, Jackie, but he couldn't catch her. She was charging around the place, yelling Olé Olé Olé Olé, not singing any more because her throat was gone.

There was Mickah Wallace, Jimmy Jr's pal, standing by himself with his tricolour over his head, like an Irish Blessed Virgin. He let Jimmy Sr hug him.

—I've waited twenty years for this, Mister Rabbitte, he told Jimmy Sr.

He was crying as well.

—Twenty fuckin' years.

He gulped back some snot.

—The first record I ever got was Back Home, the English World Cup record, he said. —In 1970. D'yeh remember it?

—I do, yeah.

—I was only five. I didn't buy it, mind, said Mickah. —I robbed it. —— Tweh-twenty fuckin' years.

Jimmy Sr knew he was being told something important but he wasn't sure what.

—D'yeh still have it?

—Wha'?

—Back Home.

—Not at all, said Mickah. —Jaysis. I sold it. I made a young fella buy it off o' me.

Jimmy Jr rescued Jimmy Sr.

—Da.

—Jimmy!

—I didn't see yeh.

Jimmy Jr was in his Celtic away jersey, with a big spill down the front. He nodded at the jacks door.

—It's fuckin' mad in there.

They stood there.

—CEAUSESCU WAS A WANKER

CEAUSESCU WAS A WANKER

LA LA LA LA

LA LA LA — LA

—Fuckin' deadly, isn't it?

—Brilliant. —— Brilliant.

They started laughing, and grabbed each other and hugged till their arms hurt. They wiped their eyes and laughed and hugged again.

—I love yeh, son, said Jimmy Sr when they were letting go.

He could say it and no one could hear him, except young Jimmy, because of the singing and roaring and breaking glasses.

—I think you're fuckin' great, said Jimmy Sr.

—Ah fuck off, will yeh, said Jimmy Jr. —Packie saved the fuckin' penalty, not me.

But he liked what he'd heard, Jimmy Sr could tell that. He gave Jimmy Sr a dig in the stomach.

—You're not a bad oul' cunt yourself, he said.

Larry O'Rourke had got up onto a table.

—WHEN BOYHOOD'S FIRE WAS IH–IN MY BLOOD —

I DREAMT OF ANCIE–HENT FREEMEN —

—Ah, somebody shoot tha' fucker!

Jimmy Sr nodded at Mickah. Jimmy Jr looked at him.

—He'll be alrigh' in a bit, he said. —It's a big moment for him, yeh know.

Bimbo tapped Jimmy Sr's shoulder.

—We'd better go, he said.

It was a pity.

—Okay, said Jimmy Sr. —Duty calls, he said to Jimmy Jr.

—How's business?

—Brilliant. Fuckin' great.

—That's great.

—Yeah; great, it is. McDonalds me arse. Seeyeh.——Good luck, Mickah.

But Mickah didn't answer. He stood to attention, the only man with plenty of room in the pub.

—Seeyeh.

—Good luck.

—A NAAY–SHUN ONCE AGAIN —

A NAAAY–SHUN ONCE AGAIN —

Bimbo gave Jimmy Sr a piggy-back to the van. There were kids and mothers out on the streets, waving their flags and throwing their teddy bears up in the air. A car went by with three young lads up on the bonnet. They could hear car horns from miles away.

It was the best day of Jimmy Sr's life. The people he served that night got far more chips than they were entitled to. And they still made a small fortune, sold everything. They hadn't even a Mars Bar left to sell. They closed up at ten, lovely and early, and had a few quiet pints; the singing had stopped. And then he went home and Veronica was in the kitchen and she did a fry for him, and he cried again when he was telling her about the pub and the match and meeting Jimmy Jr. And she called him an eejit. It was the best day of his life.

*   *   *

And then they got beaten by the Italians and that was the end of that.

*   *   *

They got in. Bimbo put in the key.

The van had a new engine.

—Here we go.

It went first time.

—Yeow!

They went to Howth.

—Maybe we should get music for it, said Jimmy Sr when they were going through Sutton. They'd stalled at the lights, but they were grand now, picking up a head of steam.

—Like a Mister Whippy van.

—Would tha' not confuse people?

—How d'yeh mean?

—Well, said Bimbo. —They might run out of their houses lookin' for ice-creams an' all we'll be able to give them is chips.

Jimmy Sr thought about this.

—Is there no chip music? he said. —Mind that oul' bitch there. She's goin' to open the door there, look it.

—What d'yeh mean? said Bimbo.

He stopped Jimmy Sr from getting to the horn.

—Yeh should've just taken the door off its fuckin' hinges an' kept goin', said Jimmy Sr.

—The music, said Bimbo.

—Yeah, said Jimmy Sr. —The Teddy Bears' Picnic is the ice-cream song, righ'. Is there no chipper song?

—No, said Bimbo. —I —— No, I don't think ——

515

—Your man, look it; don't let him get past yeh! —— Ah Jaysis. —— I'm drivin' back, righ'.

They went through Howth village and up towards the Summit to see how the van would handle the hill. They turned back before they got to the top: they had to.

—We won't be goin' up tha' far ever, said Jimmy Sr.

She was going a blinder downhill.

—Not at all, Bimbo agreed with him.

—No one eats chips up there, said Jimmy Sr.

—That's righ', said Bimbo.

They went over a dog outside the Abbey Tavern but they didn't stop.

—Don't bother your arse, said Jimmy Sr when he saw Bimbo going for the brake. —We'll send them a wreath. No one saw us.

Bimbo said nothing till they got onto the Harbour Road. He looked behind – there was no rear view mirror, of course – but there was nothing to see except the back of the van.

Then he spoke.

—Wha' kind of a dog was it?

—Jack Russell.

—Ah, God love it.

And Jimmy Sr started laughing and he didn't really stop till they got to the Green Dolphin in Raheny and they went in for a pint cos Bimbo was still shaking a bit.

—Served it righ' for havin' a slash in the middle of the road, said Jimmy Sr.

He paid for the pints.

—Can I drive her the rest of the way? he asked.

—Certainly yeh can, said Bimbo.

—Thanks, said Jimmy Sr, although he didn't really know why; the engine was his as much as Bimbo's. —Good man.

* * *

Maggie had bought them a space in Dollymount, near the beach, for the summer; she'd found out that you rented the patches from the Corporation and she'd gone in and done it. It was a brilliant idea, and a great patch; right up near the beach at the top of the causeway road, where the buses ended and started. It couldn't have been better. There was a gap in the dunes there where on a good day thousands of people came through at the end of the day, sunburnt and gasping for chips and Cokes. Except there hadn't been a good day yet.

—The greenhouse effect, me bollix, said Jimmy Sr.

There hadn't even been a half decent day.

They climbed up to the top of one of the dunes to have a decco and there wasn't a sinner on the whole fuckin' island, except for themselves and a couple of rich fat oul' ones playing golf down the way, and a few learner drivers on the hard sand, and a couple of young fellas on their horses. It was fuckin' useless. They got back into the van to make themselves something to eat and they were the only customers they had all day. It was money down the drain. Even in the van it was cold.

—It's early days yet, said Bimbo. —The weather'll get better, wait'll yeh see.

He was only saying that cos Maggie'd organised the whole thing; Jimmy Sr could tell.

—It's the worst summer in livin' memory, he said.

—Who says it is? said Bimbo.

—I do, said Jimmy Sr. —I'm fuckin' freezin'.

—It's only July still, said Bimbo. —There's still August an' September left.

One of the horse young fellas was at the hatch, on his piebald.

—Anny rots, Mister? he said.

—Wha'? said Jimmy Sr.

—Anny rots.

Jimmy Sr spoke to Bimbo.

—What's he fuckin' on abou'?

The young fella explained.

—Rotten chips, he said. —For me horse.

—Fuck off, said Jimmy Sr. —There's nothin' rotten in this establishment, Tonto.

—I was only askin', said the young fella.

Jimmy Sr and Bimbo looked at his horse. It wasn't a horse really, more a pony; a big dog.

—How much was he? said Jimmy Sr.

—A hundred, said the young fella.

—Is that all?

—You can have him for a hundred an' fifty, the young fella told them.

They laughed.

The young fella patted the horse's head.

—You'd get your money back no problem, he said. —I'll kill him for yis as well, if yis want.

They laughed again.

—Does he like Twixes? Jimmy Sr asked the young fella.

—He does, yeah, said the young fella. —So do I.

—There yeh go.

He handed out two Twixes and the young fella got the horse in closer to the hatch so he could collect them.

—He likes cans o' Coke as well, he told them.

—He can fuck off down to the shops then, said Jimmy Sr.

The young fella's mate went galloping past on his mule and the young fella got ready to go after him. He stuffed the Twixes into his pocket and geed up the horse the way they did in the pictures, even though he'd no spurs on him, no saddle either.

—Does your bollix not be in bits ridin' around like tha'? Jimmy Sr asked him.

—Not really, said the young fella. —Yeh get used to it.

—You might, said Jimmy Sr. —I wouldn't.

—Yheupp! went the young fella, and he was gone, down the causeway road; they watched him from the door of the van, his feet nearly scraping off the road.

That was the high point of the day.

—He was a nice enough young fella, said Bimbo.

—Yeah, said Jimmy Sr.

* * *

That was easily their biggest problem though: young fellas. Jimmy Sr liked kids, always had; Bimbo loved them as well but, Jaysis Christ, they were changing their minds, quickly. Everyone loved bold kids. They were cute. There was nothing funnier than hearing a three-year-old say Fuck. This shower weren't cute though. They were cunts, right little cunts; dangerous as well.

There was a gang of them that hung around the Hikers carpark, young fellas, from fourteen to maybe nineteen. Even in the rain, they stayed there. They just put their hoodies up. Some of them always had their hoodies up. They were all small and skinny looking but there was something frightening about them. The way they behaved, you could tell that they didn't give a fuck about anything. When someone parked his car and went into the pub they went over to the car and started messing with it even before the chap had gone inside; they didn't care if he saw them. Jimmy Sr once saw one of them pissing against the window of the off-licence, in broad daylight, not a bother on him. Sometimes they'd have a flagon or a can of lager out and they'd pass it around, drinking in front of people coming in and out of Crazy Prices, people that lived beside their parents. It was sad. When they walked around, like a herd migrating or something, they all tried to walk the same way, the hard men, like their kaks were too tight on them. But that was only natural, he supposed. The worst thing though was, they didn't laugh. All kids went through a phase where they messed, they did things they weren't supposed to; they smoked, they drank, they showed their arses to oul' ones from the back window on the bus. But they did it for a laugh. That was the point of it. It was part of growing up, Jimmy Sr understood that; always had. He'd seen his own kids going through that. If you were lucky you never really grew out of it; a little bit of kid stayed inside you. These kids were different though; they didn't do anything for a laugh. Not that Jimmy Sr could see anyway. They were like fuckin' zombies. When Jimmy Sr saw them, especially when it was raining, he always thought the same thing: they'd be dead before they were twenty. Thank God, thank God, thank God none of his own kids was like that. Jimmy Jr, Sharon, Darren – he couldn't have had better kids. Leslie – Leslie had been a bit like that, but – no.

The Living Dead, Bertie called them.

Himself and Vera had had problems for a while with their young lad, Trevor, but Bertie had sorted him out.

—How?

—Easy. I promised I'd get him a motorbike if he passed his Inter.

—Is that all?

—Si, said Bertie. —Gas, isn't it? We were worried sick about him; Vera especially. He was – ah, he was gettin' taller an' he never washed himself, his hair, yeh know. He looked like a junkie, yeh know.

Jimmy Sr nodded.

—All he did all fuckin' day was listen to tha' heavy metal shite. Megadeath was one, an' Anthrax. I speet on them. I told her not to be worryin', an' I tried to talk to him, yeh know —

He raised his eyes.

—Man to man. Me hole. I wasn't tha' worried meself, but he was too young to be like tha'; tha' was all I thought.

—So yeh promised him the motorbike.

—Si. An' now he wants to stay in school an' do the Leavin'. First in the family. He's like his da, said Bertie. —A mercenary bollix.

They laughed.

—He'll go far, said Bimbo.

—Fuckin' sure he will, said Bertie. —No flies on our Trevor.

—Leslie passed his Inter as well, said Jimmy Sr.

—That's righ'.

—Two honours, said Jimmy Sr. —Not red ones either; real ones.

Anyway, the Living Dead gave Jimmy Sr and Bimbo terrible trouble. It was like that film, Assault on Precinct 13, and the van was Precinct 13. It wasn't as bad as that, but it was the same thing. Jimmy Sr and Bimbo could never really relax. The Living Dead would rock the van, three or four of them on each side. The oil poured out of the fryer, all the stuff was knocked to the floor, the cup for the grease under the hot plate went over and the grease got into the Mars Bars. It was hard to get out of the van when it was rocking like that, and it was fuckin' terrifying as well. There wasn't much weight in it at all; they could have toppled it easily enough. The second time they did it Jimmy Sr managed to catch one of them and he gave him a right hiding, up against the side of the van; clobbered every bit of him he could reach. He thought he was teaching him a lesson but when he stopped and let go of him the kid just spat at him. He just spat at him. And walked away, back to the rest of them. They didn't care if they were caught. They didn't say anything to him or shout back at him; they just stared out at him from under their hoodies. He wasn't angry when he climbed back into the van. He was frightened; not that they'd do it again, not that — but that there was nothing he could do to stop them. And, Jesus, they were only kids. Why didn't they laugh or call him a fat fucker or something?

They lit fires under the van; they robbed the bars that held up the hatch; they cut through the gas tubes; they took the bricks from under the wheels.

Jimmy Sr was looking out the hatch, watching the houses go by, when he remembered that the houses shouldn't have been going anywhere. The fuckin' van was moving! It was before they got the engine. Himself and Bimbo baled out the back door but Sharon wouldn't jump. The van didn't crash into anything, and it wasn't much of a hill. It just stopped. The Living Dead had taken the bricks from behind the wheels, that was what had happened. It was funny now but it was far from fuckin' funny at the time.

Jimmy Sr knew them, that was the worst thing about it. The last time he'd walked across O'Connell Bridge he'd seen this knacker kid, a tiny little young fella, crouched in against the granite all by himself, with a plastic bag up to his face. He was sniffing glue. It was terrible – how could his parents let him do that? – but at least he didn't know him. It was like when he heard that Veronica's brother's wife's sister's baby had been found dead in the cot when they got up one morning; it was terrible sad, but he didn't know the people so it was like any baby dying, just sad. But he knew the names of all these kids, most of them. Larry O'Rourke's young lad, for instance; Laurence, he was one of them. It depressed him, so it did. Thank God Leslie was out of it, working away somewhere.

The ordinary kids around, the more normal ones, they were always messing around the van as well. But at least you could get a good laugh out of them, even if they got on your wick. One of them – Jimmy Sr didn't know him, but he liked him – told Bimbo to give him a fiver or he'd pretend to get sick at the hatch every time someone came near the van. And he did it. There was a woman coming towards them, looking like she was making her mind up, and your man bent over and made the noises, and he had something in his mouth and he let it drop onto the road, scrunched-up crisps or something. And that made the woman's mind up for her. Jimmy Sr went after him with one of the bars from the hatch but he wasn't interested in catching him. The ordinary bowsies robbed the bars from the hatch, and messed with the gas and rocked the van as well, but it was different. When they legged it they could hardly run cos they were laughing so much. Jimmy Sr and Bimbo nearly liked it. These kids fancied Sharon as well so they came to look in at her. It would have been good for business, only they never had any fuckin' money. Sometimes, Fridays especially, they were drunk. He didn't like that. They were falling around the place, pushing each other onto the road. They were too young. They got the cider and cans from an off-licence two stops away on the DART; Darren told him that. Jimmy Sr was going to phone the guards, to report the off-licence, but he never got round to it.

One night the kids went too far. They started throwing stones at the van; throwing them hard. Bimbo, Jimmy Sr and Sharon got an almighty fright when they heard the first bash, until they guessed what was happening. They were flinging the stones at the hot plate side. When he saw the dints the stones were making, fuckin' big lumps like boils, Jimmy Sr nearly went through the roof. That was real damage they were doing. He grabbed one of the hatch bars and let an almighty yell out of him when he jumped out the back door. They weren't going to throw any stones at him, he knew that; it was only the noise they were enjoying. So he knew he wasn't exactly jumping to his death, but he still felt good when he landed, turned at them and saw the fear hop into their faces. Then he went for them. They legged it, and he kept after them. A kick up the hole would teach these guys a lesson. They weren't like the Living Dead. There were five of them and when they turned and went up the verge onto the Green there were more of them, a mixed gang, young fellas and young ones, little lads sticking to their big brothers. Jimmy Sr wasn't angry any more. He'd keep going to the middle of the Green, maybe catch one of the little lads or a girlfriend and take them hostage. He was closing in on one tiny kid who was trying to keep his tracksuit bottoms up. Jimmy Sr could hear the panic in the little lad's breath. He'd just enough breath left himself to catch him, and then he'd call it a day.

Then he saw them.

He stopped and nearly fell over.

The twins. He barely saw Linda but it was definitely Tracy, nearly diving into the lane behind the clinic. Grabbing a young fella's jumper to stay up. Then she was gone, but he'd seen enough.

The treacherous little bitches. Wait till he told Sharon.

He turned back to the van. He found the bar where he'd dropped it.

His own daughters, sending young fellas to throw stones at their da. With their new haircuts that he'd fuckin' paid for last Saturday.

He'd scalp the little wagons.

* * *

—You've no proof, said Linda.

—I seen yeh, said Jimmy Sr, again.

—You've no witnesses.

—I fuckin' seen yeh.

—Well, it wasn't me annyway, said Tracy.

—Or me, said Linda.

—It was youse, said Jimmy Sr. —An' if I hear anny more lies an' guff ou' o' yis I'll take those fuckin' haircuts back off yis. And another thing. If yis go away before yis have this place cleaned properly – properly now, righ' – I'll ground yis.

He climbed out of the van.

—The floors an' the walls, righ'. An' if yis do a good job I might let yis off from doin' the ceilin'.

He looked in at them.

—An' that'll fuckin' teach yis for hangin' around with gangsters.

Linda crossed her arms and stared back at him.

—I didn't spend a fortune on your hair, said Jimmy Sr, — so yis could get picked up by snot-nosed little corner boys.

He loved watching the twins when they were annoyed; they were gas.

—Next time yis are lookin' for young fellas go down to the snobby houses an' get off with some nice respectable lads, righ'.

—Will yeh listen to him, he heard Linda saying to Tracy.

—He hasn't a clue, said Tracy.

—Righ', said Jimmy Sr. —Off yis go. The sooner yeh start the sooner yis'll be finished. Mind yeh don't get your flares dirty now.

—They're not flares, righ'! They're baggies.

He closed the door on them.

They'd do a lousy job, he knew that. It served them right though; it would give them something to think about, that and the hiding Sharon had given them last night. Veronica had had to go into the room to break up the fight.

He listened at the door. He held the handle. He couldn't hear anything. He opened it quickly.

Linda was wiping the walls, kind of. Tracy was pushing a
cloth over the floor with her foot.

—Do it properly!

—I am!

—PROPERLY!

—Jesus; there's no need to shout, yeh know.

—I'll fuckin' —

—Can we get the radio? said Linda.

—No!

—Ah, Jesus—

Jimmy Sr shut the door.

* * *

The weather stayed poxy well into July. But it was alright; the
Dollymount patch was a long-term investment, Maggie
explained. They took it easier; they only brought the van out
at night, except on Fridays at teatime for the £1 Specials. They
had time for the odd round of pitch 'n' putt, and their game
hadn't suffered too much because of the lack of practice.
Jimmy Sr always won.

They stuck close to Barrytown but they kept an eye on the
newspapers to see if there was anything worth going further
for. Maggie scoured the Independent in the mornings and the
Herald later to see if there were any big concerts coming up,
or football matches. They were going to get the van as close
as they could to Croke Park for the Leinster Final between
Dublin and Meath. They'd have to be there before the start
because all the Meath lads coming up from the country
wouldn't have had their dinners. So they had that Sunday
afternoon pencilled in; Maggie'd done out a chart. The Horse
Show was coming up as well but they weren't going to bother
with that; the horsey crowd didn't eat chips.

—They eat fuckin' caviar an' tha' sort o' shite, said Jimmy
Sr.

—An' grouse an' pheasant, said Bimbo.

—Exactly, said Jimmy Sr. —Yeh'd be all fuckin' day tryin'
to get the batter to stay on a pheasant.

There were some big concerts coming up as well.

—Darren tells me they're called gigs, Jimmy Sr told Bimbo and Maggie.

Maggie held her biro over the chart.

—What abou' this one on Saturday? she said.

—Who is it again? said Bimbo.

—The The, said Maggie.

—Is tha' their name? said Bimbo. The The, only?

—That's wha' it says here, said Maggie.

She had the Herald open on the kitchen table.

—Well?

—Darren says they're very good, said Jimmy Sr. —He says they're important.

—Will there be many there?

—He doesn't know. He thinks so, but he's not sure.

—Well —

—I think we should give it a bash, said Jimmy Sr.

—Yeah, but —

Maggie took over from Bimbo.

—You'll be lettin' down your regulars.

—There is tha' to consider, said Bimbo. —Yeah.

—Wha' d'yeh mean? said Jimmy Sr.

—It's on on Saturday nigh', said Maggie. —We always do very well outside the Hikers on Saturday nights.

What did she mean, We? She'd never been as much as inside the van in her —

—I see wha' yeh mean, said Jimmy Sr. —There could be thousands at this gig though.

—It's a bit risky but, said Bimbo. —Isn't it?

—Well, said Maggie. —It's up to yourselves —

Jimmy Sr didn't want a row; and, anyway, they were probably right. They decided just to do midweek gigs and to concentrate on the closing-time market at the weekends.

—There's a festival in Thurles, said Maggie.

—It can stay there, said Jimmy Sr.

He'd fight this one; there was no way he was going all the way down to Tipperary just to sell a few chips. But it was alright; Bimbo nearly fell over when Maggie mentioned Thurles.

—Ah, no, said Bimbo.

—Just a thought, said Maggie.

—We'll stick to Dublin, said Bimbo. —Will we, Jimmy?

—Def'ny.

Jimmy Sr felt good after that. He'd been starting to think that Bimbo and Maggie rehearsed these meetings.

* * *

Sharon had started going with a chap called Barry, a nice enough fella – some kind of an insurance man; she'd already broken it off twice and him once, but they were back together and madly in love, judging by the size of the love bites Jimmy Sr'd seen on Barry's neck the last time he'd called around. So Sharon wasn't keen on working nights any more. They tried a few nights without her, just the two of them, but it was a killer. So Jimmy Sr said he'd recruit Darren – before Maggie came up with some bright idea. Darren already had his job in the Hikers but he was only getting two nights a week out of that, so Jimmy Sr reckoned he'd jump at the chance of making a few extra shillings. But —

—I'm a vegetarian, Darren told him.

—Wha'!?

Darren shrugged.

—You as well? said Jimmy Sr. —Jaysis. ——Hang on but —

He'd been watching Darren eating his dinners and his teas since he was a baby.

—Since when?

—Oh —— Tuesday.

—Ah, now here —

—I'd been thinkin' about it for a long time and I just made up me, eh —

—Okay, said Jimmy Sr. —Okay.

He raised his hands.

—Good luck to yeh. ——Do vegetarians eat fish?

——Yeah; some do.

—Do you?

—Yeah.

—That's grand so, said Jimmy Sr. —You can just do the fish an' meself an' Bimbo'll handle the rest. How's tha'?

Darren was a broke vegetarian.

——Okay, he said. ——Eh —— okay.

—Sound, said Jimmy Sr.

They shook on it. That was great. It would be terrific having Darren working beside him, fuckin' marvellous.

—Wha' abou' burgers? said Jimmy Sr.

Darren didn't look happy.

—There's fuck all meat in them, Jimmy Sr assured him.

—No.

—Fair enough, said Jimmy Sr.

He liked the way Darren had said no.

—I was just chancin' me arm, he said. —How's Miranda?

—Okay, said Darren.

—Good, said Jimmy Sr. —She's a lovely-lookin' girl.

Darren wanted to escape but what his da had said there needed some sort of an answer.

—Thanks, he said. —Yeah; she's fine. Someone ran over her dog a few weeks ago, and she was a bit —, but she's alrigh' now.

—Where was tha'? said Jimmy Sr.

—Howth.

—A Jack Russell?

——Eh, yeah. How did yeh know?

—I didn't, Jimmy Sr told him. —It's just, nearly all the dogs yeh see dead on the road seem to be Jack Russells. Did yeh ever notice tha' yourself?

—No.

—Keep an eye ou' for them an' yeh'll see what I mean.

* * *

The weather picked up. There were a few good, sunny days on the trot and suddenly everyone was going around looking scalded.

528

—Thunderbirds are go, said Jimmy Sr.

They got to Dollymount at half-three. Sharon was with them. There was a Mister Whippy on their spot. Bimbo had a photocopy of the Corporation permit in his back pocket. Jimmy Sr took it and went up to have it out with Mister Whippy. He got in the queue, with Sharon. Bimbo stayed with the van. The kid in front of Jimmy Sr ran off with his two 99s to get back to the beach before they melted, and Jimmy Sr was next.

—Yeah? said Mister Whippy. Jimmy Sr looked up at him.

—What d'yeh want? said Mister Whippy.

—Justice, said Jimmy Sr.

He held out the permit and waved it.

—Have a decco at tha', he said.

Mister Whippy, a spotty young lad, looked scared.

—What is it? said the young fella.

—Can yeh not read? said Jimmy Sr.

—It's a permit, said Sharon.

—That's righ', said Jimmy Sr. —My glamorous assistant, Sharon, is quite correct there.

Young Mister Whippy was still lost but he was braver as well.

—So wha'? he said.

—So fuck off, said Jimmy Sr.

He took back the permit.

—It's ours, he said. —We paid for this patch here, where you are. We did, you didn't. You've no righ' to be here, so hop it; go on.

Mister Whippy couldn't decide what to do.

—Go on, said Jimmy Sr. —Yeh can go over to the other side o' the roundabout.

—No one'll see me there.

—We'll tell them you're there, said Jimmy Sr. —Won't we?

—Yeah, said Sharon.

—An' anyway, said Jimmy Sr. —Yeh can play your music an' they'll hear yeh.

Mister Whippy still didn't look too sure.

—Listen, said Jimmy Sr. —Shift now or we'll fuckin' ram yeh.

He stepped back from the van and shouted.

—Rev her up there, Bimbo!

Bimbo turned the key and then Mister Whippy got behind the wheel and did the same thing, and moved away around to the far side of the roundabout, away from the dunes.

—Seeyeh, said Sharon and she waved.

Bimbo brought the van up to them.

Mister Whippy turned on The Teddy Bears' Picnic.

—They're playin' our song, Jimmy Sr told Bimbo.

For about a week the weather stayed that way, grand and hot, no sign of a cloud. They came down to Dollier at half-three or so and stayed till half-six and went home with a clatter of new pound coins jingling away in their money box. It was easy enough going; didn't get hectic till after five. Sharon went over to the beach and got some sun and Jimmy Sr and Bimbo hung around the van and watched the world go by. Then coming up to teatime they'd climb into the van and stoke up the furnace. Then the crowds came up over the dunes and the smell hit them, and no one can resist the smell of chips.

The only bad thing was having to stare down at all those peeling faces staring up at you outside the van. Noses, arms, foreheads; it was fuckin' revolting. Red raw young ones with shivery legs would take their bags of stuff and give you their money, turn around to get away from the van and they'd be white on the other side. Sharon wasn't like that; she'd more sense. She did herself front and back and the sides as well, even.

—Like a well-cooked burger, Jimmy Sr told her.

—Jesus!

—It's a compliment, it's a compliment.

—Thanks!

The only other bad thing about the beach business was the sand. It got into everything. Even with no wind to blow it they'd find a layer of it on the hatch counter, on the shelves, grains of it floating on top of the cooking oil before they lit the

530

burner; everywhere. Jimmy Sr did a burger for himself and when he bit into it, before his teeth met, he could feel the sand in the bundie. He chewed very carefully. When they got the van back to Bimbo's they had to get damp cloths and go over everything with them, to pick up the sand, but they never got all of it. Jimmy Sr always had a shower before he went out again to do the closing-time business and there was enough sand up his hole and in his ears to build a block of flats. He couldn't understand it because he never went down to the beach, except once or twice to see if there was anything worth looking at; and there never was, hardly ever. He'd keep his eyes on the ground till he got to the beach and then he'd look around him, hoping, and all he ever saw was scorched gobshites getting more scorched. And white lines where bra straps got in the way of the sun. Dollier definitely wasn't like the resort in some island in Greece or somewhere he'd seen in a blue video Bertie'd lent him a few years ago; my Jaysis, the women in that place!; walking around with fuck all on, not a bother on them. Climbing out of the pool so that their tits were squeezed together; bending over so he could see the water dripping off their gee hairs. There were no women like that in Dollymount. It was mostly mammies with their kids. Still though, they were good for business. There was nothing like a screaming kid to get a ma to open her purse. He couldn't see the brassers in that video going mad for chips; and, anyway, they'd probably have wanted them for nothing.

* * *

It was busy, getting dark; the Living Dead were out there somewhere. Bimbo had had to dash home for a shite, so Jimmy Sr was by himself at the hatch, taking the orders. And he'd three burgers doing on the hotplate and he asked Darren to turn them for him, and he wouldn't do it.

—I'm not askin' yeh to eat them, said Jimmy Sr, trying not to sound too snotty in front of the customers. —I only want yeh to turn them fuckin' over.

Darren said nothing, and he didn't do anything either.

—Darren? said Jimmy Sr.

But Darren just started filling the bags with chips.

—Fuck yeh, said Jimmy Sr and he got back to the hotplate and picked the fish slice up off the floor.

The burgers were welded to the plate; they were part of the plate.

—Look wha' you're after doin', said Jimmy Sr.

Darren said nothing.

One of the punters outside spoke up.

—If that's my burger you're messin' with there I'm not takin' it, he told Jimmy Sr.

Jimmy Sr had had enough.

—Righ', he said. —Fuck off then. An' get your burger somewhere else. —— Annyone else want to complain?

But Bimbo came back and took over at the hatch. And with Bimbo blocking the view Jimmy Sr was able to get the burgers off the hot plate and into their bundies without doing too much damage to them. He dipped them into the deep fat fryer to make them juicy and then trapped them in the bundies before they dripped or fell apart.

—There, he said. —No help to you.

Darren said nothing.

Dunphies were out of the question as well as far as Darren was concerned and they had to go into the deep fat fryer with the fish, so Darren would stand back and get out of Jimmy Sr or Bimbo's way while they fished out the dunphies. It was stupid. Still but, they had to respect Darren's beliefs. Jimmy Sr told that to Maggie after Bimbo had told her about Darren and his vegetarianism.

—At least he has the courage of his convictions, he said.

He wasn't really sure what that meant but it shut Maggie up. Not that she'd been giving out or anything; she'd just thought it was funny that someone called Rabbitte was a vegetarian. Jimmy Sr couldn't see anything particularly funny about that.

Where Darren was way out of line, way out – just the once – was when he objected to the dunphies going into the same cooking oil as the fish.

—Wha'!?

—Part of the meat is left in the oil.

—So?

—It gets into the fish.

—It does in its hole. Nothin' would get through tha' batter. Bimbo made it.

Darren laughed but he kept going on all night about contaminating the oil and he put a face on him every time Jimmy Sr leaned over and dropped a dunphy into the fryer; he got on Jimmy Sr's wick.

No one had ordered a dunphy; he just did it to annoy Darren; he deserved it.

—'Xcuse me, Darren, till I drop this into the holy of holies.

He blessed the dunphy as it sank down and bobbed up again between two pieces of cod.

—Make sure they don't touch there, said Jimmy Sr. —We don't want any bits o' cod gettin' into the dunphy an' poisonin' someone.

Darren had one last bash at explaining osmosis to Jimmy Sr. He was halfway through it when Jimmy Sr turned on him.

—Spare me the fuckin' lecture, righ', an' just do your fuckin' job.

He flicked a dunphy into the fryer so that it would send some oil flying in Darren's direction. Darren got some of it on his arms. He said nothing but he went outside.

Jimmy Sr's ears hummed while he waited for Darren to come back. He prayed for him to come back but he wouldn't go to the door to look out; he wouldn't even look at it.

He felt Darren going past him, on his way back to the fryer.

—Sorry, he said.

He looked at Darren: he looked fine.

——Okay? said Jimmy Sr.

——Yeah.

—Grand; —— sorry.

* * *

533

They were all set to move out. It was the hottest day yet, Jimmy Sr reckoned. All they were waiting for now was Sharon.

—What's she at? said Jimmy Sr. —Jesus tonigh'.

She had Gina with her, in the buggy.

—Mammy can't mind her, she said before Jimmy Sr could ask her. —An' the twins won't.

—Yeh can't bring the baby —

—Give us a hand, said Sharon.

She went round and opened the back door. She climbed in.

—Jesus!

The heat hit her.

Jimmy Sr picked up the buggy with Gina still in it and passed it in to Sharon.

—It's fuckin' dangerous —, he said.

—We'll be grand, said Sharon. —Won't we, Gina?

Gina was looking around. She liked what she saw. She tried to free herself. Sharon sat up on the hatch counter and held the buggy close to her, between her legs.

—I don't know —, said Jimmy Sr.

He shut the door.

Bimbo went very carefully. An oul' one on crutches could have gone faster.

—It'll be fuckin' dark by the time we get there, said Jimmy Sr.

—I don't want to be responsible for an injury, Bimbo told him. —'Specially to a baby.

But they got there. Jimmy Sr got Gina to sit on a shelf and gave her a Twix to keep her quiet for a bit and Sharon folded the buggy and put it in on top of the driver's seat. It wasn't too bad that way. Bimbo showed Gina how to make batter and he got her down off the shelf and let her dip a slab of cod into it. That was a mistake because now she had to dip everything into it, including herself. But it was nice having her in the van there; it was kind of exciting, as if they were performing for her. Bimbo put her back up on the shelf out of harm's way, and Jimmy Sr gave her the other half of the Twix.

But she nearly fell into the deep fat fryer. She'd crawled nearer to it and she was leaning over to look at the bubbles and the smoke when Jimmy Sr saw her, roared and caught her. He didn't really catch her, cos she wasn't falling, but he told Sharon he did. The poor little thing was wringing with the sweat, so Jimmy Sr put her on the hatch counter to dry. She knocked the salt and pepper and a load of bags out onto the path. A load of young ones saw her and came over to look at her and say hello and wave at her but they didn't buy anything, of course.

—Get us the salt an' pepper there, will yeh, love, Jimmy Sr asked a young one.

—Get it yourself, she said.

They all walked off, laughing.

—Hope yeh got skin cancer! Jimmy Sr roared after them.

—Jesus, Daddy!

—Bitches.

—Bitis! said Gina after them.

—Good girl yourself, said Jimmy Sr.

They couldn't keep her on the counter because she'd get in the way and she was bound to fall out so what Jimmy Sr did was, he went into the dunes and found a plank. He brought it back to the van and gave it a good wipe and used up most of a milk bottle of water to clean it. It was long enough to go over the top of the chip bin and that made a seat for Gina, in the corner, away from danger. She complained a bit; the plank was wet. Bimbo put a cloth under her.

Serving was easier here than at closing time cos there wasn't a mad rush of people. It was good, a gradual, steady flow of customers. Jimmy Sr liked it. It was a good way to start the working day.

—Have yeh anny spicey burgers, Mister?

—They're on the menu, said Jimmy Sr, but not in a snotty way.

—Oh yeah, said the young fella. —How much are they?

Jimmy Sr pointed at the price on the board.

—There; look it.

—Oh yeah.

The kid was a bit simple, he could tell; the way his mouth hung open.

—D'yeh want chips as well? he asked him.

—Yeah.

—Have yeh the money on yeh?

—Me ma's comin', said the kid.

—Fair enough, said Jimmy Sr. —Will she want annythin' herself, would yeh say?

—Wha'?

—Will she be long?

—She's comin'.

—Okay, said Jimmy Sr.

Poor little sap; he'd give him the order even if his ma didn't come. He turned to get a spice-burger.

—Wha' the fuck —

—Wha'?

—Yeh can't fuckin' do tha' in here!

Sharon was changing Gina's nappy.

Jesus; if a health inspector or a guard was passing and looked in and saw the baby's little arse pointing out at him they'd be rightly fucked. Or Mister Whippy over the other side of the roundabout; if he saw what Sharon was doing he'd race down to Raheny station and report them, and he'd play the Teddy Bears' Picnic all the fuckin' way.

Jimmy Sr slammed down the hatch.

—Back in a minute, he told the kid waiting outside.

—Quick! he said. —Hurry up. An' mind nothin' drops into the chips.

Sharon giggled. Bimbo was battering away. It wasn't dark exactly; you could see everything. It was quite nice really.

—Are yeh finished? said Jimmy Sr.

—Nearly.

Sharon put the old nappy into a plastic bag and put that bag into her proper bag.

—Pity the poor fucker tha' robs your handbag, said Jimmy Sr.

536

They laughed, and Jimmy Sr opened the hatch. The kid was still there.

—Still here, said Jimmy Sr.

—Me ma's comin', said the kid.

—She's a lucky woman, said Jimmy Sr.

—Daddy!

Jimmy Sr slid the spice-burger into the cooking oil.

—Now.

He put a few chips into a bag, nice big ones, and handed them out to the kid.

—Have them while you're waitin', he said.

—A one an' one there, please.

Jimmy Sr looked to see who'd said that. It was a man about his own age, wearing a Hawaii 5-0 shirt and a Bobby Charlton haircut. Bimbo sank the cod into the fryer.

—Grand day again, said Jimmy Sr to the man.

—We're spoilt, said the man.

—What's the water like today? said Jimmy Sr.

—Shockin', said the man. —Filthy dirty, it is. Yeh wouldn't make your worst enemy swim in it.

—Yes, I would, Jimmy Sr told him. —Won't be a minute here.

—No hurry.

Sharon handed out the spice-burger and chips to the young fella. He didn't take them.

—Me ma's comin', he said.

—You're alrigh', said Jimmy Sr. —Go on. She can pay us when she comes; go on.

Gina started singing.

—OLÉ——OLÉ OLÉ OLÉ —

They all joined in.

Jimmy Sr got the cod out the fryer, shook the drops off it and put it in its bag and put that into the brown bag; a grand big piece of fish it was too. Sharon gave him the bag of chips and he slid that in alongside the cod.

—OLÉ——OLÉ OLÉ OLÉ – The works? he asked the man.

He held the salt over the bag.

—Fire away, said the man.

—Righto, said Jimmy Sr. —Say when.

The man took the bag. He handed two of the new pound coins to Jimmy Sr but stopped just short of Jimmy's reach.

—Me ma's comin', he said.

They laughed and he gave the money to Jimmy Sr. Jimmy Sr gave him his change and that was that.

—Good luck now, said Jimmy Sr. —Enjoy your meal.

—Cheerio, said the man.

Jimmy Sr watched him trying to wheel his bike and eat his chips at the same time. There was a woman outside now, trying to get her shower of kids to make up their minds what they wanted.

—Milkshake! said one of them.

They were all over her; it was hard to be sure how many kids she had with her; about six, and another on the way, now that Jimmy Sr looked at her properly.

—It isn't McDonald's, she told the milkshake kid.

—Wha' is it? said the kid.

—It's a lurry! said his sister, and she gave him a smack in the mouth, and legged it.

—Look at this, Jimmy Sr said to Sharon.

—Six singles, said the woman when she made it to the counter. —No; seven. Me as well.

—I don't want chips, said one of the boys.

—Well, you're gettin' them! said the woman. —And anyway, you, you're not even one o' mine so yeh should be grateful.

The woman looked at Sharon.

—I only own three o' them, she said.

That was all.

She looked as if she could lie down under the van and go fast asleep, and maybe not wake up again.

—Never again, she said.

—They're lovely, said Sharon.

—They're bastards, said the woman. —Every fuckin' one o' them.

538

She looked as if she felt better after getting that off her chest, and she straightened up. She patted her stomach.

—This'll be the last, she said. —He can stick it in a milk bottle after tha', so he can.

Sharon was shocked. She'd never seen the woman before.

There was a scream; the littlest lad was having a bucket of crabs and stones and water poured down his togs. The woman patted her stomach again.

—With a bit o' luck this one'll be deaf an' dumb.

She didn't smile: she meant it.

—Righ'! Jimmy Sr yelled. —Line up for your chipses!

—Me!!

—Your mammy first! said Jimmy Sr. —Get back.

—She's always first!

—Get back!

—Not fair —

—Into line, said Jimmy Sr. —Or I'll dump your chips into the sand.

He held a bag of chips up, ready to throw it.

—A straight line. —— Salt an' vinegar, love?

—Loads.

That was when Bobby Charlton came back. He threw his bike against the wall of the van.

—Come here —!!

Jimmy Sr dropped the salt.

—Mother o' fuck!

The woman yelped.

—Come here! the man said again.

But the bike slid onto the ground and he tried to pick it up but his leg got on the wrong side of the crossbar, and he'd only one hand to work with because the other one was still holding the chips. He gave up trying to lift the bike and stepped over it, and nearly tripped. He leaned against the van.

He'd given Jimmy Sr time to get his act together.

—What's your problem? said Jimmy Sr.

—I'll tell yeh —

539

—I'm dealin' with a customer here, Jimmy Sr told him. —You'll have to wait your turn.

The man was right up at the hatch now, like he was going to climb in.

—I'll tell yeh wha' my problem is – , the man started again.

—There's a queue, said the woman.

—There won't be when I'm finished here, said the man.

Jimmy Sr, Sharon and Bimbo were at the hatch. Jimmy Sr handed the singles down to the woman and she handed them on to the kids.

—Excuse me! said the man.

—Calm down, said Bimbo. —Calm down.

—Sap, said Sharon, but not loud.

—Three eighty-five, Sharon told the woman when she looked up.

—Be careful eatin' them, the man told the woman.

That sounded bad.

—Oh Christ, said Bimbo.

He looked back at the fryer.

—Righ', said Jimmy Sr, when Sharon had given the woman her change. —What's your problem?

He'd been thinking about it; he hadn't a clue what was going to happen. He stared down at the man.

—It's your problem, said the man.

—Wha' is?

—This.

He held up the bag in his hand, far enough away not to be grabbed.

Jimmy Sr leaned out to see.

—The chips?

—No!

—The fish?

The man looked very upset.

—Fish! he said.

—It's fresh, Bimbo assured him. —It was grand an' hard comin' out o' the —

—Fresh! the man screamed.

Jimmy Sr had to say it again.

—What's your problem?

—Will yeh look it.

But he still wouldn't bring his hand in any closer to the hatch.

—I can't fuckin' see it, said Jimmy Sr. —— Wha'ever —

Maybe it was maggots.

—I bit into it ——, said the man.

—That's wha' you were supposed to do, said Jimmy Sr.

This chap was some tulip.

—Wha' did yeh think yeh were supposed to do with it; ride it?

Now the man did come closer; he banged into the van.

—Oh Jesus, said Sharon.

She got back and went beside Gina.

The man's mouth was open crooked. He really looked like a looper now. They could see into the bag.

—It's not fish —, said Bimbo.

—Oh fuck —. What is it?

Hang on though —

—It's white, said Jimmy Sr.

—It's a nappy! the man told him.

—Wha'! —— Fuck off, would yeh.

—He's righ', Jimmy, said Bimbo. —It's a Pamper; folded up. My God, that's shockin'.

—Shut up! Jimmy Sr hissed at him.

—I must have put it in the batter —

—Shut up!

—What is it? said Sharon.

The man wasn't angry-looking now; he looked like he needed comfort.

—Is it a used one? Jimmy Sr asked him, and he crossed his fingers.

—No!

—Ah well, said Jimmy Sr. —That's alrigh' then.

—That's how, said Bimbo. —It'd look like a piece o' cod, folded up like. Ah, that's gas.

—Sorry abou' tha', said Jimmy Sr to the man. —We'll give yeh your money back, an' a can o' Coke; how's tha' sound? Were the chips alrigh'?

The man wasn't won over. He folded the bag into a neater package and put it under his arm.

—I'm goin' to the guards with this, he said.

—Ah, there's no need —

—This is the evidence, the man interrupted Bimbo.

He checked to see that the bag was still under his arm.

—You'll be hearin' more about this, he told them. —Don't you worry. I'll never recover from a shock like this.

—A tenner, said Jimmy Sr. —Will tha' do yeh?

—What's your name? he asked Jimmy Sr.

—I don't have to tell you tha', said Jimmy Sr.

—I don't care, said the man. —I've the evidence here.

—Twenty, said Jimmy Sr. —Final offer; go on.

—I've the evidence.

—Shove the fuckin' evidence. We know nothin' about it.

—You're not goin' to bribe me, said the man.

—It's the suppliers yeh should be reportin', said Jimmy Sr, —not us. We know nothin' abou' nappies.

Gina started singing again. Sharon put her hand over Gina's mouth, but the man wasn't listening. He was looking at the sign on the side of the van.

—Which one of yis is Bimbo? he said.

—Ask me arse, said Jimmy Sr.

He pulled Bimbo over to him.

—Get ou' an' start the van.

—But —

—Fuckin' do it!

Bimbo went to the back door.

—Go round the other way, Jimmy Sr told him.

He remembered something.

—The gas!

Bimbo lifted the gas canister and pushed it into the van. He closed his eyes when it scraped on the floor. Jimmy Sr distracted the man.

—It must be terrible bein' baldy with the sun like this, he said. —Is it?

Bimbo got to the driver's door, around the other side of the van, without the man seeing him. He got the buggy off the seat.

—I'm rememberin' all this, the man told Jimmy Sr.

—Good man, said Jimmy Sr.

He took away the hatch bars when he heard the engine starting.

—See yeh now, Baldy Conscience, he said. —Keep in touch.

And he dropped the hatch door. The salt and the vinegar fell onto the path. He shut the back door.

—Go on, go on!

The van lurched; Jimmy Sr fell forward, and grabbed a shelf. It skipped again, and then they got going.

Jimmy Sr steadied himself. He leaned against the hatch counter.

—My Jaysis —

—He'll get the registration, said Sharon.

—No, he won't, said Jimmy Sr.

—Why not?

—We don't have one. It's in the shed in Bimbo's. We never stuck it back on. Just as well, wha'.

—He might be followin' us, said Sharon.

She had a point.

Jimmy Sr opened the back door. They were still on the causeway road, and there was your man coming after them, pedalling like fuck.

—I'll get this bollix, said Jimmy Sr.

He looked back, around the van. He stepped over to the hotplate and got a can of Coke from under it. They went over a pothole or something when he was bending over. The hotplate and the fryer were still turned on.

—Jesus; I nearly fuckin' fried myself.

He got to the canister and switched it off.

He weighed the Coke in his hand, then wiped the grease off it on his shirt.

—You'll kill him, said Sharon.

She was probably right. They were heavy things when they were full. He grabbed a few pieces of cod. They were still hard enough.

Bimbo turned left instead of right at the top of the causeway road.

—What's he fuckin' doin'?

—It's so your man can't follow us home, said Sharon.

—Fair enough.

He opened the back door again and the man was still after them, but further back; his legs didn't have it. Jimmy threw a piece of cod anyway, skimmed it, to see how far he could get it. He watched it bounce off the road, well short of the man.

—There's more evidence for yeh!

He shut the door.

Bimbo brought them to Clontarf, then up the Lawrence's Road, onto the Howth Road. He went up Collins' Avenue at Killester, and to the Malahide Road.

Jimmy Sr looked out again, and saw Cadbury's in Coolock.

—We'll end up in fuckin' Galway, he said.

He threw Gina up and caught her, and again, but not too high because he'd already hit her head off the roof, and he was only doing it now to make her forget about it.

They got home. Jimmy Sr and Sharon were melting when they got out the back. Jimmy Sr had to stand in front of the open fridge door.

—We'll steer clear o' Dollier for a while, he said.

—Yeah, said Bimbo.

Bimbo was angry.

—It would never've happened if she'd —

—Shut up, said Jimmy Sr.

* * *

Maggie had a great head for ideas; Jimmy Sr had to say that for her. She got flyers printed and sent Wayne and Glenn and Jessica all around putting them into houses. Linda and Tracy did them as well, until Darren caught them sticking hundreds of the flyers into the letter-box outside the Gem.

BIMBO'S BURGERS

TODAY'S CHIPS TODAY

Wedding Anniversary? Birthday? Or Just Lazy?

Treat Yourself

And

Let Us Cook Your Dinner For You

Ring 374693 and Ask for Maggie

That was what they said, on nice blue paper.

—Four-course meals? said Jimmy Sr when she was telling them about it. —How'll we fuckin' manage tha'?

—Easy, said Maggie.

She'd stick the melon into the fridge in the afternoon so it would be still nice and cold when Bimbo and Jimmy Sr delivered it. They'd use a flask if it was soup; just pour it into the bowls and get it into the houses and onto the tables while there was still steam coming up off it. The main course was no bother because that was what they made all the time anyway.

—What abou' the sweet but? said Jimmy Sr. —The ice-cream'll be water by the time they've got through their main stuff.

He wasn't against the idea; he just saw problems with it.

—Well, said Maggie. —You could keep chunks of ice-cream in a flask as well —

—Wha'; with the soup?

—There's bound to be a mix-up, said Bimbo. —Somewhere along the line.

What they decided on was, one of them would do a legger back to Bimbo's while the customers were laying into the main course and get the ice-cream out of the fridge and hoof it back. That was Darren's job. He didn't mind; he got an almighty slagging from the lads when they saw him running across the Green with a bowl of jelly and ice-cream in each hand but it was better than having to go into the house and

545

serving the customers, like a bleedin' waiter. That was Bimbo's job.

Jimmy Sr shook the flask over the bowl and the last bits of potato slid out and dropped into the soup.

—There now —

There was nothing like a few big chunks of vegetable to make packet soup look like the real thing.

—That's great lookin' soup, said Jimmy Sr. —Wha'.

—Lovely, said Bimbo.

—It's wasted on those fuckers.

—Ah now, said Bimbo.

They were feeding the O'Rourkes tonight, Larry and Mona; their twenty-third wedding anniversary.

—We should make them cough up before we hand over the grub, said Jimmy Sr. —Fuckin' Larry wouldn't give yeh the steam off his piss if you were dyin' o' dehydration.

He took two small pieces of parsley from the bag Maggie'd given him, aimed and dropped one onto the soup in each bowl.

—Nice touch, tha', he said.

Bimbo got into his jacket.

—How's the back, Darren? he asked.

Darren rubbed down Bimbo's back, getting rid of the creases.

Bimbo put the tea-towel over his arm.

The jacket Maggie'd got Bimbo was the stupidest thing Jimmy Sr'd ever seen. He felt humiliated just looking at Bimbo in it. It was white, with goldy buttons, and the sleeves were too long. But it didn't bother Bimbo; he thought he was Lord fuckin' Muck in it – the man in charge.

—Away we go so, said Bimbo.

He checked his watch again.

—Yeah, he said. —They were told to have the table set for half-seven.

He picked up the bowls, using the cuffs to mind his fingers.

—Ring the bell for me, Darren.

—Okay.

—Good lad. Bring the candles as well, will yeh.

—Ah fuck —

—Go on, Darren, said Jimmy Sr. —You're alrigh'; they're vegetarian candles.

—Humour, said Darren.

Bimbo climbed carefully out of the van.

—Get back quick with the main order, Jimmy Sr said after them.

—Will do.

The chips were a definite so Jimmy Sr lowered the basket into the fryer. Larry and Mona wouldn't be long getting rid of the soup. Mind you, they mightn't know what it was. They put water on their cornflakes in that house; so everyone said, anyway.

Bimbo and Darren were back.

—How'd it go?

—It was embarrassin', said Darren.

—How was it? Jimmy Sr asked him.

—He started singin'.

—He's always singin'.

Bimbo took over.

—The minute he saw the candles he started singing to Mona. Tha' one, I Can't Help Fallin' In Love With You.

—Wha? —WISE MEN SAY —
ONLY FOO–ILS RUSH IN —Tha' one?

—Yeah.

—Jaysis. He's gettin' worse. Did they like the soup?

—Stop it, said Bimbo. —Their spoons were clackin' off the bowls. He was singin' an' drinkin' at the same time.

—They didn't think much o' the parsley though, Darren told his da.

—Now there's a surprise, said Jimmy Sr.

—He said if he'd wanted weeds in his dinner he'd've gone ou' the back an' got some of his own.

—Tha' sort o' thing is wasted on shite-bags like them, said Jimmy Sr.

Back to business.

—What's the main course?

—Smoked cod for Larry an' the same for Mona, said Bimbo.
—An' they both want a few pineapple fritters as well.

—And onion rings, Darren reminded him.

—Oh, that's righ'. Mona said she'd go a couple of onion rings as well.

—Jaysis, said Jimmy Sr. —They'll keep her up all night if Larry doesn't.

He dropped the orders into the fryer, except the pineapples; they only took a few seconds or they'd turn to mush.

—Do they want wine? said Jimmy Sr when he'd everything else in order.

—Yeah, said Darren.

—Black or blue?

—Blue.

Jimmy Sr ducked in under the hot plate and got out a bottle of Blue Nun.

—Do the business with tha', he said to Darren, and he held the bottle out to him.

—I'd better get back for their sweets, said Darren.

Jimmy Sr turned to Bimbo.

—There, he said. —Suck the cork ou' o' tha'.

Bimbo got working on the bottle with the corkscrew and Jimmy Sr put the two plates on the hatch counter and made a hill of chips on each of them.

—There'll be no complaints abou' the quantity annyway, wha', said Jimmy Sr. —Give someone more than they think they're entitled to and yeh have a friend for life.

—Cos they know we give value for money, said Bimbo.

—Cos they think we're fuckin' saps, said Jimmy Sr.

—The cork's after breakin' on me, said Bimbo.

—Shove it into the bottle.

The plates were full now, too full. Jimmy Sr took some of the chips off and pushed the fish further in, under the chips.

—There, he said. —Can yeh manage?

—No problem, said Bimbo. —I'll have to come back for the wine.

—I'll bring it as far as the door for yeh, said Jimmy Sr.

—Good man; thanks.

Jimmy Sr knew that Bimbo thought he meant O'Rourke's front door but he was only going to go to the van door, for the laugh.

Bimbo wasn't impressed when he got back.

—Very funny, he said.

—Ah, cop on, said Jimmy Sr.

They said nothing for a bit. Then —

—They're havin' a row inside, Bimbo told Jimmy Sr.

—Fuckin' great, said Jimmy Sr. —What abou'?

—Couldn't tell yeh, said Bimbo. —I just gave them their dinners an' got ou'.

—Ah, you're fuckin' useless.

He handed the Blue Nun to Bimbo.

—Go back an' find ou' wha' they're rowin' abou'.

—Who d'yeh think you're orderin' around —?

Darren was back with the jelly and ice-cream.

—Hey, Darren; go in an' see what Larry an' Mona are rowin' abou'.

—Go in yourself.

—Jesus, said Jimmy Sr. —What a staff; such a pair o' fuckin' wasters I'm lumbered with.

He turned to Bimbo and he was glaring at Jimmy Sr; he didn't have time to change his face. It surprised Jimmy Sr.

Eh ——are they in the front room or the kitchen or wha'?

—The kitchen, said Bimbo, back to normal.

—Fuck. We could've crept up under the window —

Larry O'Rourke came charging out of the house, trying to get into his jacket. He didn't slam the door.

—How was the cod, Larry? Jimmy Sr asked him.

—Fuck the fuckin' cod, said Larry.

He headed down the road, in a Hikers direction.

—Your jelly an' ice-cream, Larry!

—Fuck the jelly an' the fuckin' ice-cream, they heard.

He turned back to them.

—She can fuckin' eat them! Her mouth's fuckin' big enough!

—Will yeh look who's talkin'! Bimbo said to Jimmy Sr and Darren. —Who's goin' to pay for the dinners?

—Eh ——I suppose —

Bimbo looked down the road, then at the house.

—It was Mona phoned Maggie.

—Righ', said Jimmy Sr.

He went up the path, and into the house, with the wine.

Bimbo and Darren waited for him.

Jimmy Sr came back out.

—She wants her jelly.

Darren handed him a bowl.

—Better give her the both o' them, said Jimmy Sr. —She's payin' for them.

—Is she? said Bimbo.

—Fuckin' sure she is.

He went back into the house. Darren and Bimbo got the gas canister back into the van and wiped the shelves. Bimbo mixed some more batter for later that night and Darren fished some loose bits of batter out of the oil in the fryer.

—Maybe she's seducin' him, said Darren.

——Ah no.

They were shutting the back door when Jimmy Sr came out.

—Wha' kept yeh?

—I was havin' a glass o' wine with Mona.

—Is she alrigh'?

—She's grand; not a bother on her.

He waved two tenners at them.

—How's tha', he said. —An' this as well.

He held out a pound coin for Bimbo.

—Your tip, he said. —She says thanks very much. Go on; take it. ——D'yis know wha' the row was abou'? said Jimmy Sr when they were all in the van, heading home.

—Wha'?

—His pigeons shitein' on her washin', said Jimmy Sr.

—Ah, is that all?

—She's not a bad-lookin' bird, Mona, said Jimmy Sr. —If she tidied herself up a bit. Sure she's not?

Bimbo and Darren didn't say anything. Jimmy Sr wished he'd kept his stupid mouth shut. Darren was blushing beside him; he could nearly feel the heat off him, and he was blushing now himself as well. Bimbo had his mouth in a whistle but there was no noise coming out.

* * *

Although they never ran out of ways of flogging their chips and stuff, closing time outside the Hikers was still their bread and butter. Dollymount was grand on a good, sunny day but on a rainy day or even just a cloudy one there wasn't a sinner down there to sell a chip to. And there were never going to be too many good, sunny days in an Irish summer; there was always rain coming at you from somewhere. But people coming out of the pub after a few jars didn't give a shite what the weather was like, they just wanted their chips and maybe a bit of cod with a nice crispy batter on it. Anyway, rain was never that wet when you were half scuttered.

The dinners-for-two with candles and wine hardly paid for themselves. They did them for the crack more than anything else. Bimbo did them to please Maggie, because the idea had been her brainwave, and Jimmy Sr went along with Bimbo.

Only she was always having brainwaves. Sometimes Jimmy Sr felt like telling her to give her fuckin' head a rest.

They came back from Dollier on a Monday late in July covered in sand and with damn all in the money box because there'd been showers on and off all afternoon, and she was there waiting for them, swinging off the front door, with her latest: breakfasts on the Malahide Road.

—You're jokin', said Jimmy Sr, once he knew what she was on about.

She wanted them to park the van at the crossroads in Coolock every morning and make rasher sandwiches for people driving to work.

—Wha' time?

—Half-seven.

—Jaysis —!

—Eight then; it doesn't matter. Durin' the rush hour.

—Look it, said Jimmy Sr. —Maggie. If they're in such a rush they're not goin' to be stoppin' for a rasher sandwich. Or even a rasher an' dunphy sandwich.

—There's plenty of people would love a rasher sandwich on their way to work, said Maggie.

—I know tha', said Jimmy Sr. —But they'll be goin' by us on the bus or they'll be at home in bed cos they're on the dole.

Bimbo was staying a bit quiet, Jimmy Sr thought; very fuckin' quiet.

—The only people who'd drive past that way, said Jimmy Sr, —is the yuppies. An' they can make their own fuckin' breakfasts as far as I'm concerned.

—You just don't want to get up early, said Maggie.

Jimmy Sr ignored this; he wasn't finished.

—Sure, Jaysis, he said. —No yuppie'd be caught dead eatin' a rasher sandwich on his way to work. Think about it.

——You could give it a try, Maggie said to both of them, but especially Bimbo.

—Hang on, said Jimmy Sr.

He wasn't dead yet; and he wasn't getting up at half-six in the morning.

—How far is it from Malahide to town? he asked them. —Abou'?

—Five miles, said Bimbo.

—Abou'?

—Yeah.

Jimmy Sr looked to Maggie to give her a chance; she agreed with Bimbo.

—Five miles so, said Jimmy Sr. —A bit more maybe. It's not very far, is it now? You're not goin' to get hungry travellin' five miles only. Unless you're goin' on your hands an' knees.

—The airport road then, said Maggie. —That'd be better.

They'd be comin' from much further on tha' one. Drogheda, and Dundalk – and —

—Belfast, said Bimbo.

—That's righ', said Maggie. —Well —?

——I'm on, said Bimbo. —Jim?

He'd no choice.

—Okay. —— Just promise us one thing, he said. —If it works, don't make us go ou' later an' make their fuckin' tea for them as well.

* * *

It didn't work. Jimmy Sr made sure it didn't.

—Come here, he said to Bimbo.

They were on the new airport road. It was seven o'clock.

—D'you want to do this every mornin'?

—Wha'? said Bimbo.

—Don't start, said Jimmy Sr. —Do yeh?

—Wha'?

—Want to get up before the fuckin' seagulls every mornin'. Do yeh?

——No.

—Righ'; park over there then.

—Where?

—There.

—Under the bridge?

—Yeah.

They stayed there on the motorway, under the flyover, for an hour and a half. They opened the hatch and all; they didn't cheat. They made three rasher sandwiches, and Jimmy Sr ate two of them and Bimbo ate the other one, and a Twix each as well. They shouldn't have been there but the guards never came near them. They leaned out over the hatch and watched the cars and the trucks blemming past. Then they shut the hatch and went home.

—Not a word, Jimmy Sr warned Bimbo.

—No, said Bimbo. —No.

Jimmy Sr enjoyed getting back to the fort that morning. He let Bimbo do the talking.

—Where did yis park it? she asked him.

—Just there, in Whitehall, said Bimbo. —At the church; where yeh said.

—And no one stopped at all?

—That's righ', said Bimbo.

—No one even slowed down, said Jimmy Sr.

—Ah well —, said Maggie.

That was all; it was grand. Maggie wasn't pushy or a Hitler or anything; she was just a bit too fuckin' enthusiastic.

Bimbo and his kids ate nothing except rashers for two weeks after that, and Maggie brought Wayne and Glenn and Jessica and the other two kids into Stephen's Green in town and they fed seventeen large sliced pans to the ducks.

* * *

Bimbo and Maggie were the ones in charge; Jimmy Sr couldn't help thinking that sometimes. Not just Maggie; the both of them.

It wasn't that they ordered him about or anything like that – they'd want to have fuckin' tried. It was just, he was sure they talked about business in bed every night, and he wasn't in bed with them. There was nothing wrong with that; it was only natural, he supposed. He'd have been the same if it'd been Veronica. But sometimes he felt that they'd their minds made up, they'd the day's tactics all worked out, before he rang their bell.

He felt a bit left out; he couldn't help it.

When Maggie'd announced the dinners for two with wine and candles Bimbo didn't say anything but Jimmy Sr could tell that he knew about it already. He didn't stand beside Maggie and nod like he'd heard it all before, but he didn't ask her any questions either: he didn't have to. He might even have come up with the candles bit himself. It was the type of romantic shite that Bimbo always fell for.

But, again, there was nothing wrong with it; it was a good

idea. It wasn't any less of an idea just cos he hadn't thought of it himself, or because he hadn't been around when Maggie'd thought of it. And anyway, even if he didn't like it, there was nothing he could do about it. He could stay downstairs and watch the telly in Bimbo's till they were finished riding each other or whatever the two of them did when they went to bed and then go up and get in between them and have a chat for a couple of hours, but he couldn't see them agreeing to that.

There was another day; Jimmy Sr was going to play pitch and putt, against Sinbad McCabe. It was the Hon Sec's Prize he was playing him in, and Sinbad McCabe was the Hon Sec himself, and Jimmy Sr hated the cunt. So he really wanted to win it, to beat the bollix in his own cup. He was getting a few sandwiches into him – not rasher ones, mind you – and a bowl of soup, and psyching himself up at the same time. There were two things Jimmy Sr hated about Sinbad McCabe, two main things: the way he always waited till the Hikers was full before he filled in the results on the fixtures board, like it was the Eurovision fuckin' Song Contest he was in charge of, and the way you could see the mark of his underpants through his trousers. There were other things as well but they were the big two. Jimmy Sr was going to look at Sinbad's underpants lines before he took a shot; it would help him concentrate. He wouldn't talk to him either, not a word, and he'd stand right up behind him when Sinbad was putting, as close behind as he could get without actually climbing into his trousers. He was telling Veronica and Sharon this when Bimbo came in.

—What's keepin' yeh? said Bimbo.

—Are yeh comin' to watch me? said Jimmy Sr.

He wasn't sure he wanted Bimbo along with him for this one. Bimbo was too nice to everyone. He'd be chatting away to McCabe and all Jimmy Sr's work would be wasted.

—Wha'? said Bimbo.

He'd come down to hurry Jimmy Sr up; they were bringing the van to Dollier. Maggie and himself had looked out the window, seen all the blue in the sky, and stocked up the van. Only Jimmy Sr hadn't been with them, so he didn't know anything about it. They just expected him to hop. It wasn't fair. It wasn't right.

It upset him. He still beat Sinbad McCabe though.

Another thing he'd thought about a few times, and he couldn't make up his mind about it, if it was important or not: Bimbo had bought the van. Jimmy Sr'd been there beside him when he did it, but Bimbo'd paid for it. He hadn't paid much for it; he didn't think it mattered – he wasn't sure. He didn't feel guilty about it. Maybe he should have given Bimbo his half of the cost of the van. He had the money now. He was welcome to it. What would happen if he did that though? Probably nothing; he didn't know. He'd think about it, maybe talk to Veronica about it. He didn't want to do anything that would mess everything up. At the same time, he was no one's skivvy. Partners was the word Bimbo'd used at the very start, in the Hikers the day they'd pushed the van to Bimbo's. Maybe it was time to remind him of that. He didn't want to hurt Bimbo's feelings though, or even Maggie's. He didn't know.

He'd think about it.

* * *

It was great knowing there'd be money there when he put his hand in his pocket; not that he'd much time to spend it. He could go up to the Hikers whenever he wanted, if he wanted to. He sometimes got the paper in the mornings and brought it into the pub and had a quiet pint by himself but it always smelt of last night and polish and the smell that old hoovers left behind them. Except on Saturdays and Sundays; they were better.

He bought himself a suit, a grey one. Veronica liked it. She even came down to the Hikers with him the first Sunday he wore it. It wasn't flashy, and he didn't wear a tie although he'd bought one of them as well.

—Nice suit, compadre, Bertie said.

—Must have cost yeh a few bob, was what Paddy said, but you wouldn't have minded him.

Bimbo didn't say anything but he was wearing a new suit himself the next Sunday, so he must have been impressed, or Maggie'd been.

They were thinking of getting a car; they'd always had one before, or a van, but they'd always had something. Veronica was putting money away.

—We'll have a decent Christmas this year annyway, wha', he said when himself and Veronica were out having a walk alongside the seafront.

—Jimmy.

—Wha'?

—It's August.

—Yeh know what I mean, he said, but they laughed.

They all went to the zoo. Darren and the twins wouldn't come, but the rest of them did; Jimmy Sr and Veronica, Sharon and Gina, and Jimmy Jr and his mot, Aoife. They'd a great day. Gina didn't give a fuck about the animals; she just wanted to go on the slide all day. Jimmy Sr and Jimmy Jr laughed their way around the place. Aoife laughed at nearly everything they said, but especially when Jimmy Sr said that the hippo smelt like Veronica's mother used to, and Veronica agreed with him. She was a lovely girl, Aoife; lovely. They'd a picnic with them. Jimmy Jr slagged Jimmy Sr because he wouldn't sit on the grass cos he'd his new suit on him.

They had a few drinks in the Park Lodge Hotel after the zoo. It was nice in there, after Jimmy Jr got them to turn the telly down. When they were thinking of going home Jimmy Sr ordered a taxi for them, and they went home that way, in style.

—Honk the horn, said Jimmy Sr when your man, the taxi driver, was stopping at their gate.

—Do not, said Veronica.

They all got out while Jimmy Sr settled up with the taxi fella; eight fuckin' quid, but he said nothing, just handed it over to him. It was only money. He made sure he got the right change back off him though. Then he gave him fifty pence.

—There yeh go, said Jimmy Sr. —Buy yourself a hat.

Jimmy Jr wanted to give him half the taxi fare.

—Fuck off ou' o' tha', said Jimmy Sr. —Put it back in your pocket.

—Are yeh sure?

—'Course I'm sure.

He spoke quieter now.

—I remember when I was skint an' you helped me ou'; I remember tha'.

—Can I have it back? said Jimmy Jr.

They laughed up the hall, into the kitchen, and they wouldn't tell the women what they were laughing about.

* * *

It was past midnight, and hectic – mad. They were sliding all over the place but they'd no time to wipe the floor. They were used to it by now, like sailors. Sharon was with them tonight and even she was sweating through her clothes.

—My Jaysis, said Jimmy Sr.

He was getting ready to say what he wanted to say. Himself and Bimbo were at the fryer and the hotplate trying to keep up with Sharon as she called the orders back to them. Bimbo was chasing an onion ring that kept ducking away from the tongs.

Jimmy Sr wiped his brow with his arm.

—D'yeh know wha'? he said.

Here went.

He chuckled first so it would sound right, half a joke.

—This place should be called Bimbo and Jimmy's Burgers, he said.

—No, said Bimbo, very – too fuckin' quickly.

Jimmy Sr's heart was pounding.

—It wouldn't sound righ', said Bimbo.

—Yeah, Jimmy Sr agreed with him. —You're righ'.

—Too long, said Bimbo.

—Exactly, said Jimmy Sr. —I wasn't serious —

—I know tha', – still —
—No, you're righ'.

*   *   *

—You've been great pals for years, said Veronica.
Jimmy Sr nodded.
That was true. Still was.
He nodded again.
—You should try to make sure that it stays that way, said
Veronica. —The two of you.
Jimmy Sr kind of laughed.
—Don't worry, love, he said. —Anyway, it's not Bimbo
really ——I don't know. It's her.
Veronica said nothing.

*   *   *

Darren got out of the way just in time. Jimmy Sr was carrying
a brown bag that was already soggy; the arse was going to fall
out of it. He'd got his timing wrong; he'd stuck the cod and
the spice-burger into the bag but when he went to get the
chips there were none left, so while he was putting a new
batch into the fryer and waiting for them the cod had got out
of the batter and was soaking the bottom of the bag. But he
hadn't time to change it. It was getting mad outside again, and
it wasn't even dark yet; small gangs of kids had a way of
making it seem like they were big gangs of kids. There were
only about six waiting to be served but they were all shouting
at the same time, and pushing and changing their positions. It
was another hot airless bastard of a night, worse than last
night.
—Two cods, a spice, three large, Jimmy Sr checked with
the young ones who'd ordered them.
—Yeah, she said, like she'd been waiting all day for them.
He slammed in the salt and vinegar and closed the bag.
—A single an' a—
—Wait your turn! said Jimmy Sr.
He turned to Darren and Bimbo.

—One o' yis get over here.

He turned back to the young one.

—There, he said, and he handed her the bag.

—I'm not takin' tha', she said.

—What's your problem? said Jimmy Sr.

—The bag, said the young one. —It'll burst before I get it home to me house.

Jimmy Sr couldn't argue with her; she was right.

—Jesus wept!

He turned to get another bag and bumped into Bimbo. There was no damage done.

—Will yeh watch where you're fuckin' goin'!

—You watch where you're goin' yourself, said Bimbo.

—Where's Darren gone?

—Over to Flemings for water.

—He's no use to us over there, said Jimmy Sr.

Bimbo took over at the hatch.

—Yourself, he said, pointing at a kid.

—Single.

—Annythin' else?

—No.

—One single, Bimbo shouted over his shoulder, into Jimmy Sr's face. —Sorry.

Jimmy Sr handed out the new bag to the young one.

—There now, he said. —Let's see your money.

The young one looked under the bag before she handed over the pound coins, five of them. The coins were warm.

—Your hands are sweaty, Jimmy Sr told her.

—So's your bollix, said the young one, and she just stood there waiting for her change, not a bother on her. She was only about twelve. She stared up at him.

They were all laughing outside.

He took twenty-five pence out of the box. He thought that that was what he owed her, he wasn't sure.

—There, he said.

—'Bou' time, she said, and she shoved back, to get through the crowd.

She was replaced by a young fella with a pony tail.

—Righ', Geronimo, said Jimmy Sr.

—Me name's not —

—Okay, said Jimmy Sr. —Wha' d'yeh want?

—Curry chips.

—We don't do them.

—Why don't yis?

—Our chips are too good, son, Jimmy Sr told him.

—Wha'?

—We wouldn't insult our chips by ruinin' them with tha' muck, said Jimmy Sr. —They only use curry sauce cos their potatoes are bad, to hide the real taste. Now there's some inside information for yeah.

He was beginning to feel better. Bimbo went back to the hotplate and the fryer. It was about time he did a bit of real work, instead of just hiding in the corner with the fish.

—So, said Jimmy Sr. —Will ordin'y chips do yeh, or wha'?

—Okay, said the young fella. —They'd better be good though.

Jimmy leaned back and took a chip from the rack.

—How's tha' look? he said, and he held up the chip.

They all cheered. There were more of them outside now, about twenty, all of them kids.

—Yeow! Yeh man, yeh!

—They're not chips! a high-pitched young fella in the crowd shouted. —They're potato mickies!

—Gis a bag o' them! said the young fella with the pony tail.

—One single! Jimmy roared back at Bimbo.

Darren was back, with three full milk bottles.

—Wha' kept yeh? said Bimbo.

—I had to negotiate, Darren told him.

Jimmy Sr chose his next customer.

—You with the head, he said.

—A large an' a dunphy.

—Large an' a dunphy! Jimmy Sr roared.

—She was watchin' Jake and the Fat Cunt when I rang the bell, Darren told Bimbo.

—Oh oh, said Bimbo.

Missis Fleming had cut off their water supply before, when Jimmy Sr rang the bell during Coronation Street and then knocked on the front-room window when she hadn't answered fast enough for him. They'd had to buy her a box of Terry's Moonlight chocolates, and get Maggie to deliver them, before she'd given them the right of way again.

—A large, a smoked an' a spice! Jimmy Sr roared. —An' hurry up with the large an' the dunphy!

Darren filled a bag with chips and fished a spice-burger out of the fryer.

—He said a dunphy, Bimbo told him.

—It's not for him, said Darren. —It's for Missis Fleming.

He jumped out the back.

—Where's he gone now? said Jimmy Sr. —For fuck sake. We can't let that oul' bitch hold us to ransom. Two large, a bun an' a dunphy —— Stop pushin' there; you'll turn us over.

He turned back to Bimbo.

—Why can't she just get a key cut for us, like I said to her? —— Two 7-Ups with tha' last one, righ'.

Bimbo was struggling; he could tell.

Good.

Jimmy Sr lobbed in the salt and vinegar, closed the brown bag and handed it out to a young fella.

—One, eh, eighty.

—An' a Twix, said the young fella.

Jimmy Sr got the Twix and went back to the hatch and the young fella'd fucked off without paying. They were all laughing outside. Jimmy Sr had to laugh as well.

—Did yeh see tha'? he asked Bimbo.

—Wha'?

—Mister Rabbitte; here – !

—No skippin' the queue just cos yeh know me name.

—Fuck yeh.

—You're barred.

—He's after barrin' Anto, said another young fella. —He'll get his da after yeh, Mister Rabbitte.

—He can get his ma after me if he likes, said Jimmy Sr.

They cheered.

—Mind you, said Jimmy Sr. —His da's better lookin'.

—Haaaa!

They were having a great time.

—He'll definitely get his da now.

—Let him, said Jimmy Sr. —I'll let the air ou' of his wheelchair.

He turned to see what was keeping Bimbo. Bimbo was holding a spice-burger over two bags; he didn't know which was which.

—D'yeh want to swap? said Jimmy Sr.

—No! said Bimbo. —No. —— Yeah.

Jimmy Sr spoke to his customers.

—I'll have to leave yis now, I'm afraid, he told them. —We're a bit understaffed in the kitchen.

—Bye bye, Mister Rabbitte.

—Good luck now, said Jimmy Sr.

He made room for Bimbo.

—There yeh go, he said. —Make sure yeh get their money off them before yeh hand over the goods.

He'd enjoyed that, and the bit of fresh air coming through the hatch had done him the power of good. He slapped on a burger, for himself; he deserved it.

—Batter burger, large, Coke! Bimbo roared.

—I hear yeh, said Jimmy Sr.

He didn't know how anyone could eat those batter burgers; they were disgusting. You could leave one of them swimming around in the fryer for hours and the meat would still be that pink colour and you'd want a chisel to get through the batter. You were dicing with death eating one of those things. Still, they were big though, very good value. He lowered it very carefully into the fat. It was like launching a ship.

Darren was back again.

—Is she happy now? Jimmy Sr asked him.

—Yeah, said Darren. —Sort of.

—Piss on her chips the next time, said Jimmy Sr.

He passed a brown bag back to Bimbo.

—Batter burger, large.

—A Coke as well, Bimbo reminded him.

—That's righ', said Jimmy Sr.

He bent down and got a can from under the hotplate, making sure that his head didn't go too close to it. He wiped the grease off the can with Darren's T-shirt and handed it to Bimbo.

—From the back o' the fridge, he said.

—Two five, Darren told Bimbo.

—Two pound an' fivepence, Bimbo told the young fella at the hatch.

—I've on'y two pounds, said the young fella.

Jimmy Sr took the bag from Bimbo when he heard that. He opened it, got the batter burger out and took a huge bite out of it, and let the rest of it drop back into the bag. He shut the bag, and shoved the chunk of batter burger over to the side of his mouth.

—Two pound, he managed to say, and held the bag out for the young fella.

—Jaysis!! Did yeh see wha' he done!

Bimbo grabbed the bag from him.

—It's all yours, said Jimmy Sr.

They went mad outside.

Jimmy Sr chewed the burger into manageable bits. It wasn't that bad. He went back to his post and turned his burger. Darren was dipping the bits of cod into the fryer, to set the batter. He was laughing as well.

—That's revoltin', he told his da.

—They don't taste tha' bad, said Jimmy Sr, —if yeh don't look at them first. Oh, I forgot but, you're a vegetarian; that's righ'. I suppose yeh think I'm a cannibal, Darren, do yeh?

—No, said Darren. —I just think you're a fuckin' eejit.

They laughed. Jimmy Sr spat the rest of the meat out the back door. His real burger was ready. He didn't bother with sauce.

God, he felt good now.

—Large, smoked! said Bimbo.

—That's your department, Darren, said Jimmy Sr.

The meat was a good safe brown colour.

—Tha' looks better now, doesn't it? he said before he put the top half of the bun on it.

—Small! Bimbo shouted.

—D'yeh not like the smell? he asked him.

—No! said Darren. —Jaysis.

—Yeh must, said Jimmy Sr.

—I don't.

——I don't know ——, said Jimmy Sr.

He'd leave Darren alone. He passed a bag back to Bimbo.

—Large, smoked.

—One eighty-five, said Darren.

It was getting dark now. Darren turned on the lamps.

Jimmy Sr handed another bag back to Bimbo.

—Small.

—Fifty-five, said Darren.

—I know tha'! said Bimbo.

Jimmy Sr nudged Darren.

—I'm not tha' thick, said Bimbo.

—Yeh fuckin' are! said someone outside.

Darren knew the voice.

—Nappies Harrison, he told Jimmy Sr.

Jimmy Sr went to the hatch.

—Nappies Harrison! he shouted. —You're barred.

They cheered.

—Yeow, Nappies!

—Which one o' yis is Nappies? said Jimmy Sr when they'd settled down a bit.

—Here he is, Mister Rabbitte.

They picked him up, his pals, the lads that played with Darren for Barrytown United.

—Fuck off messin'! Nappies shouted.

They hoisted him up over their heads and shoved him through the hatch. He held onto the sides like Sylvester the

565

Cat but one of the lads took his shoe off and hit Nappies' knuckles with it.

—Aaah!! Fuck yeh! —— That's me guitar hand!

—It's your wankin' hand!

Bimbo saved the salt and vinegar and got out of the way. He wasn't impressed.

—For God's sake!

Nappies tumbled over the counter, over the spilt salt and the grease. His foot sent the menu board flying. He'd have landed inside on his head if Jimmy Sr hadn't caught him under his shoulders and held him up till he got his feet off the counter.

Nappies shoved his shirt back into his trousers.

—Look at Nappies' sunburn!

—Give him a job, Mister Rabbitte.

Nappies turned to face the lads outside. He took the red sauce bottle from Bimbo.

—Yaah! Yis cunts, yis!

He squeezed the bottle with both hands before Bimbo could get it back off him; gobs of ketchup rained down on the lads. The van shook. A half-empty can came in through the hatch. It hit no one but it made an almighty bang when it hit the wall and scared the shite out of Bimbo. It dropped onto a shelf and into the fryer and sent a wave of oil onto the floor.

—Oh good Jaysis —!

—Here! Jimmy Sr roared, keeping his head well down in case of more cans. —None o' tha'!

—Come on, Bimbo said to Nappies. —Out. It's gone too far. Ou'; come on.

Nappies didn't need to be pushed.

—I didn't ask to come in here, he said. —I was thrun in.

He slid on the oil.

—Jaysis!

He grabbed at the hotplate to hold himself up, but Darren knocked his hand away and he went on his arse, right into the oil.

—Get up, said Bimbo.

566

Nappies ignored him. He thought he was being cooked. He spoke to Darren.

—What'll I do?

Darren held his hands out for Nappies. He kept his feet out of the oil. Nappies' hands slid out of Darren's. Nappies looked terrified when that happened. He tried to sit up. Darren grabbed his sleeves and dragged him off the oil, to the door.

—Thanks, Darrah.

Nappies was now standing up and looking healthier, ready to start giving out about the state of his clothes. Bimbo was trying to fish the Coke can out of the fryer.

—Everythin's ruined, he said.

He could feel the oil under his runners. He gave up on the can and looked at the floor.

—Bloody bowsies, he said, and he threw a J-cloth onto the floor. —Yeh shouldn't encourage them.

—We want Nappies! We want Nappies!

The lads outside had gathered again.

Jimmy Sr stood at the hatch again.

—What's he worth to yis? he asked.

—Twopence!

Nappies didn't go out the way he'd come in. He was going to, but Jimmy Sr sent him back to the door.

—Oh yeah —

—Mind the oil there, said Bimbo. —Look it.

Nappies climbed down the steps backwards and slowly, because the oil had made his trousers soggy and it was horrible and warm.

—Seeyeh, Darren, he said.

—Good luck, Nappies, said Darren.

He was down on his hunkers squeezing the J-cloth over the chip bin.

There was no one left outside. Jimmy Sr let down the hatch door till they fixed up the mess.

They'd only the one J-cloth, and it was lifting very little of the oil.

—This is crazy, said Darren.

—It's disgraceful, said Bimbo.

—D'yeh think so —? said Jimmy Sr —

The next thing either of them said could have started a fight, so they said nothing.

It was terrible; the only noise was the shoes on the oil, and the breathing. Then Jimmy Sr remembered something.

—Did yeh ever see Cocktail, Darren? he asked.

—Are yeh jokin' me? said Darren.

—I watched it with Linda an' Tracy there earlier, said Jimmy Sr. —They've seen it thirteen times.

—That's just because Tom Cruise flashes his arse in it, Darren told him.

—Does he? I don't think he does, does he? I must've gone to the jacks —. I thought it was quite good, meself.

He saw Darren's face.

—It was shite, he explained. —But good shite, yeh know. ——The routines. Behind the bar. Between Tom Cruise an' your man from Thornbirds. They were fuckin' gas. ——Did yeh see any o' them, Bimbo?

The first stone hit the van before Bimbo could answer. It smacked the side over the hotplate, full on. The next one skimmed off the roof.

—Jesus —!!

Jimmy got the door shut.

The next one shook the hatch door.

The Living Dead were outside. They hadn't done this for a good while, more than three weeks. Jimmy Sr had forgotten that they did it.

—The cunts.

Darren knew them. Lar O'Rourke had been in his class in primary school. They knew he was in the van.

The next one hit the side again. Flakes of paint fell on top of the oil.

There was nothing they could do. They'd just have to wait till they stopped. They never did much real damage; they'd never broken the windscreen or the side windows.

The next one was lobbed onto the roof. It made the loudest

568

bang, and the rock stayed on the roof. Sometimes it wasn't rocks they threw; it was used-up batteries from their ghetto-blaster. All they ever played was UB40; nothing else, ever.

Jimmy Sr sang.

—NEARER MY GOD TO THEE —

He didn't lose his temper any more; there was no point.

Another one rolled across the roof.

They'd just have to sit it out. Only they couldn't sit on the floor because of the mess. They had to stand, away from the walls.

—Some nigh', wha', Jimmy Sr said to Bimbo.

—Yeah, said Bimbo. —I hope —

The stone nearly came through the wall.

—Good fuck! said Jimmy Sr.

He touched the dent beside the hatch.

—Someone ou' there's eatin' his greens, wha'.

That was the last one, but it was hard to tell.

* * *

They were in the front room.

—FOR GOODNESS SAKE —

I GOT THE HIPPY HIPPY SHAKE —

—Fuck; sorry, Darren.

He'd dropped the Kandee Sauce bottle again.

Darren pushed the Pause button.

Jimmy Sr couldn't get the hang of the sauce bottle. The vinegar was grand; his hand fitted around it properly. It was easy enough to catch. The sauce, though, was a fucker.

Jimmy Sr got the dollop of sauce up off the carpet, most of it. He licked his finger.

—Ready? said Darren.

—Hang on, said Jimmy Sr.

He rubbed the carpet and the stain faded and went. It was grand.

—Righ', said Jimmy Sr.

He'd the vinegar in his left hand and the sauce bottle in his right. He stood beside Darren, a few feet away, to be on the safe side.

—Fire away, Darren.

Darren lifted the Pause button.

—YEAH —

I GOT THE SHAKE —

I GOT THE HIPPY HIPPY SHAKE —

—Vinegar!

They threw up their vinegar bottles

—I GOT THE HIPPY—

And caught them, together.

—Yeow!

They laughed.

—WUUU —

I CAN'T SIT STILL —

—Sauce!

They did it; the bottles landed back down flat in their right hands.

—YEAH —

I GET MY FILL —

—The both of them!

—NOW WITH THE HIPPY HIPPY SHAKE —

And Veronica came in and caught them.

Darren managed to catch his two bottles but Jimmy Sr lost his concentration completely; he seized up and the bottles went down past his hands and onto the floor. The vinegar stayed there but the sauce bounced and rolled over and some of the goo on the nozzle came off on the carpet. Darren smacked the Pause button.

It took Veronica a while to say anything. She was more surprised than they were. The two of them were in shorts and T-shirts, holding vinegar and ketchup bottles. Maybe they'd been juggling.

That would have explained the ketchup she now saw on the ceiling.

—Ah no, look —!

—Wha'? —— Where? —— Jaysis, how did tha' get up there?

—I don't know what you two messers are up to —

—We're not messin', Veronica, Jimmy Sr assured her. —It's business.

—Well, you can do it somewhere else, said Veronica.

She saw the carpet now.

—I don't believe it —

And now the smell of the vinegar hit her as well.

—It's a routine for the van, Jimmy Sr explained. —We were workin' on it.

He followed Veronica's eyes.

—Don't worry abou' them, he told her. —They'll wash ou'.

Veronica was looking at the marks on the curtains.

—Get out, said Veronica. —Get out; go on. You bloody big eejit, yeh, she said to Jimmy Sr.

She just looked at Darren.

—Come on, Darren, said Jimmy Sr. —We'll go ou' the back, an' leave Veronica alone.

Darren wanted to say something to his mother; not Sorry – he didn't know what.

—Bring the yoke, Darren, said Jimmy Sr. —We'll be ou' the back, Veronica, if anyone calls. —— Will I open the windows for yeh there? It might get rid o' the smell —

—No, said Veronica. —Go on.

Darren unplugged the twins' ghettoblaster. He turned it on quickly to check if the batteries were working.

—SHAKE IT TO THE —

Yeah; they were grand.

There was only his mother in the room now, but he still couldn't say anything. He got out the door and followed his da through the kitchen.

He'd left the cassette cover behind him, on the couch. Veronica picked it up.

Cocktail, she read. Original Motion Picture Soundtrack. There was a picture of a nice-looking lad on the front. His mouth was shut but she was sure he had lovely teeth. She read inside to see who he was. Tom Cruise. So that was what he looked like; the twins were always going on about him.

She studied the damage again. It wasn't too bad. The curtains needed a wash anyway. A damp cloth would get rid of the ketchup on the ceiling. Darren could do that.

She went back to the kitchen; she wanted to see what they were at.

—FOR GOODNESS SAKE —

I GOT THE HIPPY HIPPY SHAKE —

YEAH — I GOT THE SHAKE —

She turned on the cold tap and filled the sink although she wasn't going to do anything with the water. She just wanted an excuse to be at the kitchen window.

—WUUU —

I CAN'T SIT STILL —

—Vinegar!

She looked.

They were standing out there, side by side, legs apart.

—WITH THE HIPPY HIPPY SHAKE —

They caught the bottles.

—Yahaa! said Jimmy Sr.

Darren looked around to see if anyone was looking over the hedge at them, and behind him into the field. There wasn't anyone, as far as Veronica could see. There was bound to be someone looking out a window though; there always was. Poor Darren.

—WELL I CAN SHAKE IT TO THE LEFT —

—Concentrate now, Darren.

—I CAN SHAKE IT TO THE RIGHT —

—Sauce!

—I CAN DO THE HIPPY SHAKE-SHAKE —

The sauce bottle hopped off Jimmy Sr's palm but he managed to catch it before it hit the ground, then got back into place.

—WITH ALL OF MY MIGHT —

OOOOOHH —

572

Darren was quite good at it, streets ahead of the other fool. They threw up both bottles and Darren did a complete spin, in time to catch them. His shorts fitted him as well. Jimmy Sr's were up at the back and down at the front, holding his belly up like a sling.

She turned off the tap.

—FOR GOODNESS SAKE—

She lowered her arms into the water – it was nice – and looked out. She wished Sharon was here, or even the twins; they'd have loved it. Darren flipped the vinegar over his shoulder, and caught it.

—Stop showin' off.

He saw her looking at him; Jimmy Sr did. She looked into the water. She lifted a hand and dropped it, as if she was doing something at the sink.

—YEAH — I GOT THE SHAKE —

I GOT THE HIPPY HIPPY SHAKE —

It got darker. She looked up. She jumped back: Jimmy Sr had his face squashed up to the window. Cold water got through her blouse. She screamed, and laughed. His nose was crooked and white against the glass. He was miming to the Georgia Satellites.

—OOOH I CAN'T SIT STILL —

He kissed the glass. She saw Darren behind him, looking around to see if anyone was looking. Veronica rapped the glass.

—Go away. You're smudging the glass.

—Ah, fuck it, said Jimmy Sr.

But he lowered himself from the ledge and backed into the garden still miming, with his hand clutching his crotch.

SHAKE IT TO THE LEFT —

SHAKE IT TO THE RIGHT —

DO THE HIPPY HIPPY SHAKE —

He turned, and dropped his shorts and wriggled. God, he was terrible. Poor Darren was bright red.

—WITH ALL OF YOUR MIGHT —

—Pull up your trousers! Veronica shouted.

Darren pointed something out to her. She leaned over the sink and saw Mary Caprani, two gardens down, hanging off her clothes-line and gawking in at Jimmy Sr's war dance. Veronica thought she'd fall, the laughing took all her strength. She was bent completely over the sink, her face was against the tap, but she couldn't get up. The face on Mary Caprani; she'd been waiting years to see scandal like this.

Darren tapped Jimmy Sr's shoulder and showed him Mrs Caprani.

Jimmy Sr ran for the back door and tried to rescue his shorts at the same time. He fell into the kitchen.

—Jaysis, Veronica! Did yeh see Radar Caprani lookin' at me?

—Never mind her, said Veronica. —She's probably just jealous.

—Jaysis, said Jimmy Sr.

He was sitting on the floor. He lifted his T-shirt, pulled in his stomach and looked down at his marriage tackle.

—Maybe you're right, he said.

Veronica's blouse was drenched. She'd have to get out of it.

The Satellites were still blemming away outside.

Jimmy Sr grabbed the hem of her skirt when she was getting past him. He joined in with the band.

—I CAN'T SIT STILL —

WITH THE HIPPY HIPPY SHAKE —

He put his head in under her skirt.

—Mammy, Darren's playin' our ghetto —

Linda ran into the kitchen.

—Jesus!

Jimmy Sr came out from under the skirt.

—Get ou'!

Linda ran, and so did Veronica.

* * *

—They didn't understand, Jimmy Sr told Veronica.

They were in bed. The light was out. Jimmy Sr had been telling Veronica about the Cocktail routine.

574

—They thought we were messin', doin' it for a laugh.

Veronica sighed. She'd thought that as well. She had to say something.

—I'm sure they didn't, she said.

—They did, said Jimmy Sr. —Maggie did annyway. She wouldn't've just gone back into the house if she hadn't of.

—Well, explain it to her.

—I will not. Why should I?

Veronica sighed again, harder this time; a different sort of sigh.

—It's not my fault if she doesn't recognise a good fuckin' marketin' strategy when she sees it, said Jimmy Sr.

—You're working yourself up again, Veronica told him. — You won't be able to sleep again.

—Ah lay off, will yeh. —— You're as bad as she is. —— Veronica ——. ——Don't start pretendin' you're asleep; come on —— Veronica? ——

*   *   *

—Get out o' me fuckin' light, will yeh, said Jimmy Sr.

Then he sort of saw himself, a narky little bollix, the type of little bollix he'd always hated. But at nearly the same time he felt better, and clearer: he'd had an idea.

—D'yeh know wha' we need, Bimbo? he said.

It was half-ten about, outside the Hikers.

He waited for Bimbo to stop what he was doing, opening bags and setting them up in little rows on the counter.

—Wha'? said Bimbo.

—A night on the batter, said Jimmy Sr.

Bimbo looked over at the pile of fish.

—Not tha' sort o' fuckin' batter, said Jimmy Sr. —Tha' just shows yeh we've been workin' too hard if yeh can't remember wha' a night on the batter is.

Bimbo didn't laugh.

—Are yeh on? said Jimmy Sr. —It'll do us good. Wha' d'yeh say?

—Righ', Jim. Okay.

575

—Good man, said Jimmy Sr.

He clapped his hands.

—We'll have a fuckin' ball.

—That's righ', said Bimbo.

They both laughed now.

Jimmy Sr wanted to check that Bimbo had picked him up right.

—Just the two of us, wha'.

—That's righ'.

—Into town, said Jimmy Sr. —Will we go into town?

—Jaysis —

—We may as well, wha'.

—Okay. —— Where in town?

—Everyfuckin'where.

They laughed again.

* * *

They wore their suits in; Jimmy Sr insisted. They were in the Barrytown DART station now. It was a horrible damp grey shell of a place with plastic wobbly glass in the doors, and a smell. He got the tickets and his change from the young fella behind the glass, a big thick-looking gobshite, and when he turned back he saw Bimbo trying to figure out the timetable on the wall.

—There's one in a minute, Jimmy Sr told him.

—No, said Bimbo. —It's the last one I'm lookin' for, to see wha' time it is.

—Never mind the last one, said Jimmy Sr.

He got Bimbo and shoved him through the door out onto the platform.

There was a fair gang on the southbound platform; a bunch of young fellas near the end probably dodging their fare, a few couples, a family that looked like they were going to visit someone in hospital.

—There's a fine thing over there, said Jimmy Sr. —Look it.

There was a young one by herself on the northbound with a

red mini-skirt and a tan and hair that made her head look three times bigger than it should have been.

—Oh yeah, said Bimbo.

—She must be goin' ou' to Howth, said Jimmy Sr.

—Wha' for? said Bimbo.

—The fish, said Jimmy Sr.

There were some things that Bimbo hadn't a clue about. Jimmy Sr could see him deciding if she was really going out to Howth to buy fish.

—I'd say she's meetin' her boyfriend or somethin', said Bimbo.

—Maybe he's a fisherman, said Jimmy Sr.

The DART was coming.

—Here we go, said Jimmy Sr. —Is there a duty-free shop in the last carriage?

Bimbo laughed.

Thank fuck, Jimmy Sr said to himself. He'd been starting to think that Bimbo had lost his sense of humour from leaning over the deep fat fryer for too long.

The trip into town was grand. A scuttered knacker and a couple having a row kept them entertained as far as Connolly. Their carriage was full of dolled-up young ones. And Bimbo began to get more relaxed looking. Things were looking up.

—What's keepin' the cunt? said Jimmy Sr when the train stopped for a minute at the depot behind Fairview Park. —Me mouth's beginnin' to water.

—So's mine, said Bimbo. —There's a few people are goin' to have to go without their chips tonigh', wha'.

—No harm, said Jimmy Sr.

The train staggered, and got going again.

—We're off again, said Jimmy Sr. —'Bout fuckin' time.

It was going to be a great night; he could feel it now. He was liking Bimbo again, and Bimbo liked him. He was leaning in closer to him, shoulder to shoulder, the two of them together. Away from the van, and Maggie, and the pressure and the rows and all the rest of the shite, they'd have their couple of pints and a good laugh, get locked, and they'd be back to normal, the way they used to be; the way they'd stay.

Bimbo started to get up when the train crept into Connolly.

—Sit down there, said Jimmy Sr.

—Wha'?

—We're gettin' off at Tara.

—Oh.

—We'll have a few in Mulligans first, Jimmy Sr told him.

—Oh, very good.

—The best pint in Dublin.

—So I've heard.

Jimmy Sr knew where he was bringing them; he had a kind of a plan.

By the time they got past the ticket collector they were really excited and they ran around the corner to Mulligans, pushing each other for the mess, and they nearly got knocked down by a fire engine when they were legging it across Tara Street.

—Ring your fuckin' bell! Jimmy Sr yelled after it, and he ran after Bimbo, into Mulligans.

There were two women climbing off their stools when Jimmy Sr found Bimbo at the bar.

—Were yeh keepin' them warm for us, girls? said Jimmy Sr.

One of them stared at him.

—We're not girls, she said.

—That's true, said Jimmy Sr when she'd gone past him.

They got up on the stools. Jimmy Sr rubbed his hands.

—Hah hah!

—Here we are, said Bimbo.

—That's righ', said Jimmy Sr. —An' here's the barman. Two pints, please.

It was a bit awkward sitting in the suits. You had to sit up straight; the jackets made you. And you couldn't just park your elbows and your arms on the counter when you were wearing your good suits; they made you kind of nervous. Still though, they'd need them for later.

578

—Wha' did you think of your women? said Jimmy Sr.

—Eh —

—Lesbians, I'd say.

—Ah, no.

—I'd say so. Did yeh hear her? We're not girls.

—Tha' doesn't mean —

—Not just tha'. Drinkin' in here, by themselves yeh know. Like men. Here's the pints, look it.

The pints arrived, and Jimmy Sr had an idea. He stood up and got his jacket off and folded it, put it on the stool and carefully sat on it.

—That's better. ———— My God, that's a great fuckin' pint. —— Isn't it?

Most of Bimbo's was gone.

—Lovely.

—A great fuckin' pint.

—Lovely.

They had two more great fuckin' pints, then Jimmy Sr got them up and out before they got too comfortable in there. They put their jackets back on, went for a slash (—The first one's always the best) and headed off for somewhere new.

—Where? said Bimbo.

Doyle's, Bowe's, the Palace; two pints in each of them. They were new places to Bimbo, and to Jimmy Sr although he'd walked past them and had a look in. He'd promised himself that if he ever had any money again he'd inspect them properly. And here he was.

—Good consistent pints, he said. —So far anyway.

—Very good, yeah.

They were in the Palace, standing up against the wall, near the door cos there was no room further in. The women were a disappointment, not what he'd imagined. They were hippyish, scrawny women. He'd expected a bit of glitter; not in Mulligans – they'd gone in there strictly for the pints – but in the other ones. That was why they were in the Palace now, in town, in their suits. Jimmy Sr wanted something to happen.

Maybe they should have gone to Howth. Still though, it was good to be just out, with Bimbo, away from everything.

—Yeh finished? he said to Bimbo.

—Are we goin' already?

—This place isn't up to much. Yeh righ'?

—Okay, said Bimbo. —You're the boss.

That's right, Jimmy Sr thought while he waited for Bimbo to get the last of his pint into his mouth; I am the boss.

It had always been that way.

They went outside and it was nice and cool.

—This way, said Jimmy Sr.

Jimmy Sr had always been the one who'd made the decisions, who'd mapped out their weekends for them. Jimmy Sr would say, See yeh in the Hikers after half-twelve mass, and Bimbo would be there. Jimmy Sr would put down Bimbo's name to play pitch and putt and Bimbo would go off and play. Jimmy Sr had rented the pair of caravans in Courtown a couple of years back and the two families had gone down in a convoy and stayed there for the fortnight.

—Where're we goin' now? said Bimbo.

—Somewhere different, said Jimmy Sr. —Wait an' see.

—I'm dyin' for a piddle.

—Fuck off complainin'.

There were huge crowds out, lots of kids—they were on Grafton Street now – big gangs of girls outside McDonalds. Not like the young ones in Barrytown; these young ones were used to money. They were confident, more grown up; they shouted and they didn't mind being heard – they wanted to be heard. They had accents like newsreaders. They'd legs up to their shoulders. Jimmy Sr did a rough count; there were only about three of them that weren't absolutely gorgeous.

This was more like it.

—There aren't any pubs up here, are there?

—Shut up.

* * *

Bimbo wanted to get out; Jimmy Sr could tell. He was murdering the Budweiser, guzzling and belching at the same time to get rid of it so they could go. Jimmy Sr wasn't going anywhere yet though. He hated this place, and liked it. It was crazy; himself and Bimbo were the only two men in here who needed braces to hold up their trousers and they were the only two not wearing them. They were also the only two that weren't complete and utter fuckin' eejits, as far as he could see. There was lots of loud laughing, at fuck all. The women though – not all of them that young either.

The crowd kind of shuffled and there was a pair of women beside Bimbo and Jimmy Sr, by themselves. Jimmy Sr nudged Bimbo.

—I don't like your one, he told Bimbo, although he did like her.

—Wha'? said Bimbo.

—Your women there, said Jimmy Sr.

—What abou' them?

—Back me up, said Jimmy Sr. —Howyeh, he said to the one nearest him.

—Oh, she said. —Hi, and they climbed back into the crowd, the two of them, the wagons.

—Stuck-up brassers, said Jimmy Sr. —One o' them was as bandy as fuck, did yeh notice?

But it was a start; he felt great.

He grinned at Bimbo.

—Wha' did yeh think of your women? he said.

—Wha' d'yeh mean?

—Don't start. Did yeh like them?

Bimbo was squirming.

—Did yeh?

—Eh —— they were nice enough —

—Nice enough? If—if Sophia Loren came up to yeh an' stuck her diddies in your face would you say tha' she was nice enough?

But he was happy enough.

A woman about his own age bumped into him.

—Mind yourself, love, he said.

—Sorry.

—No problem.

And she was gone but no matter. All he needed was a bit of practice. If she came back in an hour or so he'd get off with her no problem. Not that he'd want to get off with her. Or anyone really. He was just messing; seeing if he could click with a woman if he wanted to. He looked around.

—Over here, he said to Bimbo.

—Why? said Bimbo, but he followed Jimmy Sr. He didn't want to be left alone.

If all Jimmy Sr'd wanted to do was get a woman behind a wall and feel her up or even ride her he wouldn't have come all the way into town; there were plenty of women in Barrytown who'd have come behind the clinic with him; all he'd have to have done was buy them a few bottles of Stag and listen to their problems for a while and tell them that they were still good-looking women when they started crying. He knew them all, and some of them were still good-looking women. But he'd never even been tempted, and not because he'd have been afraid of being caught.

They were in the middle of the crowd now, not at the edge.

What he wanted was to see if he could manage a young one or one of these glamorous, rich-looking, not-so-young ones. He'd back off once he knew it was on the cards; actually getting his hole wasn't what he was after at all – he just wanted to know if he could get his hole.

—D'yeh want another drink, here, Jimmy? Bimbo asked him.

Maybe just the once he'd like to get the leg over one of these kind of women, only the once, in a hotel room or in her apartment, and then he'd be satisfied. Jimmy Sr had never been in a hotel room.

—'Course I do, Jimmy Sr said to Bimbo.

—Here though?

—Yeah, here. —— Only one more, righ'?

Bimbo nodded and slipped through to the bar.

Jimmy Sr smiled at a woman, over a little fella's shoulder. She smiled back quickly, just in case she knew him. Jimmy Sr waited for her to look over his way again, but she didn't. She was about forty but she was wearing a mini-skirt. The little fella must have been worth a fortune.

Bimbo was back.

—It's robbery in here, he said.

—You pay for the style, Jimmy Sr told him.

—Not after I've finished this I don't.

—Okay, okay. —— Watch it; brassers at six o' clock!

—Wha'?

—Howyeh, girls. D'yis need a drink?

They walked straight past him. They mustn't have known he was talking to them. They must have though; he spoke straight at them.

—Fuckin' bitches, he said. —Look at her. Her; your woman. With your man over there.

—Oh yeah.

—She's fuckin' gorgeous, isn't she?

—Yeah.

—She's got real bedroom eyes, said Jimmy Sr.

She was lovely looking alright.

—Yeah, said Bimbo.

—Bedroom eyes, said Jimmy Sr again. —An' a jacks mouth.

They laughed.

Bimbo's Budweiser was nearly gone.

—Are we goin'? he said.

—Yeah, said Jimmy Sr. —Okay.

Bimbo looked at his watch. It was after eleven.

—I could do with a proper pint, he said.

—Good thinkin' Batman, said Jimmy Sr. —Come on.

* * *

—D'yeh know how yeh click with women like tha'? said Jimmy Sr.

—How?

—Money.

—Ah yeah.

It was good to be back in a real pub.

Bimbo got two very healthy-looking pints and Jimmy Sr got two more immediately because it was coming up to closing time and Jimmy Jr had warned him that the city centre pubs were fuckers for shutting down on the dot of half-eleven.

They took over two low stools at a table.

—Yeah, said Jimmy Sr. —Nine ou' o' ten women, if they had the choice between money an' looks, they'd go for the money.

—What abou' Maggie an' Veronica?

—Not women like Maggie an' Veronica, said Jimmy Sr. —I'm not talkin' abou' women like tha'. Ordinary women, if yeh know what I mean.

He waited for Bimbo to nod.

—I mean the kind o' women we saw in tha' place back there. Stylish an' glamorous —

—I think Maggie an' —

Jimmy Sr stopped him.

—I know wha' you're going to say, Bimbo. And I agree with yeh. They are as good lookin'. But they're not like those brassers back there, sure they're not?

—No, said Bimbo. —Not really.

—Thank God, wha', said Jimmy Sr. —Can yeh imagine lettin' any o' them floozies rear your kids?

—God, said Bimbo.

Jimmy Sr sat up straight.

—But, let's face it, Bimbo, said Jimmy Sr. —They're rides, aren't they?

—Ah, I don't —

—Go on, yeh cunt. Admit it.

They laughed. That was good, Jimmy Sr thought. They weren't on their way home yet.

—That's the thing though, said Jimmy Sr, back serious. —Veronica an' Maggie. We're lucky fuckin' men. But —— they're wives. Am I makin' sense?

——Yeah.

—Those ones back there aren't. They might be married an' tha' but —— they're more women than wives, eh ——Fuck it, that's the only way I can say it.

—I know wha' yeh mean, said Bimbo.

Jimmy Sr felt so good, like he'd got something huge off his chest.

—Will I see if they'll give us another? he said.

—What abou' —?

—We'll get a taxi. Will I have a bash?

—Okay, said Bimbo. —Yeh'd better make it a short though, Jim. I'm full o' drink.

Jimmy Sr picked on the younger barman and managed to get two Jamesons out of him, and that made him feel even better.

—How's tha'?

—Fair play to yeh, said Bimbo. —Good man.

It was hard getting back down onto the stool, there were so many people around them, but Jimmy Sr did it without pushing anyone too hard. He was dying to get going again with Bimbo.

—Women like tha' —

He waited to see if Bimbo was following him.

—Women like your women go for money, Jimmy Sr told Bimbo. —They'll wet themselves abou' any ugly fucker or spastic just as long as they're rich.

—I don't know, said Bimbo.

—It's true, said Jimmy Sr. —Look at your woman, Jackie Onassis. You're not goin' to tell me tha' she loved your man, Aristotle, are yeh?

—She might've.

—Me arse. Sure, she had a contract an' all drawn up before they got married, guaranteeing her millions o' dollars; millions.

—Tha' doesn't mean tha' —

—An' Grace Kelly.

—Princess Grace?

—She only married Prince what's his fuckin' name cos he was a prince. An' Princess Diana as well.

—Wha' —

—She only married fuckin' Big Ears for the same reason.

—I always thought there was somethin' a bit odd about that' match alrigh'.

—I'm tellin' yeh, Bimbo, said Jimmy Sr. —There are some women would do annythin' for money. The women back there in tha' place would annyway.

—You could never respect a woman like tha', said Bimbo.

—No, Jimmy Sr agreed. —But yeh could ride the arse off her.

They roared.

—It's grand, said Jimmy Sr before they'd really finished laughing. —When yeh think abou' it. If you've money, that is.

——Yeah, said Bimbo. —I suppose. If you're interested in tha' sort o' thing.

—Who wouldn't be? said Jimmy Sr.

Bimbo didn't say anything, and that was good enough for Jimmy Sr. He had Bimbo thinking with his bollix.

The pub was beginning to empty. Jimmy Sr looked at his watch; it wasn't near midnight yet. It was good in a way, because now he could ask Bimbo the question.

—What'll we do now?

Bimbo looked around, like he was waking up.

—Wha' d'yeh mean?

—Where'll we go? said Jimmy Sr.

Bimbo looked at his watch.

——I suppose we'd better head —

—We can't go fuckin' home, said Jimmy Sr. —Not yet. Jaysis; it's our fuckin' big night ou'.

Bimbo was game, Jimmy Sr could tell, but lost. He let him speak first.

—Where can we go? said Bimbo.

—Somewhere where we can get a drink, said Jimmy Sr.

—Ah yeah, said Bimbo. —'Course.

Jimmy Sr spoke through a yawn.

—We ——we could try Leeson Street, I suppose; I don't know. —— Wha' d'yeh think? It might be a laugh, wha'.

Jimmy Sr's heart was loafing his breast plate.

So was Bimbo's.

——Would yeh get a pint there? he said.

—Yeh would, yeah, said Jimmy Sr. —No problem.

* * *

They were on their way.

—Hang on though, said Jimmy Sr out of nowhere. —Wha' colour socks are yeh wearin'?

They stopped. Bimbo looked down. He hoisted up a trouser leg.

—Eh —— blue, it looks like —

—Thank God for tha', said Jimmy Sr.

—Why?

—They don't let yeh in if you're wearin' white socks, he told Bimbo. —The bouncers don't. They've been told not to.

—Why's tha'?

—Don't know. Young Jimmy warned me about it. Wankers an' trouble-makers wear white socks.

—Wouldn't yeh think they'd cop on an' wear another colour? said Bimbo.

—Who?

—The wankers.

—True, said Jimmy Sr. —Still, that's wha' makes them wankers, I suppose.

—Yeah. Wha' colour are yeh wearin' yourself?

Jimmy didn't have to look.

—Not white anyway, he said.

* * *

They dashed to get into the gang of men going down the basement stairs. They were all pissed and loud, a few drinks away from being sick; business men, they looked like, about the same age as Jimmy Sr and Bimbo. The door opened; the ones in front said something to the bouncer; they all laughed, including Jimmy Sr, and they sailed in, no problem. It cost nothing, just like young Jimmy'd said.

—Thanks very much, Bimbo said when he was going past the bouncer.

—Shut up, for fuck sake! Jimmy Sr whispered. —Good bouncers can smell fear, he told Bimbo. —They're like dogs.

—I only said Thanks to him, said Bimbo.

—Ah, forget it, said Jimmy Sr. —Forget it.

They were in now anyway.

—Will we hand in our jackets? said Bimbo.

—No, said Jimmy Sr.

A suit without a jacket was just a pair of trousers; his jacket was staying on.

The wallpaper was that hairy, velvety stuff. This was a good sign, Jimmy Sr decided. There was something about it, something a bit dirty. He could feel the music in the floor-boards even before he turned into the dance and bar place. This was the business. He looked to see if Bimbo thought that as well, and caught him gawking into the women's jacks. Two women were standing at the door, one of them holding it open.

—Jesus Christ, Bimbo, d'yeh want to get us fucked ou' before we're even in?

—Wha'?

—Come on.

They were a right pair of bints, your women at the jacks door. Women like that didn't need to piss; they just went in to do their make-up.

The bar was three-sided; the barmen were done up in red waistcoats and dickie-bows, the poor fuckin' saps. It was hot. The dance-floor was over beyond the bar, not nearly as big as Jimmy Sr had imagined. The stools at the bar were all taken. Jimmy Sr led the way around the other side, nearer the dance-floor. There were tables further in, past the dance-floor; the mirrors made it hard to say how far the room went back. The only one dancing was a little daisy jumping around like her fanny was itchy. Every couple of seconds, when you thought you were going to get a goo at her knickers, she pulled down her skirt at the sides. She was very young.

—Are yeh havin' a pint or wha'? Jimmy Sr asked Bimbo.

Bimbo was looking at the young one dancing.

—Is there somethin' wrong with her? said Bimbo.

Good Jesus, there was the poor young one trying to make every man watching her come in their kaks and Bimbo wanted to know if there was something wrong with her!

—A pint? said Jimmy Sr.

—Not here, said Bimbo.

Jimmy Sr agreed with him; a pint of stout in this place would leave them pebble-dashing the jacks for the rest of the weekend.

—Budweiser, said Jimmy Sr.

—Grand.

He had to shout over the music.

There were two women at the bar, not too young and just good looking enough. Jimmy Sr got in between their stools.

—Sorry, girls.

He lassoed a barman on his way past.

—Two pints o' Budweiser, when you're ready!

—Wine bar only.

The barman looked like he'd said this before.

—Wha'?

—No beer or spirits. We've a wine licence only.

—Are yeh serious?

The barman didn't say anything; he just nodded, and went further down the bar.

—Good shite, said Jimmy Sr.

For a second he was lost. Bimbo was at his shoulder.

—Will he not serve yeh? he asked.

—He'll serve me alrigh', said Jimmy Sr. —Only he's fuck all that I want.

One of the women laughed. Jimmy Sr turned to her and grinned; it was that kind of laugh.

He was away here.

—Try the wine, said the woman.

Jimmy Sr stepped back a bit to let Bimbo stand beside him.

—Wha' would yeh recommend? he asked her.

—What's wrong? Bimbo asked him, right into his ear.

—Nothin', said Jimmy Sr.

He tried to use his eyes to point out the women to him but it wasn't easy.

—The house red's very nice, the woman told Jimmy Sr.

—Is tha' righ'? said Jimmy Sr. —Are yis drinkin' it yourselves?

—We are, yes, she said. —Aren't we, Anne Marie?

—Yeah, said her friend.

—That's grand so, said Jimmy Sr. —We'll have a drop o' tha'.

Jimmy Sr stepped back a bit more to include the friend, the one called Anne Marie, and he had a quick look at Bimbo to see if he'd copped on, and he had. He was gawking at Anne Marie.

—I'm Jimmy, by the way, he told the girls. —An' this is Bim —

He couldn't remember Bimbo's real name.

—Brendan, said Bimbo.

That was it.

—Brendan, said Jimmy Sr.

—Hello, Brendan, said the woman. —Well, my name's Dawn. And this is Anne Marie.

—Howyis, said Jimmy Sr.

He spoke to Anne Marie.

—Two names, wha'. Is one not good enough for yeh?

She didn't get it. He smiled to let her know he was only messing and turned back to Dawn.

—Better order the oul' vino, he said. —The house somethin', didn't yeh say?

He got in closer to Dawn – great fuckin' name, that – and gave Bimbo loads of room to manoeuvre for himself.

—The house red, said Dawn.

—Grand, said Jimmy Sr. —An' it's the business, is it?

—It's quite nice, said Dawn. —I think myself anyway. And it's quite reasonably priced.

—Never mind the price, said Jimmy Sr. —Let me an' Bim – Brendan worry abou' the price. Here!

He'd captured a barman.

—A bottle o' house red wine, like a good man.

This was great. They weren't bad-looking birds at all. Nicely done up; just the right side of brassy. Somewhere in their thirties. Dawn had the fine set of lungs on her, and her arse fitted nicely on the stool; there was nothing flowing over the sides. Her eyelashes were huge, but they looked real enough. He could see the dark roots in her hair; another couple of months and she'd look like a skunk. But she'd get her hair done again long before that happened. She took care of herself. She'd do grand.

There was something about Anne Marie as well though.

Bimbo edged in closer, but he wouldn't look at her for too long. He leaned on the bar.

The barman had come back with the wine.

—Just park it there, son, Jimmy Sr told the barman.

Anne Marie was fatter than Dawn; not fat though, no way. If he'd been standing right at the bar he'd have been able to see right up to her arse the way her legs were crossed. She was smoking one of those thin cigars. Her expression; it was like she didn't give a shite about anything. He was sure she went like a fuckin' sewing machine, certain of it.

—He wants to know do you want to taste it first, Dawn told Jimmy Sr.

—Fuckin' sure I do, said Jimmy Sr. —Pardon the French, Dawn.

He leaned past her, brushed against her – she didn't move back – and picked up the glass. There was only half a mouthful in it. He put his nose to the glass, and sniffed.

—Ah, yes, he said.

Dawn laughed.

—Very ginnick, said Jimmy Sr.

591

He took a sip, leaned back and gargled. Even Anne Marie laughed. He swallowed.

—A-one, he said.

He gave the barman the thumbs up.

—Pour away, compadre, he said. —How much is tha'?

—Twenty-three pounds, sir.

—Wha'?

He hadn't heard him.

—Twenty-three pounds.

——Grand —

My fuckin' Jesus —!

He handed over a twenty and a fiver. Thank Christ, his hand wasn't shaking.

—There yeh go, he said. —Keep the change.

—Thank you very much, sir.

—No problem.

If he didn't get his hole after forking out twenty-five snots for a poxy bottle of wine he'd ———— He looked at Bimbo; he looked like he'd got a wallop off a stun-gun. Jimmy Sr grinned and smiled at him, and winked. Bimbo smiled back. Dawn was pouring the drink. Jimmy Sr would have to go to the jacks in a bit to see how much money he'd left. It was a long walk home to Barrytown.

—Cheers, Jimmy.

Dawn was holding her glass up, waiting for the others to join in.

—Yes, indeed, said Jimmy Sr.

He picked up his glass. He had to shout over the music.

—Cheers, eh —— Dawn.

He laughed, and so did she.

They all clinked their glasses.

—Cheers, Brendan, said Jimmy Sr.

Bimbo looked to see who he was talking to, then remembered.

—Oh, thanks very much.

Twenty-five fuckin' quid. He could probably have got a wank in a massage parlour for that, and the fuckin' bottle was nearly empty already. He'd have to buy another one in a minute. He put his hand against the bar, across Dawn's back, just barely touching it. She stayed put. Anne Marie helped herself to another glass. She had the look of a dipso about her alright; another year and she'd be in rag order. The music was shite.

—Great sounds, said Dawn.

—Yeah, said Jimmy Sr. —Brilliant.

He nodded his head as he spoke cos it was very loud; the thump-thump-thump crap that young Jimmy used to play when he lived at home. She had to put her mouth up near his ear.

—Wha'? he said.

It was fuckin' ridiculous.

—Are the two of you out on the town for the night? she asked.

She was asking him were they married, Jimmy Sr reckoned.

—Ah no, he said. —No. ——Not really. This is nothin' special.

She nodded.

Maybe she didn't care. He put his hand in his pocket to adjust his gooter – the way she kept putting her mouth up to his ear – . Bimbo was chatting away to Anne Marie. Fair play to him. He'd thought that Bimbo might be a liability. But no, they were nodding and yapping away; he was doing his bit. Anne Marie had her glass leaning on her bottom lip. When Dawn turned to get her glass off the bar Jimmy Sr got his hand in under his gooter and yanked it into an upright position – and Anne Marie was looking at him. He pretended he'd spilt some wine on his trousers and he was inspecting them to see if there was a stain.

—What's wrong?

Dawn was looking at him now.

—Ah, nothin'.

He looked: Anne Marie was back looking at Bimbo, and the bulge was going. No harm. —He hoped it wasn't the drink. He was feeling a bit pissed now alright; that wine on top of all the pints.

Dawn got to his ear.

—What do you do, Jimmy?

—When I'm not here, d'yeh mean?

She laughed, and leaned back against his arm and stayed there.

—Self-employed, he told her. —Me an' Bren.

—Ver-y good.

—Caterin'.

—Good.

He could feel the heat coming off Dawn, he was right up against her. And there wasn't a bit of sweat on her. He wondered how she did it.

—It's great bein' your own boss, said Jimmy Sr.

—I'd say you're a tough boss to work for, Jimmy.

—No, said Jimmy Sr. —Not really now. I'm reasonable enough.

Dawn nodded.

—I don't take shite from annyone, Jimmy Sr told her —But once that's established ——yeh know.

The DJ was taking a breather, thank fuck. He'd put on a tape, but the noise wasn't half as bad. They could have a chat altogether now, and Jimmy Sr could keep an eye on Bimbo.

—Here!

—Yes, sir? said the barman.

—Another bottle o' house red wine, said Jimmy Sr. —How's it goin'? he asked Bimbo and Anne Marie.

—There y'are, said Bimbo.

Anne Marie was staring at Jimmy Sr, right into his face. He pretended she wasn't. Bimbo was grinning, like he always did when he'd more than ten pints inside in him, and swaying a bit, but not dangerously. The suit made him look less pissed than he was.

Jimmy Sr looked again. Your woman, Anne Marie, was still looking at him.

Then she spoke.

—Your complexions are very good, she said. —Considering.

—Considering what, Anne Marie? said Dawn.

—Where they work.

Bimbo! The fuckin' eejit!

—Where do they work? said Dawn.

—In a van, said Anne Marie.

He'd fuckin' kill him. Grinning away there!

He stayed close up to Dawn —— just to remember how it felt.

—Here's the wine, said Bimbo. —My twist. Twenty-three quid, isn't that it?

—They have a chipper van, said Anne Marie.

—That's righ', said Bimbo.

—Brendan's Burgers, said Anne Marie.

Bimbo and Anne Marie were holding hands.

—We're buildin' up a fleet o' them, Jimmy Sr told Dawn. —Wha' d'yeh do yourself, Dawn?

—Do you bring it to football matches and that sort of thing? She sat up, but she didn't seem to be trying to get away from him. Maybe it would be alright. He was still going to kill Bimbo though, the stupid cunt.

—Sometimes, said Jimmy Sr. —We stay local most o' the time. Our market research has shown tha' reliability is important.

He pushed Dawn's back with his arm, trying to get her to settle into him.

—The punters like to know tha' if they want a single o' chips all they have to do is go out their doors an' we'll be there outside to give them their chips.

—And do you actually make the chips and the burgers yourself?

—Sometimes, said Jimmy Sr, —yeah.

If he pushed against her back any more he'd shove her off the stool.

—Strange thing to do for a living really, isn't it?

—Not really, said Jimmy Sr. —I suppose it might —— eh —

This was fuckin' desperate; he was getting nowhere. He'd lose the rag in a minute.

Oh good shite! Bimbo was kissing Anne Marie! It wasn't fuckin' fair. Right up against her, her arms around him, moving up and down his back, then her hands into his hair.

He put his mouth up to Dawn's. She drew back.

—Now now, she said.

Like she had to cope with this all the time.

——Sorry —

Fuck it, he was a fool.

Bimbo and Anne Marie were chewing the faces off each other.

He wanted to cry, and go home. He pointed to Bimbo.

—His nickname's Bimbo, he told Dawn.

He felt really rat-arsed now. He nearly fell over. The arm behind Dawn was killing him but if he took it away that was it, over. He couldn't think of anything to say. He couldn't think. Something funny, anything. The taste of the Guinness was coming up his throat. Anne Marie bit Bimbo's ear.

Jimmy Sr went in on Dawn's mouth again.

—Stop that!

—Come on, said Jimmy Sr.

She pushed him away, well able for him; he was fuckin' hopeless.

Bimbo was going to the jacks. Anne Marie held him back and straightened his tie. Then he was gone, past Jimmy Sr.

Dawn didn't look angry or indignant, or anything. Like nothing had happened. She even smiled at him, the bitch.

He moved in again, and she pushed him away again. She pushed him back and picked up her glass at the same time.

—Fuck yeh! said Jimmy Sr, and he went after Bimbo.

The jacks was out the way they'd come in. Jimmy Sr shoved someone out of his way at the door and went in. He fell against the wall inside the door. There was another door. He got that open and there were four sinks and a big mirror in front of him. There was no one at the urinal. Bimbo must have been in one of the cubicles, getting sick with any luck.

There were three of them, two of them shut. He got over there and walloped both doors.

—Come ou', yeh cunt yeh!

One of them opened a bit when he thumped it. It wasn't shut at all; there was no one in there. Bimbo was in the middle one so.

—Come on; I know you're in there —

He gave the door a kick. Wood cracked.

—What's wrong with yeh? Bimbo said.

Jimmy Sr heard a zip going up and then the flush. He pushed against the door before Bimbo had it properly open. Bimbo didn't fall back, like Jimmy Sr'd wanted; he could do nothing right tonight. He kicked the door again.

—Get ou'!

—I'm tryin' to —

He saw half of Bimbo's face behind the door. He threw everything against it and it smacked Bimbo's face, and all of the violence went out of him.

He'd hurt Bimbo.

He wanted to lie down on the floor.

Bimbo came out and went over to the mirror. He had his hands over his forehead. Jimmy Sr followed him.

—Are yeh alrigh'?

Bimbo didn't answer.

He studied his forehead. There was a graze, and there'd be a lump. But there was no real damage.

—Sorry, Bimbo —— righ'?

Bimbo still didn't say anything.

——Are yeh alrigh'? —— Are yeh?

——It's no thanks to you if I am.

—Ah look it; sorry, righ'. —— I just lost the head —

Just now, that second, he couldn't even remember why. Then it came back.

—Wha' did yeh go an' tell them abou' the van for?

—Why shouldn't I have? She asked me what I did for a livin', so I told her.

—Well, yeh messed it up for me with your woman —

—How did I? said Bimbo. —You messed it up yourself. It's not my fault if – if she didn't like yeh, is it?

—I was away on a hack until you opened your fuckin' mouth —

—How did I?

—You told her abou' the fuckin' van, that's how.

—What's wrong with tha'?

——Ah —

Jimmy Sr didn't know how to answer.

Bimbo was looking at his forehead again.

—Is it not good enough for you now? Bimbo asked him.

—It's not tha' —

—It pays your wages, Bimbo told him.

Jimmy Sr was lost.

—If you don't want to work in it, said Bimbo, —you can leave any time yeh want to. —— An' good riddance.

—Ah look it – for fuck sake —

—I'm sick o' you an' your bullyin' —, sick of it —

They were sober and drunk, sober and drunk.

—You got off with your woman an' ——Sorry.

Bimbo slumped, like he'd nothing left to hold him up. Jimmy Sr went over and put his hand on his back.

—That's the stupidest row we've ever had, said Bimbo.

—Thick, said Jimmy Sr. —Fuckin' ridiculous.

——We'll go home, will we?

—Wha' abou' Anne Marie? said Jimmy Sr.

—I don't want —— Let's go home.

—Okay.

That was the best.

—Fair play to yeh though, said Jimmy Sr. —Anne Marie an' tha'.

Bimbo said nothing. Lucky they'd their jackets on them; they didn't have to go back.

The air was nice, nice and cold. It was heavy going getting up the steps. There was a chap passed out against the railings.

—Will yeh look at him, said Jimmy Sr.

Bimbo said nothing.

They walked down towards Stephen's Green.

—It was a terrible kip, said Jimmy Sr. —Wasn't it?

——They were teachers, said Bimbo. —The two o' them.

—Who? Dawn an' your woman —?

—Yeah. Teachers. —— Primary.

—That's desperate —

—They were married as well.

—No.

—Yeah.

Jimmy Sr slipped off the path, and got back on again.

—The filthy bitches, wha'.

They walked on. Jimmy Sr started to sing, to save the night.

—OHHH —

THERE'S HAIRS ON THIS —

AN' THERE'S HAIRS ON THA' —

Bimbo stopped to let Jimmy Sr come up beside him.

—AN' THERE'S HAIRS ON MY DOG TINE-EEE —

Bimbo joined in.

—AH — BUT I KNOW WHERE —

THE HAIRS GROW BEST —

Jimmy Sr put his arm over Bimbo's shoulders.

—ON THE GIRL I LEFT BEHIND ME.

They were at the corner. There was a taxi coming round with its light on. They stood, leaning into each other, till it came up to them.

It hadn't been a good night at all. It had been a fuckin' disaster. Jimmy Sr's head was starting to ache on and off.

They got into the back of the taxi.

—Barrytown, Jimmy Sr told the driver. —Soon home, he said to Bimbo.

—Yeah ——, said Bimbo.

He slouched down into the corner and looked out the window. Jimmy Sr did the same thing, on his side.

* * *

There was some sort of a riot going on downstairs. He was awake now. His head was killing him. His guts were groaning;

he'd be farting all day. The light behind the curtains wasn't too strong. That was good; they probably wouldn't be going to Dollymount in the afternoon. He needed a rest. He didn't want to see Bimbo. He shifted over to a cool bit of the bed. That was nice.

The racket downstairs though; they were all shouting and the dog was yipping away out of him. It didn't sound like a fight though. Maybe there'd been an accident. No; there was laughing as well.

He'd go down and investigate. He needed food inside him anyway if he was going to get back to sleep.

—Oh my fuck ——

He'd never make it down to the kitchen. He sat on the edge of the bed. —— Last fuckin' night –; God, he was a fuckin' clown. He slipped down till his head was back on the pillow and lay like that. For ages. And that was how Veronica found him.

—Look at you, she said.

She didn't sound annoyed, the way she usually did when she walked into the mix of drink and farts.

—Darren got his results, she told him.

—What's tha'?

—His Leaving results, said Veronica. —He got them.

Jimmy Sr tried to sit up.

—Well? he said.

—Seven honours, said Veronica. —Isn't that marvellous?

—Seven!?

—Yes!

—How many subjects was he doin', again?

—Guess, said Veronica.

—Seven, said Jimmy Sr. —Jesus, that's brilliant. —— Seven. He must've been the best in the school, was he?

He wished he felt better. Darren deserved better; the first Rabbitte to do his Leaving and his father couldn't even get up out of bed properly.

—Is he downstairs, is he?

—Yes. He's down there making coffee like nothing had happened, special.

—That's Darren. Cool as a —

He couldn't think —

—I'd better go down an' congratulate him —

He stood up and held onto the dressing-table.

—I got mine as well, Veronica told him.

That took a while to get through.

—Your results, said Jimmy Sr. —You did the Leavin' as well.

—I know, said Veronica.

—Yeh passed?

—Of course, said Veronica. —C in Maths and a B in English. Honours English, that is.

—Ah Veronica, he said. —That's brilliant.

—I'm thrilled.

—So am I, said Jimmy Sr. ——I'm very fuckin' hungover as well.

—You should be ashamed of yourself, said Veronica, but she didn't mean it – and that made it worse.

—We'll have to go ou' tonigh', said Jimmy Sr.

—Will you live that long? said Veronica; then —That'd be nice. What about your work?

—Fuck my work. I couldn't look at a chip. Sharon can fill in for me.

He got back to the bed.

—I'll have to congratulate Darren later, he said. —Sorry.

Veronica even made sure that the door didn't slam when she was leaving. He wouldn't sleep. There was too much —— Darren would be going to university now. He'd applied for Trinity, Jimmy Sr thought it was, to do something or other. University. For fuck sake. And Veronica – And he couldn't even get up to congratulate them. And last night —— He was a useless cunt. He groaned ——A complete and utter cunt ——

He'd bring Veronica out for a nice meal somewhere, the works; a bottle of house red wine and all.

He was still a cunt.

*   *   *

—It's for the best, Bimbo explained. —It's too messy the other way, so —— em; okay?

—— Okay, said Jimmy Sr.

He shrugged. He was afraid to say anything else. He didn't think he'd get through it.

—Okay.

Bimbo had just told him that from now on he'd be paying Jimmy Sr a wage. On Thursdays. Instead of the old way, the fifty-fifty arrangement.

—Will yeh have another pint? said Bimbo.

—No. —— No, thanks.

—Come on, yeh will. We're in no hurry. We've time for one more.

—— Okay.

—Good man.

* * *

He should have told him to stick his wages up his hole, that was what he should have done.

Veronica was fast asleep beside him, the selfish bitch.

No, that wasn't fair. She'd listened to him. She'd even told him to give up the van if he wanted to, she wouldn't mind.

He wouldn't do that though. He couldn't go back to what it had been like before they'd bought the van – before Bimbo had bought the fuckin' van. He couldn't do that; get rid of the video again, stop giving the twins proper pocket money and a few quid to Sharon, and everything else as well – food, clothes, good jacks paper, the few pints, even the dog's fuckin' dinner; everything. There was Darren as well now. How many kids went to university with fathers on the labour? No, he'd stick at it.

That was probably what Bimbo wanted him to do; give up. He probably had a cousin of Maggie's or somebody lined up to take over from him. Well, he'd be fuckin' waiting. He'd have to sack him first.

He wasn't going to call him Bimbo any more. Veronica was right; it sounded too cosy.

It was his own fault in a way; some of it. He should have bought the half of the van when he'd thought about it. Months ago. He'd thought he was cute, deciding not to bother; there was no need. He'd just been greedy. And now he was working in someone else's chipper van, like working in McDonalds or Burger King. Maggie was probably up at her sewing machine making one of those poxy uniforms for him.

He tried to laugh, quietly.

* * *

—Yes, sir, said Jimmy Sr.

—Ah stop tha', said Bimbo, —will yeh.

—Stop wha', sir? said Jimmy Sr.

Bimbo didn't answer. He lifted the chip basket out of the fat, shook it and dropped it back in.

* * *

Thursdays, he got paid. Like everyone else.

The second Thursday his pay was in one of the little brown envelopes wages always came in. He looked at it. His name was written on it.

——Where did yeh get the envelope? he asked.

—Easons, said Bimbo.

—Good man, said Jimmy Sr.

But Bimbo was busy in his corner mixing the batter.

Jimmy Sr stuck the envelope into his back pocket.

* * *

Bimbo was manning the hatch, and sweating.

—Two cod, two large! he shouted again.

He turned and saw Jimmy Sr, leaning against the shelf, pouring himself a cup of tea from his new flask. He was holding a sandwich between his teeth.

—Jimmy! said Bimbo. —For God's sake —

Jimmy Sr put down the flask and screwed the top back on it. Then he took the sandwich out of his mouth.

—I'm on me break, he told Bimbo.

Bimbo looked the way he did when he didn't know what was going on.

—I'm entitled to ten minutes' rest for every two hours that I work, said Jimmy Sr.

Bimbo still looked lost.

—I looked it up, said Jimmy Sr.

He saw that Bimbo's face was catching up with his brain.

Bimbo stood back from the hatch. Jimmy Sr took a slug of the tea.

—I needed tha', he said.

—Stop messin', will yeh, said Bimbo.

—I'm not messin', said Jimmy Sr. —I'm entitled to me break.

—Sure Jaysis, said Bimbo, —we did nothin' all nigh' except for a few minutes ago.

—Not the point, said Jimmy Sr. —Not the point at all. I was here. I was available to work.

—Hurry up, will yis!

That came from outside.

—I've five minutes left, Jimmy Sr told Bimbo. —Then I'll sweat for yeh.

—Just get us me fuckin' cod an' chips, will yeh!

Bimbo glared at Jimmy Sr.

Jimmy Sr looked back at him, through the steam coming up off his tea.

Bimbo went over and filled two bags with chips and got two cod out of the fryer. Jimmy Sr raised his arm to the small crowd outside and clenched his fist. But no one cheered or clapped or said anything. It was too cold and wet.

* * *

Jimmy Sr and Veronica had the front room to themselves. Jimmy Sr'd just been watching the News. Saddam Hussein was still acting the prick over in Iraq. Veronica had her coat on. She'd just come in; she'd been up at the school registering for more night classes – Leaving Cert History and Geography this time.

604

—Geography? Jimmy Sr'd said when she'd come in.
—That's great. You'll be able to find the kettle when you go
into the kitchen.

—Humour, said Veronica, imitating Darren.

—Fair play to yeh though, he'd said. —I should do somethin' as well.

They were talking about something different now though.
Jimmy Sr was going out to work in a few minutes.

—It's not too bad now, Jimmy Sr told Veronica.

—Good, said Veronica.

—I'm callin' him Bimbo again, said Jimmy Sr.

Veronica smiled.

—I still take me breaks though, said Jimmy Sr. —If I'm
goin' to be just a wage earner —

—You'll never be Just anything, Jimmy, don't worry.

—Ah Veronica, said Jimmy Sr. —You say lovely things
sometimes.

—Ah —

—Twice a year, abou'.

Veronica slapped him. Jimmy Sr leaned over and kissed her
cheek. It was still cold, from outside.

—I'm glad it's better, said Veronica. —It'd be a shame.

Jimmy Sr nodded and sighed.

——I can't get over it though, he said. —I wouldn't
mind —

He'd been telling her this for weeks now. She didn't mind
though; he was entitled to feel sorry for himself.

—but it was his idea in the first fuckin' place. To be his
partner – But there's no point in – It's done, wha'.

Veronica could still get upset thinking about him roaming
around the house, stooped and miserable, with nothing to do;
trying to smile at her; sitting on the front step watching the
girls go by and not even bothering to straighten up for them.
Only a few months ago. Waiting for him to creep over to her
side of the bed.

—I'll go, said Jimmy Sr.

—Right, said Veronica. —Come into the kitchen and I'll do your flask for you.

—Grand. Will I run up an' put the blanket on for yeh?

—Yes. Thanks.

They sat on the couch together for a little bit longer.

* * *

He dreaded climbing into the van. The worst part though was stocking it up, having to go through Bimbo's house, out to the back to the shed; that was fuckin' terrible. She was always there.

—How's Jimmy?

—Grand, Maggie. An' yourself?

The cunt, he hated her. It was easier than hating Bimbo. She was the one.

He paid for everything he took.

—I'm puttin' the twenty-seven pence in, okay?

He held the money over the box.

—Wha'? said Bimbo.

—I took a Twix, said Jimmy Sr.

He showed it to Bimbo.

—There's the money for it, okay?

He dropped it in.

—Ah, there's no need —

—No, said Jimmy Sr. —It's yours.

Bimbo fished the twenty-seven out and handed it back to Jimmy Sr.

—There's no need, he said.

—No, said Jimmy Sr. —It's yours.

And he left Bimbo standing there with his hand stretched out, and wiped the hatch counter. He heard Bimbo throwing the coins into the box.

He did the same thing with Maggie. He was going through the kitchen with a tray of cod. She was at the table cutting pastry into roundy shapes.

—There y'are, Maggie, he said, and he put the twenty-seven pence down on the table in front of her.

She looked up.

—I took a Twix, he told her, and he was out before she'd time to figure it out.

He hadn't taken a Twix at all.

It was enjoyable enough in a sad sort of way, acting the prick.

—Will I turn on the gas?

—Wha' d'yeh mean? said Bimbo.

—Will I turn on the gas? said Jimmy Sr.

They'd just parked outside the Hikers and climbed into the back. It was a very stupid question.

—I don't get yeh, said Bimbo, although Jimmy Sr saw that he was starting to smell a bit of a rat.

—D'yeh want me to turn on the gas? Jimmy Sr asked him.

—Wha' d'yeh need to ask me for? said Bimbo.

—Well, —— you're the boss —

—I'll turn it on meself!

He went too far sometimes, like asking Bimbo would he take the chips out of the fryer, would he put the chips into the fryer; he just fell into the habit of asking Bimbo's permission to do everything.

—You'll ask me can yeh wipe your arse next, said Bimbo once.

—No, I won't, said Jimmy Sr. —Me arse is me own.

It was at that moment – the way Bimbo had said it; the pretend annoyance in his voice – that Jimmy Sr realised that Bimbo was enjoying it, being the boss; like he was giving out to a thick lad, a thick kid he liked: he wasn't embarrassed any more.

* * *

He'd seen a photograph in the Herald of a field, like a football pitch with an embankment around it, with a sign at the side – Danger No Swimming. It wasn't a field. It was the Vartry reservoir, dried out. And the chap from the Corporation, the spokesman – the fella that used to be a runner for Ireland but never won anything – he said that there was a crisis because it was the mildest September on record. But Jimmy Sr was fuckin' freezing, and so was everyone else. He complained about it but he didn't mind it at all. The Dollymount business was over, so he'd most of the day to himself. He took Gina for walks. They brought the dog with them. He was still trying to teach Larrygogan to fetch a ball, after three years, but Larrygogan was either too thick or too intelligent to do it. Gina fetched the ball instead and Larrygogan went with her.

He'd the best of both worlds now; his days to himself and a job to go to later. He got a good wage on Thursdays, and he'd none of the responsibilities. The hours weren't bad, just a bit unsocial. He was a lucky fuckin' man; he had no problem believing that. He believed it.

So he really couldn't understand why he felt so bad, why at least a couple of times a day, especially when he was hungry or tired, he was close to crying.

* * *

He was lonely. That was it.

He was wide awake, lying on the bed, hands behind his head. He'd brought the little electric air heater up to the room with him – to read, he'd said – so he was grand and warm. It was about four o'clock, getting gloomy. He'd stretched back and opened the book but he'd drifted, awake but away from the book. The print was too small; it took too long to read a page. But he didn't blame the book. Maybe it was too warm. He lay back, not thinking, let himself wander. He didn't think about women, Dawn or ——. It was like his head got heavier and duller and then it burst out —

Lonely.

It was like he'd learnt something, worked it out for himself. He even smiled.

His eyes filled, the room and the things in it divided and swam, but he kept his hands behind his head. He had to blink. Then he could feel a tear climb out of his right eye and creep along the side of his nose. He lifted his head to see if it went quicker and blinked to feed it more water, and it went off his cheek down the side onto the pillow. Now he wiped his face; it was getting too wet. He didn't stop crying though.

He was safe enough up here.

* * *

There was a ball inside him, a ball of hard air, like a fart but too high up to get at. It nearly hurt sometimes. It made him restless, all the time. He squirmed. He sat on the jacks and nothing happened. Pressing made it worse. Hardened it more. He knew he was wasting his time but he went to the jacks anyway. And he knew there was nothing physically wrong with him, even though he could feel it. And he knew as well that he'd felt this way before; it was kind of familiar, definitely familiar. He couldn't remember exactly – . But when he'd noticed himself feeling this way, tight and small and exhausted, he'd recognised it immediately.

* * *

He chatted away to Bimbo on the way out to Ballsbridge. Shamrock Rovers were playing in their new ground, the RDS, against St Pats. It had pissed rain the night before – the first decent rain in Dublin for weeks – and again that morning, but it was clearing up nicely for the afternoon. The game was bound to be a cracker and there'd be a huge crowd there. They got a good space to park, up on the path on the river side of the Anglesea Road, and got into the back to get everything ready.

Jimmy Sr took out the letter and left it on the shelf when Bimbo wasn't looking. He took it back again – Bimbo still had his back turned – and opened it up a small bit so that Bimbo would be able to read the top part of the letter and see the letterhead. Then Jimmy Sr got down to work. If Bimbo picked it up or even just saw the top, grand; if he didn't Jimmy Sr'd stick it back in his pocket and keep it for another time.

But Bimbo saw it alright.

Jimmy Sr's face glowed, and not from the heat coming up

off the fryer. He saw Bimbo twist his head a bit so he could read the letter without moving it.

He said nothing.

Jimmy Sr left the letter there. He looked at it later himself the way Bimbo had, when Bimbo was busy at the hatch – trying to add up the price of two large cod and a spice-burger, the fuckin' eejit. He couldn't see much of it, only the letterhead and the Dear Mr Rabbitte and half the line under that. It was enough though.

They were waiting now for when the crowd came out after the game.

—Pissed off an' hungry, said Jimmy Sr.

—D'yeh want to go into the match? Bimbo asked Jimmy Sr.

—No; fuck tha'.

—It'll be a cracker, I'd say.

—How will it? said Jimmy Sr. —They're only fuckers that aren't good enough to play in England.

—Ah now —

—You'd see better in St Annes, said Jimmy Sr.

Jimmy Sr had the Sunday World with him and he gave half of it to Bimbo; the inside half, the kids' and the women's pages and the pop stuff and the scandal from Hollywood, the stuff he never bothered reading himself.

They didn't talk.

Jimmy Sr opened his window a bit. It was only a bit after four, more than an hour before the crowd would be coming out. He sighed.

—D'yeh mind waitin'? Bimbo asked him.

—I don't care, said Jimmy Sr. —It makes no difference to me. Just as long as I'm paid, I'll sit here for the rest of the season. It's your money.

—You'll be paid, don't worry, said Bimbo.

—I'd fuckin' better be, said Jimmy Sr, but not too aggressively; messing.

Bimbo kind of laughed.

Then Jimmy Sr thought of something.

—Double time.

—Wha'?

—Double time for Sundays, said Jimmy Sr.

—Now, hang on here —

—Sundays an' bank holidays. Time an' a half for all other overtime.

Bimbo's voice was very loud.

—Who says this is overtime? he said.

—There's no need to shout, said Jimmy Sr. —I can hear yeh.

—How d'yeh mean Overtime?

—That's better.

—Well?

—Well wha'?

—Abou' this overtime.

—What abou' it?

—Well —

Bimbo started again.

—Are yeh doin' this out o' spite; is that it?

—No!

—Well, it sounds like tha' to me.

—I'm just lookin' after me welfare, said Jimmy Sr. —That's all I'm doin'.

—Welfare!? said Bimbo. —Yeh get paid, don't yeh? Well paid.

—I earn it, said Jimmy Sr.

—Yeah, said Bimbo. – But why d'yeh suddenly think you're entitled to —

—That's it, said Jimmy Sr. —I AM entitled to it. I am entitled to it, he said again before Bimbo got the chance to say anything back. —I work seven days a week as it is.

—Not days —

—Nights then. That's worse.

Jimmy Sr kept his eyes on the paper and pretended that he was still reading.

—Seven nights, he said. —How many does tha' leave me? Eh, wait now till I think, eh —— None.

He snapped the paper and stared down at A Little Bit Of
Religion.

—An' now I'm havin' to give up me Sunday afternoons as
well, he said.

—You'll get paid —

—You're the boss, said Jimmy Sr. —I'll go where I'm told
but I'm not goin' to be exploited, d'yeh hear me? I want me
overtime.

—Who's exploitin' yeh —?

—You are. If yeh don't pay me properly.

—I do pay yeh —

—There's laws, yeh know. We're not in the Dark Ages
annymore. —— I should be at home with Veronica. An' the
kids.

Bimbo waited a bit.

—Is tha' wha' tha' letter's abou'? he then asked.

—Wha' letter?

—The letter inside, on the shelf.

Jimmy Sr bent forward and felt his back pocket, looking for
something.

—The letter from the Allied something —— the union, said
Bimbo.

—Have you been readin' my letters? said Jimmy Sr.

—No! I just saw it there.

The letter had been Bertie's idea. He'd got the name and
address for Jimmy Sr from Leo the barman and Jimmy Sr'd
written off to them, the Irish National Union of Vintners,
Grocers and Allied Trade Assistants, asking how he'd go about
joining up. He'd got a letter back from them, inviting him in
for a chat. He kept it in his back pocket. He wasn't thinking
of joining. He had no time for unions. He'd been in one for
years and they'd never done a fuckin' thing for him. They
were useless.

—It'll be ammo for yeh, compadre, Bertie'd said.

It was a smashing idea. They'd burst their shites laughing.
And he was right, Bertie; the letter had been ammunition, like
a gun nearly, in his back pocket.

—You've no righ' to be readin' my letters.

—It was just lyin' there.

—Where?

—Inside on the shelf.

Jimmy Sr felt his back pocket again, and looked at Bimbo like he'd done something.

—Is tha' what it's abou'? said Bimbo.

—It's none o' your business what it's abou'. It's private.

—You don't need to be in a union, said Bimbo.

—I'll be the best judge o' tha', said Jimmy Sr; then quieter, —Readin' my fuckin' letters —!

—I didn't read it.

—Why didn't yeh tell me when yeh found it?

—I didn't know you'd lost it.

Jimmy Sr leaned forward, to see out if there was more rain coming.

—Are yeh really joinin' a union? said Bimbo, sounding a bit hurt and tired now.

Jimmy Sr said nothing.

—Are yeh?

Jimmy Sr sat back.

——I'm just lookin' after meself, he said. —An' me family.

Bimbo coughed, and when he spoke there was a shake in his voice.

—I'll tell yeh, he said. —If you join any union there'll be no job here for yeh.

—We'll see abou' tha', said Jimmy Sr.

—I'm tellin' yeh; that'll be it.

—We'll see abou' tha'.

——If it comes to tha' —

—We'll see.

Bimbo got out and went for a stroll up and down the road. Jimmy Sr turned the page and stared at it.

* * *

He'd gone down to the shops himself instead of sending the twins down – they wouldn't go for him any more, the bitches

– and got them sweets and ice-creams, even a small bar of Dairymilk for the dog. It had been great, marvellous, that night and watching the dog getting sick at the kitchen door had made it greater. Even Veronica had laughed at the poor fuckin' eejit whining to get out and vomiting up his chocolate.

—Just as well it wasn't a big bar you bought him, Darren said.

It had been a lovely moment. Then Gina waddled over to rescue the chocolate and she had her hand in it before Sharon got to her. Jimmy Sr wished he'd a camera. He'd get one.

They'd had a ride that night, him and Veronica; not just a ride either – they'd made love.

—You seem a lot better, Veronica said, before it.

—I am, he'd said.

—Good, she'd said.

—I feel fine now, he'd said. —I'm grand.

—Good, she'd said, and then she'd rolled in up to him.

But it hadn't lasted. Even the next day his head was dark again; he couldn't shake it off. When Darren came into the front room to have a look at Zig and Zag on the telly, Jimmy Sr's jaw hurt. He'd been grinding his teeth. He snapped out of it, but it was like grabbing air before you sink back down into the water again.

He kept snapping out of it, again and again, for the next two days. He'd take deep breaths, force himself to grin, pull in his stomach, think of the ride with Veronica, think of Dawn. But once he stopped being determined he'd slump again. His neck was sore. He felt absolutely shagged. All the time. But he tried; he really did.

He was really nice to Bimbo, extra friendly to him.

—How's it goin', and he patted his back.

He whistled and sang as he worked.

—DUM DEE DEE DUM DEE DEE —— DUM——DEE —

But, Christ, when he stopped trying he nearly collapsed into the fryer. You're grand, he told himself. You're grand, you're alright. You're grand. You're a lucky fuckin' man.

But it only happened a couple of times, the two of them

feeling good working together. And it wasn't even that good then because they were nervous and cagey, waiting for it to go wrong again.

It was like a film about a marriage breaking up.

—The cod's slow enough tonight —

Bimbo saw Jimmy Sr's face before he'd finished what he'd been going to say, and he stopped. Jimmy Sr tried to save the mood. He straightened up and answered him.

—Yeah, – eh —

But Bimbo was edgy now, expecting a snotty remark, and that stopped Jimmy Sr. They were both afraid to speak. So they didn't. Jimmy Sr felt sad at first, then annoyed, and the fury built up and his neck stiffened and he wanted to let a huge long roar out of him. He wanted to get Bimbo's head and dunk it into the bubbling fat and hold it there. And he supposed Bimbo felt the same. And that made it worse, because it was Bimbo's fault in the first place.

Darren wouldn't work for them any more.

—It's terrible, he explained to Jimmy Sr. —You can't move. Or even open your mouth. —— It's pitiful.

——Yeah, Jimmy Sr almost agreed. —Don't tell your mother, though. Just tell her the Hikers pays better or somethin'.

—Why d'you keep doin' it, Da?

—Ah ——

And that was as much as he could tell Darren.

—But mind yeh don't tell your mother, okay.

—Don't worry, said Darren.

—It'd only upset her, said Jimmy Sr. —An' there's no need.

There was just the two of them in the van now, except maybe once a week when Sharon was broke or doing nothing better. She wasn't as shy as Darren.

—Wha' are youse two bitchin' abou'? she asked them one night after Jimmy Sr had grabbed the fish-slice off Bimbo and Bimbo'd muttered something about manners. (It had been building up all night, since Bimbo'd looked at his watch when he answered the door to Jimmy Sr, just because Jimmy Sr was maybe ten minutes late at most.

—Take it ou' of me wages, he'd said.

—I didn't say annythin', said Bimbo.

——Me bollix, said Jimmy Sr, just over his breath. And so on.)

Neither of them answered Sharon.

—Well? she said.

——Ask him, said Bimbo.

—Ask me yourself, pal, said Jimmy Sr.

—Jesus, said Sharon. —It's like babysittin' in here, so it is. For two little brats.

And she slapped both their arses.

—Lay off—!

But she slapped Jimmy Sr again, messing. He had to laugh. So did Bimbo.

—How was it tonight? Veronica asked him when he got into the scratcher and his cold feet woke her up.

—Grand, he said.

* * *

Jimmy Sr looked at Bimbo sometimes, and he was still the same man; you could see it in his face. When he was busy, that was when he looked like his old self. Not when he was hassled; when he was dipping the cod into the batter, knowing that time was running out before the crowds came out of the Hikers. In the dark, with only the two lamps lighting up the van. A little bit of his tongue would stick out from between his lips and he'd make a noise that would have been a whistle if his tongue had been in the right place. He was happy, the old Bimbo.

That wagon of a wife of his had ruined him. She'd taken her time doing it, but she'd done it. That was Jimmy Sr's theory anyway. There was no other way of explaining it.

—Look it, he told Bertie. —She was perfectly happy all these years while he was bringin' home a wage.

616

—Si —, said Bertie in a way that told Jimmy Sr to keep talking.

—She was happy with tha' cos she thought tha' that was as much as she was gettin'. Does tha' make sense, Bertie?

—It does, si. She knew no better.

—Exactly. ——Now, but, now. Fuck me, she knows better now. There isn't enough cod in the fuckin' sea for her now. Or chips in the fuckin' ground; Jaysis.

—That's greed for yeh, compadre.

—Who're yeh tellin'.

It was good talking to Bertie. It was great.

—It's her, said Jimmy Sr. —It's not really Bimbo at all.

—D'yeh think so? said Bertie.

—Ah yeah, said Jimmy Sr. —Def'ny.

—I don't know, said Bertie. —Yeh might be righ'. —— Would you let your mot rule yeh like tha'?

—No way.

—Why d'yeh think he does then?

——She's different, said Jimmy Sr after a bit. —She's pushier. She's ——It wouldn't happen with Veronica, or Vera. He's soft, there's that as well —

That was what he believed; that night. You couldn't be one of the nicest, soundest people ever born and suddenly become a mean, conniving, tight-arsed little cunt; not overnight the way Bimbo had; not unless you were being pushed. He knew what she'd said to Bimbo; he could hear her saying it, —It's either me or him; something like that. The van or Jimmy Sr.

Bimbo was opening up chips bags, getting his fingers in, spreading them inside and flicking the opened bag off them onto the shelf above the fryer. It was tragic.

Other times, he just hated him.

* * *

He missed him.

Bertie was great company but Bertie was Bertie. Bertie didn't need anybody. He was as hard as fuckin' rock. Bertie could entertain you all night and listen to your troubles all night but Bertie could never have been your best friend. Bertie didn't need a best friend.

Jimmy Sr wasn't like that though. He wished he was, but he wasn't. When Bertie wasn't around – and he wasn't around a lot – Jimmy Sr never missed him; he didn't feel a hollow. But he missed Bimbo and the fucker was standing beside him shaking the chips.

*   *   *

—Yeah? said Jimmy Sr.

He put the salt and sauce to the side, out of his way.

—Eastern Health Board, said the man outside.

Jimmy Sr was bending to point him to the clinic, beyond the shopping centre, when he noticed the piece of plastic the man was holding up. It was a white identification card. Jimmy Sr didn't take it. He stood back.

He didn't look like an inspector. He looked ordinary.

Then Jimmy Sr remembered; he wasn't the boss.

—There's someone here wants yeh, he told Bimbo.

It wasn't his problem. His heart got faster, then slowed. But his throat was very tight, like something big was coming up. It ached. His face tingled; he felt a bit guilty. That wasn't on though; it wasn't his problem.

Bimbo rubbed his hands on his trousers to get the flour off them as he came over to the hatch. He looked at Jimmy Sr and out at the man, then looked worried.

It was Friday evening, coming up to the Happy Hour; getting dark.

Bimbo rubbed his hands and made himself smile.

—Yes, sir? he said. —Wha' can I do for you?

The man held up the card till Bimbo took it.

—Des O'Callaghan, he said. —I'm an environmental health officer with the Eastern Health Board.

How did you get a job like that? Jimmy Sr wondered. Again it struck him how normal Des O'Callaghan looked. Quite a young man too, for an inspector.

Bimbo's fingers smudged the card so he rubbed it on his

shirt, looked to see if it was clean and gave it back to Des O'Callaghan.

—Is somethin' wrong? Bimbo asked him.

Bimbo looked like he needed company so Jimmy Sr moved over closer to him, but he wasn't going to say anything. Bimbo would have to sort out this one for himself.

—I'm going to have to inspect your premises, said Des O'Callaghan.

—D'yeh have a warrant? said Jimmy Sr.

Bimbo looked like he was going to fall, like he wanted to agree with Jimmy Sr but was afraid to.

—I don't need one, Des O'Callaghan told Jimmy Sr, without even a trace of snottiness or sarcasm. He was good. Jimmy Sr was impressed, and scared. —I'm entitled to inspect these premises under the Food Hygiene Act.

Des disappeared and came in the back door.

—Wipe your feet, said Jimmy Sr. —— Only coddin' yeh.

Des got down on his hunkers and looked around. Jimmy Sr nudged Bimbo. He waited for Des to run a finger along the floor and then look at it, but he didn't do that. Bimbo thought about getting down beside Des. He bent his knees a bit, then decided not to.

Des was looking under the hotplate now.

—The licence's at home, said Bimbo. —D'you want me —?

It wasn't easy talking to the back of the man's head. Bimbo gave up.

Des stood up. He wasn't taking notes or anything, or ticking things off. He looked into the chip bin. No harm there, thought Jimmy Sr; the chips were only in it a few minutes. Des looked at the milk bottles full of water. Then he touched something for the first time since getting in. He turned one of the taps at the sink and noticed that it was loose and not connected to anything.

—I'm gettin' it fixed, said Bimbo.

Des said nothing.

What was he looking at now? Jimmy Sr wondered. He shifted a bit to see. The walls; he was staring at the walls.

—Is everythin' alrigh'? said Bimbo.

Des still said nothing. Jimmy Sr decided to wipe the hatch counter, to give him something to do. His cloth was bone dry. He nearly had it in the chip bin to rinse it when he saw Des looking at him. He changed his direction just before his hand went into the bin and started wiping the outside of the bin. God, he was a fuckin' eejit; he hadn't thought – He whistled. He turned the bin a bit to see if he'd missed any of it, then stood up and went back to the hatch.

He almost didn't recognise Bimbo, the way he was looking at him. He'd never seen Bimbo look that way before, cold and intelligent. He reddened; he didn't know why. Then his mind caught up with him —

He thinks I ratted on him. He thinks I ratted on him!

He couldn't say anything.

Then Des spoke.

—Can I see your hands, please? he said.

—Wha'?

—Your hands, said Des. —Can I see them, please?

——Why? said Jimmy Sr.

Bimbo already had his hands held out, ready to be hand-cuffed. Then he turned them and opened his palms. Now Jimmy Sr understood. He did the same. He tried to get Bimbo to see him, without making it obvious to the inspector. He hadn't ratted on him. He had to let him know.

Des looked down at their palms.

—The nails, please.

They flipped their hands over. Bimbo let out a sigh. It sounded cheeky.

—Do we pass? Jimmy Sr asked Des.

If he got snotty with him Bimbo would know that he hadn't done the dirty on him.

—I'm afraid not, said Des.

He looked around again.

Jimmy Sr had to lean back against the counter. Oh fuck —

He thought he was going to shite, a cramp ran through him: Bimbo thought it was his fault.

—'Fraid not, said Des, just short of cheerfully.

Bimbo still had his hands held out. Des nodded at them.

—I'm finished, he told Bimbo.

Bimbo put his hands into his pockets. Jimmy Sr went to put his hand on Bimbo's shoulder, then didn't.

—I'm going to have to close you down, lads, said Des. —I have the power.

Jimmy Sr was surprised he could talk.

—Now, hang on —

—Let me finish, said Des. —Please. —— Thanks. Which one of you is the proprietor?

Jimmy Sr pointed.

—He —

—I am, said Bimbo.

Bimbo half-turned, to let Jimmy Sr know that he was to stay out of it.

—I am, Bimbo said again.

—Okay. Mister —?

—Reeves.

—Right, Mister Reeves. —— I have to tell you that your van poses a grave and serious danger to public health.

Bimbo looked at the floor. Jimmy Sr did too.

—I'm closing you down now, said Des.

—What abou' our fuckin' jobs? said Jimmy Sr.

—I haven't finished speaking yet, said Des.

Bimbo spoke to Jimmy Sr for the first time since this had started.

—Shut up, will yeh.

He didn't bother looking at him when he said it.

—You close down now, said Des to Bimbo. —The walls are filthy, the floor is filthy, there's no water supply—

—We're gettin' tha' fixed, he told yeh —

—the foodstuffs aren't properly covered and stored, the hotplate is dangerous, the oil in the fryer is – I don't have to tell you. You are personally unclean, especially your colleague behind you. I'm sorry but I'm empowered to make these observations. I've no wish to hurt your feelings.

Jimmy Sr shrugged.

—Your clothes are unsafe and your fingernails are what my mother would call a disgrace.

No one laughed.

—Your hair, both of you, is a threat to public health. I could go on all night. —— There are enough breaches of the food hygiene regulations in here to land you a hefty fine and even a custodial sentence.

My fuck —

Des let that sink in.

—Jail, d'yeh mean? said Jimmy Sr.

This was crazy.

—I'm afraid so, yes.

—You're jestin'! Pull the other one, will yeh.

—Shut up, you, said Bimbo. —You've done enough already.

—You're the one goin' to jail, Jimmy Sr told him.

—Just shut up —!

Bimbo looked around the van.

—— It's not tha' bad, he said.

—Yes, it is, said Des. —It's worse.

Fair play to yeh, Jimmy Sr thought. Jimmy Sr liked Des.

—We clean it, Bimbo told him.

Des scratched his ear.

—— Will I have to go to court? said Bimbo.

—A week, Mister Reeves, said Des. —What I'm going to do is —

He waited a bit.

—I'm going to give you a week to bring your premises into line with Health Board requirements. I'll provide you with a list of what you'll have to do. I'll come back in a week and if I see that you've done your homework we'll forget that I was here this week.

He smiled, then snapped it back.

—It's going to be a busy week, Mister Reeves.

Des was great.

622

Before Bimbo could thank him he started again.

—However, Mister Reeves, I have to warn you —— If you fail to carry out even one of the demands on the list I'll have to close you down. On behalf of the Minister for Health.

Now Bimbo could talk.

—Thanks very much.

Des took a pen and some papers out of his jacket pocket. He clicked the pen and went over to the counter. Jimmy Sr got out of his way. Bimbo followed him. It was some sort of a list; Jimmy Sr couldn't see it properly. Des put a tick beside nearly everything on it.

Would they have to shave their heads? Jimmy Sr wondered. He was feeling good now; he needed deep breaths.

—I'll have to get you to sign this for me, Des told Bimbo. ——Just there. —That's right; thank you. —— And this one —

He gave Bimbo one of the sheets of paper.

—That's for you, Mister Reeves, he said.

He clicked his pen again and put it back into his pocket with the other papers.

—Well —, he said. —Next week so —

—Yeah, said Bimbo. —I'll get goin' on tha'. All the things —Thanks very much.

—Goodbye, said Des.

—Cheerio, said Jimmy Sr.

—Goodbye, he said to Bimbo.

—Bye bye now, said Bimbo.

Des hopped down the steps, not a bother on him.

—Nice fella, said Jimmy Sr.

—Well ————, said Bimbo —I hope you're happy now, that's all I can say.

Jimmy Sr had forgotten.

—Wha'? he said.

It was too early to deny anything.

—You know, said Bimbo.

Bimbo wouldn't look at him.

—No, said Jimmy Sr. —Sorry; I don't know.

Bimbo scoffed. He moved for the first time since Des had gone, and turned off the fryer and the hotplate. He hesitated a bit before he turned the dial under the plate, then he did it. He took the baskets out of the fryer.

—Large an' a cod, please.

There was a young one at the hatch.

—We're closed, said Bimbo.

—We may as well get rid o' wha' we have, said Jimmy Sr.

—We're closed, said Bimbo.

—We're shut, love, Jimmy Sr told the young one. —Come back next week, he said loud enough for Bimbo to hear.

Bimbo scoffed again, and this time Jimmy Sr wanted to give him a boot up the hole; he was arguing like a woman. He let the hatch door down and it was dark except for the light coming through the back door.

—I had nothin' to do with this, said Jimmy Sr.

Bimbo said nothing.

—I didn't, Bimbo; I swear.

——Yeah —, said Bimbo.

He went out and lifted the gas canister up into the van.

—I didn't, Jimmy Sr told him. —Des just —

—Des —, said Bimbo.

—I never saw or heard of him before today, said Jimmy Sr.

Bimbo said nothing. He made noises like a strangled laugh, but Jimmy Sr couldn't see his face properly.

—Ah, this is fuckin' crazy, said Jimmy Sr. —Look it, for fuck sake, it had nothin' to do with me —

—So yeh said, said Bimbo.

Jimmy Sr could see enough of him to grab him. He pushed him back; Bimbo fell against the chip bin and the shelf behind him stopped him from going back further. The bin went over and there was water everywhere. His legs were soaked but Jimmy Sr ignored it. He had Bimbo by the shirt, and he was up over him because Bimbo's legs had slipped. He shook him.

—Are yeh listenin' to me!?

He shook him again. One of the buttons went.

—Are yeh!?

Bimbo slid back more. He was kneeling in the water. Jimmy Sr could have kneed his thick face for him. He took one hand off the shirt and grabbed hair.

—Let me up —!

—I will. I will. Just listen! —

Jimmy Sr had to calm himself. He was all set to pulverise Bimbo. If Bimbo said one thing wrong he'd destroy him. Bimbo stayed still.

——Now ——Your man comin' here —it had nothin' to do with me, righ'. I didn't rat on yeh —

He didn't want to kill him now. He stepped back to give Bimbo room. He held out his hand to help Bimbo up. Bimbo pushed it away.

—I can manage meself.

He could hear Bimbo grabbing air, like he'd been running. There was a growl in his breathing as well. Jimmy Sr was the same.

—D'yeh believe me? he said.

Bimbo began to lift the bin, then let it go.

——Yeah, he said. —Yeah. I believe yeh.

——Sorry —for —

—Forget it, forget it. —— Forget it.

Jimmy Sr was exhausted.

—We'll fix it up, don't wo –

Jimmy Sr was knocked back before he realised he'd been hit. It wasn't hard enough to throw him back against the counter but he slid before he steadied himself. Bimbo had thumped him, hard on the chest; but it made more noise than pain. His knuckles would be killing him.

This was terrible. They were coming up to the end. Jimmy Sr gasped a few times and massaged his chest. He was close to crying. And wrecking the place.

—If —, Bimbo started.

He was the same as Jimmy Sr, nearly crying.

—If it hadn't been your man, he said, —it would've been somethin' else.

—What's tha' supposed to mean?

625

Bimbo didn't say anything for a while; ages. Jimmy Sr could hear him breathing, and himself; and his heart.

A stone hit the outside of the van. They both jumped.

—Fuck —

Jimmy Sr tried to laugh but only a croak came out. Another stone walloped the wall behind Bimbo.

—Yeh were goin' to get me anyway, said Bimbo then. — Weren't yeh?

—Wha' d'yeh mean —?

—One way or another.

Another stone. It rolled over the roof.

—You were goin' to get me —

—Fuck off, will yeh.

—The union —

—Fuck off; Jaysis.

—Anythin' to get at me —

—Shut up.

—Even spreadin' rumours abou' me an' tha' woman —

—Shut fuckin' up!

——Make me.

He heard Bimbo move closer to him.

—I said nothin' about yeh.

—Yeh did.

—I didn't.

—You were the only one tha' seen me!

—Well, it wasn't me, righ'!

Bimbo'd stopped.

Just as well for himself.

He heard Bimbo giggle, forcing himself.

——Am I tha' bad? he said.

The air seemed wet.

——Yeah, said Jimmy Sr.

He wiped his nose.

—I pay yeh well, don't I? —— Don't I, Jimmy?

—Yeh do, —yeah.

——Well then?

He was pleading with him. But it was too late.

626

—When we started ou' —, said Jimmy Sr. —When we —

He tried to dry his face.

—When we got the van —

—When I bought the van, d'yeh mean? said Bimbo. — When I bought the van; is tha' what yeh mean?

He was gloating, the cunt. Trying to explain was a waste of time.

The stones had stopped.

——Forget it, said Jimmy Sr.

Gina came into the van. Sharon had lifted her in.

—Out, said Bimbo.

Sharon was in.

—Get her out, said Bimbo.

—Don't talk —

—Out!!

Gina started bawling.

Jimmy Sr was on top of Bimbo. He had him in a headlock. He tried to get at his face, to get a clean thump in. Bimbo was thumping his sides, his arse; he got Jimmy Sr in the bollix, but not hard enough. Sharon and Gina were gone. Jimmy Sr gave up on the fist and opened his hand; he got his thumb to Bimbo's face somewhere and pressed. Bimbo whined. He found a wad of Jimmy Sr's fat over his trousers and he squeezed, dug his nails into it. Jesus, it was agony – Jimmy Sr let go of him and got back. He tried to kick him but he couldn't reach. He slipped. He grazed his arm on the counter trying to stay up.

That was it; there was no mending anything now.

—I'm goin', he said.

He climbed out of the van. It was dark now. It could have been any time of night. He wiped his face. He'd go home. No, he'd walk a bit first. His eyes would be red. He'd get his breath back to normal first.

He was glad.

He turned around and headed for the coast road. He had to go past the van. He didn't look at it.

Bimbo caught up with him.

—Come on back.

—Fuck off.

—Come on —

—Fuck off.

—Jimmy —

—Fuck off.

Bimbo stayed with him.

He only wanted Jimmy Sr back so that he wouldn't feel guilty; he needed him to go back to work for him. He could ask Jimmy Sr's arse if he thought —

Bimbo grabbed at Jimmy Sr's arm, trying to stop him. Jimmy Sr turned on him, and they were fighting again, in a clinch, gasping before they'd started. Bimbo's head hit Jimmy Sr's mouth.

—Sorry —

They held onto each other, heaving. There were people coming up from the bus-stop.

Bimbo spoke.

—Let's go for a pint.

—Okay.

* * *

They drank and stared at each other. Afraid to speak. They looked away. Into their pints. Everywhere. When Jimmy Sr saw Bimbo looking at him he looked back until Bimbo gave up.

A lounge boy went by.

—Two pints, said Jimmy Sr.

His voice sounded grand now. He was dry again. He leaned over to get his hand into his pocket when he saw the young fella putting the pints on his tray and coming over to them. Bimbo tried to beat him to it.

—I'll —

—No way, said Jimmy Sr.

He took the pints from the young fella and passed one over to Bimbo.

—There.

He hoped no one came in, Bertie or Paddy. Bimbo had

finished his first pint. He held up the one Jimmy Sr'd just bought.

—Cheers.

Jimmy Sr waited. He felt good now. He was almost happy, in a very unhappy kind of way. He'd made his decision, done what he should have done weeks ago. He lifted his pint.

—Cheers.

The young fella was going by again.

—Two pints, like a good man, said Bimbo. —We may as well, he said to Jimmy Sr.

Jimmy Sr shrugged.

—Fair enough.

——For old time's sake.

—Fuck off.

—Ah, Jimmy —

—Ah Jimmy nothin'. ——I won't be goin' back, yeh know.

—Yeah.

—It's the only way.

—But – No, you're righ'.

The young fella unloaded the tray.

—I'll pay yeh your redundancy money though, Bimbo told Jimmy Sr. —Alrigh'?

—Thanks very fuckin' much, said Jimmy Sr.

He thought of something else.

—I'll buy a fuckin' chipper van with it.

They tried not to look as if they were staring each other out of it. Jimmy Sr coughed, cleared his throat, thought about going into the jacks to spit. He examined the head of his pint.

——Wha' happened, Jimmy? Bimbo asked.

It took Jimmy Sr a while to understand.

—Fuck off, would yeh, he said.

He didn't care what had happened any more. It was over and done with. He'd no time any more for that What Happened shite.

—Two pints, he shouted.

* * *

Five or six pints later – Jimmy Sr'd lost count – Bimbo was looking demolished. Jimmy Sr was holding his own, he thought; knackered, yeah, but not rat-arsed. He nearly missed the door when he'd gone to the jacks the last time but he was grand. There was still no sign of Bertie or Paddy.

Bimbo was pathetic, sinking down further into his chair, like someone had let his air out. He was licking up to Jimmy Sr now because the No Hard Feelings wankology had failed.

—Come on, Jim, —— come on.

Jimmy Sr let Bimbo keep his hand stretched out over the table, waiting for Jimmy Sr to shake it. Bimbo took his hand down. Jimmy Sr didn't have any feelings at all now but he wasn't particularly interested in making Bimbo feel any better. The cunt deserved to suffer. He should just have got up and gone home and left Bimbo on his own. But he couldn't.

Bimbo'd told him that he didn't know what he'd do now without him, told him that it wouldn't be the same without him, told him that the sun, moon and fuckin' stars shone out of his fuckin' hole; desperate for Jimmy Sr to give him a sign that he still liked him.

Bimbo put his hand out again, then forgot what he was doing. The man was demolished.

He saw Jimmy Sr.

—The best —— fuckin' – worker in the wor – the fuckin' world, he said.

Jimmy Sr looked around.

—Fifty-fifty, said Bimbo.

He sat up.

—Wha' d'yeh say-y? —— Fif'y-fifty.

—What're yeh fuckin' sayin', man?

—Fif'y-fif'y, said Bimbo. —Half for me an' —— half for
—The way it was —

—No.

Maybe though —

—No way.

—Go on. Par'ners —

—Forget it – Fuck tha'; no way.

This pint had got very warm. It wasn't nice at all.

Bimbo slipped back down. He walloped the table with his knees when he was trying to get up again. The glasses wobbled.

—Mind!

—S-sorry 'bou' —

He tried to put his hand on Jimmy Sr's leg. He couldn't reach.

——Jimmy —— you're my bes' frien' —

—No, I amn't, said Jimmy Sr. —Fuck tha'.

—Yeh are —

—Forget it, pal —— I've learnt me lesson; fuck tha'.

He knocked back the pint before he remembered that it was horrible. Bimbo was muttering. Jimmy Sr kept the glass at his mouth in case he couldn't keep it down. He badly needed a cold one; then he'd be alright.

—I'll kill it, said Bimbo.

—Wha'? said Jimmy Sr.

—Tha' poxy van, said Bimbo.

He staggered up. He staggered, but he stayed up.

—Come on, Jim, he said. —C'me on.

* * *

Bimbo drove. He went up on the roundabout near the coast road and he fell asleep twice but he got the van to Dollymount, in between the dunes and out onto the sand; through the soft stuff (—We're stuck. No —— Go on, go on; we're movin') and out to the hard sand.

They got out. The wind was lovely. The tide was out, way out.

—Come on, Jim, said Bimbo, and he went to get back in.

—Hang on here, said Jimmy Sr.

He held Bimbo's shoulder.

—What're yeh doin'?

He knew what Bimbo was doing.

—You'll regret it, he said.

—No, I won't, said Bimbo. —Not me.

Jimmy Sr got in with him.

He headed for the water. It was hard to see where it started. There were no waves, no white ones. Jimmy Sr heard it. They were in it now. He saw it now, lit up in front of him and out the side window; only a few inches. Bimbo kept going. Jimmy Sr wasn't scared. They stopped. The van coughed and died. Bimbo turned the key. Jimmy Sr looked down. There was water at his feet. Bimbo had to push to get his door open.

—Mission acc-accomplished, he said. —Come on, Jim.

He bailed out. Jimmy Sr heard the splash. Jimmy Sr did the same. He lowered himself down (—Jeeesus!!) into two feet of water, freezing fuckin' water; it lapped up to near his bollix.

—Aaaahh! Jesus; shi'e!

He'd never felt soberer.

—Where are yeh, yeh fuckin' eejit?

He found Bimbo behind the van, pushing it, trying to get it further into the water, getting nowhere.

—Give us a hand!

Jimmy Sr waded over and put his arms around Bimbo's waist and lifted him away from the van.

—Come on, he said.

Bimbo didn't fight.

Jimmy Sr let him down.

—Come on.

They waded, then walked, back to the shore. Jimmy Sr looked back. They'd only come about thirty yards. He could see the top of the van's wheels; the water only reached the bottom of the burger sign. When the tide came in though, it would disappear then.

He took his shoes off.

—I did it, said Bimbo.

He sat down. In a half inch of water.

—I did it, Jim.

—Good man, said Jimmy Sr. —Come on before we die.

Bimbo stood up. He caught up with Jimmy Sr. He put his arm around Jimmy Sr's shoulders. Jimmy Sr shrugged it off. He tried again. Jimmy Sr shrugged his arm away again.

When they got to the dry sand Jimmy Sr turned to look. Bimbo was ten yards behind him; he'd turned sooner. The van seemed to be deeper in the water.

—You'll be able to get it when the tide goes out again, Jimmy Sr told him.

Bimbo said nothing.

Jimmy Sr turned back and headed up to the dunes.

* * *

Veronica woke up while he was getting his clothes off. She smelt the sea in the room. It was getting bright outside. He sat on the bed beside her.

—Give us a hug, Veronica, will yeh. —— I need a hug.